Published by
Century Creations Printing, Inc.
5203 Gateway Drive
Grand Forks, ND 58203
(701) 746-4543

This novel is a work of fiction.
Any references to real events, businesses, organizations,
people, their actions, and locales are intended
only to give the fiction a sense of reality and authenticity.
Any resemblance to actual persons, living or dead,
is entirely coincidental.

Book design by John Loukas

ISBN 189093904-8
Copyright © 1999 Stuart G. Rice

All rights reserved. No part of this book may be reproduced or transmitted in any form by any means, electronic or mechanical, including photocopying, recording, or by any information storage and retrival system, without the written permission of the publisher and the author, except where permitted by law.

Printed in the United States of America
1999 First Edition

Fragile X

A Novel by Stuart Rice

To my parents—with love and thanks.

Everyone should be as fortunate as I.

The size of the lie is a definite factor in causing it to be believed, for the vast masses of the nation are in the depths of their hearts more easily deceived than they are consciously or intentionally bad. The primitive simplicity of their minds renders them a more easy prey to a big lie than a small one, for they themselves often tell little lies but would be ashamed to tell a big one.

A. Hitler
Mein Kampf

Prologue

It didn't hurt a little. It hurt like hell!

The sweat on Molly Loomis's brow seemed to leap through her pores as the needle pierced through the delicate, white skin on the top of her hand. She turned away and bit her lip as the welt of lidocaine obscured the small vein tracing from her ring finger to her wrist. It was terrible. It felt like a burn, or a stab; actually more like a white-hot knife carving away her flesh and leaving behind only the tattered remnants of bone and skin. This couldn't be right, she thought. It hurt too much. Then, just as suddenly as it had begun, the pain was gone. She turned her head back, looking at the anesthetist holding a gauze pad to the site.

"It's better with local anesthetic," he said.

"Thank you," mumbled Molly nervously.

His voice and eyes were soothing. "Relax. Everything is going to be *just fine.*"

The anesthetist turned away and began speaking to another nurse in thick medical jargon. Molly tried to relax. Her hand now numb and the pain a memory, she let her eyes roam through the confines of the operating room. To her right was a long table shrouded with a blue paper drape and covered with unidentifiable metal instruments. To her left was a small stand holding cautery, sterile light handles, and suction tubing. At her feet, by the edge of the operating table, she saw a nurse assembling the metal stirrups. Beyond she could see a trio of suction canisters and two glass cabinets filled with the suture.

"A little pressure here," came the anesthetist's voice again, still confident and reassuring.

With his words, Molly felt a throb in her hand, distracting her from a visual survey of the surroundings. This time it was a dull ache that seemed to gnaw at her bones, threatening to linger like a migraine. But, just as before, it quickly disappeared as if the offending needle had magically evaporated. She turned to the anesthetist and watched him inject something into the IV and secure the catheter to her hand with a clear plastic tape.

Molly started to say something, but a cloud passed before her eyes and her vision turned fuzzy. She blinked, but nothing cleared as she struggled to focus on the anesthetist. "Strange," she thought. She remembered him as tall and lean with a pleasant face, but now he didn't seem to register. He was a fog. And suddenly, she felt very, very strange.

"That wasn't too bad," she heard herself mumble.

"I do it both ways," he said matter-of-factly. "But an 18-gauge IV going through the skin really hurts. I like using the lidocaine a lot better."

"I do too," Molly replied. She shook her head. Her mouth felt weird. She knew she had said the words, but she had no idea what she was talking about.

"Without the lidocaine, the pain is just too intense."

"Ayagree."

The room seemed to move in a circular motion, with all of the operating room personnel floating between spots in their blue suits that looked like capes. Molly could hear their voices, but now the words seemed to strike her and reflect off, their meaning not registering. Her head felt numb, her body detached. She felt like she was floating, her body a thin, whispery cloud, spinning and twisting high in the air.

Suddenly she was aware of how good she felt. High. No, very high. It was all wonderful. Everyone was so nice. Everyone was being so kind. She heard herself talking. Talking about something. She was thanking everyone. Thanking them for everything. She would buy them all presents, she said. Remember them always. They paid no attention to her words, but Molly didn't mind. They were being modest. They were all so kind. She felt bliss, pure bliss.

She closed her eyes and took a deep breath. This was terrific. She had never felt so relaxed, her body floating free. It was the comfort that did it. The comfort of knowing it would soon be over. She felt even better as she considered it, the high getting higher. She opened her eyes. The room was now blue and purple and green and pink. The colors seemed to blend into one as they spun in a kaleidoscope, like tapestry in front of her eyes. She felt another surge inside herself, an exploding sensation of power and pleasure that made her gasp. She sighed and closed her eyes again. Now she knew it was the right decision.

"Good afternoon," came a voice.

The words barely registered. Molly only cracked her eyes enough to see the profile of a man standing between her naked legs, placing them in the stirrups. "Uhna," she grunted.

"We're just going to put the drapes on, Molly," came the man's voice again. "I'll let you know when we start."

Molly did not respond. She felt too good, too relieved, to talk. All the debate, all the concern, all the agony were about to end. The hardest decision of her life. At long last she knew it was right.

Her drooping eyes saw the blue drapes shield her from the doctor and his two assistants. They fumbled with instruments and talked to one another. It was more medical gobbledygook. No, it was plain English. Words she knew, but couldn't comprehend.

"You're going to feel a little pressure now, Molly."

Something slipped inside her, but it neither felt good nor hurt. It was a nothing, a slight sense of fullness in her pelvis that stretched but wasn't painful. She closed her eyes again.

"Now you'll feel me examining you."

A pair of fingers began pushing and probing, attempting to feel everything they should and nothing they shouldn't. She had experienced this before. It was uncomfortable but not painful, just like always, and she still felt far too good to even think about complaining. Her mind recalled her first pelvic exam, shortly after she was married and at her doctor's insistence. It had hurt much worse then, her whole belly aching with the cramping pain of a day-long spasm. She had tried to avoid the exams after that, but her doctors always disagreed.

"Ductuh's are too curful," she slurred. No one heard it.

"Now you'll feel a little pain."

The doctor wasn't kidding. Despite the daze, it was a ripping, shearing pain that felt like a fire melting her core. Then, it rose up further, deep inside her, and spread to her sides, her hips, and her legs. Biting her lip with her toes curling involuntarily, Molly latched onto the sides of the operating table, her grip so strong that her hands went numb.

"Uggghhhaaa."

"It'll be gone in a second," she heard him say. He was right again. She sighed in relief. It was gone. With it, she felt her body float away again.

"Now we'll start, Molly."

She felt something. It was a touch or a poke, something deep inside her that felt like a pinch and then a pull. "It shouldn't hurt now," she heard.

"Gud."

The sense of contentment had returned. The pain was gone. And more important, the agony would soon be over. The decision. The most difficult of her life. The decision that had swirled within her, tormented her, tortured her with the punishing fury of a tornado's unrelenting wake. She breathed another sigh of relief. It was good to feel good again.

She could sense something inside her and she heard a noise. She felt a cramp. Not bad.

"Suction."

There was another cramp. A sting. A poke. A scrape. None of it was bad. A push. A pull. It was easy.

"Suction."

She still felt as if she were floating, rising higher and higher into a cloudless sky. She felt dizzy. A good dizzy, content and contained. She could take any of this. Simple, nearly painless. And soon it would all be done.

"Suction."

Another scrape. Another pull. Another push and another pull. None of it mattered. None of it seemed to hurt. None of it seemed to last. She took another deep breath. She could see the blur of the anesthetist and felt him fumbling with the IV. She felt weak. No, she felt tired. Very, very tired.

"Suction!"

His voice woke her. She was aware that she had dozed off. How long, she did not know. "We're having just a little bit of bleeding," said the doctor. "But everything is fine. We're almost done. Just gotta stop this and we'll be finished."

"Good," she replied. The nap had cleared her voice, and this time they heard her.

"You've done beautifully," said one of the nurses.

"You sure have," said the other.

"Thanks," murmured Molly. "Thanks so much."

Three hours later, Molly Loomis lay on the couch in the poorly furnished front room that often served as her bed. A lone blanket was over her, and two pillows propped up her head. She was still dizzy, but the feeling of euphoria that she remembered from the operation was now long gone. Now she just hurt everywhere, torn apart, ripped in two. Her head ached. Her stomach ached. Her legs felt like noodles, her hands were like Jello. She felt herself. Another spot of blood. They had said it might be like that. She collapsed back on the pillow and wiped her finger on the tissue beside the bed. "Feel better soon," she reassured herself. "Feel better soon."

The room still seemed to spin, but the world had been spinning since before the abortion. Molly had gone round and round a million times since the doctor had first told her about the fetus's condition, a condition that would kill it, or even worse, forever leave it a vegetable.

Molly sighed. Tears came again. A baby would have been wonderful. A baby was everything she had ever wanted, everything she had ever dreamed. But that? No, not that. How could she have allowed a child such suffering or such misery? She couldn't. She abhorred abortion. But in this case, not to have done it would have been selfish. A child with no life at all. "This was the right answer," she said without conviction.

She reached between her legs. Blood. More this time. She wiped it on the Kleenex and threw her head back on the pillow. The bleeding would stop soon, she told herself. It was minor. She had bled as she drove home, staining her clothes and the car seat. That had been annoying. Next, she had stained the carpet and the floor, which she had cleaned. Then, she had stained the toilet and the shower, a rug, and a shoe. Those she had left for later. First, there had just been drops. Now, they were more. She touched herself again. Her hand was drenched in red. Her tears suddenly stopped.

She looked at the clock as she wiped her hand. 7:15 P.M. She picked up the phone and tried the number again. She would just ask them a question. Four rings, then five. Finally the voice and the menu. "If you have a rotary phone please stay on the line." It was the same as before, and in a second she was disconnected. She hung it up.

"That's seven times!" she exclaimed. "Useless!"

The doctor had said she might go through several pads, she remembered. "These operations often result in a pretty heavy flow," had been his exact words. She stood up and started toward the bathroom. It was time to change the pad. She was dizzy, but she could walk. Two minutes later, she was back on the couch. Five minutes later, the new pad was nearly saturated. Thirty seconds later, she had been disconnected an eighth time.

Molly could feel the wetness saturating her groin. She put her hand between her thighs and was shocked by what she saw. Blood everywhere. Her legs, the couch, the blanket. She gulped and picked up the phone, forgetting to wipe the blood off her hand. This was a lot of blood. A lot! It couldn't be normal. She needed to talk to someone. She heard the ring. The menu started up again. A minute later, disconnection.

"Our doctors' doors are always open." She remembered the jingle. Now she couldn't even get a live person. Again she tried. She could feel her heart begin to race. Disconnection. Again. The same. She slammed the phone down. A bead of sweat dropped in her eye. She wiped it away. More blood. She wiped it, too. The phone. Still the same. Again. Then again. Doctors' doors are always open. More blood. She looked for a different number. None. She dialed the clinic. Closed. She called ComHealth again. Another disconnection.

She threw off the blanket and stood. She felt faint and weak. She staggered away from the couch and looked in horror at the sight. Blood everywhere, covering the couch and sliding through the cloth toward the floor. Blood trickling from inside her and onto her thighs. Blood, dripping past her knees and rolling down her shins.

She labored toward the bathroom. Her legs were heavy. She could feel herself sweat and her heart pound faster. In the bathroom, she cleaned herself furiously. She could see the steady flow that kept coming. Drop after drop after drop. Glob after glob. She wiped them all and then replaced the pad again. "It's still okay," she said bravely, trying to convince herself. "Few more minutes it will be all right."

The words were said to no one. They were words to herself. Words without assurance, words without meaning. She walked to the bedroom and slouched down onto the floor, exhausted. "Few more minutes." She reached down. More blood. "This was all to be expected." More blood. And more. She felt dizzier. She felt weaker. She felt sick. All at once, light seemed to pass before her eyes. Bizarre light, like a beam carrying an angel, directly from heaven.

Molly shook her head and looked up at the clock. She had been on the floor ten minutes. She had fainted. She tried to stand, but she couldn't; her legs were now too weak to move. A pool of blood surrounded her. A sense of panic rose within her, and she could feel her heart nearly leap out of her chest. She reached across the floor and pulled the phone off the nightstand, the cord looping around her neck. She picked it up and started to dial in numbers. "To hell with any HMO rules," she thought. This wasn't normal. This wasn't right.

No voice greeted her. She punched at the numbers again. She had to talk to someone fast. 911. 911. She listened. Still no voice. Her mind went blank. Frantic. Panic. Fear. 911. She tried again. Still no voice! She looked up in front of her. The phone was unplugged at the wall! Ripped out in its fall. "God no!" Her insides seemed to explode. Her heart seemed to be in her throat.

And where was Troy? Tonight she needed to see her husband's swaggering frame. Tonight she would gladly disregard his contempt for her. Tonight she wanted to hear his key in the lock. "Troy!" she cried. She hated him. She still loved him. She hated that he hated her. "Please come home, Troy."

Molly lifted her head painfully. The room spun with the swirling regularity of a top on its final rotations. She had fainted twice within the hour; her clothing and the carpet were wet and red. She felt weak, dizzy. The pain was excruciating. She again tried to stand, but her legs seemed detached, and as she rose to one knee, she collapsed, crashing into the nightstand, striking her head on its edge and bloodying her temple.

The phone. She remembered the phone. Lying next to the cord, she picked it up and tried to plug it back in. She fumbled with it, and the open wires came into view. No! Broken! The plastic end sheared off!

Molly dropped it. She tried to cry out, but no sound came. She laid her head down and wept. The blood kept coming. Faster now. Another cramp came and curled her on the floor. Slowly it passed, then another—gripping, tearing. Finally it, too, passed, and she lay quietly on the floor, her head against the nightstand.

The room seemed to be a mirage. Through the tears, its lines and shadows waved to her. She could smell the blood's sickening sweetness and felt its cooling chill. Troy. He would not come home. If he did, he would leave her there. He did not care. It was over. She looked at the door. It did not open. She looked at the clock. It did not stop. She could feel more blood dribble to the back of her thigh. Her heartbeat felt fast, her face flush, her mouth dry. She put her head back down. She would rest. Tired. So very tired. She would clean the room later. Troy would be furious. So much blood.

Her eyes stayed open, and through the daze the room seemed to turn colors, an ebbing stream of a rainbow's progression that yielded a solid amber at the end. The room twisted, leaving her free from its bonding gravity as her body became detached. She blinked, but then she saw herself in a different light—her body dressed in silver-gray, her face hidden, unseen. No one would remember. No one would care. Suddenly, the room was white. Everything was gone.

Book One

Case White

Chapter One

June 2

The most dreaded ninety seconds of Molly Loomis's day was that brief interlude of silence between her husband's nightly arrival home and his bilious eruption that always followed. Troy's entrance was never precise, usually between 7:00 P.M. and 2:30 A.M., depending upon the number of drinks he had downed or the number of dart games he had lost. Neither criterion was reliable, but his return performance was always predictable. The usual greeting was a grunt, more a belch, resonant and ripe and full of the smell of partially acidified beer. A quick glance of indifferent recognition was next, followed by his staggering trek to the kitchen. When he returned, a fresh beer in hand, he would drop his sweatshirt next to the door and kick off his high-tops, revealing his sweat socks of the past three days. He would then settle comfortably into the midsection of the couch in a strategic fashion to assure that no one could join him. After a long, luxurious swig, he would reach for the TV remote and scan through the channels, seeking any sporting event he could find. When the evening's viewing was established, the nightly critique of Molly would begin.

To everyone else, Troy Loomis was a buddy, a friend, or a symbol of Danfield High School's glorious past. To his wife, he was a shadow, a faded icon, and a frightening reminder of her unwanted penance. Outwardly charming, his endless energy was now spent on the tedium of the day shift at Barton Machinery and the rancor of the happy hour at The Bull's Eye with his old high school teammates. He was forty pounds heavier than his fullback playing weight, but his widening waist still easily supported his thick shoulders and broad neck. His face, once a hardened iron cast of angles and cheekbones, was now fuller, with a sag beneath the chin and a softening above the jaw. His auburn hair was cut short, a quarter inch from a military crewcut, and his deep-set blue eyes, once his most alluring feature, were now perpetually red and permanently cool.

They had met ten years before as high school sophomores. He had been a boy of note in the blue-collar suburb of Minneapolis where football and a masculine image routinely merged. The football team was crucial to a community that sent few graduates farther than the local factories. As his career progressed, Troy Loomis carried with him the identity of Danfield, Minnesota, every time he touched the ball. Starting as a freshman made him a local celebrity. Winning the state championship that year only enhanced that profile. But it was the following state championships that assured his legend. As a senior, the great Troy Loomis was recruited by every major football college in the country.

Troy had inherited his physical skills from his father, a middle linebacker who had captained Danfield in the mid 1960s and dropped out of the University of Minnesota after one season. Troy had also inherited much else. His parents' marriage "out of necessity" had been ground into young Troy's mind as a warning of man's vulnerability. Ron Loomis spoke of his wife often. A woman not worthy of him. Troy's mother was supposed to have been part of the spoils, a toy, a fling. Ron Loomis had been a star. It had been intentional, his father had been convinced, calculated to snare the untouchable. Ron Loomis had hated his wife. An accident. Her fault. Catholicism had let him down, but there was no choice. Troy was born six months after the wedding, and he grew up worshipping his father, fully aware of the great man's victim status. As he grew up, Troy had come to know that no one woman would be worthy of him either.

Molly Oberg was well aware of the star fullback. She saw him in the halls and gazed wistfully as her school's most popular girls competed for the opportunity to occupy his arm. But she thought Troy Loomis would never notice her. Thin, almost frail, with a plain, porcelain face, large glasses, and limp brown hair, Molly had been slipping through high school unnoticed by anyone except for two close girlfriends. A "B" student without effort, Molly cared little for school, spending more time with her friends, dreaming of glamour and wishing for a boyfriend, but content with the understanding that college was still in her future.

Her parents had raised their only child well. Her father a plumber and her mother a part-time grocery store clerk, they had lived by the notion that education was the only trail to advancement. From her earliest years, both parents saved endlessly for the moment when their daughter would enter secondary education, something no member of their family had yet done. Molly had also looked forward to it, viewing college as an obligation to the dreams of her parents. Unfortunately, it became an experience neither of them enjoyed.

For Molly, a part-time job waitressing at Jake's Pizza, the current "in spot," helped pay for clothes and an occasional treat. Friday and Saturday nights usually produced the best tips, and Molly readily volunteered for the extra hours. Every weekend night, her class's elite would gather, ordering pizzas, joking, flirting, posturing, and preening. Molly loved to watch them, unobserved, from behind the counter as the girls alternated between coquettish and coy, and the boys between brutish and attentive. She watched carefully, detesting their shallowness yet wishing desperately to be a part of it.

Troy Loomis usually arrived late and in grand fashion, announced by the squeals of a roomful of admirers. Molly always felt the twinge of longing as she heard the room erupt. She would watch as he flirted endlessly through the evening, with many of the popular girls trading places on his lap. She wanted to hate them, the popular girls, for their manicured looks, their practiced feminine gestures, and, most of all, their access to him. She wanted to hate the boys because they did not notice her. But more than anything else, she hated herself for her desire for Troy Loomis.

It was during their junior year that they first spoke. Troy arrived late after the game and sat at one of Molly's assigned tables. "What's your name?" he asked. When she replied, he laughed in his usual manner, confident and carefree. "I was just kidding. You sit in the third row of my history class, at least when I'm there." Too shocked to talk at the revelation that he knew her, Molly had quickly taken the order, given away the table, and avoided him the rest of the night.

One week later, with a hint of makeup on her face, Molly saw him again. After another heroic three-touchdown game and amidst the noise of the restaurant, he sought her out, talking briefly about himself and the game, as she stared in awe. The next weeks were the same—a brief conversation that became regular and anticipated.

That became her romance. Short interludes of looks and idle conversation; the rest depended mainly on imagination. She looked forward to each Friday as the highlight of every week, a moment she shared, surrounded by the others, with him. Molly could not understand what he saw in her. No boy had ever shown an interest, let alone one so sought after. He was perfect—handsome, funny, and liked by all. He would never like her, but every week he sought her out.

She continued to envy the girls who held his attention and was relieved that none seemed to stay with him long. She waited patiently in admiration and paid no attention to other boys. Her girlfriends advised her to look elsewhere as high school dances came and went. But Molly remained faithful to her dream. By prom her senior year, a cheerleader from a neighboring suburb was his steady date and a football scholarship to the University of Minnesota was his future. At last, to her friends' glee, she said she had given up hope. But silently, she still hung onto those few minutes each week at Jake's Pizza.

After high school, while her friends went elsewhere for college, Molly enrolled at the U of M as well. Her parents were thrilled at the thought of their daughter in college; their lifelong ambition was realized, Molly started as an "undecided" major. Her first semester was difficult, the course work harder than expected, combined with a distracting roommate more interested in parties than homework. The second semester was harder yet, as she again crossed paths with Troy Loomis.

She had gone on impulse to a party with her roommate on a Friday night to the notorious football fraternity, Phi Kappa Theta. Their "No Prisoners–No Mercy–No Fat Chicks" party was a drunken bacchanal replete with multiple indiscretions, aberrant behavior, and four arrests, but for Molly, it was worth the trip as an inebriated Troy greeted her like long-lost family. They talked long into the night as he consumed beer after beer. She was surprised to learn about his knee pain and that he was concerned about not being the fastest back on the team. She found him simpler and more understandable than she had imagined, more vulnerable and human. He called her the next day, hung over but intent, and the next week they had their first date.

Within weeks, it was exactly as Molly had imagined. Although less attentive than she wished, he called regularly and they went out often. His drinking bothered her, but she could forgive it, rationalizing it as his stress release over the demands of being a student and an athlete. She was thrilled to discover they had so much in common. Neither had any love for college. Daily, Molly envisioned her future more as a wife and mother than as a professional, while Troy continued to want only to pursue a pro career. Their grades both suffered. But both cared little about them. Molly knew what she wanted.

They slept together for the first time after the PKT midwinter party. The moment was exactly as Molly had wished, and she knew she had become totally devoted to him. His life was hers. Her future was theirs. Molly became convinced that her parents had been wrong about her. She had neither the talent nor the desire to be a great success. A supportive role, a stabilizing force. A wife. A mother. This was her destiny. Her desire was no cop-out, she explained to herself. Most women relinquish their career anyway at the first opportunity. She was simply being realistic. A family was all she wanted. Troy was all she wanted. And now she was happier than she had ever been. In the meantime they slept together regularly, protected only by timing. She knew little of sex, finding it quick, rough, and unfulfilling. But he enjoyed it, and that pleased her.

At the first spring practice, Troy's knee gave out three hours after he had failed his third consecutive exam. Major reconstructive surgery followed one week later. Three incompletes were made up during the summer, but rehab took four hours a day and his grade point average was only 1.8. By the fall, he still could not run. To the shock and disappointment of her parents, Molly dropped out of school for a quarter to help him with rehab. He needed her, she said. But by the spring she had still not re-enrolled. Troy was forced to leave school when his knee required another operation and his academic probation expired. Three days later, Molly missed her period. On that day, he hit her for the first time.

"Good Catholics are always Catholic. Not just when it is convenient." They had each heard it since they were young. There was only one option. Angry, but accepting, like a prisoner acknowledging guilt, Troy proposed in the furious apology that followed his left hook. She accepted and forgave. She knew of his stress, his frustration, his fear. They would survive together. Happiness was created by the realization of dreams, not by the achievement of goals. She was sure he felt the same way. She knew he wanted children. He knew she wanted children. A child would bring them together, she was sure.

Troy's father greeted the news with anger and contempt, refusing to speak to Molly. Troy's mother never uttered a word. Molly's parents nearly disowned her. The wedding took place five weeks later. She lost the baby one month after that, when in a drunken frenzy, Troy pushed her down a stairway.

In the aftermath she forgave him. Scared and lonely, she told herself she had come to understand him. His sense of loss at the premature end of his football career. His grief, she told herself. She understood the pressure he felt and reasoned that he, too, had suffered with the loss of the baby.

They settled into their apartment on East St. Paul Avenue shortly after the miscarriage. Troy began work on an assembly line with his father while Molly worked two part-time jobs as a waitress. With little money and few close friends, Molly dedicated herself to the marriage. "The strong endure and the weak fail," she told herself as she tailored her life to attend to his needs. Household chores, paying bills, and compromise were her responsibility. Freedom was his assumed right. But within months, she began to suspect the worst. His hours at home became more sporadic. His drinking became worse. He became more distant, and their lovemaking, never frequent, became rougher and even more painful. She tried to remain open and warm, but she sensed his growing hostility and chose to ignore what she suspected to be true.

Two years passed with barely an affectionate word between them. But his drinking and anger continued to increase. Finally, one night she was forced to call the police after a late-night arrival when he beat her with new intensity, screaming his common adjectives of sexual scorn. When he finally finished and while she bled and cried, he collapsed into a heap of tears and apologies. She had considered leaving at that point, hurt beyond repair, but he begged her to stay. He needed her, he pleaded. Her pity for him, and her fear, made her stay.

During rehab Troy seemed a changed man. With abstinence and good intentions, he emerged attentive and supportive. But soon the pattern of money loss, late nights, and hostility reappeared. The only difference was that his outbursts were now laced with an added contempt stemming from his guilt. He rarely spoke to her. Soon, the drinking was worse than ever and he began flaunting other women openly. All money disappeared, and Molly found herself living in a world of silence punctuated only by his anger and the anxiety of her now three jobs.

Finally, after many months of building her courage, she made up her mind to leave him. But the discussion started badly and turned worse. Troy's anger turned to rage. He was possessed by the idea of desertion and the embarrassment it would cause. But as he saw her resolve, Troy turned again to an act of despair and put on a delirious and tearful confession of pure, unrequited love. She was unmoved, but her desire to leave was matched with his persistence and persuasiveness. He spoke passionately and with a sincerity she had never seen. Deep inside, she still wanted love and remained afraid to face the world alone. After hours, she weakened, and the attempted breakup ended in bed with a night of gentleness and physical delight. In the morning she cursed her weakness. Within a week, his pattern returned. Within a month, she knew she was pregnant again.

Troy was amused at the thought of a child. Most of his buddies at the plant had two or three, and his childlessness had been the source of jokes and innuendo. To him, a child was an end to the humor. Molly was ambivalent, torn between the competing impulses of the need to escape and the overwhelming, lifelong desire for a child. By eight weeks, she had resigned herself again to Troy and lived for the birth of the child. The marriage was a separate issue, she told herself. The thought of a baby elated her. Even her parents were happy.

At ten weeks, she had the first cramps. The doctor said nothing was wrong. One week later, the cramps returned, and she was back in his office. She had had abdominal cramps for years ever since a bladder infection that had required several weeks of antibiotics, but these cramps were worse, and she was concerned. They stopped the next day, but the doctor's phone call two days later confirmed the worst. The blood test had shown it, Fragile X, a rare, genetic disease passed on by the mother. Severe retardation, a lifetime of institutionalization, if not death in infancy. The baby would never even know it was alive.

Molly was devastated. A child had been her lifetime wish. But a child with no life? A child whose entire existence was suffering? Abortion was abhorrent to her, her Catholicism, her life's foundation. But how could she let a child suffer in that way? She couldn't. She knew Troy would never understand. He would accuse her of deception and killing his child. She feared him. But she also feared his reaction to such a child as well. And most of all, she feared for the lack of any meaningful life that this child would have.

Depressed but undaunted, she went for the procedure a week later. Her plan was that she would tell Troy of the miscarriage, a second—unfortunate, but plausible. The plan was perfect and well rehearsed. Drunk or sober, he would understand. It would be over in an hour, and the truth would never be told of her Fragile X baby.

At 8:45 P.M., the speeding ambulance carrying Molly Loomis blazed into the loading zone of the Hennepin County Medical Center Emergency Room. The driver hurled open the back doors, waving furiously toward the ER doors as his partner continued the CPR.

"Code 4! Full arrest!"

"Whatta ya got?" asked the breathless physician who was followed by four nurses in navy surgical scrubs.

"Mid-twenties female. Massive vag bleeding. Lost her pulse and pressure shortly after we arrived. CPR since. Got her tubed. No rhythm."

"History?" asked the oldest nurse, gray and firm in manner.

"Husband said maybe miscarriage. She's had one before."

"Pregnant?" asked the doctor.

"He says ten weeks."

"Where's the husband?"

"He's sick. Said he'd be by later."

"Beautiful," grunted another nurse.

"Whattya getting, Timmy?" asked the doctor.

"Nothin', Dr. K. Pulse with compressions, that's all."

"All right," he said grabbing the head of the gurney. "Get her into the room pronto. Continue CPR. Get me ABG's, lytes, and a type and cross for eight units. Crash cart open. Amp of epi to start. Let's move!"

Quickly the driver and the nurses pulled the gurney from the back of the ambulance and sped Molly toward the trauma room, the entire group running at full speed. The paramedic straddled the cart and continued the chest compressions, alternating every fifth with a breath of oxygen. The door to the ER opened automatically, and they were instantly engulfed in the fluorescent white of the trauma room. Ten seconds later, the paramedics swung Molly's gurney into Trauma Bed One. A respiratory therapist was waiting and hooked Molly's endotracheal tube to the oxygen container.

"One hundred percent," said the doctor, Kenneth Keating. The therapist nodded and adjusted the ventilator.

"Epi in," said the gray-haired nurse, Shirley Hammond, clearing the IV with an injection of saline.

"What do we have?" asked Keating. The room was loud as the trauma team began its organized, but chaotic, routine.

"Fib," said a second doctor, Robert Presner, as he arrived and glanced at the monitor.

"IVs wide open!" commanded Keating, nearly screaming. "And whatta we got for lines?"

"Two antecube sixteens."

"Good," he said loudly. "Blast it in. Forget the type and cross. Get me the O-neg. We need blood now! She's bleeding to death as we speak."

"Still fib."

"Shock her. Two hundred."

Hammond and another nurse poised at Molly's other side slapped plastic conductors across her chest after her nightshirt had been removed. With a swift, decisive movement, Dr. Presner swung the defibrillator paddles to the chest pads and fired. Immediately Molly's limp body rose and fell and the room stopped, everyone staring at the cardiac monitor. A tracing emerged.

"V-tach!"

"Convert her!"

"This is bad," muttered the second nurse, Cathy Taylor.

Frantically Presner changed the defibrillator to cardioversion and fired again; this time, the resulting tracing drew a cheer from the gathering crowd of nurses and medical students.

"Sinus tach!"

"You got a pulse?"

"Weak. Femoral."

"How much fluid in?" asked Keating.

"One liter."

"Faster, dammit! And where's the blood?"

"Coming! One minute," said a voice from the back of the room.

"Now!" he screamed. "STAT means STAT goddamit!"

"We're trying!"

"Shit, we lost it," said Presner, looking at the monitor. "Fib again." There was a mumbled groan in the room. "Epinepherine! One amp!"

Hammond, prepared, her hand already grasping the syringe, injected the clear solution into the vein. It worked. A more normal heart rhythm returned. "Sinus Tach. And she's got a pulse again."

"Good," grunted Keating.

"Got a pressure?" asked Presner.

"Manual of sixty," said Taylor finishing a reading. Several people cheered.

"Blood here!" screamed a voice from behind. "Four units, O-neg!"

"Yes!" shouted Presner.

"About time!" grunted Keating.

"Piggyback it in. Get me the pressure bags," said Hammond to the others, her eyes flashing and her hands manipulating the IV ports.

"I'll pack her," said Presner as the nurse handed him the equipment.

"I want those labs in two minutes," screamed Keating, "And get the blood in. Six units. Fast!"

The nurses moved with an effortless, well-practiced precision, attaching the new tubing to the established IVs; within a minute, the blood poured through the wide-open IV lines into the veins of Molly Loomis's forearms. As soon as the first units were empty, they were replaced with two more.

As the minutes passed, Molly's pulse rate, first established at 175, slowed, and her blood pressure rose as the life-saving blood circulated again through her heart and lungs. Her color, once an ashen gray, turned incrementally to a shade of soft peach-pink.

"Six units in," said Hammond, eyeing Molly's vital signs on the monitor. They were now approaching normal.

"Still bleeding like crazy," said the second nurse, watching as a pool of blood dripped from the vinyl, padded gurney onto the floor. "A unit in, a unit out."

"She needs to be explored and fast," said Presner. "We're just holding our fingers in the dike."

As the words were said, Dr. David Frissell, the trauma surgeon on call, hurried through the crowd, slipping between onlookers to the gurney where Molly lay unconscious, her body covered by a heavy, warm blanket.

"Hey, Dave," said Keating, his hand still on Molly's pulse. "Vag bleeding. Massive. Down multiple units. Got six in, so she's at least still with us."

"History?" asked Frissell, adjusting the stained white lab coat over his lanky body and ill-fitting surgical scrubs.

"We have a report, supposedly from the husband, that she has a history of one miscarriage and that she was pregnant."

"How far?"

"Ten weeks."

Frissell glanced at the blood on the gurney and floor. "Lotta blood for a ten-week miscarriage, Ken."

"I know."

"Any other history?" he asked, placing his hand on Molly's lower abdomen and running his fingertips carefully over the tip of the small uterus.

"No."

"Anything at the scene?"

"Not that we know of. Just blood."

"Family?"

"The husband found her at home. He may be on the way," said one of the paramedics.

"Dammit," said Frissell, his temper flaring. "We don't have time for maybes. Where the hell is he?"

"Really drunk," said the paramedic. "I know the guy. He's sort of a sports bar stud. He was throwing up his guts last we saw him. I'm not sure he wasn't calling 911 for himself."

"Wonderful," muttered Frissell, his jaw clenched and his almond-colored eyes narrowing to slits. "What do you think it is, Doc?" asked the paramedic. "Retained placenta?"

"No," said Frissell evenly.

"Ectopic?" asked a nurse.

Frissell became quiet. "I wish."

"OR six is ready, Dr. Frissell," came a voice from the doorway.

"Let's go," he said, turning toward the door before being stopped by an arm.

"Any chance to save it, Dave?" asked Keating. "She's young."

Frissell looked carefully at the ER physician and did not reply. He glanced back at Molly and the blood pressure monitor.

"I know," said Keating, seeing the same sight. "You'll be lucky to save her."

"I'll see what I can do," said Frissell softly. "I'll try."

Five minutes later, the circulating nurse finished the prep as Dr. Frissell backed into the operating room holding his arms aloft.

"Evening, Dave," said the anesthesiologist, Dr. Daniel Tribble.

"Danny," he said, nodding as the first scrub nurse gowned and gloved him.

"Dr. Frissell, we're low on the O-loop. Can you use something else?" she asked.

"Whatever," he said, lost in thought.

"Admission crit was fifteen," said Tribble.

"Shit. Got some more blood?"

"She's A-pos. Got eight units ready. FFP and platelets if we need 'em."

"Nice," said Frissell, fastening the drapes to Molly's exposed skin while the nurses attached the suction and cautery. "Lab is moving for once."

"What do you think?" asked Tribble.

"I'm sure it's a perforation. No other way."

"Better get going. She's pouring it out as fast as we're pouring it in."

"How are her vitals?"

"Stable, but we're living on the edge. We need the bleeding stopped."

Frissell took a scalpel and started. Switching to cutting cautery it took him less than a minute to cut through the walls of the abdomen. He opened the peritoneum, and a torrent of partially clotted blood exploded out of Molly's abdomen and onto the drapes and floor.

"Christmas," muttered a startled Frissell. "Suction! Two yankours!"

Immediately the two scrub nurses thrust the large plastic-tipped suctions into the pelvic cavity as the stream of blood flowed endlessly outward, mushrooming toward the surface like a newly tapped well.

"Whoa," said Tribble looking at the deteriorating vital signs on the monitor. "What the hell is that?"

"Major bleeding," said Frissell, already sweating heavily. "Major."

"Can you get control?"

"I'm packing. She's probably got ten units in there. It-it's bad," he stammered as he furiously packed the lower abdomen with a series of white cotton lap pads.

"You see anything?"

"Uterine, saw the fundus. It's what we figured."

"Nick an artery?"

"One or two."

With pressure from the packing, the bleeding slowly ebbed, and Molly's blood pressure, initially having dropped to 65/30, climbed again to 90/60. As they stood and watched the cardiac monitor recording the parameters, a technician arrived from the lab with four more units of blood and two units of fresh-frozen plasma for coagulation. Frissell's mind raced. His face felt flushed as he considered the options. Death was one not to be considered. She was only twenty-five, married, trying for children. Or was she? What had really happened? Drips of sweat continued to drain down the middle of Frissell's back, soaking both his scrub top and pants. He quit speculating and returned to his surgical plan.

"Ready?" asked Frissell.

"Go ahead," said Tribble, staring at the blood pressure. "She's as good as she's gonna get."

Frissell peeled the first of the lap pads out of the pelvis, his left hand gently retracting the intestines while the scrub nurses continued to suction the blood. With the removal of the third lap came a large swirl of bright red blood from deep within the cul-de-sac of the pelvis's lowest recess. Quickly Frissell pressed another into the clot and thrust his large suction against the pad, controlling the bleeding. Next, he peeled it laterally, looking for the source of the blood.

"See anything?" asked Tribble, his eyes intent on the rapidly dropping blood pressure as another percentage of Molly's blood volume disappeared into the suction canisters.

"Left lateral wall perforation. Another at the top." Frissell got only a brief look, as disaster hit quickly.

"Shit!" blurted Tribble as Molly's blood pressure bottomed out. "Big goddam trouble!" Frissell glanced toward the monitor and saw Molly's heart begin to speed. In seconds, it reached 180 beats per minute before the rhythm changed, and the tracing turned to a fine, oscillating line.

"Fib," shouted Frissell as he scrambled for the tray full of pads and gauze. He slopped a pile of the gauze into her abdomen and swung a towel over the wound. Tribble tore away the drapes and applied the defibrillator paddles to her chest. With the shock, Molly's body rose and fell.

"Damn!" cussed Tribble, as he stared helplessly at the potentially fatal heart rhythm.

"Shock her again," commanded Frissell.

"Clear!" said Tribble, applying the paddles and watching Molly's torso rise and fall again.

An instant later, the scribbling array of artifact caused by the shock left the monitor and the fibrillating rhythm of near death reappeared, running across the screen.

"Again," said Frissell, his strain obvious, but his voice weak. "We're not letting her get away."

Tribble, his right hand trembling slightly, drew up the adrenaline into the syringe and injected it into the IV. Tossing the used needle onto the anesthesia cart, he reached for the paddles and shocked her a third time with maximum current. Again the body rose and fell. The usual artifact appeared on the monitor, but when it cleared, a series of QRS complexes could be seen.

"Yes!" said Frissell, watching the heart's normal rhythm.

"Got a pressure?" asked the anesthesiologist.

Frissell felt her groin. A weak femoral pulse was present. "Yes."

"Nice," said Tribble breathlessly. "Got it on the art line too."

"Am I glad to see that!"

"Like an old friend."

Tribble adjusted his IV and turned up the dopamine drip he had started. He checked the blood pressure on the arterial line. 90/60. "She's fragile as hell, Dave," he said, automatically drawing up another drip. "She's not gonna tolerate much more of this."

"I know."

"We could lose her any time. We need it stopped."

"I know," he muttered. Frissell paused, staring at the blood-streaked drape tossed over the open wound. He slipped back into thought as the scrub nurses reassembled the sterile field, replacing the contaminated drapes and sponges. Frissell looked carefully at the patient still in his view, her eyes taped shut, her hair lifelessly on her shoulders. He saw the pale white skin and the faded, expressionless face. Who was this young woman? What secret did she hold? How had her life failed her?

He saw the clamps and the sutures positioned on the table and took a breath. There was no choice, he understood that. He had to do it. His decision now was not his own. Training had given him the knowledge to proceed with the confidence that his judgment would never be questioned. "Medically correct," the review would say. Frissell cursed the thought, a callous acquiescence to the inevitable. Medically correct, but still failure. He would save her. But he would change her life forever. He could do no more. Frissell drew a deep breath. He turned and extended his right hand. Immediately, the clamp slapped into his open palm.

At 12:30 A.M., Frissell stepped into the ICU waiting room and found a bleary-eyed young man sitting cross-legged on the floor, reading an old copy of *People* and sipping from a can of Coke. In the corner, a middle-aged couple sat beneath the dim light of an end table lamp reading a week-old newspaper. The room was silent, and the stench of alcohol was obvious.

"Molly's family?" asked Frissell tentatively.

"Yeah," grunted Troy Loomis, not looking up from the magazine for several seconds as he stared at the image of a partially clad, buxom movie star.

"We're her parents," said the woman, rising and walking forward to greet him.

"I'm Doctor Frissell," he said.

The man also rose and walked forward. Troy reluctantly came along, holding the magazine open to see the swimsuit-clad star.

"Frank Oberg," said Molly's father, a medium-framed man with thinning black hair, as he extended his hand. "My wife, Bev, and Molly's husband Troy."

Frissell shook their hands in sequence and without discernable emotion before motioning them to sit down. Molly's parents obliged. Troy also sat, but he carefully placed the magazine on an end table to keep the picture in view.

"She's a very sick young woman, but she's going to pull through," he began. "There was an awful lot of bleeding, and she required a lot of blood, but she's stable now."

"Oh my goodness," sighed a relieved Bev Oberg. "I'm so thankful."

Frank Oberg drew on his cigarette. "What exactly happened, Doc?"

"She was bleeding from the uterus into the abdominal cavity. Internal bleeding."

Bev Oberg's hand covered her mouth. "She was pregnant, you know. They've been trying for children."

"Another miscarriage?" asked Troy. "She's had that once before."

"No," said Frissell gently. "She had a uterine perforation along the posterior-lateral wall and at the apex."

"What does that mean?" asked Bev.

"Yeah?" grunted Troy.

"I'm sorry, Mr. Loomis, she was bleeding severely. We had to remove the uterus to save her life. She had to have a hysterectomy."

"Shit," muttered Troy.

Bev Oberg began to cry. Her husband put his arm around her. Everyone was stunned. "What's this about these perforations?" asked Frank.

"Two of them. Iatrogenic."

"What the hell does that mean?" asked Troy.

Frissell paused, his instincts wishing to betray his obligation to the truth. He plunged forward. "She did not have a miscarriage. She had an abortion, probably earlier today, and the procedure accidentally caused the perforations."

"Oh my goodness," exclaimed Bev Oberg, dropping her hands to her sides.

"What?" cried Frank. "What in the hell are you talking about? Are you crazy?"

Frissell shook his head.

Frank Oberg appeared to turn white with rage. "Are you sure?"

"Yes," said Frissell definitively.

Troy Loomis looked away, his jaw clenched, and said nothing, his fingers twirling his cigarette like a baton.

"For Chrissakes," cussed Frank Oberg. "Why in the hell would she do that! She wanted kids."

"I don't know," acknowledged Frissell.

"I mean, she's Catholic," Frank said, his anger barely controlled.

"She doesn't really go much to church anymore," interrupted Bev.

"We're ushers in the goddam church! It's half our lives! We give ten percent. Bev volunteers."

"She murdered my child," said Troy deliberately, seeking sympathy.

Molly's parents stopped. "Oh my God," said Bev, turning to him and gripping his arm. "I'm so sorry, Troy."

"And I wanted this one so much," Troy said, feigning emotion while looking away to steal a peek at the babe in the magazine.

"I'm sorry, too, Troy," said Frank, his anger cooling slightly. "I really am. She shoulda' treated you better. You deserve more than this."

"Thanks," he said, trying to sound upset, but secretly relieved that Molly had had the abortion and the hysterectomy.

Bev took Troy's hand, falling for his act completely. Troy realized Bev's slight movement might allow her to see the magazine. He closed it before she noticed; for added emotional effect, he hugged her.

"All these years, I'm just sorry we haven't been closer," Bev said to Troy after they broke apart a minute later.

"I know," replied Troy.

"She doesn't deserve children," Frank said disgustedly. "Anyone who would do a thing like that—"

"No, she doesn't," agreed Bev.

Troy continued to manipulate. "And a baby would have been so great. For everybody."

Molly's mother grabbed her son-in-law again, as tears streamed down on her cheeks. "She doesn't deserve you, Troy."

Frank took two steps away. His anger surged. "I don't know when I've ever felt so, so—" he stammered, grinding his fist into his open palm. "Never, never, never. She deserves whatever she gets."

"I know you two have had some trouble," Bev said, stepping back from Troy but still holding his hand.

"We now sure as hell know why," Frank snapped.

"If there's anything we can do, Troy," said Bev. "Anything."

"We'll understand," Frank nodded. "Whatever you decide about the marriage—neither of us could blame you."

"Thanks," Troy muttered, trying hard to look sad.

Dr. Frissell stood silently, expressionless, as he watched the spectacle. It was not up to him to pass judgment. He knew that. His duty to these people was over. His obligation was to his patient. His voice stayed gentle. "Molly's still very sick, and she's been through a lot. She's going to need a great deal of support to get through all of this."

They looked at him curiously, their momentary reverie broken by the doctor's strange thought.

"You can be damn sure I'll have plenty to say to her," Frank muttered, turning toward the back wall and lighting another cigarette.

Frissell ignored it. "She'll be in the recovery room for about an hour, then transferred to the ICU. I would guess she'll be in intensive care for a day or two. You can see her as soon as she gets there, maybe an hour."

"I don't even want to see her," Troy said, walking toward Frank who was now standing next to the windows.

"Thank you, Doctor," Bev said politely, extending her hand.

Frissell felt awkward. "You're welcome. I'll let you know if there's any change."

Five minutes later, Frissell stood at the foot of Molly Loomis's bed in the brightly lit recovery room. The nurse stood on his left charting the vital signs.

"You hear?" she asked.

"Hear what?" he asked, sounding preoccupied.

"Night supervisor was just here. This patient didn't have preauthorization for any of this. You know what that means."

Frissell waved at her, signaling her to quit. "Not now. Not tonight. I can't handle it."

"I never can," replied the nurse. "But it's just sad what's gonna happen. ComHealth's gonna break her."

"I know."

Frissell walked away. Words mingled in his brain. He felt grief. He felt shock and anger. What had happened? What could possibly have happened? He knew he didn't know the answer, but at the midnight hour, David Frissell grieved for Molly Loomis. Somehow he understood. Life was often indecent.

Before he left the room, he turned and looked at his patient one final time. Under the warm cotton blanket she lay still, her face pale, her eyes closed, the breathing tube taped around the corners of her mouth. Her only sign of life was the regular sound of the heartbeat as it traced across the monitor above the bed. Frissell closed his eyes. It was tragic, he thought. In an hour she would wake and in a few days, go home. She, like so many other patients, was destined to leave his life after one post-op check. But he also knew that both of their lives had been forever altered by this brief meeting. She would survive. He had assured that. But in doing so he had sentenceded her, her penance, a return to the world that had provoked her moment of horror.

Frissell left the room and closed the door. What did the future hold for Molly Loomis? he wondered. He knew that it was his fate never to know. The thought saddened him. But as he turned and walked away, he also knew that he would never forget her.

Chapter Two

June 2   7:00 P.M.

Within the Hilton Hotel's opulent Imperial Ballroom, the chief executive of Community Health One, H. Carter Hutchins, stood on top of the world. Enveloped by his shareholders' adoration, he waved his arms in a gradually widening arc. While the applause descended upon him in wave upon wave, his carefully practiced expression moved from cool temperance to unabashed joy. Methodically he waved in succession to every darkened corner of the ballroom as his flock stood before him, roaring furiously in a prolonged tribute he both expected and deserved.

As he had for ten minutes, Hutchins continued to massage the crowd. Mesmerized by the adulation, the CEO smiled to his left and then turned and pointed gracefully to his right. Following an emerging pattern, he acknowledged one section of the room, then another, and with each new gesture Hutchins was drenched in another soaking wave of cheers. Continuing to absorb every sight and sound, he appeared ready to let his glorious moment continue indefinitely, but after ten more minutes, the room finally started to tire. Hutchins, sensing their fatigue, waved his arms benevolently, pleading for their silence, and gestured for them to sit.

"In my fifty-one years, it has been my great privilege to work for a number of fine organizations, but never did I envision a moment where I would stand before a group of people to whom so much is owed and to whom I feel so much gratitude. As you know, when we undertook this mission a few short years ago, we were faced with a system of burgeoning costs, diminishing enrollment, and open market warfare over one-eighth of our nation's economy. Tonight, I say that our battle is now but a memory. We have triumphed."

As the room erupted, the CEO took a half step back from the podium and allowed the adulation to envelope him again. He smiled, nodded, and allowed the cameras a good view. He was tall, but not noticeably, his tuxedo cut to conform to the shape of a muscular man, only five pounds from ideal. His hair was perfect: thick black, parted left of center and combed backward at an angle, and accented with a gradually increasing quantity of rim gray. His dark eyes were intense, deep-set, and somewhat hidden by thick brows and an angular face. Not classically handsome, but clearly a man of profile and notoriety, he radiated an air of distinction and masculine indifference that was persuasively sexual.

When the applause slowed, he stepped forward and started again. "We stand together now on the threshold of a new era. Beseeched by the demands of a deserving public and responsive to the needs of future generations, we have created a system which will stand as a monument to enterprise, a tribute to excellence, and a gift to the needs of all Americans. In the last three years, we have taken a system floundering in the depths of disrepair and converted it to a model of stability and profitability. For this, and your support, you are to be thanked; for it is your faith and your vision which have allowed us to move forward with the ideas that will allow health care to be affordable, convenient, and progressive for all Americans for generations to come." He nodded affirmatively as they interrupted him again.

"Tonight we celebrate a landmark year—one in which we have experienced unparalleled growth in enrollment and revenues, unprecedented expansion of business contracts, and an explosion of capital acquisition." Hutchins paused for effect. His eyes narrowed as he tried to appear casual. "And not to mention that the stock value has climbed from 8 to 46 ½."

With these words, the audience leaped to their feet. Deafening cheers, liberally spiced with various calls, hoots, and yowls pushed the beaming CEO one step back. Hutchins turned again, pointing to a number that was now flashing on a screen behind the podium. His red laser pointer circled it thrice, each time with a slow, crawling arc over the top of the eleven figures and a tantalizing, rapid swoop underneath to increase his effect. With each turn, the ovation grew louder to an ear-splitting roar, and the room now stood together, even hotel staff held in Hutchins' grip.

"Ladies and gentlemen!" he roared. "Your net profits for the fiscal year—four hundred and sixteen million dollars!"

With these words, the Imperial Ballroom became a frenzy of delight and motion. Men howled and pumped fists into the air with repetitive force, fueled by the magnifying effects of their financial lust and the mesmerizing spell of alcohol. Women held both open hands to their faces, their heads toward the ceiling, feigning emotion. Dignity and discipline evaporated. In a tumultuous wave of hysteria, the shareholders slapped hands, beat their chests, hugged, and toasted. They cheered, cried, and swirled their goblets, all swallowing the contents with a tongue-swirling flourish, as if relishing a nectar blessed by the divine.

After five minutes, the roar from his wealthy shareholders lessened slightly, and Hutchins, sensing it and prepared like a conductor, raised his own goblet high into the air. He appeared to savor a reflection against the golden light above him. The room quieted as the shareholders turned toward him and raised their own glasses in preparation for the first of many anticipated official toasts.

"To ComHealthOne!" he shouted, thrusting the goblet toward the ceiling. "Tonight, to this past year! And to tomorrow and our unparalleled destiny!"

The toast, greeted with a disjointed wave of the sound of clinking glasses, was followed by a momentary pause as his two thousand breathless dilettantes sipped, swirled, and swallowed with fervor and inebriating energy. More was poured, and Hutchins quickly held his glass aloft again.

"And to you and your faith in our noble purpose!"

Again the shareholders cheered recklessly and drank with wanton excess.

Their cheers were for Hutchins, but it was their moment as well. They had grown rich with the rise of the great HMO and with Hutchins, stood poised for more. The CEO's words were all true. Destiny was no longer hyperbole, reality was no longer fantasy, potential was no longer a myth. Four years Hutchins had been given. He succeeded in less. His achievement, although not unprecedented, was merely unsurpassed. He was, as he had promised—the best.

For Harrison Carter Hutchins, it had always been that way. He stood above all even as a teenager, not by power or privilege, but by a hidden moral authority based solely on his conviction. Genius, he called himself. Strong-willed were his parents' words. Others were always less kind.

The youngest of three brothers growing up in Rockford, Illinois, the youthful Harry Hutchins was an angry loner. Friendless by design, unsuccessful in the classroom, and ignored by his high school classmates, Hutchins determined that isolation and introspection were the price of future greatness. Convinced that his peers were wasting their lives on foolish diversions such as grades, relationships, and extracurricular activities, the angry young Hutchins rationalized his youthful failures as the sacrifice necessary for his eventual prominence.

Relishing his martyr status, he occupied himself with reading. Salinger, with the misunderstood Holden Caulfield, held special appeal, but his love was biographies of business icons of the past, Rockefeller, Carnegie, J.P. Morgan, and others. These were men of significance. Titans who both built and conquered. Powerful men who rose from obscurity and achieved a lifetime of domination. Great men, as was his destiny, who achieved respect, power, fame and fortune. These were his goals. And nothing would stop him. Nothing.

High school ended quietly. So did college. In between, he continued to languish in a world of mediocre grades, isolation, and conviction that the world was foolishly failing to appreciate his celestial blessings.

Graduation was followed by depressing entry-level life at TMS Manufacturing with a small apartment and no car. He was in a hurry, and his early experiences in the business world were encouraging. He moved up rapidly, primarily because he soon succeeded in suppressing all scruples. He discovered that results were all that mattered; night and day he worked to advance, stepping over or sabotaging anyone in his way. His ruthlessness, combined with a growing confidence and political savvy, made him a force; four years and three promotions later, he jumped ship, leaping into a job no one else wanted. His instinct told him it would change his life. At twenty-six, it was time to fulfill his destiny.

In 1972, the University of Illinois medical system was in utter disarray. Academically sound, but financially struggling, it was already debt-ridden by the crushing burden of uninsured patients. Hutchins accepted a job as Director of Finance, a position unfilled for two years. Three years later, with his boss's health-related retirement, Hutchins rose to Vice President. But this time, he did so not by destroying his competition, but through his own merit. He adopted an idea about health insurance that captured many imaginations. The plan would return all the power in health care to the insurance companies. Reimbursing hospitals and doctors only a fixed amount per covered patient would force the providers to severely cut costs if they were to remain profitable.

The idea was revolutionary. To that point, medical care in the United States had been based on a fee-for-service system where physicians and hospitals were reimbursed by the insurance companies and were paid increasing sums for increasing care. The HMO concept was to prepay, so that all the money to be collected was already in the accounts of the hospitals and the clinics, meaning that the more care delivered, the lower the profit margin.

UniMedOne was Chicago's first HMO, serving parts of the south and west sides. Gradually it expanded to the north side. During this time, thirty-three-year-old Hutchins left the university to be the publically owned corporation's first chief executive. Rapidly, the subscriber base increased as Hutchins directed the HMO to seek enrollment from the wealthier, younger, and healthier Chicagoans—those less likely to consume health care. Undercutting the traditional insurance companies and appealing directly to large employers as a cheaper alternative, by 1979 UniMedOne controlled 10 percent of the Chicago market. At the same time, Hutchins' salary as CEO rose to $250,000, and the value of his stock options was estimated at $6.1 million. In 1981, Hutchins engineered his biggest coup to date, a merger with another large Chicago-based HMO, PremierCare. PremierCare was failing badly, beset by poor management and large, poorly paying Medicaid contracts. Three months later, the new merged HMO, CareOne, was profitable. It became so by dropping 75 percent of its Medicaid contracts and canceling all high-risk subscribers. His decisions were ruthless, leaving the poor uninsured, but the financial results were impressive. Hutchins' star continued to rise. At the age of forty-one, he was powerful and already exceedingly wealthy.

Several mergers with other small, regional HMOs followed, but by 1990, after eight years with CareOne, the ambitious CEO grew restless. He flirted with various insurance companies and HMOs with the hope of rekindling his earlier merger triumphs, but the Illinois market became stagnant, and no further expansion appeared possible. He knew he would need an additional triumph to realize another part of his life's destiny. In his dream, it would be a gesture of public service, an act of selfless genius at the cutting edge of medical reform that would allow him to leave his mark as the titans of industry had a hundred years earlier. The issues of the day were medical reform, downsizing, cost containment, and a return to the simpler times of less expensive, less impersonal care. H. Carter Hutchins decided he would not ride the wave, he would cause it.

In the fall of 1994, after the national elections ended any possibility of government-sponsored reform, the medical world sped forward with market-based "reform." As HMOs exploded across the country, billed as a cheaper way to deliver care and millions of subscribers flocked into the health plan, H. Carter Hutchins saw his opportunity. His idea would make his name a household word. It was novel, radical, and just happened to create enormous executive wealth. It was called vertical integration.

Horizontal integration had long been part of medical practice, groups of doctors joining together to form multi-specialty or single-specialty groups in order to share costs and reduce overhead. Vertical integration combined the services provided by the physicians, hospitals, and insurance companies into large organizations called health systems. In theory, the new organization would thrive because it would control only costs. Redundant services would be eliminated, as would redundant personnel. But in reality, the implications were more ominous: the organization would control everything, from the medicines a doctor could prescribe to the number of days a patient could be in the hospital.

To visionaries like Hutchins, vertical integration was more important than simply creating a bigger HMO. The concept allowed for corporate control of one-eighth of the nation's economy, spinning it publically that businessmen would now run health care, making it lean, efficient, and affordable. With executive know-how, the giant HMOs and health systems were the salvation of a system too ill to survive. The salesmanship was stupendous. The public and the politicians agreed. Utopia was in integration.

Vertical integration proved to be a medical blitzkrieg, and CareOne pursued it with a vengeance, buying physician practices, hospitals, and clinics throughout the region. Their ability to reduce costs created a tidal wave of employers signing up with the HMO and soon spelled doom for nearly all of their competitors. Within a year, CareOne controlled the medical care of nearly the entire state of Illinois. For Carter Hutchins, the achievement was significant; it tripled his wealth.

Hutchins reveled in his success, adding homes, yachts and airplanes to his growing arsenal of diversions. But more importantly, he soon began to prepare for his final challenge before leaving the health-care sphere. He was well aware of the rewards for the man standing behind the tidal wave. Rewards he knew were his destiny. Rewards only his wife knew he wanted. Rewards such as political power.

He first met Celia Douglas in 1973. She was twenty-eight, the daughter of old Chicago money, and recently divorced from a Chicago-based commuter pilot of modest means. Celia had married on a rebellious impulse at twenty-one and six years later found herself languishing in a quaint two-bedroom apartment far from the upscale Lake Shore Drive visions she held. The divorce was quick and painless. Shortly thereafter, she met the young executive who matched her perfectly in temperament and ambition.

Their marriage in 1975 provided Hutchins with the perfect complement he needed. She cared only about wealth and social stature. He cared only about achieving it. Their marriage was flawless, and as their wealth grew so did their reputation and social standing. She attended to a wealthy woman's role, doing very little of importance, while he attended to something significant, making more money. In between, they raised two sons, providing them private education and Ivy League access. Their time in Chicago was enormously rewarding, but when their sons left for their East coast appointments, Carter and Celia decided to leave Chicago, and CareOne, for Minneapolis and his biggest challenge yet, the chairmanship of the country's largest HMO, Community Health One.

Hutchins took the job in 1996, and within months ComHealthOne, using Hutchins well-practiced techniques, was steamrolling through the state and the region vertically integrating hospitals, doctors, clinics and insurance plans into one HMO behemoth. Even Hutchins' former employer, CareOne, fell under ComHealth's grip, merging with ComHealthOne in 1997 and adding 500 hospitals and 8.2 million subscribers to the growing empire. By 1998, most of

Wisconsin, the Dakotas, Iowa, Nebraska, Indiana, and Michigan had also come under his control.

By 1999, H. Carter Hutchins had become one of the ten wealthiest men in America and was mentioned prominently as the next Republican candidate for Governor of Minnesota. With medical inflation slowing nationally, Hutchins was hailed as a hero, a genius, and the man who had saved health care.

As Harrison Carter Hutchins gazed out across the ballroom at the landscape of admiring shareholders, he turned to his beaming wife Celia and motioned for her to join him at the podium. Together they stood in the light as the delirious applause continued to rain down upon them. Hutchins applauded the shareholders and thanked them for the opportunity. The shareholders applauded him, for he had made them rich.

Hutchins stepped back and waved. Then, as planned, he kissed his wife. The moment was captured by his photographers and the minicams that he had stationed at the back of the room. Hutchins stepped forward again and held up a fist. The cameras continued to roll. The scene seemed to go on forever. But as they applauded, no one in the audience doubted it. His wife did not doubt it. H. Carter Hutchins was indeed a man of destiny. The CEO beamed down at the crowd. He knew he had arrived at the top of the world. But he also knew something else. The top of the world was only a stepping stone.

Behind the applause one man stood alone. Hidden behind a pillar in the room's far corner he made no attempt to applaud or be seen. Instead, he stood motionless, staring intently at the CEO. The man was nondescript. His build was average, and his face was without distinction. His suit was several years old, and his manner was that of any hotel guest who happened to drop in. But this man was no ordinary spectator. He was the one man Carter Hutchins never wanted to see again.

While the CEO's canonization continued, the silent observer never blinked. Instead, his blue eyes held firm their gaze and absorbed every second of Hutchins' glory. It had been three years since he last saw Carter Hutchins, and he knew that even appearing at the ceremony was a risk. During that time he lived with the knowledge that every breath could be his last, but now the risk he took to watch the man who destroyed so many lives seemed worth taking.

He had long wished for revenge. He had planned and plotted, hiding in shadows. But until a week ago, every plan was meaningless because the proof was incomplete. Instead, they were merely the idle thoughts of a broken man. Then it had happened. A mistake. An opening. And suddenly everything was different.

He watched as Hutchins brought the crowd to its feet again. The man even briefly applauded, thinking only of his own good fortune. A hint of a smile appeared on his lips. Three years of work to avenge the one he loved, he thought, and it came to nothing. And in one instant, it all changed.

James Patrick O'Reilly turned and left, disappearing without notice into the star-filled night. He had much work to do. Lives were at stake, including his own.

As he passed through the cool, fresh, air toward his old pickup, he realized for the first time in three years he felt hope.

"Thank you, Molly Loomis," he muttered. "And pray to God I'm in time."

Chapter Three

June 15

The Third Street Clinic sat in the middle of crumbling old buildings on a dead-end street on the north end of Minneapolis. At the edge of a vista of dilapidated public housing, it stood within sight of the regal skyscrapers that composed the city's expanding skyline. The clinic was bordered on one side by a vacant brick warehouse, which contributed two rooms to the clinic for storage, and on the other side by an equally rundown series of decaying houses, home to transients and a variety of cats and dogs.

The clinic itself sat in a largely intact brick, single-story building. The entryway was three chipped cement steps, which rested beneath a graying overhang and led the way to a torn screen door and a weathered wooden door that was heavily padlocked. The two cracked windows sitting on each side of the entryway had succumbed to the neighborhood's danger six years before and now were guarded by black iron bars and a well-known alarm system.

Third Street Clinic had been founded in 1940 by Dr. Edward Berger as an independent practice serving the blue-collar neighborhoods of the north side. As Minneapolis's heavy industry had yielded to technology in the 1960s, the once robust neighborhood had moved south and west, leaving behind a trail of falling real estate values and an immigration of poverty, alcoholism, and drugs.

After Dr. Berger's retirement in 1965, the clinic faltered, leaving the area without medical service except for the emergency room at Hennepin County Medical Center three miles away. With the clinic's threatened closure, the state had deemed it a necessary asset and began providing financial assistance in the form of a yearly subsidy through federal money in the newly-formed Medicaid program. This provided some money to keep the clinic open, but left the doctor issue unresolved. No doctor in his right mind would want to practice in such a horrible area.

In order to attract doctors, the government came up with another program. Medical students who sought state financial aid could receive partial tuition waivers if they agreed to practice in under-served areas for a period of time. Marginally successful in most areas, it worked little better for Third Street Clinic. Since 1966, doctors indebted to the government had come and gone in three-year stints. Most arrived with high hopes, full of spirit and altruism. After their obligation was over they always left, overwhelmed and discouraged. Every physician had left in a hurry, except the last one, Peter Colder.

Although the Third Street Clinic did not open for fifteen minutes, Letisha Moore opened the front doors to allow inside the first of a long line of people already lined up outside. A light drizzle, that had begun just after midnight turned heavier. This, combined with a growing wind and the threat of lightning, told Letisha it was time to get the patients inside. The clinic's secretary of two years was short and heavy with shoulder length dreadlocks, a series of gold-studded earrings and light black skin. Outgoing and engaging, Letisha enjoyed her job and did it well. On this day, as always, she greeted nearly all the patients by name as they passed by into the building. Then she walked the thirty feet to the side door of the old factory and opened the padlocks, directing the remaining patients inside to wait in the ground floor hallway that the clinic used for overflow.

As they entered the factory single file, Letisha happily continued her greetings, assuring them that the wait would not be too long. Returning to the clinic, she handed out a registration form to each of the patients and took a seat behind her desk at the back of the spartan waiting room to wait for Sylvia Caspers to emerge. Caspers, the clinic's nurse was sixty-two years old, tall and graying, with black eyes and a patrician manner easily misinterpreted as arrogant or aloof. She was the clinic's greatest asset and the last remnant of its profitable years. Hired originally by Berger, she had worked continuously while raising her four children and steadfastly maintained a fierce loyalty to any doctor as dedicated as she. She routinely worked sixty hours a week, knew every patient's history by heart, and said little when her paycheck periodically bounced. She loved the reward of helping patients; little else mattered to her. Widowed for five years, she had made the clinic her central focus, and teamed with Dr. Peter Colder, the clinic had been somewhat rejuvenated.

Colder had arrived five years before from the University of Iowa, having finished his family medicine residency. Indebted to the government for his partial med school tuition waiver, he landed the job at the Third Street Clinic by losing a job lottery, but by the end of three years, he came to enjoy his niche in an area of need and had re-enlisted despite his wife's objections. His lack of interest in money or vacation cost him his marriage the next year, but the clinic provided him both a purpose and a family. The salary was poor, the hours were long, and the medical problems were staggering, but Colder never felt more needed. The neighborhood rejoiced when their doctor decided to remain.

Ten minutes after the doors opened, Sylvia Caspers ushered the first patient into the examining room, an eighteen-year-old girl with a sinus infection. Into the second room went an elderly man with a swollen big toe from his recurrent gout. With the beginning of the day, Colder slipped into the familiar fast-paced routine. Ten-minute appointments were the norm. Each started with Sylvia placing a patient in an examining room. Next she measured vital signs and took a list of medications the patient was currently using. Colder came in next; following his exam, he would attempt to answer all questions. Sylvia then escorted the patient to Letisha's desk to make return appointment. It was always hurried, but everyone was accustomed to the fast pace of the clinic, realizing the wait that all would face if Dr. Colder spent extended time with any one individual. The routine was accepted, and the clinic moved well.

After two and a half hours, Peter Colder left the first exam room, closing the door behind him, and handed the chart to Sylvia. "Right carpal tunnel. Why don't you give him a brace and have him come back in a couple of weeks."

"Small or medium?"

"Medium," he sighed. "How are we doing?"

"Letisha says there are still twenty in the factory. We've seen thirty-two."

"Okay," said Colder his thick dark hair already askew and his handsome face a bit weary, "we'll work through lunch. Why don't you run out and get something? I'll—"

"Mr. Sauer brought in a bunch of bagels for us. We can eat those," interrupted Sylvia.

"Beautiful," said a pleased Colder. "Any onion?"

Sylvia was jotting a note on a chart. "Two. He remembered that you liked those from last time."

"Gotta love the guy," Colder said smiling. "Just wish we could control his pain a little better."

"He seems to be doing pretty well. He certainly seems happy."

"We can be glad for that," Colder said. "Who's next?"

"A young mother with questions about her baby."

"How old?"

"Eight months. No English."

"Could you come in?"

"I thought you might ask," Sylvia said, grinning.

Colder entered the room, followed by Sylvia, and greeted a nervous young Hispanic girl with a round and healthy-appearing baby. He staggered through a series of questions in disjointed, self-taught Spanish, which Sylvia clarified with her more polished dialect. The young woman spoke rapidly as she described a number of routine but mystifying developments that Colder patiently explained. One by one, they answered her questions until she understood each and every aspect of her child's growth and what to expect in the coming months. At the end, she shook their hands and smiled in relief at the realization her infant was not seriously ill before Sylvia guided her to the door and Colder moved to the next room.

As the noon hour arrived, the line shortened slightly and Colder gulped down two of the bagels that Mr. Sauer had left as partial payment. Pulling a Diet Coke from the refrigerator in the office, he sat momentarily, completing some of the morning charts.

Most of the patients of the clinic were uninsured or minimally insured and often brought simple gifts designed to make up at least part of the difference. Food was a favorite, liters of soda for all to drink. Trinkets and toys were also common. Some volunteered to clean. The clinic existed largely on a communal effort and the small amount of reimbursement that Medicaid paid. Money was almost nonexistent. Colder paid himself enough to pay his bills and save a small amount, living in a simple two-bedroom house about five miles from the clinic. Sylvia,

Letisha, and Sandra Becker, the part-time accountant, were paid as generously as the monthly statements would allow. Often all four went without paychecks.

As he munched on the last of his bagel, Colder turned to Sandra Becker, who had appeared about an hour earlier and was sitting at a card table that served as her desk. Stacks of paper and two file cabinets surrounded her. Sandra was thirty-five, single, with short, blunt-cut, orange hair and thick round glasses that made her light blue eyes look enormous. She was reclusive, compulsive, an expert in Hollywood trivia, and dedicated to her four cats and a jungle of house plants. She worked two days a week for the clinic, cramming a full-time job into sixteen hours for part-time pay.

"How we doing?" Colder asked, his mouth half full.

"Well," she started, her eyes not moving from the top paper, "we have enough to buy a few Bandaids."

"That's good."

"No, it's not," she said, her hand moving gracefully over the keys of the adding machine. "Medicaid's office visits are going down another two dollars. We're gonna be in the red on everyone we see. That's seventy percent of the practice and rising."

"What about higher codes?"

"Not for the way we practice. If you're seeing them for only one problem that's all we can bill. If you start dealing with other problems you can bill more, but we'd never be able to handle the volume of patients that we have."

"Thanks to our ComHealthOne friends."

"Gotta admit they're slick," she said still staring at the figures. "ComHealth sells 'quality care for all' with a bunch of glossy brochures and then slides out of the Medicaid and welfare population knowing they're expensive to care for and have no money."

"But these people deserve care," Colder said firmly.

"No doubt, just that we're going to go broke doing it."

"Damn cherry picking," cursed Colder.

"You said it," she said, pausing to sip from her coffee. "Lots of lip service to the notion of care for all, but it's still care for profit and ComHealthOne is the best. They know that nobody can make money off a patient population that can't pay."

"The art is in avoiding them as patients."

"You said it again," Sandra sighed.

"How much do we have?"

"Total assets on paper, including the building, about $26,000, but I doubt you could get ten cents for the broken furniture in the waiting room, the nonfunctioning examining tables, or that metallic dinosaur you call an X-ray machine."

"What about in the money market?"

"Six thousand and dropping."

"At least we've got more than enough for payroll. We'll just have to increase volume."

"You see a hundred patients a day, Peter, only a third of whom can pay. ComHealth has completely cut you off from any patients with insurance. All those patients now go only to ComHealth doctors. You increase your volume, you'll just end up with more unpaid bills. The smart thing to do is to start reducing your nonpayers and send them to the emergency room."

"No way."

"We've had this discussion before."

"I know. You know how I feel."

"Without rejoining ComHealth, we'll be broke in four months."

"We've been here before."

"Never like this," she said shaking her head. "This time it's different. We're going down."

Colder looked defiant. "I'll never go back to ComHealth. I couldn't live with myself."

"Change your ways, kiss some butt. Do something."

"It's not that."

"Then what is it?"

"It's because we're not cost-efficient in their books and I don't care. We've got sick people with real problems who often don't speak English, have lots of children, have drug and alcohol problems, and who don't practice preventive medicine. You can't tuck them neatly into some damn medical cookbook that de-emphasizes care and maximizes profits."

"Peter, it doesn't matter if you're right, we're still going to go broke. We've got to fix the problem."

"I don't know," Colder sighed, finishing his Diet Coke. "All I know is I've got a factory full of patients who need care. I'll figure out the solution tomorrow."

"Is tomorrow a lottery drawing?"

"Funny."

"I'm not kidding, Peter."

Colder tried not to look defeated. "Neither am I," he muttered. Suddenly tired, he leaned back on the metal folding chair and closed his eyes, stretching his arms above his head. He knew Sandra was right, choosing to argue with her more to defend his desires than to discuss issues. He had no interest in the business side of medicine. He treated people who put their trust in him. He listened in confidence to the ailments and complaints. He treated willingly all who needed him, without regard to financial interests. Colder believed money had no place governing medicine. Corruption of care was inevitable.

"I'll think about the lottery," he said finally as he rose, buttoning his lab coat.

"I'll buy a ticket too," she said peering over her glasses.

Colder left her and walked into the hallway next to the examining rooms where Sylvia waited with a chart.

"Who's next?"

"Female. Mid-twenties. Never been here before."

"Name?"

"Molly Loomis."

Colder looked at her quizzically. "That's sort of familiar."

"She called here a couple of weeks ago wondering if we did abortions."

"I remember," he replied, nodding. "And now she's here?"

"I think she had the abortion. Wouldn't say much about it."

"She okay?"

"Seems a little shaky."

"What's up?"

"She just wanted to ask you a couple of questions."

"No problem." He looked at his nurse curiously. "But why do you say she's shaky?"

"I'm sure she's been crying. Her eyes are red. She's also got one heck of a shiner on the left and a very puffy lip. She *said* it was an accident."

"A fall?"

"She didn't volunteer and I won't speculate," she said, handing him the chart. "I'll clear you a little time for this. Some minor stuff can wait."

"Thanks."

Colder knocked softly at the door and entered without waiting for a reply. Molly Loomis sat in the corner in an orange plastic chair next to the examining table. She was dressed in blue jeans and a gray sweatshirt. Her brown hair was neatly pulled into a pony tail exiting through the back of a black baseball cap. Her sunglasses sat on a chair next to her, dangling from a small brown handbag. Her face appeared thin and worn, her pale complexion contrasting with the dark blue hue forming a crescent underneath her left eye. Both lips appeared swollen, the upper one with a small vertical cut to the right of midline. Molly's right hand trembled slightly as she rose to shake his hand, and after her blood-shot eyes returned quickly to the floor.

"How are you, Molly?"

"Fine, thank you. I'm sorry to trouble you, Dr. Colder. I know you're busy."

"Nonsense," he said. "Now what exactly happened?"

"Oh this?" she said, looking up and pointing to her eye. "Clumsy me. Troy, my husband, had been moving some things around the apartment and this carpet we have, he had rolled it up and I didn't know about it and when I came around the corner I tripped and fell right on the left side of my face. I guess I sure am ugly."

"Not at all," he said, staring at the cut on the right side of her upper lip. "I think it will heal up just fine. Mind if I look a little closer?"

"Go ahead."

Gently he felt along the rim of the eye and across the cheekbone, beneath the nose and along the jaw. "Hurt anywhere?"

"Not really."

"Were you knocked out?"

"No, I just feel so foolish," she said sheepishly.

"Any trouble with blurry vision or double vision? Ringing in the ears?"

"No."

"Trouble with taste, smell?"

"No."

"Anything drain from your ears or nose?" he asked feeling behind her ears and along her upper neck and staring at the semicircular bruises at the hairline behind each ear.

"No."

"Neck stiff at all?"

"No. I'm fine."

Colder pulled away. "You're going to be okay, but you had a heck of a fall. You have a small skull fracture."

"What?" she asked, surprised.

"Don't be worried. It'll heal perfectly, but you have a little bruising behind your ears. That's called Battle's Sign and means that somewhere at the base of your skull a small bone was fractured."

"It'll be okay?"

"Yes, but if you were to start leaking any fluid out of your nose or ears or you were to have persistent headaches, fevers, or a stiff neck you should come back and see me right away."

"I never figured it would be anything that serious."

"Falls can be dangerous. Do you remember anything else about it?"

"Not really," she said softly, still looking away.

"Well, if anything comes up, I'd like you to call me right away."

"Thank you. I will."

Colder sat back. "Sylvia told me that you had some questions you'd like to ask."

"Yes," she said as she reached for her purse and pulled a small handwritten note from the bag. "Recently I decided to have an—uh—abor—pregnancy terminated."

"Yes."

"Unfortunately, I had complications and the procedure caused internal bleeding. They had to do an emergency hysterectomy that night at HCMC."

Colder bit his lip. "Oh, my goodness, Molly, I'm sorry."

Molly tried to sound matter-of-fact. "I'm kind of okay now, but I guess I nearly died. I was pretty sick."

"How long were you in the hospital?"

"Eight days."

"I really am sorry," he said sincerely.

"No, no, I don't mean to burden you with that, I just had a couple of questions," she said, unfolding the slip of paper. "I hope you don't mind seeing me."

"I don't."

"After the abortion I lost my insurance coverage, and I was told that you saw patients without insurance."

Colder didn't pursue it. He knew the story all too well. "I certainly do."

"Everything happened a little fast, and I was a kind of confused at the hospital and forgot to ask some things."

"Understandable."

She looked at her short list of questions. "Will I have to have hormone replacements now that I had a hysterectomy?"

"No, assuming they didn't take your ovaries."

"They didn't."

"Then you won't have to."

"Okay. What about calcium? Will I get osteoporosis?"

"You will be no more nor no less susceptible than any other woman. At your age I would recommend a sound diet and no supplement."

"Good," she said, sounding relieved. "Thank you."

For a moment she hesitated, staring at the unevenly folded paper as if lost in thought before finally looking up toward his shoulders. "If I were ever to again, or if, when, I mean, sex. Will there be any problem?"

"No. None at all. Don't worry about it."

"Well, I never, um, I guess."

"Really, it will be okay."

"Thank you."

Colder tried to be reassuring. "You are perfectly healthy and normal except that you had to have a procedure that many women have for a lot of different reasons. Nothing will be any different except for child-bearing and of course, periods."

"I guess that's the good side," she said attempting a smile.

"Yes." He could see the sadness in her eyes. "But I suppose not a great trade off."

She looked down again, still shying from eye contact. "I suppose I'm a little more accustomed to the idea now. It was a shock at first. Maybe I wouldn't have been a good mother."

"I doubt that," he blurted out, sounding as much friend as doctor. "Besides. It's not impossible. You could be a candidate for in-vitro fertilization with a surrogate mother."

"You mean my egg, my husband's sperm, and another woman carries the child."

"Yes."

"I don't know, Dr. Colder. I heard about that, but that's so expensive. I know I could never afford it. And adoption, well, they look for totally stable situations."

Colder didn't push it. "If I can be of any help, Molly—"

"You have," she said looking up, her eyes moist. "Thank you." She stood and shook his hand lightly before dabbing her eyes with a Kleenex. "It's all enough to drive a girl to drink," she said embarrassed by her tears.

"Now don't start that," he said, lightly slapping her wrist.

"I won't," she said as she opened the door.

"Remember, call us if you need something."

"I will," she said as she began to walk away.

"Oh, Molly," he started as his curiosity and the missing pieces to her story got the best of him. "Mind if I ask you something?"

"No," she replied, turning to face him again, her sunglasses in place concealing the black eye.

"Sylvia reminded me that you called here a couple of weeks ago asking if we provided abortion services."

"Yes. She told me you didn't."

Colder looked at her curiously. His delicate question had opened the door. "How far along were you?"

Molly looked sad. "Ten or eleven weeks." Colder looked puzzled. Molly continued. "I gotta admit I would really have loved to have had that baby. But I had to."

"Do you mind if I ask why you terminated the pregnancy?"

"Not at all. The baby was positive for Fragile X."

Colder looked baffled. "What?"

"The baby was positive for Fragile X."

Colder paused and drew a breath. He did not want to appear stupid, but he had no idea what she was talking about. "Molly, tell me what exactly happened?"

"I had a blood test, my regular ComHealth doctor ordered it. A couple of days later I got a call from another doctor who came and visited me and explained that the blood test had confirmed the baby would have Fragile X."

"What did that doctor say?"

"That Fragile X is a horrible disease. It's genetic and that the children that have it are badly disfigured. They're also retarded and usually die before the age of two. He said that their deaths are usually painful. If they live longer, they're always in nursing homes."

Colder stood numb, his mind momentarily blank.

"He was a very nice doctor. Very professional. He also gave me a toll-free number that I could call to talk directly to an expert on it."

"And did you?"

"Yes, he explained everything in detail."

"You remember his name?"

"The doctor who visited me?"

"Yes."

Molly squinted her eyes and tried to think. "Uh, no. Oh wait. It was kind of an average name. Might have been Davis."

"You remember the phone number?"

"No, I threw it away." Molly saw Colder's perplexed look. "Is everything all right?"

Colder dropped it. "Sure," he said managing a weak smile and putting his hand lightly on her shoulder. "You take care of yourself, and as I said, call us if you need help."

"I will," she said nodding.

"And again, I'm sorry about everything that's happened. Our door will always be open for anything you need."

Molly smiled for the first time. "Thanks."

Colder paused. "One other thing. If you happen to run into that phone number will you let us know? I didn't know that service was operative. We hadn't gotten any official notification."

"I think I threw it out, but I'll look."

"Thanks, Molly."

"Thank you."

Colder watched as she turned and walked away, her small, frail frame moving gracefully and unnoticed through the growing crowd of the waiting room. In his mind he could still see the black eye and the puffy lip. He remembered her composure not concealing the lie. Sylvia walked up to him.

"What was that I heard?" she asked.

"Weird," said Colder watching her walk out the door. "Very weird."

"Thank you, Doctor," she replied with gentle sarcasm. "Now I understand perfectly."

Colder was in his own world. "Sylvia, have you ever heard of a blood test on a pregnant woman for Fragile X?"

"What? Fragile X? Are you kidding? I vaguely remember reading about the disease in a textbook years ago, but I couldn't tell you anything about it. A blood test on pregnant woman?"

"Yes. Molly Loomis says she had one."

Sylvia cocked her head. "I don't know. Could be new. We're not exactly MicroSoft in terms of technology here."

"I thought about that," he said. "But it's still not right."

"Why?"

"She got a home visit from a physician, and then a toll-free number to discuss Fragile X with a so-called expert."

"That doesn't seem so unreasonable."

"It wouldn't be," he said, turning toward her and staring her in the eyes, "except the disease that they were describing was not Fragile X."

Syvia was flabbergasted. "What?"

"It's not Fragile X."

The news hit Sylvia like a slap. "Th-the wrong disease? You've got to be kidding."

"I wish I was." Colder's mind began to spin.

"That's too weird."

Colder looked down, his face grim "It is weird. But more importantly, we both saw what this incident and, should we say *little mix-up*, did to her."

Sylvia turned thoughtful, the memory of the black-eyed Molly returning to her. "I know where I could ask a few questions about her hospitalization."

"Your friends at County?"

"Yes," replied Sylvia. "There are no secrets over there. I could do some digging."

"Start with her medical records. Then check to see if we're wrong and Fragile X can actually be tested for, et cetera."

Sylvia wrote it down. "I'll get right on it." The more she thought about the mystery, the happier Sylvia was that Colder wanted to pursue it. She felt sorry for Molly, and she was eager to start digging. As she started to walk away, Colder blocked her path. His face was unexpectedly grim, and Sylvia realized he wasn't telling her everything he was thinking.

"We have to remember the implications of a mix-up like that, if it was a mix-up."

Sylvia stopped writing. The enormity of it exploded upon her.

Colder continued. "There's a problem here. And it may be a big one. We're going to find out what it is—no matter what."

Sylvia watched him turn and walk away. She stood up straight, but her body jerked and she accidentally dropped her pen. With his words, a chill had unexpectedly run down her back.

Chapter Four

June 15

    The limousine carrying Celia and H. Carter Hutchins slipped through the thinning traffic of downtown, onto the freeway, and into a late-night rush of cars from the nightclubs on their way to the western suburbs of Minneapolis. The opera had been average, *The Marriage of Figaro*, with an overly sharp soprano and weak male voices. Bored, they had left their box at intermission to briefly attend a party with a variety of local political figures and their spouses at the governor's mansion across the river in St. Paul. After a notable entrance of firm handshakes and practiced pleasantries, they left early, at Celia's insistence, returning to the post-performance party at the Ordway Theatre, where Celia could obtain a more careful assessment of the women's gowns at the first major social event of the summer season.

    Her wish was rewarded as the elite of Minneapolis wealth responded in form for the close of the opera season, annually regarded as the beginning of summer. The men, as usual, were attired in black tie, but, as expected, it was the women who provided the show. The competition was intense, and as such their gowns were rarely from Minneapolis, a city where the social elite felt shopping consisted mainly of hunting attire and costume jewelry. Instead, most of these discerning women routinely ventured to Chicago to prepare themselves for coming seasons, with trips to the Miracle Mile in the spring, fall, and winter while on their way to the Caymans or Cancun. Some preferred Fifth Avenue or Rodeo Drive, considered superb substitutes, but a few quietly regarded any New York or Beverly Hills influence as a personal affront and an attempt to upstage.

    Celia Hutchins preferred Fifth Avenue, her Chicago society roots dictating that she shop in New York. Even as a girl, her sartorial sensibilities had been carefully cultivated, assuring her a lifetime of proper lines, tailored cuts, and coordinated color schemes. As she had matured, her loyalty had remained to Manhattan, its opulent flavor an ever-intoxicating mix of pronounced wealth and refined taste. She made four trips a year to New York, each a whirlwind tour of fashion consultants and spending orgy that satisfied all her needs for the next opportunity to be seen.

    This event had been different, however. Her husband's recent success, including articles in *Newsweek* and *Business Week* detailing his achievements, necessitated a most formidable appearance. Her gown was exquisite, an original for $16,000 and insured for considerably more. An oriental black silk with a deep V front and more daring back, its lightly padded shoulders yielded subtle waves of fabric that drew attention to her carefully accented bust. Her waiflike waist was held firmly by the smooth grip of the dress's midsection before it feathered gently to a flowing fullness, an acceptable four inches below the knee. Her necklace was new, a regal combination of diamond and emerald, a recent present from Carter to celebrate their ascent. Her ring was last year's four carat.

To her, the night had been perfect. The men had fawned over her, her darkly tanned skin highlighting her increasingly blond hair and aquiline eyes. Her weight, always minimal, had reached a new low and had been the subject of much feminine envy. Her dress had been a smash, her necklace a tower of light amongst a vista of miscellaneous metal and pearl. She had drunk little, gossiped much, flirted subtly, and with grace accepted the accolades of her envious admirers. As they sat in the back seat of the limousine, she felt dizzy and giddy, more content than she had ever been. H. Carter Hutchins simply felt drunk.

The CEO usually allowed himself little alcohol at functions of note, preferring the appearance of dignified moderation and sterling self-control. One drink, always a martini, held him for the evening. His rejection of further overtures was done with great flair, designed to maximize the impression of his importance and perfect self-discipline. His second and third drinks came later. They were always pre-prepared in the limousine, usually doubles, and they were downed quickly and frequently just as he passed out of sight of the exiting crowd.

Listening to Celia's requisite onslaught of fashion critique and society gossip after a party was always painful. He found that it was most easily dealt with by slowed neurons from an acceptable blood alcohol level. He loved his wife, but fashion talk and rumors bored him.

"Did you see Cassie Pollitt this evening?" she asked, turning on a vanity light and redoing her lipstick for no apparent reason.

"No," he replied indifferently, pouring and swirling his third drink.

"White, all white. Can you believe it?"

"Believe what?"

"For a summer dress."

"I thought white was for summer," he muttered.

"Now, darling, we've been through this so very many times. White is for weddings or I'd suppose for country western singers. That would go with their rhinestone shirts. But for anyone else? Certainly not for anyone with even a trifle of proper sense."

"I thought she looked good."

"I thought you didn't see her."

"I remember her now. Thought she looked very tan."

Celia looked startled and fearful. "Do you think she was more tan than I?"

Hutchins grimaced and looked out the window. He cursed himself quietly. It was so easy to dig a hole. "No, but it contrasted against the white."

Celia accepted it. "She probably wanted that. If you're going to wear a dime store dress, you'd better have something to draw attention away."

"It didn't look dime store."

"I was being facetious. But it was certainly no original, or even anything very good." She finished her lipstick and rubbed her hands lightly across the hair along her temples. "Do you think she's pretty?"

To a degree, Hutchins enjoyed his wife's neurotic fear of other women and its many side benefits. He had long since chosen to ignore the fantastic monetary expense her insecurities incurred. The fear kept her youthful and was thus a reflective tribute to his virility and his achievements. The neurosis also forced discussion of others that was more personal than appropriate, but sometimes titillating. "Yes, I think she's pretty, but certainly not as striking as you."

"Thank you, darling," she said, running her index finger from the side of her eyes and wiping the hint of a wrinkle clean. "I appreciate it even as a fib."

"Nonsense."

"I hear she's been sleeping with a governor's aide and that her front side got a little boost."

"Really?" he said, for once actually more curious than his question reflected. "Didn't you see them?"

"I thought that guy was her husband."

"Noooo, her breasts, silly!"

"Oh," he grunted. He went back to being bored. "How long has she been having the affair?"

"Couple of months now. He's only thirty-five. They met in the Bahamas."

"Husband know?"

"No. He's in Kentucky ninety percent of the time with their horses."

"Interesting," he said, looking out the window.

"And that name Cassie is ridiculous. She should go by Cassandra. Darling, do you think I need my eyes done?"

"Celia, you were the star," he sighed, well-prepared for this part of the discussion. "You looked absolutely dazzling. Even the governor was positively smitten."

"No, he wasn't," she giggled, barely able to control her glee. "He barely said hello."

"That's because he was afraid of embarrassing himself," he continued, grateful for the flood of vodka that was now piquing his creative senses.

"They were wonderful parties," she said, inviting more.

"I was afraid I was going to have to carry a gun to keep them away from you."

"No, no, no," she laughed.

"Those boys all looked like bulls eyeballing a tasty red target. My chivalrous duty would have been to kill them all."

"Oh, stop it," she laughed in an uncontrolled spasm of vain delight.

"I'm obviously going to have to watch you carefully, the way you look."

"You don't have to watch me," she said, leaning over and kissing him. "You know how I feel."

"You're still the most beautiful of all."

"It was the necklace that did it," she said, returning to her seat and fondling it.

"It's gorgeous."

"One of a kind. Like you."

She kissed him on the lips. "Thank you, darling."

The traffic thinned further as they headed into the wealthy western suburbs, and the lights were few when they turned from the freeway into a long, hill-laden stretch that composed the large estates of Deep Haven, Minneapolis's most exclusive suburb. A young suburb and a bastion of nouveau wealth, its sumptuous homes had been built largely on 1980s stock options, mergers, and exorbitant executive salaries. The Hutchins' estate sat atop a long, gentle slope on the pinnacle of fifty lightly wooded acres. A classic white Virginia colonial, its four great ionic columns guarded forty-five thousand square feet and twenty-eight rooms.

Five minutes later, seated on a couch in their spacious den, Celia kicked off her shoes and placed her feet on an ottoman.

"Liqueur?" asked Carter, standing behind the corner bar and in front of a wall of books.

"Chambord," she said stretching her legs.

"I'll make it two." Hutchins poured the liqueur and returned to sit down close to her.

"I never asked," she said, taking a small sip and basking in the warmth of the fireplace. "What did the governor say to you?"

Hutchins beamed. He knew his wife would sooner or later think of something other than the fact that she felt she had won all three critically important competitions: thinnest, most beautiful, and most expensively dressed. "He said I should seriously think about entering the race."

Celia sat up straight. Her triumphant reverie was broken. "What? Really?"

"Said that Simons probably doesn't want it and that I should think about it because lieutenant governors rarely win and that no one else has really stepped forward."

"Would he support you?" she asked, her eyes wide with excitement.

"He as much as said so."

"Oh my God!" she exclaimed, spilling a drop of the raspberry liqueur onto the couch. "This is positively the most exciting news! I'm breathless!"

"So was I," he admitted, his hand stroking her exposed knee. "He recommended I wait until early winter to announce, but should start forming an exploratory committee now."

"Oh, darling," she sighed, drawing a deep breath and placing her hand on his neck, loosening his tie. "This is beyond wonderful, beyond anything I could have imagined."

"Yes, it is," he said, stroking her thigh.

"I'll need another trip to Paris," she murmured, nuzzling his ear and pulling him toward her.

"Anything your heart desires," he said softly, his hands gently pulling her dress off her shoulders and his mouth lightly caressing the base of her neck.

Celia Hutchins was in heaven. "Right now, all I want is you," she whispered as she reached for his belt and pulled him on top of her. "Only you."

The familiar tears started to fall onto her cheeks as Molly Loomis wandered through the almost empty apartment. Everything was different. Everything was destroyed. Only the sound was unchanged; a persistent hum from the heating vent was the only reminder of the way things used to be. There had been no alteration in the three hours since she had returned, but she continued to survey each room as if pleading, in vain hope, that something would magically change. Her eyes searched the rooms looking for reminders and trying to assess her needs. In the living room, the couch was gone, as was the rug, upholstered chair, and television. The kitchen was equally barren. In the dining room, the table and chairs were remembered only by their prints in the carpet, and the bedroom's only piece of furniture was the guest mattress thrown onto the floor with a pillow and blanket tossed over its middle. Falling onto the mattress, Molly picked up the blanket and cried.

Since her operation, her life had been hell. For the week and a half after her discharge, Troy had barely spoken, condemning her to a purgatory of silent glances and simmering hostility. He wandered through the apartment freely, talking on the phone, watching TV, and drinking. His conversations with friends and other girls had been sympathy-seeking and riddled with hate for her. Her attempts to speak to him were rebuffed, rejected with a wave or a glance of overt spite. No physical contact was offered, and her suggestion that they at least talk was ridiculed. Finally one night, drunken with rage and filled with moral superiority, he left after a particularly vicious attack. Inside, Molly knew all too well that the abortion was simply an excuse for him to leave her, but that night's venomous verbal barrage still echoed in her mind.

Molly flopped onto her back and covered herself in the blanket. Even a week and a half after discharge she remained exhausted. The operation and hospital stay had consumed her. A slight pneumonia and vomiting had delayed her discharge, and her weight had dropped to 103, her lowest since high school. Her thin frame, weakened even more from the anemia of blood loss, looked too frail to even stand.

She opened her eyes. Tears blinded her, but the thought of what she had done returned. A life, a human life. It ate at her. Her responsibility. Her loss. How could she have been so stupid? So selfish? The questions still came. The abortion. God's will? God's wish for the baby? No, it wasn't, she admitted. But it had been for the child, she thought, and the horror a Fragile X baby's life would have been. Was it right? She didn't know that answer. She only knew she hated herself.

She rolled on her side. Her stomach ached. She couldn't see. And more than ever she was aware of how alone she felt. At first she left the hospital determined to resurrect the marriage, blaming herself for her deceit. But there was no chance. The marriage was over.

"Failure," she mumbled, restating again the guilt she felt. She failed completely as a wife. Failed in every way. It was her fault she had not made him happy, she was sure. Sexually she was a novice, with no experience other than him. Also, she had done little to learn how to please him, and even worse, had made almost no effort to make herself look more like a woman he would want. He preferred his women busty and blond. She was thin and flat-chested and regularly shied from makeup and hid from hairstyles that would make her prettier. It was a decision she now knew embarrassed him. "Ugly," she mumbled. "Ugly."

She had so many faults. She realized this now. At first Molly was hurt when he criticized her, but now she realized he was right. She asked him to help with housework and, at times, spend time with her. When his drinking was a problem, she nagged him. When he was angry, she fought back. She provoked. She frustrated. She failed.

Rolling again onto her back as the tears continued, she could see his angry face and hear the vile words again. "Slut" he called her as the back of his hand cracked into her temple. "Bitch" followed as he bloodied her nose. "Murderer" came next and was the last she heard. She remembered his fist emitting from her a shallow gasp as it pounded into her stomach, leaving her breathless and coiled on the floor. There were only sounds after that, interminable and incomprehensible, blocked by the words of her indictment circling in her mind.

Finally his haunting image left her. She lay motionless beneath the blanket. For hours she did not move, only an occasional tear and a normal rhythm of breathing hinting at life. She was broken, indecisive, not wanting to live but not wanting to die. She failed at school, failed as a mother, failed as a daughter, and failed as a wife. Now isolated from the world, her life became her sentence, her misery her penance.

Tossing aside the blanket, she stood up and walked back into the living room where only the faint sound of the fan from the ceiling air vent broke the silence. She stood before the small window that looked north toward the park. Opening the window, she heard voices in the distance, loud and laughing, interrupted only by a passing siren. She sat down under the window and leaned against the wall. Her stomach suddenly hurt. She crouched forward, her arms wrapped tightly around herself. She rocked gently back and forth and reread the letter she had received the day before.

Community Health One
IDS Center
One Tower Street—Suite 110
Minneapolis, MN 55417

June 11

Mrs. Molly Jane Loomis
2014-A N. 86th Street Apt 12
Minneapolis, MN 55419

Dear Mrs. Loomis:

This letter is written to inform you that a review of your account, claim, and medical care received during your recent hospitalization has been completed. Because your hospitalization was not preapproved by Community Health One prior to admission, all resulting care received, including all inpatient and outpatient procedures, diagnostic tests, and fees, remain entirely the responsibility of the patient and not of Community Health One.

In accordance with Section 4, part 2a of the General Subscriber's Agreement, all statements regarding unapproved care, your claim regarding your recent hospitalization has been

DENIED, *and your composite liability of* ***$113,878.94*** *will be solely your responsibility.*

This decision is final.

Sincerely yours,

Patrice Fallon
Senior Claims Analyst
Community HealthOne

cc: Gregory Alan Markham
*   Chief Operating Officer*

    As she read it, the tears that had previously stopped began dripping onto her cheeks. She continued to rock back and forth. Her stomach hurt even more, but she held tight, burying herself in the pain, the fear, and the understanding of the letter's meaning.

    Her world was gone, blown apart, shattered beyond recognition. She held no hope. Troy would not be back. Her parents' reaction was even stronger. They would not be back. Now she understood the truth of her failings and her fate. It was finished. No man would want such a woman. And worse yet, no one would care if she was gone.

    Suddenly she looked up and her eyes opened. It came to her. There was only one answer, a thought that had periodically occurred to her before. It was an ugly thought, but one that now returned.

    The sun had been down for an hour when Peter Colder opened the front door of his two-bedroom Cape Cod home. The house was empty and dark, its sparse furnishings occupied only by Mortimer, a sprawling ten-year-old tabby with a striped tail, white mustache, and a penchant for deliciously odorous feasts. Mortimer had been with Colder since the age of six weeks, slowly increasing in size to the girth of a small beagle and evolving toward the certainty that humans were designated exclusively for his servitude.

    As Peter turned on the living room light, the cat stood in the kitchen doorway adjacent to the foyer and looked sternly toward him, his eyes blinking in the bright light. Colder looked beyond him into the kitchen where the Friskies were splayed across the floor. He knew the bottom cupboard door shut poorly, and the bag of food inside was always an inviting target and convenient message whenever, in Mortimer's opinion, tardiness was displayed. The torn bag was tipped onto the floor.

    "Damn it, Mort!" he said, reaching down and scratching the cat's pleading neck gently. "You just spread it around, you never eat it."

    Mortimer didn't react, preferring to close his eyes in anticipation of a lengthy scratch. He purred loudly as his master ran his fingers between his ears. "How come you like to play with that stuff better than any of the toys I get you?"

Again there was no visible response other than a tilt of the head in order to assure each area of the head and neck was properly massaged.

The living room was still dark, and when Colder turned he saw the red light of the answering machine flashing intermittently. Leaving behind the cat, who nonetheless followed him, Colder sat down on the brown reclining chair that he had insisted upon during the divorce. The heavily beaten chair, always his favorite since medical school, had been his greatest settlement victory. He never suspected his ex-wife Julianne's well-conceived intention to exhaust his energy fighting for something she had no interest in owning.

Opening his eighth Diet Coke of the day and biting into the first of three carry-out tacos, he turned on the answering machine. The first message was from another insurance salesman wanting him to increase his life coverage. The second was from his mother. The third was from the phone company offering several more necessary options, and the fourth was from Julianne, again requesting custody of Mortimer. Colder played the message a second time and laughed at her tone, a mixture of humor and longing for a pet that he owned since before their marriage, but one that they both enjoyed. He also listened to the voice, soft but faintly sensual, in a calculated feminine manner which both knew still carried appeal to him. He missed the voice and he missed her; their marriage was a failure, but their friendship withstood the divorce. He played the message a third time and closed his eyes as the sounds echoed and momentarily held him.

The last message was from Sylvia, a regular occurrence, invariably caused because of her compulsive dedication. He slid lower in the chair, his eyes still tightly shut in fatigue.

"Dr. Colder, I just called you to remind you that you were going to call HCMC to get some information on Molly Loomis's stay. I was able to track down the basics. Surgeon was Dr. David Frissell. His pager number is 471-7534, and his home phone number is 925-6132. Molly's MP number was 465-435-985, and all of the County records are in the computer, so you can get them on-line. If not, we could have Letisha track them down tomorrow. Have a good night. Bye."

Colder sipped from the can of Diet Coke, the too-cold refrigerator having caused the soda to ice slightly, making it difficult to drink. Picking up the white touch-tone phone, he dialed Frissell's pager number, sent the page, and sat back, anticipating the inevitable ring within a few moments.

Molly Loomis's story had bothered him since her visit, running like an unsettling melody through his mind the entire day. Certainly she believed the Fragile X story and obviously so did others. But what could be the error? Was it Molly's mistake or someone else's? And if it was someone else, who was responsible? One thing was certain. It was hard to explain the error as innocent.

The questions running through his mind seemed endless, and he tried to assemble them. Sylvia's call provided one bit of encouragement. He was relieved to hear that David Frissell had been the surgeon. A medical school classmate, Frissell had been a partner in anatomy lab, compatriot in senior rotations, and a colleague during internship.

The phone rang four minutes after he sent the page, and David Frissell's tired voice greeted him with planned and acted anger. "Whattaya want, Colder?"

"You recognized the number," he said in mock surprise. "I thought you were ignoring me. You never write, you never call!"

"I have this sudden feeling of nausea gripping me. I believe it is the stench of all of the bull—"

"Body odor. You should shower more often."

Frissell, laughing audibly. "How are ya?"

Colder groaned. "Problems as always. Have to wear a club to keep the women away and the bank keeps calling, complaining that I'm depositing too much money."

"I know those problems. How do you manage a hundred different mutual funds and two hundred different women at the same time?" he joked.

"Skill and an exquisite knowledge of human anatomy."

"Only a surgeon has that, Colder."

"Fantasize all you want."

"So what's happenin'?" asked Frissell. "How you doing?"

"Good," lied Colder.

"Maybe I shouldn't ask, but how's Julianne?"

"I don't mind. New boyfriend. Geoff, good looking, studly type guy. Banker. Hate his guts."

"That's a reasonable reaction."

"You?"

"Good. Sandy's pregnant."

"Beautiful!"

"Yeah, this will be three."

"How are the boys?"

"Wild, endless energy. Can hardly believe how active a two- and four-year-old can be."

Colder laughed. "I can imagine." He took a drink from the can of Diet Coke, the ice now slowly melting. "I need to ask you a question, Dave."

"I figured this wasn't just social."

"You remember a patient named Molly Loomis?"

Frissell choked audibly. "Molly Loomis? God, how can I forget?"

"Yeah. She came to see me. But first, what can you tell me?"

"Professionally?" asked Frissell with a minor note of caution.

"Whatever."

Frissell hesitated for only a moment. Colder's question was out of the blue, but it was never unusual for one doctor to ask another about strange or terrible cases. "It happened a couple of weeks ago. Really ugly scene. She came in bad shape. Hypovolemic shock. Down a ton of units. Coded in the ER. Got her back, then took her to the OR and explored her. The vag bleeding was profuse."

"Perforation?"

"Two. Small artery, two minor veins."

"What else happened?"

"It was bad, Pete. Talked to the family that night after she was stable. Parents are right out of Ozzie and Harriet Get Religion. Their daughter's at death's door and they're screaming bloody murder because she had an abortion. Good old fashioned love, compassion, and forgiveness. Husband's a honey too. He's some sort of has-been kamikaze football hero who's now a professional drinker and cocksman."

Colder groaned. "Great. What else?"

"She woke up in the ICU, and these three gems start screaming at her. We had to practically throw them out. Parents left and never came back. I'm not sure the husband ever did either. Only visitor I saw after that was a waitress friend."

Colder sighed sympathetically. "How long was she in the hospital?"

"Eight or ten days."

"Medically?"

"She's fine. Never'll be able to carry a child, but she's alive. Psychologically, I don't know."

"She get any counseling?"

"Tried to, but ComHealth wouldn't authorize it. I think they gave her a pamphlet on grief or something."

"Great."

"In fact, my guess is that they'll probably deny her whole claim."

"You're probably right."

"Seen it a million times before."

"I'm worried about her. She seems to be a tough kid, but this was a lot. Got the feeling she was trying to make the best of a bad deal and this only added to her guilt."

"I agree," said Frissell.

"You think it's an abusive situation?"

"I never had any evidence of that. I only saw the husband once, and she never said anything about it. She was distraught and guilt-ridden. Her only concern seemed to be reconstructing the relationships."

"She tell you why she had it done?"

"No, but she did admit she never told her husband. I think she's pretty afraid of the guy."

Colder pondered the thought as he finished his drink. He changed the subject.

"Tell me, Dave. What do you know about Fragile X?"

"What?" asked Frissell curiously.

"Fragile X. The disease."

"What in the world made you think of that?"

"When Molly came to see me, she told me it's what the fetus tested positive for."

Frissell paused for several seconds. "No kidding? I didn't even know that could be tested for."

"What do you know about it? Genetics? Physical manifestations?"

"Let me think. Its been a long time," began Frissell. He paused and then slowly began speaking. "I think, maybe, sex-linked recessive, affects males, mild retardation and very rare. Am I in the ball park?"

"Yes."

"But I've never heard of it before as part of prenatal testing."

"Neither had I. That's why I wanted to know if you had heard anything around County."

"Nada."

"You know anyone who might?"

"Casey Larter," replied Frissell.

"That's a good idea."

"She's as up on anything new in OB as anyone."

"I'll ask her."

"What exactly are you looking for?"

"I want to know if Fragile X is part of routine prenatal testing, and if so, what the patient is told. I also want to know how many cases they are seeing in a year. It's weird, David. I checked the OB textbooks and did a med-line search, but I can't find anything."

"Very weird."

"I agree. Something isn't right here."

"Well, keep me posted," replied Frissell as his pager went off. "Gotta run, but I'll talk to you soon."

"Thanks."

As Peter hung up the phone, he felt a wave of anxiety bombard his body. It simply made no sense. Medicine held few, if any, secrets, and new developments were heralded, not hidden. Something else had happened, he was sure. At best it was tragic neglect. At worst it was something else. The thought chilled him. Whatever it was, for Molly Loomis, the price had been high. Everything she had.

Chapter Five

June 16

During the first hour of the workday, Peter Colder saw ten patients, varying from severe bronchitis to a misplaced peanut lodged deep within a three-year-old's nose. The sicker patient was decidedly less challenging than the mischievous child, now seen for the third time in two months with a stray item lodged within his nasopharynx. With the boy flailing in a mixture of screaming, kicking, and clawing, Colder, Sylvia, and the mother, a frail, terrified twenty-one-year-old, repeated their previously successful strategy. Not exactly textbook form, it consisted of Sylvia and the mother lying on top of the child while Colder pinned the boy's head to a pillow and fished for the peanut with a forceps, a penlight balanced between his teeth. After several deafening minutes, numerous scratches, and one near bite, the peanut finally emerged. The youngster, his torture complete and suffering no apparent ill effects, bounded to the empty waiting room to retrieve a reward. His mother followed, while Colder and Sylvia remained seated, each glowing with a thick coat of sweat.

"Should have used a general anesthetic," mumbled Colder.

"I'm sure you'll have another chance," Sylvia grumbled, starting to clean up. "What'll it be next time? A baseball?"

Colder appeared thoughtful. "I've probably dilated the nostril enough."

Sylvia glanced toward him out of the corner of her eyes. Her look was a disapproving smirk. "Funny."

"Better to plan ahead."

Sylvia tore away the sheet that covered the examining table. "Well, now that we've done *that* so well, we'll probably have about an hour break. After all of that racket, I'm sure that every patient in the county is running as fast as they can away from this building."

Colder laughed. His brown eyes flashed as he peeked out into the waiting room. Seeing only one old man sitting alone reading *People*, waiting for the results of an X-ray, he turned back to Sylvia. "You're right. They all scrammed."

"Not quite," returned Sylvia, finishing with the examining table. "You're not getting away. We're scheduled free intentionally. You have that call from Dr. Larter coming, and the ComHealth rep will be here at 9:30."

"That's not as good a story as telling people we scared all our patients away."

"Sorry." They continued to talk as she went in the other examining room.

Colder followed her. "You think I should call Molly Loomis?" she asked him. "I was a little worried about her yesterday."

"Save it for me. I want to talk to Casey Larter first, then I'll talk to Molly."

Sylvia turned away, pleased at the results of her well-intentioned maneuvering. "I'll get Dr. Larter," she said, tearing away the long paper sheet that covered the other room's examining table and tossing it into the garbage.

"Thanks." Colder picked up the phone and dictated a quick procedure note. When he was finished, he took the coding sheet and circled the number *1*, charging a minimum fee that he knew would never be paid. The mother was single, worked three part-time jobs, and made too much money to qualify for Medicaid but too little to purchase insurance. She came in often with each of her two children, for shots, colds, and checkups, always embarrassed and promising to try to pay something. She rarely did, but she was never refused. Colder and Sylvia knew that her only alternative would be the hospital, for double the cost and an endless bout with their collection department. Colder knew he was being used, but just as important, he was badly needed. He accepted both as true and the dilemma as unsolvable. His only goal was to provide care to anyone who asked for it.

The phone rang, and Colder answered it on the second ring, replacing the pen in the breast pocket of his slightly stained lab coat. "Yes."

"I have Dr. Larter for you," said Sylvia.

"Put her on."

The phone clicked audibly, and a moment later Colder heard the mildly agitated voice of Casey Larter in loud conversation with an undetermined subordinate. "Hello?" she said into the phone before muffling the speaker. "Always! Always! Plastic speculum heated to body temperature. How many times do I have to say it? Hello?"

"Casey, Pete Colder."

"Hi, Pete. Hey! No! The others. How are you?"

"Fine. You?"

"Same ol'."

Colder paused. Casey Larter, never a close friend, was more an acquaintance and colleague. Five years older, she was a large, stocky woman with a round face, ruddy complexion, and brusque manner. Casey could be alternately hostile and charming, depending on mood and topic; she swung freely between her extremes, long a byproduct of a combination of stress and chronic fatigue. She was temperamental but talented, and Colder respected her for her dedication to an area of medicine few dared enter and most had chosen to leave. She was an OB who performed abortions. She worked sixteen-hour days, believed unfailingly in her cause, and was interested only in her patient's welfare. Despite threats, burglaries, slashed tires, and two assaults, she continued on with a commitment that bordered on obsession. She had no other interests and no personal life. Her existence was her clinic, a five-room brick building located two miles south of the hospital that she shared with one other part-time gynecologist, a sixty-seven-year-old man in semiretirement. He did it out of interest and desire. She did it out of need and a sense of purpose. Together they provided a reasonable, available, and affordable option to a population with few choices.

"Same here," replied Colder.

"What can I do you for?" she asked, her tone reflecting an obvious disinterest in small talk.

"I need to know if there is anything new in prenatal testing," he said.

"Such as?"

"Genetic, chromosomal," he said, being deliberately oblique.

"I don't know, Pete. There's always a bunch of new research in the journals. In practice? I guess I need to know specifically what you're wondering about."

"Can you test for Fragile X."

The phone fell silent except for the sound of voices in the background and a nurse's overhead page of a patient. "Fragile X?" she returned, perplexed.

"Yes."

Casey took a long time to answer. "You got me there. I seem to remember, no, that was, God, Pete. I know for sure there's been nothing in the journals. And if it was being talked about, I definitely would have heard."

"That's what I thought."

"You've got me interested though. Why do you ask?"

"A girl came in yesterday. Had an AB a couple of weeks ago. Said the reason was that her fetus had Fragile X."

"She's got to be mistaken," she said firmly. "There's no way to test that prenatally. Besides, that disease is rare as hell."

"Seems weird," said Colder. "The girl's a straight shooter and appeared totally sure of the diagnosis."

"What else do you know? Could she be lying?" asked Casey.

"Her family situation is bad," acknowledged Colder. "She chose the AB apparently unbeknownst to the husband and probably her parents. Everyone's on the outs now."

"She might have picked Fragile X out of a textbook figuring it was a way to rationalize her action."

"No, she said someone called her."

"Over the phone?"

"Yes."

"That doesn't seem likely," replied Casey dubiously.

"Maybe," admitted Colder "but why would she make up something so obscure? If she was going to pick a disease, why not come up with an easy one? One that everyone knows is tested for?"

"I don't know. Sounds impressive? Lying still sounds more reasonable than someone calling her up and telling her that her fetus has some disease that really can't even be tested for."

Her sound logic silenced Colder.

"Tell you what. I've gotta run, but I'll ask a couple of others. If I hear anything, I'll call you."

"Thanks, Casey," he said, lost in thought.

"See ya."

Colder hung up the phone. Twirling his pen between his fingers like a baton, he tried to recall the details of his conversation the afternoon before. Someone had called her, she had said. An excuse? Could she be lying? Covering everything up for a baby she didn't want? Her family situation made it even probable. But why Fragile X, an obscure disease even to specialists and an affliction barely worthy of a one-line mention in most medical textbooks? Why would she pick *that* condition if she was going to lie? Colder shook his head. It made no sense.

The bedroom was filled with the heavy scent of tar. When the late morning breeze swept through her open window, a pungent mix of gasoline and exhaust combined together to amplify the already nauseating result. Molly Loomis turned over in the direction of the smell, her eyes squinting open against her wishes. Staring blankly, she saw slanting beams of sunlight streaming through the uncovered window, landing on her floor mattress and covering her exposed legs. While the stifling heat, languid air, and outside noise continued to churn her stomach, a golden curtain of dust hung like a fog throughout the room. It shifted only when the gusts of the summer breeze sent it spiraling in various coils into the far corners of the room. Molly rolled over, her face catching the breeze. She felt better as the wind evaporated a bit of sweat, but as before, its cooling effects were temporary and within seconds the curtain of fog was back to its customary spot.

She pushed the sheet from her shoulders and rolled onto her back, her legs slightly apart and her hands at her sides, while her eyes focused on the spinning movement of the ceiling. Her head hurt, throbbing like a stubbed toe seconds after impact, and her stomach ached, a combination of the healing incision and the effects of the second rum and Coke. She felt horrible, her stomach stinging in pain as if missing its inner lining, having been burned away by the alcohol. She wanted to gag, but her mouth was too dry and her body too weak. Instead she panted slowly, fighting the continuous waves of nausea.

The thought had come again the night before. Suicide. It seemed to arrive more often now, recurring in weak moments like a haunting memory. In addition, the guilt-riddled image of herself as worthless, ugly, and a failure, was now ever-present and consuming. But at this moment, she was only concerned about something else: the worst hangover of her life.

Her eyes rolled open as a screech of tires sounded on the street below. Voices sounded briefly, loud and forceful, echoing through her near-empty apartment. They were followed by the sound of a truck engine slowly accelerating and disappearing into the distance. The sound of construction then resumed with jackhammers and men's voices.

An hour passed, and gradually her stomach began to settle. Her improvement only made her more repentant. "Never, ever, again," she uttered weakly. "Never." The half bottle of rum had been the only alcohol that Troy had left. "Wuss water" he had always called it. Poison was more like it, she thought. Her panting finished, the invisible vice-grip on her head released one notch, and she finally felt well enough to stand. She struggled to her feet and after gaining her balance, staggered to the kitchen. Her head was a bit worse with the movement, but several gulps of orange juice were the needed tonic. She, at last, felt slightly human.

The carton was at her lips again when the phone rang. Not yet feeling like talking to anyone, she considered not answering, but decided against it.

"Hello?" she said weakly.

"Molly?" came a cheerful woman's voice.

"Yes?"

"This is Sylvia Caspers from the clinic. I called to see how you were doing."

"I'm okay," she replied, sounding less than enthusiastic.

"Are you sure? You sound sick."

She knew her greeting had sounded worse than she intended. She tried to sound better. "I hate to admit it, but I had a drink last night, and I think it kind of did a number on my stomach. I've been a little nauseated most of the morning."

"Well," said Sylvia putting away her nursing cap for a second, "you probably deserved a good stiff drink."

Molly laughed. She had not expected that recommendation from a nurse. "I'm not much of a drinker. Pretty much a wimp."

"You gotta do it sometimes," said Sylvia. "But don't tell the doc I told you that."

"I won't," she promised.

"Is your incisional pain better?"

"A little bit each day. It only hurts when I move fast."

"You're eating okay?"

"Not great yet."

"I think you should eat more. You're on the thin side. You don't have much in reserve, and you need to keep your strength up. Do you have enough food?"

"Well, I've got to do a little shopping. Troy kind of took everything."

"What about money? Do you have enough money?"

Molly paused, suddenly embarrassed by her ridiculous predicament. "Well, he sort of took the money, too."

"How much?" asked Sylvia, effectively disguising her contempt for a man she had never met.

"About eight hundred."

"No, how much do you *have*?"

"Well, I was planning on going back to work on Monday. They'll probably advance me some."

"Where do you work?"

"The MeDiner. I waitress. It's in Medina, on the west side of town."

"How much do you have now?" asked Sylvia again, nearly wondering out loud if Molly was in any condition to lift a tray of dishes.

"I have about fifty in my purse."

"Fifty dollars!" she exclaimed. "Forget it. Don't you move. I'm coming over this afternoon to get some things straightened out."

Molly protested. "No, really, I'll be okay. Don't bother yourself."

"Nonsense. I'll hear none of it," said Sylvia, suddenly sounding more motherly than professional.

"No, I—"

"I'll be there at three," she said, her tone reflecting a statement not open to negotiation.

Molly closed her eyes, resigning herself to the visit. She didn't wanted charity. She had no intention of burdening anyone any further. But she also had only twenty dollars, not fifty. "Thank you," she murmured.

"I'll see you then," chirped Sylvia. "Now Dr. Colder wants to talk to you. I'm putting him on."

Molly walked to the middle of the empty living room, the noontime sunlight turning the gold carpet to a bright yellow. She felt foolish standing in the middle of a deserted room, slightly hung over, unkempt, while talking to someone so attractive and charming. At least he couldn't see her, she thought. "I'd rather die," she mumbled.

"What?" asked Peter Colder.

Realizing she had spoken out loud, Molly momentarily choked, her mind running quickly for an answer. "I'm sorry," she managed. "I didn't know you were there."

"Did you say you'd rather die?" he asked quizzically.

"I meant I'd rather die than take another drink. I made myself a rum and Coke last night, and I'm still feeling it a little bit." She took a deep breath, thanking the stars she had come up with something, lame as it was.

"You want my drinking lecture?" he asked.

"I don't think so," she said tepidly.

"Fair enough," Colder said. "Then I'll tell you that I actually prefer rum and Diet Coke. Probably my favorite drink."

Molly laughed in spite of herself. "I guess I never thought about doctors drinking anything."

"Well, I tell you this, of course, as only classified information. If you repeat it, I'll be forced to inflict some horrible punishment upon you."

"My lips are sealed."

"Good. Now I heard that Sylvia is going over there this afternoon to take care of some things."

"I guess so," said Molly weakly.

"Listen, don't be embarrassed. If she didn't do it, I would."

"You have to let me pay you back. I can't accept any other way."

"Fair enough."

"But I really do appreciate this," she mumbled.

Colder paused before changing the subject. "Molly, I need to ask you something. When the call came regarding Fragile X, do you remember where it was from? Was it local or somewhere else?"

"No, I never knew. I guess I assumed it was local."

"How about the doctor when he came? How long after the call was it?"

"That same day. Maybe three hours later."

"And the number he gave you to call the Fragile X expert? It was a toll-free number?"

"Yes." She stopped, her eyes drifting back toward the kitchen. "Wait a minute. I forgot. I wrote his name down."

"Whose name?"

"The guy who came over." Molly walked to the kitchen and opened the drawer underneath the phone jack. Removing the yellow pages, she opened the cover and saw the name she had scribbled three weeks earlier. "Here it is," she said proudly. "Dr. Roland Michaels. That's the one."

"R-Roland Michaels?" Colder stammered, not bothering to write it down. "You talked to Roland Michaels?"

"Yes, he came over. He was here about an hour. Very nice."

"Did you ever talk to him again?"

"No."

Colder tried to sound casual. "How did your conversation end when you talked?"

"I told him that I was going to go for the abortion. He said he felt that was a good decision and wished me well."

"Was he an older man or a younger one?"

Molly paused for a moment. "I'd say he was in his forties."

Colder stopped, pondering a thought.

"You know him?" Molly asked.

Colder answered truthfully. "No, I don't, but it's still a good clue."

"Clue for what?" she asked, surprised.

Colder ignored her question. "Molly, can you do me a favor?"

"Sure," she replied, perplexed.

"Can you come to my office tomorrow morning at seven-thirty? I'd like to sit down with you and ask you a few more questions."

"No problem. I'll be there. I have to look for a lawyer tomorrow anyway."

"What do you need a lawyer for?" he asked, surprised.

"Divorce," she said without emotion. "That and the hospital bill."

"The hospital bill?"

"Yeah, ComHealth denied my claim. Now I owe the hospital $114,000. They called this morning. They're willing to work on some kind of payment plan, but I can't even do that. I know I'm gonna have to file bankruptcy."

Colder recalled his conversation with Frissell. He knew complaining about ComHealth would do no good. "I've got an idea. I think I know an attorney. If you could just come to the office tomorrow morning."

"I'll be there," she said sounding grateful and feeling a little better.

"Good."

"And thanks again, Dr. Colder."

"You're entirely welcome."

Molly hung up the phone and sat down on kitchen floor. She took another swig of the juice and thought about the $114,000. She had made $10,800 the year before. She knew she could never pay it off, not even over thirty years. She was ruined. She knew it. Bankrupt. Finished.

She rose and walked toward the bathroom, her thoughts still whirling between debts, divorce, and how she might end it, but suddenly she stopped, a strange and curious look creeping over her face. She had almost forgotten about why he had asked her to come back. What did he mean by "it's a clue"?

Four hours later, Peter Colder left an examining room and proceeded to his office. He glanced at the reminder Sylvia had left him before she went to Molly's. He picked up the phone and punched in Casey Larter's private number.

She answered on the first ring. "Larter."

"Hey there, it's Pete."

"Colder! What are you getting me into here?" she asked, sounding facetiously annoyed. "I made a fool of myself asking a half dozen prominent gynies and pedopods about Fragile X, and they looked at me like I'd missed a couple of doses of antipsychotic meds."

"Sorry."

"The only thing anyone had to say was one guy who had heard of a lady who claimed that she had a friend who had aborted a Lesch–Nyhan fetus."

"Can you test for that?"

"No."

"Still a long stretch," he said.

Casey sounded annoyed that the matter was slow to conclude. "I'd call it a big zero. Put it to rest."

"I would," admitted Colder, "except for one thing. I talked to the patient this morning, and she remembered the name of the doctor she talked to."

"Who was it?" she sighed.

"Roland Michaels."

"What!" Casey was incredulous, her voice rising a full octave. "Are you crazy? Roland Michaels? That's preposterous! He's been dead for almost six months!"

"That's why it's got to be true."

"Wait a minute, Pete. What are we talking about here? Dead men talking or live men imitating dead men."

"The latter of course."

"C'mon," she scoffed. "Let's get real here. We've got a girl whose life fell apart because she chose an abortion unknown to an unsupportive family. The only shot she has at damage control is concocting some excuse for the AB. So she plucks a horrible disease out of the *Reader's Digest*, not bothering to check out if it is actually tested for prenatally and then plucks the name of a doc out of a Yellow Pages that happens to be a year old. Tell me that doesn't make more sense."

Colder leaned back in his chair. "I admit it does make some."

"What else can it be? You really think it's some wild conspiracy?"

"I don't know. She seems on the up and up."

"Tell me, was she honest when she didn't tell her husband?" asked Casey.

"No," he admitted.

"It's the oldest game in the world. A lie to cover up a lie."

"I don't know."

"You have any proof? Anything in writing? Tapes?"

"No."

"C'mon, Colder. Smell the roses."

"I don't know, Casey. Something still makes me uneasy, but I'll admit you're making a good case."

"Put it to bed. Forget about her, and we'll go back to fighting our windmills."

"Hey there," he exclaimed, sounding wounded.

"You and me both, buddy. The last two crazies fighting ComHealth. Each mad in our own way."

"Thanks for the info, Casey. I owe you one."

Colder hung up the phone, holding the receiver in his hand as he depressed the button, eliciting a loud click from the speaker. The thought had never before occurred to him. Molly had seemed so truthful. So honest. Casey's assessment made sense. Molly had a motive to lie and an opportunity to prepare it. A glance through a textbook relating diseases that no family member or nonmedical husband would ever comprehend. Then, exaggerate the details, locate the name of a physician, and the lie was ready. Obviously it made sense. The fib didn't even have to be a great one, because that was simply a backup plan. The real story was a miscarriage like the one before. Only if confronted would Molly need to lie. It was perfect. A failing marriage, a child that would complicate the divorce. She had planned it all. Suddenly he felt disgusted, frustrated, and used. "Stupid," he said to himself. "Idiot."

Two hours later, he drove home through the thick downtown traffic of rush hour. He had seen ten more patients, with Letisha acting as his assistant. All had been the same. People in need, some sick, some not. Arriving at the house, he fed Mortimer, cooked dinner, and then turned on the Twins–Yankees game, eating on a TV tray in his living room. Within minutes of finishing his meal, he was lying on the couch, a gentle whisper of summer wind through the open window caressing his face. He was tired. The day, like most others, had been long. He was no longer thinking about Molly Loomis. His mind had moved elsewhere as night neared, beaten into submission by the day. In a moment he dozed off.

At 10:15 P.M. the phone rang. Shaking himself awake, he found the phone beneath a stack of newspapers. "Hello?"

His ex-wife's voice greeted him. "I want him, Peter."

"Hi there," he sighed.

Julianne Purcell's voice was soft and almost seductive. "He likes me better."

"Does not," he said, scanning the room for the cat, but unable to locate him. "As always, he's lying right here on his back, paws in the air begging for his belly to be scratched."

"Liar, but I want to hear him talk."

"You know he won't do that. Great dominant male lions are above speaking to females. They reserve their precious discourse only for other dominant males."

"When did you get another cat?"

"Funny."

"Oh, I do miss him so," she sulked. "I made such a horrible deal. I should sue my lawyer."

"Julianne, you are a lawyer and you had a great lawyer. You got the house, the furnishings, the cars, and the money. I got the cat and a TV."

"See what I mean? Horrible."

"Look, that new boyfriend of yours could buy you a thousand cats."

"I only want one."

"What's his name?"

"Mortimer."

"No, your boyfriend, or should I say, that phallic symbol you wear wrapped around your finger now. It rhymes with goofy, doesn't it?"

"Funny," she said, equally adept at feigning hurt. "And it's Geoffrey."

"What does he do? Help little old ladies deposit their Social Security checks for a little cut, like fifty percent?"

"Close. He makes money. Unlike some. Investment banking."

"Ah yes," said Colder, now awake and warming up. "Charge seventeen and pay out two. A Harvard MBA to realize a fifteen percent profit."

Julianne winced audibly. "Ouch, I relent. You win."

"Sorry," he replied. Despite their divorce, they remained on good terms and enjoyed the verbal jousting to the extent that neither one was ever hurt.

"You have a bad day?" she asked.

"Long and bad. I'll tell you about it sometime."

"Work?" she asked gently.

"Yeah," he groaned.

"Any contracts forthcoming?"

"No, we're living on cash and breaking even on Medicaid. I need some patients with insurance or it's over in about three to four months. But with ComHealth controlling the market, I don't see how I can make it."

"That's really ugly."

Colder listened to his ex-wife's voice again, realizing how empty his life seemed without her. Each independent and caring, but with matching work habits, their relationship crashed over the mechanics of commitment, priorities of young adulthood, and the details of daily life. Together they were unworkable. Apart they felt closer.

"Yeah it is, J," he replied. "I may have to leave."

Julianne sounded sad. "Where would you go?"

"I don't know. Maybe a small town. People think the big cities have all the good medicine, but it really isn't true anymore. Not with managed care. Some of the best medicine is in the rural states now. The corporations haven't really gotten there yet, and it's hard to consolidate power in a cluster of small towns. HMOs can't make it on Main Street because in small towns everyone knows everyone. The insurance salesman has to eat dinner at the town cafe with his subscribers."

"And they're not too excited about watching a bunch of custom-tailored profligates dining from their gold-plated trough of subscriber money." Julianne's thought was interrupted by a loud sneeze.

"You got a cold?" he asked, gladly changing the subject.

"Little one. It's better."

"Eat your soup."

"I will. By the way, the reason I called is that Geoff's bank has a luxury box at the Twins game Saturday. Basically it's a schmoozing session between my firm and the bank, but these are the guys to talk to about loan ideas."

Colder knew where she was headed. "No. No loans. It's either in three months with smaller liabilities or six months with larger ones."

"Just a thought. And there will be a lot of single wom—"

Colder scolded her. "Julianne, you know that's a *no* zone."

"You have to start, Peter. Your life is slipping away."

"My business, J. Even if you're right."

"C'mon. How long has it been? Six months? A year?"

"What? A date?" he replied. "One week."

"Come off it," she scoffed. "I'm not talking about a trip to Samson's Subs with Letisha and Sylvia. I'm talking about a date with details."

"Well—" he started.

"Look, you're a wonderful guy," she said tenderly. "Witty, bright, fun, and a wonderful lover. You shouldn't waste it."

"I appreciate your lying on that last one," he chuckled. "You can't lie to your ex."

"Beepers and thirty-six hour shifts are the most effective birth control known."

"The desire was always there though."

"Thank you," she laughed. "You know that I just worry about you."

"I do know it, and I appreciate it."

"Call if you even think about calling."

"I will."

"Night."

Colder hung up the phone, a sense of regret and frustration sweeping over him. She complicated and enriched his life, making him alternatively miserable and ecstatic, angry and joyous. Now in their time of relationship clarity, none of the extreme emotions ever came to pass. He glanced toward her pictures still sitting atop the TV, her graduation from law school and the two together in Yellowstone. He missed her. He missed what they had had. He wished for what they didn't have.

The phone rang again, and Colder looked at the clock, his thoughts stolen from his reverie. Ten-thirty. Closing the window, the warm June evening having cooled slightly, he again punched the talk button, knowing it would be Sylvia. He sat down again on the couch as Mortimer appeared from the kitchen and leaped into his lap.

"Hi there," he said.

"Hi," Sylvia replied. "I just finished with Molly. I'm glad we did this. Her place hadn't been cleaned in three weeks, she's still very weak, there wasn't an ounce of food in the place, and the only piece of furniture is a mattress."

Colder remembered his conversation with Casey Larter. "I think she's lying, Sylvia," he grunted.

"What?" she asked incredulously "Lying about what?"

"Her story. A to Z. Fragile X and all."

"Are you kidding?" she asked, sounding like she thought Colder was a complete dunce. "Not one chance in a million. I don't think this girl could step on an ant right now without crying, let alone stick to a pack of lies. Besides, why would she do it?"

"Denial."

"You're wrong, Peter," she said, using his first name, as she occasionally did in private. "She's got a twelve-inch scar on her abdomen, a broken marriage, an estranged family, a hundred thousand dollar debt, and an infertile future. She just spent the last six hours crying, blaming no one but herself. If that's denial then I'm the Queen Mum."

"I don't know," said Colder, voicing his uncertainty.

"I got the whole story today, and it's as ugly as you can get." Sylvia hesitated. "Let me say it this way. If somebody puts you down enough, you start to believe it. I know that's not what you're asking, but it does explain her."

Colder slouched into the couch. "She said it was Roland Michaels that she talked to."

"I know. She told me about it."

"So what does that tell you."

"That she is telling the truth. She's no actress. She couldn't tell a lie this big. I don't know who this guy was, but I do know she was downright proud of the fact that she came up with the name."

"Does she know that we're fishing?"

"She knows something. We'll have to level with her soon."

"If she's lying, she'll have to come clean. There's no point in carrying it any further."

"She's not lying, Peter. I *know* it. I've raised four children and have been a nurse for nearly forty years. I can smell B.S. a hundred miles away. Believe me, there's no scent here."

Colder sighed. His instincts about Molly were the same. "For some unknown reason, I hope you're right."

"I know I am."

Colder sat up straight, the cat leaping to the floor. "I'm meeting her in the morning."

"That's what I wanted to talk to you about. I changed the schedule, if you don't mind. Letisha got her in to see her cousin, the lawyer, tomorrow morning."

"Tyler Briggs?"

"Yes."

"I thought he was a trial lawyer."

"He is. But he'll do the divorce and whatever else is necessary for free. Courtesy of our Letisha."

"That's great. I was going to suggest someone I know, but this should work out fine."

"We have one new patient I added at ten to eight. After that, it's chaos the rest of the morning."

"I'll be there."

"Get some sleep. You sound tired."

"I am a little."

"See you then."

Colder stood up and walked to the kitchen. Removing another Diet Coke from the refrigerator, he opened it and watched as the great cat Mortimer stared quizzically at his two-legged master drinking from another odd-shaped dish. Disinterested, the beast walked into the living room and plopped into a well-lit spot in the middle of the floor. Colder followed. As he approached the couch, the phone rang again. He chuckled to himself, the routine well-known. At least half the time, Sylvia called back with one final thought.

"Do I get to guess?" he asked.

At first there was no answer, only a strange silence and an unidentifiable sound in the background.

"Hello?" asked Colder.

"At long last we talk, Dr. Colder," came the male voice, firm and resonant. "I have much anticipated this moment."

Caught off-guard, Colder's mind was blank. "Who is this?" he asked.

The man spoke softly and deliberately. "Someone you do not know, but someone you can trust."

Colder was vacillating between irritation and curiosity. "You have a name? Or a reason for calling?"

"I am a friend," he said. "The rest you need to discover."

Colder paused, running through his mind voices from his past. He did not recognize it. He cursed himself for not having caller ID. No, he thought. Too simple. This man had called prepared. *At long last we talk.* Colder felt his heart suddenly skip a beat. The man had been watching him! He knew him! The skipped heartbeat was followed by a wave of fear. What would he want? Why would someone watch him?

"Who the hell are you?" demanded Colder.

"I have told you." The voice was soothing. "A friend. A friend who can be trusted."

Colder was still skeptical. "Okay, why do I need your friendship?"

"For reasons you do not yet know."

Colder decided to play along. "Then why not tell me?"

The voice paused as if carefully guarding a tightly held secret. "Because then they will kill you, too."

Peter Colder's eyes widened and his heart began to pound at the sound of the words. Although he didn't know what he had been expecting, it wasn't this. Perhaps a joke, a hoax, a gag from an old college friend. But this was no joke, and Colder knew without asking. The threat was real.

The man continued. "I have called you to tell you of my presence and warn you at the same time. The forces that surround you, you do not know or understand. As of this moment, their discovery becomes your quest. And your future, as does mine, now comes to rest upon it. Realize that they will watch you, and that after this call, I will never call you this way again."

"Why do you call now?"

"To warn you. And to tell you the truth."

"What is the truth?" Colder asked, swallowing hard.

"What you heard from your patient, you must believe it. All of it is true."

Peter was confused. "What are you talking about?"

"What she says," said the man, "is true."

"Molly Loomis?" he asked

"Yes, Molly Loomis."

"What in the hell are you telling me?"

"You must seek that truth, as you must seek me. Find me, and you find the answer."

"The answer to what?"

"You are bright enough, Dr. Colder. Consider this conversation carefully. Remember every detail of every word from now on. As I said, I won't contact you this way again. But be prepared to talk to me within twenty-four hours, for I know your routine well. Open your eyes, your mind, and your imagination. You need me. And I need you."

"Who are you?" asked Colder again.

"I am the answer to the question you have asked all day. I am the only link to what you have stumbled onto." His voice trailed to a whisper. "I *am* what happened to her. I—am Fragile X."

Chapter Six

From atop the IDS Tower, the view extended twenty miles in any direction. Looking east past St. Paul into the lush woodland of western Wisconsin or south along the St. Croix River basin, the eye encountered only the majestic green plumage of early summer and a beautiful aquamarine sky, accented by a few glossy, white clouds drifting lazily in the early afternoon. To the north, past the smaller buildings of downtown industry, the city extended only a few miles, yielding to the rolling hills of old country estates, new developments, and an irregular pattern of heavily settled lakes. To the west, the heights of downtown could be seen, icons of brick and mortar lifting lifelessly toward the sky while beyond, the city sprawled interminably, repeating itself in an endless pattern of mirror-image suburbs, shopping centers, and bisecting cement thoroughfares, representing the formerly small city's graduation to the late-twentieth-century ideal.

ComHealthOne offices occupied the top five floors of the IDS Tower. H. Carter Hutchins' recently renovated citadel sat immediately beneath the roof, one story above any of the other ComHealthOne offices. His office was huge, over seventy-five feet in length and one hundred feet in depth, complete with a century-old oak desk, mahogany bar, and numerous overstuffed leather chairs. The carpet was a rich, dark blue. Three walls were glass. The nonglass wall contained recessed bookshelves filled with trophies and personal memorabilia. Adjacent to the bookshelves was a sprinkling of pictures, carefully selected, beautifully framed, and seen by anyone exiting the room. There was Hutchins with Gingrich and with Dole. Pictures of Trent Lott, Pat Robertson, and a golfing George Bush. Friends or mementos, they stood as his tribute to himself, an enduring image of power and a framed decoration intended to add ego to his vanity.

At precisely 1:00 P.M., the four top ComHealth executives reporting to Hutchins arrived and entered the office. The exactness in the timing was a traditional ritual of precision that Hutchins insisted upon with the terse, dogmatic vigor of a football coach. As usual, the CEO greeted each with a firm handshake and quick visual examination. They were all flawlessly groomed, clean-shaven with closely cropped hair. They were dressed in navy, their suits custom-tailored. Their shoes were heavily polished and their stomachs a disciplined flat, their bodies having yielded to the new ideal of the businessman, that beauty and success were inevitably linked, symbiotic, and mutually dependent.

Hutchins had chosen them all carefully. Men like himself, only slightly younger. They were competitive, polished, ambitious, and university-pedigreed. In business they were sharks, blood-hunting animals that consumed anything in their way. Privately, they were doting husbands, at least on the surface, and always discreetly concealing the numerous affairs that they felt great men deserve. They succeeded in their disguise because their wives were distracted, bored women of wealth, travelling between homes and continents while hired hands raised their children. Spending money and social acclaim were their favorite and only real interests.

Carter Hutchins finished eyeing his men and tossed a folder containing the results of a study on Medicaid patients' utilization of health-care services back onto the desk. He slipped into his chair and glared at the four as the other executives sunk into their chairs in front of his desk. "We needed to spend $500,000 to find this shit out?" Hutchins asked incredulously. "Any seventeen-year-old cheerleader whose bloodstream is being diverted from her brain to her gum-chewing jaw would know that!"

"At least we have it on paper," answered Gregory Alan Markham III, the Chief Operating Officer, a sandy-haired man with a square face and deep-set eyes.

"Well, for God's sake, don't show it to anyone."

"It won't leave the room," he assured him.

"It just confirms what we've been saying," replied Stanton Ross, the Chief Financial Officer, a short man with a weightlifter's neck and legs. "We don't want any damn poor people. They never work. And they lay around procreating and consuming health care at twice an acceptable rate. We'll never turn a profit on them."

"I agree," said Preston Cooley, the Executive Vice President of Sales and Marketing. Cooley was tall, fair, and muscular. "We should be out of Medicaid completely."

"It's not that easy," said Hutchins. "Appearances count. The trick is isolating the nonconsumers, then raising the co-pay on the others and stopping them before they get in the doctors' offices."

"I don't know, Carter," said T. Wilson Bolger, Executive Vice President of Human Resources. "If they get in that door, it gets mighty expensive. Some of these mamas are having a half dozen kids, bringing 'em in twice a week for every stuffy nose."

"Then the co-pay should be a hundred bucks," said Ross.

"No," Hutchins responded. "The governor would have a fit. Remember, we're talking about Medicaid. These are taxpayer dollars."

"But with a co-pay of twenty, they're in every week."

"It's still easier to tighten the locks on the front door. Make it difficult for the patient to get to the doctors. It's harder for people to see that we're restricting care."

"I agree," said Markham.

"Where are we with the Cost Incentive Plan?" Hutchins asked Bolger.

"The squawking has nearly died down. The primary care docs are set to fall in line. There are still a few bleeding hearts who are whining about cutbacks, but they're smart enough to see that they don't have any choice."

"Good," said Hutchins, nodding approvingly.

"What are the particulars again?" asked Ross.

"Each primary care physician is allowed eight specialist referrals per month. Beyond that, his income starts dropping. For every additional referral to a specialist, the doctor's income is reduced one percent."

Hutchins eyes lit up. Bolger's words were magical. "What about bonuses?"

"Base salaries will be about sixty-five. If they meet all incentives, they could probably make ninety."

"The base still seems high," said Markham. "What's the median?"

"Seventy-five. We'll be at the thirtieth percentile, but only one-half a deviation below the mean. Trust me, the doctors will take it. They all know that they can't make it as an independent. We'd crush them."

"Remind me of the bonus program," said Ross.

Bolger handed him a sheet of paper as he talked. "If a doctor prescribes only the medications on our accepted list, he will get a monthly bonus of ten percent of his monthly base. If they hold their ordering of blood tests, X-rays, and CT scans to the lowest twenty percent of their peers, they get a bonus of ten percent of their monthly gross. This is in addition to the specialist referral pattern I described. If they meet all three bonus criteria, they can get their income up to about the national mean.

"The bonus plan is reasonable," said Hutchins. "But with respect to specialist referrals, I'm hopeful that we can keep them to one or two per week. Just enough to say we're doing it."

"I agree," said Markham. "It's the only way."

"In terms of Medicaid," said Hutchins, "our contract with the state runs through December. Right now our accountants are analyzing heavy-usage individuals. Most of these could easily be eliminated on technicalities like unapproved providers or pre-existing conditions. We're going to ID them now. After the new contract, we'll target them for cancellation."

"Won't the governor squawk then?" asked Markham, his eyebrows raised.

"We'll do it quietly. We'll demand two and a half percent more in block money to cover our losses in their sacred Medicaid cows, and then when they agree, we raise the co-pay to seventy-five dollars on those we ID as overutilizers. We take them back, the governor gets to crow about how his Medicaid kids still have the same access to doctors as those privately insured, and we turn red into black."

"Beautiful," gushed Markham.

"Meanwhile, we make sure these patients have to work like hell to see a doctor."

Ross laughed out loud. "The door to the doctors is locked, and the door to the specialists has twenty-five deadbolts, all with no keys!"

"Exactly," said Hutchins, his eyes glowing as he took a sip of coffee with a smug, self-satisfied smirk.

"What about our internal reviews?" asked Ross, turning toward Bolger.

"We've completed cardiac, GI, and musculoskeletal. We're shooting for twenty-five percent less angioplasties, forty percent fewer bypasses, fifteen percent fewer scopes, and fifty percent fewer joint replacements within twenty-four months."

"What do the surgeons say?" asked Hutchins.

"Same. A few of those same bleeding hearts like to quote Hypocrites like it's the damn Bible, but they're falling in line."

"Salaries?"

"Again at the thirtieth percentile with incentives."

"Give me some specifics," Hutchins ordered.

"A heart surgeon will be allowed to do five bypasses a month. After that, he'll hit his penalty. Each additional operation will cost him one percent of his salary."

"What about this thirtieth percentile?" asked Ross.

"It'll probably become a regional standard because of our position. That's what I anticipate. There'll be room for cutting further next year when everyone else adjusts. Quite frankly, if we correct the doctor's salaries at five percent per year, our profit margin overall will increase two percent."

"Combine that with the two and a half percent I was talking about, plus the expected cost reduction from access containment and we might see a twelve percent rise overall," said Hutchins.

"Eleven point eight is what I project," said Markham.

"Beautiful," said Hutchins. "I'll tell that to the board tomorrow night. Get it into the shareholder minutes."

"Where is the stock right now?" asked Bolger.

"Forty-six and a half as of one hour ago," said Markham, glancing at his watch before running his fingers over his short, styled hair.

"I'd like to see us get to fifty."

"At twelve percent, we'll get to sixty," gushed Ross enthusiastically.

"We'll make our shareholders filthy rich," Markham said.

"We'll make out reasonably well ourselves," Bolger said, thinking about his four million shares purchased as options at thirty cents.

"Thank God for free enterprise," laughed Markham.

"Thank God for managed care," cheered Bolger.

They all laughed louder. Hutchins stood and shook the others' hands. Concluding the brief meeting and patting each other on the back, they agreed on cocktails at six at the Minnesota Club, to be followed by a black tie Cerebral Palsy Benefit with the Vice President as the honored guest. They continued to joke as they headed out Hutchins' door.

"Celia going to wear something special?" asked Bolger, the last to leave.

"I'm sure she will," nodded Hutchins with a practiced male expression of combined rue and pride.

"She always looks lovely," said Bolger.

"Thanks. I'll tell her you said so."

"Not too loudly," he said closing the door. "Diedre would be a little unhappy."

"See you tonight."

When the door closed, Hutchins strolled back across the office floor, his body ambled with an exaggerated bounce of contentment and satisfaction. The boys had been right. The stockholders would get rich. He would get rich. He paused thinking of the math, then stopped, realizing there was no need. The math was simple. Twenty million shares. If the stock hit fifty, he knew what he would make.

He became more pensive as the quiet of the office began to sink in. He thought of himself as he closed in on his life's ambition. He thought of the biographies that sat in his case. Great men, like himself, who had changed the world. Hutchins turned again toward the windows, the southwestern view showing the wealthy western suburbs. He saw trees, roads, and buildings, the blending of man and nature and his travels in between. Above, he saw the sky, blue and crystalline with a long pattern of white, like a skein of rolling silk spreading across the heavens. His eyes turned directly to the west, following the cloud to its natural end—one spot, dark and gray. It was a blemish to the eyes of perfection. He turned and walked away, choosing to ignore the odd, dark cloud on the horizon.

Tyler Briggs's office was located at the southeast corner of the fortieth floor of Daley Towers, the four-year-old paired white edifices that represented the eastern edge of downtown proper. Located five blocks from the Metrodome, his windows offered him the appealing glow of the great dome's roof when the Twins played on summer nights. During the day, it offered a clear view of the campus of the University of Minnesota. The office was large, with two sets of tables and chairs, three couches, and a well-concealed refrigerator hidden amongst a wall of impressive-looking law books. It was elegantly furnished in a recurring theme of chrome, gray, blue, and glass, with two large mirrors on each of the open walls. On the desk was a picture of his wife and two children in a sailboat near a beach. Behind the desk were his diplomas, University of Minnesota and Northwestern Law, encircled by a ring of photographs. The pictures were of himself in uniform, standing at the side of others. Michael. Spike at the Garden. Coz and Whoopi. Halle Berry. Barry Bonds. Oprah. Muhammed Ali.

Briggs stood behind his desk, talking on the telephone as Molly Loomis entered the room. She could see he was tall, at least six foot three as he towered over the glass surface of his desk. All Molly knew from Letisha was that he was thirty-four years old. She did not know that he was so handsome. His light black skin contrasted sharply with his dark eyes, but fit easily with the fine features and slim physique of a body one easily envisioned as a model. He wore round wire-rim glasses, the lenses so thin that the glasses looked more for effect than correction. His olive green suit was formal, but did little to hide the lawyer's subtle, sartorial flair.

His manner was less formal. He was animated as he talked, with gestures, expressions, and a wildly swinging dialect that varied from slang to courtroom legalese. He motioned for Molly to sit in one of the upholstered chrome-framed chairs that faced the desk while he listened to a high-pitched male voice. As she sat down, he made the gesture of one pouring coffee while he wedged the phone between his shoulder and his chin. Molly mouthed, "No, thank you," and he returned to the conversation. Two minutes, later it ended with Briggs laughing heartily and dismissing the caller with a booming "Later." He collapsed into the chair directly facing Molly.

"Sorry," he said, standing again and shaking her hand. "Tyler Briggs."
"Molly Loomis."

They sat back down and Briggs began to size up his client. Molly was dressed neatly in a sun dress; her hair was slightly curled, and her face had a hint of makeup. Her purse trembled slightly as she held it to her waist, her eyes roaming over the pictures of the celebrities before landing on the coal-black eyes staring over a cup of coffee. She was unimpressive, but not at all unappealing.

"Letisha told me a little bit about your situation," he began.

"I really appreciate your taking my case. I know you're very busy."

"My cousin's my friend. Her friends are my friends," he said warmly.

"I'll pay you what ever you normally charge," she said determinedly.

Briggs waved. "Forget it. Not this time. It's on me."

"Seriously," said Molly. "I insist."

"No, I'm under orders."

Molly insisted. "I won't do it any other way. How much per hour?"

"Fifty dollars," he lied.

"Letisha said two-fifty, and I dragged it out of her."

Briggs grinned. His smile was easy and slightly charmed. "There is a little flexibility in the fees."

"I'll take customary," she said trying to sound fierce. "I don't have it now, but I'm going to make it back. I promise you."

Briggs leaned back. He was surprised, taken slightly aback by the dogged determination of the young woman whose story he had only heard the night before. He had imagined a basket case, a crushed flower wallowing in self-pity, not someone who by all appearances was at least capable of a semblance of poise.

"Deal," he said.

"Deal."

"You need a divorce," he started.

"Yes."

"I'll tell you honestly, Molly. I don't do many divorces. I'm strictly a trial attorney. If there's something complicated we may need to get help."

"I don't think there will be."

"Is there anything to contest?"

"I want the engagement ring and what he left in the apartment. He agreed to that."

"Nothing in dispute? No children, property, vehicles, or bank accounts?"

"No," she answered.

"Nothing?"

"No."

"You're kidding. Absolutely nothing?"

"Yes."

"You're right," he said, "then it should be easy."

"I'm afraid that's only the half of it though," she continued. "I'm broke. I think I need to file bankruptcy."

"What?" he said, leaning forward. "I didn't hear about this."

"Letisha doesn't know."

"What do you owe?" he asked.

"One hundred fourteen thousand."

Brigg's jaw dropped open. "No way. You're kidding."

"No," sighed Molly. "I wish I was. My insurance claim was denied."

Briggs shook his head sympathetically. He pulled out a pencil and opened a legal pad. "I'd better hear this. Let's start from the beginning. Tell me the story."

For ten minutes, Molly told him about her life. She started with her basic background, her work, and her marriage. She then proceeded into greater detail of her past two years, from the problems in the marriage to the miscarriage and the news about the fetus that led her to the abortion. She did not mention the beatings. She told him of the bleeding, the operation, how disappointed her family had been, and Troy's departure. She told him about ComHealth's letter denying her claim.

Briggs took notes and listened intently, writing down every detail. How she talked about her life was as revealing as what she said. He suspected abuse instantly as she talked, choosing to confront it later. He saw that the hallmarks were all there. The apologetic and needing-to-please nature, the low self-esteem. She did not need to admit it. She said it without words.

He listened even more carefully as she talked of ComHealth's letter of denial, the bill, and the money-seeking creditors already calling twice per day. Briggs knew something of ComHealthOne. His cousin, Letisha, had talked frequently about their "slash and burn" tactics. And he knew of the CEO, H. Carter Hutchins, from his famous TV ads. Briggs's mind wandered for a moment as Molly paused in her story. He thought of the ad he had seen the night before. Hutchins was speaking paternally, standing in a nursery surrounded by smiling nurses and a mother with her child. "You're number one with ComHealthOne," the great businessman had said, pointing toward the cameras.

Briggs's thought was interrupted when Molly found the ComHealth letter in her purse and handed it to him. Tyler read it, laughing once in spite of himself at its intrinsic horror. He strolled a few feet to the copy machine. When finished, he returned the original to Molly and sat back down. "A remarkably sensitive literary work," he grunted.

Molly shook her head back and forth. "I'm totally screwed. I made eleven thousand last year. I'll owe them for the rest of my life."

Briggs knew she was right; bankruptcy was probably inevitable. His thoughts, however, went elsewhere.

"Was the policy your husband's?"

"Yes."

"Do you have a copy of it?"

"Someplace. Actually no, I think Troy has it."

"I want to look at it," he said. "I'll have to get one."

"I'll get it," she said. "Why?"

Briggs didn't answer, his mind springing ahead.

Molly saw the strange look in his eyes and was curious. "What are you thinking?"

Briggs was silent for nearly a minute. Then he looked up and tossed the letter back onto the table. "Molly, I'll make you a deal," he began. "We do it your way, it's two hundred fifty an hour. Or we do it my way. It's contingency. Only a percentage of what we make."

"Make?" she asked, confused.

"Call it my trial lawyer's instinct," he said, sipping his cooling coffee. "But I think there's something in here."

"You mean sue them?"

"Maybe. I want to look at that contract with a microscope. Remember, a loophole is open to both sides, and even something airtight has air all around it just waiting to get in."

Molly's surprise and delight were obvious. "I'll take your approach," she said with a smile.

"Very good," he replied. "If nothing else, we'll raise a little stink. Maybe ComHealth will cut a deal with us."

"I'll get a copy of the contract right away," she said.

"Bring me any brochures, newsletters, subscriber information, or advertisements that you had as well. I'll have my paralegal look, too."

"I might have a brochure."

"Also, I'll need to talk to your doctors, review your medical records, and obtain copies of any X-rays. We'll get you a release for those."

"I'll do it this afternoon." For once Molly had hope.

"And one last thing," he said. "I want to see you again at ten o'clock tomorrow with all that we talked about, and at that time I want to know the truth about you and Troy. I want to know everything. Not the fairy tale."

Molly looked down, her face reddening against her will. "Fair enough," she mumbled.

"Good," he said rising and reaching across the desk for her hand. "Now let's go kick some ass."

Molly's blush lessened. She was both shocked and pleased that this man had taken such an immediate and substantial interest. The thought of suing the HMO had never occurred to her, knowing that she had a signed agreement. ComHealth policies had always been confusing, she admitted to herself, but she knew her signature was on it. For a moment, it did not matter. Even if it was only for a second, entertaining the thought of the bill being paid was enjoyable.

"I'll see you tomorrow," he said warmly, shaking her hand.

"I'll be here at ten."

"Good."

When she was gone, Briggs refilled his coffee cup. As he sat back down, his feet rose automatically to the ottoman. He relaxed and thought about Molly's story. For many years he had known that the instincts of the trial lawyer were based on olfaction. And her story and ComHealth's letter had a scent. He knew it. Even in the turbulence of a gusting summer wind, putrid remained itself, putrid. The scent of decay. The scent of death. This letter had it.

He sipped the coffee again and pulled toward him the small figurine of a bloodhound that sat on his desk. His mascot, his idol, his raison d'etre, had been given to him by his wife years earlier. He positioned the small porcelain creature in front of him and stared at the long nose swinging close to the ground. They both now had the scent. It was the scent neither had known before. "It's the scent of a dragon," he said, recalling the image of ComHealth's famous symbol atop the IDS tower. "Now lead me to it, Mr. Bloodhound. All we need is the trail."

Peter Colder finished with his last patient and retreated to the storage room, the largest of the four back rooms. The other employees, who had reacted with nervousness about the news of Colder's strange caller the night before, were already seated and talking.

"So this guy knew your name?" asked Letisha before he could even sit down.

"He knew everything," said Colder forlornly. "I'll bet the guy knows my pant size."

"You think the phones are tapped?" asked Sandra.

Colder had known right away that his phones were tapped, because the caller had known about his doubts about Molly's truthfulness. This could only have come from his conversations with Casey or Sylvia. "I'm sure they are."

"What about your home?"

"There too."

"What are you thinking, Peter?" Sylvia asked him. "Do you think it's a hoax?"

"No way," he said assuredly. "This guy has a plan and we're part of it."

"He called himself Fragile X?" asked Sandra, trying to calm herself.

"That's what he said. 'I *am* Fragile X.'"

"What the heck does that mean?" asked Letisha.

"Is he perhaps responsible?" asked Sandra. "Maybe he's the guy who claimed to be Roland Michaels."

Sylvia had doubts. "Wait a moment. Let's slow down. Right now we don't know anything conclusive. All we have with respect to Fragile X are the statements of a very distraught Molly and a strange phone call."

Colder agreed. "I know, but I haven't been able to come up with anything else."

"On the other hand, to think that this is all a prank is almost certainly wishful thinking," acknowledged Sylvia.

"Does Molly know?" asked Sandra.

"No," said Colder. "But it's time to tell her."

"We rescheduled her to this afternoon," said Letisha.

"We got a message to her as she left Tyler's office. She should be here any minute. She was getting some information at the hospital."

"He's definitely going to represent her?" asked Sylvia.

"Yes," said Letisha proudly.

"I'm glad. I know he's a good lawyer."

"The best."

"We'll have to tell him too," said Colder. "In fact, he might even have some thoughts."

"I can set up a meeting for tomorrow," said Sylvia.

"No, I'll call him in the morning."

Colder paused, his mind wandering back to the conversation of the night before. His mind had raced so quickly during those few moments that many of the details had continued to filter back to him throughout the day. "The man said he'd call me today."

"What?" asked Sylvia.

"Mr. Fragile X," replied Colder. "He said, 'Open your mind, remember every detail of every conversation we have from now on.'"

"What else did he say?"

"He said he'd never call me at home again."

"If he were a threat, he'd never say something like that," said Sylvia.

"I know," admitted Colder. "The man has to be a friend of sorts, warning us. Otherwise it makes no sense. But why would he never call me at home again?"

"He's afraid of being detected," said Sylvia, the realization striking her one moment before the others. "He needs all the calls to appear random."

"Of course," grunted Colder. "Perhaps some computer is checking for patterns of numbers or something like that."

"Whatever, it means that he's the one who doesn't want to get caught," said Letisha.

"That's right," Colder said. "He's worried about himself getting detected, not us."

"You think he's running?" asked Sandra.

"We'll have to consider that."

Sylvia nodded her head unconsciously, lost in thought. "Did he say anything else?"

"Yes. When I asked him something about why he couldn't tell me anything, he said it was because then they would kill me too."

"That's right," said Sylvia agreeing. The others shifted nervously, but Sylvia pushed on as if Colder's last statement had been insignificant. "So then it is safe to assume that he knows one or more who have been killed *and* that it's somehow linked to Fragile X."

"Yes," replied Colder.

"Ohmigod," slurred Letisha as Sylvia said the word "killed."

"So what do we have?" Colder asked no one in particular. "We have a man who holds a secret. His code name is Fragile X. He has knowledge of deaths, perhaps murders. He is afraid and cautious. And he has carefully plotted some link-up with us."

"Plus he obviously knows of Molly," chimed in Sandra. The others looked at her, recognizing the accuracy of her statement.

"That's right," said Letisha.

Sandra continued. "So he must know something about how her situation evolved."

"Yes," agreed Sylvia.

"But how would he know about her?" asked Letisha.

"The blood test that Molly had," offered Sandra. "The one that detected Fragile X."

"No," said Colder. "It doesn't exist. I checked. There is no prenatal test for Fragile X."

"But that doesn't make sense. Somehow Molly got diagnosed as having a baby carrying Fragile X," protested Sandra.

"Yeah," agreed Letisha.

Colder and Sylvia turned to one another, the cold realization striking them simultaneously. The nonmedical people, Letisha and Sandra, *were* right. If Molly's story was true, then something *had* been diagnosed. No other explanation worked. "You're right," said Colder. "You're absolutely right."

"What do they test for in the blood?" asked Sandra.

"At six weeks?" said Colder. "Not much, except maybe HcG and glucose."

"That doesn't take us anywhere," said Sylvia.

"It will at least take me back to Casey Larter," said Colder. "I'll call her tonight."

"Couldn't Mr. Fragile X have found out about Molly when she went for the abortion?" asked Sandra.

"That's the only other thought," acknowledged Colder. "Perhaps the story passed to him when Molly went to Women's Health, or maybe he has access to her medical records or tapped into a computer."

"Either way, whatever this whole thing is, it carries a threat with it," said Sylvia.

Colder guided the discussion away from their fears and took control, "Tell you what, let's do it this way. Sandra, can you run me a med search on anything on Fragile X in the last five years in the medical literature? Then run a second one on prenatal testing. Use the key words 'prenatal' and 'serum.'"

"Consider it done."

"Letisha," he said, turning to her, "Don't you know someone over at Women's Health?"

"Tammy Marsten."

"Good. See if you can get anything out of her about the goings on there. Find out if they send out any blood tests. Ask about employees. See if they had anybody fired, die unexpectedly, threats, anything."

"She'll tell me," assured Letisha. "Talking is her hobby."

"Sylvia," he continued, "I need a copy of Molly Loomis's medical records. See if you can pull some strings."

"I'll call Dolores Smith at County. I'll have it in an hour."

"That's not legal," Colder grinned.

Sylvia Caspers was grim and a little pale. "Neither is murder."

One hour later, the four gathered again, taking the same seats as before, with Molly Loomis now among them. After arriving, she thanked Letisha profusely for her meeting with Tyler Briggs. Turning to the others, Molly spoke with glowing praise for her attorney. "He's terrific," she said three times.

Letisha beamed over the kudos for her cousin. "I know."

"He thinks we should at least contest the bill with ComHealthOne. He's hoping at minimum to reduce it and perhaps file suit if there has been an error."

They were all pleased, happy that she would be well represented and encouraged by the thought that perhaps her bill could be reduced or eliminated. They also noticed that she seemed upbeat and steady, more vigorous than in the days before.

When Molly had finished, Colder began the long story of his suspicions about her Fragile X story. He related his previous doubts about her and his conversations with Dr. Larter, although modifying her confidential opinions. Next, he told of the phone call from the man claiming to be Fragile X and the conclusions they had drawn.

Molly Loomis stared at him, her eyes wide in amazement as he completed telling the details of their deductions. She said nothing, only periodically shaking her head. Finished, he looked her directly in the eyes with obvious regret. "I'm sorry to admit that I doubted you a little, Molly," he said sincerely.

She looked embarrassed. "Don't be. Why should you believe a story so crazy as this?"

Colder was solid in his affirmation. "We all believe you, Molly. Completely."

Molly looked Colder in the eyes. "Thank you."

"And Tyler?" interrupted Letisha. "You're gonna tell him?"

"Yes," replied Colder. "Tomorrow. In fact, I may go with you, Molly, if you don't mind."

"I think he wanted to talk to you as well."

"Perfect."

Colder turned to the others. He was still slightly chagrined to have had to admit that he had doubted her even though Molly seemed unaffected. He plunged on. "Okay, team, what did you all come up with in the last hour?"

Sandra spoke first. "I have a list of articles on prenatal testing over the past five years," she said, handing them to him. "All these medical terms look like Greek to me."

Colder scanned the three-page list, seeing nothing even hinting of a clue.

Sandra continued. "Then I have a list of all articles about Fragile X in the past three years. There were twenty-two. Twenty of them were about, like, mapping the genes. The other three were just talking about the disease."

Colder took the second list as well and within a minute had confirmed the accountant's suspicions that this list was also useless.

"Damn," he said.

"Sorry," mumbled Sandra. "I didn't think it looked too good."

"Don't worry. It's not your fault."

Letisha started talking. "Women's Health had one employee leave three months ago. A secretary who got married and moved to Denver with her husband. Good employee."

"That doesn't sound like much," said Sylvia.

"No other turnover and no real problems to speak of."

"What about ex-employees?"

"Nothing that she knew anything about. They have daily protests like all abortion clinics, but nothing unusual lately. She doesn't know if their phones are bugged, but doubted it because they run a monthly check for confidentiality reasons so that women couldn't be targeted."

"That sounds like a dead-end," said Colder. "What about the computers?"

"She said that they put in a very expensive security system a year ago. They had a couple of break-ins a few years ago, but now the system is supposedly tight."

"Maybe there's still a weakness?" offered Colder.

"But we're looking for something reasonable. Think about it. This guy is wary as a cat. Unless he was a computer genius, he'd be crazy to try to break into a heavily guarded system," Sylvia argued.

"You're right," sighed Colder. "Probably another dead-end." His eyes caught Letisha's. "What about the blood?"

"They do some of their own stuff. CBC's, electrolytes, HcG, estrogen, progesterone, and tox screens. But they send out all other labs and paps."

"About what we do here," said Colder.

"Where do they send it?" asked Sylvia.

"Most labs, cultures, and the path go to Doyne. Rare labs they'll send to U of M." Colder shook his head, frustrated by the dead-end. "That's exactly what we do here."

"What is Doyne?" asked Molly.

"A private firm that does lab tests in the city," said Letisha.

"Why are you concerned about the blood?" asked Molly.

"We're thinking that a blood test might have been the link to Fragile X," answered Sylvia. "The man that called Dr. Colder knew that you were involved. The only three possibilities we could think of were through the blood tests, your records at Women's Health, or your records at County."

"Or your friends," corrected Colder, looking at Molly. "Did you tell anyone about it?"

Molly shook her head side to side. "No. Most of my friends were more Troy's. I almost told Tracy, she's a waitress friend of mine, but I decided against it."

Colder looked down again, burying his chin in the palm of his right hand.

"I'm still confused about the blood," Molly asked. "Why were you worried about where Women's Health sends the blood?"

"Because we needed to know where your blood might have gone," explained Sylvia.

"But I had my blood drawn at the ComHealthOne clinic, not at Women's Health," protested Molly. "This Dr. Michaels came to see me as a result of the blood I had drawn when I thought I was pregnant."

Colder leaped to his feet, his mind ablaze. "Yes! What was I thinking?"

"I did it just like ComHealth wanted me to," Molly continued. "When I thought I was pregnant I called them. I got this OB nurse who authorized the pregnancy test. Then I went to their clinic and had the blood drawn. A few days later Dr. Michaels called me."

"That's how ComHealth works it," agreed Colder. "No visit to the doctor. Saves them money."

"Wait a minute," said Sylvia. "Who's your primary care physician, Molly?"

"Dr. Tim Schmidt."

"Did he know any of this?"

"I doubt it. He's really tough to get in to see."

"So the pregnancy test was ordered over the phone, got drawn at ComHealth's clinic, sent to Doyne, and some guy named Michaels appears a couple days later."

"Yes," agreed Molly.

Colder's eyes were locked with Sylvia's. "A-plus weird," she said.

Colder allowed himself a hint of a grin. "I think I need to pay a little visit to our friends at Doyne, first thing tomorrow," he said.

"I'll go with you, if it will help," offered Molly.

"You're on."

"Will they be closed on a Saturday?" asked Sandra.

"Just enough to be useful," replied Colder thoughtfully. "Fewer people around may be to our advantage."

"I'm supposed to meet Tyler at ten."

"Then we'll go at eight-thirty. It will be just enough time."

"How about if I meet you here at a little after eight?" asked Molly.

"Beautiful."

Colder finished the meeting. "You four go home," he said turning, looking at his watch. "It'll be past your dinnertime if you don't get going now."

"What are you going to do?" asked Sylvia.

"I have to go get a phone call from our friend."

They all suddenly realized they had forgotten about the Fragile X man's promise to call. "You know where he's going to call?" asked Sandra incredulously.

"I think so. He said, 'Open your mind,' What does that mean to you?"

"That's like that ad on TV to read a book."

Peter Colder nodded. "My 'creature-of-habit' life has made it easy for him to track me. I think he's probably got about ten places where he knows he can get hold of me."

"What's this one?" asked Sylvia.

"I stop at Browbeater's Books almost every night, usually just to chat with the owner. We went to college together."

"You think he's been following you?" asked Letisha.

"I think he knows everything about me. In fact, I'm sure of it. He's way ahead of us. He's just giving us everything in clues in case someone else is listening."

"Why doesn't he just tell you what this is all about?" asked Sandra.

"That I don't know. But it's something I think we need to find out. Hopefully tonight."

Twenty minutes later, Peter Colder opened the front door of Browbeater's Books, a cramped, musty, one-room bookstore in an old brick building along a depressed strip of Lake Street. Mark Henning nodded as Peter entered, the bookstore owner's tall frame balancing atop an extended ladder.

"That guy get ahold of you?" he asked Colder as he stretched toward a book.

"Who?" asked Peter.

"Some guy. Didn't leave a name. Said he'd call back."

As he said it, the phone rang.

"Go ahead and get it," said Henning, dusting the cover of his prize.

Colder walked behind the counter and picked up the phone. "Browbeater's Books."

"You have done well today, Dr. Colder. You have exceeded my expectations."

"Why don't you just tell me what you know?" demanded Colder coolly.

"You know the answer to that question. You simply won't admit it to yourself."

With these words, Colder felt a chill.

"I will call again tomorrow," said the voice. "What is your favorite Beatles song?"

"Uh—*Hey Jude*," struggled Colder.

"Mine is *Yellow Submarine*."

Colder thought of another question, but it was too late. The line was dead.

Chapter Seven

The next morning, Molly Loomis knocked on the front door of the Third Street Clinic and peered through the shades. Colder, smiling brightly, opened the door and guided her in. But as soon as he saw her, he realized something had changed. Something was wrong. She was dressed casually in slacks and blouse but her hair was no longer curled and she again looked tired and worn. The life he had seen in her face the night before was gone, and her skin now looked faded and without texture. Her brow was lined and her lips quivered as she looked at him. He noticed that her eyes were reddened and partially obscured by the dark glasses she wore. Trembling noticeably, she walked past him toward Letisha's desk as if in a daze, her hands clutching her bag.

"What's wrong?" he asked.

"Troy has a lawyer, too," she replied, handing him a single sheet of paper. "This was at home when I got there." She pushed the sunglasses back and nervously brushed the sides of her head, "He couldn't even tell me when I was over there yesterday. I stood right in front of him, and he wouldn't even say a word!"

Colder glanced at the hand-written note, but did not read it. He turned his attention to Molly. "What exactly happened?"

"He won't even talk to me," she mumbled, not answering.

Colder paused. As Molly stood dazed, he peered at the note and suddenly he understood. He walked toward her.

"He wouldn't even tell me," she mumbled again.

Colder felt odd, knowing that he was still technically her physician but realizing that his instinct to maintain a professional distance might be counterproductive. She needed a shoulder and a friend more than a doctor's psychological probes. He was determined to provide whatever was necessary.

"He wants it back?" he asked.

"Yes, my engagement ring."

Colder bristled but held his tongue. He had long before learned to never be too critical of a spouse no matter how flagrant the violation. He understood that in the human psyche the emotions of love and hate stood side by side and often in shadow of one another, as the sun, like the mind, rendered different light upon the two. It was safer to cajole, stimulate, and support. He would provide this.

"I know he just wants to sell it. He's trying to buy a truck."

"What a prick," said Colder, in three words violating a lifetime's worth of brilliant psychoanalysis.

Molly didn't hear him. Instead she was lost in her own thoughts. "He wants one of those huge trucks with the big wheels and the gun rack in back for when he goes deer hunting." She stopped and pulled something from her purse "Oh, and I found this in the paper today." She handed him a small want ad that had been cut out. "It's his new phone number," she said. "He's selling things. I just thought maybe Tyler should know."

Used Essentials: Mounted Buck Deer busts, Collector Beer signs, 1997 Snowmobile. Mint! Really Fast! 612-428-3501.

Colder read the ad and returned it, his face without expression, but he suddenly felt that this man's procreative failures might actually be a hidden societal blessing.

"He always thought all those deer busts would be worth something," said Molly. "He used to pick them up at garage sales. He kept them in storage."

"They—" started Colder.

"I hated them," continued Molly. "The signs too. They were always dusty and junky, and most of them made noise."

"You probably won't even miss them," he said.

"But not the ring," she protested. "Not my diamond. I can't. It's mine, and I may never—" Colder came to her and held her tightly as she started to cry. "Who's ever going to wa—" she did not finish, instead burying her face in his chest. Gently he rocked her back and forth as his arms clutched her firmly.

Colder felt ashamed. He knew that to him and his coworkers it had all been a mystery that had become a threat. A problem to be solved. A problem with an origin and an answer. To Molly Loomis, there was no solution, no answer. The problem was simply her life, irreparably altered and her future hopes forever dashed.

Colder continued to rock her gently, letting her cry. He started to speak but then held back, refraining from the automatic 'doctorly' reassurance that still tried to slip off his tongue. He knew he was crossing a line slightly as he held her, but he made no attempt to stop.

"We'll talk to Tyler," he said soothingly. "I doubt Troy'll have claim on it."

She shook her head back and forth, tears flowing freely. Finally, she gently pushed herself away, and then laughing nervously she wiped her eyes. "I'm making myself a mess."

"You look fine."

"I appreciate that," she said, reaching for a Kleenex on an end table. "But you still better hide the mirrors."

He laughed at her joke. "You certainly don't look any worse than anyone else who ever walks in here, myself included."

"You're a wonderful liar," she laughed as she continued to recover and put herself together.

"It's true, what I said." Colder was surprised at how easily the words came to him. A compliment of sorts, perhaps undeserved, but heartfelt. She was frail, but not meek; feminine and without any insecurity that saw emotion as weakness.

"We'll talk to him," he repeated.

"Thanks."

Colder thought it would be good to get her mind on something else. "You ready?"

She, too, was ready to leave thoughts of Troy. She sniffled and nodded. "Let's go."

Doyne Laboratories had been started by Charles Doyne in 1983 in Kansas City. The premise, high-volume laboratory analysis at cost savings, had initially been coolly received by clinics and hospitals dependent on the revenue, but as health insurance evolved, several HMOs began contracting with the expanding organization. Doyne promised the HMOs a low price. The HMOs promised Doyne a large volume. The combination was wildly profitable. With the HMOs as an ally, success was automatic, and by 1993, Doyne Laboratories was the largest chain of comprehensive medical lab services in the Midwest. With last year's revenue over $350 million, their explosive growth was continuing. Recently, Doyne had announced expansion plans into Ohio and Pennsylvania, and rumors placed them in Tennessee and Virginia by the end of the year. Wherever they went, competition appeared to melt.

Colder pulled his car into the parking lot, stopping in front of the single-story brick building. The two walked through the front door and found an entirely renovated structure, probably once apartments, but now an open expanse of glass-walled rooms. Machines and computer terminals were everywhere, and a handful of employees dressed in white lab coats ambled between the rooms. Peter and Molly stopped at a receptionist's desk that was only a few feet inside.

"May I help you?" asked the receptionist, a pretty and petite brunette, about twenty, with a large name tag that said Randi.

"My name is Dr. Peter Colder," he said easily, "and this is my assistant Joan Freeman."

Molly blinked, but said nothing. "I often send labs here from my clinic, the Third Street Clinic, and I was concerned because it appeared that one I sent over a few weeks ago got lost. I was wondering if there had been a problem."

"It's certainly nice of you to visit," said Randi pleasantly, "but to save you a trip in the future, I can let you know that we also offer an automated telephone service."

"Thank you," he said nodding. "We often use it. But I just wanted to see the place. I've sent a lot of blood here. It's only six blocks away, and I had never bothered to stop by."

"Certainly," she said. "I'll get Mel. He'll be able to help you."

When Randi disappeared through a glass door and down a hallway, Molly turned to Peter, a slight hint of smile on her face. "Joan? I didn't know I got a new name."

Colder was happy that she appeared to be feeling better. She said little on the trip over, but now he continued to try to draw her out. "I thought it would look less strange than me bringing along a patient."

Molly appeared to put the morning's tears behind her and relax. "Well, if I get a new name, how about a fancy one then?"

Colder paused. "You mean like Chantel or Monique?"

"Yes. Those are good."

Colder rolled his eyes. "Because you look like a Molly and I look like a Peter. If we were Beauregard and Monique, we would have come in a limo and dressed in evening black."

Molly managed a short laugh. "Okay, but if we're going to do detective work I want to pick my name."

He smiled back at her. "Fair enough."

They turned toward the offices. In the distance, they could see the receptionist navigating through a series of glass passageways followed by a short, bald, heavy-set man with a five o'clock shadow, an oversized tie, and a broad grin. He walked past Randi and extended his hand. "Mel DeLorme."

"Peter Colder," he said, shaking the burly hand. "And my assistant, Joan Freeman."

DeLorme nodded pleasantly to Molly. "Nice to meet you both."

"We're here about a patient's lab work."

"That's what Randi told me, Doc," he said turning and motioning them to follow.

"I can assure you that that's a rare one. We pride ourselves on both accuracy and efficiency."

"I've never had any trouble before," he said, walking one step behind the man and in step with Molly.

"We'll go to my office and check the computer," he said.

They walked through a winding series of glass-lined halls with the colored carpets acting as trails. They followed a navy carpet past several rooms, each housing large computers. DeLorme led them around two more turns and finally to an inconspicuous office hidden behind more computers in a neighboring alcove. Following him, Peter and Molly went inside and took two chairs that faced his cluttered desk. DeLorme fell into his seat, pulled the keyboard out from under the desktop, and turned on his computer. "Let's see what we got," he said.

Colder scanned the room. All four walls, like the rest of the building, were glass. They were thick, but crystalline, allowing little sound and perfect vision. The rest of the office consisted of two waist-high filing cabinets, each with a realistic-looking plastic green plant and a few scattered trinkets. Behind the desk was a wooden cabinet that looked much like a TV console. One door was partially open, and Colder noticed a box of Triscuits and a bag of Chips Ahoy. On top of the cabinet was a series of pictures. One family portrait with a wife and two teenage sons. Others appeared to be of parents and friends.

"What was the patient's name?" DeLorme asked.

"Loomis. Molly Loomis."

"Two *o*'s—*m*—*i*—*s*?"

"Yes."

Mel DeLorme typed in the number and frowned as the screen showed the file.

"That's strange," he said. "There is no record of us receiving it."

"I'm sure we sent it," said Colder without threat.

"We have some stuff from a few years ago. CBCs, cultures, but nothing recently."

"We sent a CBC, Sed Rate, and pregnancy."

"Seems weird that we would have no record of it."

"Yes," acknowledged Colder.

"Let me try the log file. What date did you say it was?"

"May sixth. We usually send them over late, around 5:00."

"Means it should have been received at about 5:30," DeLorme said, punching letters and numbers on the machine. "This might take me a minute."

Colder looked at Molly, who was still gazing in different directions throughout the building.

"Here we go," said DeLorme staring at the screen. "May sixth."

His expression quickly turned again to a frown as he scanned the long list of names, numbers, and times. "Not here either. You sure on the spelling?"

"M-o-l-l-y-l-o-o-m-i-s."

"That's what I typed in. Let me try the seventh. Maybe by chance it didn't get registered until the next day."

Five minutes later, they had tried the fifth, sixth, and seventh, as well as various spellings of her name. They had also reviewed all of the old lab values from two years before. There was no sign of the blood.

"I don't know what to tell you," he said finally.

"Could it have gone to another of your offices?" asked Molly.

"It would still show up in this computer," he said pleasantly.

"The only thing I can think of is that the we never got the blood."

"That must be it," said Colder. "We might have erred."

"It's bound to happen once in a while. By the way," he continued," you wouldn't know if the patient got a bill for the service would you?"

"No," replied Molly immediately. "I'm sure she didn't."

"Well, that should help," said DeLorme. "Then we almost certainly didn't process the blood, because the computer automatically bills as soon as the lab is run."

"We must have lost it."

"Sorry I couldn't be of any help," said DeLorme rising.

"No, you have," smiled Colder. "I think my office must have dropped the ball. We're a pretty low-tech operation compared to this. I'm afraid it's probably us."

"If you have any other questions though, I'd be pleased to help."

"Thanks again. We can show ourselves out."

They shook hands, and Mel DeLorme waved to them as they followed the navy carpeting back through the maze of glass rooms and to the foyer where Randi greeted them as they passed. "Get everything settled?"

"Yes," said Colder. "Thanks for your help."

"You're welcome."

A moment later, they stepped outside into the brilliant sunshine of the Saturday morning. "What do you think?" asked Molly.

"Very interesting," said Colder as they walked toward the car. "You had someone call you about a test result that doesn't even exist or has disappeared."

"You think that's what happened?"

"Yes," Colder said. "At least I think so. What else could it be?"

"Maybe they just wouldn't tell you because you weren't from ComHealth," Molly said.

"No. They had that lab work you had done four years ago. And that was ComHealth."

"True."

"Let me think," Colder continued as he opened her door. "First of all, we have no explanation of how this Fragile X issue came about. And now, secondly, we have no idea where your blood went and where this 'positive Fragile X' test came from."

"Yes."

Colder stroked his chin and looked thoughtful. "Let's look at this differently. Say you worked for ComHealth and you decided to hide the lab."

"Okay."

"If you were ever going to hide a fact like that, where would you do it?"

They stopped next to the car and stood without opening the doors. Molly caught his train of thought. "I'd bury it deep in a computer. And in a room with enough computers to run the world. A room like they had here at Doyne."

"That's what I was thinking too," he said unaffectedly.

"Do you know much about computers?" she asked.

"Not enough to take on those," he replied as he glanced back at the building.

"Maybe our Fragile X friend can help," said Molly. "When is he going to call?"

"Noon."

Molly looked perplexed. "You figured his clue out?"

"Yes. I'm pretty sure his reference to my favorite Beatles song and *Yellow Submarine* has to do with my usually stopping for a sub sandwich on Saturdays."

Molly looked slightly alarmed. "I think he's been watching you."

Colder nodded and tried to appear unconcerned. "We'd better get to Tyler's."

Molly saw through his act, but said nothing. He, too, was still a little worried. They climbed into the car and drove off in silence.

Tyler Briggs looked elegantly casual in an ensemble of cotton pullover, button-down shirt, and cuffed trousers. As before, he stood behind the desk talking on the phone while squeezing a spring-grip strengthener in his right hand. He motioned them to sit down as he continued the conversation, obviously with another lawyer, as a barrage of legal terms suddenly spewed forth, followed by the hilarious laughter of an inside joke. One moment later he was formal, followed by another laugh and a quick goodbye.

"Sorry," he smiled, turning to them and tossing down the plastic-handled trainer.

"No problem," said Colder.

"Tyler Briggs," he said extending his hand.

"Pete Colder."

"How are you, Molly?" he asked.

"Better."

"Good," he said. "Sleep okay?"

"Pretty well."

"Did you bring everything?"

"Yes," she said proudly, laying records and X-rays on his desk.

He began to flip through the items. "Excellent."

"I think that I can be of some help in interpreting the records," said Colder.

"I'm counting on it," Briggs replied. "I'm not big on the medical lingo."

"Do you think there's a case?" Molly asked, not sure if she was ready for the answer.

Briggs fingered through the HCMC record, pausing only briefly as he fanned through the pages while the others took seats. "Don't know yet. But I have learned a few interesting things about our friend ComHealthOne in the past day."

"No friends of mine," Colder mumbled.

"That's kind of what I wanted to know."

"Why don't you tell us what you know first. Then Molly and I have a lot to let you in on," Colder suggested.

"Fair enough," said Briggs, removing his glasses and kicking his feet up on the ottoman. "Let me start you with this. Your friends at ComHealth in the span of the last three years have moved from the eighteenth to the largest HMO in the country. With their pending acquisitions and mergers this year, they will again almost double in size. At this point, they control the health care of over twenty-six million people, and that is expected to grow to forty million by the end of next year. Their gross revenues last year were in excess of $4 billion. Their profits exceeded $400 million. The company's net worth is greater than the GNP of over half the countries in the world."

"It's a machine," Colder admitted.

Briggs continued. "They now contract with, or perhaps better said, 'own,' over sixty thousand physicians, four thousand clinics, and two thousand hospitals. Their legal team alone is over two hundred attorneys on an annual budget of $14 million."

"Incredible."

"The five men running the company have personally made over $300 million in stock options in the last eighteen months. If that company's stock were to hit one hundred, which is entirely likely at a ten percent growth, it's quite possible that Hutchins himself would be worth a couple of billion dollars."

"Business is business," Colder said with a touch of sarcasm.

"There's a down side to this," started Briggs. "And it's a big down side. They've *never* lost a case on anything to do with a patient contract dispute." Neither Molly nor Colder reacted. Somehow they had expected to hear that. "In addition, we have four attorneys in our firm. We're small, but growing. We have four paralegals, six secretaries, and one night watchman. Our annual gross revenues are probably about a one-month salary to one of their top attorneys. In other words, to take these guys on, if we actually got to trial for something, it might break us. In fact they could probably do that with motions and continuances alone. A five-year delay to them means nothing. To us—"

"Are you saying no?" blurted Molly fearfully.

"I don't know what I'm saying yet," Briggs said tentatively. "I don't even know if there is a case. I just want to hear what you have to say."

"We'll tell you everything we know," Colder offered.

"Good," Briggs said. "That's what I was hoping for." He reached into his pocket and pulled out a Certs, popping it in his mouth.

Briggs's eyes started glowing. "Let me toss some numbers at you. In the last three months, ComHealthOne has registered somewhere over 500 official complaints, varying in nature from long delays to difficult access to doctors. They have also systematically canceled the contracts of over 11,000 people, all apparently legally, but these poor souls were also all heavy users of health care services."

"Good business practice," Colder's words dripped sarcasm.

"Apparently so."

"What do you think, Tyler?" asked Molly.

Briggs was gazing out the window at a cloud high in the sky. He appeared to be deep in thought. "I'm interested," he said finally. "The old saying is behind every great fortune is a great crime. And, well, when you have two hundred lawyers working for you, my suspicion is that you're living on the edge."

Colder nodded and took a deep breath. "Now let me tell you a few things."

"Please do."

"I contracted with ComHealth until eighteen months ago and continued to do a bit of work for them until a few months ago. Now I just see patients of theirs if they are getting jerked around and can't get in to see a doctor."

"Why did you stop?"

"I couldn't stand what they were doing. Cutbacks in care, lying about it, huge profits at patient expense. It was unbelievable. And finally there was the last straw."

"What was that?"

"They were starting something new. They called it an 'incentive-based compensation plan.' I refused to go along with it, and they essentially forced me to resign or be fired."

"Start from the beginning," said Briggs, pulling out his yellow pad.

"It really requires a brief review of the history of medical economics."

"Go ahead," said Molly, apparently stealing the words out of Tyler's mouth.

"You see, it used to be that most people were insured by indemnity plans, like Blue Cross/Blue Shield. The way that worked was the doctor treated the patient, sent in his charges, and the insurance company in turn, out of money collected from patient's premiums, reimbursed him. This system, where the incentive was to provide more care, was then blamed for the increasing medical costs, the logic being that the doctors were ordering too many tests and treating too long because they profited from it."

"Isn't that true?" asked Briggs.

"A lot less than people think. First of all, rarely does a physician directly profit from ordering a lab, an X-ray or a CAT scan, because they usually don't own the machines or provide the service. Now it is true that the physician would make more money by seeing a patient more often, taking a more detailed history, confronting more medical problems, or doing a more detailed examination."

"For more in-depth care."

"Yes."

"What about operations or procedures?"

"The same. In the old system, if a surgeon operates more, he makes more money."

"So there was a financial incentive to operate more."

"True. But to blame that as a real factor in medical inflation is really to play on people's most cynical fears. The equivalent would be for me to say that you're going out and encouraging people to get divorced so that you could make more money."

Briggs laughed. "Lawyers have been accused of worse."

"But more importantly, while aggressive medical care is probably a bit inflationary, it's also good care and what people need. Heart catheterizations and bypasses, neurosurgery, and joint replacements. Intensive care medicine."

"That was the old system," said Briggs.

"I think I wish we still had it," Molly said ruefully.

"I agree," acknowledged Colder. "It was imperfect, but the motivation was at least parallel to, if not completely in step with, a patient's best interest."

"What about now?"

"The prepaid concept used in HMOs is exactly the opposite. A subscriber pays in a monthly fee. There is no deductible on most policies so other than a co-payment each time a patient visits a doctor, usually like twenty dollars. They are responsible for nothing more."

"How are the doctors paid?"

"The HMO pays each doctor or clinic a capitated rate, a certain amount of money for each subscriber, no matter how much service is provided."

"So providing service is now an *expense* rather than revenue generating."

"Exactly. The only way to make money in a prepaid system is to either receive large capitated payments, which obviously doesn't happen, since it is a cost-containment system, or to reduce the amount of service provided."

"And how have they done that?"

"Originally the HMOs were quite subtle. Several years ago, when they were trying to sell themselves to the country as less costly alternatives with no difference in quality, their tactics were primarily internal. What they did was take control of all care. They set up elaborate algorithms, or cookbooks, that physicians were supposed to follow in order to control how a patient was cared for. Standardization sounds good, but the truth was that the real motivation was to reduce the number of tests ordered, the number of specialists seen, and the number of operations performed. They did it by setting up a great roadblock to care, something called 'preauthorization.'"

"I know about this," Briggs said. "You have to call your insurance company to get anything authorized before you get it done or they won't pay for it."

"Yes. So the HMO controls what gets paid for and realistically controls what care is delivered."

"But if you disagreed with ComHealth and felt a patient needed a test, couldn't you still get it?"

"Yes, by negotiating over more roadblocks—phone calls, forms, appeals. With enough effort, a physician could usually get a necessary test or do a necessary operation."

"You said 'usually.' So their restrictive efforts did ultimately affect patient care?"

"Certainly it did. They are in business to make money. Pure and simple. And that's what they did. Their strategy was twofold. First, raise the bar. Make it difficult to get into the system. Next, restrict care even if the patient goes into the system. It was inevitable that it affected patient care."

"What's different now?" Molly asked.

"Well, the first thing they did was make an enormous amount of money. They wrung what they call 'savings' out of the system like crazy. Most of this was from restricting tests that most physicians would agree were probably near a point of being excessive. As an example, say a post-op blood count when the patient had bled very little. Some of these things had been done for years, based on not much more than physician's habits."

"So these cutbacks doctors agreed to."

"Anything that was truly unnecessary? Certainly."

"Then what happened?"

"Well, what the HMOs discovered was that the best they had likely achieved was really a one-time savings. The fact is that people are still being born, getting sick, and dying. They still need care. There is only so much 'savings' you can wring out."

"So there was a new strategy?"

"Yes. And this is where the problem starts. When a publically traded corporation's initial profits are huge, shareholders simply raise their expectations. They want even greater profits. But more importantly, when the corporate executives discover that there are no more magic savings within the system to fatten their bottom line, they're left with few options."

"Like what?" asked Molly and Tyler simultaneously.

"Like they had to change the system."

Briggs was writing furiously. "How'd they do that?"

Colder sat back. "The first strategy was the loophole strategy. Find every fine line you can and deny any claim possible."

"But that's nothing new," protested Briggs. "The old indemnity companies did the same."

"But never to this degree. Old indemnity companies like Blue Cross made three cents on the dollar. They did so for seventy-five years. They never tried to increase their profit margin at the expense of patient care. Since these HMO guys are publicly traded corporations, they *have* to return better than ten percent growth per year to their investors. Corporate reality."

"I believe you. Go on." Briggs' pen was poised, ready to take more notes.

"The second strategy was to systematically attempt to insure only those least likely to use the service. They use any means necessary to void a policy."

"Like they're doing now with Molly."

"Yes. But it's their third and fourth strategies that really start to get them into questionable territory."

"Go on."

"By using typical techniques, undercutting and accumulating market share, ComHealth obtained great leverage within the system. By 'vertically integrating'—buying clinics, physician practices, hospitals, lab facilities, et cetera—they control everything and everyone. They used this not only to ratchet down reimbursements, but to eliminate competition *and* further increase their control of how doctors and hospitals did business."

"Sounds a little scary to me," said Molly.

"It is, but what's worse is that when they get that kind of grip on the healthcare system, they're also gaining control of how many tests are ordered on patients, when they are performed, when patients are admitted to hospitals, when they are discharged. They not only move onto a slippery slope, they dive onto it."

"I see."

"But it's the fourth strategy that is the least well known and the most terrifying," said Colder. "Now they're trying to make the physicians a part of the HMO financial equation."

"How so?"

"A physician is paid a salary, usually less than what would be considered an average salary for his specialty. Then they tack on incentives so that the practitioner can make up the difference or even more. The incentives are quotas. For example a family doctor like myself would be allowed to refer only a certain number of patients a month to specialists. After that he would be penalized, with less income."

"Whoa," said Briggs, his eyes widening. "So doctors have a financial incentive not to refer more than their quota?"

"Not only that, but they would be rewarded for referring less. A perfect employee would be one who didn't refer at *all*."

"What about surgeons?"

"Same thing, so many operations in a month. Beyond that, they would be penalized."

"So they are paid more for not using their skills?"

"Exactly so. That's how perverted the system is becoming."

Briggs sat back, stuck his pen in his mouth, and clasped his hands behind his neck. He was looking more interested all the time. "Tell me, Pete, why'd you leave?"

"Simple. I wouldn't practice like that. I trained to be a doctor, nothing more. I couldn't stand the idea that money was more important than the patient."

Briggs stared at him curiously. He had heard about Colder's financial troubles. "Are you an idealist, a rebel, or a fool?"

"Probably all of the above."

Briggs chuckled as he rose and poured cups of coffee, handing them to Molly and Peter. "Tell me," he said as he returned to his seat. "Why don't the doctors fight it? It would seem to me that they still hold the cards. They deliver the care."

"For the doctors to complain publicly would be impossible. Doctors are seen as Lexus-driving country clubbers, one step removed from the real world. To even raise the issue would be impossible. The public is cynical, and with the history of high salaries and the prestige that medicine has enjoyed, people would view physician complaints as little more than sour grapes. Physicians have no power in the court of public opinion, and, therefore, have no real power at all."

Briggs and Molly listened intently while Colder continued to talk. Briggs still occasionally wrote down ideas as they tossed around in his brain. When Colder finished, Molly was shaking her head. "ComHealth's certainly created an empire," she said with an exaggerated admiration.

"That they have."

Briggs was ready to move on. "And now this stuff about Fragile X and Molly. What can you tell me?"

For the next twenty minutes, Colder related to him all of the details of the past week, including his phone calls with the man who called himself Fragile X, his speculation as to why the man was wary, and the missing blood. Briggs continued to listen carefully, jotting more notes, rising once to refill his cup of coffee. Finally finishing with a review of Molly's medical history, during which time Molly interjected periodically to clarify details, Colder stopped, nearly out of breath.

"What do you think, Tyler?" Molly asked. "Overall."

Briggs was staring at the ComHealthOne policy that Molly had placed on his desk when they had first come in. Running his fingers along the fine print as if he were reading Braille, he squinted, mouthing some of the words silently. He paused, holding the contract at his side, and looked blankly past them. "I don't know," he said finally. "As I see it, there is some sort of mystery with disappearing blood. Then, there is a diagnosis that can't be established and some wacko that keeps calling claiming to be a disease. To make it even more complicated, there is an insurance contract here with Molly's signature that can be used to invalidate her claim. A contract held up by innumerable courts."

Molly looked downward. Colder also looked deflated. "Then you don't think that there's anything to all this?"

Briggs shook his head for no discernible reason. His gaze turned pensive. "It could break us," he whispered only to himself.

"What about the contract?"

Briggs turned away, staring out the window. He was now off in his own world. "If it got big, they'd come after us with fifty attorneys, a hundred assistants all working twenty-six hours a days. They'd have five, ten million to spend, easy. They'd fight to the end, to the death."

His last words were inaudible as he leaned against the wall, lost in a reverie of his own. "It's a long shot," he said finally. "We'd probably all go down."

"Then you believe the story?" asked Colder.

"The wacko caller, you mean?" questioned Briggs.

"Yes."

Briggs turned away again and picked up the small porcelain bloodhound that he had placed on the bureau behind the desk. He fondled it, running his fingers over the various curves and edges. It was there again. The scent, faint, but real. He turned to them, placing the small animal on the desk facing away. "It's all pretty crazy. And I'm not sure I'd believe any of this, let alone even think about taking on ComHealthOne if it weren't for one thing."

"What's that?" asked Molly.

"One little thing I haven't told you yet."

"What's that?"

"A little piece of trivia that might interest you."

"What?" they asked together.

Briggs smiled glibly. "Did either of you know that ComHealth owns Doyne Labs?"

Colder's mouth fell open, his eyes wide. "No."

"Yes. For a couple of years."

Molly fell back in her chair. Both she and Peter were speechless.

Briggs continued talking. "I think we might be interested to know what else they own."

"I- I agree," stammered Colder.

"Then you think there's a case?" asked Molly eagerly.

Briggs looked down, refolding the documents that were splayed across his desk. "Yes, I think there's something. At very least, we can raise a little noise and create a little stink."

Molly looked relieved. She stood and hugged Tyler. "Thanks," she said as she released him.

"You're welcome."

Colder rose and shook Briggs's hand. "Thank you, Tyler."

"You're welcome as well. But I'll need to talk to both of you again soon."

"What are your plans, Tyler?" asked Colder

"Quite simple," said Briggs. "We'll nip at them and hope they don't bite back. Raise enough stink and maybe they'll pay. That's the goal. Just get them to pay her bill."

"What about this Fragile X stuff?" asked Molly.

"We might use it to put a little fear in them. Right now, though, there's nothing there. And truthfully? We don't have the manpower to investigate it well."

"So use it as a threat?"

"In a subtle way. It could be very helpful in getting them to pay your claim."

"But what if we prove it's real?" asked Molly.

"You mean if ComHealth were actually involved in some sort of criminal conspiracy?"

"Yes."

The thought was like a sweet drink to a parched attorney. Briggs swallowed and couldn't stop his grin. "You know ComHealth's symbol? The one that sits atop the IDS Tower."

"That great big dragon?"

"Yes."

"If we found that, then we could slay that ugly monster."

No one said another word. The thought was simply too electrifying.

Molly crumpled several Kleenex into her purse, and minutes later they sat in Peter's car, winding their way through the morning downtown traffic.

Chapter Eight

Forty-five minutes later, Molly and Peter sat at a back table of Samson's Subs, a small downtown deli that catered mainly to off-campus university students. The walls were decorated with old rock and roll memorabilia as well as small shrines to James Dean, Marilyn Monroe, Jimi Hendrix, and Kurt Cobain. Overall, the restaurant represented a fascinating mix. It was part a '50s soda fountain, part yuppie nostalgia, and part Generation X schizophrenia.

Most tables were taken at the noon hour, occupied by grunge-worshipping, Bohemian-looking university students intently discussing a number of deep thoughts. The usual discourse revolved around social upheaval, world peace, and the artistic expression of human suffering inherent in contemporary rock music. Just as frequently, however, it was about beer and sex.

Samson's was famous for its submarines, eight inches long and overstuffed with meat, cheese, and lettuce. Its reputation, however, came from a liberally used secret sauce that was more carefully guarded than the combination to Fort Knox. Colder munched on a club sub with extra cheese while Molly had turkey and cheese. An order of fries sat between them, with a Diet Coke in front of Colder and a chocolate shake near Molly.

"Is it good?" he asked.

"Yuh, yuh," she tried to say, her mouth full.

"I insist you eat everything," he chuckled. "Doctor's order."

"I'll try," she managed as a hunk of sauce fell on a napkin. "Thanks for buying."

"You're welcome."

Molly swallowed and wiped her mouth. "Sometime you'll have to let me buy."

"I'll hold you to it."

Her eyes sparkled as he said it. The appealing gaze struck him, but just as quickly his doctor's mind returned. He wondered how long it had been since she had sat for a meal with someone, engaging in simple, nonthreatening conversation. He looked at her willowy frame and her thin, but delicate, face. He wondered what her life had been like. How many times had Troy hurt her? How many blows? How many words? How many threats and how many insults? The ugly thought occurred to him—wouldn't it be natural to begin to believe the words heard over and over again? The mind stripped naked, then twisted and broken. In the end, a sense of worthlessness replacing the fear, while a dependence grew upon the abuser, the paradoxical side effect. Colder saw it all in her: weakness desiring to be strong, failure wishing to succeed. But at this moment she seemed to have no thoughts of the past. She was simply herself. For a moment she seemed better.

"I really like Tyler," she said.

"He's an exceptional attorney. I've heard it from more than Letisha."

She sipped on her shake. "I'm sure of something else too. As I listened to you two talk today, I was trying to remember what Dr. Michaels, or whoever he was, said to me. I was so shocked by all of it; I admit I wasn't too clear. But I know that it was the blood test that had led them to the diagnosis. I'm sure he said so."

"You're sure?"

"Absolutely," she affirmed.

"Then we have to find out where the blood went. It's only logical. If Doyne is owned by ComHealth, then you have to figure that everything is controlled and monitored by the dragon."

"Right."

"The problem is, I have no idea how to get into their computers."

"I do," Molly said without missing a beat.

Colder was almost speechless. Part of his sub fell. "You do?"

"Not me, actually," she blushed. "The kid who lives across from me."

"Who's that?"

"His name's Reggie Tan. He lives with his mother. He's in high school and he's awesome with computers." Colder just listened as Molly went on. "He got in a lot of trouble last year because he hacked into his school computer just before one of their newspaper issues went to print. He replaced all the articles about homecoming with some pictures from *Playboy*. The police came in the middle of the night and hauled him away. The next day, the principal gave a speech on the front steps of the school surrounded by three preachers."

Colder laughed out loud. "What about the school paper?"

"I heard that fifteen hundred were printed, but no one could even get a copy. After the principal's speech on TV, kids from other schools were calling, trying to buy them."

"What happened?"

"The papers started turning up in other suburbs a couple of weeks later. Reggie outsmarted everyone. When those guys were on TV every night talking about how evil they were, the price was going up all the time. Reggie actually had 'em, and he sold every one."

Colder threw his head back. "Oh yeah. I remember that now. It was in the paper. Then they made the kid give the money back."

"No, actually they let him keep it. His mom is an invalid, and he used the money to buy her an electric wheelchair."

"Really."

"He's a good kid. A little bit of an original, but I bet he could do it."

"Somehow, I believe it."

As he said it, the pay phone on the wall behind him rang. Colder rose and answered it before it rang again.

"Hello?"

It was the voice. "You have done well today, Dr. Colder."

"Thank you," he answered reflexively, motioning for Molly to listen as well.

She pressed her ear next to his.

"Mr. Briggs will do quite nicely. In fact, you could not have done better."

"I'd like to know who you are."

"In time, Peter. At this point, you have no need to know. I also want to tell you that at this moment you are in no danger. When that changes, I will warn you."

Molly shook her head back and forth, answering Colder's question as to whether it was the same man she had talked to a month before.

"The only things you need to know right now are the following: One, the trail is warm; you are correct, the blood was at Doyne. And two, you must find a copy of a journal. *The British Journal of Developmental Genetics* from July of 1997."

"What do you mean, the blood was there?" he asked.

"I will not talk to you now for a while. You will need time."

"Why will I need time?"

"Do you enjoy beer, Dr. Colder?" came the voice, ignoring his question.

"Occasionally."

"I have a preference for local beers myself. Cold and on tap."

The phone went dead. Molly and Peter sat down, gazing at each other.

"When is he going to call again?" she asked.

"Once a month, I go to a happy hour at a place called the Down Under to meet some old resident friends. He'll call then."

"What did he say we need to get?" she asked.

"*The British Journal of Developmental Genetics.* July 1997."

"That should be easy," she said.

"Sandra's going to the library this afternoon. I'll ask her to pick it up."

"He also said that the blood was at Doyne," grinned Molly. "We were right!"

Colder nodded. "I think we're going to need your computer friend."

"I'll talk to him right away."

Molly stopped, and the smile slipped from her face. The man's other words had struck her. "He also said we weren't in danger—yet."

Colder was fixated on the same remark. "I know."

"I don't think he was kidding," she said, her enthusiasm evaporating with the thought.

"Neither do I," he said glumly. "Neither do I."

Reggie Tan's computer did the conventionally amazing things. It played music from a CD, worked as a telephone, stored a ton of information, and scanned pictures into files. But most impressive to computer novices Peter Colder and Molly Loomis was cyberspace travel. Reggie took them to the Louvre in Paris, traveled to the Smithsonian, and then took a tour of the White House. Lastly, Reggie visited the Third Street Clinic and broke into the computers, just for fun. Colder and Molly sat in amazement watching him work. An artist of the keyboard with flying fingers, Reggie floated through cyberspace like a child enjoying the freedom of no gravity.

Reggie looked like any kid from the mall on a Friday afternoon. His thick, black hair was two inches long over the top of his head, but cut short on the sides and back. His Eurasian face was tanned and handsome, with only one small blemish on his right cheek, hinting at a fading acne problem. Blue jeans, gold loop earring in his left ear, and a T-shirt with the name of a rock band that Colder had never heard of made Peter suddenly feel very old.

The walls of Reggie's room were covered with posters, one of Bruce Lee in *Enter The Dragon*, a second of the Minnesota Twins 1991 World Series team, and a third a life-size, full-length image of Marilyn Monroe from the *The Seven Year Itch*. Colder glanced back and forth from the computer to the poster, trying not to look at the blowing dress and legs for more than carefully timed, short bursts.

Molly sat on the edge of the bed, staring at the blonde bombshell. "You think she was that tall?" she asked.

"Marilyn?" asked Reggie.

"She looks about six feet tall there," said Molly, sounding slightly envious.

"I think she was about five-five," replied Reggie matter-of-factly, his fingers still tapping effortlessly on the keyboard.

"It's a disgusting image really," she continued. "You should be ashamed of yourself, Reggie."

"I am," he said, his turned back hiding his mischievous grin. "I'm very ashamed."

Colder laughed.

"Does your mother know?" Molly continued as Reggie stopped typing, staring at the computer screen.

"She hates it too," replied Reggie. "What do you think, Doc? I think it's something about estrogen and estrogen being like magnets of the same polarity."

Colder grunted a nonanswer. "It's almost obscene," said Molly.

Reggie turned to her, the grin no longer hidden, his dark eyes flashing. "Now wait a minute, Mol," he protested. "Who's that hunk-o-rama, stud muffin, cherry-cheeked beefcake that you and Tracy have hanging in the back of the restaurant. What's his name? Brad Pitt?"

"That's different," she mumbled, knowing she had overplayed her hand.

"Different? No shirt, lots of pecs, and a big cowboy hat?"

Colder was enjoying himself. "Who is it?"

"The guy from a bunch of movies. They have an old poster from *Legends of the Fall*."

"It's art," Molly said feebly, almost mocking her own words.

"It's ob-*scene*," contradicted Reggie with an exaggerated twist of his neck.

Colder bowed his head solemnly and spoke in a reverential tone. "Men as objects. The great tragedy of the twentieth century. I feel used."

Molly turned and pushed him away with both hands, trying not to laugh. "Give me a break! So, he's good looking!"

"We're all just hunks of meat," Reggie continued.

"I know," Colder said, happy to see Molly come further out of her shell. "It's tough being a sex symbol, isn't it?"

"Yes, to be wanted only for sexual powers."

"Then shamelessly discarded."

"Like a used rag." Reggie grinned and watched Molly cover her ears.

"Like the black widow who kills the male after she mates," Colder offered.

They both broke into laughter and Molly stood up, shoving them both gently.

"Stop it!" she giggled. "I think I'm going to throw up!"

They all started to laugh, but before they could enjoy it, the computer's screen changed. Seeing the new image, Reggie stopped and grunted approvingly. "Yes. We're in."

Colder's eyes opened wide. "Doyne?"

"Yes."

"How did you learn how to do all of this?" asked Molly, again seated close to Colder and looking over Reggie's shoulder at the screen full of numbers and codes.

"Got my first computer when I was eleven, was a used one from the school. Some of the teachers upgrade every couple of years, so I just asked if I could have the old stuff. Even if they wouldn't give it to me, I could usually buy it at a cheap price."

Colder watched with admiration as Reggie continued to type in commands that were illegible to him. The screen slowly scrolled downward. Peter was rapidly taking a liking to the teen. Molly had told him Reggie's story on the way to the apartment. His father was an engineer, killed in a car accident eight years before that had also left his mother quadriplegic. Reggie cared for her with the help of a home health aide that he paid for by working two jobs, one on weekday afternoons and the other on weekends. Reggie worked hard; the county helped a little, but money was always very tight.

"I got a good modem about a year ago," he continued. "After that, I could really do more stuff."

"I heard you were pretty good," Colder said. "Molly told me about how you earned the money for your mom's wheelchair."

"Yeah," chuckled Reggie. "But it got me in a little trouble too."

"It was for a good cause," said Molly.

Reggie laughed at himself. "Should have known it was illegal."

"You have that rebel streak, Reggie," said Molly.

"I'm just glad you're on our team, Reggie," said Colder.

The screen flashed again. "Okay, labs, May sixth."

They all stared at the screen, looking at the log-in times, names, and numbers. On the left was each individual's name, sequenced by time entered in the next column to the right. The third column contained abbreviations for the tests ordered, and on the far right were the initials for the point of origin for the specimens. One by one they passed through the list, over two hundred specimens in all, logged in between 5:00 P.M. and midnight.

"Not there," said Colder.

"No," Reggie agreed.

"Try other days," Molly encouraged.

For fifteen minutes, Reggie searched the Doyne files for the week following May 6, as well as billing records. There was no record of the blood having ever been at Doyne Labs.

"Can you go back to the original screen?" Colder asked.

"Sure."

Ten seconds later, the long vertical columns reappeared and Colder pointed to a name. "That one."

"Stephan French."

"Yes. Can you open that file? He's an old patient of mine."

"Sure."

Reggie opened the file to find a long list of labs dating back over four years. "Go back to early 1995," Colder directed.

The screen changed as Reggie typed in the commands, and a moment later another listing appeared. "That one," Colder said, pointing.

A moment later a line appeared.

HIV—confidential.

"HIV," said Reggie, surprised. "You want me to get it?"

"No, I just wanted to see how it was listed."

"Confidential," said Molly.

Colder ran his hand through his hair. He looked puzzled. "So they openly list the world's most confidential blood test in the computer. But Molly's vanishes without a trace."

"Let's think about it logically," began Reggie, turning toward them. "Mr. Fragile X tells us that the blood was there. Assuming that he's telling the truth, it means that the blood probably would have been logged in the conventional way."

Colder's cell phone rang. Pulling it from his back pocket, he appeared annoyed by the interruption. "Hello?"

"Dr. Colder?"

"Yes." Peter answered, recognizing Sandra's voice and remembering he had asked her to call.

The accountant seemed out of breath. "I just got back from the library."

Colder's eyes wandered from the computer screen. "What did you find, Sandy?"

"You said the *British Journal of Developmental Genetics* from July of 1997, didn't you?"

"Yes."

"That's weird."

"Why?"

"Because that journal was discontinued in June of 1997."

Colder never expected this. "Really?"

"All of them are there right through the June issue, but nothing beyond. I checked at the desk, and they looked it up. It's for sure. The last issue was June 1997."

"Odd."

"You think the guy could have made a mistake?"

"I doubt it. This guy's running circles around us."

"Do you want me to check out any of the other issues?"

"No, that's okay," said Colder. "I don't think they'd be helpful. Do this though, if you don't mind. Find out who the publisher was and confirm that it ceased publication after that issue. Also, see if you can find out why."

"I'll get right on it."

"Thanks, Sandra."

"Any luck with the blood?" she asked.

"None yet."

"I hate to be a wet blanket," she said gingerly, "but we still don't have any evidence that anything this guy has said is true."

"I know, Sandy. It still may be a wild goose chase."

"I'll get on it anyway."

"Thanks."

As he hung up the phone, he turned away from the Bruce Lee poster that he had been gazing at absently. He returned to the others. Reggie was hunched over the keyboard while Molly moved closer to the screen. "The journal doesn't exist?" she asked.

"Quit publication the month before."

"Weird," said Molly. "None of this makes sense."

"What are you working on, Reggie?" asked Peter.

Reggie did not move. His nose was inches from the screen as his eyes scanned back and forth. "What I figure is that they use a pretty simple system. Each person appears to be entered as a separate file. If that's true, there should have been some record of Molly's new entry within her old file, since it's not likely that they would have created a new file."

"You see anything?" asked Colder.

Reggie shook his head. "Nope. I don't see a thing."

"So the only explanation that's possible is that they created a separate file that they then deleted."

"Why would they do that?" asked Molly. "Wouldn't that be redundant?"

"Not if they were interested in hiding something," said Colder.

"Doc, do you know any patients whose blood you sent over there for a pregnancy test plus additional stuff?"

Colder thought carefully. "Yes," he said, the name popping to mind. "Debbie Scarborough. She'd been trying for three years. She had gamma knife for an AVM when she was nineteen and takes Tegretol."

Reggie grinned back at him. "I have no idea what you just said, but I got the name."

"Sorry. We sent her blood for pregnancy and Tegretol level."

"No problem." Reggie typed in the name, and seconds later the listing came up.

Scarborough, Deborah M.   48642721
Scarborough, Deborah M.   48642722   *Pregnancy test*

"Two files," Molly exclaimed.

"And one for pregnancy," said Colder

Reggie opened the second file, the screen showing the positive pregnancy test. The other file followed, detailing a handful of labs from the patient's past as well as the current Tegretol level.

"What do you say we try Molly again?" Reggie asked.

"Good idea."

Reggie entered the name, and the file appeared.

Loomis, Molly J.   *43599647*

"Not there." Molly sounded disappointed.

"I expected that," admitted Reggie. "Let's try something different." He exited the file. After a pause, he typed in the file number, searching for it. "Scarborough's pregnancy file was one number higher. Let's see if that file existed for Molly."

As he typed in the number, the screen changed.

File 43599648 has been deleted

"It *was* there!" exclaimed Colder.

"Yes," mumbled Reggie still working furiously on the keyboard. "Something was."

"Is there any way to get it?"

"It'd be tough," admitted Reggie. "I'm sure it's backed up somewhere or copies exist, but the truth is if they're real concerned about hiding a secret file, they'll make it almost impossible to find."

"True."

Reggie searched through the computer intently. Two minutes later, he turned to them disconsolately. "No way."

"But it was there," said Molly optimistically. "Which means our Fragile X friend is definitely telling the truth."

"Yes," admitted Colder.

Reggie looked perplexed. "So, what was in it that needed to be deleted?"

Colder nodded. "There's the real question."

"I think it's what we're looking for," Molly offered.

"I agree," Colder nodded. "And then the next question is, Who deleted it?"

"Someone at the lab?" Molly asked.

"That's the best guess," said Reggie.

Colder bit his lip. "I'd agree with that, except for a couple of things. First of all, we're no longer talking about an accident. That automatically means it's some sort of conspiracy. If that was the case, the people actually running the labs and entering them into the computer would need to be involved. That involves three shifts of workers every night and day of the year. That becomes a lot of people and makes it difficult to keep quiet."

"You're right," admitted Reggie. "It would make much more sense *not* to have anyone know. Say program the computer to automatically delete a file if it came up with a certain result. No one other than the programmer or whoever got a copy of the data before it was destroyed would know."

"Can a program like that be written?" asked Colder.

"A third grader could do it."

"Thanks," chuckled Molly and Peter in unison, both knowing they could barely turn on a computer.

"Really, not to insult you guys, but I don't think it would be difficult at all. In fact, I could probably find it in their system with a little time to browse."

"I wish we had another blood sample," said Colder.

Molly agreed. "I thought of that. That would be the other way, wouldn't it?"

Colder frowned. "But we'd need someone with whatever they detected, and you can't detect it beforehand."

"I don't see how that would work," said Molly.

Colder turned to Molly. "Let's run through this. The blood that they tested was yours. Sounds simple, but it makes a big difference, because the fetal and maternal circulations do not mix. Therefore *you* must have whatever they were testing for in your blood."

"What?" asked Reggie.

The thoughts continued to come to Colder. "There are only two possibilities. Either something about Molly that they detected or the marker is something of the fetus's that crossed the placental barrier."

"What difference would it make?" asked Molly.

"Because for some reason, that blood test led whoever to advise you to have an abortion. The result of that test led them to tell you of Fragile X."

"Then we should test my blood again," said Molly firmly. "If the marker is there now, then that's what they were looking for. If it's not, we know it's related to the pregnancy."

"And if it's there, we can trace where it goes by watching it as its run through their computer."

Colder was becoming excited. "Beautiful!"

"And if it's not there?" asked Molly.

"Even then we still have a chance," Reggie said. "I can probably work their computers to trace a positive test. Figure this. If a positive test gets acted on, that means someone had to have looked at it and relayed it to this Dr. Michaels, or it goes directly to him while it is being deleted. What I think I can do, if I can figure out the program, is make it send the positive result elsewhere, to someplace I can retrieve it."

"You can do that?" asked Colder.

"I think so. My guess is it happens quickly. Like, someone running the test, putting the blood in the machine, the computer reading the test, the test being positive, the test being sent and then deleted." Reggie paused. Another possibility crossed his mind. "Do the technicians read the results?"

"No, it's all automated," Colder replied.

"So after they put the blood in the machine, they really have no contact with it?"

"Only to take it out and throw it away."

"So a positive test for whatever they're looking for could be identified, recorded, sent, and deleted without anyone ever really knowing about it."

"Yes, it's possible," Colder said.

"But, then we should be able to track where the blood test went just by checking where they sent information that night. Can we do that, Reggie?" asked Molly.

"There usually is a log file," Reggie replied, fading into thought. "Not everything is saved, usually just a log, but it depends."

"In the meantime, we need to take some blood."

Molly did not look excited. "What a wonderful way to spend the afternoon."

"I'll buy you a sub afterwards," Colder offered.

"Actually a taco sounds better," she smiled. "But you're on."

"I gotta go to work at seven," Reggie said, rising from the chair, "but I'll see if I can come up with something before then."

"Thanks."

"Hey, Mol," Reggie said turning to her, "my mom wanted to say hello. She's in the living room."

"Great. I wanted to see her too," she said, slipping out the door.

When she was gone, Reggie quietly closed the door and turned toward Peter Colder. "She's a good lady. I'm glad she seems better and has all you guys as new friends."

"Everyone at the office likes her a lot and really wants to help."

"I don't know how she ever got hooked up with that loser or why she loved him so much."

"What do you know about it?" asked Colder now wantonly crossing the professional line.

"It was bad," sighed Reggie. "Happened all the time. Probably twice a week he'd come home drunk as hell. Then you'd hear it. She'd scream for him to stop, then you'd hear her crying."

"He'd beat her?"

"Not just that. I mean a slap, a punch or two, probably. He's a big guy."

"What do you mean?" Colder asked, not comprehending.

"Wasn't just him beating her. It was more that that."

Colder was getting Reggie's drift. He could feel his anger surge inside.

"No way you could call it *making love*," continued Reggie. "These walls are so thin. I could always hear her crying after."

"What a piece of shit," Colder cursed, his face flush. "And this is the guy her parents sided with?"

"Oh, he's a piece all right. A man's man. Stud. You know the kind."

"I'd like to kick the—"

"Don't even think about it, Doc. He ain't worth it. The only thing we have to worry about now is that for some reason she still believes she loves him."

"No way. That's crazy!"

"I'm serious. Beneath everything, she does. Watch it with that wedding ring. She'd die before that comes off. She's sure no guy will ever want her again."

"That's not true," Colder empathized.

"You explain it. You're the doctor."

Colder said nothing. As he said it, his conversation with Sylvia returned again, *You hear it enough, you begin to believe it.*

Reggie continued. "But despite that, she's really a wonderful person."

"I believe it."

"And one other thing. That story she told you about how I got to keep the money from selling the student newspapers and bought the electric wheelchair for my mom?"

"Yes.

"It's mostly a fairy tale. They made me give the money back, to a school board-determined charity. Molly paid for most of the wheelchair. Troy had a shit-fit when he found out."

Colder shook Reggie's hand and thanked him. They walked into the living room of the small apartment where Molly sat in a lounge chair next to Reggie's mother Cynthia Tan. Dark-haired, occidental, and frail, she sat in her wheelchair, her body largely wasted away from the years of disuse. She talked through a tracheostomy tube that was next to a horizontal scar from her old neck operation to stabilize her spine.

Colder said hello, and they talked briefly, Molly sitting beside Cynthia and lightly stoking the woman's useless hand. During the greetings and small talk, Colder watched as they joked, kidded, and laughed. He looked at the chair, its electric motor and joystick that she could manipulate with the crude movements of her arm. He watched as Cynthia Tan pleaded with them to stop by again, and he nodded in appreciation as she thanked him for coming. He memorized the scene without effort. His eyes did not need to be told to look. No matter what the topic of conversation, his gaze seemed to always return to Molly.

Chapter Nine

Early Sunday morning, Reggie Tan sauntered into the Third Street Clinic carrying one sheet of paper and a bag full of fresh bagels. Sylvia opened the door, introduced herself, and gratefully took the bag. After sniffing inside, Sylvia pulled out a plain bagel and escorted Reggie to the back room where the rest of the office staff, Colder, and Molly had gathered. The window blinds were open, and the bright sunshine of the June morning made the overhead lights unnecessary. The building was warm. Reggie pulled off his jacket, draping it over the lone open chair, apparently saved for him. The others greeted him like a new member to a club, with handshakes and smiles. Molly hugged him briefly, with a friendly firmness.

"Thanks for the bagels," offered Sandra, her normally nervous and dour affect momentarily lapsing as she tore into the oversized onion roll.

"Cream cheese is there," said Sylvia, pointing.

"Got 'em at Dough Girls," replied Reggie.

"Mighta known," interrupted Letisha. "They've got that *soul* taste!"

"Then why is it attached to the Hunan Kitchen?" Reggie asked with a devilish smile.

"Give me a break!" Letisha exclaimed, realizing he was kidding. She turned to Molly. "Girlfriend! Why'd we invite this kid?"

They all laughed. Sylvia rose and filled coffee cups while the others gathered in a circle. Reggie pulled out the single sheet of paper he had carried with him. "'Fraid it's not great news. Molly's new blood all went into the old file. Negative pregnancy and all the other stuff."

"Should have figured," said Molly glumly.

Colder paused, trying to swallow a large bite of a bagel. Choking down the inadequately chewed last bite, he managed to speak. "That's actually not bad. We now see a pattern emerging. The blood comes in, it's tested and placed within one file. If the pregnancy test is positive, it goes into a second file and then must be tested for whatever. If whatever is there, then the entire group of labs in both files gets deleted as if it never happened, the company then claiming it never got the blood."

"Sounds likely," admitted Reggie. "That's how I was looking at it."

"But she still was notified that she was pregnant," said Sylvia.

"Exactly. So we know that the tests were run, used for interpretation of a condition, and that someone, as a result, recommended that she abort the fetus. We also now know that they are taking the positive pregnancy tests and testing them additionally."

Reggie nodded. "Yes—and can I have a bagel?"

Sandra rose and offered him the bag containing the half dozen that remained.

"Reggie," started Peter, "were you able to check their computers and see if something is there?"

"I was gonna try last night. Ran out of time. I'll try after work today."

"That's fine. Anytime you can."

"You think we should go back to Doyne and ask around again?" asked Molly, focussing her attention on Peter.

"No, actually I don't. But there's something that our friend Mr. Fragile X said that bothered me."

"People getting killed?"

"Yes," he admitted.

Molly was thoughtful. "If it's true, this really is dangerous."

"And we now have no reason to believe it isn't," Sylvia interrupted.

Colder decided to change the subject. He knew everyone in the room had experienced more than a tinge of fear, but no one yet had told him they wanted out.

"Let's think about this lab stuff again. As I see it, the only way that this could have been pulled off was if almost no one knew. Everything would have to appear random and be impossible to detect. No other way it could happen."

"In other words, you don't think that the people at that place know anything," said Letisha.

"That's right. The manager is just a straightforward guy who likes to play golf and eat a little too much. The rest of the employees look like a bunch of young people right out of their med tech degrees. No, I don't believe any of them would know."

"It would be much smarter and safer to hide something in the computer," Molly agreed.

"But if you did go back and snoop around," Reggie said, "the manager might report it to someone who did know something. We could track that, and that might be helpful."

"The other way to look at it though, would be his superior knows nothing, blows it off, and we gain nothing. Or he knows something, and we're now seen as a problem. And, like our friend said, people have been killed. I'm afraid I see only a downside to going back."

"You're probably right," Reggie admitted. "It's up to me. I can work on it today."

Sandra stood, opening the folder she had been carrying, her usual nervous twitches instantly returning. "I found out a couple of things," she stammered, looking at all of them. "First of all, the *British Journal of Developmental Genetics* was originally owned by Chesapeake Publishing in London. It was a company that had been in business for over one hundred years until it was purchased by Manheim Publishing in 1989. Manheim is a large European publishing company that ran into trouble in the early 1990s and sold off some of its assets. Some of its money losers were academic journals that they published on contract with different societies."

"Was this journal a medical society journal?" asked Colder.

"No, it was, I believe what you call a—um—"

"Throw-away journal."

"Right," she said, pointing toward him. "That's what the woman said."

Colder leaned his chair back, relaxing. "That just means that one of the big genetics societies did not use it as their primary journal. It was a lower-prestige journal that paid for itself with advertising rather than subscription money."

"Apparently it had been marginally profitable for a while, but then began losing money. Manheim sold the rights to it, but it was discontinued in June 1997."

"When did they sell it?" asked Sylvia. "And to whom?"

"I've even got the official date," grinned Sandra proudly. "June 14, 1997."

"So, no July issue was ever published?" asked Molly.

"No," said Sandra.

Colder was silent, his mind twisting in the midst of various thoughts. "Never published," he said finally, "but most certainly *planned*."

"What do you mean?" Letisha asked.

"It averages about a year to get an article published in most journals. If you look at the date of acceptance and compare it to the date of publication, it is rarely less than nine months. In other words, there was almost certainly a planned July issue, as there would have been August, September, and so on for several months."

"Plus," interrupted Sylvia, "the date, June fourteenth. That is late to stop a publication. Most of those journals arrive before their month of publication."

Sandra nodded. "Like June arriving the last week of May."

"Yes," Colder agreed. "In other words, we can almost be sure that the July issue was completely planned, even to the point where the presses might have been running."

"Maybe there are some copies," Sandra offered.

"I doubt it," said Colder. "If anyone had them, it would be listed as being in print. Academic Internet is well established. We can look, but I doubt it can be found."

"But what about their inventory of articles? Records?" asked Sylvia. "If they had planned a journal, there had to be articles they were going to publish."

"That's our best bet," agreed Colder. "And it may be what we're actually looking for. We need to track down what happened to all of that."

"I'll get right on it." Sandra was determined.

"I never asked, Sandy," said Colder. "Who bought Manheim?"

"Waverland Publishing in Los Angeles."

"Interesting," said Reggie. "An American company."

"See if you can find out more about them too."

"I know a little," Sandra acknowledged as she grabbed another bagel. "They do publish a few throw-away journals."

"Why would they suddenly stop this one?"

"I'll keep digging."

Reggie rose, finished with his bagel. He looked at his watch. "Hey, I gotta run."

"Call me later," said Molly. "I'll be checking on your mom this afternoon."

"I will. And thanks," he said giving her a quick hug.

After Reggie had departed, Sylvia began cleaning up the office, and Sandra retreated to her desk. Letisha walked Molly and Peter to the door.

"You're off to Tyler's?" Letisha asked Molly.

"Yes."

Letisha looked fierce. "Tell that boy he's in trouble. Was supposed to call me last night."

Colder laughed. "We'll make sure he knows he's in it deep."

"He is," she said, the affection for her cousin shining through.

Tyler Briggs was dressed casually in a champagne-colored, button-down shirt, and tweed, pleated trousers. In front of the glass-topped desk, a little girl about four, dressed in a pink dress, sat on the floor playing with her dolls. She glanced toward Molly and Peter as they entered the room, but returned as quickly to her toys. Briggs stood behind the desk immersed in a handful of papers, his glasses no longer present, but the ubiquitous coffee cup was dangling in his free hand.

"C'mon in," he said jovially. "Meet my daughter Denisa."

"Hi, Denisa," said Molly, bending to one knee.

"Are you going to play with me?" the little girl asked, her coal black eyes sparkling excitedly. "My daddy's busy."

"What are you playing?" Molly asked, rising and perching herself on the edge of the chair.

"I'm getting her dressed," Denisa replied, holding a doll out for Molly to see.

"She looks wonderful," said Molly.

Briggs stood behind his daughter, a smile stretched across his face. "She likes to come on the weekends and run around the office."

"She's beautiful," said Molly, looking up at Tyler for a second.

"I like to think so," he replied, trying to sound humble.

The little girl beamed at the words, knowing their focus was exclusively on her. "Do you like my dolls?" she asked, waving at the other dolls and their clothes.

Molly nodded approvingly. "They're very nice."

"First-born," Briggs said almost apologetically at the extent of the array. "I'm afraid we overdo it a little."

"Hard not to," Colder said.

"You have a son, too, don't you?" Molly asked, looking toward the pictures on the desk.

"Tyler, Junior. He's nine and a half months younger. A little too wild for work mornings at the office."

"Daddy, are we going to watch Dalmatians tonight?"

"Yes, honey, we'll watch it tonight."

"Good," she said returning to a red dress.

"She likes *One Hundred and One Dalmatians*," Briggs whispered, loud enough for everyone to hear.

"I like that one, too," Molly said, still gazing at the little girl.

"Do you want to come over then?" Denisa asked.

"No," said Molly gently. "That's for you and your family. But I'll play with you now for a while."

"Okay."

"Now, Denisa," Tyler began, his tone a gentle reprimand, "don't you be bothering Molly. We have to work."

"Okay," replied the four-year-old.

"I'll play with you a little later," Molly whispered into her ear. Denisa's eyes grew big, and a smile lit up her face.

The three adults made their way to chairs. "I'll tell you what I've got," said Briggs, getting right to the point as they all took seats. "We went over the contract with a microscope last night. Marcus, oh, you haven't met him. Marcus Sanders, our other senior guy, crunched through it."

"Find anything?" Molly asked.

"Well, it's carefully written to say the least. It reeks of expense and care. These guys did their homework. They've written every clause with enough exceptions and exclusions to baffle almost anyone but another contract lawyer."

"Is there something there?" Colder asked.

"I doubt it. Self-protection may not be pretty, but it is the law."

"But aren't there some vague areas in the contract that might be probed?" Colder wondered, trying to sound like he knew something about the law.

"Not really. It's essentially written so that they will cover their patients very narrowly. Beyond that, they have a parachute. They're basically trying to exclude anything that they can. It's a business, nothing more. These guys are just a little more hard core."

"You're being nice," Molly said.

"What about her specific case?" Colder asked.

"Her name is on the contract. She signed the contract, and the contract says that any services received must be preapproved."

"But this was an emergency!"

"Doesn't matter. They specifically state that nothing is covered unless preapproved."

Molly looked shaken. "I tried about a thousand times, trying to get approval!"

"Actually, it was about fifteen," said Briggs. "I have the records."

"What more could I have done?"

Briggs sighed. "They'd also say that your illness was the result of an unauthorized procedure. They'd fight you there, too. That part is a weaker argument, but they'd probably try it as well."

"Unbelievable," said Colder sadly. "A life-threatening emergency, and they don't have to pay for the care because the patient hasn't jumped through their two million hoops."

Molly handed Denisa the doll. She looked depressed. "Then there's nothing there. I should have figured."

Briggs stroked his chin. He looked quizzical. "Well, not necessarily. Every medical contract is written using the terminology 'fair and reasonable.' It's essentially an acquiescence to the fact the medicine is rarely neat and tidy. The law tries to build into the system some sort of protection for people."

"Huh?" asked Peter.

"I'll be honest with you. That's the tactic that a lot of people have used to try to sue HMOs. This, and unconscionable treatment, impossibility of performance, like your having to get preapproval for an ER visit, have been tactics. But nothing's ever been successful in a trial. Because of that, the only real hope is a settlement."

The thought seemed inconceivable. "A settlement?" Molly wondered out loud.

"Sometimes the company pays to avoid the publicity of a trial. Other times they'll pay because it would cost more to defend themselves."

"But if there's no settlement?" Colder asked.

"If not, well, the court has just not looked favorably on this argument, fair and reasonable."

"In other words, in a trial there is no chance," said Colder.

"Basically, yes," Briggs admitted.

"Unbelievable," muttered Molly.

Tyler continued. "So if we file suit, we'll really be trying to slide between those two words and stir up enough action to make them settle. We have little else."

"Let me say this," said Molly. "I was bleeding to death, and I couldn't get through to them. I tried to follow their rules and yet I couldn't."

"Yes," Briggs acknowledged, "and that's partly what we're thinking. Like Peter said, if 'fair and reasonable' are not broad enough, it gives them a license to deny almost any claim they want to, and certainly any claim where preauthorization was not granted. In emergency cases like yours, that is carte blanche. They could deny absolutely *everything*. Heart attacks, strokes, accidents."

"And they are," Colder added.

Molly's eyes were fiery. "Tell me the truth. Do either of you believe what happened was fair and reasonable?"

The two men stopped. Her question was basic, but still provocative. "No," Colder said shaking his head.

"Neither do I," said Briggs.

Molly appeared resolved. "Then I say we try anything we can. Sue them."

Tyler Briggs stood and looked out the window toward the Metrodome. "You realize, Molly, that if this somehow, remote chance as it might be, ever came to trial, they'd fight you to the end of the earth. They'd never settle." He turned back and looked at her carefully. "What you are talking about is their lifeline, the blood of the entire system. Fair and reasonable, without being so, but justified in the law. In a trial, they'd try to humiliate you, crush you, annihilate you. Every detail of your life, every thought in your mind, everything you ever said or did would be exposed and challenged."

"I know," said Molly softly.

"They can't just win. There is no victory in that for them. You must not only be shown to be wrong, but to have wronged them. The only way to do that is to destroy you."

"I understand," she mumbled.

"There would be more lawyers than you've ever imagined. You'd be seeing dark suits in your sleep. If this case gets attention, they'll have press conferences more often than the nightly news, and you'll hear about yourself like you never have before."

"I know."

"They have the money to buy the press and paint the picture they want the public to see. You'd be portrayed as the dropout who couldn't hack school. The woman who drove the man who loved her away. The wife who had an abortion but didn't tell her husband. The woman who broke her contract but wants them to pay. You'll be a bitter, hostile, little tramp who destroyed her own life and now wants someone else to pick up her pieces."

Molly didn't visibly react as the words cut her mind and heart. "I know."

Briggs turned back to them and returned to his seat. The room was silent. He sipped from his cup, looking over its brim and staring at the grim determination in Molly Loomis's face. "There is one other thing," he said finally, looking directly into her eyes.

"What is it?"

"You have one thing in your favor. It's only one thing, but it's important," he continued, not breaking his stare. "You're also the kind of defendant they fear the most."

Molly was surprised. "Why's that?"

"When you've taken everything from someone, when you've stripped them naked and stolen their world, then they become their most dangerous. Any attorney knows why."

"Why?" asked Colder.

Briggs looked solemn. "Because then they have nothing left to lose." He stopped talking, letting the thought resonate in all of their minds. Half a minute passed.

Molly Loomis stood, a spark of fight lighting her eyes. "I want to do it."

Briggs did not respond. His eyes narrowed. He reached into his desk and pulled out a small, stapled pile of papers. He tossed it on the desk. "Then here it is."

Molly looked at the top sheet. She had no idea what it was. "What is it?"

"Two counts. Breach of contract and bad faith denial of coverage, with a request to pursue punitive damages. And most importantly, a demand for a trial. Marcus already has it ready."

"The lawsuit?" asked Colder.

"You bet."

Molly picked it up, staring at the cover sheet. Colder put his hand on her shoulder. Both saw that in official terms, the lawsuit was called a complaint. Briggs held up his coffee cup as if he was making a toast. "We'll file it. Molly J. Loomis versus ComHealthOne."

Molly's eyes widened.

"Are you ready?" asked Briggs.

"Yes," she said without hesitation.

"Then it's time to go to war."

A few hours later, Peter Colder opened his front door and was greeted by the scolding yowl of Mortimer. It was a verbal reprimand for inattention and a delay in the great beast's desired dinner hour. His chastising complete, the great tabby turned and ambled toward the kitchen, his nonverbal instruction to follow and feed, unmistakable. Colder dutifully obeyed, opening a rank can of miscellaneous meat mix that Mortimer greeted with possessive fury. Growling heavily between bites and in the spirit of his carnivorous heritage, he looked at Colder savagely, as if daring him to try to steal his feast. Colder slipped a plastic sealer over the can and plugged his nose before burying it deep within the refrigerator.

He had dropped Molly off after lunch. They had eaten together at a Chinese buffet. She had seemed more upbeat and optimistic, even with the knowledge that the lawsuit could be futile and the consequences severe. She seemed more talkative, less distant as their friendship emerged and her level of comfort grew. He was no longer her doctor, simply a friend, a good friend with her best interests at heart.

There was something very appealing about her, Colder thought. She made no apologies for what she was not, nor any for what she was. Her life had been simple, her aspirations simpler, and her soul never plagued by the contradiction offered by some as the modern ideal of woman. Molly Loomis's life was to have been rich in purpose and free from the self-deception of the "have-it-all" mindset. But now it was gone, the life she had envisioned burned beyond recognition.

Colder sighed out loud. She had informed him that she would be returning to work in the morning. It seemed unfair, he thought. Her life all the same, yet her life completely different.

Colder was surprised at himself. He found he was thinking of her often, more so than he should. There was a charm and a sly, shy humor. A personality without great self-confidence, but of surprising core strength. A radiant honesty, a natural zest, an allure they were all there. Colder was very surprised at himself. He suddenly found himself looking forward to her company again for lunch the next day.

He lay down on the couch and opened a Diet Coke. He had the remote and turned on *ESPN's SportsCenter* and began watching the highlights from the day's games. The score crossed the screen, and he saw that the Twins had won. He raised his hand in triumph. Mortimer saw the hand movement as an invitation, and instantly the great beast leaped onto his chest, purring loudly and positioning himself within inches of his treasured master's face.

"No, no, Morty," said Colder gently swiping him onto the floor. "You smell like that stuff!"

The cat gazed at him despite the setback of unintended rejection and awaited a second chance. Colder sat back up. "Don't even think about it." Mortimer put one paw on Colder's arm. It was effortless, accompanied by a look of contentment, curiosity and assurance, a gesture of bonding that only a great cat would understand.

The phone rang and Colder grabbed it. "Hello?"

"Dr. Colder?"

He recognized the voice. "Yes, Sandra. How are you?" The accountant's voice was shaky, but not more than usual.

"I think I might have found something."

"What have you got?"

"I got ahold of a secretary who works in the academic division for Manheim in London. It took a while. And sorry, I'm afraid I might have run up a few bills."

"Don't worry about it."

"Anyway this woman had come over from Chesapeake when they merged with Manheim, and she had worked for the guy who was sort of the editor of the *Journal*."

"How did you find her, especially on a Sunday?"

"She works Sunday through Thursday. I just got lucky. I started asking around, and they connected me to her. She's apparently the only one still around who knew anything about that journal."

"What about the editor?"

"The editor's job was really kind of bogus. Some guy out in the country who approved articles and sent them in after they had been approved. He read them, or skimmed them, or sent them out for colleagues to review, then sent the final copies to her after they had been approved. I say bogus because she didn't seem to think he ever really did anything other than stamp 'Approved.' She said she never saw corrections or changes."

"What about the July issue?"

"What we suspected was true. They had articles for four more issues, and the July issue was on the press when they shut down."

"Any printed?" asked Colder excitedly.

"A few. Seventeen to be exact."

"What happened?"

"Some guys came in the middle of the day and shut the whole place down. Took all of the work in progress—files, articles, archived tapes, everything. All gone in less than an hour. I guess it was like a military assault."

"So everything is gone."

"Yeah, at least she thought so, but—"

"There's more?"

"About three days later, one of the guys came back, looking around. She asked him what he was looking for, but he wouldn't exactly tell her. Finally she got it out of him. They had checked the numbers and discovered that seventeen journals had been printed. The problem was that they only had *sixteen*. There was one missing."

"Yes!" shouted Colder sitting up straight.

"Don't get your hopes up," said Sandra. "I have no idea where the thing is, but she thinks that it still exists."

"Why?"

"About every month, someone still drops by and asks her about it. Last time was only two weeks ago. She said to me that she wasn't surprised that someone else started asking about it. She figured that there was something in it."

"What about the editor?"

"Died about two months after they shut the journal down. Heart attack."

"Anything suspicious?"

"I asked that, but she didn't seem to think so. He was in his late sixties and had had two attacks before."

"What about typists, typesetters, copy boys, anyone who might have read it."

"You're a little old-fashioned, Doc!" she exclaimed affectionately. "The way they do it is simply by typing the editor-approved manuscript into a word-processing program. The computer assembles it. The only other parts are the cover, which never changed except for the date and volume number, and the ads, which were digital and merged electronically."

"So no one else read it?"

"I don't think so."

"Damn."

"I think that's pretty much a dead end, except for the fact that somewhere in this world a copy of that journal exists."

"Hmmm," said Colder, his mind racing. "What about Waverland Publishing?"

"I was just going to get to that. Waverland Publishing, founded in 1931. Morris Waverland. Started the business in Hollywood. Published a little bit in nonfiction, some star biographies and some 'B' novels that were a sort of pre-World War II smut. Did well for a while and made a good bit of money, but then watched as a couple of useless sons tried to spend it all on fast cars and fast women."

"Wonderful."

"In the '50s, they were nearly broke, but the senior Waverland resurrected the company by almost single-handedly inventing the dime store romance novel. Even wrote a couple himself. It put them on sound footing, and he took the company public in 1960, bailing out with a big, well-lined parachute."

"The sons?"

"Still useless, I presume."

Colder laughed. "What happened to the company then?"

"Waverland got bigger when it went public. Took over some of Hearst's old stuff, a few magazines, few newspapers at very low prices and started to expand. They also got bigger into books, both fiction and nonfiction. They've grown steadily. Now they're the fourth largest publisher on the West coast. Company is solid and reputable, with about a six-to-eight percent growth per year. Revenues are a couple hundred million a year."

"What about academic journals?"

"That's the curious thing. Because it's a public corporation, I could get a lot of information, but I couldn't find another single journal that they had ever purchased. In fact, they don't publish anything that is even remotely close to one. Then I checked a little further, and the weird thing is that the purchase of the *British Journal of Developmental Genetics* is mentioned in a one-sentence blurb in shareholder minutes, nothing more."

"Wouldn't you think that if you wanted to launch a new direction for the company you would do it with a little more fanfare?"

"I would. It's almost as if they wanted to buy it, but didn't want anyone to know about it and had no plans for it," admitted Sandra.

"Why in the world would anyone do that?"

"My thoughts exactly. There had to have been something in that issue that someone didn't want to come out. The way they assure it is to snatch up every copy and every record and make them vanish from the earth. Except for one problem, a copy may still exist."

"And one other problem," said Peter. "There's more than one guy out there who knows about it."

"You think Mr. Fragile X could be the author of the article?" asked Sandra.

"The thought crossed my mind."

"Then who are the people that he said are dead?"

"Anyone who knows what was in the article."

"Probably all except him."

"That theory works perfectly, except for one thing. We might be totally wrong."

"True."

"And another thing," he continued, "why Waverland Publishing? They've got no connection to anything."

Sandra chuckled. It was a self-satisfied, confident sound that Colder had rarely heard from the nervous accountant. "That's where you're wrong, Peter."

"Why?"

"Because I saved the best for last."

"Give it to me."

"A thought occurred to me. Maybe it would be interesting to see who serves on Waverland's board of directors."

Colder picked up his Diet Coke but stopped before he took a drink.

"I'll give you one guess," said Sandra slyly.

Colder's mind spun. It took several seconds, but when the thought hit him he dropped the nearly full can on his foot. The carmel-colored liquid spread over the carpeting, but Colder paid no attention. "No way!" he exploded.

Sandra Becker couldn't hold it in any longer. She was ready to burst. "You got it, Doc! None other than the best. The big man himself. H. Carter Hutchins!"

Chapter Ten

June 30

At mid-morning on Monday, Marcus Sanders settled into one of the guest chairs in front of Tyler's desk and loosened his tie. Thirty-six years old, married with one child, Tyler's partner was of average build but with a memorably handsome face and pleasing demeanor that easily carried a room's attention. He was also tireless, good on his feet, and great in front of a jury. Tyler had always been glad to have him as an ally. The two partners, having completed their journey to the Hennepin County Courthouse, waited eagerly for what they were about to hear. When the irate call came, Briggs picked up the phone on the second ring, "Tyler, what the hell is this shit?" asked Paul Mercer, his sandpaper voice blasting through the microphone. Mercer was the oldest junior partner at Barnes and Whitfield, the largest law firm in Minneapolis and the advocates for ComHealthOne.

"You nuts?" Mercer, known as Pokey, was a caustic, late-forties mediocrity, with an immaculate toupee and severe short-man syndrome. He was a man who felt his bulldog demeanor and knowledge of off-color jokes entitled him to a place among the nation's legal elite. Both wives had wearied of him, neither of his children spoke to him, and all of his girlfriends enjoyed his lavish gifts, but Mercer's true joy in his middle years now came from serving as an enforcer on a legal team that Briggs and Sanders referred to as "Hitler's Henchmen."

"How are you, Pokey?" Briggs asked, amused.

"Think you can just walk in there an' plop down some piece of shit like that, like you're buying a damn cheeseburger?"

"Not at all, Pokey," said Marcus. "We're completely serious. We were, in fact, looking forward to your call."

"I shoulda known you'd be there too, Sanders. The Dynamic Duo. Laurel and Hardy."

"We just want what's she's due," Briggs said, determined not to take any of the baits that were coming. "You cheated her, and you know it."

"Aw bullshit," said Mercer, sounding annoyed. "You know it and I know it. That contract is so solid you couldn't open it with a nuclear warhead."

"You're wrong, Pokey. It's impossible to perform and unconscionable."

"You guys are crazy!" he exclaimed. "What do you even take a case like this for? You know we can beat the shit out of you just with numbers. Then the chick, your client, she's just a little wench who couldn't keep her legs together who now's pissed off because we're playing by the rules."

"Not that at all, Pokey," said Marcus.

"Oh, I get it," he said with a sarcastic, enlightened tone. "Times a little tough for Batman and Robin. No rich colored boys to keep the coffers full, so you drag up some little tart to take on the big, bad white guy. Should have known, always boils down to that."

"She's as white as yo mama, Pokey," said Sanders grinning.

"Really," said Mercer doubtfully. "I'm surprised—seeing this is a breeding-type case."

Sanders and Briggs instantly broke out laughing, Marcus slapping his thigh as if Pokey's provocative conversation was exceeding even his finest expectations. "Forgot to tell you, Pokey. We're sitting here with Don Fogarty of the *Star Tribune* and June Thomasson of KSTP and they were wondering if they could use this tape for a special they're running on the social conscience of Barnes and Whitfield."

"Fuck you."

"Hey, Pokey, you know that cross you have burning in your front yard. Is that symbolic or another girlfriend's going away gift to you?"

"Screw yourselves. Both of you."

They both continued laughing. Even Pokey Mercer chuckled briefly.

"Pokey," said Sanders finally. "We want the money."

"You guys are serious?" said Pokey incredulously. "Two million dollars? You got some horny little girl as a client who's pissed because she can't pup and you take that on contingency? How hard up are you?"

"Take it to Henrich and the rest of the SS. Have 'em cut the check this afternoon and we'll even go have drinks tonight. If you can spare time from the harem, we'll buy."

"You guys are totally crazy!" he exclaimed nearly shouting. "You've lost it! You know we'll never pay that bill. She broke the rules."

"Fair and reasonable."

"Something you guys don't seem to know anything about."

"Breach of contract—bad faith," chimed Marcus. "We want it."

"You're really serious. I can't believe it."

"Of course we are."

"Don't hold your breath," Pokey growled.

Marcus strolled toward the window. "Call us back. Tell us what Goerring and Goebbels say."

"I know what they're gonna say," Pokey grumbled. "And a civilized man like me doesn't use shitty language like that."

"We'll be talking to ya."

"Don't say I didn't warn you," Pokey said hanging up.

When the phone clicked signaling the disconnection, Briggs and Marcus were no longer smiling. The battle had officially begun. They knew that Pokey would take the case to one of the senior partners, the men that with Mercer composed the group they viewed as the equal of the Nazi's Gestapo. High-profile, high-pay, and equally skilled, their reputation for ruthlessness and success were parallel points of pride. They rarely played fair and more importantly, they never lost.

"When do you think he'll call?" asked Briggs.

"About two minutes to five."

"He's right, you know," said Marcus. "They'll never settle this one. *And* our case is weak as hell."

Briggs slid deep into his chair. His posture reflected his mood. The thought of taking on a firm as formidable as Barnes and Whitfield was intimidating enough, let alone with a case as weak as theirs. Briggs closed his eyes, the upbeat mood of moments before already a distant memory. "I know, Marcus. I know."

Sylvia Caspers knocked on the examining room door, opened it, and peeked her head around the corner. "Excuse me, Dr. Colder," she said with an apologetic smile. "I need you for a moment." Colder, immersed in a one-year-old's inflamed left ear and nearly deafened by the infant's wailing, was glad for the break.

After apologizing to the mother, Colder slipped out the door where Sylvia was waiting for him. "Casey Larter on line two."

"Thanks," he said, not breaking stride. Colder closed his office door and for a few seconds collected his thoughts. He thought about this call he had expected for forty-eight hours, but he remained somewhat indecisive about his approach to her. He knew that whatever his plan, Casey with her blunt and forceful manner would probably dictate the discussion.

"Casey?"

"God, Colder. What is this? Three times in a month. People will talk!"

"We should be so lucky." Colder laughed effortlessly, concealing well his horror at the thought of a romantic evening with a woman twice his size, sporting the complexion of a beet and a manner as appealing a pit bull.

"I know you didn't call to charm me."

"No. I know I couldn't do that."

"Many lesser men have tried."

"But I wanted to let you know something. The patient I talked to you about."

"AB—hyst—no coverage,"

"Yes. She's going to take ComHealth to court, trying to cover the bill."

"Good," Casey hissed. "Hope she collects $50 million or at least what Hutchins has in his Christmas fund. They should be roughly equal."

"I'm not sure—"

Casey interrupted. "Man, I'd love to see her win. Then see it followed by a stampede of lawsuits from patients figuring out how little care they were actually getting."

"It's going to be a tough case. I don't know if there's much of a chance,"

Casey sighed. "On that count, I'm sure you're right. ComHealth's lawyers bath themselves in oil. Trying to get one would be like trying to catch an eel with a greased hand."

"I know."

"One of my patients tried to sue them last year. She had a drive-through delivery. The baby was discharged eight hours after birth and came back two days later septic as hell. Nearly died. Three weeks in the ICU. Company denied coverage because the parents took her to a suburban hospital that ComHealth doesn't contract with, and they hadn't gotten authorization."

"But it was an emergency."

"Yeah, so then they tried to blame the parents, saying they should have recognized earlier that the child was that ill. If they had brought her in a day earlier, most of the hospital stay would have been avoided."

"Just shoot me," groaned an appalled Colder.

"Ultimately ComHealth paid some of the bill, but their contract reads that if you received care outside their chain of hospitals they are only accountable for half, so this family was still stuck with about fifty thousand. From what I hear, ComHealth ended up paying the hospital about a third of what they were supposed to, but the hospital decided to eat it, figuring it would cost what they were owed just to recover it."

"That's a familiar tactic."

"I hope she wins, but I won't be holding my breath. They don't lose when they don't want to. And they don't want to lose much."

"I know."

Colder paused before speaking again. "Casey, I need to ask you another question."

"Shoot."

"The AB itself. Uterine perforation. How often does it occur?"

"Rare, but not unheard of. It's not malpractice, if that's what you mean."

"That's kind of what I'm getting at."

"Who did it?"

"Fred Fielding."

"Naw," she replied. "He's a bit of a pompous ass, but he's good. I actually even reviewed his numbers a year ago on a routine QA for the state board. Nothing out of the ordinary. It doesn't happen often, but when it does it's awful."

"Just wanted an opinion."

"That's natural," she said, concluding that part of the discussion. She changed the subject. "How are you doing financially, Colder? The truth."

"One word? Bad."

"That's what I was afraid you'd say."

Colder decided to address a rumor he'd heard. "I hear you're thinking about joining ComHealth."

Casey was forthright. "I don't know. Financially, I may have to give this up. The clinic breaks even, but my gyn practice is like yours. Losing money."

"Tell me about it."

"ComHealth's had a standing offer on the table for me to join them. But then it would give them total control of OB/gyn in the city, except for my partner, who'd probably retire."

"Ugly."

"Yeah. Even though that idea makes me sick, I don't know."

"It's a big decision," Colder sighed.

"They just want control so they can start to get rid of us. I know the rumor is that they want to get fifty OB/gyns out of the city by the end of next year. They want to shift almost all of it to family practice and nurse practitioners. Even high risk."

"Unbelievable. As if family docs like myself or nurse practitioners should be doing high-risk obstetrics."

"No, but it would sure save them money."

"Screw them."

"But get the latest, Colder. Now I hear they want no prenatal testing or visits after pregnancy is established, until one visit in the third trimester."

"Ridiculous."

"The logic is that cavemen had babies and didn't need technology, so why should we?"

"Unbelievable."

"The dumbing down of medicine," Casey sighed. "I just don't know if I have the energy to fight it anymore."

"I know."

"If I went with ComHealth, they'd guarantee my job for five years, and the salary isn't bad."

Colder realized her dilemma. He hated to see her even contemplate joining them, but he understood why she was thinking about it. "It's hard to pass up."

Casey sounded torn. "I know."

"Tell you what," said Colder, trying to sound upbeat. "I'll keep you posted on the lawsuit."

"Wish her luck. You know how I feel."

"Thanks, Casey. And whatever happens with you and ComHealth, you're a woman of integrity and a good doctor."

"Thanks, Colder."

"Talk to you soon."

"Bye."

Depressed, Colder hung up and went back to work.

Tyler Briggs's phone rang three minutes earlier than he had predicted. Marcus Sanders, sitting across from Tyler gave his senior partner a "you win" look. Tyler punched the speaker phone button and heard his secretary's voice. "Mr. Mercer on line one."

"Thanks, Mary. Put him on."

An audible click was heard and then the monotonous background noise of a cellular phone. "Pokey!" exclaimed Tyler.

"Hello, boys, I hope your day was as good as mine!"

"Talk to me."

"I even talked to Whitfield himself on this one," said Mercer obviously chewing something, either a cigar or gum.

"What did Adolf say?"

"Told me to offer you the usual two."

"Guillotine or noose?" Marcus asked.

"You got it. Withdraw or go down. No negotiation."

"Sorry."

"How's this boys? Whitfield was playing golf with Judge Van Gilder out at Minnekada this afternoon. They both wanted me to tell you that there'll be no bullshit allowed from you guys."

"Funny."

"See you at the hearing, boys!"

The phone went dead and Marcus and Tyler stared at each other without expression. An unpleasant silence descended upon them. Everything they had anticipated was coming true, and aside from the inevitable excitement that goes with a battle, their only other sense was fear. It was now becoming all too clear that they had willingly signed on for the fight of their lives. They knew ComHealth's attorneys would first seek to dismiss the case with a summary judgment. It would also be ComHealth's first in an endless series of motions. Unfortunately this motion was also one that Van Gilder might just grant.

When Peter Colder arrived at the Tan apartment, Molly and Reggie were busy preparing dinner. The planned meal was to celebrate the day's two events—Molly's twice-delayed return to work and the filing in court. An Italian meal of antipasto and rigatoni was the menu. Molly had arrived home at four, having worked the day shift without a hitch. Her stomach had been a bit sore, and by the end of the eight hours, she had felt tired, but her coworkers had welcomed her back with a small party, and the event had made any physical discomfort substantially less painful. In addition, the owner had agreed to advance her two hundred dollars and allow her to pick up extra hours as soon as she felt well enough. Cutting the sausage for the antipasto, she joked with Reggie and Cynthia about her day.

"I nearly dropped the first tray," she said. "Major klutz. Swung it like a drunk."

"Did you hit anyone?" Cynthia asked, her wheelchair at the edge of the small kitchen.

"No. Thank goodness I wasn't carrying soup. It would have gone all over the windows!"

They all laughed. "I did spill one cup of coffee though. Fortunately it was my own."

"Where did it go?"

"On my arm."

"Ouch," said Colder.

"No burn," she said turning and smiling at him. "But like I said, major klutz."

The phone rang, and Reggie put down the spoon he was using to stir the sauce and walked to the living room. A moment later he returned to the kitchen, motioning to Molly. "For you. It's Tyler."

Molly put down the knife and moved to the phone, her conversation easily audible from the kitchen.

"Hello?—Hi—Really?... That sounds great!—Two weeks... Okay.—Next Monday?—Yeah—I'll make sure.—Okay—Thanks—Bye."

Molly returned to the kitchen, her expression even, and returned to the sausage.

"What did he say?" asked Cynthia.

"The divorce will be final in two or three weeks."

"Yes!" exclaimed Reggie.

Molly showed no emotion. "Troy agreed that I can keep the ring."

Reggie looked disappointed. "No. Just give it to him, Molly. It's the only thing that will still link you to the guy. He'll never let you forget it."

"No," Molly said firmly. "I want it."

"Don't bother her, Reggie," Cynthia said. "It's her business."

"Mom," he grumbled.

"What else did he say?" asked Peter, not missing anything.

"They filed the lawsuit. There will be some kind of hearing soon. He said it looks like it's going to be a fight."

"We figured that," Reggie said.

"Yeah," Molly said distantly.

"Hey," Colder said, breaking the mood, "all of this is good news. It's what we have to do. The next step. No need to be depressed. C'mon, I'm opening the wine."

"Good idea," Cynthia agreed.

Colder opened the bottle of wine and poured half glasses for all but Reggie. The eighteen-year-old was forced to sip a few drops from a glass that Colder slipped him almost out of the sight of his mother, who pretended not to notice. Cynthia's glass was attached to a brace on her arm, and she managed to drink without spilling a drop.

Within minutes, the mood lightened as Cynthia began relating tales of Reggie's escapades as a child and his penchant for mischief. They roared in laughter as she told of the times he was sent home from school for the practical jokes that he had played on the other grade school children. Despite her severe disability, Reggie's mother seemed cheerful, talking proudly of her son's school work, and how he had worked to keep them afloat after the accident.

When dinner was ready, they moved to the small dining room where a white table cloth held a central candle and four place settings. Cynthia Tan was again able to eat with the aid of a brace. Even though her hands were immobile, her arms had enough smooth movement to coordinate the feeding with a spoon.

The Italian dinner was outstanding, and after numerous compliments from Colder and Cynthia, Molly and Reggie traded barbs, each in a teasing manner attempting to secure more credit. Colder mentioned his contribution of the wine, which was loudly booed as being inconsequential, requiring no skill or work. Throughout the dinner they laughed, joked, and ultimately left the table too full to remember that they had once been starved.

"You get an 'A,' Molly," said Cynthia. "You need to come over here more often."

"Mom! I'm the great chef."

"I know you just stirred the pot. Molly's the genius," she said, smiling.

"I'll come anytime," Peter offered.

"We'll hold you to that," said Molly, turning to him.

"C'mon," said Reggie, starting to bus the dishes. "I have to show you what I found."

"I'll help with the dishes," offered Peter. "I'm good at this."

Twenty minutes later, the dishes were done. While Cynthia listened to an audio book, Reggie took Peter and Molly into his bedroom, closed the door, and motioned for them to sit while he retrieved the computer printout.

"We were so right," he said softly as if he were afraid of being overheard. "Last night I messed around in their system for about three hours. It's exactly as you figured."

Molly and Colder each held copies of two pages of computer commands—

a mixture of punctuation and indecipherable phrases. "I hope you know what this means," said Molly. "Because I have no idea."

Reggie beamed. "I have more than an idea. I know exactly what it means."

"Enlighten us," said Colder.

"The Doyne system works pretty much like we guessed. The blood gets logged in and is assigned to one file and given a number. If a pregnancy test comes back positive, that blood is tested at the same time for something that is identified as 7K3. I don't know what 7K3 is, but it must be what we want, because the way the program is written, if they find 7K3, the file is transferred and then deleted, just as we thought."

"Where is it transferred to?"

"The program lists a terminal number dd697, but I don't know where that is. That could be in the next room or in Nebraska. I have no idea."

"Can you track it?"

"Not unless there is a physical network map in the system. But I can at least try."

"This is really helpful, Reggie," Colder said appreciatively. "Great work."

"Thanks. I'll try for more when I get back from work."

"Where do you think it goes?" Molly asked.

"I'd love to think it leads right into Hutchins' office. But I doubt it will be anything that obvious," said Colder.

"I'll bet you're right," said Reggie. "It will probably be a terminal that any number of people could use. I'll also bet that there isn't a record anywhere of this data."

Molly nodded. "That seems logical. Why would they save anything?"

"Exactly," said Colder.

"So we'd never be able to prove anything," said Molly.

"Seems remote," Colder acknowledged.

"I had an idea," said Reggie, his mischievous grin returning. "What if we entered a positive test?"

The idea surprised Colder. It took a few seconds to process. "Yes! Good idea!"

"We may not be able to follow it all of the way through the system, but we may just get a phone call and a visit."

"Perfect!"

"We put in a positive test. Positive pregnancy with a positive 7K3. We'll run it with someone we know and then let them make contact. That way we can track it backward and maybe even meet this doctor."

"If we had someone who could have contact with the doctor," said Colder thoughtfully. "Hey, Letisha could pull it off. No doubt about it."

"She'd be perfect," said Molly.

"I'm liking this," said Reggie.

"Let's do it," said Colder.

Reggie was ready. "I'll snoop around again later tonight and see if I can find the system map and that terminal."

"Tomorrow we could send the fake. I'll talk to Letisha in the morning."

"Cool!"

Their evening concluded five minutes later. After saying goodbye and thanks to Cynthia and Reggie, Colder stood with Molly outside her door across the hall. Both of them suddenly felt a pleasant uneasiness. Colder paused and then awkwardly touched her on the shoulder. "You're a great cook," he said.

"Sometimes. I have my share of disasters too."

"Well, tonight was great."

Molly's lack of self-confidence threatened to overtake her. She bit her lip and shifted her weight nervously. "Thanks. We'll do it again?"

"You can count on it."

It was the answer she wanted to hear. She smiled and hugged him briefly. "Thanks for everything, Doc."

Colder kept a hand on her shoulder. "I think it's time you stopped with the 'doc' stuff. I always hated that, and besides, I'm not really your doctor anymore."

"Okay." She blushed as she said it.

"And—it makes me feel old. I'm only a few years older than you."

"Pete or Peter?"

"Your choice."

"I'll sleep on it," she said, opening her door across the hall and returning his gaze.

"Most people call me Pete," he said formally.

Her eyes were twinkling. "Good night, Peter."

A magnificent sunset was emerging when H. Carter Hutchins, sitting in the splendor of his office high above the city, poured his two guests a snifter of brandy. Jackson Barnes and Harley Whitfield took their glasses, and Hutchins offered a toast. The CEO, radiant with magnanimity from his two previous martinis, lavished a heap of superlatives upon his distinguished friends. The two attorneys, who had spent most of the evening fawning over the potential governor, graciously accepted the compliments and then returned to their seats. Inside, both men considered the remarks, including "the finest attorneys of this generation" obvious truths. Barnes and Whitfield, easily the two most notable attorneys in the Twin Cities area, were each sixty years old, former law school classmates and lifelong friends. Graying, but within a carefully cultivated image of distinguished power, they were each well-maintained and always perfectly groomed. They had founded their firm in 1964 after brief careers as assistant D.A.s in Hennepin County. The experience, disillusioning but enlightening, had informed them quickly that the only money in law was in defending rich clients, never in prosecuting. With wisdom gained, their first years were spent in personal injury and medical malpractice, where they soon gained reputations as tenacious and relentless fighters with a hunger for large settlements and larger publicity. Their tactics were effective. Since most of the accused preferred to shy from the spotlight, out-of-court settlements became the norm. As Barnes and Whitfield expanded, they employed a variety of new approaches to the law; the most notorious was hiring a series of "informants" to help them find cases. The most famous incident involved the employment of a number of operating room nurses throughout the city whom they used to identify potential malpractice cases. The strategy was controversial, but the program was wildly successful and made Barnes and Whitfield "names" in the Twin Cities.

As they grew, associates were added, two in 1974, two more in 1976, and four in 1980. During the following decade, they expanded rapidly, and with revenues booming and the firm's emphasis broadening, Barnes and Whitfield themselves concentrated more on the business end of law, reserving their courtroom expertise for the few cases promising wide exposure. Their biggest break came in 1988, with the settlement of a class action asbestos case involving forty thousand workers. In that case, they won over $75 million. Of that, they collected $30 million, while each worker got enough to pay a month's electric bill.

The verdicts had left them rich men, and the suddenly civic-minded partners began to focus strictly on profile. They gave to charity and to their churches. They concentrated on benefits and causes of public note, always close to a camera and never far from a microphone. They flirted with owning a professional sports team before simply negotiating the deal for another. Their fee, naturally high, was paid by public money. By 1995, they had largely retired except for the occasional case that interested them. They no longer drew salaries; their seven-figure yearly income was strictly tax-free in well-structured accounts that eliminated annoying liability and allowed them to concentrate on their civic pride and their public persona.

In 1995, the giant HMO, Community Health One, had hired Barnes and Whitfield, who were now large enough to handle nearly any type of crime or criminal. It was a natural fit for an insurance company operating on the fringe. A group of twenty partners with two hundred associates worked full-time for the HMO. The firm's revenues from the HMO each year neared $15 million, but Hutchins always felt the cost had been well worth it: they never lost a case.

"It's a slam dunk, Carter," said Barnes.

"Same old thing," said Whitfield, swirling his glass and enjoying the comfortable spin of the vodka. "Go to the guy with the deep pockets."

"There's positively no case there. They start sliding between words on a contract and Van Gilder's likely to have them thrown right out on their asses."

Hutchins paused, standing and looking out over the lights of downtown and allowing himself one more drink than usual. "I understand the legal implications," he said. "I just don't understand why."

"What else could it be?" asked Barnes. "It's part black and white, part rich and poor."

"That's the problem with success," said Whitfield. "The envy that it generates. That's all it is, envy of those who have achieved and prospered. The leaders, the visionaries, the people that make this country work and allow the others to enjoy the fruits of their labors."

Hutchins disagreed. "They see it differently. These little people can never see the responsibility that comes with making decisions for large groups of people. They truly view themselves as important. Living off the system, one way or another, while the successful pay the bills. My God, a girl like that probably doesn't even pay a dime of federal tax."

"It's true. We pay millions of dollars per year, provide the jobs, fuel the growth of the economy, and yet they have no hesitation in biting the hand that feeds."

"How many babies would these girls have?" Hutchins asked, starting to roll with the alcohol in his veins. "Babies they really can't afford, babies never destined to be productive members of society. Just more people to live on the system. And worse yet, what will these babies cost us in medical expense?"

Barnes splashed down the last of his drink, the glow of the evolving sunset invigorating him. "But they want us to pay, Carter," he said, with a satisfied smile. "They'll go to work or on the dole for ten grand a year, but when they have six kids, the money's tight, and they don't have a big screen TV, it's always somehow the rich guy's fault."

"Dammit!" shouted Hutchins, slamming down his drink and feeling better by the minute. "I will not be blackmailed by some little bitch who can't do a fucking thing other than get herself knocked up. The system is supposed to be designed to protect those of us who try to make this world a better place. It's supposed to reward those of us who try to make health care affordable, who create jobs, and increase everyone's standard of living. Shit! Can't these women with their precious wombs think of anything other than themselves and the damn babies they can't afford?"

"I don't think so, Carter," said Whitfield. "They view pushing puppies as almost an obligation, a rite of passage to womanhood."

"Dammit," hissed Hutchins.

"It's true though," agreed Barnes. "All of 'em look at it that way."

Hutchins eyes were flashing. "It's nonsense. Our system can't afford that kind of freedom anymore if people are going to still have care. We have to start to make the difficult choices. Value to society and affordability to society." Barnes and Whitfield both nodded.

"There *is* no other way," continued Hutchins, his voice lowering menacingly.

"When freedom becomes an instrument of tyranny against the greater good—then we *must* restrict it, control it, or better yet, eliminate it."

"That's where we are."

For a moment they stopped, the room consumed by silence, punctuated only by the distant sound of an airplane high in the sky.

Hutchins swirled the drink. A brilliant plan was emerging in his mind. "Harley, tell those coon lawyers of hers that there will be no settlement. And that if this so much as appears in the want ads, I promise them, they'll never practice again."

"They'll buy that," said Whitfield confidently.

"If they don't, then they are the only thing I didn't think they were—stupid."

"And the girl?" Barnes asked.

Hutchins leaned over the desk, sneering with contempt. "If this so much as gets a peep on the airwaves, I want everything about her floating through the air like the wind. I want fifty guys out in front talking about how she screwed them, and how much she liked it. Also the husband. Pokey's boys have already found out that he used to rough her up a little. The public will need to know how much she liked that too. A Catholic, a little S 'n M, an abortion, and a husband who didn't know."

Whitfield roared approvingly. "You should have been a lawyer, Carter."

"We'll crush the little bitch," the CEO grunted.

Barnes finished his drink. "We'll get 'em. Just another day at the office."

"Exactly," agreed Hutchins. "That's exactly how we want it."

Five minutes later the two attorneys left after a flurry of handshakes, mutual admiration, and promises of more drinks when the issue was finished. A moment later, Hutchins' private line rang, the line used only by his wife.

"Celia," he cooed warmly. "A nice surprise."

"I'm sorry you're so late."

"I won't be long."

"Good," she said as if by reflex. "I'll be taking a car."

"That will be fine."

"I do hope that we can raise some money for those poor Negro children tonight. They so rarely have both mothers and fathers. Do you have your tux?"

"Yes. I'll change in a minute."

"Good," she said again as if by reflex and not hearing. "I thought I'd wear black. What do you think? I know black is always right, but this is summer after all. Do you think another color would be better?"

"You'll look fine no matter wh—"

"Do you think anyone else will wear black? I would so much like to be the only one wearing it, and I have the new dress that I bought just last week."

"I'm sure that will be lovely."

"I'll see you there, darling. Love you. Bye-bye."

With a flourish she was gone, and Hutchins hung up the phone, only to notice his second line flashing. "Hello," he answered, slightly annoyed.

"I need a minute," said Gregory Markham, the Chief Operating Officer whose office was one story below. "It can't wait. You need to know tonight."

"Make it fast."

"On my way."

Two minutes later, Gregory Markham carefully shut the heavy bronze doors of H. Carter Hutchins and took the seat formerly occupied by Jackson Barnes. Markham was composed, but earnest.

"What is it that can't wait?" asked Hutchins, rising from the desk and undoing his tie. "I'm at a benefit in forty minutes."

"A problem has come up."

"I've had enough problems for today. Why the hell do I pay you a million dollars a year? To come into my office at eight o'clock at night like a whimpering hound wanting a pat?"

"You need to know this," Markham replied, accustomed to the moods of the boss.

"Spill it then."

"She's one of them."

"Who's *one* of *what?*" Hutchins barked.

"Molly Loomis."

"What about her?"

"She's a Fragile X."

Hutchins paused and stopped, his shirt half unbuttoned and his fingers fondling a cufflink. "You're sure?" he asked, his tone instantly changed.

"No question. It's in my log. The name rang a bell and I checked on it."

"Shit," said Hutchins, his hand rubbing his chin. His habit was to become both profane and formal when confronted with a problem. "Unfortunate. That complicates things a little."

"A lot, perhaps."

"There's no way to trace it though?"

"None. It ends at Doyne."

"And all records are gone?"

"All except yours and mine."

"What about the Doyne system?"

"It's a lock. Anyone tries anything, we'll know."

"Good."

Markham wasn't through. He lowered his voice even though no one else was listening. "But there's still the wild card."

Hutchins bristled. It was as if someone had stung him. "That son-of-a-bitch. Where is he?"

"Still no idea."

"Shit. He has it?"

"I'm sure he does."

"We have to have him, Greg. You know that. Whatever you need to do."

"I'm on it."

"Like I said," growled Hutchins, his eyes narrowing. "What*ever* you need to do."

Markham nodded in affirmation, the message clear. "I'll find him."

Hutchins patted him on the shoulder and walked by. "Good," he said, as if he now considered the case closed. "That's what I wanted to hear."

Chapter Eleven

Reggie was tired, but elated, at 2:00 A.M. when he typed the last of Letisha Moore's positive pregnancy test into the computer. He had begun two hours before, having first negotiated through the maze of security traps built into the Doyne system. But even with the security gone, a second problem remained. Entering a fictitious test had proven difficult because the data was recorded automatically by the computer as the samples were analyzed rather than manually entered by a user. To overcome this problem, Reggie modified the original program slightly to accommodate a second point of data entry. After modifying the program, Reggie entered the positive result, including the 7KS, and then erased his tracks, changing the program back to the original before logging off. His entire time in the system was less than an hour, and for additional safety if a problem was ever detected, he implicated one of the technicians, borrowing a password he had found and decoded within the system.

Finished and feeling satisfied, he lay down on the bed and set an alarm for 3:00 A.M. The one hour was only a guess, but he figured that it would take only a few minutes for the information to be sent and then deleted. These functions were dependent on the second computer's program, which he had not been able to trace. He lay back on the pillow and shut his eyes. Within minutes, it seemed, the radio alarm woke him up to the strains of old Simon and Garfunkel. He shut off the radio and wiped his eyes, the music having disturbed his first dream of the night, and turned on the computer again. The room was instantly converted to a shadowy glow of neon gray as the black-and-white screen of the virus-checking program ran quickly through his system. Finished, he activated the modem, and within two minutes he had his answer.

Reggie beamed when he saw it. Perfect, he thought. Seeing the new files, he realized immediately that the computer had taken the bait. Letisha's file was gone, completely erased as though it had never existed. The plan had worked masterfully. Now they would wait for any contact with Letisha. She would be their link, because according to the computer, she was now a Fragile X.

His task complete, he again disconnected from their system, signing off this time as a different technician using another borrowed password, and shut off the computer. Lying down on the bed, he found himself at first no longer tired, invigorated by his victory and the anticipation of what they would find. He thought of the possibilities. Who would call her? Who would come? Would it be the same guy who had visited Molly? Or would they use some other means?

Reggie knew they had them either way. Any method that they chose would be recorded or kept, establishing proof of a definite link of the Fragile X to Doyne and, ultimately, to ComHealthOne. He was elated and rewarded himself with the Snickers bar that he had on his nightstand as he stared at the ceiling in the darkness. He decided against telling the others. Too late, he thought. He would call them in the morning. The candy finished, he found his eyelids heavy. Moments later and without another thought, Reggie fell into a deep, contented sleep.

The evening of the fourth of July was flawless, and after an afternoon of running errands together, Molly and Sylvia, groceries in hand, arrived at Peter's house. When there was no answer at the front door, they walked around the side and into the fenced back yard where chef Colder, spatula in hand and coals waiting, sat in anticipation of the meat and corn. After greetings, they sat down and began preparations for the feast. The grocer had advertised the sweet corn as being the first of the year in Minnesota, but with its large ears and robust yellow-orange color, all agreed that it probably originated much closer to San Francisco than Minneapolis. They shucked it and wrapped it in foil, and Colder placed the wrapped cobs on the edge of the grill. Continuing to act like he knew what he was doing, he seasoned the meat and, finally, tossed eight thick, red hamburgers onto the grill. The two women *oohed* approvingly when the burgers, which appeared to be oozing fat, shot smoke into the air after hitting the hot steel. Colder flipped the burgers with a dramatic flair, creating another blast of gray, and then sat back to relax on an old folding lawn chair. Molly and Sylvia sat next to him on the picnic bench that was attached to the wooden table, already draped in a red-and-white checked table cloth. Sylvia poured them all some lemonade and started to relate the day's events. Just as Reggie's name was mentioned, he turned the corner, holding a large bag of potato chips, grinning broadly.

"Finished my part of the cooking," he exclaimed, holding the chips aloft like a trophy.

"Booo!" the others shouted, waving him away with their hands.

"We have to have vegetables," he pleaded.

"Way to go, Reggie," laughed Molly. "There'd be no nutrition without you."

"I know, I know," he said taking a seat next to Molly and bowing his head twice as if having been honored. "It's hard to be humble."

Molly swiped at his exposed arm with her hand. "I'll ignore that. And besides, you're late. We've been slaving all day."

"I'll bet," he laughed, looking over his shoulder at the hamburgers on the grill.

"Well, at least ten minutes."

"How's your mom?" Sylvia asked, handing him a glass of lemonade.

"Good. She eats dinner with her friend Dottie on Wednesdays. She comes over and makes something."

"Brave lady, your mother," Sylvia commented.

"Yeah, she's come a long way. The computer has been great for her. She uses it all day to read and talk on the phone. She can draw with it, too."

"I've seen a couple of her drawings," said Peter. "She's good."

"She's quite a lady. My source of inspiration."

Sylvia decided to brave the area. "How long ago was the accident?"

"Seven years next month."

"Do you mind if I ask how it happened?"

"Not at all. It was a dark night, and a drunk driver was speeding."

Sylvia shook her head disgustedly.

"My dad was killed. Mom hung on. I didn't think that she'd make it for a long time. She was in bad shape, on a respirator with pneumonia and other infections. They had to fuse her neck, the sixth and seventh vertebrae, and afterward she was in a halo brace for three months. Finally she stabilized enough to go to rehab. She was there six months."

"How did you do it financially?"

"Dad had pretty good life insurance. He was an engineer. But that was pretty much used up in a couple of years with all the bills. Medical was harder. Our original insurance company got bought out by ComHealth. They had our policy canceled within six months. Medicaid saves us now. They pay for most everything. The rest of it I can take care of with my jobs. If it wasn't for Medicaid though, we'd be on the streets."

Reggie opened the bag of chips and took a handful. He talked of the tragedy with the quiet confidence of someone touched by it but neither bitter nor blame-seeking. "Hey! The burgers!" he cried suddenly.

Colder bolted up, his concentration having lapsed with thoughts of Cynthia Tan. A cloud of gray-black smoke was billowing high into the air, far above the grill. He scrambled for the spatula, dropping it once on the ground before clumsily flipping the meat, as the others laughed hysterically at his uncoordinated routine. One patty was tossed too close to the edge of the grill. It teetered perilously toward the coals, rocking with any gust of air or surge of heat from below. Colder stabbed at it with the flat front end of the spatula, attempting the rescue. Instead he pressed too firmly, cutting off the inner third of the burger while the remainder fell into the coals, resulting in another explosion of smoke and sizzle.

"Damn," muttered Colder disgustedly.

"Now that was a work of surgical precision," giggled Sylvia. "Very impressive."

"You get that one," laughed Molly.

"Very well done."

"Man, that one's history," chuckled Reggie, peeking in to look. "That was like an execution."

"Funny," Colder said, trying not to show his own amusement at his feeble culinary efforts.

"We're down a burger," said Reggie as the overly hot grill continued to smoke furiously. "I could run down the block to Mac's."

"No, we're okay," said Sylvia. "Dr. Colder wasn't that hungry anyway."

The first blast of smoke was only a warning. The grill was too hot, and quickly the smoke reappeared and then turned to fire. The threesome laughed even harder when Colder frantically tried to control the incineration. He scrambled to rearrange of the grill's contents, wildly flipping burgers, spinning corn, and shoving all the food to the edge. At first it barely seemed to help, but after two minutes, the smoke and fire finally relented.

With the inferno gone, the view of the grill was clear. Everyone could see that the foil on the corn was completely black. Some of the corn was exposed and burned beyond edible. Colder rolled one charred ear, frowning sheepishly as smoke surged out of it. The hamburgers were worse. They were rock-hard, black as night, and shaped like the coals. When he touched them, they also emitted a spiraling trail of smoke. Feebly, he rolled each of them side to side.

Chagrined, Colder turned to the others. "Maybe Mac's isn't such a bad idea after all."

His admission nearly put the others into convulsions. It took minutes, but when they had recovered, they assured him politely that they preferred his burnt golf balls to precisely cooked, premium meat.

"You don't do any surgery, do you, Doc?" asked Reggie.

"I could certainly try."

"Glad we got some good lawyers on our side."

Just then Sandra turned the corner and waved hello, an unexpected grin flashing on her face. Perspiring slightly, with her red hair pulled into a pony tail, she appeared hurried, her usual nervous twitches even more pronounced. She nodded to each of them, tossed her purse on the picnic table, and removed her windbreaker. Still not speaking, she returned to her purse and began rummaging through it.

"How are you, Sandra?" Sylvia asked of her slightly neurotic, but incredibly efficient friend.

"Good, good, good," she murmured. Looking up, she glanced at the grill.

"Those look good," she said sincerely, not having actually seen what she was complimenting.

They all broke out laughing again and Colder, reseated in his chair, held the spatula aloft in triumph. "Redemption!"

Sandra, spying the burnt offerings, sized up the situation instantly. "You know I'd never say anything else, Dr. Colder," she said diplomatically.

Peter tried hard to look hurt, but he was having far too much fun to succeed.

"Thank you," Sylvia said. "We've been working on his humility."

"I'm humble, I'm humble," Colder begged. "I've completely surrendered to the barbecue gods."

Sandra returned to her bag and then the lone manila folder she carried with her. "Any word from Letisha?" she asked.

"Didn't hear anything today," said Colder. "She's at home now in case someone calls."

"I think it was five to ten days after the test that I was called. So if the pattern holds, it should be soon," Molly explained.

"They have the work number, don't they?" Sylvia asked.

"I put it in," said Reggie.

Sandra sat down, no longer fiddling with her purse and papers. She pulled an envelope out of her purse and withdrew a piece of paper from inside. Her action seemed slightly unexpected, and they all turned to her as if by reaction. Her nervousness seemed to evaporate. The quirky accountant suddenly looked at the others with a smug look of complete self-satisfaction. She said nothing, but the others noticed.

"What is it, Sandra? You look like the cat that swallowed the canary," asked Sylvia.

Sandra's smirk became a grin, and she tossed the sheet of paper onto the table. From their seats, none of them could read it. The only print on the paper was located in the center and was quite small. Reggie picked it up and saw it was simply a name.

"James Patrick O'Reilly?" he asked. "Who's this dude?"

Sandra reached across the table and grabbed the glass of lemonade that Sylvia offered her. "Thanks," she said softly, still grinning uncontrollably.

Colder's eyes narrowed as he looked at her.

"You bet," Sandra said. "That's our guy. Dr. O'Reilly is Fragile X."

Colder leaped from the chair, bounding toward Sandra and closing the distance in one stride. He took the paper in his hand and stared at the name as if the printed letters would provide additional insight into the man.

"You're sure?" he asked, sounding breathless.

"Positive."

"WAY cool!" yelled Reggie.

"Wonderful!" exclaimed Sylvia.

Sandra looked down, her natural shyness overtaking her with the acclaim. "It's only a start. I don't have the article. Just the name."

"Don't even think about being modest," Molly said warmly. "You deserve a lot of credit. This is a major break!"

Colder agreed. "She's right, Sandra. It's fabulous. How exactly did you find out?"

"In April of that year, the *British Journal of Developmental Genetics* listed the authors who were expected to publish articles in the second half of the year. This was put in so that anyone looking for a particular author would have some idea of when their next publication would come out. Turns out I was able to track down the authors of all twelve of the articles that were to be published in that issue of *BJDG*, and I got ahold of someone for eleven of the twelve. It seems that all eleven of those articles were published elsewhere within a few months."

"Really? You talked to the authors of eleven of the twelve articles that were to be published in the missing journal?" asked Reggie.

"Yes."

"Great work."

"What did they say had happened?" Colder asked.

"Each author's story was the same. They got a call from the *Journal*, explaining that it was ceasing publication and that their articles had been resubmitted for publication in other journals. Unfortunately, none of them knew any of the other articles in the *Journal* and none of these articles are even remotely close to anything we would be looking for. Ant genes, sunflower genes, and so on."

"Then what we're looking for is the last article," said Colder.

Sandra agreed. "Yes. And from the list of authors expected to publish, I was left with four names. I checked them out. Interestingly, they never published another article."

"Are they all British?" Colder asked.

Sandra grinned. "I'm getting to that. I talked to a couple of the British authors and asked if they knew of any colleagues who had been killed, disappeared, or died under mysterious circumstances. They all said no."

"That would fit. This guy I talked to sounds American. If all of them had been young and from England, you would think that it would have been a little strange that none of them had heard of a bunch of people dying."

"You're right."

"What were the four guys' names?"

"Mark Stevenson. He was from Tulane. Phillip Wyland from Wisconsin-Madison and Stephen Schmitz from Michigan. And then O'Reilly from UCSF."

"What happened to them?" Reggie asked.

"Like we figured. All dead," Sandra said, matter-of-factly. "O'Reilly's the only one left. Wyland died in a house fire with his wife. Schmitz died in a car accident. Stevenson and his wife and child died from carbon monoxide poisoning. Faulty furnace."

Colder's face was grim. "I'll bet. What about O'Reilly?"

"Disappeared. Not a trace."

"All those people dead?" asked Sylvia incredulously.

"As far as I can tell, they are still considered accidents. Investigations may be ongoing, but they all happened within about a two-week span in June of 1997."

"This is getting a little spooky," said Molly.

"No kidding," Reggie acknowledged. "Someone really didn't want this coming out."

"What about the authors' bibliographies?" asked Peter.

"Zilch. They didn't list anything."

"Anything in the past that might clue us in?"

Sandra withdrew another paper from the folder and handed it to Peter. "I printed a list of their previous articles, but it doesn't look helpful."

Colder scanned it and in less than a minute tossed it back onto the table. "You're right. There's nothing there."

Colder walked to the grill and removed the corn and the very well-done hamburgers, tossing them onto a large plate and delivering them to the table.

"Where do we go from here?" Molly asked, looking up at Peter.

"Our friend Dr. O'Reilly said he would call me tomorrow night. I think I may have some questions for him."

"Like the title of his article?" Reggie asked.

"That, and two other things," Peter said, his mind spinning in a myriad of concerns. "Who does he think killed his friends?"

"What else?" asked Molly.

Colder looked worried. "How can we help him save his life?" His voice trailed off, and no one else spoke, preferring for a while to dine in silence.

Chapter Twelve

July 21

By midmorning, Tyler Briggs and Marcus Sanders had already been at work for hours, and Tyler's office, the adopted war room, was a mess. The desk and tables were full of legal references, CDs, notes, and piles of paper strewn everywhere. While impressive in quantity, the legal research had been depressing in content. The discouraged looks on the partners' faces were entirely appropriate.

What they had learned to this point had given them no real reason for optimism. Pokey Mercer had been completely right. In similar lawsuits, the courts nationwide ruled almost exclusively along the narrow lines of the law, rarely choosing to interpret contracts or the breadth of the services covered. They found no examples of someone successfully suing under the famous clause of "fair and reasonable." All litigation based on this statement was soundly defeated. In fact, they found few examples of HMOs being successfully sued for any reason. One, a boy in California whose bone marrow transplant was eventually covered, was originally denied because the care had been labeled experimental. The court ultimately ruled that the HMO would have to pay since the care was no longer simply an experimental therapy. The other victories they found had been small and generally with a common theme, an aggressive cost-cutting HMO trying not to pay for services it had contracted to pay for. There were no victories in cases like Molly's.

When the phone rang, Tyler answered on the second ring. "Briggs."

"You know everything you need to know, boys?" Pokey Mercer was obviously on a cell phone and trying to talk above the traffic noise.

"We know everything, Pokey," Sanders said, straining to sound optimistic.

"I doubt it," he laughed as a passing truck nearly drowned him out. "Your little girl tell you all about her past?"

"Of course she did," Briggs said, sounding weaker than he had intended and looking across his desk at his partner. "But I doubt she told you."

Pokey was halfway between patronizing and condescending. "You guys are nice boys. I really hate to see you embarrass yourselves and waste your time."

"You call it embarrassing when five hundred clones wearing fine wool suits walk out into the light dripping in egg?"

"Nice try. You know you ain't got shit, and plus, you don't even know what we know about your girl."

"You got a reason for calling us, Pokey, or you just standing in front of some bar impressing a short skirt with your cell phone?"

"You boys are going down. We've got about twenty thousand precedents and we could probably come up with about two million more if we wanted to. You might as well admit you're wasting your time and the court's time. I doubt Van Gilder will even give this ten minutes."

Tyler and Marcus hesitated. They knew that as much as Mercer revolted them, he would not call ever simply to chat. He was delivering a message, a message that they knew to be true: every precedent was in ComHealth's favor. The second message was even more ominous, an implication that he knew something about Molly that Tyler and Marcus did not.

"I don't know, Pokey," Marcus said, recovering. "Think they'll let you keep this job after the fall? Your firm likes only blue bloods married to vintage Victorian women. You'll be the guy assigned the blame."

Pokey was surprisingly quiet and calm. "Go ahead and insult me, Sanders. It doesn't matter to me. I'm being more of a friend right now than you know."

"Thanks," Tyler replied, suddenly aware the phone was dead.

Tyler hit the button for the speaker and stood, loosening his tie, having felt a sudden warmth. "What the hell was that?"

"I don't know," admitted Marcus, concern etched on his face. "The guy may be a lot of things, but he wouldn't say that just to blow smoke. What else do you know about Molly?"

"Only what I told you." Sanders shook his head. "There's got to be something else. He as much as told us."

"He's bluffing. Just jerking our chains."

"Maybe."

Tyler sounded confident, but he wasn't. "Still, I need to talk to her. A real heart-to-heart. If there is something there, we'd better know it now, or it'll be exactly as Pokey says."

Marcus disagreed. "No. It'll be way worse than that."

Molly was alone at her apartment when Tyler arrived. Having worked the night shift at the diner, she was now eating a breakfast of Kix and toast before going to bed. Briggs called her right after his call from Pokey Mercer and she agreed to see him immediately, sensing his concern. Dressed in sweatpants and a T-shirt and sitting across from him in the living room, she nibbled on a piece of toast as Tyler pulled from his briefcase a series of papers, laying them on the barren floor.

"Molly," he started, taking no time to get to the point. "Like I told you, I had a call from one of the ComHealth attorneys this morning. He implied very strongly that they had something on you that they intended to use against you personally. I need to know."

Molly looked shocked. "Really?"

"I wouldn't be here if I wasn't serious. And they wouldn't have said that if they didn't think it was enough for us to want to withdraw."

"There's nothing I haven't told you," she said earnestly.

"What about old boyfriends?"

Molly looked away, thinking. "None really. A couple of dates in high school, but no one that I would call a boyfriend."

"What about Troy?"

"Just as I told you," she said, moving her hand in a gesture of curiosity and concern.

"What about your sex life?"

Molly did not react noticeably, but it pained her to answer. "You really want the truth?" she asked softly.

"Yes."

"It was awful, at times almost violent."

Tyler bit his lip. He hated to ask. "Violent? Did you object?"

Molly's face turned white. "You mean if I didn't object, you think that they would—"

Tyler didn't say it, but he knew Barnes and Whitfield had routinely done worse. "I don't think that there is anything about you that they won't know, anything that they wouldn't use if it aided their cause."

Molly was instantly shaking, her voice quivering. "But that would mean that Troy would have to get on the stand and lie."

"Not really. Just tell it in a way they want the jury to see it."

"Oh my God," Molly murmured, her lips tightly curled in a grimace of mental anguish and her brow furrowed with worry.

"First of all, let me say this. What they intend to do will be to get this thing dismissed. What they're doing now is just rattling sabers, trying to intimidate you. But if it ever comes to a trial, we know for a fact that they will try to attack you personally. You'll be portrayed as angry, bitter, and money-hungry. You know that, but they'd also like you to look sluttish and manipulative, if possible."

"I think they can get me on being 'stupid' pretty easily," Molly said sheepishly, "but it would all be lies. I admit I have my faults. I am angry and a little bitter, but not in that way. I'm the one who went for the abortion. I'm the one who has to live with the consequences. All we've been saying is that this was emergency care and that they should have to pay for what they say they pay for, emergency care and things that are fair and reasonable."

"I agree, Molly, but I need to know. Is there something there? Is there anything to what they're saying?"

"No," she said firmly. "They can call me a slut if they want, but the truth is that that part of my life has been more like—pathetic." She looked completely perplexed. "And they can claim I'm money-hungry but that's not true either. It isn't about being greedy at all."

Briggs stared at her, convinced that she was telling the truth. "Then what is it that they have?"

"I don't know," she muttered, putting her plate on the floor and curling into her borrowed couch. "I have no idea."

"They must be bluffing."

Briggs knew that this would just be one of many problems designed to throw them off the trail. Innuendoes, hints, and false accusations designed to distract and consume their time. They would do it in a way to take directly from the preparation of their case, and it was just the first example of what their superior resources, money, and manpower could afford. For Barnes and Whitfield, it would be nothing more than an afternoon's work for a handful of junior associates. For Tyler and Marcus, it would be several nights' worth of work to research any rumor or to dismiss any hint. The reality was that it would be guerrilla warfare, but any overlooked problem could cost them the case. A case that was already weak at best.

"What about your parents, Molly? Any skeletons? Business problems, money problems?"

"No. Not a chance. They're as honest as can be."

Briggs shrugged and began picking up the papers from the floor and replacing them in the folder. As he did so, he recalled again what Mercer had said. They definitely had something on her. Maybe it was a bluff, but Tyler tried again, running through the possibilities about her life. "What about your medical history, Molly? Anything?"

She shrugged, her mind still on her parents. "A little bit of asthma. I use an inhaler if I need it. Nothing else."

"What about the miscarriage?"

Her attention returned with the question. "It was right after we got married. It was during a fight. Troy pushed me down some stairs."

Briggs closed his eyes, the sight too vivid. "Did you try to get pregnant right away again?"

"Yes. I wanted a baby, but the doctor wanted me to wait for a little while."

"Why?"

"I had developed this little infection that needed to be treated. He didn't want me pregnant until after it was controlled. Said it could affect the baby."

"What did you have to do for that?"

"Antibiotics."

"That took care of it?"

"Yeah. My doctor was concerned about it for a while, but the antibiotics finally got it taken care of."

"Were you okay?"

"Yes, er, sort of. After the miscarriage, I kept having this abdominal pain. I think part of it was the infection. But my periods got bad too. I guess I just became one of these women who have organs from hell."

"What about now?"

"Well, everything is gone with the hysterectomy."

Briggs flushed, feeling foolish for such a question. "Sorry."

Molly dismissed it. "Forget it."

Tyler leaned back, his thoughts racing. For a moment, the sudden sound of children's voices distracted him, and he gazed toward the open window, seeing only the brick building across the street. The summer breeze blew across his face as it sent the half-drawn shade floating into the air. An instant later, the voices stopped and his concentration returned. As it did, he turned toward her and stared at her intently. She was huddled, but relaxed, in the corner of the couch. Her look was a mix of confused, innocent, vulnerable, and determined. She, too, struggled to make sense of Mercer's message.

Briggs was confident that his client was truthful. She had no reason to lie, but he also feared that the truth posed a dilemma, because he knew that Pokey Mercer would not be Barnes' and Whitfield's man of deception. He was as subtle as a charging bull. They would never use him as the spreader of misinformation. Subtlety was an unknown to Pokey. He was a bomb thrower. The thought startled him, and a sense of fear crept over him as its meaning sank in. Molly Loomis was telling the truth. Unfortunately, perhaps, so was Pokey Mercer.

Briggs scratched his brow and wiped away two beads of sweat. Molly said nothing at all, gazing at him, their thoughts suddenly the same. Even if Mercer was lying, the task was becoming more difficult. Lies and truth, rumor and innuendo so easily blend into fact. A skilled lawyer could make Molly look like a scheming, greedy nymphomaniac without ever presenting a shred of evidence. More than ever before, Briggs was convinced that ComHealth would stop at nothing to win. And now more than ever, he doubted that Molly would ever have a chance.

In continued silence, Tyler stood to leave and Molly rose with him. Pensively, the two said their goodbyes. Briggs left the apartment more depressed than ever.

At 10:00 P.M., Reggie Tan opened his apartment door and stepped inside. The room was dark, and turning on the light he saw that his mother's door was closed, a signal that she had gone to bed early. A small light over the stove guided him into the kitchen, and he opened the refrigerator and pulled out a 7-Up. He opened his mother's door, seeing her sleeping soundly against the moonlight in the window and then shut the door quietly. Retiring to his room, he turned on his computer. He had spent all day waiting for a call from Colder regarding any contact about Letisha's pregnancy test, but still none had come. Nearly two weeks and no contact. Reggie was convinced he had made a mistake. He decided that he would check the files again.

Logging into the Doyne files had now become simple. He had recorded all of the passwords of the employees into his system during his visits into their operating system, and now he simply rotated between employees to divert any possible suspicion. This time he used a new word, "Redhead," from his list, and within a minute he was again looking at Letisha's file. There appeared to have been no change, the files still missing as if never there. He searched for the file, re-entering the missing file numbers, but the screen said "File Does Not Exist."

"Same as before," he muttered, shutting down the modem link and then the computer. He gulped the soda in three large swigs and then lay down on the bed, opening his economics book. He was frustrated. He knew that they had contacted Molly between five and ten days after her test, and since they had planted the positive test on Letisha, two weeks had passed without a word. He was now a little worried. Something had gone wrong. But how?

He turned to his homework. His plan was to study for an hour before sleeping and then again for an hour in the morning before school. He also understood himself well enough to know that his mind would be on Letisha's test and not macroeconomic theory. He opened his book, and for ten minutes he tried to concentrate, his eyes aimlessly wandering from page to page as if the print was illegible Sanskrit while his thoughts circled between Molly, Letisha, the Doyne computers, and the link to ComHealthOne. They needed proof of the link. They needed the trap to work.

Faster than he expected, the fatigue of eight hours of class and six hours of sweeping floors began to erode at his thoughts, and he lay his head on the pillow and closed the book. He looked at the clock, 10:10. He was disappointed. He had expected to study for an hour, but he felt exhausted, his efforts useless. He undressed, turned out the light, and climbed into bed, feeling more drained with each passing minute. As his head hit the pillow again, he noticed that his head hurt slightly, but the bed was warm and the softness comfortable. His thoughts stopped with the favorable sensation. He instantly fell sound asleep.

Peter Colder's phone rang. Startled by the noise, the great cat Mortimer leaped from the couch and bounded toward the kitchen. Colder sat straight up on the edge of the sofa, his eyes fixed on the TV where the sportscast showed highlights of the second Twins victory in a row. He picked up the phone reflexively, a look of annoyance on his face from the interruption, without looking at his newly purchased caller ID.

"Hello," he grumbled, as if hoping for a dial tone.

"Dr. Colder," came the voice.

Peter fondled the remote and turned off the TV, his mind turning instantly to the caller. "Very clever," Colder said with only a hint of sarcasm.

"One can not be too careful, my friend."

While at the happy hour at five o'clock, Colder had been paged by the County Hospital operator, the message being that he would receive a phone call after ten from an old friend. Looking at the number on the caller ID, he recognized it as one from a local restaurant, a number that no one would suspect.

"So you are in the city?" asked Colder.

"Not for long."

"Have you been here long?"

"You don't need to know, but the answer is no."

"When will we meet?"

The voice stopped for a moment. "Not soon. There is no need. I am here only to check on some things for you."

"Such as?" asked Colder, surprised.

"They will begin to follow you soon. By my estimation, within days. Anyone who searches for the journal will be watched. And you, my friend, will be watched carefully."

"Because of Molly?"

"Yes, and they will follow her too."

"I had expected that," Colder admitted.

"That is the only reason I call. To warn you. They will be bugging your phones and following you."

"What about you?"

You will not hear from me for a while now. Maybe a week or so," said the voice.

"You removed all the bugs from my office?" asked Colder.

"Yes,"

"I thought my leaving the door open would make it easier."

"My thanks," he said with a chuckle. "There can be no hint that you have heard from me."

"I understand."

"I will be watching, and I will find you."

"When?"

"Like I said. Maybe a week. But certainly when you need it."

"Why not now?"

"Tell me. What could you prove with what you have?"

"I don't know. I don't even know what we have yet."

"You don't need to know yet. I can tell you that they did it, but you need to prove that they did it."

"What exactly did they do?"

"Not yet. What and why, is for later."

"When?"

"Like I said, I will contact you."

Colder kicked his stocking feet up on the couch and slid up against a large pillow he often slept on. He felt a combination of intrigue, fear, and strange exhilaration as he talked to the man, the same nagging sensation of nervous anticipation that he both detested and thrived upon. "The journal won't do it, you know. They could say it was a fake."

The man coughed audibly, his hand apparently muffling the noise. "I have the original data," he said finally. "Trust me. I have everything you'll need."

Colder smiled to himself, now leading this friend and determined to take his shot. "I should have known. Every geneticist I've known has been a compulsive planner."

There was a pause, followed by another muffled cough. "Very good," said the voice, surprised. "I'm impressed. Tell me more."

At that moment Mortimer reappeared, leaping onto the couch and looking quizzically at his master. "What would you like to know, Dr. James Patrick O'Reilly?" he said smugly while starting to scratch the great cat's neck.

There was a long pause. "I'm very impressed," O'Reilly finally said. His tone changed. His voice almost sounded grateful that his cover was now exposed. "How did you find out?"

"Not for you to know," chuckled Colder. "We all have our mysteries."

"Touché."

"Seriously," Colder said. "We tracked it back through the abstracts. Process of elimination."

"I figured," said O'Reilly.

"Can I ask how many are dead?" Colder asked.

O'Reilly came clean with the information. "Five, including my partners' wives."

"That's what we thought. And you?"

"I've been lucky. I was to go in a car accident, but the two cars that had planned to assist me over a cliff collided and locked fenders. I had just enough time to get away."

"You've been hiding for three years?"

"Yes. They found me once, but I had an alarm system that warned me and gave me a second narrow escape. I've been running ever since."

"Why do you reappear now?"

"Because the precedent is dangerous, computers are dangerous, and men of power are men to fear. This needs to be stopped. It has to be stopped."

"We can stop it?" Colder asked.

"I'm sure you already have," said O'Reilly. "They'll know that Molly Loomis was one."

Colder sat up straight, the thought catching him off guard.

"They would stop it instantly with something like this case," O'Reilly continued. "The risks would be too great."

Colder wiped his tightly closed eyes, more in frustration than fatigue. "I never thought of that," he admitted.

"These guys are very smart. They won't take chances. They're too good."

"Damn," Peter muttered.

"These guys are gonna be tough to get, Peter. They're well insulated."

"I know," Colder admitted. After a pause, a question came to him. "By the way, Jim, how did you find out about Molly and this Fragile X business?"

"I knew that when my partners were killed and then in the aftermath *BJDG* was purchased by Waverland, there had to be a reason."

"Your paper?"

"Absolutely. I'll tell you, never once when we were working did it occur to us that this was anything more than a medical advancement. But I guess everything is bass-ackwards these days in medicine."

"Tell me about it."

"Anyway, I began to realize that Hutchins had to be behind things, since he was on the Waverland board. Through a little computer piracy, I've become a pretty good hacker, and I was able to confirm that Hutchins was the main force behind the purchase. After that, I got even more scared when I realized what an aggressive, omnipotent HMO could potentially do."

"How did you find out about Molly?"

I'm getting to that. For quite a while, I couldn't do anything other than theorize and hide. I hacked into Hutchins computer on several occasions. I never found a thing until one day when he got an e-mail from someone close to him, probably one of the other executives. It was a very strange message. All it said was 'Fragile X operative.'"

"That would seem weird."

"What really got me thinking, though, was that Hutchins erased the message immediately. Normally he saves his messages for a couple of weeks."

"I see."

"After that, I took a chance. I tapped into a couple of the local women's clinics' computers. It didn't take me long to find a woman who'd had an abortion because of Fragile X, Molly Loomis. I was pretty sure of what I was on to. I followed her a little, saw her go to you, tapped your phones, and confirmed my suspicions."

"Can you prove anything?"

"A little. But the real problem is tying the big boys to it as well as figuring out the way the blood goes through the Doyne computers. I haven't been able to do that. The security system is way too tricky."

"Damn," grunted Colder. "It was a good try."

"What was a good try?"

"Well, we set a trap in the Doyne computer, logging in a positive result on a pregnancy test, one that we passed off as a Fragile X. We were going to try to locate the man who contacted Molly."

"What?" exclaimed O'Reilly, horrified. "You're kidding! When?"

"Maybe two weeks ago," Colder said, confused.

"You broke into their computers?" he asked, his voice rising with anxiety.

"A friend did. He's slick as can be."

"Oh God," shuddered O'Reilly. "I should have warned you. He may be slick and thought that he was undetected, but that security system is so complicated that unless you were one of the original designers, you'd never have a chance. They can track anything with that system."

Colder's eyes widened in horror. "Oh, God we walked right into it."

"Check on your friend right away. Right away!"

"I will," muttered Colder, his mind on Reggie.

"Remember," he warned "They'll be watching you now."

"I know."

As the phone went dead, Colder leaped up and began to pace the floor, waiting several seconds in order to assure a new connection on the phone. He punched in Reggie's number and with his heart racing, waited for an answer. Colder knew that Reggie would be home, the teen's work schedule etched in his mind. After seven rings without an answer, Colder hung up the phone and redialed, his fear rising. Certainly Cynthia would answer he thought, her speaker phone activated by a large button at the head of her bed. Nothing. Eight rings, then ten, then twelve. No answer.

"Damn."

Colder felt panic, with sweat springing through his skin and dripping down his back. He hung up the phone and dialed Molly's number, his hand shaking as he punched in the numbers. He misdialed the first time, his index finger slipping from the eight and instead punching the zero. Redialing, a moment later he heard the ringing start, and he tried desperately to collect his thoughts. On the third ring, Molly answered.

"Hello," she said tiredly.

"Molly."

"Hi," she said, her voice sounding pleasantly surprised.

"Molly, I need you to go over and check on Reggie and his mother right away."

She could easily sense his concern. "What's wrong?"

"Do you have a key?"

"Yes."

"Use it. If you don't get an answer, try to break it down. I'm on my way."

"Peter," she said, her voice stopping him. "What's wrong?"

"Reggie might have walked into something. O'Reilly says that the Doyne computers are rigged."

"Oh God."

"I called there, but haven't been able to get an answer."

"I'll go right away," she said, still sounding calm.

"I'll meet you there."

Colder tossed the phone on the couch and sprinted to the door. Leaving the door unlocked, he ran to the car parked in the driveway and a moment later sped toward the apartment building four miles away. As he wove through the darkened residential streets lined with parked cars, racing far above the speed limit, he cursed at himself for having been so stupid. Of course they would guard the secret with their lives. A secret that now threatened to take more lives. There would be no simple access to it or easy trick to reveal the mystery. They had all been fools, naive and gambling with more than they knew.

Five minutes later, his car was at maximum speed as the apartment building came into view. In the distance, he saw the familiar line of parked cars lining the street. Seeing an open spot in front of the building, he slammed on the brakes and swung into the opening. Leaping from the car, he bounded up the steps in seconds. The front door to the brick building was propped open, and Colder raced up the two flights of stairs to the second floor and then to the end of the hall. A small crowd of people was gathered in front of Reggie's door. Colder pushed his way through, elbowing several people out of the way. Entering the apartment, he saw Molly on the living room floor, kneeling next to Reggie. Colder's heart fell. Reggie was lying on his back. His skin was a dark cherry-red, and he was motionless. "Shit," muttered Colder, as he dropped to Reggie's side.

Reggie was unconscious, but breathing very weakly. Molly, tears running down her cheeks, continued the mouth-to-mouth resuscitation. Colder stopped as Molly gazed up toward him, her look one of anguish.

"Get him out," said Peter, commanding the others in the doorway. "And clear the building. It's carbon monoxide."

"What?" came a voice.

"CARBON MONOXIDE!" screamed Colder. "Everyone! GO!"

"An ambulance is on the way," said one, an unconcerned-looking middle-aged man with a large belly stretching his T-shirt.

"Carbon monoxide?" exclaimed a woman.

"I got a headache," said a child to his mother.

"Yes. Do it fast. Everyone! Out now!"

"Are you sure?" asked another.

Colder ignored her, reached down, and grabbed Reggie, looping his arms underneath Reggie's arms and dragging him forcefully into the hallway. Molly followed and kneeled down again at his side, giving him another breath.

"Get him out onto the grass and keep breathing for him if he stops," Colder said pausing to check Reggie's pulse and breathing—both weak, but steady, Colder looked at Molly as the large man grabbed Reggie by the shoulders and began tugging him toward the stairs while the rest of the crowd stood idle, watching.

"Cynthia?" Peter asked Molly.

Molly Loomis grabbed his hand, shaking her head as tears rolled off her cheeks. She tried to speak but couldn't. Colder pulled her toward him, and she collapsed into him like a limp rag. Half dragging her, he made his way toward the bedroom. Inside there was no odor or color, and the lights were all on. Molly's face was buried in his shirt, not wanting to look again. Peter broke her hold and rushed to the bedside. Molly turned away. Cynthia's legs and torso were covered by a white sheet. The skin of her face was a pale red, and her eyes were open but vacant. Colder felt for her carotid pulse, already knowing the answer. The skin was cold, the pulse absent.

Colder turned and walked out, leaving the room undisturbed and burying Molly under his arm. Sinking into him, tears continued to stream off her cheeks as they left. Outside, they could hear the ambulance's siren nearing, and in the hallway, a few of the residents continued to mill about until an angry Colder drove them from the building. "She's dead. There's nothing to see. It's carbon monoxide. Now *GO!*"

With the word "dead," they finally began to leave.

Ten minutes later, the ambulance sped away, leaving a growing crowd of police, another ambulance, and the coroner. Molly and Peter rode in the back with Reggie, now intubated and breathing 100 percent oxygen under pressure. He remained unconscious, but his vital signs were stable. Neither Molly nor Peter seemed able to speak as they wound through the streets and then onto Hennepin Avenue, the deafening ambulance sirens screaming overhead. Molly leaned her head into his shoulder. She was no longer crying, her emotion having yielded to anger and fear.

Nearing the hospital, even the joy of seeing the first movements of Reggie's hands was tempered with grim reality. For the first time, they both realized the true nature of the world they had stepped into. There would be no more excitement or intrigue, mystery, or acts of reckless indiscretion. Their foolishness had meant danger. Unnecessary, unwanted, and now costly. Reggie would survive, the effects of the carbon monoxide diminishing as they rode. But the pursuit of Fragile X had claimed its sixth victim. Cynthia Tan was dead.

Chapter Thirteen

July 28

The week following Cynthia Tan's death yielded three new developments, only one of which was positive for Molly and her friends—Reggie's discharge from the hospital. He was released from the hospital after a four-day stay. The day after his release, he buried his mother. The service, in the same church where Reggie's father's funeral had been seven years before, was attended by several hundred people. Friends who knew Cynthia before the accident, those who knew her at the hospital and rehab, as well as those who knew her from her volunteer days at the Spinal Cord Injury Center after her accident, were all present to pay their last respects to a woman whose unwavering optimism and endless fortitude touched them all. The service was lengthy but moving, with the receiving line at a reception afterward taking two hours to pass.

The day after the funeral, Reggie moved in with Sylvia, the arrangement scheduled to last until the end of the school year. The same week, the police investigation began and unofficially concluded, a rusted pipe in the air conditioning unit being blamed as the cause. There had been no clues to suggest otherwise, nor had there been any witnesses. Privately, the police had assured Reggie that they would keep investigating, but publicly the official cause appeared to be an accident.

To make matters worse, the legal problems continued to mount. After the funeral, Barnes and Whitfield filed six more motions, all prepared as potential reasons for dismissal, but at the very least serving to delay the case for weeks or months while they were argued. The motions were expected, and Tyler had warned Molly that their stall tactics were only beginning. The attorneys' strategy would be in part to wage an old-fashioned battle of attrition, using their greater resources and staff to concentrate on minute details and nuances that would effectively use up time and consume Tyler's and Marcus's energy. The motions were just a few of the many more that were expected to come, and with their filing Tyler knew that most of his office would now be focused on only one case, a gamble Briggs was already beginning to regret. He knew that the partnership had the money to work for a short time, but a protracted course prior to trial would strain their firm to its limit. If the delay was six months or more, there was little likelihood they could continue. The dilemmas were impossible. They needed time to prepare for the trial, but they needed the trial to be early. They needed to defeat the motions, but they needed to spend their time preparing for the trial itself. There was too much time, too little time, and nowhere near enough money. Ideally, they would have twelve lawyers researching medical contract law and six investigators probing into ComHealth. They would want a team of professionals deciphering the mystery of Fragile X and a handful of experts delving into every aspect of the lives of the ComHealthOne board of directors and its chairman.

Each morning before sunrise, Briggs and Sanders, along with their two junior partners Stephon Reed and Michael Barker, met in the conference room and then continued to work until they could stay awake no longer. The junior partners, who had been with the firm less than five years, were still handling a few outside cases. For all four attorneys, the hours had become exhausting, and within two weeks of accepting the case, the strain and fatigue were already noticeable. They were frustrated, angry, and at times, fearful of what they were up against. For all their wistful idealism, the intense preparation was a practical necessity. If they made it past the motion phase, the trial was undoubtedly going to be ugly.

By 9:00 P.M., the remainder of the Chinese dinners that were scattered throughout Briggs's office had cooled, leaving behind only the hardening remnants of sauce-covered rice and a mixture of once-delicious aromas. The center of the room was occupied by a large temporary table brought in the day before. The four partners sat around the rectangular structure amidst piles of papers, coffee cups, and used dishes. A single overhead light illuminated the room.

Briggs was dead tired, having spent most of the night before on the phone with a friend in California who had twice sued HMOs over care restriction issues. Unfortunately, both cases had been failures. His friend's advice had been to steer clear unless the case was a slam dunk, noting that no court had been sympathetic to plaintiff complaints, instead opting for a very narrow interpretation of contract language. The conversation left him disappointed, but not discouraged. His conversation with his wife earlier in the morning had left him discouraged.

Tina Briggs was everything that Tyler had ever wanted in a woman. Equally bright, talented, and outgoing, she was a good companion, great friend, and a valued opinion on all matters, even the law. She had an innate ability to grasp the complex easily and analyze correctly even matters on which her fund of knowledge was limited. She was coolly objective, frank, and confident in her opinions, which often led to many of the heated discussions that had punctuated their nine-year relationship. They also remained very much in love.

They had been a couple since their undergraduate days at Northwestern and married before his second year of law school Tina used her degree in social work until the birth of their second child. Since that time, three years before, she worked as a tireless mother and an author of several children's books. She maintained a close circle of friends, generally the wives of the other partners and a couple of old college roommates. She guarded her children and her marriage fiercely, knowing that the pressures of the law were pressures that opposed her and her children's interests.

"Tyler," interrupted Stephon Reed again, his eyes looking at Briggs humorously. "You dead?"

Briggs shook his head, returning his gaze from the window. "Think so."

"How much did ol' Tina take out of you last night?" asked Marcus. "Anything we should hear about to squeeze our glands and give us a little lift?"

"God no," Briggs shrugged. "Just screaming."

Michael Barker, a short, round man with extremely dark skin and a few flecks of gray around his ears, looked excited. "That sounds good. I can live with screaming."

"I'll rephrase it," Briggs said.

"No," Reed interrupted, his long, thin body rocking back on his chair and his hand running over the smug grin on his face on its way to adjust his glasses. "We want to hear about the screaming."

"At me boys, not with me."

"Right, yeah, I'm sure," offered Marcus with a wink. "Ever since you insulated those bedroom walls, you've been coming in dead in the morning. I'm worried about you."

Briggs rolled his eyes and flipped a used plastic fork onto in Marcus' lap by slamming its teeth to the table. "Argh," grunted Sanders as a gob of rice stuck to his shirt.

"Better than coming home with lipstick on," Stephon said, trying not to laugh too hard.

"Not much," Sanders grunted, only mildly amused, wiping at the rice on his shirt with a napkin.

"We're getting punchy," Barker said. "I'm a wimp for these twenty-hour work days."

"So am I," Briggs said. "I can't do it like in law school."

"Getting old?"

"Very."

"Seriously, Tyler," Michael asked, demanding the truth. "Tina all over you?"

"Problem is that she's right," Tyler started. "If she was wrong, that would be one thing, but she knows me like the back of her hand. She knows all of us, and she thinks this case is all an unnecessary gamble."

"It is a gamble," Marcus admitted. "But that's law."

Briggs continued. "But what really bothers me is that she's not anywhere near as sympathetic to Molly as you'd expect her to be."

"That's natural though," Reed interrupted, his black eyes meeting Tyler's. "Women are always harder on other women. It's because they have a much narrower definition of success and responsibilities."

"That's a man's opinion," said Marcus, still fiddling with his shirt.

"No, it's true," said Reed disagreeing. Although the younger partner had a habit of being wrong and right equally, he was nonetheless always authoritative. "Women have a much clearer understanding of their sex and because of it are much less tolerant."

"I thought the opposite was what they said. Women sympathize with their own," Barker said.

"No, everyone wants to make men out to be Neanderthals and women as naive. But you know, neither is true. With respect to their own sex, you ask people to tell the truth and they're always harder on their own kind. It's easier to transfer their own values."

"That's what I'm worried about," Tyler said. "We're going to need a male jury."

"The jury consultants would agree," said Marcus, finished with his shirt. "Give me twelve educated white males for this one. Or a bunch of women who've been abused."

"Fat chance for that one," Reed muttered. "Whitfield will DQ those on sight."

"You agree on white?" Briggs asked.

They all nodded. "Father-daughter identity," said Marcus. "I agree."

"Yeah."

"Where we going to get an educated white male jury around here?" asked Tyler. "This is downtown, Hennepin County."

"Got to try."

"Himmler and Goering will want black women."

"No way. They'd kill us. They'd just see a little white girl scheming for money and complaining about her life."

"What about the abuse angle?" asked Reed.

"No way. Black women are the least sympathetic to that."

"I agree," said Marcus. "We need white men, preferably ones with daughters who are dating beer-guzzling jocks with permanent erections."

"Amen," said Tyler. "Give me a hive of WASPS."

"We'll never get it."

"I agree. Noncatholics."

"Naw," said Marcus. "The Catholic angle doesn't matter. Most aren't anymore anti-abortion than the Protestants. That's just a church thing."

"Maybe," said Tyler.

"Give me a bunch of liberal Catholics who feel the church has done 'em wrong."

"Risky," said Stephon. "Molly's vulnerable on the abortion issue. Abortion goes right to people's souls. Maybe three people in ten, you know how they're gonna feel. Always pro-life or pro-choice. But the other seven? They're busy looking at both sides of the coin. They could go either way."

"I agree," said Tyler.

Sanders pulled apart a fortune cookie that said, all good things come to those who wait and tossed it onto the table. "What else does your wife think, Tyler?"

"She's worried about the firm."

Stephon Reed shook his head. The four partners, concerned themselves, tried reassurring their wives that both Reed and Barker were still working on other cases. "Firm's fine. At least for now."

"About the case?"

"Tina thinks Molly was wronged."

"Grudgingly?"

Tyler paused. "No. I don't think so. She's not ready to jump up and grab a banner, but she's supportive of her."

"That's what I was wondering. I'm getting the same message at home. You know that women also have a tendency to be intrinsically fair when on juries."

"Are you saying we want them, or to not worry?" asked Stephon, still focusing on the jury composition.

"I don't know," admitted Marcus. "We definitely want white males, but I don't think it's going to be as predictable as we might think."

The phone rang, and Marcus turned. It was a line forwarded from his office, and for the next five minutes he discussed several family issues with his wife Dorene. The others pretended to work while Marcus tried to balance a conversation between candor and diplomacy. It worked poorly, and Marcus, obviously the recipient of his wife's frustration, blushed as he hung up the phone. "Going to be ugly," he sighed.

"The wives aren't wrong," said Tyler, closing his eyes and leaning back. "I hear the same every night. There will always be lawyers and people who've been wronged. But you'll never have another family."

"You agree with that?" asked Barker.

"You have to," admitted Tyler. "That's the problem with most of life. Right and wrong are rarely options. The choices are just between hard and harder. Here we're taking harder."

Barker grinned and swallowed the last of his fortune cookie. The chunky junior partner was always eating, and had a long history of dysfunctional relationships. None of the other partners ever took his advice on women seriously. "Are you a lousy father if you choose harder?"

"No," said Stephon. "Just a better lawyer."

They all laughed uneasily and then turned as if on cue to the papers before them, their dinner now over. Stephon Reed lifted from the table the top sheet of paper from a file he had pulled from his briefcase when Marcus was on the phone. "Let's start with this," said Reed.

"Good idea," said Marcus. "We're sitting here talking about jury composition, and we don't even know if we can get past their motion to dismiss. Right now my bet is we're S.O.L."

Barker nodded. "S.O.L. is looking more real."

"What do you have there, Stephon?" Tyler asked, ignoring their comments and arranging his own papers.

Reed was expressionless. "Not much. Just ComHealth complaints, the actual numbers."

"Really?"

The others paused as if seeing something they had not been expecting. No one had expected getting the ComHealth dirt to be easy. "What?" asked an incredulous Marcus Sanders.

"You're kidding me."

Reed had been coy all night. Now he was leading them to his prize and proudly wearing a smug grin. "Not really that hard, at least to an investigator of my skills." The three other attorneys pelted him with Chinese food.

"What do you have?"

"Give it to us," Tyler said, his arm still cocked with a hunk of chicken.

Reed seemed oblivious to the fact that almost an entire dinner was sticking to his shirt. He swung his head haughtily and tried his best to appear both pompous and hurt.

"You really got the complaints data?" Marcus asked. The senior partner could not believe it. All of them had expected the ComHealth numbers to be impossible to obtain. For weeks, they had received hints and "unofficial" numbers, but they had been stymied beyond that.

Reed finally started to talk. "Damn right I got the numbers. But listen to this, boys. I'll go you one better. I got us a witness!"

Reed was giddy. The partners flushed. Their mouths fell open. Tyler dropped his entire stack of papers. "A witness? What? Who?" asked Tyler.

It was the news they had all been waiting for. Stephon had been holding out. The other partners weren't upset. They were ecstatic.

"Before I tell you, I just want you to know that I want to renegotiate my contract. I'd like a hundred million over four years, with a jet and a signing bonus."

"Get real," groaned Tyler.

"Get lost," moaned Sanders.

"All right, all right. But tell me. Who would you like to have, most of all, as a witness if you could get him?"

"Someone who could get us past a summary judgment motion. Someone who could get us past S.O.L.," said Barker.

"Who?"

"Hutchins."

Stephon laughed. "Almost that good."

"Another executive," Marcus offered.

Reed's eyes lit up. Sanders had guessed it, but no one could believe it.

"No way," screamed Marcus. "No damn way!"

"Yes way."

"No way!"

"Yes! Way!!!"

The news was too good to be true. A willing, candid executive's testimony could be devastating. "Who?" Tyler nearly screamed.

"Name is C. Boyd Messenger. Hutchins fired him several months ago. Was an Executive VP."

"Oh my God! What does he say?"

"Brace yourself." The others barely breathed. They had the looks of hungry dogs. For weeks, they had languished without even a hint of good news. This was unbelievable.

Reed reached under the table. His hand emerged with a bottle of cognac and four glasses he had been hiding. The others grabbed them, and Sanders poured the drinks. After a sip, Stephon began his tale of the ComHealth executive while the others listened in amazement. The booze and the thrill went to their heads with equal speed. It was even better than expected. The fired executive had told Reed every dirty secret of ComHealth's business operation. "The bottom line is this," he concluded. "This guy is willing to testify about every money-making technique, claim denials, exceptions, exclusions, revoking policies. Everything the HMO had done. He was part of it. He was one of the developers."

No one could believe it. No one could breathe. Tyler's eyes felt like they were spinning. "How the heck did you find him?"

"He approached me. He's still friends with one of Barnes and Whitfield's junior partners and was tipped off about the lawsuit."

"It's beautiful," gushed Sanders.

Tyler was thrilled. "And he gave you the data too?"

"Yes."

Tyler reached across the table and pulled a piece of chicken off his partner. "Stephon, you can't play out your option. Forget it. You're too valuable here."

Reed was still holding something back. "One thing though—"

"Why was he fired?" asked Barker before he could finish.

"He's a boozer. Big time."

"Is he credible?"

"Yes. But he says it's all over his file that he lied to cover up his alcoholism."

"That's a problem," Marcus admitted.

Briggs was not going to let the executive's downside bother him. The news was too good. "Is he telling the truth to you?"

"Absolutely."

"We can work with him then. It's a hell of a lot better than nothing."

"And best of all," said Sanders, "no way Van Gilder grants a motion to dismiss if this guy is willing to testify."

Reed rubbed his hands together as if anticipating a delicious meal. "That's kinda what I thought."

There was no question that their witness had a possible credibility problem, but they also knew that for the first time they had someone who could substantiate a charge that the entire ComHealth system had been constructed as a money-making scheme that restricted access to doctors and medical care. Reed had given them the mother lode. It was the perfect present at the end of a long week.

"It's beautiful."

"And one more thing. He gave me the names of a couple of key players. The first is an old maid. Head of claims that makes the Dowager Empress look like Mrs. Santa Claus. The other is a Sergeant Schultz type who devised the whole toll-free number 'dial-a-voice' access system that never lets anyone get to a doctor."

Optimism reigned for the first time. "This is toooo beautiful," slurred Marcus.

Tyler took another swig of the cognac. He couldn't believe his ears. He pointed at the pile of papers. "Go on, Stephon. Tell me. I gotta know. How many appeals are there?"

Reed flashed a broad toothy grin. "Thought you'd never ask. ComHealth in Minneapolis processes on average two *thousand* appeals per day. They insure in the metropolitan area about a million people and on average have about five thousand patient visits per day. Of those, *forty-eight percent* end in appeal."

They all gasped. "That's damn unbelievable." Sanders was incredulous.

"That's what it is. Just an elaborate scheme to control how much care is delivered."

"Are the number of appeals going up or down?"

"That's the scary part. They're actually going down."

"Which means that the physicians are not fighting as much."

"Yes. You can see why. ComHealth has 'em by the balls. They're losing salary. You can only expect a certain amount of altruism before reality kicks in."

"Wrong," contradicted Marcus. "I expect more and so does my baby girl."

"So do I," said Tyler.

"We all probably do," Stephon admitted.

"How do you change the system?" Michael asked.

"Only the patients have the ability to do it."

"The patients are everyone."

"Exactly," said Stephon.

Sanders lit a small cigar and inhaled it halfway, savoring its strong taste before sending a series of rings across the room. He was formulating a plan. "The only thing I see here is groundwork. We can show that ComHealth systematically engages in a pattern of bad faith practices that are designed exclusively to discourage the utilization of services."

"That's putting managed care on trial," said Tyler. "That's a big dragon."

For a moment they were silent before Michael Barker spoke again. All four partners were quivering with excitement. "The whole system? That's the big-big time."

"Any objections?" asked Marcus.

They all shook their heads. They were all in agreement.

"Good."

The four men stood up. Tyler held up his glass and the others followed. The news of the witness erased any doubt. "We've got a trial, gentlemen!"

"Yes!"

"Yes!"

They all sipped and savored their drinks. The miracle had happened. For the first time, there was a crack in the ComHealth wall, and they had slipped through it.

Chapter Fourteen

July 30

Just after 8:00 P.M., Molly Loomis picked up her tip from the table that had contained two very dirty truck drivers. She swooped it into her apron pocket and retreated into the restaurant's back room. Safe within the tiny locker room, she took a seat on a small metal chair, wiped her brow, and collapsed, exhausted, into a heap. A cup of two-hour-old coffee at her side, she sipped it and enjoyed her momentary respite, ignoring the sounds of the full restaurant. The shift had been long, an extra four hours because Tracy Timlin's husband had called at four, needing her at home. Both of their children had come down with fevers and spots and he was concerned about chicken pox. Tracy left to join her family at the doctor's office after Molly agreed to cover the extra four hours. Molly had not been excited about the idea, but carefully hid her reluctance from Tracy and said nothing about having to cancel dinner with Peter, instead telling her friend that she would be glad to earn the extra money.

The dinner hour was an array of male truckers. Two large-bellied beer truckers, one from Budweiser and one from Miller, playfully spent two hours trading insults and barbs and fighting with food. The rest of the beer-drinking customers played right in, siding with their favorite beverage. By the time they left, the restaurant looked as though it had been caught in a crossfire between a hurricane and a tornado.

The episode left Molly exhausted. She was used to passing truckers' cracks about her body but this group particularly enjoyed themselves. It depressed her. She did not need to be told again how she was too skinny and flat-chested. She knew it. But the comments still hurt. The only positive about the night was that one man had left a ten dollar tip and the other a five, raising her nightly total to eighty-five dollars, almost forty more than she originally figured.

Still in a trance, she took off the apron and slipped the change and the bills into her pocket. Next, she tossed the apron into a laundry bag, a large coffee stain from early evening stretched across the front. Hearing a noise behind her, she turned and saw Gus LeClerc, the owner and former chef, looking at her.

"Thanks for staying," he said mopping the top of his bald head.

"You're welcome. It was worth it."

"Those boys had their fun," he said, shifting his bulking frame closer to her. Molly hid her hurt well. "No problem, Gus. They tipped well."

"You sure?" Gus's black eyes peered closely, studying Molly's face for the truth.

"I can listen to anything as long as they pay me. I have no scruples. And besides being told you're as flat as day old beer is better than being told you look like a whale."

"I shoulda punched the one out," mumbled Gus.

She shook her head and laughed briefly at her defender. Gus LeClerc, a famously gruff exterior with a soft interior, was like a father to the six waitresses. "Gus, he weighed about three hundred pounds and he ordered three meals for himself. Now that's a good customer," she said bravely.

"As long as you're okay."

"I'm fine," she said, her diplomat's act nearly perfect.

"Molly, I know you had to break your date. I appreciate it."

"It wasn't really a date," she said, rising and slipping into the windbreaker she would wear home.

"You were going out." Gus studied the thin figure in front of him, amazed at the changes that he had seen in her since her husband had left. That SOB leaving was the best thing that could've happened to her, he thought. Now maybe she can have a life instead of a living hell.

"Just to get something to eat," she returned, not wishing to hint at her own eagerness.

Gus would not drop it easily. "I'd call that a date."

"No, it wasn't."

"Anyway, I know you were looking forward to it."

"Don't worry. He understood."

"Have I met him?"

"Not yet."

"Got a name?"

Molly tried not to blush. "Dr. Peter Colder."

Gus extended his head back in surprise, his double chin rippling with the movement. "Whoa. A doctor?"

"Yes."

"What kind."

"A witch doctor," she said with a ridiculous smile. "He carries voodoo dolls in his black bag."

"C'mon." Gus was pleased to see Molly laughing and joking around.

"Family practice. He works at Third Street Clinic."

"Good for you. Is the divorce final?"

Molly looked down but without expression. "Soon."

Gus gazed at the left hand where the wedding and engagement rings still sat. "You should be happy about that."

Her tone was flat. "Yes, I am."

Gus said nothing, not believing her, but choosing not to debate. "You reschedule your date?"

"Later this week."

"Good."

As they spoke, there was a knock at the back door. The service entrance, used for supplies and employees, opened into the parking lot. Gus furrowed his brow with an annoyed look. He lifted the latch and began to pull the door open. The heavy steel door swung slowly as if on a conveyor and as it did, the humid blast of a July night greeted them. Gus stepped back and two men came into view. They were in dark suits, both fortyish, with short dark hair, unremarkable faces and ideal body weight. Neither showed any expression and one held a briefcase. The first, a bit taller, extended a badge toward them. To Molly's surprise, Peter and Reggie stood one step behind.

"Keith McWilliams, FBI," said the first, swinging the badge in front of Gus and motioning to his neighbor. "My partner, Tom Hastings."

Gus looked stunned. "Please come in, gentlemen."

"Thank you," McWilliams said, his black hair and eyes only accenting his placid, cold demeanor. Hastings stepped in first, without a word.

As the four entered, Molly looked at Reggie, who did not make eye contact. She then turned to Peter who raised his eyebrows in an expression that she didn't understand. Gus closed the door once everyone was inside.

"Mr. LeClerc," Hastings began as he carefully surveyed the room, "do you have an office in this building?"

"Yes, sir," he replied.

"May we use it? There are a number of things that we need to discuss with Ms. Loomis."

"Certainly," he said with a nod and pointing. "It's on the other side of this wall. But it's no bigger than this."

"Thank you. That will do nicely."

Gus guided them through the small doorway to the back room, and one minute later, all five people sat in LeClerc's private office, gathered around his desk with a fresh pot of coffee and cups provided by the owner. Having served them, Gus departed, closing the door with one last glance at an anxious-looking Molly. As soon as he was gone, McWilliams began to speak. The agent was a muscular man with bright blue eyes and a rugged jaw that gave him an appearance of anger and intimidation. "First of all, Molly, let me tell you what this is about."

"Please do," she murmured, sitting down next to Peter.

"We are here investigating the death of Cynthia Tan."

"You are?" asked Molly, surprised.

Hastings jumped in. The second agent's frown, etched upon his muscular face, also seemed to indicate that any emotion other than anger was impossible. Molly could feel herself shake. "Yes. We feel that there is a strong possibility that Cynthia Tan was murdered."

"What?" asked Molly, surprised. "But the police—"

"We're not at liberty to say more at this time," Hastings replied, his dark eyes giving Molly an intimidating look. "But we do have a witness and a videotape that put two men at the scene within an hour before she died."

"Videotape?"

"Your landlord has a small camera that shows the main floor hallway. He says he put it in a year ago after he was robbed."

"I didn't even know," mumbled Molly.

Reggie, appearing relieved that the investigation was continuing, sighed. "I didn't either. But it helps here."

"Who is the witness?" Molly asked.

"Mrs. Macon," McWilliams answered.

Molly frowned, disappointed. Beverly Macon was eighty-seven years old, with failing eyesight and a tendency to drink at least a pint of a forty-proof "cure all" every day. "I don't know," Molly said, "I want to catch them too, but you should know, Mrs. Macon has trouble deciding which is the dryer and which is the washer."

Peter disagreed. "She ran right into these guys, Molly."

"And the tape matches her description of the men."

Molly put her hands up in surrender. "That's great."

Hastings continued, his laser-like gaze not relenting. "It probably would not be of any interest to the FBI except for the fact that these two men identified from the video have been sought in the investigation of some other deaths from a couple of years ago in other states."

Molly glanced at the others and her eyes widened in comprehension. "The scientists?"

"Yes. One and the same."

Molly emitted a short gasp, but tried not to act too surprised. Reggie and Peter had obviously been told earlier. McWilliams opened his briefcase and pulled out a folder and handed her two photos of a man. The first was an eight-by-ten blowup of two men standing by a car. The one facing the camera had his face circled by a red magic marker. The second was a police photo of the same man, round-faced with long, scraggly hair and several days of stubble.

"Recognize him?" asked McWilliams.

Molly stared at the images for only a moment before returning them. "No," she said firmly. "I'm sure. Never seen him before. I would remember that face."

"Fine," said McWilliams. "How about this one." He handed her another picture. It an eight-by-ten of a man in a suit with neatly groomed black hair and a handsome but nondescript face.

Molly nearly fell off her chair. "My God!" she exclaimed. "That's him! That's the doctor, Dr. Roland Michaels. He's the one who came to visit me!"

McWilliams nodded at Hastings as they all stared at the picture. "Actually his name is Luke Henry, but he has about two dozen aliases. He's not even close to being a doctor."

"He sure sounded good," Molly said. The sight of the phony doctor made her squirm in her seat.

"Oh, he's pretty familiar with medical lingo," Hastings said. "He was in med school for a year in the Caribbean, and he once did time in Arizona for impersonating a doctor."

"For something like this?"

"No, it was a big scam on narcotics using a tactic that might have been used here."

"He totally fooled me," Molly said sheepishly.

"The scam is to use the names of recently deceased doctors to fill prescriptions. This usually happens in the bigger cities for three or four weeks or so until the red flags go up. Roland Michaels just happened to be a name they used. But apparently now the scam has moved on to other things as well."

"I'll say," Colder commented grimly.

"Who's the other one?" Molly asked.

"Larry Stephenson," McWilliams said, again removing the picture of the pony-tailed roughneck from the manila envelope. "Nicknamed the Electrician."

Molly's face took on a sardonic look. "I'm afraid to ask how he got that nickname."

McWilliams was running the edge of the photograph between his fingers. "You're right. He's slick."

"Do you know that he killed them?" she asked.

"Again," started Hastings, "the investigation is ongoing and there are things we can't tell you, but I can tell you that we are very interested in discussing some matters with them."

Reggie interrupted. "In other words, yes." The two FBI agents did not disagree.

Hastings withdrew the two photographs and put them again in their folder before turning to Molly. "Ms. Loomis, the reason we need to discuss this with you is that it is quite possible that you were also a target the night that Cynthia Tan was murdered."

Molly blinked and swallowed, but showed no discernible expression. She had somehow expected the statement. "I was afraid you might say that."

"The furnace ducts in your building were repaired last summer. In the process, your apartment was connected in with the upstairs furnace instead of the basement one. I don't think that they knew that. Because of it, only the Tan apartment and two vacant ones were affected."

Molly's dejected eyes hid her fear well.

Reggie held copies of the pictures in his hands. "I'm going to kill them both."

"Easy," said Hastings, putting his hand on Reggie's shoulder.

"Why are we targets?" asked Molly, managing a question that she thought she already knew the answer to.

"Mr. Tan was in the Doyne Lab computers," McWilliams said with a note of disapproval. "And you are a threat as well apparently."

No one in the room feigned surprise. Molly looked down at the floor. "What do we do now?"

"We need information. Dr. Colder has filled us in as to much of what has gone on to this point."

"About Fragile X?" she asked.

"Yes."

Molly knew the agents probably had already heard her entire story. She was more interested in what the FBI knew. "What can you guys tell us?"

The two agents glanced at one another. "Only that we are closer now than we have been and that your suspicions are probably true."

"How many women do you think have been affected?" Colder asked.

"Offhand I would guess in the hundreds, but there is no way of actually knowing. I am sure that Fragile X was just one of their many code words."

"Do you know any others?" Colder asked.

"No," Hastings admitted.

"How about proof?"

Up until now, the agents had been restrained, but suddenly McWilliams became more talkative. "Not much. What we do know is that we can trace these two guys to the same areas where the others were murdered. Unfortunately, we can't put them at the scene."

Hastings interrupted. "We've got one other thing. We may have a lead on another Fragile X woman."

"Really? Did she see this Dr. Michaels or whatever his name was?" asked Molly.

"Luke Henry. And no. It was all done by phone, just like your first contact."

"Did she have an abortion?" Molly asked.

"No," Hastings replied.

"Could you track the call?" Reggie asked.

The FBI agents clammed up. "Tried. Dead end."

Colder looked puzzled. His thoughts were elsewhere. "How did you hear about it?"

"We got a call from an obstetrician in the area."

Colder's face turned stoney. His instincts were taking over. "It might help if I knew who."

Hastings and McWilliams looked at each other as if debating for a moment the implications of releasing the information. Apparently deciding that the benefits outweighed the consequences, McWilliams turned to him. "Your friend Casey Larter."

"She lied to me," grumbled Colder, recalling a conversation days earlier when she again had denied any knowledge of Fragile X.

"I'm not sure she did so willingly," said McWilliams.

Colder looked perturbed. "I'll sure as hell find out."

"The important thing," Hastings continued, "is providing protection for both Molly and Reggie and establishing proof."

The thought of the danger distracted Colder from his thoughts about Casey Larter's lie and returned him to Molly and the others. He nodded in agreement.

"We will be providing surveillance for both of them from this moment on. We'll install some security equipment in your apartment, Molly, as well as in Mrs. Caspers' house. Also there will be some marshals that will guard you. They won't be in your way. You'll have to look for them to see them, but they'll be around," McWilliams said.

"How long will you do that?"

"As long as we feel it's necessary."

"Good," Colder said, relieved and looking at Molly.

McWilliams continued. "In the meantime, we need the proof. We need O'Reilly."

Colder looked disappointed. "I haven't heard from him since before Cynthia was murdered."

Hastings was unperturbed. "I'm sure you will. We'll be ready."

"He's freaked out," Reggie said. "He watched three of his friends die."

"He also holds the key," Hastings said, his manner barely sympathetic.

"Can you protect him?" Molly asked.

"If we can get ahold of him."

There was a knock at the door. It was followed by the entrance of Gus LeClerc with a tray full of apple pie and ice cream. He brushed off the thanks that greeted him and departed, but not before a glance at Molly assured him that everything was all right. Once the door closed again, Hastings continued.

"We need the journal or at least some hard proof of what went on."

"What do you think O'Reilly knows?" Reggie asked.

"We're not sure," McWilliams admitted. "But maybe Dr. Colder would care to speculate."

Colder swallowed a piece of pie, then put down the plate while the others looked at him as if staring at an instructor awaiting an assignment. Caught off-guard by the request, he wiped a small piece of crust from the corner of his mouth and swallowed before beginning. "Let me say this. ComHealth's whole motivation has been cost containment. It's only natural that they would take some sort of next step. I'm sure that what they have is some sort of antigen or marker that crosses into the mother's blood that can identify a fetus that is bound to suffer some debilitating disease."

"Such as?" asked Molly.

"Could be anything. Could be anencephaly where the baby is born without a brain or biliary atresia where the liver is horribly malformed. Could be severe heart defects or one of many blood disorders that are essentially incompatible with life. Could be a demyelinating disease, where the baby's nervous system is destroyed within a couple of years, or another genetic syndrome where the physical defects are devastating."

The medical lingo was boggling, but they all let it pass. "Go ahead and speculate, Doc," Hastings urged.

Colder looked confused. "The problem I have with this is that I don't think what I just said is right."

"Why?" asked Molly.

"Because if Fragile X was any of those conditions, where it is well known that the baby is going to die or be condemned to a horrible life, then the issue is simply a debate on abortion. Irrespective of anyone's feelings about that, abortion is a legal procedure, and if any of these diseases were suddenly able to be detected with their devastating consequences, people might welcome it and then it would simply be a matter of choice. Realistically, a debate on abortion would not be worth multiple deaths and all of these threats."

"What are you suggesting?" asked McWilliams.

"I think it's something else."

"Money?"

Colder nodded. "I think that is the basis. First of all, the only research that the HMOs sponsor are studies that try to figure out ways to save money. New technology and new medications cost money, so they don't sponsor research in those areas. Therefore, if you find that they are interested in something new, it has got to be because it saves them money somehow. Secondly, if it were legal, popular, advantageous, or even morally acceptable, they would make it public. So, by exclusion, it can't be one of those."

"Where does that take us?" Hastings asked.

"Ethics in medicine is a slippery slope," Colder continued. "One man's benign neglect is another's smoking gun. One woman's free choice is another's murder. I think what they have done here is take one step further along the continuum. One where more would object than approve, and they've done so in the interest of economics."

"Give me an example."

"Say they figured out how to detect a fetus that would as a child develop diabetes or as an adult develop heart disease or a certain type of cancer. These diseases may not be as deadly or as debilitating as a baby without a brain, but they are infinitely more expensive to take care of."

"My God," Reggie exclaimed. "They're advising abortions just because someone will be expensive to take care of?"

"Maybe. Like we said, I'm speculating."

"I guess that would be considered preventive medicine," Molly said darkly.

Bemused, Colder turned to look at her. "Precisely. Maybe that's what they think we've come to, no longer able to afford the chronically ill, and their type of *prevention* is the best way to solve the problem."

"It makes some perverted kind of sense," Hastings admitted.

"If it was less far out, there wouldn't be a reason to hide it," Reggie agreed.

Colder continued. "The trick is to get the public to slowly buy into the notion. A majority of the population would agree that an abortion for a baby without a brain would not be unreasonable, but most would say that an abortion for a fetus with a high risk of having an expensive, but treatable, disease would not. The strategy would then be to slowly sell the public on the expense of chronic disease, and gradually the public buys into the concept. First it's a secret, then it's a 'discovery,' and then it is a 'difficult choice.'"

"It's immoral," Reggie accused.

"Not to be contrary," Colder said softly, "but it's already going on. Economics plays a role in decision making from the day of conception to the day of death. It's sick, but true. The drive toward cost containment has only amplified the trend."

"You can't apply the laws of business to medicine," Molly said.

"Not without casualty," Peter admitted.

Hastings stood and stretched before swallowing the last of his pie. "Take a shot, Doc. What's your best guess? What is Fragile X?"

"I don't know. I really don't. But it has to be genetically based, a marker passed into the maternal circulation, not apparent at birth or on a standard ultrasound during pregnancy. My guess would be something like diabetes."

"Could be," McWilliams said, also rising. "It seems to makes sense."

Colder looked dejected. "But we need O'Reilly to tell us and prove it."

Hastings scrutinized Colder. "Just how much do you know about Dr. O'Reilly and his friends?"

"Not much," Peter admitted, facing the piercing dark eyes of the FBI agent.

Hastings' grim face was replaced with an enlightened grin. "Then let me tell you something that you might not have known."

"What's that?"

"Did you know that he and the others worked for ComHealthOne?"

Colder's fork dropped to the floor. Molly's jaw fell open. Reggie Tan shook his head and laughed. All of them were convinced of one thing. Nothing could surprise them anymore.

July 31

The following night was the first time that Colder had actually set eyes on the man that the press had begun to call the "probable Republican nominee for Governor." The "Minnesota Man of the Year" banquet was now thought by most to be the likely coming out of the man being actively groomed as the successor to the two-term Governor Alan Carlton. For weeks, the press releases of the state Republican chairman had hinted that the party mantle now belonged to the man credited with saving the state's health-care system, and his expected appearance had garnered interest in a usually unnoticed public ritual. Suddenly, the award that Hutchins had quietly solicited with a number of generous donations from ComHealth's treasury became a media event, carefully orchestrated and attended by the luminaries who would be needed as contributors in the now inevitable campaign.

As the honored guest, H. Carter Hutchins arrived on time, leading an entourage of fifteen, including his four lieutenants, their wives, and a handful of reporters. As always, he was camera-ready, resplendent in a black tuxedo and his wife Celia in a dazzling new sequined gown. Walking to the head table, they were escorted by the governor and his wife. After several hundred handshakes and smiles, they took their seats, Hutchins next to the governor's wife and Celia next to the governor.

From the back of the room, an ill-at-ease Peter Colder stood on his toes to see the entrance before returning to his seat when the commotion died down. The invitation to the Minnesota Man of the Year banquet at the downtown Radisson had come late, at noon that day courtesy of Casey Larter. It was as an olive branch offered in response to Colder's irritated phone call to her that morning. The invitation had distracted him and he told her yes without thinking. Four hours later, he found himself in attendance, with a rented tuxedo courtesy of Sylvia Caspers. It was the closest thing to a suit that Colder had worn in over two years.

After the grand entrance, Colder sat down. Next to him, Casey Larter was clad in a long, royal blue dress that hung loosely over her large body. Her long, gray-streaked brown hair was tied neatly into a bun. She appeared tired and to have gained even more weight since Colder had last seen her. Her usually red face was pale, her eyes were dark, and even her mannerisms and speech suggested anxiety and fatigue. Colder knew her untruths had a reason, and that his accusations earlier that day had resulted in their date. He had never known Casey Larter to tell a half-truth or even engage in diplomacy, let alone lie. After his earlier anger had faded, he was more curious than irritated and determined to find out what she knew.

The applause finished, and the mayor of Minneapolis stood at the podium and began to introduce the head table. Colder turned to Casey, his glare not subtle.

"You lied," he said, leaning toward her out of earshot from the table's other six guests.

"I'd prefer you use a different word," she whispered.

"Call it what you want."

Casey turned to him. "It was a lie," she admitted.

Colder sipped on his water, listening half-heartedly to the introduction of several local big shots who were each receiving awards in exchange for their contributions. "Why?" he asked.

Casey ignored his question, turning her head as Gregory Alan Markham III, the Chief Operating Officer of ComHealthOne was mentioned. "You're a better doctor than me, Peter. You always were."

Colder leaned over and whispered in her ear. "That's bullshit and you know it. We already got too much hot air in here to maintain a snow job. Just give me the facts, Casey." Momentarily distracted by the applause, Colder looked toward Gregory Markham, who had taken the microphone and was busy thanking the other ComHealth executives, each destined for awards themselves. He couldn't help but notice Celia Hutchins applauding furiously with a light, birdlike motion. "Why am I here?" he asked Casey finally. "I feel like I've gone to hell."

"I want to talk to you," she said crossing her legs and leaning in her chair even more toward him. "I didn't lie to you. I had planned on telling you."

"I'm listening."

"I heard about it a few weeks ago. A girl, here in the city, got the same message that Molly Loomis did."

Colder didn't acknowledge that he was aware of the other patient. Instead he looked at her suspiciously. He still had no idea why she had lied to him and until he had some understanding, his trust of her would be limited. "What's the front page on that patient?"

"Twenty-six. Little education. Welfare. Drug addict. Was high when she got the call."

"Did she have an abortion?"

No," answered Casey.

Colder's face lightened with an idea. Casey shook her head. "I thought of that. I ran her blood at our place. Nothing. Whatever is being tested for, I don't know."

"Then what did she say?"

"She wasn't reliable enough to tell you the time of day, but her story matches Molly's perfectly."

"Is she your patient?"

"Was." Suddenly Casey Larter looked almost scared. "Her car went into a lake a few of nights ago. She's dead."

Colder stopped staring blankly into space as the statement sank in, feeling both anger and fear simultaneously. The implication tore right through him. In an instant, he realized he had missed a very important point. If a woman had the marker and chose not to abort, then she could be seen as a threat to ComHealth because the real disease would be revealed with the birth of the child.

"This is serious, Peter," Casey said, still looking at the head table.

He grimaced at the thought, closing his eyes in resignation and fear, realizing that Molly's choosing an abortion had perhaps saved her life.

"No one is going to stop them."

"It's all about money," he said in a mumble.

"Of course it is."

"Have we lost all sense?" he asked, burying his head in his hands.

"C'mon, Peter. You know that one man's morality is another man's vice."

"What have you done?" he said, convinced that at this moment she was telling the truth.

"Taken the logical step."

"What's that?"

"I'm joining ComHealth. We're closing down the Rosewood Clinic."

"Oh no."

"I can't fight it anymore. They're killing us financially, and truthfully, it's like they own the world. I don't know what will happen if I stay independent, but now with this, and me knowing about it—" her voice trailed off.

Colder knew the decision was logical. Given the same circumstances, he would probably do the same. "I understand."

"Thanks for not beating on me."

Colder just shook his head. "Forget it. You don't deserve criticism."

"Yes, I do, but that's not what I want to talk about. I want you to know that I met with Markham about this."

Colder was shocked. His eyes widened. "What? You checked it out with the ComHealth brass?"

"Yes, I thought it would be best to confront it. And, I thought like you did. The whole thing was too weird. So, yes, I checked it out."

"What happened?"

"At first I didn't specify what I wanted to see him about, and no one returned my calls. But two days later, I mentioned Fragile X, and within an hour Gregory Markham III paid a visit to me."

At that moment a large applause broke out. The crowd stood and cheered as the mayor finished a toast to the executives of ComHealthOne, describing them in what now appeared to be a campaign slogan—the ones who had returned affordable health care to Minnesota. Two minutes later, the applause stopped and Colder, clapping his hands like the others to avoid notice, turned again to Casey.

"What did Markham say?"

"What do you mean, what did he say?" she replied coldly. "Think about it, Peter. He's the damn COO of ComHealthOne and he's talking to me about an anonymous patient he seems to know as well as his daughter. I barely asked anything more. It scared the hell out of me."

Colder nodded in understanding. "What else happened?"

"He gave me and my partner an offer on the Rosewood building. Three times its value. I could practically retire with the profit."

Colder wiped his brow. "You're kidding me."

"I don't kid," she said seriously. Her ferocious look confirmed her statement.

"Anything else?"

"Before he left, he told me how glad he was to have me as part of the

ComHealth team and that they wanted me there for years to come. He said that he knew that sometimes every team has a few problems, but that they are best solved internally and he would always be available if anything ever bothered me."

"That was it?"

"Yes."

"What Markham said could have meant anything," Colder said weakly.

Casey Larter shook her head in disagreement. "Do you take comfort in naiveté?"

"No, you're probably right."

She leaned toward him. Colder could smell the mint she had been chewing on. "Look, let's face facts. Fragile X is real. Molly and this other woman aren't lying. And—several people are dead."

"Maybe more than we know," Colder said.

"Yes," Casey sipped on her water. "I read about Molly's neighbor."

"It was intended for Molly and that woman's son."

Casey Larter looked somewhere between disgusted and afraid. "I may have no scruples, Peter, but I want to keep my own hide intact. This stuff scares the hell out of me."

Colder ignored it. "You invited me here to warn me then?"

"Sort of."

"What aren't you telling me?"

"One last thing. Markham mentioned you by name."

"What?" he whispered. "When?"

"Two days ago, he called me again. Said he knew that we were friends. Also that he knew that you were having financial trouble and that your bitterness toward the organization was part of the basis of Molly's lawsuit. He did try to sound magnanimous though. He said he hoped everything worked out well for you, and that his door was always open if you wanted to talk."

"Great. I've never even met the guy."

"Doesn't matter. Don't miss what he was really saying."

"In other words, beware," Colder said, masking his fear well.

"Yes."

Colder's face was grim and ashen. He felt confused, paralyzed by the weight of an invisible force riding down upon him. He had never planned on risking his life or placing others in danger. He had no idea of the extent of the Fragile X tentacles now threatening to ensnare all that had contact with it. He was simply a doctor, knowledgeable, but naive. "Where to we go from here?" he muttered to himself.

Casey managed to hear it. With a curious look, she asked "Have the reporters talked to you yet?"

"What?" he replied loud enough to cause the rest of the table to turn. Peter looked sheepish. Disapproving, the others gazed at him, then turned back to the podium as the mayor began to introduce Hutchins.

"A reporter from the *Star Tribune*. She came around two days ago. Somehow she got wind that the Bureau was snooping around Reggie Tan's place and thought it was weird that the FBI was investigating a local matter."

"You're kidding."

"I'm not. She's been asking around. She'll get to you."

Colder sighed audibly. It all seemed like too much. "What exactly did she ask?"

"A lot. I think she might know something."

"Did you talk to her?"

"No, but I let her ask questions for a few minutes to see what she was talking about."

"Let me guess. You did it in your office so that if any inadvertent audio equipment happened to be around your innocence could be assured."

"You're getting wise quickly, Doctor."

"What do you think she knows?"

"She was fishing, but I think she knows that the FBI is looking into ComHealth for something and that there have been multiple deaths that may be linked somehow."

"Fragile X?"

"She asked me about it. I didn't tell her anything."

"The geneticists?"

"Didn't say anything."

"Molly?"

"No."

"Did she say anything else?"

"Only that she would be back."

As he heard Casey's answer, Colder picked up his glass and drained the last of his water. At the same time, the mayor finished his hyperbolic introduction. While the mayor panted and moved away from the podium, H. Carter Hutchins rose to greet the standing ovation. He put down the enormous plaque he had been given and waved in his usual practiced fashion to the crowd and moved gracefully to center stage. Colder stood and applauded lightly. He tried to say something, but the noise was too great. He tried again. "We're lambs in the lion's den," he shouted in Casey's ear.

She nodded in agreement. "Listen carefully to what he says," he saw her lips say.

Colder turned to the head table. It was a scene he felt he had seen a million times. Only the names and faces were different. The most twisted ritual of politics, the speech, was about to begin.

Colder watched with a curious detachment as Hutchins began. He focused on the audience. They appeared in love, consumed by the admiration that arises within the allure of charisma. Colder heard Hutchins' patriotic words about the noble mission he had undertaken and the financial achievement of managed care and the greatness of market-based "reform." Colder winced as the audience applauded. The cynical reality of Hutchins' half-truths stung him as the soon-to-be candidate thundered on. He now knew how medicine had lost the battle. It was simply that truth and good intention were never a match for the spellbinding quality of a smattering of patriotic fervor, a myriad of half-truths, and a welcomed easy solution to a difficult problem. Medicine had never known these men before. The entrepreneurs and the politicians. Men in need of fortune and fame, irrespective of all else. He stared at Hutchins, the words no longer registering. The CEO was the minister at a funeral, believing the words that all wanted to hear. The tragedy was that the funeral was not his, or Casey's or, any other doctors'. The funeral was for the patients.

The masterful speech lasted nearly an hour. While Hutchins accepted the ovation of the crowd, Celia joined him, her well-practiced smile now perfect as well. In the back, reporters scribbled notes to themselves while the news cameras captured the happy couple embracing the governor and his wife.

Colder signaled to Casey and together they walked out. They said nothing as the pushed through the doors and out into the night, escaping the sounds of political bacchanalia.

"Sorry I lied to you," said Casey, preparing to leave.

"Forget it. I shouldn't have yelled at you earlier today."

"Ever seen anything like it?"

"Never. It's over, Casey."

"I know."

Colder did not want to talk any more. He was as depressed as he had ever been. "I'll see you. Thanks for the invite."

"You okay?" she asked.

The festivities had distracted him. Now the fear and anxiety began to return. He was worried about Molly, Reggie, and the others. "Yeah, I'm fine."

"Call me if I can help."

Peter nodded and walked away. The evening air was unseasonably cool. He felt even chillier. As he walked along the short sidewalk between the hotel and the parking lot, he tried desperately to convince himself that the whole situation was something other than hopeless.

Chapter Fifteen

As he walked away from the hotel, Colder's thoughts returned to Casey Larter. Her words about ComHealth's subtle message to him seemed more terrifying with every step. But as he walked, he was increasingly aware of the sound of footsteps behind him, and he turned to look. Standing under one of the parking lot's bright lights was a thin young woman. She was in her mid twenties, with dark hair cut in an unflattering pageboy style and a steely, insolent face that seemed to gaze at the world with a primed and critical eye. She carried no purse; instead her hands were buried in the pockets of her faded blue jeans and her arms lost in the volume of the oversized white cotton sweater. She made no attempt to move when Colder saw her; instead she slouched forward, her head tilting down and her deeply recessed eyes watching him with the curious detachment of a cat eyeing a prey.

"Dr. Peter Colder?" she asked in a manner reflecting the fact that she knew the answer to her question.

"Who are you?"

"A friend," she said walking toward him.

"I'm not up for any games," he replied, turning away and taking one step forward.

She walked the five yards toward him. "Marcia Sullivan. *Star Tribune.*"

Colder turned back and shook her extended hand. Her grip was surprisingly strong. Up close she was prettier, but only by nature, having made no attempt with makeup or clothing to appear anything other than discreet.

"Peter Colder."

"Didn't like what you heard in there?" she asked. "I saw you leave."

Colder did not answer right away; instead, his eyes wandered through the parking lot to see if any others watched them. Casey was gone, and other than a few people mingling in front of the hotel, the lot was deserted. He ignored the reporter's question. "You know, Ms. Sullivan, it scares the hell out of me that you're standing here in the middle of a parking lot knowing my name and what I was doing here."

"I'm no threat," she replied. "And it's Marcia."

"Fair enough. But you also know I can't talk to you."

"It's a free country."

"I don't know anything."

Marcia Sullivan laughed suddenly and loudly, with the assurance of a parent whose child had told a lie too large to be believed and too humorous to be ignored. "I'm sure that's not true."

"Why are you here?" Colder sounded weary.

"Same as any reporter," she answered. "I'm searching for the truth."

"Searching for a story."

"Whatever," she replied. He began to walk, and she moved with him.

"I don't know any stories."

"C'mon," she scoffed. "Insult me, and I don't mind. But don't lie. It's unbecoming."

"I don't have to talk to you."

"No," she admitted. "But sooner or later you probably will be."

Colder pondered her statement, realizing that she was probably right. For a moment, he considered leveling with the young reporter, telling all that he knew and thought. His mind wandered to a blaring headline of greed, deceit, and murder with a Hutchins mug shot staring out toward him. It was appealing, deliciously appealing. But he had no proof, only innuendo, and without proof he was merely a dangerous accuser. "I'll take that chance," he said finally.

Marcia wasn't swayed. "How do you think Hutchins will be as our next governor?"

Colder stopped again. "I'm sure he'll be wonderful."

"I'm sure you do," she replied, her cat-and-canary smile reappearing.

The reporter's manner was annoying him. She had the typical self-assurance of a recent college grad whose wall was littered with awards and whose classroom insights would solve all of the world's problems. Smug and glib with an effortless sarcasm. He had figured her instantly for print journalism, her standards not bowing to the superficial world of the electronic media. Colder guessed her to be politically informed, probably liberal, maybe conservative, whatever was fashionable among the young, iconoclastic intellectual elite. He instantly both disliked her and respected her, for he knew her critical eye was probably seeing more than anyone else around.

"No one says he'll win."

"Polls run him ten points ahead of anyone the Democrats throw out there."

"Then maybe he will. It's still a year away."

"He's a very complicated man," said Marcia.

"That's a fair statement," Colder replied, allowing himself to be drawn into a bit of a conversation.

"Very busy too. Like serving on all of those boards. Boards of corporations that buy up journals." Colder said nothing, but his startled reaction was obvious. Marcia continued to talk. "I can't imagine why anyone would want an obscure, unprofitable medical journal as an acquisition, can you?"

"I don't know what you're talking about." Colder shivered at the words, not knowing whether it was the weather or the reporter's surprising knowledge that produced the effect.

She kept on. "You know the real interesting thing is to see which of his men in waiting get to wear the next crown. Gonna be like an old feudal war when the king is gone. The four disciples all wanting to be Jesus."

"Interesting way of putting it."

"My money is on Markham. Where's yours?"

"I don't know. I don't know any of them well."

"He was the one who fired you."

"I resigned," Colder said, not really caring about the difference anymore.

"I forgot."

Colder shrugged. "He's probably a good guess."

"Markham is Hutchins' closest ally."

"Then you're probably right."

She stared at him with indifferent eyes that seemed to wander through his brain as they searched for an open avenue. "Dr. Larter won't talk either," she remarked.

"Did you expect her to?"

"Actually I'm more curious as to why you haven't told me to get lost," she replied.

Colder laughed. "I probably should."

"Let me guess. You like my company?"

Colder chuckled again. She was physically attractive in her own way, uncompromising and freely original, but he was more concerned by the fact that his appeal to her was more like that of the black widow to her ill-fated mate, allure for a purpose. "Yes. That's it. I like your company. How did you know?"

Marcia didn't pursue the banter. "Why haven't you left?"

Colder kicked at the ground aimlessly. "I guess I'd like to know what you know, and how you know it."

"I thought you'd say that," she replied.

"And?"

"Not that easy, Colder. You have to feed a poor, starving girl." She shifted her weight to her right and tilted her head back. Her gaze was relentless.

"You don't impress me as helpless, Ms. Sullivan."

Marcia pulled a cigarette out of her jacket and lit it. Appearing to revel in the smoke, she took a long drag and blew a series of concentric circles into the air with an air of Gen X sophistication. "Let's be straight. We wouldn't still be talking if we didn't both understand that we might help the other."

Colder cocked his head. "True."

"Honestly, Colder. I won't make any value judgments about ComHealth or any of the other blood-sucking HMOs. That's not my point."

"Then what is?"

"I know your angle is Molly Loomis and saving the Third Street Clinic. They've got you on the outs, and your financial sheet reads like a page from a Stephen King novel."

Colder was too stunned to even form a reasonable reply, his eyes blinking multiple times. "Where do you get this stuff?" he managed feebly.

"I've seen the lawsuit." Marcia saw Colder's shock. "It's not the Shroud of Turin you know. You can get you're eyes on it. But more importantly, you don't throw stones at H. Carter Hutchins without getting noticed, and you're getting noticed."

Colder sighed. "What's your angle?"

"That's obvious. I want the story."

"What do you know about Molly?"

"She's the plaintiff. Talked to a few people at her work and found out about her bum of a husband, the abortion, the hospitalization, the denial of the claim, and the suit. I mix that in with the fact that the FBI shows up to take over a police matter, Cynthia Tan's death, and suddenly it occurs to me. There might be a little more to this story."

Colder's shoulders dropped. "That all you know?" he replied, now almost disappointed that she had nothing more.

"I know that your assistant, Sandra Becker, went fishing in England for an obscure journal and that she did it after Molly Loomis came to see you. I know that the company that published the journal was purchased by a Hutchins-influenced company based in L.A."

"The journal does not exist."

Marcia Sullivan suddenly looked angry. "At least give me the truth. Tell me you won't talk to me or tell me the truth. But don't lie."

Colder momentarily closed his eyes. He sighed and shook his head. "You're right, I am sorry. You don't deserve that. The truth is that we don't have the journal."

"Now that I believe."

"What else do you know?"

"I know about Molly's run-in with this fake doctor. And I know several geneticists that used to work for ComHealth are dead and one is missing. The word is that you know where the last one is."

"Lord," muttered Colder, amazed. He started walking again, and she followed. "Where did you get all that?"

"Am I wrong?"

"I didn't say that."

"Couple of cops were a little peeved when the FBI took over the investigation into Cynthia Tan's death. They have their ways of getting even."

"Like talking to you?"

"You said it, I didn't."

"So you know that the official report about Cynthia Tan was fiction?"

"Yes."

"Then why haven't you printed it?" He stopped again.

She finished the cigarette and leaned comfortably against the back of a blue Honda Accord. "Everyone knows that isn't the story, and there's no proof of anything yet."

"That may be all we ever know," said Peter.

"Look, Colder. We need to be straight with one another. There are a couple of pieces that I don't know yet, and I need them. You're in the same boat. I'm offering you a trade."

Colder fell silent considering the offer. The truth was he knew little more than the reporter, but he felt certain that she was concealing something as a means of getting him to talk. He also knew that with her contacts, it would only be a matter of time before she found out all that he knew. He thought about it for a moment and decided it would be better to have her as an ally of sorts.

"Okay, Ms. Sullivan."

"Marcia."

"Okay, Marcia. What do you need to know? Off the record."

"What's Fragile X?"

Colder laughed out loud. "You won't believe me when I tell you. We don't know."

"I believe you," she said, not sharing his amusement.

"But you're right. It's the link."

"Then tell me what you know."

"Off the record?"

"Off the record."

Colder didn't hesitate. He almost found himself glad to be talking about it. For the next five minutes, Colder detailed everything he knew. He spared no details and openly speculated as to what Hutchins and ComHealth had been doing. She took notes infrequently and listened intently, looking past him most of the time as if immersed in thought. When he finished, she put her pad of paper back in her pocket and the pencil behind her ear.

"So you think that Fragile X is some disease that would cost the HMO a lot to treat?"

"Yes." Colder continued, reviewing with the reporter his theory that Fragile X would more likely be a *costly* disease to treat rather than a lethal disease for which the public might support the use of abortion.

"Interesting," the reporter said. "Your theory makes sense."

"It's still just a theory," he admitted.

Marcia was gratified. "All right, you stepped out on a limb, and I appreciate it. I'll pay you back. I owe you. What I said earlier about the four disciples wanting to be Jesus is no joke. These guys may put on a good front of unity, but the battle to succeed Hutchins is a true tale of the lust for gold."

Colder loosened his tie. He was finally starting to relax. "I don't know much about it."

"Bottom line is that only one man can do it. The old problem of the air getting thinner at the top. Here's the scoop. All four of them are smart, ruthless, and incredibly ambitious. Probably none of them is more talented or deserving than the other, which leads to a natural competition of amazing intensity. I know it's already ugly, but out of that ugliness one survivor will emerge."

"I think I must be missing something," Colder said, looking puzzled.

"The guy who gets the crown walks off with the treasure of King Midas. Last year alone, Hutchins made $12 million in salary and $40 million in stock options. That's not even counting what he's already made. Can you imagine how rich a guy of forty would be if he took over that spot?"

"Healthy checking account."

"But here's the problem. Hutchins is no stooge. And he's got a problem. He's got this little Fragile X matter that hangs over him like a cloud. Think about what happens when suddenly three guys don't get the job. They lose their chance at the golden egg. Hey, they could even get the ax. The new Caesar probably isn't going to want Brutus and Cassius hanging around."

Colder's back straightened, the realization hitting him like cold water. "Only one of them knows about Fragile X."

Marcia Sullivan smiled. "We think alike, Colder."

"And you think it's Markham," he continued, not even hearing her.

"Markham was on the letter sent to Molly."

"Form letter. Doesn't mean anything."

"Markham is the COO and bought ComHealth's computers. He's the only one of them who knows anything about the security system they have."

"Might not be in their computers. Or at least not in their system."

"Markham contacted Casey Larter."

Colder said nothing, his eyes narrowing and a slight grin crossing his lips as he realized she was right. "Still doesn't prove anything though."

"That's true."

"When did you figure it out?"

"Couple of days ago."

"It's good work," Peter admitted.

"Thanks. But it doesn't take us all the way."

"How do we get Mr. Markham to cooperate?" Colder asked.

"I don't know that. But I do know one thing else. A while back, Hutchins ordered a major overhaul of their computer system. My guess is that it was just an excuse to get rid of any trace of Fragile X."

"Then we're dead," Colder said.

"Not quite. My guess is that Markham saved it somewhere. He's got it on disk."

Colder's mind was spinning. "Why would Markham even keep it on disk?"

"Decent insurance. I'd say because those disks are worth about $30 million a year."

"You're right again," he said. He was embarrassed that the reporter was thinking so much faster than he.

"Tell you what," she said. "You hear anything, call me."

Colder chuckled at her words, laughing more at himself and his former determination not to talk to the reporter. He was now finding himself now actually enjoying his slightly sarcastic new friend. "How will I get hold of you?"

She handed him a card with phone and pager numbers. "Here."

"If I see one word of this in print—" he started.

She interrupted him "Not until we have what we are looking for. Everything is off the record."

"Good." He started walking toward his car. He noticed she did not follow, but he heard her voice.

"You know, Colder," she said, now from about twenty feet. "Making moral judgments isn't my job. But what ComHealth has done is despicable. All these cutbacks in care while the executives get rich. And then lie so constantly about it. It's unbelievable."

"I know."

"And as for Molly Loomis. I gotta admit I would like to think that I would have the guts to do what she's doing, taking 'em on."

He turned to look at her, walking backwards. "I'm sure you would."

"Usually I'm not real big on going to court, but if Sanders and Briggs can get it to the courtroom, or if I can help, I'll be there."

"Thanks."

"I just hope we get to watch the bastards fry."

With those words, she left. As Colder watched her disappear into the darkness, he found himself both amused and excited at the information as he struggled to get his key into the lock. Two minutes later, he drove off, leaving the Radisson behind. His mind was still on the conversation with Marcia Sullivan and the possible existence of the Fragile X disks.

Molly was scrubbing the last of a ketchup spill from the far corner table of the MeDiner when Tracy Timlin walked up to her with a strange grin that nearly stretched across her entire face. A different smile on the outgoing Tracy's face signaled something new. Her blue eyes had a mischievous glow, and she cocked her eyebrow in an exaggerated fashion designed to attract attention. Molly, stooped over the linoleum and still furiously wiping at the stained table, only glanced toward her and missed the show. "Grab a rag, Trace," she panted. "I think they painted this stuff on."

"You got a call, Molly," she said, trying to sound mysterious.

"Who is it?" she grunted, but making an attempt at humor, "Ed McMahon? My sweepstakes entry?"

"What?"

"Tell him I'm pretty busy, but that I did want the red Ferrari."

Tracy ignored her. "I think it's Peter."

Molly stopped scrubbing and looked up her good friend standing over her. "How do you know?" she asked, wiping the sweat from her brow.

"Because he asked for Molly Jane Loomis, dragon slayer and waitress par excellence. That's a quote."

"That doesn't sound like Troy," she admitted.

"No, I remember what he sounded like. Kind of like Schwarzenegger in *The Terminator*. Is Mowwy dare?"

Molly tried not to laugh as she walked to the back room. "He wasn't that bad."

"No it was worse," said Tracy, taking hold of the rag.

Molly unconsciously straightened her dress and fiddled with her hair before picking up the phone. Peter had called her each day for the past several weeks, and despite the fact that they had been unable to meet for anything more than lunch, she found herself looking forward each day to the phone call. They had done nothing but talk and eat, but she found the conversations easy and the "dates" fun. Colder was both intelligent and entertaining, with a constant string of medical stories that often left her laughing nearly to tears. She found him less intimidating than she would have thought. Despite the differences in education and life experiences, they had more in common than she originally expected. Their failed marriages provided an easy topic, and they spent hours talking about their failures and the frustrations. Over the weeks since her visit to his office, she had come to depend upon him as a friend, respect him as a doctor, and want him as a part of her life. He was also terribly attractive.

"Hello," she said, picking up the phone.

"Hey you," said Colder warmly. "How's the night going?"

"Oh, God," she sighed, both happy to hear his voice and wincing at the thought of the "family from hell" that had just finished tearing apart the diner. "Had this maniac family that nearly burned the place down. Just left. Ketchup, mustard, salt, sugar. You name it, we're out of it."

"Get a good tip?"

"A dollar," she exclaimed. "Forty-dollar bill and a one-dollar tip."

"Just shoot me," groaned Colder.

"No, shoot them. How was the banquet?" Molly asked, changing the subject.

"Hutchins is a master. He could sell life insurance to a dead man."

"Did he get his award?"

"More like he was anointed."

"Please," she replied, "I think I'm going to be ill."

"It was quite an evening."

"What happened?"

"I met with a couple of interesting people tonight." Colder proceeded to tell her of the meeting with Casey Larter while Molly listened in disbelief.

"They killed someone because she didn't have an abortion?" she asked incredulously.

"Yes."

Molly sat down. She could feel herself start to sweat. She was beginning to understand how O'Reilly must have felt for the past three years. "You know, Peter, it's absolutely critical that we get O'Reilly in safely. This is getting really scary."

"Yes."

"Have you heard from him?"

"Not a word. But he's clever. He'll reappear."

One of the marshals who were Molly's constant companions peeked into the room. Molly waved. She was more grateful than ever that they were guarding her. With the wave the man disappeared again. "I talked to Tyler about three hours ago. The first hearing is next Wednesday."

"That's a motion to dismiss—er, summary judgment, isn't it?"

"Yes. He's still a little worried, but this new witness sounds helpful."

"We're all going to go with you," he said. "I closed the office that morning, and Sylvia, Sandra, and Letisha are all going to go too."

"Oh, you don't have to," she said, still sounding relieved despite her protestation.

"We want to, Molly," he said sincerely. "I want to."

Molly blushed. "Thank you."

"How's Reggie?"

"Better. He went back to school yesterday and said his teachers are being very reasonable. Most of his missed assignments can be made up at his leisure."

"Has he said anything else?"

Molly paused, thinking about her answer. "Let's put it this way. He's not interested in buying his insurance from ComHealth."

"He's not in the computers, is he?"

"He assured me he isn't."

"Good."

Molly got up and walked to the counter where a candy bar she had nursed throughout the night sat half eaten. She decided she was no longer hungry and tossed it in the wastebasket. "You said you met with a *couple* of interesting people."

"Yes," replied Colder, telling her the details of his conversation with Marcia Sullivan.

"My God!" she exclaimed. "She knows all that? Why haven't we read about it?"

"She's waiting, looking for the big story."

Molly sat back down. It was all dizzying. "We need O'Reilly," she said.

"She has a good point though," he continued, "thinking that Hutchins is probably working with only one of his underlings. More than one would make it more difficult to keep it a secret, especially if the other three got aced out for the top job."

"It is a good thought. Who was she thinking?"

"Markham."

Molly groaned recalling the letter of denial. "My buddy."

"It's certainly possible," said Colder

"I agree. It is."

Colder's pager went off. After a long pause, he grunted. "There it is. Gotta run."

"ER?"

"Hospital, but not an emergency. Say, I called for a couple of reasons. One, I'm kind of in the mood for a sub again. How about you?"

"Sure," she said, feeling herself blush again.

"Good. I'm working through lunch tomorrow, but how about the day after?"

"Perfect."

Colder sounded happy. "Great. Secondly, I was thinking about this reporter and how she might help us. I think I have a way we could kill two birds with one stone."

"What's that?"

"It would take the heat off a bit as well as increase the temperature in the ComHealth offices."

"This sounds good."

"Actually a couple of doctor friends of mine proposed it to me."

For the next couple of minutes Colder gave her the details. She thought it was brilliant and agreed they should proceed. Both felt Briggs should be involved, so she hung up and called the lawyer. Tyler gave his enthusiastic blessing. The attorney told her he, too, had been trying to think of some such plan, but had not yet come up with anything. Thrilled, she called Colder back and set the plan in motion. "He says do it," she blurted.

"I'm on my way."

Molly could hear her voice quiver. "This is hardball, Peter."

"It's the only way we can play it."

"Those were Tyler's words exactly."

Colder paused for a moment before double-checking with her. "You sure you're okay with it? It could get ugly."

"Absolutely."

"I'll see you soon."

"I'm looking forward to it."

"See you then." Colder hung up. He realized he was looking forward to seeing her as well.

Two hours later, the six doctors gathered briefly outside the emergency room of the Hennepin County Medical Center. They all arrived on schedule at precisely the designated hour, and the entire meeting lasted less than one minute. They came dressed in a mixture of shorts and shirts, jeans and baseball caps, wandering down the sidewalk outside the cramped ER, each handing the sixth man a single sheet of paper. They made no acknowledgment of one another, instead passing by one another as if unnoticed and then disappearing quickly into the night.

The first had been Casey Larter. The second was Daniel Garland, an internist. The third was Mark Everson, a dermatologist. The fourth was David Frissell, who had once operated on Molly Loomis. The fifth was Kevin Tigen, an oncologist. Each handed Colder a sheet of paper containing a single name and a medical record number that their nurses provided. Colder pocketed the names without expression as if accepting an illegal payment and then he walked unnoticed toward the parking lot. No one had seen the six of them together. If they had, no one would have known what they had seen. The moment passed without a hitch. With one brief meeting, unnoticed by the world, the operation the five young physicians facetiously called "Overlord" officially began.

Chapter Sixteen

August 4

It was early evening when Peter, Molly, and Tyler sat in the living room of Jayne McCall, the first patient of "Operation Overlord." Her residence was a one-bedroom apartment near downtown Hopkins, a blue-collar suburb on Minneapolis's west side. The second-story flat overlooked a quaint neighborhood of 1920s homes. In the tidy living room, Molly sat with Peter on a battered couch, a hand-knit afghan draping its back side. Briggs sat across from them in a worn upholstered chair. Between them, a chipped, wooden coffee table sat with a plate of snacks and sodas. In the corner, a small color TV sat propped on a file cabinet, and in the room's far corner, an old red bean bag chair was home to a cocker spaniel named Raymond. The walls were empty except for a print from a Guthrie Theatre production in 1992 and an old prom picture of a much different-looking girl of several years before.

Jayne McCall sat on a folding chair a few feet away from the others nearer the kitchen. By her appearance, her age could have been anywhere between nineteen and thirty without causing surprise, although they all knew it to be twenty-four. Since they had arrived and taken their seats, she had crossed and recrossed her legs at least eight times in a nervous gesture that was both curious and sad. McCall might have been attractive, but her sandy-colored hair was limp and unstyled and her face was pale and drawn. Her eyes rarely made contact with the others; instead, she stared almost continuously at the floor and spoke softly in a voice barely above a whisper. An unflattering plaid smock hung loosely over her jeans, concealing a figure that was at least thirty pounds over ideal.

In twenty minutes, Molly, Peter, and Tyler had learned a great deal about Jayne and why Colder had been given her name. Single, she lived alone with her dog and worked as a night cashier at the SuperValu grocery store ten blocks away. She had grown up in Minneapolis, having graduated from high school six years before. Two semesters of college had led nowhere, and she had dropped out when her life had completely fallen apart. Now, she lived in planned anonymity in her tiny apartment in a deliberate attempt to hide from the world. That part of her life had not been stated. There was no need. The scars on her face had told it all.

Jayne continued to rock back and forth nervously as she told the story, her eyes shifting continuously between the feet of her three guests. She made little attempt at eye contact, and whenever she did, it was soon followed by a self-conscious nod and a hand covering the lower half of her face. Molly felt an intense bond with her, a woman only a few years younger, whose life had been filled with such pain. Colder asked most of the questions while Briggs and Molly sat in disbelief.

"When did it start?" Colder asked, trying to gaze discriminately at the lower half of her acne-riddled face.

"When I was seventeen. Maybe a little when I was sixteen."

"Was it bad then?"

"Not too bad for about a year," she replied softly, still not looking up at them. "I was pretty then."

"You still are pretty," Colder said, lying.

All three guests stared at the scars, innumerable, deep, and consuming the lower half of her face and upper neck. Each of them was a small, star-shaped crater with tiny tentacles reaching out toward the skin. Some were small and nearly black. Others were nearly dime-sized and several millimeters deep. Surrounding them the skin was red, like a fiery crimson that was only partially masked by makeup. None of her lower face was unblemished. Only her forehead was normal.

Jayne ignored his polite remark. "It was horrible. Once it started it couldn't be stopped."

"Did you take medicine for it?" Molly asked, concerned.

"Everything," she said shaking her head. "I started with this solution that I rubbed on three times a day. After a few months it only seemed to be getting worse, so they put me on Tetracycline. I stayed on that for six months, and it didn't get any better so we tried another antibiotic."

"Erythromycin?" Colder asked with the slightest hint of sarcasm in his voice.

"Yes. And then doxycycline and then ampicillin and then monocycline. Each for about six to nine months. It seemed endless. Nothing worked." As she said it, her voice quivered slightly. "The pimples became so big they were like cysts. Then they would pop, and as they healed, a scar would form."

"Didn't anything work?" Briggs asked.

"Nothing," she said, a tear falling down her cheek. "It seemed like each day I would wake up and there would be a new scar on my face. I couldn't believe it. Each day another one. My face disintegrated before my eyes. Before I knew it, there wasn't a single spot below my eyes that wasn't affected."

Molly handed Jayne a tissue, and for a moment they all sat gazing at each other and around the room. The old prom picture was the only remnant of the clear-faced girl who seven years before had smiled happily at her future. Now she sought only to hide from that memory.

"Did you try anything else?" asked Colder.

"Septra," she choked back.

Peter turned and glanced at Molly, offering her a roll of his eyes, and then gazed thoughtfully into the streak of light beaming through the curtains. "The algorithm treatment again," he muttered, inaudible to anyone but Molly. "Damn cookbook."

"Now they say that there's nothing that can be done," Jayne uttered. "Not even dermabrasion will do anything. The scars are permanent."

"No kind of plastic surgery?" Molly asked, looking up at Colder who was shaking his head back and forth.

"Probably no," returned Jayne. "'Live with it,' was all they said."

Colder's blood boiled as he watched her. Jayne McCall's face and life had been ruined by a force she did not even know. A conspiracy, achieved by preying upon the patient's trust. "Did you ever have Accutane?" he asked as he leaned toward her.

"No," she replied. "Would that help?"

Colder shook his head. "No, I wish it would."

Tyler Briggs sat straight up in his chair, his eyes narrowing toward Colder. "Why do you ask?"

"Because that's what she should've had."

Jayne looked up at him, her red eyes making contact with Colder's for the first time. Molly glanced at Tyler and then at Colder. They all seemed surprised.

Colder took a deep breath. He knew it was time to cross over the line and start flinging stones. "What you have, Jayne, is a condition called nodular cystic acne, the most serious form of acne. People don't think of acne as a serious disease because it is not life-threatening, but if untreated or inadequately treated, it can result in severe scarring and—"

"What do you mean *should* have had?" interrupted Jayne.

"Exactly what I said. That is the drug you should have had. If you'd been given it early enough in your course, you wouldn't have any scarring today."

Jayne looked as though she had been hit by lightning, her shoulders convulsing involuntarily at the sound of his words. Molly emitted an audible gasp, her hands rising in a reflex to cover her mouth. Tyler was expressionless.

"Are you sure?" Jayne asked as if not believing.

"Positive."

"Go on," encouraged Briggs.

Colder took another deep breath as if preparing to exorcise a great demon from deep within his long-troubled soul. In a curious way, he felt rejuvenated by the thought of finally telling the truth to those outside the fraternity of medicine in the same way that his colleagues had talked behind closed doors.

"You were treated by a managed care protocol, based on using the cheapest medicine first. Then if that doesn't work, go to the next cheapest. If that doesn't work, then another. The reason that you didn't get Accutane is that it is the most expensive drug available, and ComHealth doesn't want its doctors to use it even though it's the most effective. What they are banking on is that by the time you get to the end of the algorithm, you'll have outgrown the disease. A lot of the time they are right, the disease does go away. Sometimes they are wrong."

"You're saying that if I had been given that drug right away, I wouldn't be like this?" she asked incredulously, her hands and lips trembling.

"Yes, I am," he replied.

"But I trusted him!" Jayne exclaimed. "How could he?"

Molly stood up and walked to the kitchen where she took another of the kitchen chairs and placed it next to Jayne. Molly put her hands on Jayne's shoulders and rubbed them comfortingly.

"It wasn't your doctor, Jayne," Colder said carefully. "I've known him a long time. He's a good man. Remember, he's the one who gave us your name."

She glanced up at him, her look one of obvious distrust mixed with curiosity and the recognition that what Colder said could possibly be true.

"He's the one who is doing the prescribing, but it's the insurer behind the scenes who is controlling what is really prescribed."

"Then why didn't he tell me? I would have paid *anything* to avoid this."

"He can't. He's bound by his contract not to say anything to you about alternative forms of treatment, and if he prescribes unapproved medications he is financially penalized. If he does it too much he gets fired."

"My God," said Molly. "Just how callous can you get?"

"This is just basic managed care."

"Yeah, but this is me!" Jayne exclaimed. "This is my life! My face! The only one I've got. And look at me now. I'm like a damn Halloween mask!"

She buried her head in her hands, now weeping uncontrollably as Molly continued to hold her by the shoulders. They said nothing, instead gazing intently at one another with Briggs catching Colder's deliberate glance.

"I trusted them!" she sobbed.

"I know," Colder soothed. "And I wish I could help."

For a moment her body shook as the frustration of the years of failed treatment, the depth of her disfigurement, and the now-exposed lies poured from her. She trembled, her hands vibrating with a series of fine but uncontrolled movements as she struggled to breathe. Molly held her tighter. Suddenly her entire body appeared to collapse as she leaned forward and fell silent. An instant later, she rose again and looked at Colder, her eyes badly stained by the tears and from the rubbing of her eyes. "Then why are you even here?" she asked harshly. "To make fun of my misery? To visit a leper just to see how one lives? To see the elephant girl?"

"No," said Molly.

"Not at all," Briggs agreed.

"We want to help," Colder said.

"How can you? You already said that you couldn't."

Colder measured his words carefully as Jayne struggled to regain her composure. "I can promise you this. There are many more people that care about what has happened to you than you can imagine. Many who would do anything to see you helped. The truth is that your doctor has even risked his career by giving us your name."

"How does that affect me?" she asked.

"We may not be able to find a cure," Colder said, "but we may be able to get justice."

"How?"

Colder shifted on the couch even further toward her, his knees now nearly in contact with hers. He glanced at Molly, whose expression was a mixture of anger and sorrow, and then he turned to Jayne. "As you know, Tyler is representing Molly in a lawsuit against ComHealth. She, like you, was victimized by a system out of control, and like you, it has nearly ruined her life. The problem is that because the suit hinges largely on a technicality within the contract, there is a very strong possibility that we will lose the lawsuit."

Jayne glanced at Tyler, who nodded his assent.

"With that in mind," continued Colder, "the best possibility of a meaningful outcome is if people begin to understand the truth about what ComHealth has been doing. To do that, we need people to talk publicly about what has happened to them and to tell the truth about how this HMO has been operating."

"You want me to go public about this?" she asked, still recovering from the shock.

"We'd just like you to tell the truth," Colder reassured her.

"Oh, my God," Jayne muttered, her look turning to one of terror. "My face on TV and in the newspapers? I can hear the laughter now. No way. No way. I can't do it. I just can't."

"There won't be any laughter," Molly encouraged. "There won't be a person in the city who won't admire you for your courage."

Jayne looked up at her, the fear in her eyes fading slightly. "Do you really think so?"

"I know so."

"What about you?" Jayne asked.

"I started out just wanting to get them to pay my bill. But then I realized that this is so much more than me. That's why we need you, Jayne. Even if we lose the case, we're still right. And change can start when people begin to tell the truth."

Jayne continued to stare at Molly, feeling an almost sisterly bond with the person who more than any other shared her misery.

Molly continued. "I can't undo the past any more than you can. But what we do from now on may make a difference in the lives of many others."

"I'm no crusader." Jayne was doubtful.

"Neither am I," Molly admitted. "I'm nothing more than a simple waitress."

"You're both a lot more than that," Briggs interjected. "You're human beings with dignity and rights. And what happened to you both was wrong."

Jayne turned back to Colder. "What exactly would happen?"

"A reporter would contact you."

"He wouldn't take any closeup shots of my face would he?"

"No, this reporter would honor any request that you have. I know that for sure," said Colder.

Jayne dabbed her eyes and blew her nose into a Kleenex. Embarrassed by the noise, she laughed at herself and then sneezed uncontrollably before laughing out loud again while her faced turned crimson.

"Believe me," Colder said, deflecting the moment. "I can make a much more ridiculous noise than that."

"I certainly hope not," she managed, still wiping at her nose. "You think it would really help?"

They all nodded.

Jayne paused, but only for a moment. "Then I'll do it."

Molly squeezed her tightly. Briggs rose and shook her hand while Colder followed. "Many people will thank you," said Briggs. "Many."

"I don't worry about thanks. Just so it helps."

"We'd like you to come with us then," Colder said.

"Go out?" There was fear in her voice.

"Yes. We're going to meet some new friends."

"Who?"

"The first is a woman about your age. Her name is Lisa Bowman."

"Does she have my problem?" asked Jayne, trying to piece herself together.

"No, not your problem."

"What does she have?" asked Jayne.

Colder faced the ground, and his eyes narrowed as he spoke, the harsh truth still not easy to reveal with candor. "She has cervical cancer. She's going to die."

Lisa Bowman lived with her parents in the suburb of St. Louis Park on the western side of Minneapolis. The three-bedroom brick home was in the heart of an old, working-class neighborhood that boasted neatly kept lawns beneath a rich canopy of hundred-year-old elms. The house was at the apex of a small cul-de-sac that contained similarly sized houses. The front yard was tiny, but the property fanned out as it reached toward the back, its far border a large hedge that concealed the back alley. The house itself was simple, with a slanting roof diving toward the front-facing living room and a yard light that illuminated the entryway and the single-stall garage.

By the time the group arrived, Peter had told Jayne, Molly, and Tyler about Lisa Bowman's medical history. She was twenty-six, married, with a son whom her husband currently cared for. She had moved in with her parents as her condition worsened. Her husband lived nearby, in the house they had purchased two years ago. In good health until the summer one year before, her abnormal pap smear had led to the diagnosis that would sometime in the near future take her life.

As the six others gazed at the frail, thin woman lying on the couch wrapped in a blanket on the living room couch, they felt nothing but pity, recognizing that the cervical cancer had spread too widely for even a ray of optimism to penetrate the conversation.

Lisa greeted them with a gentle wave as they entered and were escorted to their seats by her attentive parents. Dick and Ellen Holmberg offered their guests cookies and coffee and disappeared briefly to locate the planned refreshments. The others looked in awe and horror at the failing figure of a once pretty girl who now looked nothing like the teenager in a cheerleader uniform and graduation picture that adorned the wall. Her black hair was clumped and drawn loosely into a pony tail. She was sweating, and her eyes appeared tired. Her skin was a lifeless white.

Lisa motioned the group toward her. Despite her fever, chills, and sweats, she smiled weakly at them. Without great effort, Lisa appeared genuinely content and in no great pain as the morphine pump circulated the drug continuously throughout her system. She nodded to each as they introduced themselves and even managed a little chuckle as Peter told her of the purpose of their visit. Just as he finished, her parents returned from the kitchen, having heard all that had been said, and placed the tray of refreshments on a center coffee table.

"Please," said Ellen Holmberg motioning to the chairs. "Sit."

The others obeyed, each taking a chocolate-covered cookie and a cup of the steaming hot coffee. "You want to try some, honey?" Ellen Holmberg asked her daughter.

Lisa shook her head no, grimacing as if her stomach was aching.

"She doesn't eat much," said Dick Holmberg. "They had to start her on this stuff."

"TPN," Colder said. "Total parenteral nutrition."

Molly, sitting next to Peter on a folding chair, gazed up at the white liquid that dripped through an IV line and into a large vein under Lisa's clavicle. "What is it?"

"A full day's nutrition that is already digested. Just given in the vein."

"It doesn't taste very good," Lisa joked.

Jayne looked ill, her eyes wide and her hand covering her mouth while looking at the fluid that appeared like milk disappearing under the girl's gown.

"Can you eat at all?" asked Briggs, feeling guilty with a cookie in his hand.

"Not really," she replied. "The steroids ate away my stomach lining, and I really haven't been able to eat since."

"When was that?" Colder asked.

"A month ago."

"Have you been able to keep your weight up?" he asked.

"Gained two pounds in the past two weeks." She was proud of the accomplishment.

"We keep trying to feed her," Ellen Holmberg offered. "The doctors tell us that that's okay."

Colder nodded. "It sure is."

"I want to thank you for coming," Lisa said, changing the subject. "I think I understand what you are thinking."

"No," Briggs protested. "We thank you."

"Dr. Larter called me yesterday," she continued. "At first I was a little reluctant, but now I don't know. I just wouldn't want anything to happen that would hurt her."

"We have the utmost respect for Dr. Larter," Dick Holmberg said. "Her father delivered Lisa, and if it wasn't for her, well, I don't know that Lisa'd be around today."

"We know what happened," Ellen said. "No amount of money could change that. We're angry, but we're not vindictive. Our only thoughts have been with Lisa and how to make her comfortable."

"What exactly happened?" asked Molly.

"Pap smear," Lisa answered. "I missed one."

"When?" Colder asked.

"Dr. Larter became my OB when I changed from my pediatrician when I was seventeen. I had my first pap when I was eighteen, and she continued it yearly after that. When I was twenty-two I had an abnormal one, Class One they called it. Dr. Larter assured me that it was okay, but that I needed to continue to get tested each year because I had had an abnormal test. The year after was normal. The following year when I went to see her, the spring I got married, Dr. Larter said that she thought that I should have another since I had had the atypical cells two years before. But now that I was covered by ComHealth, they wouldn't pay for a test each year in women under thirty-five. I could have it only if I paid for it out of pocket."

"How much was it?" Jayne asked.

"Put it this way," she said sadly. "It was the worst money I ever saved. I was stupid, and naive, and too busy to think about it."

"You had one the next year?" Briggs asked.

"About ten months later, I had Brady without trouble, but something was wrong. I was spotting a little bit and had some pain. When I went back, Dr. Larter found the cancer."

"She operated the next day," Ellen offered.

"They took out my cervix, uterus, and tubes, but the cancer had spread even beyond that. They also had to take out part of my colon and rectum and give me a colostomy. After that, I had radiation and chemotherapy and was in the hospital for three weeks."

Jayne gasped.

"I did pretty well for about six months. It's been a struggle since then."

"A lot of pain?" Colder asked.

"The cancer came back where they said it might. It's all over my pelvis. My stomach and back hurt most of the time, but the morphine helps. The dose is pretty high now, but most of the time I'm comfortable."

"Dr. Colder, do you think that the missed pap smear did it?" Ellen asked.

"Yes, the cancer would have been detected."

"That's what Dr. Larter said too," Ellen said.

"It was my fault. I should have just paid for it," Lisa mumbled.

"Not to be argumentative," Tyler started, "but that is only part of it. People should not be placed in conflict with their health care. The very fact that the insurance company denies coverage that a doctor recommends is a statement that the *insurance company* views the service as unnecessary. This places you in the position of becoming a consumer, not a patient. It forces you to make a decision that you do not have the knowledge to make and take an unnecessary gamble. The fault here doesn't lie with you. Those who enforce arbitrary guidelines on vulnerable and unsuspecting people are at fault."

"I'm not interested in suing anyone, Mr. Briggs," she said.

"Neither are we," said Dick. "Rich or poor won't change what happened, and, well, everything we'd have to go through, we don't want it."

"I understand," said Tyler looking at Lisa's weary eyes. "I would never even suggest for you to pursue any action against your wishes. I am here simply to gather information and to discuss with you what we are currently doing and why."

Lisa sat up a bit and pulled the blanket down slightly, revealing a flannel shirt beneath, her forehead still lined with sweat. "What did they do to you?" she asked Molly.

It was all they needed. Molly and Jayne each took turns relating their histories and the events that had led them all to meet. They did so in a matter-of-fact manner that was neither void of nor packed with emotion. They gave both medical details and the effects on their lives.

"You poor girl," said Ellen Holmberg, looking at Jayne, who had spoken second.

"Don't feel sorry for me," she said with a growing resolve. "I only want my experience to stand for something."

"The same here," said Molly.

"How do you feel about going public?" Ellen asked Jayne.

"A little scared," she said with a nervous laugh.

"Molly," Dick Holmberg asked, "would you also be speaking to the reporter?"

"No," she answered. "Not until the trial."

"It's better that she stays silent for now," Briggs acknowledged.

Lisa coughed heavily, raising some phlegm and wiping it away from her mouth with the tissue that sat at her side. For over two minutes, no one spoke; each person in the room appeared to be contemplating everything they had heard. Finally Lisa broke the silence. "I wouldn't want anything bad to come to Dr. Larter. I'll always be grateful to her. The night she told me, she sat right here and cried with all of us."

"I know how she felt," Colder said.

"But what would you gain, honey?" Ellen asked.

"Nothing," Molly said. "None of this is really for any of us."

Lisa turned to her parents. She coughed again, and when she cleared, she spoke. "If it's true I only have a couple of months left, maybe I can do some good for someone."

"It's up to you, honey," her mother said.

"I don't know," Dick said. "You're awfully weak."

"Maybe this would give all of this some meaning, Dad. Maybe it would help someone else avoid this same moment. Maybe it will give my son something to remember me by."

Her father said nothing, bowing his head and struggling for control. Ellen Holmberg reached out and held her husband's hand. Lisa's eyes filled, but her voice remained steady as she turned to Tyler. "Call the reporter," she announced. "I'll talk."

Three hours later, Peter, Molly, Tyler, and Jayne had completed their journey. Following the visit with Lisa Bowman, they had met with Shirley Mitchell, a sixty-four-year-old grandmother whose widely metastatic breast cancer had been missed because of ComHealth restrictions on mammograms. The gaunt, dying woman, whose attorneys had advised her that there was no legal case against the HMO, also agreed to talk to the press.

The last patient had been Rudy Jalowicz, a fifty-five-year-old grandfather living in a hospice overlooking Lake Calhoun. Jalowicz, dying of metastatic kidney cancer, had been healthy until a year before when the cancer had been diagnosed. Lucid, Jalowicz referred to himself as a "managed care sacrifice," since his cancer could have been diagnosed at an early stage with either a blood count or a urinalysis, tests that once were a part of yearly physicals. Eliminating these yearly tests had saved ComHealth millions, but also cost a number of people their lives. Rudy Jalowicz was one. He, too, agreed to talk.

At ten minutes after midnight, the four people began driving back toward Jayne's apartment. Traffic was still fairly heavy, and the journey was longer than expected, but throughout the drive, no one spoke. For the first time, they had all seen the faces and the names of ComHealth's success. They had seen the people broken by the weight of the profits. They had seen death. The experience had left them drained and numb, and their silence seemed an obligation. There was nothing left to say.

Chapter Seventeen

August 5

Troy Loomis awoke, instantly aware that one of the two women in the bed with him had vomited, leaving a sticky sensation over most of his naked body and a pervasive stench of acidified bile and half-digested rum hanging in the room. The smell was horrible. It made him gag, but after belching twice, his nausea seemed to pass. Better yet, his equally pungent breath seemed to neutralize the aroma.

He lay on his back, covered by a single sheet. Its pattern was a spinning mixture of stripes, and its lower half was soaked in a mixture of fluids from a prolonged night of drunken excess. Trying to see between eyelids that were nearly cemented together, he saw the ceiling and wall twist and turn and as he rolled onto his side. He was able to recognize only that he was not at home. Other than that, he didn't know. It would be a morning of mystery. Again.

He didn't recognize either of the women. The first was blond to the shade of white, with roots that matched the color of her eye shadow and hair extensions that spread like the tentacles of an octopus over most of her body. Her naked leg was slung over his waist, leaving her torso and her head draped over the side of the bed. Her body was ample, her chest enormous, with "Love" tattooed on her ankle and a set of five gold bands piercing each ear. The second woman snored loudly. Her once formidable mane of black hair lay on the floor beside, revealing a short cut of dishwater blond hair. She was thin, but physically flawless. Her arm was draped on his chest, her head face down and turned away.

He kicked away a bottle of cheap rum that rested between his legs and sat up, the movement of the leg and arm causing the women to stir, but not wake. He sank his head into his hands and waited for the pain to relent and the spinning to stop. He was angry. Not at the others, but at himself. Drinking men didn't have hangovers, only nondrinkers did. He prided himself on never being sick. "Must have been the cheap shit," he mumbled to himself.

After five minutes of sitting, he felt better and stood, fumbling through the mixture of clothes. Reaching for a sock, his left foot struck an empty bottle of Budweiser, his little toe sticking in the orifice and leading him to cuss wildly into the air. One woman stirred momentarily, but fell back asleep. He flung the bottle away and picked up the sock. Then he picked up his underwear and his other sock. His balance barely steadying, Troy stumbled into the clothes.

It came to him slowly. Oh, yeah, he thought. I remember these babes. The two with the black guy sitting in the corner. The one with the wild black hair and the one with the tits. "Ha!" he laughed as he recalled the sight. Look who the chicks had taken home with them. Always the same, he congratulated himself. Once more, *he* was the man.

Moving through the apartment, and struggling to avoid a collection of beer cans, wine bottles, and empty bags of chips, he finally found his shoes. One was positioned half underneath a purse, and the other one was abutting a chair. He noticed one woman's purse was open, its contents spilling onto the floor as if kicked by accident. On the floor were three tens and a five. He pocketed them without hesitation.

Troy pulled his keys from his jeans front pocket. He walked down one flight of stairs and then out the front door of the apartment building and onto a sidewalk. The sun was high and the morning warm. Near noon, he figured as he looked up and down the street, searching for his truck. Not seeing it he began ambling north, when suddenly he remembered the ride to the apartment. It was in a Jeep with a sun roof. He had stood and shouted into the night air, beating his chest against the wind. They had been on a lawn. Whose lawn? Where? He couldn't remember all of it. He continued to try. Slowly it came back, piece by piece. He had left the truck. Left it at the bar. Parked behind in the usual spot. He had figured it out. He looked up and saw the street signs. He was six blocks away.

He started walking. His mind went back to what he had been thinking about for days. The time since the divorce had been outstanding, actually better than that. It was the stuff of legends. There had been girls every night. Girls, girls, and more girls. Short, tall, black, white, young, and younger. They all wanted him, he knew that. He accepted that. It was the charm. It was the look. The penetrating eyes, the muscles, and his allure of strength that made them melt. He was sure that the girls talked about how great he was in bed. He was an incredible lay. Who wouldn't want a piece of Troy Loomis?

He congratulated himself on his penetrating insights into the female psyche and reviewed his theories. It was best if they were married. Of this, he had become convinced. The married girls loved the risk and never talked. They just wanted a piece of something else. It was his manly obligation to show them what great sex could be and make them happy. And he was happy when they were happy. Nah, he laughed. He didn't care if they were happy. It was just about fucking. No one could do it like he could. Five drinks and he was better, six and he was unstoppable. Too bad he couldn't get paid. He was a fucking artist.

As he walked, his mind seemed to clear, the prevailing fog of alcoholic slumber lifting like the haze of the morning being burned away by the sun. He felt good, well, decent at least. He crossed the road onto Second Street and noticed that the bounce in his step had returned. His knee did not hurt, and he bounded like a thoroughbred frolicking in the morning sun. An old and beaten convertible passed, occupied by a couple of teenagers smoking cigarettes. They missed him by a few feet, and he flipped them off for coming so close. They looked disinterested and then sped away, returning his gesture with a convulsion of laughter and a cloud of exhaust. Second Street was old apartment buildings, hidden in the shade of surrounding trees. A few children played in the streets, but only an occasional car bothered them. He walked along the sidewalk, picking up a stray tennis ball and bouncing it like a yo-yo. A brown dog approached, barked once, and then sniffed his foot. Troy kneeled and scratched its neck as it licked him. Walking away, the animal followed him for a few steps. Apparently bored with Troy, it turned and went back to its nap in the shade.

Troy Loomis almost felt content as he emerged from the shade. Life was pretty good. The boys all talked about him again at work. How lucky he was. How much he was getting. He was again their idol, *the man*, the legend they wished they could be. It felt good to know that they thought that of him. He had returned to the limelight, a man able to do things others could only dream about doing. But it still wasn't right. Something was wrong.

He had first felt it when he signed the paper and saw the name. She had been around so long. It seemed weird not to have her there. He missed her. He thought about her as he walked. She wasn't pretty, but that was okay in a wife. It kept others from looking at her and made her feel indebted to him for his courtesy. She was a pretty good cook, and the apartment had always been clean. The money she had made had not been bad, even though she probably could have worked another job. His mind stayed on her. She hadn't been a bad wife, he admitted to himself. In fact, she had been a pretty good wife.

He did miss Molly. It was true. He did. "But not the sex," he laughed to himself. She was useless. He'd rather sleep with the dog. It was almost as if she didn't like it. And he really didn't like to be around her much either. She liked to talk about intellectual things like current events and even history. She read books and never talked about anything important, like sports. And worst of all, she never liked to party.

He laughed when he thought about the abortion, how he had used it to dump her. He wouldn't have wanted some retarded kid that needed all kinds of attention and special schooling. He didn't care about the Catholic bullshit about abortion. He had paid for three already, what would be one more? No, he only cared that she couldn't have his kids, and he had always wanted a boy who could play football.

He stopped and bounced the ball like a basketball, then tossed it with a high arc against a branch of an old elm that hung over the sidewalk. The ball struck it squarely and bounded back to him and he raised his arms in triumph. None of that seemed to matter now, he thought. Who the hell cared about kids now anyway? Maybe someday when he was older. Then he would find the right chick and she'd do it for him. Right now he needed time. He needed space. He wouldn't mind being married. But in the right kind of marriage. One with freedom and a clear set of rules. One like he had before.

But he did miss her. He knew his life had become incomplete. Maybe they could just live together. She could take care of the things she did best and he would keep her happy as he had before. She would be the envy of her friends, the girl they all wanted to be. He smiled at the thought and tossed the ball in the air, catching it behind his back with a flourish. He would call her tonight. He knew the necessary words and phrases. She was a nice girl, but not as smart as he was. He would have her again. For his needs. For his desires. He would forgive her and take her back. He had made up his mind. He definitely would call her.

August 6

Just before noon, Judge John Van Gilder's well-used gavel signaled the end of the first pretrial hearing. It had lasted only twenty-five minutes, and in that time, the distinguished-looking, silver-haired judge of the First District Court had managed to spend almost all of it looking as if he was sucking on a lime. His decision, denying the summary judgment motion, had been without comment, but his glare toward T. Quentin Cox, the ComHealthOne attorney, could not be read as anything other than "Don't waste my time again."

Cox, a junior partner at Barnes and Whitfield, was one of their anonymous group of perfect suits, coiffures, and colognes. Their main job was to obfuscate, frustrate, tie up time, and consume resources. They were also unofficial experts at guerrilla law. This group of about ten in number would represent ComHealth on the motions and even perhaps perform some direct and cross-examination at the trial. But they also knew that if or when the trial generated much publicity, their big boys, Barnes and Whitfield, would arrive to take over.

The first hearing was only a formality, a legal exercise and an annoyance. Cox's persuasively spoken argument was passionately felt, beautifully acted, and utterly irrelevant. Van Gilder had twice rolled his eyes in a manner easily seen by everyone in the court. Within seconds of T. Quentin Cox's fist-raised, crescendo finale, Judge Van Gilder ruled in favor of Molly Loomis and exited the courtroom in a huff. In twenty-five minutes, it was assured that the case would go to trial.

Earlier, Tyler provided a concise and well-planned two-minute argument that Van Gilder liked. With this and the news of the ex-ComHealth executive as a witness, the ruling was expected. No one showed any great excitement. Instead they now all had an air of expectation. A huge hurdle passed. The great HMO was going to court. All of them knew though, that from now on, the task would only become more difficult.

Molly, sitting between Tyler and Marcus, turned and looked at her group of friends sitting in the front row, a smile emerging when she came to Colder. He returned the look. The others stood up and swarmed around her.

"Way to go," grinned Letisha, her black eyes flashing as she shook Tyler's hand.

"Ain't done nothing yet," he reminded her, nonetheless pleased.

"You kicked his ass," she whispered loud enough for the departing T. Quentin Cox to hear.

Tyler and Marcus shut their briefcases and started to say goodbye to the group. Molly hugged them both. "We gotta run," said Tyler. "We have to talk to Cox."

"Talk to you later," said Marcus to Molly.

"Thanks."

The two lawyers left the courtroom, leaving the others to mingle and discuss what they'd seen. Briggs ran ahead and flagged down the ComHealth lawyer, who was halfway down the hall. "Wait up," Briggs said to Cox. The perfectly groomed attorney, who looked like a part-time model for *GQ*, stopped.

"Waddya want, Tyler?" he asked, sounding annoyed.

Briggs pulled up beside him, a sarcastic grin cutting its way across his lips. "Where's the A team?"

"Eat it. You know they won't be here for any of this crap."

Marcus joined them and the three started walking "No. I mean Pokey." Tyler replied, ready with the insult. "Oh, that's right, it's Wednesday, the brothels are open."

"Funny," said Cox, walking out the front door of the courthouse and into the sunshine.

"Where'd you learn those gestures you used in there? That hand in the air. That was Michael Jackson. It was beautiful. All you needed was the glove."

"Have your fun now," he scoffed, the banter not appearing to bother him at all. "I'm still waiting for the witness list."

Sanders continued. "Sure, sure. Hey, is it really true that Barnes is Herman Goering's nephew? I swear I saw his face on a KKK commercial when I was in Birmingham at the ABA last month."

Cox started to walk away. He seemed to have no interest in playing along. "You guys can't even insult me well."

"Look, Timmy," began Briggs.

Cox stopped and spun around. "Mr. Cox to you, Ty."

Briggs walked up to Cox and stopped close enough to count his eyelashes. Despite the jokes, Briggs hated the ambitious junior partner. He was a perfect Barnes and Whitfield attorney. His activities had bordered on criminal for years. When Cox tried to walk away again, Tyler grabbed him by the arm and stopped him. It was time to send a message.

"Listen, Tim. I know that you sold dirty laundry on your former friends McMaster and Blake to get this job. I know your wife likes to take monthly trips to that shrink center up on the hill because you can't seem to keep your pants on, and I know that you keep most of your money in your girlfriends' names so any possible alimony payments would look more like the electric bill. But I don't care about that."

Cox's face turned a shade darker, and his teeth became a bright white bar across his lower face. He glanced at the passers-by, relieved to see that they hadn't heard.

"That's bullshit and you know it," he fumed, his voice not convincing.

"Oh, really," retorted Briggs with dubious delight. "Just so it works. Sound familiar?"

"Is there a point to this?" Cox replied, his face changing shades like a mood ring.

"Look," Sanders said, jumping in, "we know that some of your SS boys have been talking to the guy Molly dated once in high school."

"That's not quite how I understand the relationship," he chuckled.

"You guys pull any shit," Marcus started.

Tyler interrupted. "If that guy shows up with a new car or a stereo so big that it scrambles brains, I'm going to ask for an explanation."

"Are you accusing us of bribing witnesses?" Cox asked innocently.

Tyler stepped closer. "I'm only wishing that I owned stock in some of the companies that your firm does business with."

"You mean represents."

"You know what I mean."

Cox stepped back. "I don't get you boys. What motivates you here? You really believe in apple pie and motherhood?"

"We at least believe in integrity."

"Give me a break. Now the law is about virtue? You think your little girl is about virtue?"

"I'm just saying no bullshit," said Marcus.

"All right. We talked to the guy. That's true. We talked to many of her friends. But why would we need to break the law? We'll win this case easily anyway. Even you guys know that."

"Don't be so sure." Briggs backed down. The argument made sense. For once in his life, Cox might be telling the truth.

"C'mon, Tyler. Give it a rest. Cash in your chips, and we'll go have a beer. It's a loser. You know that."

"We'll see." Sanders shifted positions and spoke as forcefully as he could.

Cox stepped away, waving his free hand and shaking his head as if amazed he was even having the conversation. "I'll see you guys soon. And by the way, just wanted you boys to know. All those motions we filed last week?"

"Yes," said Tyler tentatively.

"We're pulling them. We want the trial as soon as possible. We don't want to delay it. Have the trial tomorrow if possible. Justice delayed is justice denied you know."

Briggs' and Sanders' mouths fell open. Cox beamed as he watched his verbal arrow bury itself deep in their chests. "What?" asked Tyler.

"No way," mumbled Marcus.

"Got it from Barnes and Whitfield themselves. We're ready."

"You gotta be kidding," panted Briggs.

Cox walked away. "I never kid," he shouted over his shoulder.

"When?" asked Tyler.

"Week of August twenty-fifth. Three weeks."

"What?"

"I already checked the calendar. The date is open." Cox stopped and turned back toward them. His satisfied mug looked like that of a man who had just won the lottery. "You boys will be ready, won't you?"

"Any time, any place," Marcus grunted.

"I'm glad we see things the same way. Now if you'll excuse me." Cox bounded down the steps to his awaiting limo.

Marcus and Tyler were too numb to talk. For a month, they had assumed that if they got past the summary judgment motion that the suit would be drawn out forever, consuming all of their time and resources. It was a tactic they had anticipated and tried to prepare for. It was so obvious a tactic, it was almost obligatory. Never had they anticipated the opposite.

"Are you kidding me?" asked Marcus of Tyler.

"I don't believe it."

Neither man answered the other. They started walking, but did not speak. Both felt consumed by the agonizing combination of nerves and adrenaline.

The news of the day was better than anything they could possibly have hoped for. Not only would there be a trial, but it would happen soon. Molly J. Loomis versus ComHealthOne. It was simply too terrifying and too good to be true.

In the parking lot, Sylvia, Letisha, and Sandra piled into Sylvia's Bonneville. After shaking hands with Molly, they took off to get the clinic ready for a full afternoon of patients. They each promised that they would call her that night. As Molly waved goodbye, watching the car drive off, she realized how grateful she was for her new friends. Jayne left a moment later. She had been up all night working her shift at the SuperValu and the fatigue showed on her face. She hugged Molly, promised a phone call that night, said goodbye to Peter, and departed in her old Datsun.

Molly and Peter waved to her as the car disappeared. Gone, they walked together along the sidewalk toward mid downtown. "Lunch?" he said.

"Yes," she said facetiously. "Every time I'm in court I get hungry."

"A sub?"

"Samson's it is."

"I'm buying."

She shook her head disapprovingly. "You always buy."

"I like to."

"Sometime I get to."

Colder stopped and looked at her light green eyes, radiant against the high, midday sun. "Deal. I'll hold you to it."

They began moving again, and after a few more steps Molly broached the subject she most wanted to know about. "What do you think?"

"I think today was a good start. Van Gilder was obviously impressed by that witness that Tyler found. Boyd Messenger."

"No, no. About Lisa, Shirley Mitchell, Rudy Jalowicz."

Colder was morose. "None of them has a chance."

"And they absolutely would have lived if ComHealth's rules were different?"

"If they had had proper care, yes."

Molly just shook her head. "What about Jayne?"

"I know of some stuff a few plastic surgeons are doing out in L.A., Beverly Hills. But it's expensive, and there's no way she could afford it."

"ComHealth should have to pay for it. That poor girl's scars are hideous."

For a moment they walked in silence. The noontime sky was a beautiful blue and the temperature was a perfect seventy-eight degrees. Molly glanced at Colder, who seemed lost in thought. She thought about how much she enjoyed every moment she spent with him. She had even come to feel slightly dependent on him. Her only frustration was that she still couldn't convince herself that he could ever care for her.

"You know, Peter, you've never told me about your family," she said.

Colder realized it was true, and he didn't hesitate. "My dad owned a contracting business. He died six years ago. My mother and brother still live in Arizona. Bryan's three years younger. He's a pilot."

"I'm sorry about your father."

"He was a good man, good father. He took care of my mother, left her well off, and then helped me through college and medical school. In many ways, it was a great source of pride for him. He had come from a large family, and I was the first person ever to go to college, let alone go to medical school."

"He must have been proud."

Colder paused to think about it. "Yeah, I suppose he was."

"It sounds like there's a 'but' in that statement, the way you said it."

Colder looked briefly into her eyes. "No, no 'but.'"

"You should be proud. You're a doctor."

Colder laughed at her statement. "You could do it. You'd probably be better than me."

Molly laughed "No way. But thanks for the compliment."

There was a break in the crowd as they crossed the street. Peter grabbed her arm and guided her through the opening. As he released her, he leaned closer and spoke to her in a serious tone. "I'm not kidding, you know."

His remarks caught her off-guard. She spoke without thinking. "I should have stayed in school."

Colder had been waiting for such an opening. "Why didn't you?"

Molly hesitated. She realized he was asking more than a simple question. "I think people get programmed early in life. They come up with their plans often before they've really considered all the implications. Then everything starts to happen, and they've gone down this path with no way to get back. I guess that's where I'm at."

Peter watched Molly as she spoke. The sunshine highlighted her hair and helped illuminate her face, bringing a vitality to it Peter hadn't noticed before.

Molly continued. "There were a lot of things I thought about when I was younger—what I wanted to be or do. But now I don't know. Its like—maybe it's too late."

Colder stopped and turned her toward him. He placed his hands on her shoulders and stared determinedly in her eyes. "No! Never say that. Life is never over. Even the statement 'life is over' doesn't make sense. Think about it, Molly. The past is only for those who don't realize the potential of the future. Everything is open to you, Molly. Everything."

Molly was both embarrassed and skeptical. "I look at what all these people have done with their lives—famous, you know, and I think about how little I've done."

Colder still held his hands on her shoulders. "Fame may be the tale of the age, Molly, but it's an empty one. Celebrity is almost never achievement."

"I suppose."

Colder let her go and they started walking. "You think the woman who makes millions singing songs in skimpy suits has achieved more than a night nurse with a ward full of patients?"

"No."

"Or the air-brushed magazine cover princess has done anything as meaningful as a single mom?"

They stopped again. This time he put one hand on her shoulder. "Molly, you have it all—brains, looks, determination, and strength. Forget about the spilled milk. Forget about what others have done. Let it all go and dream big. Because there are no limits for you."

She laughed nervously, and they started walking. She felt herself flush. His words and the way he said them stirred her. Even though she was sure he was just being nice, they were the nicest things anyone had ever said. "Thanks," she said, "but it's kind of tough."

"Why?"

"Well, everything's kind of mixed up right now."

"Troy?"

"That's a big part of it."

Colder tried not to sound too curious. "What happened there?"

"I was stupid. Sometimes that saying is true, you think that love will conquer all. Troy was the guy every girl in our school would have killed for. They used to make fools of themselves just to sit near him in a class. When college came, it was like fate that we came together. I think I was just lost in this magical world of make-believe that only I visited. I really believed he was something he wasn't."

"And now?"

"I suppose I still love him. Er, maybe. Actually I don't know what I feel. It's a mixture of things really. I don't feel attracted to him like I once did, but I care about him and I care about the relationship we had. I want him to succeed and to be happy, but I want the same for myself and I'm not sure that could ever be with us together. I guess more than anything, I know I probably hurt him, and I hurt my parents too. I know I'll always feel bad about that."

Colder decided not to press, noting that the wedding ring still was on her hand. He was disappointed to hear she still had feelings for Troy, but he also understood the confusion that went with failed relationships.

"Have you heard from your parents?" he asked as he again guided her by the arm through an opening in the crowd.

Molly shook her head. "No. That will never be the same. All of this nearly killed them. My dad. He'll never accept something like this. The church, well, there are things that people just simply don't do. Abortion is one."

"What did he say?"

Molly measured her words. "You know you don't really debate a person who has the answers that they want. My dad is comfortable with his beliefs. He has no need to question what he thinks. He has no fear of being wrong or even any thought that he could be wrong." Molly stopped and then started again. "But I do think that's how he learned to judge."

"How's that?"

"People are always judging each other, all while claiming they're not. I think that's where they get it, from being taught that there are answers to everything and that if everyone just thought the same, it would all be okay."

"What about you?"

"My dad always said that there are things that only God could understand or forgive. This would be one."

"But you're his daughter."

Molly scoffed. "That doesn't matter. It's about principles and morals. He would see it as having disgraced God, disgraced him, and myself. I'm not deserving of his forgiveness."

"Only God's?"

Molly's eyebrows went up involuntarily. "Yeah, I suppose. But only with appropriate punishment."

Colder dropped it. "What about your mother?"

"She started in pro-life about fifteen years ago. It has been her life. Meetings, fund-raisers. For me to do this? It's worse than if I died. If I'd died, there'd at least be some kind of strange glory for her, but with this, there's only embarrassment and anger."

"What about her though?"

Molly paused and scratched her head. "I think life is simple when you make it simple. She believes things like, The poor are poor because they don't work hard enough. Your life is bad because you screwed up. To her, it all boils down to hard work and faith. If you follow those two, bad things don't happen unless God somehow intended it."

"And how do you fit in?"

"I don't any more. I really don't. But, in this, I learned that everyone needs a reward. Sometimes the only reward in a situation is the ability to sit in judgment and to pretend to suffer its consequences. Like martyrdom. And here I am a consequence. It's a matter of principle for them."

Colder held his tongue, choosing not to say anything about the principles of piety that allowed the sacrifice of a daughter.

"No," she mumbled. "They'll never be back."

"Principle more important than people?"

"Actually, I think it's pride. One thing I learned is that when people say it's principle, it's usually pride."

The crowd began to thicken even more as they neared the corner deli that advertised the largest sub sandwiches in Minnesota. The noontime rush seemed to begin fifteen minutes early, and a crush of power suits and high heels suddenly descended upon them. Hurrying to the curb, they beat a large rush that appeared poised to invade the next half block and fill the half-dozen restaurants that catered to the noon traffic. Colder timed the light, and two seconds before green, he grabbed her by the arm. They bolted across the street and into the deli, claiming the last remaining table.

"Nice move," panted Molly as she sat down.

"You can do that when you're in Olympic shape like me," he said puffing up his chest.

She reached underneath the round table and grabbed at his midriff, her fingers locating at least two inches more than he would have liked. "Well, almost Olympic shape," he laughed.

"I know that condition well."

A waitress was there immediately, her manner pleasant but hurried, as if to hint that they wanted a quick turnover during the noon hour. Molly ordered a club sub and Colder a seafood. Each had chips and Cokes. The orders appeared almost before they could restart their conversation, and one minute later, the waitress had left them the check. In ten minutes, their leisurely lunch was over and they rejoined the army of migrating power suits and high heels marching in the noontime sunlight.

As they walked, Colder thought about their conversation earlier. He wanted to get back to it. "What's next for you, Molly? After all this? I mean, your plans. Or bigger, what's your dream?"

"I don't know," she laughed. "I'm still working on it."

"Seriously."

Molly's smile evaporated. It had been so long since anyone had shown interest in her life that she didn't know how to react. "I suppose happiness, success, good health, like everyone else."

"That's your dream?"

"I suppose." It was a feeble lie, but it was all she could muster.

He scolded her playfully. "That's got to be part of it. But you have to think bigger."

Molly laughed weakly. "I'll try."

Colder looked philosophical. "How about—"

She interrupted him. "No-no. Enough about me. What about you—your dream?"

Colder laughed. "Now that was a good escape."

Her eyes shone. "Thank you. But that was no answer."

Colder turned serious as they continued to walk amongst the crowd. "I don't know. I suppose I dream of making a difference. Doing something to stop this managed care insanity."

"Like crushing ComHealth?"

"Yeah, right," he chuckled.

"It's a good cause, though. A good dream."

"I've thought a lot about it," he said. "It really is something I believe in. And even if it's all probably futile, well, sometimes a cause is still worth fighting for."

"Yes."

They stopped. Molly stood close to him and looked into his eyes. She could see the conviction and the passion. With every moment and word she felt more drawn to him. "I understand that," she said, "but what about happiness and success?"

Colder was pensive. "You know, when I was a kid, I dreamed of being a great man. I suppose all little boys have that dream. But as I got older, I realized that there was nothing special about me. I was just like everyone else. I also learned something about life, that happiness is only in the heart and success is only in the mind. And it was up to me to find both. And I will."

"I'm sure your mother thinks she has a great son."

He laughed. "She thinks she has a great dog, too."

Molly slapped his arm, "C'mon."

"No. It's not me. Greatness occurs only when fate meets a person willing to sacrifice all, not for glory, but for the knowledge that the pride earned by sacrifice may be the only consolation. Posterity over the present. People over personal interest." Colder looked glum. "No, it's beyond me. I just hope that whatever happens to me, and the clinic, that someone better and stronger than me will pick up the baton."

Molly barely resisted her desire to hug him. "I think many others are starting to carry the baton, too."

Colder's sad look faded. He glanced at his watch. They both remembered what was about to happen. "I think you're right."

A moving car pulled up about twenty feet behind her. "We've got company," he said.

She turned and watched as the young driver put two quarters in a meter before ambling toward them. "Is that her?" she asked, gazing at the pretty, slim, brunette.

"Yes."

It would be his first meeting with the reporter since the awards dinner a week before, but in the meantime Colder had learned a great deal. The morning after their meeting, he had asked Sandra to track down any information she could on the erstwhile reporter who had trailed him the night of Hutchins' award dinner. Sandra's college roommate still worked for the *Star Tribune* newspaper, and within four hours, anything he had ever wanted to know about the cigarette-smoking, Gen X critic with an armor-piercing tongue was available to him.

Marcia Sullivan was twenty-four and originally from Yankton, South Dakota. The youngest of three daughters, she had gone to the University of Iowa with majors in journalism and political science. Her father owned a liquor store; her mother was a homemaker; her sisters, a lawyer and an engineer. The *Star Tribune* had been her second job. The first was with the *Minot Daily News* in North Dakota.

The reporter came to Minneapolis with glowing recommendations, but to the editors, her first year proved to be a bit of a disappointment. Her latest review said that she seemed to lack the aggressiveness needed to succeed in journalism. Following the negative review four months before, she was placed on probation. Apparently always viewed as a talented writer, the hard stories seemed to elude her. According to Sandra's friend, two months ago the managing editor threatened Marcia with her job. The experience left Marcia frustrated and angry; now the young reporter seemed to be practicing the caustic, crusted affect of the jaded veteran who sees conspiracies like McCarthy saw communists. According to Sandra's friend, the manner was an act, a deliberate effort to save her job. Sandra also learned something else about Marcia Sullivan. She was scrupulously honest, reliable, and deserving of a break. Peter Colder was pleased. Marcia Sullivan was perfect.

"How are ya, Dr. C?" she asked like a seasoned pro.

"It's nice to see you again, Marcia," he replied, shaking her hand.

"You must be Molly Loomis," she said, turning toward her. "Marcia Sullivan."

"Pleased to meet you."

Marcia shook her hand and gave Molly a quick glance, her eyes instantly processing everything from clothes to posture. She then returned to Colder.

"I understand that Judge Van Gilder ruled in your favor this morning, Molly. The summary judgment motion was rejected, and there will be a trial. Any comment?"

Colder and Molly stopped, each looking at the reporter's eyes that hid nothing. "Sorry," Molly said.

Colder had asked the reporter to join them, not telling her what the meeting would be about.

Marcia was polite. "Well, it's very nice of you to ask me to join you here at precisely 12:45, but maybe I might know why?"

"In a second," Colder replied. "Let's walk."

As they started moving into the thick crowd, Marcia began talking. "You know, Dr. Colder, in all fairness, I'm not sure we were quite even the other night. You were quite generous, so maybe I'll offer up something I've learned."

Colder was surprised. "I'm not sure that's true, but anything you know I'm glad to hear."

"Stanton Ross. One of Hutchins' four disciples."

"Yes."

"I have it from a good source that each of the past four weeks, he's sold over two hundred thousand shares of ComHealth stock."

Colder stopped, bumping into Molly and setting off a chain reaction of minor collisions before the crowd began moving around them. "He's sold two hundred thousand shares in four weeks?"

"I thought you might be interested."

"How much does he own?" asked Molly, as the crowd forced them to start forward again.

"Don't know that. Probably millions."

"Two hundred thousand shares?" Colder was calculating their value and the numbers were boggling his mind.

"It gets better," continued Marcia. "He's got a sell order at forty-two."

"What are they at now?"

"They're up four in the past week. They're at fifty now," she replied.

At Third Avenue, they turned and the crowd thinned to the point where they could stand unbothered. Colder leaned back against a brick building and rocked back and forth. "What do you think that means?" he asked.

"May not be Markham," said Marcia. "It may be Ross. He's a Hutchins' favorite and just as capable of eating his young."

Molly looked confused. "But couldn't that mean nearly anything? Leaving the company, needs the money, worried about the price?"

"Yes, it could," admitted Colder. "It could also simply be the first time that he's been able to sell his options. It might be a red herring."

Marcia Sullivan's smile was irrepressible. "Except one thing," she continued. "He sold the shares short."

Colder grinned sickly. "I have no idea what that means. The only stock I ever owned was one share of *Playboy* when I was fifteen."

"Selling short means that the shares you sell are borrowed instead of your own. You can make a nice, healthy profit if the stock drops and you buy back at a lower price."

"He's taking his money and running," said Molly.

"And," continued Marcia, "it would also appear that he's betting that the stock will drop."

Colder was thoughtful. "Anyone else doing it?"

"Nope."

"He may be worth watching," Colder said, understating the obvious.

"I thought you might say that."

They began walking again, moving past a publishing company and an old warehouse that was being renovated into an art gallery. For a few minutes, they walked in silence before Colder stopped. "Marcia, I want you to know that I did a little checking on my own about you."

The reporter did not appear surprised. "I'd have told you if you asked."

"I think it's only fair that you know that—and that I know almost everything—"

"Please, not everything," she interrupted, the look of mock horror on her face quickly destroying the brass image she had labored to cultivate.

"Well, probably not everything," he admitted.

Her eyes narrowed as if preparing to question them. "Okay. Quiz. What was my biggest article?" she asked.

"'State Dog Show at the Metrodome.'"

"Oh, God," she mumbled. "I'm so embarrassed."

"Don't be," replied Colder. "My confidential source thinks highly of you."

"Then you know—"

"Yes."

She turned away and walked a short distance before pausing and coming back. Her tough exterior was completely gone. "Maybe journalism isn't for me—really."

"Don't say that. I think there's room for more than the stereotype," said Molly.

"I don't know," replied Marcia. "Sometimes I just don't know."

Colder stepped forward. "I was always told that honesty and integrity counted for something."

She laughed. "I think they do, as long as you combine them with results."

Colder pulled the slips of paper from his pocket and handed them to her. It was the names of the four patients they had visited, plus six more that Colder had visited on his own.

"What are these?"

"The names of people with addresses and their phone numbers. In each case, ComHealth's tactics led to unnecessary, severe complications or terminal illness. The medical record numbers are there, and all of the patients have agreed to talk to you. If you need assistance, I will corroborate the medical details."

Marcia's knees buckled and she struggled to talk. "I don't know what to say."

Colder patted her once on the shoulder. "I only ask one favor."

"Anything."

"Make it the best work you've ever done. For some of these people, this is their epitaph."

"It will be done," she managed. "I swear it."

Colder took Molly by the arm, and they began walking away. "Keep in touch," he said.

Marcia did not reply. Her eyes filled with tears, and emotion threatened to overtake her. She struggled to formulate a single thought. She took a deep breath and dabbed at her eyes as Molly and Colder disappeared into the crowd.

She looked down at her trembling hands and the slips of paper with the names and phone numbers of the ComHealth patients. The enormity of what was happening continued to sweep upon her. She felt weak and dizzy, unable to even breathe.

    She staggered back and gazed down at the slips of paper. She knew that Colder had given her a miracle and also the greatest challenge of her life. But more importantly, Marcia suddenly recognized what she had in her hands. The first was obvious—her career. But the second was what caused her knees to buckle. It was the atomic bomb.

Book Two

Overlord

Chapter Eighteen

August 11

Five days later, the bomb exploded when the first of Marcia Sullivan's articles splashed across the front page of the Minneapolis *Star Tribune*. Marcia told the story of Lisa Bowman and her impending, but once preventable, death from cervical cancer, as well as promising in the following days the story of Shirley Mitchell and her breast cancer, Rudy Jalowicz and his renal cancer, Jayne McCall and her disfiguring facial scars, as well as several others She had lit the fuse and watched the bomb detonate. The paper promised two consecutive weeks of articles, including not only those Marcia referred to in her first article, but also a man whose stroke had gone untreated with the new drug TPA, resulting in major disability, and two men whose heart attacks had resulted in death because their symptoms did not fit ComHealth's over-the-telephone criteria for an ER visit. "Death In the Great HMO" the series was called. Her writing was potent. The stories were true. The implications were overpowering.

Shortly after the morning paper began circulating, the activity started. First local radio stations began reporting the story, catching thousands of stunned commuters on their way to work. Within an hour, local television cameras arrived at the IDS building and stationed personnel at every entrance. By 9:00 A.M., the Community Health One offices were receiving over five hundred calls a minute and the overwhelmed ComHealthOne telephone system ceased to function, converting to an emergency recording that pleasantly led all callers through a circular touch-tone menu and ultimately to disconnection. Quickly, within the offices of the largest HMO in the country, chaos reigned. Ten receptionists quit in a huff, forty repairman were called to try to fix the battered phone system, and more importantly, H. Carter Hutchins, having avoided the reporters to this point, called an emergency meeting of the top executives.

Preston Cooley arrived first at the IDS Tower, but when his white limousine was immediately accosted by a battalion of screaming reporters, he drove off without even stopping. Other executives suffered the same fate, finding themselves unable even to get to their offices. By cell phone, Cooley reached Hutchins. The CEO was at breakfast with the governor. Cooley's news sent Hutchins into a fury, and within an hour, as reporters' calls continued to come like rain, all five of the top ComHealth executives gathered at their favorite hangout. Harley Whitfield and Jackson Barnes joined them.

The hundred-year-old Twin Cities Club sat as an offshoot of Kellogg Avenue on a small expanse of downtown real estate that amounted to more than an entire city block. Located within a thick grove of trees sitting at the top of the hundred-foot slope to the Mississippi River, the back of the club offered a perfect view of the skyline of St. Paul. At the end of a private cul-de-sac, the club was Minneapolis's most exclusive, with membership admission rules unpublished and subject to intense speculation. The only known facts were that a combination of birth, wealth, or substantial notoriety was a well-established and absolute necessity. To the upper crust of Minneapolis society, membership was a requirement. At the moment, though, it was merely a convenient hiding spot.

"Who the hell did it?" thundered Hutchins, his eyes red with anger.

"We don't know," replied T. Wilson Bolger, the ComHealth Executive Vice President of Human Resources.

"I'm sure it was the doctors," said Markham. "Who else?"

"Fire them all," said Hutchins, trying to control his anger, but swiping at a stack of papers sitting on the polished oak table and sending them flying. "By sundown."

"I don't know, Carter," Cooley said. "We don't have any proof of breach of contract and it may make the situation even worse."

The lawyers were unusually quiet. The junior partners accompanying them waited for the two senior men to speak. Jackson Barnes was calm. He was combing his hair leisurely and looking at himself in a mirror at the room's far wall. "As your legal counsel, I would agree with Preston."

Hutchins paid no attention. He was busy raging away. "And who the hell is Marcia Sullivan? Who is this little bitch?"

"I talked with Ed Weinshel at the *Star Tribune* about an hour ago," began Stanton Ross, the ComHealth President.

"Great," Hutchins scoffed, tossing a wad of paper onto the floor. "The editor? Son of a bitch. Like he's a friend. Goddam liberal communist. He never met a man with a dollar that he liked."

Ross continued. "Weinshel told me Marcia Sullivan is their chief medical reporter. She's only been with them a year, but she's already the head of her department."

"Shit. What else?"

"She only did two years of college because as a reporter for the student newspaper, she kept exposing corruption in the administration."

Hutchins rolled his eyes.

"She speaks seven languages, has a tongue that could slice a diamond, the mentality of a hungry pit bull, and her nickname is 'Jaws' because she likes the taste of very rare meat."

"Christ," Cooley mumbled.

"Weinshel even told me she has 'Bitch' tattooed on her biceps."

"Unbelievable," Hutchins grunted.

"Goddam lez, I'm sure," Whitfield said.

"Gets worse. Weinshel told me her senior thesis was entitled 'Fingers in the Dyke: The Fall of Heterosexuality and the Coming Lesbian Revolution.'"

"I think I'm going to puke," Hutchins groaned.

"Wait a minute," Cooley said. "I thought you said he told you she only did two years of college."

Jackson Barnes finished combing his hair and then leaned close to the mirror to inspect his teeth. "I tell you what the little bitch needs."

Markham had his doubts. "You sure any of this is right? I talked to Penny Wickman at KSTP, and she said that Sullivan is twenty-four, has a boyfriend, and was hanging on for dear life at the paper."

"As if TV is our friend," Cooley said.

Hutchins ignored both and looked at Ross. "What else did Weinshel say?"

"He asked me why we didn't just shoot our patients. He said his cousin could get us bullets wholesale."

Bolger groaned, gazing out the second-story window toward the river. "I can see the media is determined to be fair about this entire thing."

"They just smell blood on successful hands." Whitfield massaged his vanity by preening the silver hairs at his temples. "It happens now—or later. It doesn't matter."

Markham looked annoyed. "Sorry to be so stupid, Counselor, but I'd like to hear your thoughts."

Harley Whitfield rose and took one of the toasted bagels that had been left on the silver tray in the middle of the table. He took one bite, and appearing to savor it, held it in his mouth for a moment before swallowing. "Simple, really. The truth is that they can't win this case in the courtroom, so they'll take a few shots at us in the media and when they lose, they'll be able to proclaim that the system failed and walk away with a ton of publicity. That's all it is. Nothing more."

"You think it's all about this Loomis thing? There wasn't a single word about her!"

"Certainly. And it will blow over. These things always do."

"What about the individual cases?" asked Hutchins, still pacing and not convinced. "Are we liable?"

Bolger stood. He took a computer printout from his briefcase and laid it on the table. "I've only had an hour, but some of the boys were able to get me a little on them. Apparently there were no red flags on the charts when they went for review. It appears, to this point, that every procedure was followed perfectly."

"Who are these people in the articles?" Markham asked. He was the last to arrive and hadn't read the paper.

Hutchins sipped at his coffee, his anger finally waning. "They only published one today, but they have 'em coming throughout the week. One's a girl who's pissed because she's got a couple of scars on her face. She claims we're at fault because we wouldn't authorize the right medicine. Then there's a woman with breast cancer who says she should have been allowed to have a mammogram before age sixty."

"Christ. One in eight women get it. Someone's got to be the one!"

Hutchins continued, "A girl who skipped her pap smear and now has cervical cancer and a guy who has kidney cancer who says he should have gotten a blood count or a urinalysis."

"Who cares what the patients say? They don't know what's going on anyway," said Ross.

"Did the same doctor corroborate their statements?" asked Harley Whitfield.

"Yes," said Hutchins.

"Told you," said Whitfield. "This Loomis thing."

"I knew it," said Markham pointedly. "None of ours would even dream of doing that. They know the consequences."

"That damn Colder," Hutchins muttered.

Barnes, finished with combing his hair and flossing his teeth, turned and ambled to the table, where he picked up a cherry Danish and began cutting it into fourths. "It doesn't matter. I know what Harley's thinking, and he's right. Colder's just one guy who has an ax to grind with us. It actually works out well for us. He can easily be discredited."

"This isn't a trial, Jack," said Hutchins. "This is business. It's PR."

Barnes' brow became lined as he unleashed a devilish grin. "That's what makes it even easier."

There was a knock at the door, followed by the entrance of four more attorneys, each in uniform navy suits and fashionable ties. A cross-looking T. Quentin Cox led the pack, followed by three associates.

Whitfield shook Cox's hand and nodded to the other lawyers, who chose to stand near the wall. From the associates' manner they were clearly the slave labor, each hoping for a partnership one day, but now merely workers hoping to impress. They all appeared to be in their late twenties with suits they could not afford and tired, but attentive, looks. They stood as if at attention, notepads in hand, poised and ready.

"What do you have, Quentin?" Barnes asked.

"I've prepared a press release to be handed out two hours before our press conference at one o' clock. It will emphasize the slanderous nature of the allegations, affirm that in each of these cases, standard practice was followed throughout, and reaffirm our commitment to quality care for each and every patient."

"What about legal action?" Bolger asked.

"My recommendation would be that we suggest it may take place against Dr. Colder and the newspaper."

"Exactly," said Barnes. "Only a suggestion, not a threat. We want benevolence with vindication. We express our deepest sympathies to the families and the patients for their misfortune. Then we rattle a few sabers behind the scenes."

"When is the second Loomis hearing?" Hutchins asked. "Isn't it at the same time?"

"Yes," Barnes replied. "One o'clock."

"Good thinking," Markham said, appreciating the tactic.

"You're deciding on witnesses today?" Stanton Ross asked.

"Hopefully."

"We just want to get this Loomis thing over with as fast as possible," Markham said.

"Agreed," said Hutchins.

"One thought I had," Cox said. "I think we may need to consider how we would like to portray the good doctor's role in this thing. A suggestion could be made that his affair with Ms. Loomis is both a conflict of interest and another basis for these allegations."

"Is that true?" Hutchins asked.

"Not substantially," Cox admitted. "But not a total lie either, and it might make for interesting reading."

"Then just suggest it," offered an associate.

"And one final thing," said Cox. "We use the press conference as a pulpit to categorically deny that any illegal, inappropriate, or unusual action was taken in the case of Ms. Loomis. We say that we sympathize with her, profoundly regret the course that her life has taken, but that we simply behaved in a way that was not only within our rights but in keeping with the best interests of all of our subscribers."

"God, can this guy toss it," Bolger salivated to no one in particular.

Cox continued as if he hadn't heard the compliment. "If we don't make the connection, the press will. We should anticipate it. Be proactive."

"I agree," Markham said.

The two senior partners waved their hands, forcefully disagreeing. "No way," Whitfield said. "Don't connect them."

"The Loomis thing is a nonissue," Barnes replied. "Save anything we have for a trial if it comes to that. Right now we don't bring her up. Remember, she doesn't have a case. Saying anything more just gets the media interested. Connecting Colder with Loomis? Too risky. Right now no one's paying any attention to Molly Loomis, and we want it that way."

"The best thing we can do with Loomis is get it over with," said Whitfield. "And fast."

It was clear from the senior partners' tone that there would be no debate from their juniors. While Cox sizzled from the rebuke, the ComHealth executives accepted Barnes' position.

Barnes looked straight at Hutchins. "Carter, it would be my recommendation that all of you make an appearance at the office as soon as possible. Just say a few words to the press on your way in, and then tell them that everything will be discussed in detail at the press conference. We'll take it from there."

"How would you like me to handle it, sir?" Cox asked Barnes. He was already burning, but now he was approaching combustion as he realized what was happening.

"Harley and I have quite a bit of experience in dealing with the press. Perhaps we should handle the press conference while you and Ace finish with the Loomis hearing."

"Very good, sir," he said.

"You've done wonderful work on such short notice," Hutchins said to Cox, in a skillful attempt to diffuse the moment.

"Thank you, Carter," Cox replied, taking full credit as his three exhausted associates watched recent history be rewritten. "I try."

"We'll convene after the press conference. Somewhere around four."

"The hearing will take about three hours. I should be there by four," Cox commented, making sure he was included.

"Good."

A moment later, Cox left, as did the associates and all executives except Hutchins and Markham. Barnes and Whitfield remained. Hutchins suddenly seemed edgy again. "Jack, Harley, there's one other little thing. Tell them, Greg."

For twenty minutes, Markham obliged, telling the stricken attorneys everything about Fragile X while the lawyers listened in horror. When Markham was finished, he plopped back into a chair, exhausted. "That's the whole of it, gentlemen. Not a single thing else."

"Where are the files?" Barnes asked, his indigo eyes staring fiercely at the young man.

Markham leaned back as if moved by the intensity of the glare. "There are none."

"None at all?" Whitfield asked.

"No," Hutchins assured. "The only copies were in the hard drives of two computers within the offices. They're all gone."

Markham nodded, confirming his boss' statement.

"Any chance anyone could have gotten them?"

Hutchins sipped again at the drink. "None."

"Good," said Whitfield, rapidly adding up the number of laws that had been broken. "Then it won't matter what happens. As long as there is no direct link, they have no connection to you."

"What about the journal?"

Whitfield was skillfully formulating a plan. "What about it? A company whose board you happened to sit on bought it, but didn't feel it would be profitable and junked it. A few, or one copy of the obscure final issue contains an article that a few wishful thinkers would like to think ComHealth took to heart, but it can't be proven. It's a nothing. It doesn't mean anything."

"Good," said Hutchins, relieved.

"Again, though," Barnes asked. "is there any way that this guy, O'Reilly, could link you to it?"

"No," Markham said.

"It doesn't even matter legally," said Whitfield.

Barnes, too, was preparing the stonewall. "I agree with that. From a legal point of view, there is nothing to worry about. But I think we all know that if this guy came forward, he could raise quite a stink."

Whitfield shook his head in disagreement. "It would be merely wild, unsubstantiated charges. No threat at all."

Barnes put down his pen, wiped a few beads of sweat from his upper lip and looked toward Hutchins. "Maybe. But what about the guy, Carter?"

"He won't be coming forward. I can assure you."

Barnes nodded, accepting the statement at face value, and said nothing more.

"Another question," said Whitfield, having taken no notes and now massaging his drink. "Why did you do it?"

"We're merely at the cutting edge," said Hutchins. "The public is going to have to accept the fact that the days of red ink are over. Were it not for cost containment, there would be no chance for health care in the future. Although the beginnings of any revolution appear draconian, the results are necessary. Here it is no different. The fat is coming off the calf."

Markham nodded in approval. "'Wisdom denotes pursuing of the best ends by the best means,' Frances Hutcheson."

Hutchins gazed out over the river as a small collection of gulls swirled in the wind. "I prefer the abridged version of that comment, despite the bleeding hearts' objections."

"The end justifies the means?"

"Yes." Hutchins launched into a harangue. "Think about it. We are at a critical point in our history. We can no longer pay for what we want. Millions have chronic conditions for which their premiums would never cover their costs. Millions with lifestyle-induced disease, cancers, arteriosclerosis, arthritis from obesity. Individuals all demanding care without the ability to pay. And their only option? To have others pay for them. The system we now know can no longer exist. Our only hope lies with cost containment. Controlling access, creating incentives to provide less care and perhaps, most importantly, minimizing risk factors that would expose the system to unnecessary costs."

"What exactly does that last one mean?" Whitfield asked.

"Fragile X would just be the beginning. If not now, sometime in the near future. If not us, then someone else. Maybe the country's not ready now, but it will be. The truth is that that reality we just mentioned will dictate policy, and cost will dictate reality."

Barnes sat back, rubbing his eyes from the combination of the long day and the alcohol. "I think this conversation should represent the end of the discussion of this Fragile X subject, gentlemen. It is, and should remain, a closed matter."

Whitfield nodded and then looked squarely at Markham. "We'll be ready should anything unexpected arise," he said. "However, it sounds as if there is little chance of that."

Markham remained silent, his confident expression radiating assurance.

Five minutes later, with their plan to smother Fragile X complete, they shook hands and the attorneys left. As the door closed, Hutchins turned and faced the window, Markham at his side. Hutchins and Markham remained edgy in the face of Marcia Sullivan's article and their admission to their attorneys. "Any word on our friend?" Hutchins asked.

"No."

"There will be soon."

"I'm sure you're right." said Markham.

Hutchins turned to face him. "Dr. Colder is becoming quite a problem."

Markham said nothing for a moment, instead looking at the emotionless face. "Yes, he is."

Hutchins nodded. "I'm glad we see things the same way."

Markham remained cool. He was finishing a donut and wiped his napkin across his mouth to make sure no crumbs remained. "I'll take care of it."

Hutchins nodded again, opened the door, and left.

James Patrick O'Reilly watched the press conference from his trailer, deep within the woods near Annandale, Minnesota, sixty miles west of Minneapolis. The dilapidated brown structure, its peeling paint no longer concealing its numerous holes, was hidden within the lush underbrush of the McClintock

Forest, a nature reserve accessible only by a single gravel road that wound through a treacherous course of deep ravines and a series of fallen trees. The seldom-used road was the only public access to Cedar Lake, an unoccupied lake too shallow to support game fish. It was declared part of the reserve in 1948. Since that time, it had become a sanctuary to various birds and mammals, rarely visited by man. Although a handful of abandoned cabins still surrounded the lake, their structures were all failing badly and overgrown with weeds. Only the gradually deteriorating gravel road hinted at a once-vibrant area.

O'Reilly's cabin sat six hundred yards back into the woods to the west of the lake, completely hidden from view. His part-time home for the preceding two years, the decaying structure erected sixty years before had no running water or phone. Only a carefully maintained well and a smoldering split-stone fireplace gave the casual observer any indication of human habitation. The wood structure was nearly covered with ivy. Its north end, dented from the fall of a nearby tree the summer before, had housed O'Reilly in the summer, the thick wood surroundings providing a nearly perfect cover. But it was deeper in the woods, hidden well within an old wooden barn, that he did his work.

Inside the barn was his rust-colored 1964 Chevrolet pickup. A relic that gave every appearance of abandonment, it was caked with dirt, bordered by bales of hay and without a front left fender. Rust covered the body, and little paint remained, but the vehicle started on command and daily made its trip into town. In the back of the barn, the hay bales concealed a small room, carefully constructed, insulated and accessible only from a tunnel underneath the truck. A trap door led to a four-step ladder and body-sized tunnel that he had carved through the clay soil. The tunnel, only twenty feet long, led to a second trap door and then into a ten-by-ten room where he had spent much of two years, hiding, watching, and waiting.

A television hooked to a satellite dish concealed in a nearby tree, its cable buried, provided his look at the outside world. This pirated signal was of secondary importance and merely for entertainment. A second dish, five feet away, allowed him to monitor cell phones and cordless conversations.

The rest of the room held an old, tattered couch on which he often slept and a small school desk he had picked up at a local flea market. The desk appeared to have no use, as its chair was too small for an adult and its top appeared not to open, having been bolted shut from the underside. But to O'Reilly, the old desk was of great importance. Inside were the two things that threatened yet at the same time could save his life—a series of computer disks and the last copy of the July 1997 issue of the *British Journal of Developmental Genetics*.

James Patrick O'Reilly had greeted the morning paper with glee, its screaming headline of "Death in the Great HMO" bringing tears to his eyes. The scathing article itself and its promise of additional installments over the next two weeks were only part of his reason to celebrate. Almost lost in Marcia Sullivan's stories was the small article on page three that she had also written on the continuing investigation of the mysterious deaths of three scientists over two years before. Three scientists who had worked for ComHealthOne.

O'Reilly trembled as he read the paper. His morning trip into the small town of Annandale had brought him food for the day and a newspaper whose headline had nearly scalded his eyes. He had waited two years for the moment to come and in the electrifying black print stretching across the front page, he saw hope for himself for the first time. For years he had hidden, his future destroyed by a discovery they had turned against him. For years he had run, twice nearly dying, by car and by bullet, only to survive by divine providence. The scar on his forehead was a testament to his luck. The crushed and partially paralyzed left hand was a badge of honor in his ongoing war.

He read and reread the articles. They were wonderful, thoroughly riddled with a talented journalist's flair for skillfully mixing fact with innuendo while presenting the blend as an evolving story. They were beautiful. Finally putting the paper down when the press conference began, he watched as Jackson Barnes, Harley Whitfield, and H. Carter Hutchins took turns spinning a yarn with pleading explanations of personal hurt, individual indignity, and calculated compassion. They even spiced each triumphant spin with a blast of managed care salesmanship that would make even a used car vendor blush. In amazement, O'Reilly watched as the three men whose daily fashion bill exceeded the average American monthly wage took turns forcing each other from the microphone, competing for leadership in sound-bite potential and ridiculous exaggeration. They pontificated about the needs of mothers and children. They preached about the needs of the elderly. They reverently nodded in synchrony as each talked about the hope for the future and the sorrow they felt for these tragic patients who had neglected to care for themselves.

Hutchins' voice cracked with emotion as he spoke. "It is my sincere hope that we can make sense of this sadness and understand that these tragedies have occurred not because of managed care, but in spite of it. Disease prevention remains the cornerstone of the managed care philosophy. It is only with prevention that we truly find a cure."

O'Reilly found irony in the words. As Harley Whitfield took the microphone and rambled on about the virtues and accomplishments of ComHealthOne as a provider and innovator, O'Reilly removed the screws from the bottom of the desk and opened its wooden top. No longer listening to the diatribe, he sat on the couch and thumbed through the pages of the journal that had changed his life and cost five others theirs. He looked at the title. It was not pretentious or even notable. It merely mentioned a protein, a single strand of amino acids that threatened to change the world.

Hutchins talked of prevention. O'Reilly shook his head. Prevention. No, there was more than irony in the word. There was an incomprehensible injustice. O'Reilly knew that the pursuit of Fragile X was indeed preventive medicine. Hutchins spoke the truth in that regard. It would prevent illness and it would save money. But what Hutchins had failed to mention was that Fragile X was also designed to eliminate over ten million Americans.

At 5:00 P.M., Judge John Van Gilder's gavel struck for the second time in the matter of Loomis versus ComHealthOne, and within seconds the small courtroom was deserted. The hearing had been two hours long. Two motions had been argued, the witness lists had been presented, and, most importantly, a trial date had been set. To Tyler Briggs's and Marcus Sanders', as well as ComHealth attorneys T. Quentin Cox's and Ace Farnsworth's slight surprise, the hearing had also been apparently unnoticed by the press.

A. J. "Ace" Farnsworth was another of ComHealth's band of young, talented and marginally corrupt lawyers. But to law-abiding attorneys, Farnsworth was the champion. He was thirty-five, good-looking, and redefined ethics on a daily basis. Receiving alimony from three impoverished ex-wives and paying less in taxes than an unemployed mother of five, Farnsworth prided himself on being Barnes and Whitfield's rising star. Seen as both clever and ruthless, he had managed to quickly amass a fortune by robbing ex-spouses and aggressively trading in the stock market with what struck seasoned pros as impossible luck. Neither Briggs nor Sanders had been surprised when the Ace, articulate and sociopathic with a telegenic charisma, showed up as their newest opponent.

Both Cox and Farnsworth were under orders from Barnes and Whitfield to avoid the press despite the junior partner's protestations that it would be better to "proactively" deal with the Loomis lawsuit. That rebuke was made worse by the fact that both of the junior partners felt slighted by the senior attorneys' unwillingness to share the public glory that was arriving with the media attention surrounding Marcia Sullivan's articles. However, as soon as the two ComHealth lawyers left the courthouse, they realized that something had changed. The reporters had noticed. Glory was everywhere. The cameras had arrived.

To the first questions, Cox and Farnsworth declined comment, following the orders of their bosses. But realizing that the press had already made the connection between the Loomis lawsuit and the newspaper articles, and certain that Briggs and Sanders were feeding the press freely, Cox and Farnsworth eagerly gave up their silent acts and launched into sermons that contained everything from moral decay in America to their own special relationships with God. The score of reporters listened eagerly, wrote furiously, interrupted frequently, and occasionally attempted to offer questions to the filibustering pair.

"There is only justice when justice is sought," Farnsworth had roared when asked why it wouldn't be cheaper for ComHealth to pay the claim than to fight a lawsuit. "It is this abuse of the legal system that contributes to the rising costs for all law-abiding citizens. Someone must assume the high moral ground and someone must speak the truth about what our founding fathers had intended for the justice system in this country. That justice is blind, affordable, available, and not influenced by indecent threats that border on blackmail."

"What about the ComHealth patients in the newspaper?" came a question.

Cox stole the microphone. "I can't comment on that. But I can say that all patients within the ComHealth system receive nothing but the finest care and that all cases are reviewed with careful scrutiny and the most demanding of standards. The cases to which you are referring have undergone rigorous review, and in all instances, all standards of care were noted to have been met. What we have here is a tragic situation of dying, desperate people, with whom we can all sympathize, taking out their frustrations against the organization that has stood by them during their time of need. Although we bear no malice and share their grief, we understand that our company's reputation is its most precious commodity and that we may need to seek legal relief."

"Is that a threat?" asked the reporter.

Ace Farnsworth stepped in front of his partner. "Yes. It is true that we are contemplating legal action against the paper and several others. Our damages related to this libelous action may be substantial. In any action we pursue, we may need to ask in excess of nine figures."

The flock of reporters gasped. "How much?" asked a young woman.

"Over one hundred million?" asked another reporter.

"Possibly."

The reporters wrote even faster as Cox continued, detailing the various charges of slander and libel that he was spontaneously considering. His adrenaline continued to pump at the sight of the live TV. Inside, he was glad that the press had made the connection between the Loomis case and the newspaper story. Farnsworth felt the same way. He depicted the Loomis case as historic and monumental.

"Mr. Farnsworth," followed up a reporter, "if this case has no merit, then how can it be historic and monumental?"

Farnsworth ignored the question, but roared on. "With regard to Molly Loomis, I say this. She is an angry young woman with a deeply checkered past who has suffered greatly as a result of her poor judgment. We sympathize with her in the fact that she has hurt herself, but despite our sympathies, we cannot allow injustice."

"Injustice?"

"Yes. And more importantly, despite our generosity, we cannot allow greed to punctuate the system."

"Greed?" asked a reporter.

"Generosity?" asked another.

"With Molly Loomis, ComHealth simply followed the contract as it is written. The company has stayed with the other patients throughout treatment. All of the bills have been paid."

"Isn't that your responsibility and not an act of generosity?" asked the second reporter.

"Er-um, technically, yes, but we have also been most generous," mumbled Cox.

Marcia Sullivan emerged from the crowd. "Actually it is my understanding that Jayne McCall, one of the patients to be cited in the *Star Tribune* article, went outside the HMO for treatment she should have had in the first place. Because of this, her bill has not been paid, and she is now in debt over $3700."

Cox's eyes flashed. "I'm confident that represents an accounting error."

Marcia continued "Well, actually, no. I have copies of the appeals that her doctors filed with the board of review regarding her care and her personal appeals regarding her bill. Would you care to comment?"

"I'm sure that there is a simple mistake," Farnsworth said, sounding annoyed.

"And with Molly Loomis—"

Cox again took the microphone. "The point here is that there may have been an administrative error in a single case. Any of us would admit to that. Community Health One serves million of clients. We will occasionally make the unintended error. The salient issue is ComHealthOne's absolute commitment to the highest-quality care at every level. From preventive care, to prenatal medicine, to critical care, surgery, and geriatric medicine, our client's sole concern is the well-being of every patient."

"What about the report that over twenty doctors have called the paper this morning to confirm that they are now being forced to accept incentives to not provide care at the threat of their jobs?" asked another reporter.

"Nonsense," scoffed Farnsworth. "Our client's physicians are all board-certified or board-eligible and come with glowing recommendations of personal integrity."

It was a perfect answer to a question not asked. "What about the disincentives?" he tried. "Do you deny they exist?"

Cox grabbed the microphone. In the background, he could see two more trucks of TV cameras as well as another half-dozen reporters. He looked at Ace. All at once, both realized that they were rapidly climbing out on a limb. Cox tried to recover. "Have any of these supposed physicians come forward? Gone public?" Cox asked pointedly.

There was a brief silence before Cox, pleased with himself, continued. "The issue here is integrity. Our client's integrity, the integrity of the system, and the trust we place in our physicians. Frivolous suits like this one undermine the public's confidence in our treasured institutions because of the cynicism that they generate. We feel for the dying, empathize with the ill, and pity those whose lives have been plagued by an unfortunate turn of events. But our client is a business, and more importantly, our client has an enormous public responsibility. It is a responsibility that they take seriously and an ideal they intend to fight for vigorously. In this regard, we will be vindicated."

The well-spoken drivel only seemed to invigorate the reporters. Marcia Sullivan stepped forward with six others. "But Mr. Cox, about Molly Loomis—"

It was too late. Cox and Farnsworth had turned off their microphones. The two lawyers, satisfied with their sound bite, ended the press conference just as the new group of reporters appeared. In a flash, the two attorneys waved goodbye and disappeared. The impromptu press conference was over.

Five minutes later, safe within the confines of a Lincoln Town Car, the two junior partners began to seriously consider all that had happened. Despite the thrill of the moment, the further they drove, the less convinced they were that the day had gone well. The plan that Barnes and Whitfield had mapped out that morning, not to connect the cases in the paper with the Loomis case, had been blown to shreds.

"It was inevitable," Farnsworth said.

"Yeah," Cox murmured. "We should have been proactive like I suggested. I knew it would happen. Reporters aren't stupid."

Both lawyers poured themselves stiff drinks as they headed to their offices. They seemed to sense the growing problem and neither talked again as the Town Car blended into the traffic. They each considered the issues. They knew their senior partners would be upset and that Hutchins would be livid. But they also knew that Farnsworth's rationalization for speaking so freely was also right. The Loomis case becoming public *was* inevitable.

The two continued to sip their drinks as they drove toward the office. On the radio, they heard a replay of Barnes and Whifield's press conference, followed by a replay of their own. For the ambitious pair, it was both thrilling and worrisome. The case that three hours before had seemed minor league was now dramatically different. It was expanding rapidly. What bothered Cox and Farnsworth was that rapid expansion was always risky. Both of them knew that the case might very well explode.

Peter Colder was deep into the third chapter of a book entitled *Fragile X Syndrome* when the phone rang at 10:30 P.M. Growing gradually disinterested, he put down the heavy volume and turned toward the phone and checked the caller ID. The sight was welcome as always. His ex-wife, Julianne.

"How are you?" he asked.

"There's something strange about that caller ID," replied Julianne. "If sometime you don't answer, should I assume I am no longer welcome. At least to call?"

"You're always welcome."

"Thank you, Peter. Now, how is he?"

Colder glanced at the cat. Mortimer was crashed on the couch next to him. "He's out tomcatting."

"He's neutered. I'll bet he's on the couch right next to you."

"You seriously need to get that checked out, those powers you have. Can you take the garbage out just by gritting your teeth or anything useful like that?"

"I never should have let you have my cat, Peter. I'm concerned for his welfare, with that irregular schedule you keep. Cats are creatures of habit. I'm sure that he's becoming overtly dysfunctional."

Colder looked down at the great beast, lying on his back, his four paws stuck straight up. "He looks almost psychotic at the moment. I'm concerned too."

"I raised him from when he was a kitten."

"I bought him from a neighbor. And he was four years old when we met."

Julianne pretended to whine. "You have such a distorted way with history. It's all those Latin terms you were forced to memorize in medical school."

Colder knew his ex-wife liked to tease him with fictitious stories of how Mortimer was actually hers. It was part of their usual conversation, but when she called late at night, he knew she usually had another motive. "So what's up?"

She sighed. "The party last Saturday. You didn't come."

Without any sound of regret he answered. "I was busy."

"That's the third time in three months I've tried."

"I know."

"I talked to Geoff. He will loan you the money you know."

"You know I don't want the money."

"Yes, I know."

Colder knew that his party attendance record could still not be the real issue. "J, seriously, you know I love talking to you, but when you call at ten thirty, I know it's your thinking time."

Julianne blurted it out. "Geoff wants me to marry him."

Colder was shocked by the suddenness, but not surprised. "Congratulations."

"Stop it," she said with a single laugh. "You know if you told me that I wouldn't say congratulations."

231

Colder felt strange. "That's just because you're more honest than me."

"No. Just more candid."

Colder didn't care about the difference in the words. "What did you say?"

"I said he *wants* me to. I didn't say I was going to."

"Then what are you thinking?"

"I don't know. Relationships never seem to be right. You and I were great lovers but never great friends."

"Correction," echoed Peter. "We were never great lovers, but we were in love."

"That's better said. But now we're great friends."

"It's easy to be great friends when you're not sleeping with someone, just like it's easy to be in love when you're rarely around each other. Illusion and romance are never disappointing like reality."

"Do you think it is harder to fall in love when you're older, Peter?

"You're not old. You're only thirty-one."

"That's not an answer."

"I think that the problem with emotions is that they lead us astray from our real mission in life, our real purpose."

"Oh God, where did that come from?" scoffed Julianne. "*The Marines Basic Training Manual?* I know you better than that. You figured out a long time ago it was foolish to have as your legacy some irrelevant medical eponym as a reward for a life of complete self-sacrifice. You're smarter than the fools caught up in the game of ego and glory."

"Think so? Where am I now?"

Julianne stayed the course. "Talking to me and not able to refute my statement."

"No, almost broke, on a sinking ship, and overloaded with idealism that sailed into a storm."

"Peter."

"I don't know if love is harder with age," he sighed, relenting. "I think love's peaks and valleys are kind of modified with experience and age. I suppose that there is a tendency, a bit patronizing perhaps, to view young love as crushes, college love as lust, and beyond, the truly mature emotions of adulthood."

"That sounds deep enough to be right or wrong depending on who you ask."

He ignored her. "But I'm not sure that maturity even exists as a state. People simply change from tolerant as children, to intolerant as teens, to moderately tolerant as adults, to intolerant as aged. Maturity then becomes largely a children's trait."

"Thank you for the advice, Doctor."

Colder slid lower into the couch. The movement disturbed the cat, who promptly plopped down on the floor. "What are you going to do?"

"No idea."

Colder sighed. Jealousy prevented him from wishing her with another man. Envy prevented him from wishing her happiness without him. Logic, as usual, won out. He knew it was time to let go. His voice sounded weak. "It's hard. I really do wish you well."

"I know." Julianne coughed. She had heard the rumors that her ex-husband had been seen frequently with the woman suing ComHealthOne. Jealousy and envy affected her the same way. Logic, as usual, barely won. "The whole office is buzzing about this Molly Loomis case."

"The whole town is."

"What's she like?"

Colder knew his ex too well. "J, is that what you really want to ask me?"

"Not really."

"Truth? She's either of us in a different life. Good person, bad luck, and a couple of bad decisions. But you'd like her."

"Pretty?"

Colder stopped. He had been waiting. He knew this was the ultimate feminine question. Everything she really wanted to know was loaded into it. To phrase the reply as anything other than a comparison to Julianne would tell her everything she really wanted to know "Yes, she is, J. She's pretty."

Julianne paused. "I'm happy for her," she said finally. She coughed again. Her voice was sounding slightly stuffy, and Colder remembered her allergies always acted up in late summer. He was sure Julianne wanted to ask more, but he knew she wouldn't. He wanted to change the subject.

"Did you see the press conference?" he asked.

"Yes, I did. Tyler and Marcus have an uphill battle."

"I know."

"Every attorney in the office would love to have a crack at one of these HMOs, but they're like the tobacco companies. No one can ever get 'em."

"They finally got tobacco."

"Only after ninety years and then only on tobacco's terms."

"I know. That may be what happens here."

Julianne sneezed. "Sorry. Allergies."

"I remember."

"I remember a lot of things," she said softly.

"Julianne."

She interrupted. "I hear from a reliable source you've been with her a lot."

"Look. You know how I feel about you and I know you feel the same way."

Julianne sighed. "Then why is it I somehow don't like her?"

"Believe me, you would."

"You're always nicer to my consorts than I am to yours. Why is that?"

"Because of my great depth of character," he joked.

"That may be true," she said seriously.

"It's not true, and you know it," he replied. "But you'd like her."

"You like her, don't you?"

Colder reached down and scratched Mortimer's belly. He had been wrong. Julianne was being more insistent than usual. He thought about his relationship with his ex-wife. He would always care, but the crossroads for both was obviously at hand. "Geoff's a good man."

"I know he is," she replied. "But you didn't answer me."

Colder stopped again, confronted by his long-standing weakness his ex-wife knew almost all too well, talking about feelings. He drew a deep breath. Carefully he prepared the answer, a well-conceived deflection that would allow things to pass to a different day. But just as fast, he thought about Molly. Molly Loomis. He thought about the eyes and the face, the brief moments they had shared. Molly. The thought of her struck him. He started to dodge, but the wrong words came out. "Yes, I like her, " he said, admitting it to both Julianne and himself for the first time. "I really do."

Chapter Nineteen

August 12

When Molly stepped inside her front door, the smell of fresh flowers was everywhere. It was a fine, fragrant scent, hinting of spring, but rich like summer. Puzzled, she turned and saw two dozen roses, red and pink, sitting in vases on the kitchen table. As she moved toward them the flowers' scent was even more powerful, crashing upon her, enveloping her, and tickling her nose like a fine wine. She unwrapped each dozen and held the vases aloft. The odor was majestic, and it seemed to increase exponentially with each passing second.

Looking around, she could see no card. They were lovely, floral perfection, but it nagged at her. Who would send them? Peter had said nothing, and she had been with him the entire day. She hoped it would be him, but she doubted it. He was just being nice, a friend, a good friend. She put them back down. Still, they were beautiful. She had never received roses before. Even if it were a mistake.

Glancing down, she found the card on the floor, apparently blown there by the breeze. Next to it was a small note written by her landlord explaining that he had let himself in. She opened the card and read the handwritten note. "I'm sorry for everything. Love, Troy." She slapped it shut, not wanting to read it again. "Troy." The name slipped off her tongue. He had been calling her frequently. Each time, she had put him off, not wanting to talk to him. She couldn't believe he would send her roses. But more importantly, she couldn't believe he really cared.

In the time since the split, Molly fought to kill the lurking thoughts she still had regarding Troy. Tracy, Gus, Sylvia, and Reggie all told her numerous times that Troy wasn't worth it. Yes, he had hit her. Yes, he had hurt her. Yes, he drank, and yes, he was unfaithful. He was all of that and worse. They were all right, she knew that now.

She put down the card and smelled the flowers again, closing her eyes to fully embrace their splendor while the languid air of her apartment seemed magically transformed. She loved them. Then she thought about him again. Yes, her friends were right. Love was blind. Love was ignorant. Love was foolish. She had been all of those. But love was also what had kept her going, been her guiding force and her purpose. She had not been perfect, nor had he. She had not been blameless, nor had he.

No, she thought. She did not want him. The wounds were too deep, the memories too real. They were all right about him. There had been more women than she would ever know. The drinking and the gambling. How could she even consider it? Why did she still even care?

She sat in front of the flowers enjoying them, her mind wandering as they seemed to blend together before her eyes in a mosaic of colors. Tracy had said it best. It was because she was vulnerable that she still thought about him. "Vulnerable and stupid" had been her exact words, but Molly knew Tracy had emphasized vulnerable for effect. She said it was the combination of everything. The lawsuit and the operation. The divorce and the debt. The loss of family. The combination was wearing. The effect was dangerous.

Molly thought about it. Tracy was half right. But part was the memory. High school, when he walked above the others. College, when he arrived like a man of glory. Being with him, she shared it too. And although she had come to understand its shallowness, she had also come to understand its allure to him and its destructiveness when it was gone. No. Troy Loomis was no saint. But then again, neither was she.

Quit it, she thought to herself disgustedly. "You're rationalizing again," she said out loud. The two could not be compared. Her fault had been to lie once. His was to be a liar. Was there a difference? she asked. Of course there was. Everyone knew that. Those who lie chronically lose the ability to see truth's edge, whereas white lies speak of need and conscience. There was a difference. But she knew she was not blameless. It would have been his child too. And now he sent her roses.

She could not go back to him. Her life had been miserable. She remembered when he had spent all their money on a new truck that he promptly crashed before he had it insured. She remembered the DUIs, the women, and the bar fights. She remembered him coming home wounded. Yes, he had needed her, she admitted. He would probably be lost without her.

Molly chided herself out loud. "Don't be an idiot!" But the thought faded. What would be her future with men? she asked herself. Pretty? Hardly. Dynamic? People never knew she was in a room. She could never be like some other women. Like Julianne, Peter's ex-wife. Letisha told her she was tall and beautiful, a woman with an educated vocabulary who could converse about anything. She also said Julianne was outgoing and witty and could draw men like a magnet. No, Molly thought about herself, she was nothing like that. She should forget about Peter. He should be with someone like Julianne, someone more like himself, a light against darkness, not invisible like her.

She thought about Troy. He needed her. But that was not enough, she told herself again. Maybe Troy did care. Colder would never need her. An independent man with a job that took all his time; she had enjoyed every minute they had spent since they had met two months before, but his responsibilities were so many, his time so little. Plus, he would never want her. He would certainly want someone as beautiful as Julianne.

She smelled the roses again. "Troy." It hurt to even say it.

"Troy, Troy, Troy," she sighed. It would not hurt to at least talk, she convinced herself. She could not go back to him. She was sure of that.

In a cramped office on the second floor of the FBI building in downtown Minneapolis, Agent Tom Hastings sat behind his desk enjoying his third cup of coffee for the morning. Agent Keith McWilliams sat across from him, transcribing the notes he had made of the press conference they had watched together. The television sat on the desk between them. McWilliams finished reading the second of Marcia Sullivan's articles, this one about Shirley Mitchell and the neglect that had led to the spread of her breast cancer. He tossed the paper aside and looked at his partner. Hastings, his eyes clear despite not having slept in twenty-four hours, appeared thoughtful as he thumbed through the file amassed on James O'Reilly.

"When do you think he'll call?" asked McWilliams without looking up.

A gust of summer wind filtered through the open window, with it the noisy street sounds from below. "He's a smart guy," replied Hastings. "He knows it's time."

"Evidence?"

"If he has anything that has something to do with Loomis, Tyler Briggs has to have it now. Barnes and Whitfield have to see it. They've got the final hearing soon. Have to have it before that."

"Yep."

"You know," Hastings sighed, "both sides will probably want to delay it."

"They say they don't," McWilliams laughed.

"I don't believe it."

"Neither do I."

"Actually Briggs might like the trial soon. The city is hot as hell right now."

"I agree," McWilliams said. "And it may be for a while."

The phone rang, and Hastings picked it up. "Yes," he mumbled after he saw the words "pay phone" scrawled across the caller ID. McWilliams did not look up, having returned to his notes. "Okay," continued Hastings. "Yeah, sure." He hung up.

"What the hell was that?" McWilliams asked.

"Wife's at home. She's trying to make some torte or something. I'm supposed to pick up some sugar."

"Gimme a break," McWilliams scoffed. "You guys live two blocks from SuperValu. Why can't she just get it?"

Hastings glared at him. "Never comment on wives."

McWilliams put down his pen and waved in surrender. "Sorry, sorry. I just thought, you've been up thirty-six hours, and all she's got to do is bake, well."

"Keith," Hastings started, "we've been friends a long time. We've done it by following the rule. No religion, politics, or relationships."

"Sorry."

Hastings drew a deep breath, his eyes showing a bit of fatigue. "Apology accepted."

"Thanks."

"But you're also right."

They both laughed.

The phone rang again. The caller ID read "unavailable."

"Hastings."

"Agent Hastings?" came O'Reilly's voice.

"Dr. O'Reilly," the agent replied, signaling McWilliams to pick up the phone.

"Don't bother tracing me. It's blocked and run through another location."

"Fine," he said, picking up a pen. "But we've been hoping you'd call."

"I'm ready to get this done."

"We need to talk to you," McWilliams interjected.

"Hello, Agent McWilliams. And yes, I need to talk to you."

"And?"

"Look. I haven't survived for two years because I was foolish," he began, his voice sounding slightly frightened. "But you know what I need."

"What?"

"This is a billion dollar operation in a multibillion dollar industry. They definitely give a damn about me."

"We need to know what you have," McWilliams said, preparing to scribble notes.

"I have proof that ComHealth was using a discovery in order to induce women to have abortions. I have the article, the data, and the computer disks that show it in their records. I'll give it to you for my life."

"Protection?" McWilliams asked.

"Of course."

"It can be arranged."

"How long will it take?"

"Twenty-four hours," Hastings said, jotting down several scribbles on an empty sheet of paper.

"It will be done on my terms," O'Reilly said.

"Security will be airtight," McWilliams assured.

"I don't trust anyone."

"Probably wise. But I can assure you, it will be fine."

O'Reilly paused as if suddenly lost in thought. "Tomorrow I will give you a list of one hundred different spots around the state. One of those will be the site that you will pick me up at on the assigned day."

"What?" asked Hastings. "We can't possibly cover one hundred sites."

"I know. I don't expect you to. Only local police can do that."

McWilliams thought he understood. "Okay. Then we'll pick you up from them?"

"Maybe."

"When will you actually come in?"

"I'll let you know that later."

"If I may," Hastings began.

"No. No negotiation. This is the way it has to be."

"Fine." Hastings relented.

"I'll call you," O'Reilly said, hanging up.

Tom Hastings looked across the two desks at his partner. "Very wary."

McWilliams nodded. "I would be too."

"It's not a bad idea. No one else could cover that many sites."

238

"I agree."

"I'll make some calls."

"And don't forget the sugar," McWilliams mentioned as he rose to leave.

The hors d'oeuvres were shrimp cocktails. The dinner was lobster, the first she'd ever tasted, and the dessert was crepes suzette. Molly loved every course of the finest at Manny's Restaurant.

Tracy had screamed into the phone when Molly told her that Troy was taking her to dinner; the fact that it was one of Minneapolis's best restaurants did nothing to convince Tracy that Troy remained anything other than a complete bum. The conversation had been ugly. "I don't care what you do, Molly," Tracy had hollered. "Shoot him, stab him, or boil him in oil. They're all fine. But don't go out with him!" Still, Tracy had not dissuaded her. Molly decided she would at least talk to him.

What did she see in this man? He had lied to her, cheated on her, hit her, and yet she could not seem to help the fact that she still felt attracted to him. Why? she asked herself. She felt angry, guilty. How could she feel this way? Everyone was right about him. And she was just stupid. There was no other explanation.

Men were born stupid, Tracy said. Women only chose to be so. Molly wasn't sure about that, knowing Tracy to be biased after a bad first marriage and occasionally, a troubled second one. But at times, it made sense. Two things were unquestionably clear: she was being stupid, and the dinner had been wonderful.

The restaurant was nearly full as they dined. Molly and Troy sat along the far wall, their booth abutting the lush paneling that lined the entire dining room. A dim red glow enveloped the room, a product of a ceiling chandelier and auburn table lights. White linen tablecloths, elegantly cut, covered tables spaced casually to assure both privacy and quiet. The waiter, dressed in white dinner jacket and black tie, delivered the check as Molly nibbled nervously on the last of her crepes.

"You know I love you," Troy whispered, leaning over the table.

Molly's mouth was full, but she mumbled and waved at him as if not wanting to hear it. "No, Troy."

"Why not?" he pleaded.

"Which one of the ten thousand reasons?" she asked.

Troy looked hurt. "That's not fair."

Molly tried to be firm. "How about the time when you broke my nose?"

"I know," he said. "That was bad, but I couldn't help it. I was drunk."

"Or when I came home and you were in bed with that girl from the bowling alley."

"We had too much to drink."

Molly shook her head. "Like that's an explanation?"

"I'm human, Molly. And you know that women want me."

Molly finished the desert and pushed away the plate, determined only to give him his say. "Troy, you took me for a complete chump. You humiliated me and used me."

"I know," he admitted, interrupting her. "I made some mistakes. But I've changed."

Molly rolled her eyes.

"Seriously," he continued. "I have. And I got a promotion."

"What?"

"A week ago. Assistant manager in tools."

"That's good," she admitted.

Troy tried to look earnest. He raised his right hand. "And I've only been going out once a week. Swear to God.

"Troy—"

"Seriously, Molly, I thought about everything you said. You were right. *Everything*. A to Z. I admit that now."

"Troy."

"I was a shit. I can admit that. I'm a man. And a man can admit when he's wrong."

"That's not the point."

"I know. But I still mean it. And besides, you lied to me too."

Molly shook her head, disagreeing. "Troy, c'mon, don't give me that. You never cared about a baby. That was just an excuse so you could get out of the relationship and go screw around with a hundred thousand women."

"That's not true." He paused. "At least not totally."

"You know all I ever wanted was to have a baby. A healthy, happy baby I could call my own and raise. A home and a family."

He reached for her hand but she drew it away, the recollection flaring her anger. "You're right, again."

She remained composed. "Look, Troy. I've moved on. I'm happy for you that you've gotten a promotion and that you've changed, but the divorce is final tomorrow, when I sign the papers, and it's the best thing. For both of us."

"No."

"Yes."

"Molly, you're broke. You have a terrible job that isn't going anywhere and—"

"Don't say any more."

"C'mon, Mol."

"I'm getting on with my life."

"With who? The doctor?"

Molly looked surprised. "How do you know about him?"

"I keep on top of things," he replied.

"He's a friend," she said, her eyes falling to the table.

"Look. I know about this guy. I checked him out. He works twenty-four hours a day and his ex-wife, who's still in the picture by the way, is this lawyer who looks like Julia Roberts. You really think this guy is gonna be in your future?"

Molly did not look up, stung by the fact that for once his words rang true.

"He may be a great guy but—"

"He's a friend," she interrupted.

"C'mon, Molly."

"Troy, I didn't come here to get back together. I came only because we've barely talked throughout the divorce. I thought I at least owed you that."

"I owe you more than that."

"True."

"Besides, you look great," he said, sounding sincere.

Molly closed her eyes. She would have preferred he argue with her. Apologies and compliments were always more difficult to handle. "Thank you for the dinner, Troy."

"You're welcome. I'd like to do it again."

Molly said nothing.

"Can I ask you a question?" he began, looking at her diamond.

"What?"

"If you don't love me and don't want to see me, then why do you still wear the ring?"

Molly flushed. "I think it's because I'm stupid."

Troy laughed out loud, his deep voice resonating throughout the restaurant and causing several heads to turn. "Then you're just what I've been for a very, very long time."

The waiter returned and picked up the check and the credit card. A minute later, he returned, and Troy signed the check, leaving a fifteen percent tip. After thanking the waiter, they walked from the restaurant where the valet retrieved the truck.

Driving her home, Troy talked about his new job. Assistant manager. A good raise and bigger responsibilities. Molly listened. He was saying all she had ever wanted to hear from him. And saying them in the right way. One after the other. Responsibility, motivation, apologies. It was almost unreal. She remained strong. At least on the outside.

When he dropped her off at her apartment, he did not kiss her. Instead, he walked her to the front door and lightly squeezed her hands. Then he waved goodbye as she let herself into the building.

Long after he was gone, Molly sat alone in the darkness of her apartment, wondering about what she had done. She felt lost and confused. Much of what Troy had said was true, especially about Peter Colder. Colder was nice to her and they had gone to lunch and dinner many times. But he had never really talked to her about "them," and he had never even tried to kiss her. It was obvious. He did not want her. She groaned out loud. Why had she gone to dinner with Troy? He always did know how to get under her skin. Was any of the rest true? Was it remotely possible? Could he be a changed man?

Her living room window was open and she sat on the floor beneath it. She listened as the sounds of the highway less than a mile away provided a distant backdrop to the otherwise quiet night. She was mad at herself. Tracy Timlin was right. The dinner was a mistake.

August 13

Tyler Briggs jogged along First Avenue through the muggy air of August on his way to the FBI building. A heavy coat of sweat emerged after only three blocks and he held his side, fighting the ache that was becoming increasingly severe with every step. Still trying to go fast, he grabbed the four inches of extra skin that seemed to be holding him back. He laughed at himself when he felt it, recalling a day when his side was as taut as a drum and a half-mile run meant a cooldown rather than a frightening proposition and a last resort because of a car with a failed starter.

The downtown was beginning to awaken and as he turned onto Fifth Street. He passed by a series of small shops whose proprietors were sweeping away the residue left by the street cleaners that had passed by two hours earlier. He ran by a small crowd gathered outside a corner bakery and caught a whiff of some freshly baked cinnamon rolls. After a brief pause to consider a purchase, he decided against it, recalling his thick side, and jogged on, determined to keep on the diet he had started the minute he had grabbed his extra four inches.

He turned onto Fourth Avenue and slowed his jog slightly. He wiped the sweat from his eyes and loosened his tie as the morning sun descended upon him and the humidity threatened to overwhelm his fragile conditioning. A small crowd in front of a bagel stand stood open-mouthed as he passed by, each wondering if he was running from a heart attack or an attacker. Finally, he slowed to a crawl as he passed through the revolving door of the FBI building and headed directly for the bathroom to towel off.

He looked at his watch. Ten after eight. "Damn," he thought. "Been ten minutes late all morning." He took a handful of paper towels from the container and standing in front of the mirror, wiped himself furiously as the sweat seemed to ooze forth like sap from a maple tree. For five minutes, he repeated this pattern, wiping off the perspiration and then waiting as it reappeared as he stood in the old bathroom underneath a vent with an air-conditioned breeze blowing down upon him. Finally, the perspiration relented and he headed for the second floor.

The Minneapolis FBI Building, long in need of renovation, was a dilapidated relic of J. Edgar Hoover's robust budget. Twice slated for repair in the 1980s, the projects had fallen victim to funds shifted to Star Wars and B-1 bombers. Now the four-story building was cold in the winter, warm in the summer, and plagued by a computer system that worked like a radio built by a seventh grader. The once beautiful marble floors were badly chipped, and the walls were a fading mix of avocado green and pumpkin orange 1970s wallpaper.

Feeling better, Tyler sprinted up the back stairs to the second floor and found Room 212. The old wooden door with the translucent glass window was ajar, and he walked in.

"Hey, keep the door open. It's the only air we get," Hastings complained.

"Will do," Tyler replied, releasing it.

The small office was twelve-by-twelve, with two metal schoolteacher's desks connected to each other at their front sides and positioned against the far wall underneath a closed window. Shoulder-high file cabinets were located in each corner, and on the walls was a mix of diplomas, certificates, and a calendar. A small TV and two laptop computers were on the desks. A printer was behind Hastings.

McWilliams sat across from Hastings, chewing on red licorice. He nodded as

Briggs entered. Colder sat on a folding chair facing the window, his back turned. He was reading the latest of Marcia Sullivan's scalding articles, this one, the third in the series, on Rudy Jalowicz and his kidney cancer.

"Anyone else hot?" Briggs asked as he pulled up the vacant chair positioned next to Colder.

"How are you, Tyler?" Colder asked, shaking his hand.

"Only hot. Otherwise okay."

McWilliams was businesslike, his crewcut showing his glowing scalp, but he appeared determined not to complain. "O'Reilly called us yesterday."

"What did he say?" Briggs asked.

"Not much," Hastings said. "Only that he's gonna come in."

"When?"

"I suspect very soon. I think we'll know today or tomorrow."

"He's calling today?"

"Possibly."

"Perfect," Tyler said.

"He sent us a fax first thing this morning. It detailed a few things," McWilliams started. "Tyler, you're to be involved as an attorney. Dr. Colder is to be involved, I presume, because he's the only one O'Reilly fully trusts."

"Fine," Briggs said, unbothered.

McWilliams stood and took a sip from a carton of orange juice. "His plan is this. On the morning he comes in, Dr. Colder will receive a message from O'Reilly. They have been communicating and apparently they have it worked out."

Colder nodded, recalling O'Reilly's instructions from the night before. "All you guys will have to do that morning is follow me."

Briggs was dabbing at his forehead with a Kleenex from the desk. "Sounds good."

"Basically it is," Hastings admitted. "After that message is received, we'll go get him."

"I'm pretty sure it'll be in the city," Colder said.

"We agree," Hastings said.

"The only weakness is that we won't have any time to secure the area."

"That should be made up for by the fact that there is almost no way anyone could know where he is going to be."

"Really, the only chance for someone to get him is if he's followed," McWilliams admitted.

Colder took a drink of his orange juice and smiled. "I like it."

McWilliams sat down again and tossed his carton in the garbage.

"Did he say exactly what he has?" Briggs asked.

Hastings nodded. "A copy of the data and the journal as well as the computer disks that confirm that ComHealth was using his discovery."

Briggs ran his hand over his face, a wave of uneasiness sweeping over him. Colder saw the change. "What is it, Tyler?"

"It's a legal matter. It may be hard getting his journal and disks into court. We lack foundation. In fact, he is our only foundation."

"But it's his research," Colder protested.

Briggs was off in thought. "True, but it was never published, and was only slated to be published in a now defunct journal. They'd also argue that even if it had been published the journal wasn't authoritative."

"Oh God," Colder moaned.

Briggs continued, "We have to prove chain of custody. Where has all of this evidence been? Has it been altered?"

"And worse than that," Hastings said, clearly aware of many legal nuances, "the article by itself may not prove anything."

"True," Briggs admitted.

Colder sighed. "Then how does this stand for Molly?"

"We have two minor hearings left. Those will be in the next ten days. Then we'll pick the jury, and the trial will start right away. Van Gilder has it on the calendar for August twenty-fifth."

"That's coming up awfully fast."

"When they withdrew all the motions, it put this thing in overdrive. The fact that Van Gilder's court is the only one around that isn't backed up for two years also helps."

"What about this stuff? O'Reilly's stuff?"

Tyler sighed. "If it's a bombshell, we'll have to have a continuance and disclose it. Van Gilder won't even have to think twice about that, because Barnes and Whitfield will want time to try to destroy it."

"How long?"

"Month or two, minimum. Probably more."

"And if not?"

Briggs loosened his shirt, still trying to cool down. "We'll know as soon as we talk to him. If he wasn't a material witness, he'd be useless in this civil trial; although he'd still have value in a criminal case."

"Then?"

"Well," Briggs offered, "I would say it will start about as scheduled. I talked to Pokey Mercer yesterday afternoon. They know that Marcia Sullivan and the *Star Tribune* are going to run all these articles on patients who got shafted, maimed, or killed by this HMO. They want the trial soon. They're taking a public relations beating."

"They want it as a soap box," said Colder.

"Yes."

"How do Loomis's chances look?" McWilliams asked, his crewcut scalp still glistening in the heat.

Briggs looked forlorn. "It's a long shot. These guys were smart. They wrote these contracts and these rules for just these situations. They're way ahead of the patients."

McWilliams grunted "It sucks. We may not get them in criminal either."

Briggs sighed. "The disks may not be admissible there either."

"Shit," Colder cursed. "This guy's been running around for two years and now everything he has may not be of any use?"

"It's possible."

"Unbelievable."

"We don't know that," Briggs said. "It also quite possible that everything he has was obtained legally. In that case—"

Colder smiled. "Say a prayer."

"Exactly," Hastings muttered.

McWilliams stood again. His phone rang and he began talking to another agent. Hastings stood also and shook Briggs' and Colder's hands. The meeting was over. "Dr. Colder, we'll be in touch."

"Fine."

"If anything changes, I'll let you know."

"Sounds good."

Briggs and Colder waved to McWilliams, who was engrossed in a conversation. The agent waved back.

A minute later, Briggs and Colder were walking together outside

"Tell me the truth," Peter said. "What do you think is going to happen?"

"My gut feeling is that it's going to be real, incriminating, but inadmissible. I smell a zillion technicalities coming and a zillion dollars and delays finding them."

Colder looked discouraged. "What then?"

"After that, it's strictly a criminal thing."

"I mean about Molly?"

"Truth?"

"Yes."

"Marcus and I have been working day and night on this for the past six weeks. We've found only one case where an HMO lost on anything like this and realistically, it was more a red-tape screwup than a real point of contention. The truth is, they've never lost on anything they've chosen to fight full bore. These contracts are like steel."

"What about Molly?"

Briggs put his hand on Colder's shoulder. "She's a good kid. Has got a lot of guts. I like her, and, well, we're going to fight like hell."

Colder was still forlorn. "I think I hear what you're saying."

"We've played hardball with them because we had to. Even if we lose, this fight is still worth fighting. It's bigger than us and it's bigger than this case."

"But it's going to be ugly."

"They're going to come after her with everything they've got. Realistically, I know there is no chance that they'd settle now. But with all this press coverage, maybe something good will happen to her."

"I understand." Colder looked down. "How long do you think the trial will take?"

"Three days. Four max. It won't take long."

"Four days of hell."

"Probably," said Briggs.

Colder looked thoughtful. "Would more time be helpful?"

Briggs knew what he was getting at. "Truthfully? No."

Colder could feel himself start to sweat. "What about for them?"

"I gotta admit their strategy still baffles me. I thought they would want to delay this as long as possible. It's a risky strategy to go to trial when the heat is on."

Colder stopped. Tyler's office and Third Street Clinic were in different directions. He shook Briggs's hand. "Thanks."

"Don't give up," Briggs said. "I'm not."

"Neither will I." Colder tried to sound confident.

"Fragile X may still be a bombshell."

Colder sighed. Again he felt deflated. "But maybe an inadmissible one."

"Maybe." Colder waved goodbye. It was an ugly thought, but one that both men knew could possibly be true. James Patrick O'Reilly might risk his life for almost nothing. As they left each other, the hot August day seemed suddenly even hotter.

Chapter Twenty

August 14

By the fourth day of Marcia Sullivan's articles, Minneapolis–St.Paul was sizzling. The stifling late-summer heat refused to relent, and there was now a constant haze surrounding the ComHealth offices that most in the city swore was steam. The fourth article in Marcia Sullivan's series dealt with Jayne McCall. Carefully describing how the ComHealth doctors were forced to prescribe her medications based on an algorithm of cost savings rather than on efficacy, Marcia hammered home the message. The verbal image of the young woman's scarred face was poignant and powerful; and Jayne, gaining confidence from the support she received from friends, appeared on the local news in anticipation of the article. Further pictures of her appeared in the paper. In this case, a picture was worth a thousand words. The result was even more trouble for ComHealth.

Newspaper, TV, and radio coverage, already extensive, was continuing to grow as each of Marcia's articles appeared. But as expected, ComHealth was fighting back with all its might. Sensing the opportunity for immediate glory, Jackson Barnes and Harley Whitfield seized the lead from Ace Farnsworth and T. Quentin Cox and were now actively taking on the role as lead attorneys. To counter the paper's allegations, they promised the press daily conferences and insisted on equal coverage in the name of fairness. The local networks were happy to oblige. The summer had been slow for news.

By Thursday, a constant press presence was established outside the HMO's offices and on the streets in front of the IDS Tower. Talk shows dominating the airwaves were flooded with angry callers. In the meantime, a few small protest groups advocating patient rights began to appear in front of the ComHealth offices and in front of the governor's mansion across the river. The protests at both sites were peaceful, at first little more than a handful of professional activists, but by early afternoon on the fourth day of the crisis, over one hundred people had gathered at the IDS in anticipation of H. Carter Hutchins' expected statement. The local press continued to cover it thoroughly, interviewing each protester and gathering even more personal stories on the cutthroat HMO. Hutchins, largely reclusive since the stories began to hit the papers, preferred to let his lawyers talk while he confined himself to the Twin Cities Club, his office, and his home. He had attended no social functions, and this afternoon's press conference would be his first time with reporters since Monday.

Hutchins had much to address. The night before, Reggie Tan had ordered a keg of beer and three Strip-O-Grams to be delivered to Hutchins' home. After the press received the anonymous tip, the pictures of Hutchins in front of the keg and flanked by the veil-clad women landed on page three. The viewer could not tell by the look on the CEO's face whether he was tanked or ticked, but within hours, the image became a favorite of all the local TV stations.

At 2:10 P.M., H. Carter Hutchins stepped into the sunshine to begin the press conference flanked by an entourage that included the attorneys and his fellow executives. The members of the local media were packed together in front of him on the steps of the IDS as a smiling Hutchins strode confidently to the podium. With the cameras rolling, he began with a five-minute dissertation about the struggles of his grandfather as a young Irish immigrant. Next, he talked of his father's struggles in the Depression, trying to make ends meet as a young businessman raising his family. Then he continued with a dissertation on affordable, quality health care. As always, Hutchins was a brilliant speaker. Even the jaded reporters who stood in front of him taking notes listened in admiration as he spewed forth the familiar refrain about quality and cost control as if they were parallel concepts. Even those who knew the truth were forced to admit that Hutchins truly believed his lies and delivered them skillfully. His speech was sound-bite-riddled, his manner beautifully affecting, his conclusion a soaring vision of hope. It was a masterpiece.

Hutchins spoke for half an hour without stop. When he finished, with tears in his eyes and looking hurt that anyone would imply his organization would ever consider any motive other than the elimination of human suffering as reasonable, Hutchins left the podium, appearing too shaken to take questions. Harley Whitfield and Jackson Barnes stepped forward to answer the reporters. Hutchins and his assistants left to return to their offices.

Colder stood across the street behind a TV van. With him was David Frissell and Dr. Eric Johnson, whom Frissell introduced to Colder as a ComHealthOne doctor. They listened to Hutchins' latest harangue on the speakers set up to serve the several hundred people who gathered.

Frissell had had enough. He pulled the others away.

As the three perspiring doctors walked off, they could hear the ComHealth lawyers at the microphone disputing the *Star Tribune's* article of the day. They started by talking about an "intrinsic press bias" and criticizing the way the case had been presented. This was part of their usual strategy: slam the article, deny they had done anything wrong, and obfuscate like crazy. As it had been in the preceding days, it was a worthy effort, but not lost on the audience was the fact that never once had a doctor appeared to dispute what Marcia Sullivan had written about any of the cases.

"The tragedy of a young woman like Lisa Bowman," Harley Whitfield boomed, his carefully groomed silver hair shining like a light against the darkness of his navy Brooks Brothers suit, "is that her cervical cancer could have been prevented. And remember, *prevention*, is a mission of managed care and a core concept of ComHealthOne." The statement made the three doctors stop and turn around again.

The journalists were even less impressed. A young male reporter for the *St. Paul Pioneer Press* jumped right in. "How do you say that prevention is the mission when one of the first programs the HMO instituted was to eliminate yearly physicals, routine EKG's, chest X-rays, pap smears, mammograms, blood counts, and urinalysis? The very action that contributed to these people's diseases?"

Whitfield appeared to bless the question with an affirming nod. "The issue is cost effectiveness. Obviously, we cannot perform every test on every patient, every year. This is why we leave it up to the doctors, amidst the sanctity and care of the doctor–patient relationship to decide which tests are indicated and which are not. Our mission as an organization is to provide for the services that our physicians feel are necessary for the patients as they see fit."

The reporter was not swayed. He pushed on. "Isn't that merely a rationalization to thrust the blame onto the physicians when the truth is that ComHealthOne is exerting pressure on physicians not to provide care by tying their income to cost savings?"

"Our physicians make patient care decisions. They write the algorithms. They follow them. We do not exert pressure."

Another reporter stepped forward. "But how do you explain the fact that each of these cases was a direct result of restrictions that your organization has imposed and that only two years ago would have resulted in early detection and possibly a cure? Lisa Bowman's cervical cancer, Shirley Mitchell's breast cancer, and Rudy Jalowicz's kidney cancer."

Wthifield didn't bat an eye. He continued to weave and dodge. "First of all, I disagree with the premise of the question. Our efforts to allow for affordable care for all do not cause cancer. Secondly, as I have stated before, individual care decisions rest with the physicians, never with the insurance company." Colder and the others walked away, no longer listening and unable to stomach anymore of it.

Rounding the corner of the Dayton's department store, Casey Larter nearly decapitated them as she hustled in the direction of the press conference. Her white lab coat tucked underneath her arm and her navy-colored summer dress looking more like a wrinkled tarp, she appeared haggard, hot, and pale.

"Casey," Frissell shouted, grabbing her by the shoulders like a lineman would a halfback as she plowed through them.

She stopped, looking surprised.

"Oh, hello boys," she grunted, jerking to a stop.

"What's the hurry? asked Colder, watching her perspire. "You aren't missing anything."

Casey wiped her upper lip with the side of her wrist and gazed at the press conference. The rim of protesters around the periphery was quiet, allowing Whitfield to speak. The dozen cameras sprinkled throughout the crowd were fixed on the silver-haired lawyer as he continued his diatribe about Lisa Bowman's tragedy. Near the back of the crowd and across the street were the television vans, seven in all.

"How many people are here?" she asked.

"I'd say about two hundred," Johnson answered.

"That's about a hundred more than yesterday."

Frissell turned back to the crowd. "And three more TV stations today. One from Fargo, one from Duluth, and one from Des Moines."

"Anything new?" Casey asked.

"Naw," replied Colder. "Hutchins is already gone. Gave a speech about God, motherhood, and apple pie. All with a tear in his eye."

Casey closed her eyes. "So sorry I missed it."

"It's just going to be the Barnes and Whitfield show from now on. We're going to get back to work."

She looked at Johnson and Colder. "I didn't know you guys knew each other."

"I just introduced them," Frissell replied.

Casey had a strange look on her face. "You have some things in common."

The remark puzzled Colder, and he started to speak, but Casey didn't appear to be listening. She looked upset. "This is driving me crazy. You know that ComHealth's stock has actually risen the past two days? These guys are making more money off this!"

"Yeah," Colder replied. "The rumor is that their quarterly report is going to show a five percent growth, and there's talk of buying two more clinics in the northern part of the state."

"Unbelievable," Johnson muttered, gazing back at the lawyers. The sandy-haired obstetrician looked physically ill. His face was a pale sheet of white, and his eyes had dark stains beneath them.

Casey shook her head. "I thought this might affect Hutchins' popularity, but it hasn't touched it. *Star Tribune* poll this morning listed him as the seventy percent favorite for the Republican nod."

"It's only been three days," Colder countered.

"But if you watch the news each night, all you're seeing is Hutchins talking platitudes and the lawyers talking about ComHealth's bringing down health-care costs. This is nearly turning into a damn commercial." Casey looked exasperated. "Look. Even the protesters appear mesmerized."

"These guys are good," Frissell admitted. "You explain away every death or act of neglect as an aberration. Then talk about how much money you're saving the consumers and finish by reciting the rigged polls that claim to represent patient satisfaction, and Hutchins still walks away looking like the savior."

"I make a prediction," Casey said, standing with the three in a line facing the press conference, "that they sail through this unscathed. In the next few days, we'll see fewer people and cameras."

"No way," Colder said.

Frissell stepped forward. "Maybe."

Casey continued. "Within a week, Hutchins is back to his usual, wanting to be a Republican governor, so he can be part of their scene. Fox hunting, polo, country clubbing, and cutting welfare benefits to children."

"I doubt it." Johnson was more optimistic. "The talk shows are going crazy, the letters to the editor are anti-ComHealth, and the public is talking about it like crazy. That reporter is gonna be publishing cases all next week too. This is just warming up."

"I agree," Colder said.

Frissell was focused on something else. "This isn't about politics, Casey."

"Sure it is. It's still ultimately about politics and money. The Republicans with their naive and undying faith that the market can do no wrong. Ideological fools. Remember, capitalism is about win–win only in political speeches. On the street, it's about beating someone. And when it's applied to medicine, it's deadly. This is what the market brings."

"You're a Democrat?" Frissell laughed.

Casey was watching Harley Whitfield talk to the cameras. "Hardly. They're just as bad. They offer nothing, but instead use the poor and the dispossessed for political gain. They do nothing but pander to their voters. Lip service to everything, while off the record admitting that 'government can't do everything.' Talk about a cop-out and philosophical defeat."

"So?" Colder wondered where she was going with this.

"The Republicans always offer a simple answer that's wrong. They're naive. The Democrats are hypocrites. They think they're ideologically pure *and* correct while knowing that their pet theories of economic redistribution have already been shown to not work. What do you say? Pick your devil."

"Then you're a communist?" Frissell asked. "Or a fascist."

Casey shook her head. "No. Democracy is still the best. It offers freedom. But its weakness is that it mandates political expediency and creates intellectual corruption."

Johnson was not listening. He didn't care about politics. He moved forward, staring at the crowd and the lawyers, lost in thought. His eyes were glazed and his face seemed to grow only paler. "And the meek shall inherit the earth," he mumbled to himself. "If only it were true."

The others grew quiet. They, too, had no interest in discussing politics with Casey and instead turned their attention again to the speaker, Jackson Barnes. After ten minutes, the press and the crowd appeared to grow slightly disinterested. By both filibuster and finagling, he successfully dismissed Lisa Bowman's case as a fluke and was now busy reciting statistics of patient satisfaction almost exactly as Casey Larter predicted.

"Ninety-five percent of our customers were satisfied," Barnes roared.

"You know how they make their patient satisfaction surveys look good, don't you" Casey asked.

"How?"

"HMO clientele are basically younger and healthier, so figure that nine people in ten have minimal contact with a doctor during the year. They're obviously going to have no complaints about anything, so they're essentially starting with a ninety percent approval rating. Anything beyond that is gravy."

Jackson Barnes finished his description of ComHealth's sterling patient satisfaction rating, and for a moment there was silence amongst the reporters. Colder and the others watched. After an awkward second, the crowd turned at a sound and Marcia Sullivan stepped forward. The doctors could make out her slim physique emerging from the shadows of her fellow reporters. "Have you ever heard of Fragile X?" she asked.

Colder laughed to himself, watching as his friend stepped back into the crowd that faced the two lawyers. Even from one hundred feet, they could all see

Jackson Barnes frown. "No," he replied. "Never heard of it."

Marcia asked nothing more, but the other reporters leered at her with a mix of curiosity and jealousy. She had become a celebrity of sorts, and peer envy was the obvious price. Harley Whitfield took the microphone and began another harangue about patient satisfaction surveys. He was eloquent as always, and his redundancy and exaggeration were also useful tactics. After another minute, no one seemed interested. He completed his two-minute soliloquy and the press conference broke up with the lawyers scurrying into the IDS Tower.

Colder and the others walked away. After a few steps, Frissell turned to Colder. "That was our reporter, wasn't it, Pete?"

"Yes."

"Was she talking about Fragile X? Our disease?"

"Yes."

Casey smiled, recalling her earlier conversations with Colder about Fragile X. Her grin was devilish. "And then again, boys, everything I said about this being over could be wrong."

Long after nightfall, James Patrick O'Reilly's 1964 Chevrolet pickup chugged down Minnesota Highway 55 at just under the speed limit. On the seat beside him was the manila envelope he had purchased at the supermarket and would use to carry the journal and the disks. On top of the envelope was a pack of Marlboros with one cigarette missing. He had never smoked before. He had tried one and liked it. He would have another later. It was something he always wanted to try.

The two-lane highway that connected the northwest side of Minneapolis to the lake country was heavily traveled and the old, orange pickup was completely immersed in a line of cars commuting from downtown into the country. The highway stretched east–west through a series of small towns, Medina, Buffalo, Rockford, each with many new buildings and burgeoning economies, benefiting from the gradual migration of Minneapolis to the west. Each still showed signs of the quaint towns that they had once been: family-owned hardware stores, bakeries, and markets. Now, however, each little town clearly showed the advance of civilization; each possessed a McDonald's and a Wal-Mart.

Early that morning, O'Reilly had faxed the FBI the list of one hundred places around the state that he might appear. He did so because he trusted no one. He did not trust local police. They could easily be trumped by corrupt superiors or Feds. He did not trust the FBI, knowing that the investigation into his colleagues' deaths had been stymied long ago. He trusted no one. No one but Peter Colder.

Ninety-nine of the places were nonsense. One was real. In the brief conversation with Colder, O'Reilly told him where, using a reference from an earlier conversation. Colder understood instantly. As O'Reilly drove along with the commuting traffic deep into the lake country toward his hideaway on the edge of the wildlife refuge, he reflexively lit another cigarette. He thought about his life. He thought about everything he had seen. He thought about the future. He thought about tomorrow. It had all been so long.

"Will it work?" he wondered aloud.

He reached over to the passenger seat and fondled the envelope, flipping it between his fingers. He had calculated it all carefully. By the time he told Peter Colder the exact location, there would be less than half an hour for the two FBI agents, Colder, and the others to get there. There would be witnesses and zillions of people. It was perfect. No way anyone else would have a chance. No one except Colder knew they were even part of it. And it was in public. Very public. He hoped it would work. He prayed it would work.

O'Reilly took a drag on the cigarette. This one didn't taste as good. He threw it out the window. He was nervous, and his hand trembled noticeably. He knew he was enjoying his last days of freedom. In less than forty-eight hours, he would enter the lion's den. On Saturday morning, he would surrender himself to Colder and the FBI in the most public place in the state—the Mall of America, the largest shopping mall in the United States.

Colder called Molly shortly after the press conference to ask her to go out for dinner, but she was scheduled for a night shift and had only two hours to spare before work. They decided that instead of going out, he would bring over Chinese. She was excited at his call, not having heard from him in two days. He used the need to talk as an excuse, as he was looking forward to seeing her too.

For the two hours, they traded stories about the day and laughed until they were nearly sick. They made fun of the buffoonery of Ace Farnsworth and T. Quentin Cox and nearly became apoplectic with laughter when they recalled Tyler's stories about the esteemed ComHealth lawyer Pokey Mercer and his million-dollar toupee and two million girlfriends.

It was an enjoyable evening and one that neither wanted to see end. But the clock killed it for Molly and the pager destroyed it for Colder. Molly left for work, and a half-hour later, the beeper's annoying sound brought Colder firmly back to reality. Having returned home, but no longer using his own phones for contacts with O'Reilly, he drove to a pay phone and called the number. Ten minutes later, the wheels were started in motion. The directions were given.

When he hung up, Colder took a deep breath. The pleasant evening with Molly was now just a memory. Even worse, O'Reilly's arrival loomed and the realization caused his entire body to suddenly go numb. Had they covered everything, he wondered? Would he be safe? The worries were of no use, Colder concluded. There was no going back. In less than forty-eight hours, it would be their equivalent of D-Day, where the real "Overlord" had happened, and Germany's "Case White," the planned conquest of the world, had begun to crumble. Colder closed his eyes and said a silent prayer that this time the result would be the same.

Chapter Twenty-one

August 15

Sitting in one of the heavily cushioned chairs that were scattered throughout his palatial office, Gregory Alan Markham, ComHealthOne's Chief Operating Officer, couldn't conceal his fear. A fine line of perspiration had begun to form under his hairline, while a light mist appeared to be dampening the upper rim of his shirt collar. He was motionless, staring blankly out his massive south wall window like a blind man oblivious to the light.

The first phone call had been an annoyance, coming in the middle of the night, but the second one, arriving as soon as he sat down at his desk in the morning, terrified him. The night before, the caller had spoken only one sentence, too fast for him to understand in his sleepy state, but the second time, the words were clear. Each time the caller, a high-pitched male voice, had said, "Watch your back."

The words had struck like an electric shock, sending a wave of fear through him that left him feeling paralyzed and slightly nauseous. He closed his eyes and fingered the pen he had been carrying for half an hour. It couldn't be happening, he told himself. It was as if his worst fears were suddenly coming true. Markham tried hard to think objectively, but the rising sense of panic made it difficult.

Trying to reconstruct each twenty-second event, he knew he didn't recognize the voice. That didn't bother him, realizing that someone was trying to warn him and remain anonymous, but the call the night before had been to his home number, which was unlisted. That was somewhat worrisome, but even more troubling was the fact that the morning call had been on his office's private line, a number that only his secretary, his wife, and fellow executives had access to. It didn't take a genius to figure out that the person who had called him had significant access, probably from inside ComHealth.

Markham reopened his eyes and again stared blankly out the window while his mind continued to jump between fears. Who had it been? Hutchins? No. That made no sense. Bolger? Doubtful. Ross? Cooley? None of them seemed right. Markham shook his head disgustedly and stood up, walking to the window. He knew the who question was irrelevant. The pertinent question was, Why? To that, he had no immediate answer.

Markham let the events of the past few days flow over him again, searching for any clue. It had all been ugly. He knew that despite their lawyers' public protestations and spin, ComHealthOne was taking a major blow. The Marcia Sullivan articles were having an effect. ComHealth's own press conferences and press releases had been helpful, but any check of the local TV or radio confirmed that public opinion was shifting against them. Every night in the six-thirty time slot, the local stations preempted the national feed to run specials, while radio covered it even more extensively. When interviewed, person after person continued to describe ComHealth as "greed merchants," "murderers," or "butchers." One had even called Hutchins a "hybrid of Michael Milken and Jack Kevorkian." Others had been more succinct, simply calling them evil. Markham knew that even with the most adept spin they could put on it, they had suffered a hit, primarily because the one thing they could not allow to happen had happened. The public had come to understand that managed care companies made their money by providing less care, and no amount of lying could alter that fact.

The only good news for ComHealth was that the problem remained local. None of the networks or the national papers picked up the story, except for a brief mention in *USA Today*. For once, the ComHealth executives were glad that the national media largely viewed Minnesota as a suburb of the North Pole. Because the story remained local and only one-sixth of ComHealth's subscribership was from Minnesota, its stock hardly wavered, continuing to hover around fifty, keeping intact the fortune created by Markham's huge position.

What worried Markham and the other executives was that the whole organization now seemed to be teetering on the edge of a cliff. Hutchins schmoozed his way through a meeting of the board of directors the night before, but despite his reassurances to the largely out-of-town board, the core group of executives knew that all hell could easily break loose. Privately, after the board adjourned, Hutchins gathered them together for an impromptu meeting. Markham joined the lawyers, Cooley, Ross, and Bolger in Hutchins' office as they talked of the "three-pronged fork," the three possibilities that could endanger the organization.

The first was if the story became a national sensation. Hutchins said he doubted it would, feeling that if the national media had not yet picked up the story, they weren't going to. All agreed. The second prong was if a new scandal were to hit the organization. Hutchins was sufficiently vague, but Markham knew exactly what he meant, Fragile X. The other executives, Cooley, Ross, and Bolger, had never known anything about it and missed the real meaning of the CEO's statement. The third prong was the Loomis trial. All agreed that they must do anything necessary to win. Markham felt a sense of relief after the meeting, and the other executives appeared to feel the same way. They shared brandies and cigars before their drivers took them home. It was shortly after he arrived at his suburban home that Markham first began to wonder about his future. Maybe it was paranoia. Maybe it was real. Either way, he slept poorly, and after the phone call, he didn't sleep at all.

Since Markham had joined ComHealth five years before, H. Carter Hutchins always assured him that he was the natural successor to the CEO spot. Bolger was too dumb, Hutchins often said. Ross was "a little too smart and a little too nice," while Cooley was "a wonderful number two man." Markham heard these assessments many times over five years, private conversations where Hutchins appeared to confide in him. Markham took those thoughts at face value and largely agreed with them. He also knew that Hutchins' phenomenal success with ComHealth allowed him to control the board of directors easily and that in all likelihood, he would hand-pick his successor. Markham's own work was praised by both Hutchins and the board.

He had no reason to doubt his eventual accession. His relationship with Hutchins was friendly, and there had never been a professional conflict. They golfed together regularly and vacationed together occasionally. Their wives were the best of friends, and their business philosophies seemed to mirror one another. Markham often said, "Patients mean dollars. Dollars mean power. Power means expansion. Expansion means more patients." Markham obsequiously called it "Hutchins' Circle." H. Carter Hutchins had not disagreed. Similarly, Hutchins once said that "Quality equals dollars." Markham had liked it so much that he had it made into a bronze paperweight that he gave back to Hutchins as a gift. Privately they loved to joke, saying, "Really it's dollars that equal dollars—and only money matters."

Personally Markham admired the unique blend of talents that had clearly been Hutchins' reason for success. Possessing the charisma and disarming charm of a politician, a scientist's analytical mind, and the ruthlessness of a Salvadoran death squad, Markham knew that H. Carter Hutchins was that one man in a million whose destiny was limitless. Markham merely hoped to follow in his footsteps.

Hutchins was his mentor, but he had also been helpful to Markham in other, somewhat darker ways. The first time was four years before. While playing golf one day, Hutchins mentioned how much he liked the look of an obscure, over-the-counter stock, MinDak Health. At the time, MinDak Health was a small, struggling HMO covering western Minnesota and the Dakotas. Markham said nothing in reply, and Hutchins never mentioned it again, but over the course of the next month, Markham acquired over one million shares of the company, then trading at just less than seven dollars a share. Six months later, ComHealth's board of directors announced a buyout of MinDak Health and with the news, the stock jumped to $17 per share. Markham's profit for that round of golf was $11 million. He had no idea what Hutchins' profit was.

Technically no violation occurred. There was no law that forbade Markham from owning stock in another HMO, and since he was not a member of the board of directors, he had no direct knowledge that a takeover was imminent. Also, there was no paper evidence of any irregularity. It was strictly legal. Or at least not able to be proven. The SEC never said a word.

Markham was extremely grateful, the incident nearly doubling his net worth at the time. It was also the first time he had been introduced to the hidden side of Hutchins. From the moment it happened, Markham was afraid that a favor of that magnitude would require repayment. He was right. It did.

About four months later, Hutchins asked Markham fly to the Bahamas to meet with the chairman of Redlin Medical, headquartered in Nassau. Markham knew Redlin as an offshore corporation that bought surplus medical equipment from suppliers below cost and then in turn sold it to ComHealth at a deep discount wholesale price. The reason for the visit was purportedly to negotiate a pharmaceutical purchase, but when he arrived in Nassau, Markham became aware of a much more detailed scheme. Expecting to find a large office building when he arrived, instead he found an abandoned building with a mailbox. Outside the building was a white limo that took him from his cab to the spacious home of Carter Hutchins' lifelong friend and wealthy Nassau resident, Redlin Pierce.

Markham met with Redlin Pierce for over three hours that day. During that time, as he sat on a long, third-floor balcony of Pierce's sprawling mansion, he began to appreciate Hutchins' innovation and his own foolish naiveté. Redlin Medical was a dummy corporation. Its legitimate business involved the purchase and reselling of equipment and pharmaceuticals. However, its only buyer was ComHealth, and its profits were shared by the two "stockholders," Mr. Green and Mr. Black. The silver-haired, patrician Pierce, who made his money in investment banking, was Mr. Green. Hutchins was Mr. Black.

Their scheme was simple. Redlin would buy something such as pharmaceuticals nearing expiration for a deep discount, ten million pills for $100,000 or one penny per pill. The pills were then resold to ComHealth for two cents per pill or $200,000, netting Redlin Medical $100,000. ComHealth subscribers were happy because their prescriptions cost less, usually fifty to seventy-five percent less, not realizing their medications were a little older. Since the medications were not expired, everyone appeared to win, and no questions had ever been asked.

That part of Redlin Medical was sound business and perfectly legal, but the rest was absolutely the opposite. After the sale, the profits were placed in an account of a local branch of a Swiss bank and aggressively invested. The account was administered by Redlin Pierce under the pseudonym of Mr. Green.

What Hutchins and his friend had constructed was an elaborate insider trading scheme. The profits from Redlin Medical were then invested in companies that Hutchins knew were about to be taken over. Since Hutchins was prohibited by law from buying stock in a company about to be acquired, Pierce, acting as the mysterious Mr. Green, would buy shares of the company to be acquired months before the takeover became public. When the notice of acquisition hit the streets, the stock would soar, and Hutchins and Pierce would reap enormous profits.

Markham, shocked at Pierce's candidness, listened as the old banker told of how they always bought only enough to avoid IRS red flags and then laundered their profits through a second set of transactions between ComHealth, Redlin Medical, the bank, and a local investment brokerage. Markham had been overwhelmed by the plan's extent and its complexity. There was no way of knowing how much Hutchins and Pierce made over the years while they perfected their scheme. The information was not volunteered, but a conservative estimate would have been a half-billion each. It was at that very moment that he first felt something different about H. Carter Hutchins. Before it was respect and admiration. Now, it was also fear.

Markham knew that his being let in on the scheme meant that Hutchins implicitly trusted him. That fact was at first flattering, but soon Markham realized it was less a compliment than a statement. Markham guessed what Hutchins had actually done, doctoring records to make it appear that Markham knew well in advance of his stock purchase of the proposed buyout of MinDak. The realization was an epiphany, because for the first time, Markham knew that Hutchins owned his soul. Hutchins and Pierce enlightened him merely to use him for their own ends.

"Carter has great hopes for you," Pierce said.

"He's a pleasure to work for, and I hope to continue the tradition he has set forth," was his reply.

Pierce gave him one brief assignment. On his way back to Minneapolis, he would deliver two suitcases to a man named Nick staying in the Waverly Hotel in Atlanta. Each suitcase contained a million dollars. Pierce told him he would recognize Nick by the fact that he was a black man with one brown eye and one green eye. He would also say the code phrase, Fragile X.

After the delivery, Hutchins openly told Markham what the money was for: the deaths of several scientists. Hutchins also told Markham what else he expected of him: to coordinate Fragile X. "We're just ten years ahead of the mainstream. Soon the country will accept this type of preventive medicine easily. They know we can't afford to take care of everyone anymore."

Markham was less sure, but he did as he was told, and within two months the plot to identify the carrier fetuses was in place, hidden deep in the Doyne Lab computers. It worked perfectly, and after six months Hutchins was so pleased that he tossed Markham another tip. Regent Health. There was no point in saying no and there was no going back. This time Markham made a reluctant $13 million and with it chalked up his third felony. He became a criminal without a choice.

For two years, it worked beautifully as one after another Fragile X fetus was aborted. No one ever caught on, and with great care, they thought, no one ever would. It was twenty-four months of peace, prosperity, and perfection. And then came Molly Loomis.

As Gregory Markham looked out the window, another drop of sweat slid from his forehead onto his temple. Never in his life had he imagined it. His only real crime was ambition. But now, it seemed more a fleeting ghost, disappearing into a cloud of murder, insider trading, and a complete destruction of public trust. He was as guilty as sin. Perhaps once unwitting, but certainly not unwilling.

He cursed his stupidity as he realized the truth. They had all been pawns. Hutchins' methods, ingenious, tried, and true. Favors bought control, control bought fear, and fear bought loyalty. To himself he now wondered what the other executives owed Hutchins. He knew the others traded on inside information, as did their lawyers. Several, like Ace and Bolger, bragged about it after a drink too many. But then he realized it really didn't matter what anyone owed Hutchins, because the CEO owned all his lawyers and executives.

Markham walked away from the window, sat down at the desk, and stared at the phone. He had few choices. He knew that there were cracks in the ComHealth foundation. Big cracks, with reporters everywhere looking into them. Markham shuddered at the thought.

The phone call had been a wake-up call to a notion he should have seen before. If it all came apart, H. Carter Hutchins would need a fall guy. Markham punched in the number, his hand trembling slightly. The question began to sink in. Was he the fall guy? He didn't know. Nor could he answer the other question that plagued him. Who was warning him?

On the first day of reasonable temperatures in a week, the downtown streets were loaded with shoppers, businessmen, and cars. Reggie and Molly jogged across Hennepin Avenue as the last automobile passed by them. Landing on the sidewalk along the far side, they slowed to a leisurely pace as they walked toward the Third Street Clinic. The sun-streaked morning yielded a warm afternoon, and both removed the windbreakers they were wearing, tossing them over their arms.

"What time is it?" Molly asked, wiping a strand of hair from her brow.

"A little after two, but don't try to change the subject."

"I shouldn't have told you."

"You told me because you wanted me to disapprove," Reggie replied as he dodged an older woman with a large shopping bag.

"That's probably true."

"I swear to God that if you go back to that guy I will personally string you up by the nostrils from the highest tree I can find."

"Gross," Molly muttered, flattered by Reggie's macho musings.

Reggie continued, "Look, you like the doc. Just admit it."

Molly stopped in her tracks. "That's not true," she pleaded, her face turning red.

Reggie laughed and put his arm around her shoulder, tugging affectionately on her pony tail. "C'mon."

"It's really not," she tried again.

"Molly, you're face is like a living polygraph," he chuckled.

"He's older than me," she said, looking away.

"How much?"

Molly didn't hesitate. "Five years, three months."

Reggie laughed again. "My God! A real sugar daddy."

Molly playfully pushed Reggie away. "Shut up."

Reggie was undeterred. "Molly, the best thing that's happened to you in five years is that divorce becoming final. I wanted to drink champagne when I saw that paper."

Molly frowned. "Besides," Reggie continued, "I know who you really want."

"Enough," Molly said, slapping his wrist. She was embarrassed, but not unhappy to talk about it. "I don't want to hear another word."

Reggie lifted his arm from her shoulder, and they continued walking side by side. "Waddya really think, Molly? You think Troy just woke up one day and said, 'Okay, today's the day I quit being a beer-drinking, skirt-chasing, woman-beating bum'? Forget it. Guys like him feel entitled to that life. It's like part of their manhood. They don't really see what they do as wrong. And they'll say anything to get what they want."

Molly both hated and loved Reggie's wisdom beyond his years. He was right. She brought the divorce up to hear his thoughts about Troy. "What if he really has changed?" she asked. "Wouldn't he deserve another chance?"

Reggie rolled his eyes and turned away from her.

Molly continued. "I mean it's not as if I'm lily white here."

Reggie groaned audibly. "Get real, Molly. What are you, *desperate* to feel guilty?"

"No."

"Look, his lies were like drool out of a baby. He cheated on you more often than you could count. He broke your nose at least once, and every time he came home drunk he would—"

Molly stopped again and raised her hands, stopping him. Her face was even more flushed. "How did you know about that?"

Reggie looked sheepish. "Cheap apartments. Thin walls."

Molly started walking. Reggie trailed one step behind. It was a full minute before she spoke again. "You know he never considered it that."

"What did I say earlier? Entitled? Manly man?"

Molly said nothing as they turned onto Third Street. The crowd was decidedly thinner, and they could see the clinic at the end of the cul-de-sac. She could dispute nothing that Reggie said, and worse yet, she knew it all already. She felt angry at herself. Angry at her temptation. How could she be so stupid as to even think of going back to him?

"Let's change the subject," she said finally.

"I said what I wanted to," he replied. "Hope I didn't offend."

They were three steps from the front door of the clinic when Molly stopped. She turned to Reggie and faced him. "You didn't. And thanks. You're a good friend."

"Don't ever think about him again," continued Reggie.

Molly leaned over, kissed him on the cheek, and then walked inside.

The waiting room was full with an assortment of patients ranging from a large pregnant woman to a little boy screaming and holding his ear. The noise was extreme from a group of little children playing in the corner with a set of Legos and two little girls playing with some balls with bells. Sylvia stood behind the reception desk talking about a prescription to an elderly man who cupped his hands to his ears to help him hear. Letisha was attending to the pregnant woman, taking her temperature in the waiting room, as the examining rooms were obviously full. Sandra scurried about the back hallway, talking on a cordless phone and carrying a large handful of computer printouts.

Molly waved, and Sylvia saw them, nodding with a smile and signaling them to go into the back office. They wove their way through the crowd and past one of the large balls that careened away from the girls. Letisha slapped Reggie on the thigh as he walked by, eliciting a grin.

"Busy?" asked Molly as she slipped past Sylvia.

"Unbelievable."

"We'll be in his office."

Five minutes later, a harried-looking Colder threw open his office door and took a seat on one of plastic chairs. Reggie stood looking at the diplomas lining the wall. Molly sat in a corner, wedged between two file cabinets.

"Hi, wish I had more than two minutes," Colder said. He sounded and looked exhausted as he popped open a Mountain Dew.

"You look tired," Molly said, trying not to look too happy to see him.

"I think we saw about eight hundred this morning."

"You've got about eight hundred still out there," Reggie added.

Colder closed his eyes, relishing the cold crispness of the drink before emitting a sigh. He had been working harder than usual and that fact lined his face. The financial pinch was growing ever greater, and Sandra told him it was now nearly hopeless. "You guys throw on some white coats. It'd go a lot faster."

Reggie laughed. "There's an idea. Molly and I could go to work for ComHealth. They'd probably like that. Since we wouldn't know any tests to order, we'd really save them some money."

They all laughed at the black humor, each knowing all too well that the confrontation with the powerful HMO was looming ever closer. Despite everyone's prediction that ComHealth would seek to delay the trial for months or years, no such request had occurred, and they all knew that there would be nothing that would be funny about that battle.

Colder stood and shut the door. Molly stopped laughing and looked at him carefully. He was suddenly serious, his manner controlled and methodical.

"It's on for tomorrow."

"What?" Reggie asked.

"I got the second call. He's coming in."

"O'Reilly?"

"Yes."

"When?" Molly asked.

"Sometime late morning."

"Where?"

"A public place. He'll let me know all the details tomorrow."

Molly was ecstatic. The thought of meeting the man who could prove ComHealth's link to Fragile X was electrifying. Her voice quivered as she spoke. "You talk to Tyler and the FBI?"

"Yes," Colder replied, catching her gaze. "It's arranged for him to be guarded."

"Then what?" Reggie asked. His enthusiasm matched Molly's, but for different reasons.

"Tyler figures he'll need a couple of days to go over everything, including all the evidence. Then the evidence will need to be examined by the ComHealth lawyers and they also have the right to interview him."

"Oh, God," Molly muttered.

Colder was reassuring. "Tyler's sure he's safe the minute he's in our hands and we have the journal and his data. At that point, the whole thing is sure to be public. For him to suddenly have a car go off a bridge, well—"

"He's right," Reggie agreed. "Every reporter in the country would be on it."

"Not to mention every cop. Once he starts telling his story, I think that the ComHealth guys are going to run for cover."

Molly turned away, suddenly struck by a realization. She shook her head, silently cursing herself. How selfish she had been. Throughout her ordeal, she thought only of herself, her loss, her predicament. But here was a man who had lost everything, his family, his career, and his freedom, all because of an innocent discovery. And now he risked his life again, for her, for those who had died trying to bring the killers to justice. As she considered what his life had been like, living on the run, in fear, her euphoria faded, replaced by a sense of responsibility.

"We've got to get him in," Molly said solemnly. "If for no other reason than to give him his life back."

Reggie nodded in agreement.

"There'll be both FBI and local police," Colder said. "And it's going to happen fast. From the time he tells us where he'll be, we'll have less than a half hour to get there. If we're late, he'll be gone."

"In other words, no one would have time to set up a hit," Reggie said.

"Exactly."

"Any idea where?" Molly asked, turning back toward them.

"Like I said, it'll be a public place. He'll find us. Once we have him, the agents will surround us and get us out of there."

Molly hesitated for an instant. There was obviously some danger to the plan.

"I think we're the only people he trusts," said Colder, looking at her.

Molly tried to look brave. "Then that's what we'll do."

"I'm going too," said Reggie.

Reggie's fearlessness was welcome. Colder grinned. "I was counting on that."

"I've got a lot of work to do tonight," Reggie said. "But I'll be ready tomorrow."

Molly turned to Reggie, confused. "But you said you weren't working tonight."

"Not my job—my—should I say, hobby?"

Colder's eyes took on an amused glint. "May I ask what exactly your hobby is?"

Reggie remained evasive, "That information is on a need-to-know basis only. Right now, only I need to know."

"Does your hobby have a name?" Molly asked.

"At the moment, I'm just calling it Project PITA. Pain in Their Ass. Right now, it's Mr. Markham that's sweating a little. Couple days ago, it was someone else."

"You wouldn't by chance have something to do with that picture in the paper of Mr. Hutchins with the keg of beer and the strippers would you?"

"I assure you," he chuckled, "I would never, *ever*, participate in anything like that."

They all laughed, but Colder reminded Reggie to be careful. "Remember what we're dealing with. When we went into their computers—"

Reggie interrupted him. "I will."

Molly started to speak when the door opened and Sylvia stuck her head inside. "Dr. Colder?" she said, emphasizing the title as a reminder that there were patients waiting.

Colder nodded and stood up, ready to leave. "Be here at 9:00 tomorrow morning. We have to drive to the phone where he's going to call. Then we'll go get him."

"FBI?" asked Molly.

"They'll be with us."

Reggie could barely contain himself. For the first time, his excitement boiled over. "We're gonna get these bastards!" he exclaimed, pounding his fist into his open palm.

Five minutes later, Reggie and Molly walked back along Third Street toward Hennepin Avenue. Their pace was brisk, fueled by a combination of adrenaline, expectation, and fear. "I can't wait," Reggie said.

"It's almost terrifying when you think of it," Molly said, ignoring him. "Think of what O'Reilly's been through."

"Tomorrow he's free."

"Yes," Molly agreed.

"And tomorrow we shoot the first bullet at ComHealth's heart."

For the first time all day, Molly permitted herself a smile. "Yes."

Suddenly Reggie stopped, his face turning grim.

"What?" asked Molly, confused.

"I don't like it," he said quietly.

"Like what?"

Reggie looked down at the ground. "Like the way—"

"The way what?"

"The way Colder looked at you. I think he likes you."

With the words, Reggie cackled loudly and ran several steps ahead of her. Molly's face flushed. She took two quick steps but then stopped realizing she would never catch him in a race. "Reggie Tan!"

"It's true,"

"I'll kill you!"

Reggie bounded easily ahead of her. "You gotta catch me."

Molly stopped. She had no interest in catching him. She was too busy thinking about what he had said, wanting it to be true.

As midnight neared, Markham was still sitting at his desk in an office now lit only by the single light at the corner of his desk. The ice in his drink was nearly melted, he sipped at the scotch tentatively, as if drinking slowly would disguise his boozy breath when he returned home. The long day was filled with the familiar ritual of damage control. He hadn't talked to Hutchins or any of the other executives, preferring to spend most of the day in the office.

As he peered out at the lights of downtown, he became with every passing minute more convinced that his theory of the morning was correct. If Fragile X exploded, he would be the fall guy. It only made sense. His were the only fingerprints directly on it. He made all the arrangements and the contacts. He delivered the money. It mattered little if anyone else had known. He was the one who would be implicated.

As the day progressed, he figured out who had given him the warning. It was almost undoubtedly someone close to Hutchins. That was the Hutchins way, and the message was unmistakable—solve the problem and you're safe; lose control and you're finished. Markham spent the entire day doing what he needed to do. He needed to solve the problem.

The phone rang. Markham was expecting it, and he answered it on the first ring. "Tell me," he said.

"I don't know yet."

"Damn it," Markham growled, his voice trailing to a seething whisper. "That's not good enough. We've got to know, and we've got to know now."

"Look, Greg, nobody knows. Not even the doctor."

"You sure?"

"Positive."

"Then how can you guarantee anything?"

"I'm telling you this guy is smart. He's gotten away from us for two years. But we'll get him."

"You didn't answer my question," Markham hissed, barely controlling his temper.

"I'm telling you, tomorrow night you'll be sipping champagne."

"You'd better be right."

"Trust me. You'll have everything in your lap. You can have a bonfire."

"Like I said, you'd better be right."

"I'll talk to you tomorrow."

When the line went dead, Markham hung up the receiver and finished his scotch. Trust, he thought. How appropriate. No one was worthy of that.

He poured himself another drink, no longer worrying what his wife would say. She would never complain if she had any idea how much was at stake. Markham picked up the phone. He slammed down half the scotch and took a deep breath. He had one final call to make. It was a call he had been waiting to make, a call that could determine his fate.

Chapter Twenty-two

August 16

The day James Patrick O'Reilly had waited for arrived with a cool morning fog that lifted a half hour after the dawn. As the sun rose in the east, the lush woodland that had been his home for so long offered a symphony of birds and wildlife, while a faint breeze passed through the leaves, sounding at times like a flute and at others, an oboe.

He lay awake all night, his feet propped up in the back end of his pickup, staring at the stars and listening to the gallery of nature's sounds. He knew today would be his final act of freedom, mere hours in the course of a lifetime, but his movements now were the last few efforts of a man about to face destiny. He always imagined how it would end. Press conferences, a trial certainly. It all seemed so foolish in reality. A crazy discovery that was meant to be more a curiosity than anything else. Now it was the focus of his world. The end point for some. A beginning for others.

He had long since decided what he would do. It would have been safer to disappear. But they had killed his wife, his unborn child, his friends, and he could never have lived with just letting their deaths go. Justice was not revenge, but it did offer hope. What happened from here was his destiny. He would tell the truth of what happened to the world.

In the rearview mirror above the dashboard, he carefully stroked on the make-up. First his hands, then his neck and face. His skin shade would be a light black, a carefully chosen tone to hide his fair complexion but not look artificial. It took time to apply it evenly, but finally finished and satisfied, he turned to his hair. The wig was a loose curl of a young black man, long in the back. He fitted it carefully over his own short, reddish hair. Then he pulled a gray Charlotte Hornets sweatshirt over his head and finished with a Chicago Bulls cap and sunglasses.

Gazing at himself in the mirror, even he didn't recognize his face. Realizing he had not yet done his eyelids, he finished the makeup. Satisfied, he picked up the manila envelope containing the magazine and the disks and tucked it into his belt underneath his sweatshirt. Finished, he took a deep breath and began his journey.

He drove from his hiding place in the woods into Rockford where he stopped at a Standard Oil station. A moment later, he was talking to Colder.

"You know how to get the next call?" O'Reilly asked.

"Yes," Colder said, his voice a touch nervous. "You'll page me at exactly ten o'clock. You'll be at a pay phone."

"Correct. When you answer, don't talk to me. Just listen. I have no doubt that someone will be watching you, and they will probably try to mike you from a distance, but as long as you use any random phone and don't talk, they'll never know.

"Got it."

"And carry the cell phone. Anything goes wrong. I'll call you on that."

"Check."

"And, Peter," O'Reilly said, his own voice now quivering. "Thank you."

"Don't mention it."

"I—"

"We're gonna have a bunch of agents, and we have a safe house set up for you. It's all downhill from here," Colder interrupted, sounding confident.

"Thank you."

O'Reilly hung up the phone, holding on to the receiver and closing his eyes. It was about to happen. His mouth felt dry. His heart raced. His palms were wet. Two years he had waited. Two years he had planned. Had he thought of everything? He worried. Could there possibly be a slip-up? It was possible. Covering everything was nearly an impossible task. He was sure of only one thing. They would definitely try to kill him today.

Colder hung up the pay phone at the SuperAmerica and drove the three miles back to the Third Street Clinic. He went inside, and Sylvia handed him a cup of coffee; they both took seats in the waiting room.

"Okay?" was all she asked.

Colder nodded yes.

Molly and Reggie arrived five minutes later, ten minutes ahead of time. "You hear from him?" Reggie asked.

"Yes."

Molly could see that Colder was concerned. His usual good humor was absent, replaced by a pale and somewhat distant look. His greeting was warm, but his manner was subdued. She interpreted it as the same fear that she was feeling.

"When are we going?" Reggie asked.

"As soon as everyone is here."

They sat in silence contemplating James Patrick O'Reilly as they waited for the FBI agents. There was no nervous or black humor spoken to break the tension, only the recognition of all that O'Reilly had gone through and the worry they still had for him. Reggie sipped on a cup of coffee. Molly declined. Colder let his sit and grow cold.

At precisely 9:45, the two FBI agents arrived, as did Briggs and Sanders. Seeing the cars pull up outside the clinic, all except Sylvia got up. She was staying at the clinic to continue with a few chores.

"I just have a few stitches to take out," Sylvia said to Colder as he headed for the door.

"I'll call you when we're done," he replied.

"Good luck," she added, trying not to sound afraid. Colder closed the door behind him and joined the others, who had moved outside.

Everyone was silent except Colder as the FBI agents, Tyler, and Marcus stepped out of the cars. "Morning."

"Dr. Colder," Agent Hastings said.

"Who are they?" Colder asked, without a greeting, pointing to another gray sedan with four men in it parked fifty yards away.

"More agents," Briggs replied.

Marcus approached Molly and put his hand on her shoulder. "How you doing?" he asked, his voice reflecting genuine concern.

"Good," she said without hesitation.

"Attaway."

The two FBI agents were in no mood for small talk either. "Dr. Colder," began Agent Hastings. "You're the only one who has ever actually talked to him about this. And you, Molly, and Tyler are the only people he apparently trusts."

"He is very careful and distrustful."

"Speaking on behalf of the bureau, I must say that we remain somewhat uncomfortable with today's arrangements. We are not accustomed to utilizing untrained personnel in a situation such as this."

"There isn't a choice," Molly said pointedly. "He'll never come in unless he sees us."

The two FBI agents looked surprised at her resolve. They had thought of her as mousy, but by the tone in her voice Molly was almost taking charge. McWilliams cleared his throat. "I express my reservations from both personal and professional points of view."

Colder stood behind her. "We appreciate that, but as Molly says, there really is no choice."

"Would it be helpful if—" Agent McWilliams started.

Colder interrupted, shaking his head negatively and waving his hand. "Forget it. This is the only way he'll do it."

The two agents fell silent and looked at each other. Hastings finally spoke after what seemed like five minutes. "Well, I guess we're at your disposal."

"Then let's go," Peter directed. "Everyone in the cars."

Five minutes later, the four cars exited downtown Minneapolis on Highway 35W heading south. Colder led, his car carrying Molly and Reggie. The two FBI teams followed, and the lawyers trailed. Turning west toward the western suburbs, Colder kept watching in his rearview mirrors. He saw that no one appeared to be following.

As they breezed through the light Saturday traffic, Reggie also looked out the windows, straining to see anyone who might be trailing them. "Someone's watching us," he said. "I can feel it."

"I agree," said Molly softly. "It's not even ESP. It's more like something crawling on my back."

Colder exited on Nicollet Avenue and turned south, driving past an endless stream of small businesses and strip malls. O'Reilly had told him only to pick a place where they couldn't possibly have tapped any phones. This was it. The

Nicollet business district was perfect.

Colder looked at his watch. One minute to ten. His heart seemed to leap into his throat as he realized the call was one minute away. He carefully eyed the area and pulled to the side of the road. One gas station and a laundry. Then he saw it, a pay phone outside a Dunkin' Donuts. "Perfect," he thought, stepping outside.

"That one," Molly said, pointing to the phone,

Colder looked at Molly and smiled. "Just what I was thinking."

The other three cars pulled to a stop behind them. Colder ran the thirty yards to the pay phone and exactly as he arrived at the booth, the pager went off. The agreement had been that he had to call back in thirty seconds or they would try again five minutes later. Two misses and the deal was off. Colder made it easily and O'Reilly answered immediately.

"Peter?"

"Yes."

O'Reilly recognized the voice as Colder's and he continued. "The place is the Mall of America. Twenty minutes. Camp Snoopy. You walk toward it from the north. I'll find you."

The phone went dead. Colder was struck by the fear in O'Reilly's voice. He was a man who was paranoid for a reason. But what could go wrong? he asked himself. His question did not help. He, too, was fearful.

Colder walked to the cars and slipped into the back seat of the first group of FBI agents' car. "Mall of America. Twenty minutes."

"Where?" said Hastings.

"We go in from the north and head toward Camp Snoopy. He says he'll find us."

"Let's go."

Colder bolted out of the car, and minutes later their four cars raced toward the Mall of America. "It's a good spot," Reggie said. "He's a smart dude."

"There'll be a million people there today," Molly added.

"We only care about one," Colder said without being contrary. "Only one."

"Yes." Molly could see on Colder's forehead the first hint of sweat begin to appear.

Marcia Sullivan stared through the binoculars at the four cars parked three hundred yards ahead. Her windshield was dirty, but she could make out Peter Colder easily as he made his way back from the phone booth to a tan Ford Taurus.

"Something big is going down," she said.

"How do you know?" asked Kenny Mellum, her boyfriend of three years and a cameraman for KSTP-TV.

"I just do. That's the FBI with Colder and the lawyers are in the last car."

"How do you know that's the FBI?" Kenny asked.

"I don't," she replied, allowing her binoculars to wander over all of the cars between them. "I'm guessing."

"Marsh," Kenny began, almost whining, "just what in the hell are we doing? FBI?"

"I'm doing Colder a favor," she answered, still looking carefully at every passing car. "I owe him big time, and he asked me to help him."

"That wasn't what I asked you."

"He asked me to follow him this morning at a distance. He wanted to know if anyone was following him. If so, I'm supposed to call him on his cellular."

"What's he doing?"

"I don't know, but I have a pretty good idea."

Mellum groaned and asked no more questions. He was accustomed to his girlfriend's relentlessness and absent-minded evasiveness. He knew he would never get a straight answer. "We've got exhibition football on TV this afternoon, Marsh. We better be done," he said, still whining.

"Go," she exclaimed as their cars took off, pointing furiously at them.

"Oh God," he groaned as he shifted into gear. "What am I in love with? Half Cagney and Lacey and half Woodward and Bernstein."

"Just drive," she said patting him on the thigh, holding the binoculars in her other hand. "I promise you it'll be worth your while."

Kenny groaned and obeyed, convinced his girlfriend had lost her marbles.

When H. Carter Hutchins boarded the corporate jet, a brand new Gulf Stream V, he did so with a slight jaunt in his step, a playful reminder of the success the day would bring. A meeting of HMO executives in New York had been a good excuse for Celia to shop and for him to miss any events in Minneapolis that might occur on that day. Pausing at the top of the stairway and gazing across the sun-streaked tarmac like a royal surveying his kingdom, he stood with a look of confident satisfaction. He knew that when he returned, the problem would be solved.

Satisfied that all was on schedule, he turned and entered the airplane, where an attendant gathered his coat and handed him a glass of champagne. Hutchins took it gleefully. He killed it in two gulps. He felt better yet. The sun was shining, the champagne was exquisite. The buzz was invigorating. It was going to be a good day.

Colder's worries began to lift as soon as their four cars screeched to a halt in front of the north entrance to Mall of America. Realizing they had made the journey in less than the allotted time relieved him. Knowing that unless someone had been tipped off that the site was the world's largest shopping mall, there would never have been time to arrange for anyone to beat them there. For the first time, he was confident that O'Reilly would be safe.

The Mall of America, or Mega Mall, had been built in 1992 on the old site of Metropolitan Stadium, the former home of the Minnesota Vikings and Twins. Easily the largest shopping mall in the United States, it housed over five hundred retail stores on over four million square feet. With forty-nine restaurants of ethnic varieties, eight nightclubs, a fourteen-screen movie theater, and a seven-acre amusement park called Knott's Camp Snoopy at its center, the Mega Mall had become within a few short years the single greatest tourist attraction in the state, drawing more tourists annually than Disneyland, Graceland, and the

Grand Canyon combined. On an average day, it attracted one hundred thousand visitors. Near the holidays, that total was near three hundred thousand.

James Patrick O'Reilly had chosen wisely. Colder knew that by ten on a Saturday the mall would already have nearly 40,000 people inside. Tracking any individual walking in or out would nearly be impossible. Camp Snoopy was also a good choice. Centrally located and on the ground floor, the amusement park had a fifty-foot balloon of Snoopy at its entrance. The area was always jammed with parents and children wandering through the shops or waiting for the rides. Trying to find anyone alone in that area on a Saturday would be next to impossible.

Moving swiftly to the doors, Colder stopped and opened one, allowing Molly, Reggie, Tyler, and Marcus to pass. The FBI agents spread out as if on command, planning to go in other entrances. As they had driven, the FBI quickly mapped out a plan. Two men would occupy the third floor overlooking the amusement park. One would be on the north side, the other on the south. Two more would be on the second floor. One on the west, the other on the east. Two would roam through the amusement park. Two would be with main group. As they drove, the FBI arranged for fifteen members of the mall security force to meet them in the amusement park. The plan was to blanket O'Reilly with an army of men the minute he appeared.

Colder let the door swing closed and jogged a few steps to catch up with the others. He glanced at his watch. 10:12. He grabbed Molly by the arm as he passed her and caught her determined glance. He was struck by her courage. She seemed so purposeful and calm. Much calmer than he.

Colder passed the rest of the group, walking arm in arm with Molly. They moved through the crowd, dodging many groups of loitering people. It took them less than two minutes to arrive at Camp Snoopy and another thirty seconds to position themselves on the west side of the merry-go-round. Colder looked at the watch again. 10:14. Molly and Reggie leaned into him to see the time. Their hearts all skipped a beat.

Briggs and Sanders stood with two FBI agents ten feet away. Both attorneys knew that this man was the key to their cause, his information critical, his testimony essential. Tyler looked at Marcus nervously and then at the large clock overhead. One minute had passed. Beyond the clock, which stood as a tower in the middle of the park, he could see one of the agents arrive on the second floor. Immediately the agent pulled a cell phone from his pocket and began talking. Briggs could see the agent nod his head and hang up. Gazing in other directions Briggs was unable to see the remaining agents, his view obscured by the rollercoaster and the various buildings of the amusement park. Happy to know they had arrived, he began to look through the crowd for any sight of O'Reilly.

Molly hung onto Peter's arm tightly, her left shoulder leaning into him. She could feel her heart rate increase and her palms grow sweaty. Scanning through the crowd, she saw only a mass of people mingling, talking, and laughing. There were babies in carriages and toddlers scampering about. Parents and adolescents, couples and elderly. No one appeared to pay attention to them. There was no sign of O'Reilly.

They all guessed he would appear in some sort of disguise. He never admitted that, but it only seemed logical. What would it be? Teenager? Old man? Woman? They all seemed good options, and looking through the crowd Molly knew they would probably not identify him until he was right upon them. One minute later she checked the clock again.

The mall security force seemed everywhere, meandering back and forth, trying not to draw attention despite their numbers. Molly easily counted eight as she stared through the crowd. It relieved her to see them, and her mind wandered to a possible disguise. "Old man?" she whispered.

"Maybe," answered Reggie. "But I don't know."

"Neither do I," admitted Colder, still leaning into Molly.

All of them understood O'Reilly's unwillingness to specify his appearance. Any breach of confidence would be critical. If something went wrong, he would certainly need a way out. As much as he trusted Peter and Molly, his experiences led him to such measures of extreme caution.

An old man walked toward them. For a moment, Molly loosened her grip as his gray eyes met hers. Then he turned, blending into a large gathering of parents watching their kids. It wasn't O'Reilly.

Another man appeared to approach them. He was tall with a leather pilot's jacket. He looked squarely at Molly for a second, but then his gaze passed them and he walked by, disappearing into the crowd.

"What time is it?" Reggie asked.

"Ten-eighteen," Colder replied.

"You think he's watching us?" Molly asked.

"Maybe," Colder said with a crack in his voice. "But I'd hope he'd just come out. Every extra moment is just another for others to get here."

Sanders walked over to them. "Anything?" he asked.

Colder shook his head.

"Everybody is in place," Marcus said.

"Good."

A group of wild squeals heightened the noise in Camp Snoopy as the Whirlaway, a ride with spinning seats started up. This was followed by a deafening roar as the rollercoaster came barreling by, and for a moment no one could hear anything as the entire mall seemed consumed by the noise. Molly plugged her ears and turned gazing into the mass of people behind them on the other side of the merry-go-round. It was 10:19.

It happened quickly. He appeared from the crowd, one hundred feet away. A man, unquestionably O'Reilly. One man, alone. Walking toward Snoopy, the giant centerpiece of the amusement park. Made up as a black man with a baseball cap and a Chicago Bulls jacket, his head was down, his hands in his pockets. He walked rapidly, purposefully, not looking at anyone else.

The noise, still deafening, Molly tugged on Colder's jacket and he turned. Reggie, seeing them move, turned as well. Colder waved to Tyler, and within seconds everyone had spotted him, and they began to head toward him. Marcus, Tyler, and the agents were the closest, but they were blocked by a throng of people. Molly and Reggie, catching a natural seam in the crowd, took off. Colder was right behind. They jogged twenty yards, pausing at the base of one of the roller coaster's dips. They lost him in the crowd for an instant, but a security guard joining them pointed, and each saw the flash of the Bulls jacket through the people. The four of them moved swiftly toward the spot where they had seen him. Pushing furiously through the crowd, they paid no attention to the complaints they left behind. Colder forged his way into the lead, and the others followed winding their way through a crushing burden of bodies. As they passed a group of four teenagers, Colder could see him clearly. He was walking slower and at an angle away from them.

Colder and the others stopped. Peter cursed to himself. They had taken a bad approach to him. He could see Tyler, Marcus, and the agents suffered the same fate. While O'Reilly walked a straight line, each group had swung out, looking for a cutback lane. None had materialized, and O'Reilly was no closer than he had been.

O'Reilly continued to walk toward the giant balloon character. His head was down, but he appeared to be watching everything carefully from beneath the cap. He was sixty feet away. Colder raised his hand and waved. O'Reilly did not see them. Tyler, Marcus, and the agents could be seen in the distance, also trapped behind people. O'Reilly was now directly between them. Colder could see Briggs waving furiously at their man as well.

O'Reilly paused as he neared the crowd surrounding the merry-go-round, the last obstacle before Snoopy. Needing to veer toward one group or the other, O'Reilly swung toward Colder's. At that instant his eyes caught Colder. O'Reilly moved quickly, cutting sideways into an open area behind the crowd. Colder, Molly, and Reggie cut the same way, moving parallel to him, attempting to get around the mass of people. It was impossible. They had underestimated the number that would be in the mall's amusement park, and no one could move. O'Reilly dodged an older couple and walked into a small clearing. He was still fifty feet away. His eyes caught Molly's. A tiny smile appeared on his face.

The overhead rollercoaster roared by again as he moved toward them. Reggie, catching a small break in the crowd, sprinted toward O'Reilly. The others followed. Reggie was only ten yards away when O'Reilly appeared to stumble. As if tripped, he dropped to one knee. Reggie stopped. O'Reilly's hand swung to his left shoulder and his baseball cap flew off. Colder and Molly stopped, nearly crashing into Reggie. O'Reilly tried to stand, but suddenly his chest appeared to be driven forward, as if pushed from behind. He landed on his stomach, his face pounding against the floor. They all watched, horrified as blood appeared all around O'Reilly's chest spreading out on the floor. One woman screamed, then another, then many.

Colder pushed Reggie away and tried to get to his prostrate friend, but the scattering crowd blocked him. At the sight of the blood, a few realized what was happening. Two women screamed, followed by several children. The immediate crowd began to scatter as O'Reilly lifted his head and tried to crawl along the cement with his arms, his legs seemingly uncontrolled. Reggie and Molly tried frantically to slide through the mass of people, but they were paralyzed by the spreading frenzy. Suddenly another bullet appeared to strike O'Reilly as his body shook in a spasm and blood flew into the air. This shot was loud and easily audible. The crowd, realizing it was gunfire, began to run. Screaming started everywhere. It was bedlam, and every person in the crowd was nearly trampled in a wild race to get away.

Colder could see Briggs's group. They, too, were blocked and pushed back in the melee. Colder's eyes turned to the second floor. Two of the FBI agents were running in the direction of the food court, the area directly behind O'Reilly. As the crowd passed him in a random stream he could see O'Reilly's body fall still. Frantically Colder threw a large teenage boy aside, only to be blocked by two parents running with strollers. Colder tried to slide by the people, but made no progress; O'Reilly was only a few feet away but remained unreachable. He was still motionless, the pool of blood surrounding him widening.

With anger and fear surging within him Colder drove past two teenagers only to be pushed right back by the crowd. Colder glanced toward O'Reilly in time to see a man in a long coat arrive at O'Reilly. The man, only there for a second, reached into O'Reilly's jacket and removed a large manila envelope. An instant later, he disappeared into the crowd on the far side. Colder was frantic. He jumped back up onto a split rock wall and bounded in three large steps to its end, leaping high into the air. Colder's daring move parted the crowd below, the people lunging out of his way as he landed on the cement. In two more steps he was at O'Reilly's side. Screams continued in the crowd, but now instead of running in a stampede, the people began to slow, blocked by the exits, and trapped against one another. There were no more gunshots to be heard and some people even began milling about, gawking at the downed man and the blood.

Colder flipped O'Reilly on his back. He was unconscious but breathing weakly. His pulse was thready. Reggie arrived and then Molly. Tyler, Marcus, and the agents were a second behind.

"He's alive," Colder managed as he cradled O'Reilly's head.

There was blood everywhere and O'Reilly's eyes had the terrified look of a man fearing his own death. Molly buried her face in her hands and leaned into Reggie.

"We need an ambulance," Colder said, his voice shaking, not knowing that two of the security guards had already called for one.

Sensing that the danger had passed, the crowd began to quiet and slowly encircle the group. More security arrived every second and quickly held the people at bay. O'Reilly lay on his back. His color was gray and he appeared to choke on blood. There had been three gunshot wounds. One in the left shoulder, one in the left chest, and another in the abdomen. Blood oozed freely through his clothing at each site.

Tears formed at the corners of Colder's eyes. "You're okay, Jim," he murmured into the wounded man's ear. "You're okay. Hang in there. You're going to be just fine." Colder knew differently. The wounds were bad. "We need an ambulance!" he screamed at the crowd.

"Two minutes," said one of the guards.

Colder continued to hold O'Reilly's head, cradling it against his chest. "Hang in there, buddy," he whispered. "They're coming."

The FBI agents and security police were flying about, screaming into cell phones as they searched the building for the gunmen. The others stood by. Briggs looked pale. Marcus looked faint. Molly was still buried in Reggie's arms, her sobs audible to anyone near.

O'Reilly coughed weakly and a drop of blood appeared at the corner of his mouth. He took two shallow breaths. "You're okay" Colder repeated, still rocking his cradled head.

With the words, O'Reilly opened his eyes. The gaze was distant, but clear. "Colder," he managed.

"I'm here, Jim. Ambulance is coming."

"Collllder," he stammered, his tongue thick.

"Don't try to talk," Peter whispered in his ear.

"I always liked you," he replied, his voice a bit stronger, but his eyes closed again.

"You're going to be okay, Jim," Colder was unconvinced.

"I re-re-re-spected you," he choked, blood pouring from his mouth.

Molly heard his voice and bit her lip, trying for control. She dropped to her knees on O'Reilly's other side. With tears still streaming down her face, she took his hand. "Molly," he managed weakly, cracking his eyes open again.

"Don't you worry. You're going to be just fine," she somehow managed to choke out.

"I want you to get them."

"We will," Molly assured, holding O'Reilly's limp hand.

Colder did not survey the wounds nor bother applying pressure. The problem was internal. He knew O'Reilly was bleeding badly. "Colder," he choked as more blood appeared at his mouth.

"I'm here," he whispered. "You don't have to talk."

With great effort, O'Reilly tried to speak clearly. His eyes were open, and he seemed to look at the group around him before he refocused on Peter. "I respected you because of you—your life—and Julianne."

"What?" asked Colder, astonished that she would enter into the conversation at this moment. "Julianne?"

"Y-Y-Yes," he stammered.

"Don't talk," he said, convinced O'Reilly was delirious from low blood pressure. But for an instant he was stronger, his eyes burning. And he sounded almost healthy. "Because, you know, the best measure of a man is in the feelings of those he leaves behind."

Colder was flabbergasted. He did not know what to say.

"Take care of everything," O'Reilly mumbled, his eyes closing and his strength fading. "I always knew I would leave it to you."

"Don't talk like that,"

"Jim," Molly cried, seeing his eyes close.

"Jim!" Colder screamed as O'Reilly became gray.

A moment later, the ambulance crew arrived but Colder waved them away. He continued to hold O'Reilly's head in his arms. Molly, her tears flowing forth unabated, held them both. The once-screaming crowd was now silent, and only the sounds of the operating rides punctuated the eerie quiet. Above them, the clock read 10:25. It was one minute past hope. James Patrick O'Reilly had died at 10:24.

Chapter Twenty-three

By the time Marcia Sullivan arrived forty-five minutes later, the arguing had already started. Two off-duty policemen came upon the scene within two minutes of O'Reilly's death, and an additional fifteen investigators from the Minneapolis police department descended on the mall as well. Combining the locals with the mall security and the eight FBI agents had proven a volatile mix. Within minutes, bickering over procedure and jurisdiction had taken over.

O'Reilly's body lay curiously alone, covered by a black tarp in the center of the amusement park. The area looked clean, the surrounding blood cleaned up as soon as the police photographers finished with their pictures. The officers continued to interview a few bystanders who had witnessed the man in the trench coat remove the envelope from O'Reilly's jacket.

No one from the press was at the scene. The police had stonewalled them. Marcia Sullivan was allowed in only because she knew Colder's cell phone number. Briggs sneaked her in, and she spent her time roaming among the officials, eavesdropping on their conversations.

Marcia tried to comfort Molly, but it had proven to be a nearly impossible task. Witnessing O'Reilly's last breath was the proverbial last straw, and Molly's emotions poured forth endlessly. Colder stood with her, holding her tightly, his own tears of sorrow and anger buried in her hair. For forty minutes, they stood together, neither making any attempt to break away and neither one giving any thought to the loss of a witness or possibly the case. What mattered was that they had lost a friend. And more importantly, a friend had lost his life.

Two of the FBI agents approached Colder, who was still holding Molly tightly.

"Stupid damn plan," said the one. "We should never have let him do it. We should have called the shots."

Colder's temper flared and he broke Molly's grip. "What do you mean?" he asked angrily.

McWilliams looked at him with paternal condescension. "If we had organized it—" he started.

Colder stepped forward to a point less than six inches from the crewcut agent's face. His cheeks were flushed nearly purple. "O'Reilly gets killed and all you guys can do is tell me how smart you are? Just what the hell is this? You and I both know there are only two possibilities. Either you guys couldn't guard shit from a fly or someone in your group is a mole."

McWilliams' jaw clenched, his ex-marine's discipline trying to give way to his ex-marine's temper. Colder continued. "Only O'Reilly knew, and then only you guys knew. Either they got lucky as hell and just happened to have a gunman sitting up on the railing or one of your guys leaked the site as soon as we got it."

McWilliams' urge to break the doctor's nose was powerful, but so was the doctor's logic. His anger barely suppressed, the FBI agent backed off. The scenario Colder presented was also one his group was considering. McWilliams forced himself to be calm. "Dr. Colder, can I walk with you for a minute?"

Colder rubbed his eyes, trying to regain his composure. He nodded, and they walked off toward the other side of park. "Peter," Agent McWilliams began as soon as they were out of earshot. "What you just said, unfortunately loud enough for the entire world to hear—"

"Sorry."

McWilliams continued. "—is something we are considering. Obviously there was a leak. Either someone caught our transmission, or—"

"Do you have any ideas?"

"No."

Colder paused. They were now far from the others. He could see Molly with Reggie. Marcia was talking to Briggs, and the other investigators still appeared to be arguing. McWilliams lit a cigarette in the nonsmoking building and blew smoke away from Colder. "The locals have got to do their thing here. They've got a dead guy who was murdered in a very public way. They need an answer to the question: Who? You and I need an answer to the question: How? We already know why."

Colder's anger was still simmering. "Any word on the guy with the envelope?"

"We found a coat matching the description on a bench near the west exit. Empty. He got away."

"Great," Colder grunted. "How about my idea?"

McWilliams bristled. "It's under advisement. But remember, I work with these men. I trust them."

Colder dropped it. He had stated his case and McWilliams had heard it. The damage was already done. He changed the subject, trying to be reasonable. "What now?"

"Locals will want to interview all of you. Publicly they will be the primary investigators."

"What about you?"

The gruff FBI man took a long drag on his Winston. "Most of what I will be doing I can't tell you about."

Colder nodded as if to say "fair enough." He was still angry but realistic; the agent appeared to be doing all he could and saying more than he probably should. "I'm sorry about losing my cool," Colder said.

"We're all sorry about what happened."

Colder shook slightly. The memory was too vivid. He tried not to tear up. "He died right in my arms. He looked right at me."

McWilliams was sympathetic, but still every bit the investigator. "Did he say anything to you?"

"No," sighed Colder. "Mostly it was gibberish. I don't think he was lucid. The only thing that seemed to make sense was some stuff about us continuing on, trying to get them."

"Nothing else?"

"Something about a man's character and something about my ex-wife. Like I said, he wasn't lucid."

McWilliams nodded. "Did he say if he saw anything?"

"No."

As they talked, a police sergeant walked up to them. Stocky, balding with a double chin and a scar above his upper lip, he motioned to Colder. "Doctor, we're going to need to interview you."

"Yes. I'll be right there."

McWilliams extended his hand, and Colder shook it. "I'll be in touch," said the FBI man.

"I'll be waiting."

Briggs and Sanders knew the lieutenant who arrived to take charge of the investigation, and that acquaintance allowed them to make arrangements to be interviewed by the police later in the day. After a long and difficult goodbye with Molly and the others, they made their way to the north entrance and left in the car they had parked in the loading zone two hours before. A large crowd of television and newspaper reporters surrounded their car, but they answered no questions and drove away without even a "no comment."

Neither Briggs nor Sanders even thought about the effects on their case. They had never seen a man die before, and watching O'Reilly struggle against death, his desperate eyes pleading for help, left an unforgettable impression. Thinking clearly was impossible. Briggs drove the car onto the freeway and headed for downtown. They would go to the office first and then to the police station. Beyond those two events, they had no immediate plans. Marcus opened the passenger window a crack, letting the breeze swirl though the cab. "God, I'm hot," he managed weakly. Tyler nodded in agreement, but did not reply. He felt dazed and ill.

Their car sped ahead, merging into the traffic heading downtown. They did not speak further, each finally beginning to consider all of what had happened. O'Reilly had died. The journal and the records were gone. Fragile X was gone. There was no need to say anything. They both knew the case was gone as well.

Molly was still trembling when Marcia sat down next to her on a bench facing the merry-go-round. The police were interviewing Reggie and Colder. Seeking a moment by herself, Molly found the empty bench fifty feet from the main group of investigators. She continued to stare off into space, her lower lip quivering as if wanting to yield more tears, but her eyes remained dry. Her hands, folded on her waist, shook slightly, and her face remained noticeably pale.

Marcia made no attempt to be cheery, her own anger too close to the surface to allow any superficial conversation. She reached over and took one of

Molly's hands, squeezing it lightly. Molly turned to Marcia, her eyes filling. "They killed him."

"Did you see anything?" asked Marcia, sounding like a friend, not a reporter.

"No. Just blood. And him trying to breathe."

Marcia tried not to think about it. She already nearly fainted at the sight of his dead body. "I want you to know that if there is anything I can do—" started Marcia.

Molly sighed. "Thanks."

Marcia continued to hold her hand. Although Molly was a few years older, she could feel a kinship with her. "I really mean it," Marcia repeated. "Please call me for anything. I was human long before I became a cynical reporter who knows everything."

Molly tried to laugh, but coughed instead. "Thanks," she said as she squeezed her friend's hand.

"Don't mention it."

By evening, the police interviews were concluded. Preliminary interviews were conducted at the Mall of America, but then all witnesses returned in the afternoon to police headquarters for a more lengthy questioning. Colder's interview lasted the longest, and when he departed the police department the others were already gone, having driven ahead to Sylvia's house where they agreed they would meet for dinner. Colder returned first to the clinic to pick up the briefcase he had forgotten and then left. He planned to stop at his house to change clothes before going to Sylvia's.

A light rain was falling as he drove the downtown streets. The Minnesota Twins were hosting the Cleveland Indians in a baseball game at the Metrodome, and the streets were filling fast for the game that was an hour away. Instead of driving through the traffic, he swung onto some back streets, and in less than fifteen minutes, he was parked outside his front door.

Mortimer greeted him as soon as he stepped inside. With an air of disenchantment from his master's prolonged absence, the large orange tabby waddled away from him toward the kitchen as if to direct him to where food should be placed. Colder followed, but before obliging him, picked him up and scratched his neck. His purring was restrained, but a moment later some Fancy Feast lightened the great cat's mood.

Colder ambled though the house still largely in a haze. He had answered the questions each a million times. No, he had no idea who had done it. No, he had no idea how the gunman had found out. Throughout the interview, he told the truth and speculated freely. He didn't know who had actually shot O'Reilly, but he knew who he thought might have been responsible. He told the police about Fragile X, the journal, the previous deaths. They asked questions, took notes, and did their jobs thoroughly, but it left him even more discouraged and sad. He was now convinced more than ever that the entire episode was about to end. There was no proof that Fragile X existed. No one even knew exactly what it was. There was no provable link to ComHealth and no evidence to even imply a link. Colder sat limply on his couch and opened a Diet Coke. It was over. He was sure of it. Hutchins had won.

The phone rang just as he took a swig of the Coke, and he answered it on the second ring. "Hello."

"My God, Peter," Julianne exclaimed, obviously relieved to hear his voice. "Are you okay?"

"Shaky." He wasn't afraid to admit it.

"I just saw all of it on the news. You weren't hit were you?"

"No."

"They released video from the surveillance cameras. It's cloudy, but they have some footage of the shooter and the guy who took something from him."

"It was *the* envelope," sighed Peter.

"The journal?" asked Julianne, piecing it together.

"Yeah."

"Oh, God, no."

"Yes," he replied, without trying to avoid sounding disappointed. "On the videotape, where was the shooter?" asked Peter.

"In the food court on the second floor. Right behind a pillar."

"Dammit." He fought anger, frustration, and exhaustion simultaneously.

Julianne struggled to find words. "You want me to come over?"

Colder recalled that his ex-wife had had an important dinner with her boyfriend. "Aren't you going out?"

"Geoff and I were going to go, but when I heard about this I begged out. He knows I was worried."

"You know I don't want to come between you two."

"Peter."

"Seriously, you should go. I'm okay."

"You know I still care."

Colder did not reply immediately. His ex-wife had an infuriating habit of wanting to discuss serious topics when he was at the height of tension or emotion as if his lesser reserve would yield a more truthful discussion. He had no intention of discussing his feelings now. He had just watched a man die, and he needed time to recover and reflect. But he was torn. He didn't want to punish her for her feelings and her habits. "I care, too. You know that. This just isn't a good time."

"I'll come over."

"No," he said firmly. "I'm heading over to Sylvia's. Everyone's gathering there. We've got a lot to talk about."

Julianne hesitated. "I'd imagine."

"I was actually just going to call you though. I knew you'd want to know."

"It scared me."

"Me too," he replied softly, the haunting thought returning. "It was really ugly. He died right in my arms."

Colder could hear Julianne crying lightly. Neither spoke for nearly two minutes. "I was really worried." Her voice cracked slightly as she said it.

"Thanks."

"You know I still love you," she said.

"Love you too," he said without hesitation, but with mechanical precision.

"I know."

"What about Geoff?" Colder was glad to change the subject. He was still seeing the look in O'Reilly's eyes as death neared.

"I love him too. You're just different. You're like a sick addiction."

For the first time all day, Colder smiled. "Oh, great. Now I'm like heroin or LSD."

"Yes."

"I'm flattered," he replied

"What about Molly?" she asked.

"She's taking it hard."

"I really do feel bad, but you know that's not what I asked," she replied.

"What?"

"How interested are you?"

"Julianne, please, not now."

"That much, huh?"

"Julianne. Please. Not now," he whined without remorse.

"You know she'll never ask you," she said, her voice still wavering.

"I—" he began.

"Say hi to Morty, and I'm glad you're okay."

"Julianne," he started, but he heard the click, and the phone went dead. He hung it up and slunk further into the couch. Mortimer, purring contentedly, curled up on his lap and fell into a deep sleep. He closed his eyes and grunted. It was classic Julianne. Always ahead of him and always getting him to feel guilty for their mutual failure as if his telling the truth assigned him the blame. He loved her for her intellect. He hated the way it possessed her. And he hated feeling guilty when he had done nothing wrong.

He reached down and scratched the orange beast's neck and watched as the great ball of fur turned in his lap onto its back. "Morty, I want to be a cat too." The big beast just purred louder.

H. Carter Hutchins' G-V touched down in the Twin Cities at 9:27 P.M. The day was an unequivocal success, unparalleled in recent memory. Riding in the limousine toward the IDS Tower he realized he was already slightly high from the champagne he and Celia had shared on the flight home from New York. Pouring himself a scotch on the rocks, he looked forward to an even greater high.

In New York, they were met by Marvin Cook, the Minnesota state Republican chairman, and his wife Beverly. While Hutchins and Cook met regarding his potential candidacy and lined up some money from the national organization, their wives had gone shopping. After spending just under seventy-five thousand for five new outfits and one winter coat, Celia was euphoric. Not to be outdone, Hutchins was positively giddy when the state party was given nearly two million dollars by the national committee for his expected campaign. But the best news of all was Markham's call late in the afternoon. His message was ominous and cryptic. "Checkmate." With the word, Hutchins uncorked two bottles of Cristal and celebrated all the way home.

At the airport, Celia and the Cooks had taken one limousine, their homes only two miles apart. Carter Hutchins, planning to meet Markham at the office, took a second. The ride downtown was pleasant and easy. The Saturday night traffic was light, and the limousine flew down the freeway as Hutchins contemplated the moonlit night and his future. The worst was unquestionably over. Fragile X was dead. Oh, yes, he admitted. There would be those who would speculate as to what it actually had been, but now all shreds of evidence were gone. Without it, no one could ever do more than guess. And it would never be public.

In addition, the newspaper had taken its best shot. Soon the stories about mistreated patients would be over and then it would be ComHealth's turn. He formulated his plan. On Monday at a press conference he would announce an internal investigation into the practice habits of the physicians responsible for the care of each of the patients identified by the paper. As suggested by their lawyers and their media consultants, they would respond to the criticism by impugning the doctors and claiming ComHealthOne was leading the fight for increasing discipline against bad doctors. Given the public's general confusion about managed care and their innate cynicism, he knew it would sell.

The second part of the plan was a new $20 million advertising campaign featuring high-tech medicine and aggressive inpatient care. Hutchins knew it was laughable, recognizing that ComHealth was doing anything it could to keep people from utilizing high-tech medicine; but the public now fed itself on television, and $20 million would buy enough air time to eat away any problem. The plan was perfect. It was over. Even Molly Loomis. He knew what they would do to her.

The scotch was sixty years old and smooth. It seemed to flow directly into Hutchins' blood and then to his brain, transforming him into a picture of corporate contentment. Sliding deep into the seat, he gazed at the moon. He had never felt so good.

In Hutchins' office at the top of the IDS Tower, Markham waited expectantly. He had downed two gin and tonics without effort and now, with third in hand, he stood at the window overlooking the skyline, waiting for Hutchins. His euphoria had not yet faded. The end of Fragile X was one of the greatest moments of his life. The trouble was gone. Fragile X was only a memory. And most importantly to Markham, with this success he was now unquestionably Hutchins' heir.

He fingered the unopened manila envelope nervously and laughed at himself. The envelope was heavy. Medical journals always were. He thought about the journal. Men had died for this one remaining copy. It cost two years and over $2 million, but it was worth it. On this night, Fragile X would officially end, ignominiously burnt to an ash in a wastebasket.

H. Carter Hutchins strolled into the office with a look of glee. "Gregory," he said, shaking Markham's hand furiously. "Fine, fine work."

"Thank you."

"Where is it?"

"On the desk."

"Perfect."

"I thought we might watch the news and see what our press friends say while we celebrate with a little champagne."

"Wonderful," laughed Hutchins, collapsing into a seat in one of the plush chairs. Markham turned on the big-screen TV that had appeared from behind a cabinet along the far wall.

"What are we drinking?" asked Hutchins.

"Dom Perignon."

"I love it."

Markham retrieved the bottle from the refrigerator and opened it with the skill of a wine steward. Pouring the champagne without losing a drop, he brought the two glasses to the center of the room and pulled his chair next to Hutchins. A remote on the end table next to Hutchins' chair allowed him to dim the lights just as the news started.

"What's been the word so far?" asked Hutchins lighting a cigar.

"Not even an ID on O'Reilly, let alone speculation. They have nothing; it will die."

Hutchins downed half the glass. "Police will have to come up with some bullshit story to cover themselves. Drug deal, Mafia, or something. Just wait."

"You're right."

The news started, and the lead story was O'Reilly's murder. It began with the surveillance camera footage of a man said to be the gunman firing from behind a pillar. Next they showed O'Reilly fall, and finally Colder and Molly cradling him in their arms. The reporter then showed footage of a late afternoon press conference where the chief of police answered questions pertaining to the murder.

"At this time," the police chief said formally, "we cannot rule in or out any possibilities, but I would say that this has all the traditional hallmarks of an underworld hit, although it could also have been a drug deal gone bad."

Hutchins and Markham hooted with laughter and polished off their glasses of champagne. Markham refilled them right away and they continued to cackle at the television. Now on the screen the studio anchors looked concerned and talked of the tragedy that so many children had witnessed. Hutchins turned it off and concentrated on a cigar. "Beautiful," he chuckled. "Fucking beautiful."

"It was like a charm."

Hutchins rose and walked to the window. He savored the cigar, letting its smoke swirl through his nasal passages like a perfume from an irresistible woman. The champagne was grand. The light buzz it gave him made his feet numb and allowed him the sense of floating. He took a self-satisfied breath and looked out the window. Below he could see the city, the lights of the night sprawling in every direction. It was his domain, soon his kingdom. He couldn't feel better. Finally, amidst the ecstasy, he thought of the fateful journal. "Let's see the damn thing."

Markham grinned and handed his CEO the envelope. Hutchins tore open the end. Flipping it upside-down, he tried to dump out its contents. The journal was stuck, but three disks fell out onto the desk. "Stick 'em into the computer," said Hutchins, putting down the envelope without taking out the journal.

Markham obliged, and in a moment the computer's A-drive displayed the disk's contents. "No files found" was the message.

Markham's eyes widened, and Hutchins put down the champagne flute he had retrieved. "What the hell?"

Markham quickly rechecked, but the message was indeed correct. The disk was blank. Furiously he removed the first disk and checked the second. It, too, was blank. He tried the third with the same result. Empty.

Markham looked at Hutchins with the panicked face of a first grader late for class. Both men lunged for the journal. The envelope fell to the floor in the scramble for the disks. Hutchins dropped to his knees, retrieved it, and stood up, his usually perfect hair now standing straight up. He tore at the envelope and violently yanked the journal free. It folded open in his hands.

Markham saw it first, and fell backwards into a chair, nearly fainting. Hutchins stood holding it aloft like a tennis shoe with manure stuck to its sole. His hand trembled. His lips quivered. His eyes appeared ready to explode. He turned to Markham and tossed the magazine hard at his chest.

"Shit! Fucking shit!" roared Hutchins with a volume that nearly blew out the window.

Markham's impassive eyes belied his inner convulsions. The game was not over. In death, O'Reilly had had the last laugh. The disks he had been carrying were indeed blank. The journal was still missing. The star of the magazine was no scientific article. Instead, it was a very beautiful playmate of the year.

Chapter Twenty-four

The mood was worse than somber at Sylvia's house as Colder's group gathered for the ten o'clock news. It was total depression. Finished with their mandatory police interviews, they had all driven to Sylvia's suburban home, where she prepared a light dinner and hors d'oeuvres. Reggie, who was still living in Sylvia's basement, was the first to arrive, followed by Sandra, Letisha, and Molly. Colder had been last. Briggs and Sanders declined, deciding instead to spend the evening with their families.

They gathered around the television set in the living room, watching as a live report outside the Mall of America recounted the tragedy. The video from earlier in the day vaguely showed the shooter and clearly showed Molly and Peter holding the head of the dying O'Reilly. They all stared at the painful images, hanging on every word the reporter said. The young reporter was careful, mentioning the names of Molly and Peter as bystanders. He did not speculate as to who was responsible or why the killing had happened. Nor did he mention the contingent of FBI that had been in the building. The reporter did his job well, stating only the facts that were established and not indulging in any open speculation.

Using a remote, Sylvia turned off the TV the minute the report ended. She turned to the group sitting in a semicircle surrounding the television. The public had been given the on-the-record version. But none of them had any interest in the official word.

"The FBI had to be the leak," said Sandra, the only one eating the hors d'oeuvres.

"Maybe," Peter admitted disconsolately. "I essentially accused them of that, but who knows? Maybe O'Reilly just slipped up."

Molly stood and walked to a spot next to Sylvia. The earlier emotion had relented and turned to logic. "It's actually a better explanation than a conspiracy. Whoever was chasing him was doing it for a long time. Sooner or later, they were bound to get him."

"No way," Letisha said, disagreeing gently. "That boy had them on the run for two years. No chance he slips up on something he's been planning that long."

Reggie nodded vigorously. He was convinced that O'Reilly had been the victim of a conspiracy. "I think we can even figure out where the leak is."

"How?" asked Sylvia.

"We can probably be safe in assuming that O'Reilly's call to Peter was the first time that anyone had ever heard where the meeting would be."

"True."

"That leaves only two possibilities. First, and most likely, would be someone was listening on their radios or phones."

"They were talking by phone," Colder said.

"The second would be if an FBI guy actually made a call to tell someone."

"Doubtful," Sylvia said. "I can't see anyone being that dumb. And besides, no one there, an agent or any of you, were alone, were you?"

"No," Reggie admitted.

Colder leaned back on the vinyl-covered kitchen chair he was sitting in and rubbed his tired eyes. "Actually, guys, I'm not even sure it matters. So there's a crooked agent someplace. Or so they picked up the transmission and beat us there. What are we going to do about it? They got the journal. They killed O'Reilly. Finding out would be nice. But it won't change what happened."

The others fell silent for a moment, realizing he was right. Reggie finally spoke. "I kinda feel compelled. For his sake."

"I think we all feel that way," Molly said.

Colder agreed. "I know. I just mean it probably doesn't influence the case."

Sylvia walked into the kitchen where the coffee was brewing. Neither she nor any one else wanted to talk about the damage that had been done to Molly's case. It seemed improper in the face of a death. "Cream or sugar anyone?"

"No."

"No thanks."

"Sugar, a little," said Reggie.

Just as Sylvia returned with a tray filled with cups and saucers, the phone rang. She put the tray down on a coffee table and answered it on the second ring.

"Hello?"

Without another word, she handed the phone to Molly. "Troy," she said evenly. "Gus at the restaurant told him you were here. He said he's been calling all over for you."

For five minutes, Molly talked to her ex-husband while the others pretended not to listen. She was polite and lukewarm, relating the day's events to him while the others talked softly enough so that they could still hear every word Molly said. Reggie and Letisha leered at her, their looks confirming their disapproval. The others, including Peter, showed no discernible reaction.

"Really, I'm okay," she said as she tried to wrap up the conversation. "Thanks though."

Reggie moved to the phone and threatened to hang up with the push of a finger. Sylvia slapped his wrist, and Letisha laughed out loud.

"I'm fine, Troy. But thanks for calling."

Reggie stuck his index finger deep into his mouth and feigned a gag. Letisha and Sandra both laughed and struggled to not be heard.

"See ya," Molly said. As she hung up the phone, she waved at the others as if to say "I don't want to hear it."

Reggie opened his mouth, but Molly glared at him. She turned to Colder, whose look turned to that of a calculating professional. "It was nice of him to call," he said, with his best attempt to sound objective.

Reggie groaned. Letisha hissed. Molly stared at Peter, trying to read him as Sylvia put a stop to the commentary. "Enough."

Colder's ambiguous eyes softened to something impossible to read. Molly looked away. She did not know whether she wanted to talk to Troy or not. She did know she didn't want to talk to him in front of her friends. "Sorry for the interruption."

Sylvia returned to her spot leaning against the TV and changed the subject. "Did O'Reilly have any relatives?" she asked.

"No," Peter answered. "I know his wife was killed, but I'm not sure about the rest."

"Tragic," Sylvia mumbled.

"Yes."

For nearly an hour, they talked about this man they had never met and the tragedy that consumed his life. They agreed that they would share the responsibility of arranging a funeral service and decided upon Sandra's church, St. Michaels, for the wake and the funeral.

Over an hour and a half after first arriving, weary and still numb from the day, they all agreed it was time to go home. Rising to retrieve his coat, Peter was caught off-guard by the sound of his pager. Still attached to his belt, it had not gone off all day. He reached for it and checked the number. 527-9494. Not recognizing the number, he replaced it on his belt.

"You're not going to call it?" asked Sylvia, returning from the closet carrying jackets.

"I never answer numbers I don't recognize," he replied. "It's usually wrong numbers, guys looking for their drug dealers."

Reggie grimly laughed at Colder's bit of beeper insight.

Peter's respite from the device was momentary. The pager went off again. This time the number was ominous.

527-9494—911.

Colder gulped at the sight of the 911, the emergency number, and headed for the phone. The others caught his surprised look and watched him run.

He got to the phone and punched in the number. "Dr. Colder," he said firmly.

The group could see Peter's eyes widen and his lips start to quiver. "What?" he exclaimed. "No! What! Oh, shit! I'll be right there." His face as pale and seemed to have lost all expression. His legs appeared about to buckle. Reflexively, he searched his pockets for his keys. "No—no—no," he mumbled.

"What is it?" Molly asked.

"I—I don't believe it."

"What?" asked Sylvia, moving to his side.

"I gotta go—now. That was the police." Colder found the keys, dropped them, and picked them up again. "They—they—um—had my pager number from today."

"What did they say?"

Colder appeared stunned and frantic. He looked at Molly. His eyes were wild. "They called me to tell me my house is on fire. It's burning to the ground."

Three cars barreled toward Colder's house at a speed at least twenty miles per hour over the limit. The residential streets that offered the shortest route from Sylvia's house were deserted except for an occasional parked car, and in a few minutes they were within two miles of the blaze. Hurrying along a straightaway, they could see in the distance an orange arc stretching into the night sky. The glow was eerie, with its orange-amber hue that could only represent a major blaze. Speeding through a rapid series of turns, they found themselves less than six blocks away. Colder's car containing Molly and Reggie surged down the street, past several bystanders' cars and came screeching to a halt across the street from his flame-riddled house.

At least fifty people stood milling on the street and in the neighbors' yards watching the blaze. Two fire engines were parked in the street, and pairs of firemen stood on three sides of the house, each firing heavy streams of water through broken windows. Three police cars stood by, the officers talking with each other and interviewing a handful of neighbors.

Colder leaped out of the driver's side and dashed across the street. He was stopped by a young policeman, but after identifying himself as the homeowner, he was shown to one of the firemen, a lieutenant, who was apparently in charge. Molly and Reggie followed, their eyes wide in horror as new flames burst from an upstairs window with an explosion, sending a shower of glass and ash into the front lawn.

"You Dr. Colder?" asked the lieutenant over the noise.

"Yes," Colder muttered, still staring at the blaze.

A short, sturdy-looking man in his mid forties, he appeared genuinely sympathetic. "I'm Lieutenant McKenzie."

Colder shook his hand weakly, but watched as the entire two-story house seemed to be consumed by fire despite the three hoses working continuously. The blown-out upstairs windows seemed to stoke the flames, and now waves of fire swept out the windows, across the wood siding, and onto the roof.

"I'm afraid it's going to be a total loss, Doc," said the lieutenant sympathetically.

"What about Morty?" asked Colder weakly, his body rigid but, wavering.

McKenzie's face stretched in horror. "Is someone in there? We were told you lived alone."

Colder looked down and shook his head. Tears filled his eyes, and, staring at the ground, he hid them from the others. "No. Morty's my cat."

Molly slid to his side and took his arm gently. Colder looked away from everyone. "Sorry, Doc," McKenzie said.

"Wonderful old guy," Colder choked. "Ten years."

Molly moved next to him and squeezed his arm. For an instant, she leaned her head into his shoulder. Colder turned toward her and managed a grim face that was halfway between smile and frown. One lone tear fell from the corner of his eye. "I'm so sorry," she whispered. Colder shook his head and held her hand.

"Shit," Reggie cursed, as another round of fire waves cascaded from the upstairs windows onto the siding. The firemen, who had been standing in the front yard firing water into the living room, now moved the stream into the upstairs bedroom, directly into the teeth of the blaze. Sylvia, standing behind Colder, put her hands on his shoulders and watched the house burn. "Oh God, Peter. I'm so sorry." Letisha and Sandra joined them, both watching with expressions of horror and anger.

"When'd it start?" Colder asked, struggling to think logically, his mind still on his pet.

"We got a call about twenty-five minutes ago from a neighbor, a Mr. Hatcher."

Colder nodded knowingly. Ross Hatcher lived across from him. He was an elderly widower and a night owl who always walked his two dogs late at night.

"He was apparently out for a walk when he saw flames on the ground floor."

A loud crash jarred them as half of the ground floor's ceiling fell. Great flames billowed out from the living room and surged past the whispery waves of flame still flowing forth from the upstairs windows. Dust and smoke obscured some of the inside flames, but moments later the fire was larger than ever, and the entire house seemed to disappear in a thick veneer of orange-rust. Holes began to appear in the roof, and fountainlike surges of flames sprang forth. The firefighters' efforts were obviously futile, and the water could only to keep it from spreading to neighboring homes.

Sylvia released her grip on Colder's shoulders and stepped forward. Her earlier anguished look had turned to anger. Reggie's face was cold and impassive. Letisha and Sandra were quiet. Molly stood with her arm in Peter's, watching as the savage fire continued to envelope the home. The burning shingles were emitting a thick black smoke that turned the highest flames to a flickering auburn stream, and they all watched as piece by piece, the roof began to fall into the gutted inside and the white exterior turned a ghastly black.

The firemen continued to furiously spray, showering both the exterior and interior. Their efforts succeeded in controlling the heat and avoiding the spread, but with every passing minute, the house came closer to collapsing.

With nothing more to say than to express his sympathy, Lieutenant McKenzie walked away to talk to one of his fireman manning the first truck. Colder and his friends continued to watch the house burn. Despite the late hour, more neighbors and spectators appeared in the street to watch as the house continued to be consumed by the swirling flame. Relentlessly, it ate at the north wall, then the south, and soon a large area of burning living room could be seen where the front wall had once stood.

For Colder, the sight was devastating. Everything he owned and every tangible memory he possessed was evaporating before his eyes. It was too much. His practice nearly bankrupt, his faithful pet gone, O'Reilly murdered, and his house burned. It was too much. He choked up, and tears began to drop onto his cheeks.

Molly gently stroked his arm. She was also on the verge of tears. "Oh, God, I can't even think about Mortimer."

"Neither can I," Colder managed to choke out.

As they stood watching the fire now erode more of the remaining outside walls, Ross Hatcher walked up to Colder and put his hand on his shoulder. "I'm sorry, Peter."

Colder turned to the gray-haired old man, his two beagles attentively sitting by his feet, and shook his hand. Gathering his poise, he eyed his friend. "Thanks for reporting it, Ross."

"It's such a shame," he continued. "I remember when it was built. Back in '35. Old man Miller. And you had done such a nice job with it."

"Thanks."

Ross Hatcher's eyes narrowed. The horrible thought struck him. "Your kitty okay?"

Colder shook his head.

"Oh no! Not Morty!" said Ross looking stricken. Colder knew how much the old man loved animals, especially Mortimer. He had often taken care of him when Colder was gone.

With the news, Ross Hatcher was overcome. He tugged on the leashes, and the two dogs rose obediently. The old man had suffered much tragedy himself, with his wife dying less than a year before from cancer. He was a good friend, but there was little anyone could say now.

Another section of the front wall suddenly caved in, and with it another blast of smoke and flame exploded into the night sky. All four walls and the roof were now consumed, and the flames hung like great orange curtains over the entire house, reaching deep into the darkness.

Molly, too, was overwhelmed. "Why would they do it?"

Peter did not respond, instead his tear-filled eyes stared into the orange inferno. He stepped forward as a huge chunk of the roof fell into the nearly consumed house. For a moment, the fire slowed by a fraction as some of the blaze was smothered by the falling material. The control he fought to maintain gave way and tears streamed freely forth. Molly continued to hold his arm, and they watched together as the brief muting of the fire ended and the blaze resumed in full force.

Colder then stepped closer, Molly at his side. Now they were close enough to feel both the heat and the mist from the water. One of the firemen signaled them to move back, and they complied. As he turned to the group, Colder saw their looks of anger, awe, and curiosity, and suddenly the thought struck him. He turned to Molly, still at his side, her face only inches away. "What do you mean, why did *they* do it?"

"Just that," she said matter-of-factly. "Why did they do it?"

"Who?"

"You know."

Colder stepped away from her, allowing her question to jolt him into logic. "You're implying you don't think it's an accident?"

"You think it is?" she asked.

"Yes. At least, I thought so." Colder was struggling. His brain seemed paralyzed.

"Did you have anything valuable in the house? Anything they would want?"

"No," replied Colder. "Upstairs was clothes and bedding. In the attic was my old kid stuff. Ground floor was kitchen. Den had a TV and stereo."

"What else?"

"Living room with furniture. Basement was tools and equipment as well as books, computer stuff, journals—"

Colder did not finish the sentence. The others had pulled up close to him and

Molly, and collectively they all gasped as the word "journals" slipped from his tongue.

"Oh, God," Reggie panted.

Colder ran through the possibilities. Appliances, electronics, stove. He knew they had all been turned off. The wiring was good, checked a year ago when he upgraded the outdoor outlets to 220-volt. Gas lines were fine, the furnace barely a year and a half old. Could it be?

Colder's thoughts raced. His house. Why? Finally, his mind seemed to process his thoughts again. But what had happened? He had nothing they would want. It seemed ridiculous that they would burn his house. But then he realized that *they* did not know that he didn't have anything important. But if so, why now? Why would they burn the house when they already had what they wanted?

"Unbelievable," Reggie muttered.

"They don't have it," Molly gulped.

Sylvia was placid and analytical. "But do you really think O'Reilly would have sent it to you, Peter?"

"No way," Colder replied, convinced. "That's why they burned it. They looked though my mail, and it wasn't there. Then they got into my basement and found about ten thousand journals that all look alike and an equal number of computer disks. It was a hopeless task. They just torched everything."

"But then," said Sandra, "they can't be sure they eliminated it. In fact, they're probably still looking."

Colder looked around and saw a dejected-looking Ross Hatcher, with his two beagles, still watching the house burn. He signaled the old man to come over.

"I can't believe Mortimer's gone," Ross said, his frail hands trembling as he approached them. "I shoulda gone right in there."

"Ross," Peter asked, "was there anyone leaving my house around the time of the fire?"

The old man nodded. "I told it to the police. There was a dark van. I noticed it parked in the street, oh, maybe five minutes before the fire started."

"Did you get—" Reggie started.

Ross Hatcher waved him off. "No. I looked out the window and it was there. I have no idea how long it had been there. Then it was gone. I never saw anyone and I never saw the plates." The old man looked shaken. "The poor kitty," he muttered again.

Suddenly Colder began to boil. His house, his belongings, his pet. "Shit."

"I'm sure that's it," Reggie said. "Too many coincidences."

"Maybe they're just punishing you," Sandra said. "Maybe they do have it. We saw the guy get the envelope."

"Possible."

Reggie disagreed. "But why burn a house? That's not how these guys have behaved. They usually deal directly with the problem, like kill someone."

Sylvia agreed. "So we know, or at least are pretty sure, it was arson and probably for the reason we think."

Colder's face was crimson and his chin twitched as he tried to control himself. He suddenly felt consumed by a desire to kill with his bare hands. He clenched his fists so tightly his hands ached, and his arms shook as if in spasm.

"But if he didn't have the stuff, and they couldn't find it inside—" Sylvia struggled with the thought. "Well, if O'Reilly didn't send it to you, then to who?"

Beneath the anger, Colder was tired. "I have no idea."

"He had to have given some clue. Any clue."

"Figure this," Letisha said. "The guy, O'Reilly, comes out wearing the stuff, but it's a fake. He's figuring they still might get him, so the only way to deliver it is to have hidden it somewhere and then give a clue as to where it is. Sylvia's right. He had to have told someone."

Colder was still trembling, but he closed his eyes and tried to hold his anger in check. He drew three deep breaths and opened his eyes. He looked at the charred remnants of the house with the fire now beginning to relent. Tears of anger filled his eyes as he saw it, and his lips quivered again. Suddenly Molly grasped his hands. He did not look at her, but she tugged at him as if seeking his gaze. When he looked at her, Molly appeared faint, weak, and her eyes seemed to tremble. "O'Reilly did tell us, Peter."

"What?"

"He told us," she repeated. "We just weren't listening."

His mind becoming clear, Colder's knees buckled. "Oh, no," he gasped, realizing she was right. "Oh my God!"

Another small explosion rocked the house. All but Molly turned to see. Another wall fell, and fiery smoke was launched high into the air. When the others turned back, Colder was gone.

Chapter Twenty-five

While his house continued to burn, a frantic Colder flew away in his car. Reggie and Sylvia called to him as he roared off down the street, but he did not stop. Sandra, standing a few feet apart from the others, looked baffled.

"What the heck is going on?" she asked.

Molly had been holding Colder's hand tightly. She had let him go with the hesitation of a parent seeing a child off to school, but she knew how he felt; it was something he had to do. She started to answer, but another large crash of burning embers muted her first response. She coughed as smoke descended on them. They all moved farther away, and she tried again. "He knows where the journal is."

"Where?" Reggie asked.

"It was what O'Reilly said to us. We should have figured it out."

"What?"

"He sent it to Peter's ex-wife."

Letisha's mouth fell open. Despite the grim nature of the night, she allowed herself a half-hearted laugh. "Love it. No one would ever have thought of that."

Reggie took a step back. "Oh, man."

Sylvia looked at them as if they were crazy and Molly shook her head in contradiction. "Don't you get it?" she asked. Seeing Reggie's and Letisha's confused looks, she knew immediately they did not. "If they burned the house, then there are only three possibilities. One, they came here first and don't know about Julianne. Two, they knew about it being sent to her and went there first, God forbid. And three, they came here first, couldn't find it, and then…"

Reggie's lips quivered. In the furor of the day, no one was thinking clearly, least of all himself, but now it suddenly all became clear. "Oh, shit," he groaned. "And Peter said that he told the FBI guy that O'Reilly's last words were about Julianne."

Letisha was horrified. "And the FBI may be the leak!"

"Yes," Molly said, her voice trembling.

They paused for a second as the danger sunk in, but Sylvia was way ahead of them. She was moving as fast as her body would allow, swinging her arms wildly and running toward the policeman, trying to draw attention to herself. The others followed. The police were stationed behind a barricade a hundred feet away.

Running right behind, Reggie turned to Molly. "You know where Julianne lives?"

"No idea," Molly replied, nearly hyperventilating in the smoke

"I do," Sylvia chirped, trailing them. "It's only a few miles. I can get us there."

Within three minutes, they piled into a police car and blazed away from the fire. The policemen had initially offered slight resistance, but Sylvia was forceful and persuasive. Combined with the day's events and the rampant speculation that was running through the police force about O'Reilly's murder, they quickly relented, eager to avoid any other murders under their noses. Sandra and Molly sat in the back seat of the first car. The others sat in the second.

As the two police cars raced from the smoldering scene, Molly closed her eyes and slouched deep into the seat. Her eyes seemed to burn, and tears welled up and began to fall onto her cheeks. O'Reilly, Fragile X, the house, the cat, now Julianne. Everything going wrong. Everything burning, dying. But now, worst of all Peter. She knew he still cared for Julianne. They had shared a life together. Now he wasn't thinking rationally. No one was thinking rationally. They had all underestimated. They had all been stupid. There was danger everywhere.

In the front seat, the policemen talked between themselves and with others on their radio. Sandra gave them directions. Molly barely listened. The rapidly passing darkness was only a blur as the tears continued to obscure her eyes. She knew whoever was looking for the journal and disks would have no hesitation to kill again. The thought made her choke. "Peter, please God, no," she whispered to herself. "Please, please, no."

Julianne lived five miles further west in the Minneapolis suburb, Edina. It was nearly a straight shot from his house and figuring that most of the local police were preoccupied with the fire, Colder floored the accelerator and sped down the empty streets toward his ex-wife's home. He tried her number on the cell phone, but there was no answer, and for the first time in his life he found himself hoping she had spent the night at her boyfriend's.

It all seemed so obvious now. O'Reilly dying, but talking about Julianne. Carefully, obliquely, as if someone might be listening. Colder ground his teeth thinking about his own stupidity—accusing the FBI of a leak and then promptly telling everyone O'Reilly's clue. "Peter, you idiot," he continued, verbally beating himself. "You're such an idiot!"

He was suddenly thinking little about his house. His mind seemed consumed by a tangle of emotions and thoughts. How could he have let it happen? His fault, he was sure. Not careful enough. First Cynthia Tan, then O'Reilly, and now Julianne in danger. Lost in the middle was Molly's case and everything he owned. "Screwed everything," he muttered. "Every damn thing."

The deserted streets of the middle of the night offered no resistance as he flew into Edina. Hitting seventy miles an hour, he blazed down 66th Street toward Ridgeview Drive. What if the van Ross Hatcher had seen was there? He still struggled to control his rage and map out a logical plan. It wouldn't be, he assured himself. They would have gone to her house first, then his. It was only logical. And she had to be safe, staying at Geoff's.

Suddenly the realization hit. It seemed like days ago, but he had talked to Julianne less than seven hours before. She had told him she was staying home, not going out to dinner as she and Geoff had originally planned. *And now there was no answer!* No! No! No! he thought. His finger shook as he pushed the redial on the phone. He flipped the phone to speaker and swung the car onto Ridgeview Drive, the last street before Julianne's. It rang six, then seven, times. *Still no answer! And no answering machine!* A surge of panic hit him, and momentarily the car swerved, the front right tire careening over the curb. Regaining control, he floored it again, swinging past a lone parked car and screeching onto Limerick Lane, Julianne's street. God, no, he thought.

Immediately he could see the house in the distance, sitting at the end of the dead-end street. Two lights. The living room and a bedroom upstairs. No cars in front. Maybe everything was okay, he thought. His car surged to eighty miles an hour and covered the one and a half blocks in less than five seconds. He slammed on the brakes and his tires screeched loudly against the cement, but only for a second as he skidded right through the angled driveway and came to a stop on the grass in the front yard.

Flying from the car, he leaped over the shrubs that guarded the narrow sidewalk and lunged toward the door. Bounding up the three steps, he threw open the outside door and tried the inside. Also open. "Jules!" he screamed. No answer.

The living room was to his left, and he ran through it. Empty. Circling into the dining room, he continued into the kitchen and headed toward the den, flipping on lights as fast as he could. "Jules! Julianne!"

The den was empty. He turned around, retracing his steps to the kitchen. Opening the basement door, he saw that it was dark. He closed it. "Jules!" he yelled toward the front foyer. He stood motionless, but heard nothing in response. His heart pounding wildly, he bounded through the hallway that led back to the foyer and the front door, and raced up the stairs. "Julie?" he said more weakly, as he turned left and approached the bedrooms. The guest bedroom light was on, and when he looked in he was surprised to find it also empty. Suddenly his heart leaped. Why were these lights on? He turned and threw open Julianne's adjacent bedroom door. "Julianne?"

As soon as he turned on the light, he saw her. She was fully clothed, lying next to the bed, face down. Her right arm was skewed laterally. Her left arm was buried under her.

Colder gasped audibly and lunged toward her. Falling to his knees, he rolled her limp body and felt for a pulse in her neck. It was present. He leaned over and listened for a breath. Also present. Slow and shallow. She was alive.

"Thank God," he murmured as he shook her lightly. He could see a small cut near her left temple where she had apparently been struck with something blunt. Moist blood covered the left half of her face and neck. "Julie," he said softly, shaking her gently by the shoulders.

She did not move, still unconscious. He held her wrist, feeling every beat of her still-present pulse. Relieved she was alive, he managed to think like a doctor. Pulse strong and normal rate, not hypovolemic, probably no internal bleeding. Breaths slow and regular, normal rate. Unconscious. He scanned her body quickly. She was dressed in a T-shirt and jeans, and he saw no other obvious signs of trauma. He opened her eyes. Her gaze was conjugate, and the pupils constricted briskly in the light. "Thank God," he said again, feeling better by the minute.

His left hand moved back to her wrist while his other wiped a bit of the drying blood off of her face. "Julianne," he said, stroking her cheek.

With the sound of her name, she stirred slightly and then opened her eyes with a painful grimace. Her right hand rose to her face reflexively, swooping across her mouth in an uncoordinated fashion. "It's okay," he soothed. "It's okay."

Suddenly, she shook her head, and her eyes and mouth popped open. She swung her arms wildly, striking out at him as if fending off an intruder, but he was quicker, and he easily blocked the blows. "Julie, it's Peter."

She emitted a low grunt and then a cry as if in pain and swung again savagely with her right hand, striking him hard on the shoulder. "Julie," he said, gently pinning her arms to the ground. "Julie!"

Her name stopped her, and she relaxed under his power. Her eyes saw him staring down at her and her face changed in recognition. She started to cry. "Peter," she choked.

Colder reached down and lifted her up, taking her into his arms. "It's okay," he whispered, holding her tightly. "You're gonna be fine."

Julianne sobbed for several minutes, letting the tears fall onto Peter's shoulder. He rocked her back and forth and stroked her hair. "They're gone now. You're gonna be okay."

The words didn't seem to register, and she continued to cry, more from fear than pain. She tried to control herself, but seemed unable to talk as he continued to hug her like a cocoon. "No one's gonna get you now," he said.

Colder scanned the room as he held her. Her bedroom was basically neat. The bed had been turned back, but had not been slept in. Mail was scattered all over the fluffy, white comforter. In the middle was a manila envelope, torn open and empty. "I had it, Peter," she sobbed as if knowing he was looking at the bed. "I had it."

"Don't worry."

"I-I didn't get a chance to see it," she said, pulling back from him slightly to wipe the tears from her eyes. "But it was the journal and two disks."

"Forget it," he said firmly and almost in reprimand. "What's important is that you're okay."

"They were right there," she continued, trembling at the recollection. "I had it in my hand, and then this guy grabbed me by the neck from behind. I dropped it, and then—I don't know." She felt the right side of her head and winced. "They must have hit me."

"Yes," he agreed dabbing his fingers on the side of her head.

"I saw something," she said as her thoughts became clearer. She pulled far enough away that she could face him. "It was one of those journals where the articles inside are listed on the front. Something about a protein."

Colder wasn't interested. He put his hand over her mouth, a gentle gesture to tell her to be quiet. Although he admired his ex-wife's courage, he was too relieved at seeing her alive to give any thought to the journal. "I don't want to talk about it now. You need to be checked over."

Julianne nodded and tried to stand. Helping her raise herself up, he guided her to her feet. Her legs wobbled like a new colt's, and she her body wavered wildly. She stood for only a second before collapsing onto the edge of the bed. "Light-headed," she panted.

"Hurt anywhere else?"

Julianne slouched her shoulders and rolled her head. "My neck's a little stiff, I guess."

He crossed his middle fingers over his index fingers and put them in her palms. "Give me a squeeze." Opening her eyes, she could see some of the soot on his hands and for the first time was aware of his smell. She squeezed his hands firmly but looked at him with curiosity as he continued to act as her doctor. "What's with you?" she asked. "You smell like a fireplace."

"My house burned tonight."

"What?"

"My house. It burned."

"No!"

"Yes, it's all gone."

"Everything?"

"Yep."

"What about Morty?"

Colder shook his head.

Julianne turned away. "Oh, God, no."

Colder looked down, but suddenly Julianne turned back toward the nightstand and glanced at the digital clock. She grabbed him by the hand. "Is that the right time?"

"1:04. I think so," said Colder, confused.

Julianne was frantic. "Peter, the last thing I remember was the time. 12:58. They might still be in—" Julianne's eyes were wide open and pleading, but before she could continue, she emitted a gasp. Her eyes were looking past him, and she started to scramble to her feet. "Peter!"

Colder realized too late what was happening. He raised his hand as the blow from a small club slammed into the side of his head.

"*No!*" screamed Julianne as Peter staggered to a knee. The two men dressed entirely in black stood before them. The first held the club. The second a gun.

Colder, staggered by the blow, tried desperately to stand, but fighting unconsciousness, it was impossible. He was an easy target. Again the club found its mark, blasting into the side of Colder's head and knocking him to the ground face down. With methodical precision the gunman, who had been waiting behind his partner, stepped forward. Drawing the gun, he fired two shots into the middle of Colder's back directly at the heart. With each well-placed bullet, there was a grotesque explosion of blood.

"NO!" Julianne screamed again. She stood and desperately tried to swing at the gunman, but her coordination was off, and she missed. The first man stepped toward her and swung the club at her. The blow to the head was savage. It spun her in a semicircle and caused her to fall hard onto her back. Still slightly conscious, she writhed on the floor. She cracked open her eyes and tried to stand, but her mind was foggy, and her eyes were unfocused. She struggled to see, but she couldn't. There was only a black blur above her. Another crushing blow landed on her skull and there was a flash of light with the pain. She felt the cold steel of a long pistol barrel enter her mouth.

"Thank you for your help," she heard someone laugh. "But the rest of this is none of your business."

Julianne tried to scream. Her head hurt. The room spun. The two men stood above her. The one with a gun rammed the barrel deep into her mouth. "You should have minded your own business." Again she tried to scream, but no sound came out. There was a bright light. There was pain. Then there was nothing.

The trauma team at the Hennepin County Medical Center was ready in less than four minutes when the call came through. Doctors and nurses, standing in a room where the unbelievable was the norm, couldn't believe what they were hearing. An army of medical personnel huddled around the radio to listen as the paramedic team called in again.

"It's Dr. Colder all right," crackled the voice.

"I got that much," Dr. David Winfield, the chief resident in surgery grunted. "I want the details this time."

"Double GSW. Both entries are in the back. Exits are in the front. One in the chest, the other in the upper abdomen. Looks to me like they were aiming for the heart and just missed."

Winfield had no time for irrelevant speculation. "Give me his vitals."

"Pulse one-twenty. B.P. seventy over thirty, and he's bleeding like hell."

"Airway?"

"Eight endotracheal. He's on a hundred percent and his SAT is ninety-eight."

"Access?"

"Two fourteens and a sixteen."

Winfield approved. "Good. Now what about the other patient?"

"His ex. She took a few blows to the head but they didn't shoot her. She's conscious and seems to be all right. She's coming in the other unit."

"Gimme your ETA."

"Four minutes."

"We'll be ready," Winfield said, signing off.

The trauma room was hushed as the tall figure of Dr. Winfield stood before them, his thick glasses exaggerating his black eyes. "Listen up," he said, taking command. "I want five units O-neg up here *now*! and a twenty-unit cross. And I want ten of FFP the minute he hits the door."

"Yes sir," came a voice.

"And if some idiot in the blood bank so much as utters a word of complaint, I want the pencil-neck brought here so I can personally rip his tongue out of his mouth."

"Done!"

Winfield continued to bark orders as the entire fifteen-person team scrambled to assume their positions in the trauma room. "Tell the OR to crack the trays. We're coming straight through."

"X-ray? CT?"

"Forget it."

"Asadourian? Wessman?" asked an intern.

"Called," said a nurse. "Five minutes."

"Then let's be ready," muttered Winfield.

With these words, the trauma room flew into high gear. One nurse called the OR while another called the blood bank. True to form, the blood bank squawked, but when the nurse invited the technician to come to the Trauma 1 and have his tongue removed, he obliged and sent the units of O negative without another peep. The OR was easier, their well-oiled machine ready for any case within minutes. A third nurse opened line trays just in case.

In the middle of the fray, David Winfield took a deep breath. The anger the others were seeing was really his anxiety. He knew Peter Colder. He liked Peter Colder. But he also knew trouble when he heard it, and this was big trouble. "Say a prayer," he mumbled to himself. "Say a damn prayer."

The intern standing next to him heard what Winfield had said. He started where his chief resident had left off. He, too, knew big trouble when he heard it. "Hail Mary, Mother of God—" he started.

Molly and Sylvia arrived with the others at the hospital shortly after 2:30 A.M. The policemen had bent at least a dozen rules in transporting them, but in the chaos of the night and the emergency room, no one seemed to notice or care. As always, a large crowd milled in the entrance, the usual mixture of drunks, police, nurses, and doctors.

Sifting through the maze of people gathered near the front of the enormous ER, Sylvia led them toward the reception desk. She was perilously close to collapse, her usual stoic reserve melted at the sight of Colder's bleeding, unconscious body. Molly and Reggie followed, walking arm in arm, unable to speak or even cry. Letisha and Sandra were last, wavering as they walked.

None of them were first-hand witnesses. The police had entered the house and found Peter and Julianne lying in the upstairs bedroom. Julianne was unconscious, Colder bleeding badly. The friends had seen him only when he was carried out on the gurney, gray and unconscious.

A nurse guided them to a darkened, but empty, waiting room on the second floor where they sat without speaking. A few minutes later, a harried-looking intern arrived.

"How bad is it?" Reggie asked, not even bothering with introductions.

The intern, a tired-looking young man, was polite. He told them that he had not been in the OR, so he could only tell what he knew from the three minutes Peter had been in the trauma room. "They were bad wounds," he said honestly. "One in the left chest, the other in the abdomen. He's lost a lot of blood."

Molly broke down. Sylvia, Letisha, and Sandra buried their heads in their hands. "What are his chances?" Reggie asked.

The intern hesitated. "I'd only be speculating. We'll know much more in an hour or two."

All of them realized that the intern was sent there merely to greet them. He had no real information. Reggie thanked him politely, and the young doctor left. Sandra and Letisha moved to Molly's side, and the three cried together, each still haunted by the sight they had seen and the thought of Colder near death. Sylvia stared blankly out the window that faced the downtown lights. Reggie stared at the floor. The horror was too great for all of them, and it seemed impossible that it could have happened. Peter Colder dead? None of them could even think of it.

Tears welled in Reggie's eyes as he listened to the others cry. He felt nauseous and angry, tired and beaten, grief-stricken and incredulous. "How? How?" he thought to himself. He looked up at Molly, crying, huddled with Letisha and Sandra.

Peter was such a friend. Selfless to a fault. The world would never be the same without him. How could he possibly die?

Dr. Melvin Wessman was elbow-deep in blood as he tried desperately to stop the bleeding in Peter Colder's chest. As soon as the thoracic surgeon had made his incision in the fifth intercostal space, an explosion of arterial and venous blood nearly soaked him. Dripping in blood, he continued. Cutting feverishly, Wessman spread the ribs and slammed in some lap pads in a vain attempt to stem the flow. Below him, the trauma surgical team of Dr. Winfield and Dr. Charles Asadourian were also deep in blood, buried in Peter Colder's abdomen.

"Trouble," Dr. Fred Schantz, the anesthesiologist said. "Pressure's bad."

All three surgeons looked over the drape at the arterial tracing. The weak pulsations yielded a blood pressure of only 60/30, and the pulse remained nearly 180.

"More damn blood," growled Asadourian, a giant Armenian with a bass voice and thick black eyebrows. "We need more damn blood."

"We got four pressure bags going," Schantz replied. "Any chance you can just pack?"

"No way," Winfield answered.

Wessman looked up from the chest. Blood was dripping from his surgical mask. "Here either," he announced. "This is big trouble. I've got a bad lobe, an intercostal, a bad PA, and he's forming an aortic pseudoaneurysm before my eyes. The only thing I've stopped is the intercostal. This is deep shit."

Asadourian was equally blunt. "Our bullet took out a renal artery and vein, calyx, ureter, and half the kidney itself. It also got the spleen and maybe a bowel."

The anesthesiologist only shook his head. He turned to one of the three circulating nurses. "Tell the blood bank to send us twenty more STAT. And tell 'em STAT means STAT! I want the fresh-frozen now!"

"DIC?" asked Winfield.

"Probably. You see a clot?"

"No."

Asadourian took a deep breath and plunged back in. He and Mel Wessman were the two finest trauma surgeons in Minneapolis. Vietnam veterans with three years at a frontline MASH unit, there was no type of human injury they had not seen. Wessman was small, wiry, and volatile. Asadourian was enormous and as cool as an arctic night. Both were mentally sharp, proficient, and extremely profane.

"This is a damn mess." grunted Wessman, struggling to see. "No. Suck here. Shit!" he screamed at the scrub nurse.

"I'm taking the kidney," Asadourian said evenly, without asking the resident for his opinion. "Clamp the vessels. We've gotta just stop the bleeding."

"I agree," Winfield said, offering an opinion that had not been needed.

Shantz's voice was wavering. "Blood pressure fifty."

"Shit!" Wessman screamed. Asadourian looked up at the chest and saw a silver-dollar-sized stream of pulsatile red blood blasting out of the wound. The aorta, the largest artery in the body, had given way. "Aorta!"

"Take the kidney," Asadourian commanded Winfield. "I'll help Mel."

"Yes, sir."

Charles Asadourian shifted his hulking body to the head of the bed and reached his hand into the chest. The hole in the aorta was the size of a fifty-cent piece, but the entire vessel wall had been weakened by the shock of the bullet and was dilating like a balloon.

"Aortic clamp!" Wessman commanded.

The scrub nurse slapped the long metal clamp into his hand while Asadourian coolly grasped the entire artery with his hand. The maneuver made the upper portion of the vessel visible, directing the blood downward.

"I've got no pressure!" Schantz yelled. "Zero!!"

The surgeons said nothing. Wessman and Asadourian had only seconds, and they knew it. Colder had lost over a liter of blood in less than thirty seconds and was already perilously low on blood volume. They had to stop the bleeding now. Wessman gripped the long clamp and swung it into the chest as Asadourian tightened his grip. "There," Asadourian grunted. "Take it."

Wessman opened the clamp, gripped the vessel above Asadourian's hand and closed it. It didn't work. Instantly the vessel exploded in blood.

"No blood pressure!" Schantz warned.

"Shit," Asadourian grumbled.

Wessman did not flinch. The scrub anticipated his command. Without a word she slammed the second aortic clamp into his hand. Wessman, his eyes never leaving the approximate site of the target deep in Colder's chest, swung the clamp into the wound and tried again.

"V-tach!" Shantz yelled, watching the monitor and squeezing in a unit of blood by hand.

The first clamp had fractured through a part of the injured aorta that had appeared deceptively stable. The move caused everything to blow. The only positive was that the sudden total loss of blood pressure had nearly stopped the abdominal bleeding and allowed Winfield to clamp off the injured renal artery and vein. "Clamped here," the chief resident panted.

The two surgeons heard him, but ignored it. Stopping the aortic bleeding was a must, and it was now or never. He had to get the healthy part of the aorta clamped, or Colder would be dead in seconds. He knew he had one last chance. Wessman eyed the target. The bleeding vessel was deep within the chest and hidden by the expanding pool of blood. "Now!" Shantz howled. "We need something now!"

Wessman didn't flinch. One bead of sweat fell on his forehead, but it was the only hint of stress he showed. Asadourian pulled harder on his retracter and adjusted his suction. "Get it," he whispered.

Colder's heart appeared to be quivering instead of beating. Wessman glanced at the organ, its strange rhythm more like twitches than healthy contractions. He turned his eyes to the great vessel, the blood still pouring forth. He moved the clamp toward it, its teeth zeroing in on the vessel wall.

"There," Asadourian said, verbally guiding him.

Wessman eyed the pinkish vessel and slid the clamp past the lung. Moving it with a steady hand, he passed the clamp over the vessel. He closed his eyes for an instant and said a silent prayer. "Please don't let it fracture again."

"Now," Asadourian grunted. Wessman squeezed the clamp. For a moment, the two surgeons held their breath, expecting the vessel to explode again with a giant blast of bright red blood. But the prayer appeared to work. The vessel held. The clamp had stopped the aortic bleeding. "Better," Asadourian grunted.

Wessman exhaled deeply, allowing himself one second to gather his thoughts. The maneuver had given Peter Colder a blood pressure, but with it the blood supply to the body had been cut off. In addition, it had caused the pulmonary artery to bleed again.

"Pressure of forty. Sinus tach," Schantz sighed.

The surgeons could see that Colder's healthy heart had converted back to its normal rhythm, but was beating as fast as it could in a reflex to try to elevate the blood pressure. Asadourian and Wessman began operating furiously. The pulmonary arteries, always thin and fragile vessels, were bleeding profusely. Wessman packed the area with lap pads while Asadourian prepared to take out the left lung's upper lobe. "Lobectomy. Take one. Preserve the other."

"Yes."

"Bypass?"

"No time."

"I agree."

Their hands worked in perfect synchrony, and they operated with little verbal communication. Even the scrub techs, their skills hardened from years of trauma, knew exactly what to expect next. In less than two minutes, Peter Colder's left upper lobe was gone, and with it part of one pulmonary artery.

Shantz leaned over the curtain. His voice was slightly less frantic. "Pressure of fifty. Got back the coags. They're bad."

"How bad?" Wessman asked the anesthesiologist.

"PT and PTT off the map. DIC panel is way pos."

The surgeons didn't reply. This was another piece of bad news. They knew that even if they could get Colder through the operation, the overwhelming likelihood was that he would die within twenty-four hours from a coagulopathy. The blood loss and administration of blood products in massive amounts lead to a condition where the blood can no longer clot, and the patient begins to bleed everywhere. It could very well be a case where the operation succeeds, but the patient dies.

"FFP. As much as they can give us," Asadourian barked.

Wessman eyed the second pulmonary artery. "I'll repair it," he said. "You graft the aorta."

Winfield, working on resecting the damaged kidney, groaned. "Spleen is bleeding again."

"Can you repair it?"

"Doubtful."

Asadourian did not hesitate. "Take it, too," he sighed.

As Wessman and Asadourian undertook the repair of the aorta and the pulmonary arteries, Colder began to slide into the depths of the horrible coagulopathy. Every IV site began to bleed, and blood began to appear at both nostrils and the corner of his mouth. Nowhere in the wound was a clot forming. Dr. Shantz slammed in three units of fresh-frozen plasma rich in coagulants and called for more. The anesthesiology resident pushed in two units into a central line and then pushed in another unit of blood. His blood pressure steady, he needed both blood cells and coagulant factors as fast as they could possibly be brought in.

Wessman had the second pulmonary artery repaired in four minutes, a running proline suture performing the trick. Meanwhile, Asadourian picked out the aortic graft and cut it to size. Each man was sweating profusely, but their eyes were steely and determined. No one was giving up.

"Any more arrhythmias?" Winfield asked.

"No," Schantz replied.

Winfield lifted out the shattered kidney with its attached vessels and proximal ureter. Less than two minutes later, the spleen was gone. They were the fastest nephrectomy and splenectomy he had ever done. "Done here," he gasped. "Bleeding is better."

Asadourian glanced up at him. A circulating nurse wiped his sweating brow to prevent anything from dripping into the wound. "How's that colon?" he asked the resident.

"Nicked but no perf."

"You sure?"

"No mucosa. Positive."

"Good," the big man said, grateful for the first bit of good news. "Make sure you've got all the bleeding and get the hell out of there. Let's at least give him a chance to die of something else."

"I'm on it."

Five minutes later, Winfield was closing the abdomen while the anesthesiologist poured in blood and fresh-frozen plasma. For the first time, volume going in exceeded blood loss. Colder's blood pressure began to slowly rise.

One hour after the operation had begun, Dr. Wessman took a deep breath. The room fell quiet. The aortic graft, a twelve-inch segment of the body's largest blood vessel, was complete. The old trauma surgeon eyed the aortic clamp uneasily. Every surgeon's greatest fear was about to be confronted, removing the life-maintaining clamp and testing the suture line. If the suture line blew, there would be no saving Colder. Any further up on the aorta and the great vessels that supplied the brain would be involved, making the repair impossible. Wessman turned to Asadourian. The giant Armenian raised his burly eyebrows and nodded. Wessman sighed. "Well, boys, the moment of truth."

The tired-looking intern, who had watched the surgery from the corner of the room, closed his eyes and quietly finished the prayer he had started earlier. He had never seen someone survive an injury like this.

Wessman closed his eyes, his mind flashing back to the explosion of blood he had seen a half hour earlier. His momentary reverie finished, he bit his lip, opened his eyes, and put his steady hand on the clamp. Dr. Schantz turned away, not wanting to look. Winfield took a deep breath. The nurses gritt their teeth. The lead scrub picked up another aortic clamp as the intern started another "Hail Mary."

"Do it," Asadourian said, his usually calm voice wavering slightly.

Only the buzz of the clock could be heard punctuating the nervous silence. The sweat that had been wiped from Wessman's brow reappeared. Cautiously, the surgeon unlocked the clamp and gradually began removing the occlusive pressure on the aorta. Instantly, the blood started streaming past the clamp and into the graft. So far so good. Wessman slowly pulled the clamp back, sliding its teeth over the pulsating vessel. Bit by bit, he removed it. As he did so, the last bit of security was gone.

A moment later, Wessman pulled the long metal instrument out of Colder's chest and held it in the air. Everyone in the room gasped audibly. The surgeons did not react. They looked at the graft and then at the blood pressure monitor. With blood flow restored to the body there was a momentary drop in blood pressure registering in the right arm's arterial line, but there was no bleeding to be seen. The graft had held.

The two old army surgeons sighed deeply, relief flowing through their bodies. Winfield groaned, his relief audible. Wessman and Asadourian closed their eyes and gently tapped their foreheads together. It was a gesture of thanks, pride, and happiness. "Looks good, Mel," grunted Asadourian. "Looks damn good!" The entire room cheered.

Twenty minutes later, an unconscious Peter Colder was wheeled from the operating room directly to the ICU. He was still in florid DIC, and his blood pressure was low. Renal failure, multiorgan failure, respiratory distress, and sepsis all remained potential hurdles to be crossed, but for now, the greatest challenge had passed. They all knew that for nearly an hour Peter Colder had lived on the edge of death, but thanks to the hospital, the skill of three surgeons, and a team of many, he would at least live a few more hours. More importantly, he still had a chance.

There was no fanfare at 3:00 A.M. when the journal and disks arrived at Gregory Markham's office. Placed unceremoniously in a kitchen garbage bag, they had been dumped in the mailbox by the courier and retrieved personally by Markham. Holding them aloft in the dim light of his office, Markham looked at them more as a curiosity than a trophy, the last remaining link to his future and ComHealth's past.

Markham opened the journal and stopped on the article's cover page. James Patrick O'Reilly was listed as the second author of the seventh article. Markham skimmed the title and focused on one phrase. Protein B1B. That was what it had all been about. He closed the journal and put it on his desk. He didn't want to look at it. Markham turned on his computer to check the disks. One by one, he ran through their files. In less than a minute, he assured himself they, too, were real.

He picked up the phone and called Hutchins, who answered on the first ring, sounding awake.

"Yes?"

"Got them," muttered Markham

"Good," said Hutchins, sounding relieved. "You're gonna burn them?"

"Crush and burn."

H. Carter Hutchins exhaled deeply into the phone. Markham guessed he was still up, probably sitting in his den. "Good work, Greg. Forget about anything I said earlier. It was just heat-of-the-moment stuff."

"I understand."

"Very good work."

"Thanks."

The phone went dead, and Markham hung it up. Sitting alone in the depths of his office, he grabbed the journal again and fingered it like a fine cloth. Retrieving it had saved his career.

He stood and walked to his coat, which was hanging behind the door. In the breast pocket was a small can of lighter fluid. He retrieved it and then returned to his seat. He had drunk nearly a bottle of champagne earlier, but now his mind was anything but intoxicated. It spun with questions. How? Why? What had he become? "Men have died for this," he muttered out loud. And he was responsible.

Oh, he thought, it could be justified. Like when a murderer goes free, the system can be blamed—the high standard of proof, or other self-deceptions lawyers use to make their face palatable to their eyes. Markham closed his eyes, but he could not deceive himself. Nothing could erase his guilt or his shame. It was orders, he told himself often, the old argument of weakness and fear. Or, it was entrapment. He tried that one too, an argument of incompetence. No. He knew nothing could save him from himself. He was guilty. Pure and simple. He allowed everything to happen.

The euphoria of recovering the journal died. Markham continued to sit alone in the office, brooding about his life. He thought more about his child and the lessons he would teach her, the lies he would have to tell. He thought about his wife and his betrayal of her dreams. And for what?

Markham rose from his seat. He felt dead, destroyed, like an addict at the end of a trip. His body seemed limp, his head hurting. How had it happened, he continued to wonder? What had he become? Markham knew that the questions asked were themselves indictments, ignominious inquiries into the essence of a life gone wrong. And he had been witness to it, he thought wishfully. "No," he said out loud after a moment of reflection. He was active in it. He could never deny that. He wasn't a fool.

That old cliché of the slippery slope came to his mind. That lethal combination of ambition, amorality, and acquiescence. The ethic that made men wealthy and allowed them to rationalize all that its attainment required. But no, it was more than that. It was money. Money controlled them. Money, worshiped as prosperity. Money, rationalized as security. Money, cleansed as philanthropy. Money, the fragile fiber of the needy man's soul.

He walked to the mirror and gazed at his face, thinner than it should be, uglier than he would have wanted. He thought of his daughter and his wife. He thought of his life, his future, his past, and his secret. He knew now what he had become—a willing victim of himself, a willing prisoner of the lies that so subtly deceive. But he could still not answer the other simple question. What was it all for?

He looked again at the mirror, but now he no longer saw himself. The image changed. A metamorphosis. His face became a negative, dark where it should be light. He searched for his old familiar features, but they were gone. The face was now a gross distortion, an aberration, a hideous reinvention of himself. No, it was real, he told himself. It was the face of his new character, the face of his soul.

Markham closed his eyes. He knew he could not answer the question that rang in his mind. He still did not know. But the face in the mirror told him who he was. He couldn't deny it. The ambitious business student had succeeded. He got what he wished for, everything. But in doing so, he became a different man. He became H. Carter Hutchins.

He took the lighter fluid and soaked the pages. Then, with one match, he lit them on fire. Tossing it into the wastebasket, he watched it burn, the pages flaming two feet into the air. After the print began to disappear, he took the plastic disks and broke them with his hands. They, too, he tossed into the fire. Minute by minute, he watched the fire burn, occasionally stoking it with more lighter fluid just as the flames began to retreat. First the outer pages burned and soon the inner pages began to disappear while the plastic seemed to melt before his eyes. He watched as the flames licked at the sides of the metal wastebasket, leaving it untouched and further serving as a metaphor for his body and soul. Finally, the deed was done. He did not know why he had done it. He only knew it was right.

When everything was burned, he began moving more quickly. He picked up around him, threw some papers into the wastebasket to cover the extinguished ashes, and opened a window and to let the smell pass. A few moments later, all traces were gone and he left the office.

As he took the elevator down to the garage, he was still thinking about the fire, the journal, and the disks. There would be no trace. No identifying marks. To all concerned Fragile X was but a bad memory. A problem that nearly destroyed them. A problem for the future to work out. He asked himself the question again. Why had he done it? Again he couldn't answer. He fondled the envelope and glanced at it briefly. But suddenly he felt a bit better.

Markham walked out of the elevator and then out of the building. He stepped into the street. Downtown was quiet. The air was warm and humid, with fog partially obscuring the streetlights. Markham paused and looked up at the hazy glow of the moon. He breathed a little sigh of relief and began to walk again. After the furor of the day, his mind at last began to clear. He thought about the journal again. Fragile X was gone. At least to the world. It was a disaster. Nothing went as planned, but in the end they succeeded.

Markham was now resolved. His decision comforted him, and he felt better with every step. Tomorrow he would act, hide them in a place no one would ever see. Perhaps there would never be a need. Maybe it really was over. But if a day ever came when the secrets of his past threatened to destroy his future, he would have a surprise for the world. On that day, Markham would let everyone know that he finally disobeyed orders. In the depth of this horrible night, he had done the unthinkable. He saved the journal and instead burned the *Playboy* and the three blank disks.

Chapter Twenty-six

August 17

Throughout the rest of the night, Colder's condition held steady. He remained heavily medicated, unconscious, and on life support, but his blood pressure and pulse had stabilized. The severe bleeding of earlier was resolving, and to this point, most of his laboratory values were normal. Privately, however, his doctors worried. They knew he had been a victim of very low blood pressure for a long time. This left most of the body starved for blood, and during that time he could have suffered a stroke, heart attack, or injury to his surviving kidney as well as damage to any other organ. Even in the glow of a surgical success, Wessman, Asadourian, and Winfield were dubious of his chances for survival.

Colder remained in the surgical ICU on the second floor of the HCMC in a private room. At 5:30 A.M., the three surgeons who had operated joined Colder's friends in a large conference room and began an explanation of all that had happened. Marcia Sullivan, the last to arrive, sat with Molly. Sylvia sat with Sandra and Letisha. Reggie stood alone, looking out the window into the darkness. The mood was somber.

After introducing themselves, the doctors talked of where the bullets had entered and exited and what tissues were injured. They described the surgery in detail, but avoided the most gruesome details and the truth of how close Peter Colder had actually come to dying. All three men were experienced at giving both bad and good news. They neither overdramatized nor underplayed the events that just happened. Wessman talked at length, while Asadourian was more succinct. Winfield remained largely quiet, instead deferring to his superiors.

"Our biggest worry now," Wessman continued after about twenty minutes, "is what we may have to fight through. In a few days, we'll know for sure if he has had a stroke or heart attack, and if so, how bad it is. Also we'll know if his kidney has been damaged."

"Which of those do you worry about most?" Reggie asked.

"The body has an intrinsic mechanism that preserves the most vital organs if the blood pressure becomes low. The first thing it does is to shunt blood away from less vital tissues like muscle and bone to important ones like the brain and the other organs. In this way, the body attempts to prevent damage even in situations like this. The flip side of that, though, is that the brain, heart, kidneys, and liver all require significant blood flow to keep healthy." Wessman paused, realizing he wasn't really answering the question. "I guess I would worry most about a stroke. After that, I suppose, the possibility that his remaining kidney may fail."

"What if he's had a stroke?" Sylvia asked. "Paralysis?"

"We don't know," Asadourian replied. "We've just got to wait and see."

Letisha was shaking. "And if his kidney fails? Dialysis?"

"Possibly, but that's a worst-case scenario."

Asadourian and Wessman continued to answer questions while walking along a narrow fence that bordered unrealistic expectations and undue gloom. They wanted to be truthful and convey their worry, but communicate that not all hope was lost.

"It's going to be a long haul," Asadourian said. "I would say that in the best of situations, he will be in the ICU for a couple of weeks and then in the hospital several more." Everyone nodded in understanding.

The surgeons continued to discuss their concerns and, after almost an hour more, the room finally fell silent. Everyone was spent. Realizing that all questions had been answered, the three tired surgeons stood to leave, and one by one the others stood and thanked them. "We'll check with you if anything changes," Wessman said to Sylvia.

"Thank you."

When the doctors left, they walked away from the waiting room toward the elevators that would take them to a long-awaited cup of coffee. "I have a bad feeling," Wessman admitted.

"You always do," Asadourian teased his friend.

"So do I," Winfield said as they arrived at the elevators.

Asadourian stopped and turned toward Winfield, a knowledgeable man who was less than a year from completing his training. "Why?"

"Because he lost six inches of his aorta, a lobe of his lung, a pulmonary artery, a kidney, not to mention his spleen. He's gone through forty-five units of blood and fifteen units of FFP. He's unconscious; he's probably prerenal and he may have had an MI."

Asadourian grunted. There was nothing wrong with what Winfield had said. The chief resident was ready to graduate, but the old trauma surgeon had something else in mind.

"You're just forgetting one thing," Asadourian retorted.

Winfield nodded, knowing what was coming. Asadourian was a "half-full" kind of guy and Winfield had heard it a million times over five years. "I know," he muttered. Asadourian's face lit up with a toothy grin. "You're forgetting the most important thing of all. After all that he went through, all of it, Peter Colder is still alive."

No one could disagree.

After the conference, everyone returned to the waiting room, which was otherwise empty in the early morning hours. They used the phones to call people, talk among themselves, and try to make sense of everything that happened. A nurse relayed news that Julianne Purcell had been admitted and was on ward 3W. She suffered a concussion, but the CAT scan of the brain was normal, and she was now resting comfortably under light sedation. Everyone was clearly relieved. After a few minutes Sylvia, Sandra, and Letisha left to visit her.

Moments later, a hospital volunteer arrived with a tray of pastries, coffee, and juice and as she slipped them into the room, she was nearly run over by Tyler Briggs and Marcus Sanders. In the commotion of the fire and then the shooting, everyone had forgotten to call the attorneys until Reggie remembered about an hour earlier. The two men looked stricken as they flew into the waiting room.

"How is he?" Tyler asked breathlessly.

"Critical."

The two men, panting and pale, flopped down on chairs and listened as Molly gave them a medical update. They were too preoccupied to realize that they both had their shirts incorrectly buttoned. The lawyers listened in horror as they heard the details of the wounds and the surgery. Numb and anguished, they were unable to speak.

Sylvia, Letisha, and Sandra returned after a brief visit to Julianne. With Geoff at her bedside, she slept while her family talked with relatives on the phone. The three Third Street Clinic employees felt slightly awkward and cut their visit short. When Sylvia and the others returned to the waiting room, Molly stood, waved to them, and walked toward the door. She offered the lame excuse of needing to go to the bathroom, but everyone clearly saw she was crying. The others pretended to pay no attention.

Slipping out of the glass-doored waiting room, Molly turned out of sight and ambled along the empty hallway with her hands across her chest. She stopped and leaned heavily against the wall. She knew that none of them blamed her. Peter's friends were objective and fair. But that didn't matter. She blamed herself, knowing that without her, none of it would have happened. She knew that Peter would have cared that the case was gone, evaporated in a whirlwind of gunfire and flame. But she did not. This was about Peter. Peter Colder, fighting for his life. A man she was falling in love with. A selfless man, a son, a brother, a friend to so many. A man who lived in a world where self-sacrifice was standard and self-interest did not exist; where money meant nothing, and wealth resided in the soul. It was so unfair, she thought. He *could not* die!

Molly staggered into another dark and empty waiting room at the end of the hallway and closed the door. Taking a seat near the window, she paid no attention to the first hint of sunrise. It seemed impossible that the sun would ever shine again. Instead, she buried her head in her hands and continued to cry.

One hour later, Briggs and Sanders walked out of the Hennepin County Medical Center and paused on the sidewalk. Peter continued to remain stable. Having promised everyone that they would return before noon, the attorneys slid unnoticed out of the building. Marcus picked up a newspaper inside and they glanced together over the headlines and the text. The front-page article was about O'Reilly, but it offered nothing new. Having trouble locating his relatives, the police refrained from releasing O'Reilly's name. Nothing in the front page or the rest of the paper mentioned Peter Colder.

Finished, Marcus tucked it under his arm, and the two men began walking toward their office eight blocks away. Tyler never remembered feeling such rage. Even in the heat of athletics, when the mind stops and anger's impulse begins, he had never felt such hatred. His prevailing thought was to walk into ComHealth's offices with a shotgun. Only after a battle with his logical side did he decide against it.

"Someone's got to bring these bastards to justice," he hissed.

Sanders did not miss the thought. "But it won't be us, will it?"

Tyler kept on walking. He did not look at his friend. "You know, in this friggin' world, there really isn't such a thing as right or justice. Only wrong and injustice."

"What?"

"I was just realizing that."

"What are you getting at?"

"The law really doesn't provide justice. There's no justice ever for O'Reilly. No justice for Peter. No justice for Molly, Jayne McCall, Lisa Bowman, or their families."

"No."

They jogged across the street, dodging a couple of other pedestrians. A morning shower had passed, but the wind continued. As they emerged out of the shadow of the buildings, the air was surprisingly cool. Marcus buttoned up the jacket he was wearing. Tyler did the same. "Just what are you thinking, Ty? You and I both know this case is over. It's history."

Briggs didn't move. They stood on the street corner as others passed by. "Marcus, ask yourself what this case is really about."

Sanders responded immediately. "It is about a powerful insurance company hiding behind cleverly written clauses that make them a ton of money by denying care."

"I would phrase it differently. It is about being sleazy and shitty. The sharp edge of capitalism that cuts deep."

"What in the hell are you talking about?"

Tyler's eyes were on fire. "Remember the biblical story of David and Goliath?"

"Sure, who doesn't?"

"Well, David's slaying of the Philistine was in itself a metaphor for life. The reality that good will ultimately triumph because of evil's inherent and persistent weakness."

"What's that?"

"That people will always come to see evil for what it really is."

Marcus chuckled. "I think you're losing it, or maybe I am. I have no idea what you're talking about."

"We take the stone and we begin to swing it. One by one, the people will see. See what we are aiming at, and see why."

"You don't really think we should contin—" Marcus stopped. His face told all. He was sure one of Tyler's oars had slipped out of the water. "Listen, Tyler, we should walk right over to Jack Barnes' office and apologize for even bothering him. Without Fragile X, we've got nothing but an old executive that drained his liquor cabinet every day. Nothing!"

Briggs was nonplussed, his burning eyes slicing right through Marcus. He looked almost psychotic. "Forget it. By the time we're done, they'll be begging us for mercy."

Sanders laughed out loud. "My God, buddy! What have you been smoking?"

Briggs ignored him. He walked even faster. "As I said, begging us for mercy."

Marcus struggled to keep up. "I don't see how."

"Van Gilder let the case *in* without Fragile X because it had merit. With that, we're halfway there."

"What are you talking about, Ty?"

Briggs appeared almost too preoccupied to continue to talk. He kept looking back and forth as if he were expecting someone, but kept walking at an ever-accelerating pace. "I have a plan," he whispered over his shoulder. "I have a helluva plan."

"What is it?" asked Marcus, struggling to stay with him.

"It's called, 'Goliath's Achilles Heel.'"

"Just what the hell is that?"

Sanders looked as if his he was sure his friend was at least a dozen cards short of a deck. Briggs kept on walking; all the while, his thoughts were becoming arguments, arguments he knew would draw blood.

"It's time to sharpen the knives, Marcus. Time to sharpen them good."

Sunday morning was wonderful for H. Carter Hutchins. Markham's middle-of-the-night phone call had been a relief, and when he awoke at seven, he found a beautiful late-summer sun gazing at him through his bedroom window. After showering and throwing on a robe, he joined his wife in the east-wing solarium, where the maid brought them a breakfast of tea, fresh fruit, and eggs benedict.

Sitting amongst the splendor of the recently redecorated room, Hutchins allowed himself to relax. For the first time in several weeks, he had little reason to worry. Fragile X was finally gone. O'Reilly, too, was gone, and nothing could ever connect ComHealth with anything. In addition the company's stock price continued to hold despite the negative publicity. And fortunately, the issue remained a local.

Hutchins sighed as he sipped on his tea and reviewed the coming schedule. Tomorrow the ComHealth public relations effort was poised to kick into high gear. This strategy was critical, pacifying the board of directors at their Friday meeting, as did the reassurance that the annoying little lawsuit that several reporters seemed interested in would be taken care of soon. Things had definitely turned for the better.

The morning paper contained nothing of the incident. Hutchins knew it never would. There was no proof whatsoever linking ComHealth with any mischief, and the only people who knew anything, his executives and lawyers, were completely beholden to him. Hutchins took a bite of kiwi and leaned back. The day was going to be a good one.

After breakfast, the chauffeur drove him and Celia to United Presbyterian, their church since moving from Chicago and the church of the upper crust of Minneapolis's western suburbs. Every week was the same, half fashion show and half good "Christianship," where the economically successful merged their calculated piety with their politics and congregated to offer judgment upon the world.

Each Sunday, Celia and Carter attended the Bible study at 10:00 A.M. followed by the service. This week, Celia looked particularly radiant in a new Givenchy original she had purchased the previous week in New York. After the service, the congregation took turns exchanging pleasantries, talking of clothes, children's accomplishments, and their latest vacations. This lasted nearly an hour, until finally bored with the act, they all went home.

Hutchins spent the rest of the day watching a preseason football game and talking on the phone with fellow executives and a few board members. The executives all thought as Hutchins did. It was over. They could relax.

At dinner, he and Celia dined lightly, veal and vegetables, and afterward they watched a tape of *Dr. Zhivago*. The ten o'clock news offered nothing new, and after a dip in the hot tub and a small glass of amaretto liqueur, they both went to bed.

By 11:00 P.M., H. Carter Hutchins was comfortably asleep at the end of a perfect day. He had no idea that everything he said and everything he thought was entirely wrong. Nothing was perfect. Nothing had been solved. Nothing was even close to being over.

At midnight Sunday, a sleepy Molly stirred. In the corner of the darkened waiting room where she sat leaning against a wall, she cocked her head to see who had entered. She could see Phyllis Colder talking to her son Bryan in the hallway outside the glass wall of the waiting room. Peter's mother and brother had arrived in the middle of the day from Arizona and were still trying to come to grips with what had happened. Their first reactions were predictable, but they managed to steady themselves and spent much of the time in Peter's room. They treated Peter's friends like family, but often kept to themselves, apparently trying to make sense of it all.

Molly shook herself and looked around the room. Sylvia, Letisha, and Sandra were asleep across from her. She could see by looking at Reggie's face that nothing had changed. Shaking herself awake, Molly saw the silhouette of Marcia Sullivan coming toward her. The reporter, who had stayed with them all day, now looked equally tired when her features came into view.

"How you doing?" she asked Molly.

"Okay."

Marcia looked exhausted. Not even the darkness of the room could hide the sagging of the eyes and the drooping of the face. Looking at her, Molly realized that none of them had slept in nearly thirty-six hours, including the reporter, her friend. "You need to get some sleep, Marcia," she said.

"So do you."

"Anything new?" Molly asked.

"No. He's still unconscious, but they've quit giving him blood. I took that as a good sign."

Molly sighed. Marcia's face changed slightly and Molly picked it up. "I gotta talk to you," the reporter said.

Molly did not respond at first; instead she turned and gazed out the window toward the lights of downtown. After a minute, she turned back to Marcia. "Let's walk."

They left their group of friends, reassuring them that they would be back shortly, and strolled past the ICU. Her emotions hidden just beneath the surface all day, Molly began crying again the minute she saw the ICU door. "You know, I've never felt like this," she began, as if talking would make her feel better.

"Neither have I," Marcia confessed.

"There are so many things I would do differently. I would never have allowed—"

Marcia interrupted her. "It's not your fault," she said firmly, taking a strong hold of Molly's forearm. "It's not your fault. Period."

Molly stopped. She knew that was technically true, but no amount of discussion could change what happened or how she felt about it. She also had no interest in debating levels of guilt or why she felt as she did. That was a discussion she would need to have with herself.

They started walking again and without thinking found their way to the nearly empty cafeteria, where the two sat down. Marcia had a forlorn look on her face, the appearance of a person plagued by guilt. Molly knew the look. In just a short period of time, she had come to be able to read the reporter well. It was indeed guilt she felt. Guilt over having to do her job.

"Molly, you know how I feel about you and Peter. Just a week ago, I was a struggling reporter in risk of losing my job. You guys saved me."

"That's not true," Molly interrupted.

Marcia dismissed it. "Yes, it is. And I just want you to know that I would do anything to help you."

Molly heard the sincerity in the reporter's voice. "I appreciate that."

"It won't be long before the trial starts."

Molly waved her hands. "I don't know where that stands now. I haven't talked to Tyler or Marcus and—"

"I have." Marcia's face was a weird mix of stern and philosophical.

"You have?"

"In fact, I've talked to them a great deal."

Molly was slightly surprised, but not upset. "What did they say?"

Marcia was straightforward. "They seem more determined than ever. They're planning on going ahead. Jury selection and maybe even opening arguments next Monday. The twenty-fifth. Unless you want to delay it."

"But he thinks that ComHealth will delay it, doesn't he?"

"Yes. Probably."

Molly looked spent. Her body was hunched forward and appeared to tremble. "I don't know. I'm just trying to think."

"I understand. Believe me, I do. But try this on for size."

Molly tried to gather her thoughts while Marcia described her conversation with Briggs earlier that afternoon. "I'm sorry to tell you this now," Marcia finished. "I guess you're the last to know. But I thought this could be helpful to you."

Molly sighed. In the corner of the cafeteria, she could see the agent who had been following her at a distance, as always. It all seemed unreal. All she could think about was Peter. The legal issues, the danger, even the thought of a trial, seemed incomprehensible. First, she never thought her case would get this far, and secondly, there was Peter. "I don't know if I can do it."

"I understand. And so do they. Tyler and Marcus will be talking to you tomorrow. The trial could almost certainly be delayed if you want."

"I-I don't know," she answered. "I just haven't thought of it."

Marcia opened a bite-sized Baby Ruth. After offering it to Molly, who refused, Marcia gobbled it down and then returned to the proposal she had offered Molly's team. "Molly, in the next couple of days, things are going to get sticky. Like we talked about before, people are going to want to hear from you. Your story and why the lawsuit."

"I know," Molly admitted.

"Dealing with reporters, dealing with TV. It's not easy."

"I'm sure."

"They're taught to look for the story within the story. Extract every drop from the well and drink from it until it's dry."

"That's not a pretty thought."

"No, I'm sure it isn't."

Molly looked across the table into Marcia's eyes. She knew without saying it that the stakes were rising before her eyes. For the past week, she had shied away from the publicity as all the other ComHealth victims took the stage. Now it was her turn join in, and if the suit continued, she knew there would be no turning back. No aspect of her life would be left unknown. From her school failures, to her failed marriage, to her failure to tell her husband about the abortion; it would all be there for the public to see and analyze.

"I want to help," Marcia said.

Molly looked away from the reporter and toward an elderly woman drinking a cup of coffee across the cafeteria. She had met the woman earlier in the day. Her husband, a retired teacher, was suffering from complications of bypass surgery and had been in the intensive care unit for two weeks.

"I don't know," Molly heard herself mumble. It was so tempting to drop the suit completely. What chance did they have? Fragile X was gone and with it their only real hope. It was probably over before it started. But Peter and O'Reilly. She thought about what they would want, what they said, what they sacrificed.

The old woman across the room raised her cup of coffee, acknowledging Molly. It seemed strange, the curious bond of friendship strangers feel when sharing the worst moments of their lives. She liked the old woman. The woman smiled at Molly, a smile of friendship and understanding. Generations apart, they were no different. They knew what the other was feeling.

"What exactly did Tyler say?" Molly asked.

"That it would be okay. He wants you to."

Molly nodded. "He told me there would be a time."

Marcia was firm. "That time is now."

Molly stood up. She needed a minute more to think. "You want a soda?"

"Pepsi," Marcia said, taking the change out of her pocket.

The trip to the vending machines lasted ten minutes, but Molly returned with Pepsi and Diet Sprite in hand. She sat down, opened her can, and took one long swig. Her thoughts and feelings finally controlled, she took a deep breath. She closed her eyes as if trying to recall the wording of a story she had always known she would one day have to tell to the public. "Let's start from the beginning," Molly began. "Once upon a time…"

Three hours later, Marcia Sullivan hung up the phone. Her conversation with the *Star Tribunes'* managing editor complete, she took the elevator to the ground floor and headed home to type the article. The twenty-minute conversation told her what she could and could not print, but even with some limitations, she knew full well what she was carrying in her pocket.

When she arrived at her tiny apartment, she went directly to the computer. Six hours later, she finished and e-mailed the copy in to the paper. As she fell into bed for a two-hour nap, she ran through the article in her mind. Every word, every phrase. She wanted to do Molly justice and tell it the right way.

In the silence of Marcia Sullivan's efficiency flat, the sleeping reporter dreamt a pleasant childhood image of snowsledding with her brother, while at the hospital, Peter Colder clung to life and Molly Loomis huddled in a waiting room. Across town, H. Carter Hutchins passed through an uneventful Monday while the cities swirled with rumors and speculation about O'Reilly's murder and Colder's shooting. None of them knew that for all of them, it would be their last day of freedom and the end of their former lives.

On Tuesday morning, August 12, the Minneapolis *Star Tribune* containing Marcia Sullivan's article hit the streets. In the following hours, Minneapolis–St. Paul erupted in a frenzy previously unseen in the sedate midwestern area. The reaction was an unprecedented explosion of outrage. Throughout the state, the blast's heat made the sun look like a forty-watt light bulb.

By the end of the day, H. Carter Hutchins knew for the first time the extent of his miscalculation as all of ComHealthOne was rocked by the intensity of the article's shock wave. But this article had caused more than just a local earthquake. These tremors were felt elsewhere. Now the battle would be played out before a much larger audience. The story of Molly Jane Loomis versus ComHealthOne had gone national.

Chapter Twenty-seven

Tom Brokaw and NBC slated it as the third story of the evening news. Dan Rather and CBS pitched it as fourth, as did Peter Jennings and ABC. Each newscast featured a correspondent from Minneapolis offering a synopsis of Molly's story printed that day in the *Star Tribune*. They stationed themselves outside the Hennepin County Court Building and showed an old picture of Molly from her freshman year at the University of Minnesota. NBC and CBS interviewed Tyler Briggs, while ABC spoke with Marcus Sanders. ComHealth refused to comment. In their brief answers to the camera, the two lawyers reiterated the confrontation they were determined to create. The ordinary citizen against the executive money-making machine of managed care medicine.

Each correspondent began a review of the medical histories of some of the ComHealth patients that the Minneapolis area knew from Marcia Sullivan's articles. They talked of Rudy Jalowicz and his bout with kidney cancer. They mentioned Lisa Bowman and her battle with cervical cancer. And they talked of Jayne McCall and her savagely scarred face. Lastly they mentioned Shirley Mitchell and her inadequately treated breast cancer, and Lester Cummings, the man whose widespread colon cancer would have been detected by a screening test no longer offered by ComHealthOne.

But the correspondents noted that the *Star Tribune* series promised other patients as well. Each day, the paper offered previews of the upcoming stories. On Wednesday, Marcia would be reporting on two patients who had suffered heart attacks and died after ComHealth refused to approve an ER visit. On Thursday, NBC and CBS reported, the *Star Tribune* article would focus on a middle-aged man whose stroke and paralysis went untreated with the new drug TPA. On Friday, she would detail the death of Zach Lawton, an eight-year-old who died of a splenic rupture when ComHealthOne mandated his discharge from the hospital. The little boy partially ruptured his spleen in a fall from a bicycle. Watched in the hospital without needing surgery, Zach was discharged from the hospital against the surgeon's advice. The surgeon recommended several days more of observation before the boy could be safely discharged, but ComeHealthOne authorized payment for only two days. Fearing a massive bill, Zach's mom took him home. The boy died that night.

Following their stories on Marcia's patients, the correspondents concentrated on Molly Loomis. They finished their reports by describing her coming lawsuit as the first major legal test of managed care tactics. All of them mentioned that local interest was enormous, but none of them mentioned O'Reilly or any of the numerous rumors about his death.

The Minneapolis–St. Paul reporters were far less restrained or charitable. For the first time, O'Reilly's name was mentioned publicly after an uncle, notified of his nephew's death, allowed public disclosure. They mentioned that he was an acquaintance of Dr. Peter Colder, who was shot and critically wounded shortly after his house burned. The reporters openly speculated that the death was linked to Molly Loomis's case and therefore to ComHealth.

The city reacted in astonishment and anger. The radio talk shows whose calls about ComHealth had slowed slightly with the weekend, were now overwhelmed. Every station devoted extensive coverage and commentary, and the local television channels immediately began preparing specials at 6:30 and 10:30 each night through the length of the trial. Tyler Briggs and Marcus Sanders were smothered with requests for interviews. They declined all but the major networks and one each for the local channels. Molly Loomis was also besieged with requests. She declined them all.

August 20

On Wednesday morning Tyler, sitting with Marcus in his office, hung up the phone. His update on Colder's condition from Molly was not good. Over the past twenty-four hours, Colder's condition had worsened. As the doctors feared, his remaining kidney ceased to function. This "shock" phenomenon, a result of the low blood pressure, necessitated a round of dialysis and would require another one in about twenty-four hours. The condition could be temporary or permanent. In addition, Colder's liver was now failing slightly. The only good news was that a heart attack had been ruled out. A stroke remained a possibility, as he had not regained consciousness, but a CT scan and an MRI were both negative.

Marcus listened to Tyler's conversation with Molly from a distance. "No go?" he asked.

"Nada," he said, shaking his head. "She sounds half dead, but she wants to go ahead."

"She's got guts," Marcus mumbled.

Tyler nodded in agreement. He knew Molly understood their predicament. They had spent weeks preparing the case with two strategies in mind. The first was with the presence of the Fragile X link. In that scenario, they played to win and in doing so, bring down ComHealth and Hutchins. The second strategy, in case the Fragile X link did not materialize, involved making a lot of noise, but all involved knew there was no real chance of winning. They were now stuck with the second strategy. In reality, despite the horrible timing, there would never be a better time for the world to hear the truth about how ComHealthOne had "saved" health care.

"I know she'd love about a year continuance," Tyler continued. "She's totally exhausted. But she's convinced that this is what's best for everyone."

"What about that other call?" Marcus asked. "What did Pokey say?"

Briggs looked confused. "Well, he swore about a thousand times and talked about his new Corvette. But delay it? I guess I always assumed that if this exploded, they would delay automatically. But I'm surprised. Pokey didn't say anything like that."

"They will tomorrow," replied Marcus. "Why the hell would they possibly try the case now? To this point, it has been like a parking ticket case. I don't know if they've even taken it seriously until now."

"I believe that."

"They'll definitely delay it. Most likely for about a decade."

"Yeah, but Pokey didn't say that," Briggs commented.

Marcus scoffed. "How could they possibly go ahead?"

"I don't know." Briggs wondered the same thing but without coming up with an answer. "Maybe they feel that they can come up with some positive PR out of it if they take the center stage. Barnes and Whitfield are both pretty persuasive guys. Maybe they feel they could turn it around if they just got a chance to talk into a microphone with a big audience listening." He finished his thought, knowing it sounded lame.

Marcus dismissed that thought with a wave. "Forget it. They'll ask for a continuance tomorrow. This business about withdrawing the motions and 'justice delayed is justice denied' is just BS, and everyone knows it. They'll come back with a zillion motions tomorrow. Enough to delay it a hundred years."

Briggs picked up his cup of coffee. "You're right."

Marcus slid a little lower in his chair. "Really, what does it matter?"

Tyler didn't respond. He knew what his partner meant. Whenever they tried the case really didn't matter. Ultimately, the written law would decide the outcome, irrespective of their criticism of managed care.

"I suppose it doesn't."

"But what if?" began Marcus taking a sip of orange juice. "You ready if this trial happens?"

Tyler rolled the styrofoam coffee cup between his fingers. For four days, his thoughts and emotions seemed to run continuously out of control. From the anger to the anguish, from the electrifying excitement of talking to the networks to the growing fear of a crushing public defeat. "Yeah," he grunted. "I guess so."

"When it's done, we're gonna need a vacation."

Briggs turned in his chair to see out the window. The day was sun-streaked and flawless. "That's sort of what bugs me," he said. "The cloud will pass, and we'll go on with our lives. We'll be better off because of this case no matter what the outcome. But what about Molly, Pete, and O'Reilly?"

Marcus knew what he was feeling. "We can only do what we can do."

Briggs did not reply. There was no need. He knew that they were now just philosophizing. That meant they were both ready for the trial.

"You think they'd ever offer a settlement?" asked Marcus.

Briggs only shook his head. He knew at this point there was no chance of that.

The ComHealthOne board of directors convened an emergency meeting on Wednesday morning. The sixteen men and four women filed into the paneled and polished boardroom with looks ranging from grim frustration to overt hostility. In the preceding twenty-four hours, ComHealth stock declined eleven points, reducing the company's market capitalization by nearly twenty percent and creating an avalanche of complaints from stockholders. In addition, the scathing reports appearing on TV news programs and in newspapers raised the blood pressure of nearly every director. For the first time, many were quietly wondering about H. Carter Hutchins.

As he took his seat and began the meeting, the CEO, as usual, appeared unflappable. "First of all, I would like to thank all of you for coming. As you would expect, I have a number of issues I would like to address."

With those introductory words, Hutchins began a half-hour dissertation that attempted to reassure the directors and place blame everywhere else. As always, his oration was skillful and his salesmanship superb. When he finished, he felt confident that the problems were solved.

He gazed around at the faces in the room. Most directors looked at him curiously. Some took notes and seemed to be jogging their memory by reviewing them. Others appeared deep in thought. Finally, Frederick Wyman spoke. The recently retired CEO of ATA Security Systems was the newest member of the board and the one Hutchins knew the least well. "Carter," Wyman began. "That all sounds well and good. But I need to ask you something. I, and I think I speak for everyone, need to know if it's true?"

"Excuse me?" asked Hutchins, sounding weaker than he intended.

"If it's true, what the papers are saying. What the news is saying."

Hutchins was ready for the question. "The press will never be our friend. We all know that. There isn't a corporation or an executive in America that the press doesn't look at as somehow exploiting the people. If they didn't print that, they wouldn't have anything to print."

Wyman was not swayed "Look, Carter. It's not like they're accusing Coca-Cola of being a witting accomplice to what amounts to murder."

Wyman's tone rattled Hutchins. He looked around. The other directors were now glaring directly at him. Hutchins remained calm. "That's not at all an accurate representation of what has happened."

Rebecca Melton spoke next. An attorney and senior partner at Melton and Stearns and a member of the University of Minnesota Board of Regents, she was Hutchins' least favorite board member. Cold and impersonal, she rarely spoke, but was always harsh when she did. "Mr. Hutchins," she began formally, "in the past week, since the first of these case reports became public knowledge, our firm has fielded inquiries from over five thousand people, all ComHealth subscribers, regarding the care they received. These people are aware that they used to get X-rays, blood tests, and other tests and now they're not. After talking with some, I would say unequivocally that these people are less angry than scared. I, like Mr. Wyman, want to know what's going on?"

Hutchins bristled. He knew he was entering shaky ground. He knew full well that the board knew that much of the cost savings were a result of decreased testing on patients. It infuriated him that they would imply surprise at that now. But he also knew that the board's job was to control the direction of the company, including firing executives if necessary. He forced himself to show restraint and control.

Hutchins sounded confident and sincere. "All of the restrictions in access were carefully structured and based exclusively on what is considered a basic standard of care. The physicians did much of the work themselves. We merely followed it." Hutchins sipped his coffee. He was sure he knew what the directors wanted to hear. "The changes in medicine in the past few years have been enormous. But we must always assure that in our eagerness to obtain control of the spiraling cost of medicine we at no time allow vital services to be restricted or curtailed."

"That's what I wanted to hear," she replied.

Another director broke in. "Specifically, Carter, what are you proposing?"

"I'll let Mr. Markham tell you about a quality assurance review we are initiating."

Markham stood obediently and began a twenty-minute explanation of the study. As he spoke, all of the executives and many of the board members sensed that the whole thing would probably be looked at for what it was, an inside whitewash, but no one had a better idea. It became clear that a serious public relations effort was going to be needed, and an internal review they could control was far better than an external review they could not. Even if a few people in the press called it a sham, it wouldn't matter. It would be a good sham.

Hutchins returned to analyzing the board as Markham spoke. In the time he had spoken, and in the brief exchange he had had with Rebecca Melton, he was now sure of the board's tenor. One thing was certain. He had underestimated their anger and concern. Hidden right beneath the surface was the implication that unless the problems were solved now, major changes would be made. In all likelihood, his job.

He flushed as Markham continued talking. It infuriated him to even think his job could be in danger. He had given this company everything. Never in the stockholders' wildest dreams had they anticipated the return they had received. His success was unimaginable, unprecedented. It enraged him that the directors now covertly threatened him, the man who made it happen. Incredible.

Hutchins listened carefully as Markham finished. The board of directors seemed pleased with the proposal for the quality assurance study, public relations effort or not. Markham reiterated that each individual case brought to light would be investigated and their doctors would be publicly blamed. But with these words, the board was less impressed.

"Are we, or the public, really to believe that these doctors are intentionally not acting in their patients' best interest?"

"That's not what we said," Markham replied. "Our official position is that these patients became ill because they were neglected. The physician is responsible for ordering the tests."

For the first time, Rebecca Melton's temper flared. "Mr. Markham, that is not what I asked. What I want to know is if you're really going to tell the public that these doctors suddenly decided to quit ordering all these tests because they, out of the blue, got brain rot?"

Markham gulped. Hutchins boiled. The other executives looked uneasy. Rebecca Melton's menacing eyes burned into each of the executives, one by one. "Who in their right mind would believe that? I don't believe it, and anyone with an IQ above ten knows that these doctors are being pressured."

"Ms. Melton," Hutchins began.

"No," she interrupted, "take this morning's article for instance—this Mr. Ellis McGovern."

"I haven't seen it yet," one director said.

Rebecca Melton summarized the article. "He's an older man. A few weeks ago his wife calls our nurse line, telling the nurse that her husband has had a paralyzed arm for over an hour. Somehow, despite her calls, we don't give him authorization to go to the ER, and when he falls into a coma it's too late to give him the drug that would have stopped the stroke. Now he's in a coma in a nursing home. So, Carter, tell me how we can justifiably blame that on the doctors?"

Hutchins started to speak, but Melton interrupted him again. "To say that the doctors are responsible may not technically be a lie, but it's deceptive at best. There is no question, given the recent articles and what I'm seeing on TV, that the public has come to understand this deception."

Several board members cleared their throats or coughed. All looked at Hutchins. The crux of managed care was to limit access to specialists and apply direct pressure on doctors not to treat or test. To deny it any longer would be ludicrous. Candor and honesty were his only option now.

"This has been discussed extensively with counsel," the CEO replied. "Everything that has been done has been entirely, and I would stress *entirely*, within the limits of the law."

There was a murmur in the room. Hutchins continued. "Change is never pretty. Change is never easy. But America, consumers young and old, businesses, industry—they have all demanded cost control. And we have delivered. We have acted within the law. Period."

Hutchins' demeanor was controlled. His words were reasonable, his logic was true. For the first time the board seemed a bit more at ease. They had had no reason to doubt him before, and Hutchins' reassurances appeared to placate many of the board members. The words "within the law" were what they needed to hear. The board remained a bit nervous, but their tone changed.

Melton remained a bit skeptical. "Financial accountability, but no clinical accountability."

"And no legal liability. That's the law. Period."

Everyone was breathing easier. Rebecca sat down. "So, what about this lawsuit?" asked T.J. Johnson, the CEO of a local bank. "It's been getting a lot of press."

Hutchins was eager for the change of subject. "It's a little thing, really. A tragic young woman contesting a bill. Our counsel was disappointed that it was not dismissed."

"What about Fragile X?" asked another board member. "A local reporter claimed that the guy murdered at the Mall of America was connected to Molly Loomis."

Hutchins laughed out loud. "There have been some wild rumors. Loomis has made up this wild story about being coerced into an abortion. Her story is that she was told by some 'mystery' doctor that her child had a lethal disease, Fragile X Syndrome. The problem is Fragile X isn't even a lethal disease."

"She made it up?"

"Probably. We know she lied about the abortion to her husband and family."

"But why would her lawyer spend the time and money to bring it to trial?"

Hutchins coughed once. "ABC, NBC, CBS, CNN. He'll never have more free publicity in his life."

The board appeared to understand. "What about the murdered man?"

"He was a guy who disappeared a couple of years ago. A scientist. Geneticist I think," Hutchins replied.

"No connection?"

"None that we know of."

"I heard he used to be employed by ComHealth," another board member stated.

"Two years ago, yes. He was doing some research for us. Mediocre research, I might add. So mediocre that we discontinued the program."

"I heard something about his wife dying," one added.

"Yes, his wife died under mysterious circumstances, and he disappeared shortly after he collected the insurance money. As I understand it, the police and FBI had been looking for him for a long time." Markham's eyes widened in surprise. The lie was new, but it sounded good.

Hutchins' fiction appeared to satisfy them. "I heard a rumor that Boyd Messenger is going to testify," Rebecca Melton said, changing the subject.

Hutchins allowed himself a cup of coffee. "Yes. The fact that they have an ex-ComHealth executive willing to lie and exaggerate is the only reason Judge Van Gilder didn't throw it out."

The board stirred. "Who else is testifying?" asked a former airline executive.

"They've subpoenaed our head of accounting and claims. They've also got a doctor. Maybe a couple of others."

"You've seen their witness list?"

"Yes."

Rebecca Melton kept pushing. "Who do we have on it?"

"Well, we're fortunate," Hutchins began. "Normally a case like this would be assigned to an associate of a junior partner, but at my request both Jack and Harley have been involved from the beginning."

"I assume you'll ask for a continuance, six months or so?"

"Possibly. Jack and Harley are considering that." Hutchins was indefinite, and the board members picked up on it.

"Why wouldn't we ask for a delay?"

"Both Mr. Barnes and Mr. Whitfield feel that the case is extremely straightforward. It could possibly be utilized effectively to our advantage. This girl has some interesting sidelights to her life, and when they become public, it may actually make us look sympathetic."

Several board members laughed out loud. "That I'd have to see."

"Precisely," Hutchins said. "That may be the strategic advantage."

"And the fact that our opponents are almost certainly expecting us to delay," Markham piped in.

"Exactly."

Frederick Wyman looked unsure. "Are we still sure that it wouldn't be better to drag it out over a couple of years. Let it die of attrition?"

Hutchins stood up. By the tone of the questions, he knew that he was back in control again. The inquisition was over. "The case has generated enough publicity in the past few days that if we did that, every time there was a delay or a new motion it would be on the news. Tyler Briggs or Marcus Sanders would be on-screen talking about how this huge law firm with all of its resources was using stall tactics to avoid a trial. Then, when the trial finally came, it would be the same as it would be now. Despite the recent events, our counsel feels it would be better to simply use this as a springboard to bigger and better things."

The board members were in agreement, and no verbal dissent was offered. They'd heard enough. They remained wary but supportive, and the conversation drifted to a number of more minor issues. Ten minutes later, the meeting adjourned, with the members heading toward cabs that would take them to offices or to the airport.

An hour after the meeting ended, Hutchins sat alone in his office with his tie loosened and an Irish coffee in his hand. Professionally, it was the closest call he had ever had, and he knew that the doubt lingering in boardroom was not yet fully resolved. The press would be merciless. They would continue to harp on the cases that Marcia Sullivan had written about. The editorials would be scathing. The scrutiny would be intense. But Hutchins knew that his plan was a good one, a winning one. The trial would be the first step, and within that public spectacle would be the most important part of the plan—the destruction of Molly Loomis.

Chapter Twenty-eight

August 21

Thursday morning, the news about Peter's condition was no better. He continued to languish in a coma, and the doctors remained concerned about his poor kidney function and the possibility of infections. The news did little to discourage Molly. She continued to spend every waking moment at his bedside.

At mid-morning, the sun was halfway up the skyline as Molly sat in her usual position, leaning against his bed with her back to the door. The cardiac monitor showed the usual rhythm trace, and the oxygen flow from respirator's cycles provided the only sound in the room. Molly, as she had been doing since his surgery, talked to Peter as if he were awake.

"You'd be happy if you could see what was happening," she began. "They're talking about Jayne and Lisa and Rudy on the radio and on TV. It's even bigger than that, really. It's national." Molly leaned back and kept talking. "Hutchins and his lawyers have been on TV all the time. They're giving it their usual spin. And they've got a couple of younger attorneys who are nearly killing each other over who gets to be on camera. They're pretty funny. But overall, it's like I've been telling you. It doesn't look good."

Molly hesitated. She stood up, adjusted a blanket that was no longer covering his feet, and tucked them in. Finished, she sat back down. "But you know, Peter, I'm not really worried. I know you'd be pleased at what's going on. Whatever happens with me, so be it. I'm just glad that you believed in me. I don't think you'll ever know how much that meant."

A technician appeared, whom Molly had seen several times. It took him only a couple of minutes to he draw the necessary blood out of the arterial line and leave. Molly did not move. The earlier squeamishness she felt at all of the necessary procedures was long gone.

"Just another blood draw, Peter," she started. "They're still checking on your kidneys and other things." She laughed at herself. "Like I should explain medicine to you."

Molly sat back and crossed her legs. She sighed as fatigue seemed to creep up on her. "You know, Peter, I think that's kind of what I miss the most about you. Just the way you would talk to me, like explaining medical things. It was so nice to have that. I don't think I've ever had a friend like you before. Not Tracy. Not even Troy. Never Troy."

Molly shifted slightly in her chair and leaned forward, picking imaginary lint from the blanket. "Peter, what would I have done without a friend like you? You believed in me, encouraged me—like no one else has ever done. You gave me back something that I had lost."

Molly paused. She could feel herself choke up, but for the first time she felt able to speak from the heart. It was as if weeks of emotion were finally boiling over "When I met you, Peter, I don't think you knew how bad things were. It was really bad. In fact, it was worse than that. I don't even want to say what I was thinking about. I was seeing my life as though it were already over—like I was dying, with no one to help and no one who cared. But walking in your office that one day, with you taking an interest in me and treating me like I was important, well, it gave me something back. It's really true, Peter. You don't know it, but you saved me, you really did. And the weird thing is, that when I thought about all that happened to me, even as bad as it was, in a strange way it was good. Because I met you."

Molly stopped again. Even though she knew he could not hear or comprehend what she was saying, she still felt the need to make her thoughts clear. "I said earlier, Peter, that you were my friend. You are. But you're also much more than that. You're the answer to the question you asked me a while ago. My dream? It's easy. You, you are my dream." Molly wiped away a tear, and she dabbed at one that had fallen on the blanket. "Listen to me," she scolded herself. "I'm talking in past tense, and we'll have none of that around here." The reverie over, Molly sat back with a rueful smile. "Anyway, Colder, you have to get better. I owe you a whole lot of sub sandwiches. And more than that, I've got a surprise for you—"

Reggie and Marcia started the morning by walking through the commotion of downtown to gauge the reaction of the city. Nearly two thousand people protested outside the ComHealth offices on Wednesday, and by the time Reggie and Marcia arrived Thursday morning, the crowd was already nearly double that number. By nine, the downtown area became such a clogged mess of protesters that the police were forced to block off over six square blocks and create detours. The protesters, able to walk freely along the streets, virtually set up camp in front of the tower, beneath the well-known ComHealthOne dragon.

Reggie and Marcia arrived just in time to see CNN and Court TV arrive, as well as the day's first speaker, Elizabeth Lawton. The mother of the boy who died of splenic rupture when discharged too early stepped to the makeshift podium. After her emotional retelling of the story, the crowd gave her a thunderous ovation. Her speech, combined with the growing media presence, only energized an already boisterous crowd.

Marcia and Reggie carefully analyzed the people. Only a handful of the protesters were the usual mixture of "cause-of-the-day" types. Most were housewives who traveled from the suburbs, workers stepping out of their downtown offices, and college students from the three nearby universities. A few shoppers stopped by to gawk, but most in the crowd were there to mingle and listen. Two law students from the University of Minnesota organized an impromptu program and were circulating fliers throughout the crowd. After each grabbing one, Reggie and Marcia pocketed them, planning to return later in the day when Lisa Bowman's parents were scheduled to speak.

After listening to one speaker, Elizabeth Lawton, Reggie and Marcia slipped away from the crowd, but not before they paused to see the workers frantically setting up the Court TV booth in anticipation of next week's trial coverage. As they walked back to the hospital, they also noticed that CNN was broadcasting live. They marveled at the sight. Four days before, Molly Loomis had been completely anonymous. Now she was the focus of a trial that would receive national coverage. The thought was both chilling and electrifying. They expected a local reaction, but never in their wildest dreams or nightmares had they anticipated national fallout.

Their adrenaline flowing, they returned to the hospital where they nestled into a corner of the hospital cafeteria. Reggie picked up a newspaper on his way into the hospital and quickly read Marcia's latest article. This one was about the two men who died of heart attacks when their chest symptoms were not sufficiently alarming to force the ComHealth telephone nurse to allow them to be sent to the ER. Now almost numb, Reggie tossed the paper aside and gazed at the relaxed reporter sitting across from him. "Amazing," he grunted. Marcia was slouched deeper into her chair. She did not reply. Her mind had long since left the article. She was still analyzing what they had seen and making plans. Getting no reaction from her, Reggie picked up the paper again and pointed at one of the other headlines. "'ComHealth Officials Announce Multimillion Dollar Quality Assurance Plan.' Why'd you write that?" he complained. "Why not 'ComHealth Beaurocrats Announce Stock Price Propping Scheme' or 'ComHealth Executives Announce Latest PR Whitewash.'"

"I didn't write it," she protested. "Reporters never get to write headlines. The editors do that. Besides, I don't think the bosses would approve of either of those."

Reggie was undeterred. "They're closer to the truth than the one they wrote."

Although unimpressed with his argument, Marcia enjoyed his eighteen-year-old enthusiasm. "I'll take it under advisement," she laughed.

Reggie put the cap back on the pen. His joking stopped. "You know, Sandra Becker told me that Third Street Clinic will probably be in the red as of next week."

"I think it's actually worse than that."

"Broke?"

"Yes. Sylvia feels that even if Peter recovers they'll never be able to reopen."

"Damn. Isn't there anything they can do?"

"No."

"That really sucks."

The melancholy thought was interrupted by Marcia's pager. After leaving for five minutes to answer a call from another reporter, she returned. Her dejection was gone and the newly twinkling eyes did not escape Reggie's notice.

"What are you grinnin' at?"

"My friend Ted at the *Star Tribune*, the Strib," began Marcia. "He said that there's almost five thousand people downtown now."

"Five thousand! Whoa," exclaimed Reggie.

"*Time* and *Newsweek* reporters are there now, and the rumor is that Brokaw is coming to Minneapolis for the *Nightly News* next week, for the trial."

"No way," Reggie gasped.

Marcia was excited. "Yeah, but it goes way beyond that. You know those two law students who are organizing things?"

"Yeah."

"Well, after last night's newscasts, they set up a toll-free number hotline for ComHealth victims, and now they have almost sixty people lined up to talk to the crowd. Some are coming from as far as California. And MSNBC is live, covering everything."

"Whoa."

Marcia looked pleased. "This is getting big."

Reggie took the cap off the pen and began to chew on it again. "What about Molly?"

"That's the only thing. They all want her to speak."

"Who's they?"

"The press. The organizers of the protests. Everybody."

"No way," replied Reggie. "No way."

"It doesn't matter. I talked to Tyler last night. He won't let her, and she doesn't want to. She's got enough to think about. He may issue a prepared statement, but that's it."

"Good."

"The trial will come soon enough."

"Right." Reggie was puzzled. Marcia had a strange expression. It was a classic cat-that-swallowed-the-canary look. "What else gives?" he asked. "You're looking at me weird."

"Just an idea," she offered.

"What?"

"Remember a while ago when we talked about how some of the ComHealth executives were selling their stock?"

"They were smart. It's dropping like a stone."

"Well, Ted told me that there is a story coming out in the *Wall Street Journal* tomorrow that the SEC is looking into those transactions."

"That was just a couple of weeks ago," Reggie said.

"Exactly. SEC usually gets interested when executives dump millions of shares and then two weeks later the stock takes a nosedive."

Reggie laughed gleefully.

"But it gets even better than that. That's the only story they're printing, but there's also a rumor that several of the ComHealth executives and their lawyers have made some serious money over the past three years trading HMO stocks."

"What?"

"In fact, the word is that a bunch of these health-care executives nationwide are under investigation and it's been going on for over a year and a half. All these mergers, many clearly knew in advance. They made millions."

"Pinch me! I love it."

"Either they were the greatest stock pickers on earth or the luckiest," she said.

Reggie was giddy. "I doubt it."

"Either way, somebody knows something. It sure looks like they may have been tipped off to pending mergers and they made a fortune. All illegally."

"Yes," Reggie quipped, wiggling in his chair. "I think I'm gonna wet my pants!"

"You probably won't, but I think some of those ComHealth boys might when the SEC completes its investigation."

Reggie laughed even harder, but then his grin evaporated. He had a sour thought. "But wait a minute. This is insider trading stuff. These guys aren't stupid. They know that the SEC may be going to look over all those transactions."

"You're absolutely right," Marcia admitted.

"So how will they ever prove anything?"

Marcia's eyes bored into him. "*Wall Street Journal's* a paper of record. They don't publish anything unless they've got their information right. I can assure you."

"You think they've already got them?"

"I think they've got something and they're close. It won't happen tomorrow, but something is coming down."

Reggie's mind was now blazing ahead. Her confidence in him was flattering, and he decided to confide in the reporter. He changed the subject and confessed. "I need to tell you. I've been in Markham's computer."

"Reggie," she scoffed, trying hard to sound miffed.

"I know," he admitted. "You're going to tell me it's dangerous."

"That's because it is."

"Granted," replied Reggie.

Marcia knew from his tone that there was no chance she would change his mind about playing around in Markham's computer. And besides, she was too interested in what he had done to chew him out. "What did you see?"

"The entire thing is clean. Not a single reference to Fragile X."

"We figured that."

"The only thing I was able to do was leave him a couple of calling cards. Phone messages and e-mails."

"What did you say?"

"Told him to watch his back."

"But he'll know it was you," Marcia protested.

"No. I routed it through their phones and one of the secretary's computers. He'll think it came from inside."

"What was your plan?"

"Just to shake him up a bit. But I came up with something new. I thought maybe we should tell him that we had the journal and the disks."

Marcia looked perplexed. "Why would you do that? He knows that's not true."

Reggie's mouth curled into a devilish grin. It was the bomb he waited to drop on his reporter friend all morning. "No, he doesn't."

Marcia looked puzzled. "What?"

"Think about it. All along O'Reilly gave the impression that there was only one copy of the journal and one copy of the disks."

"Yes."

"But no one really knows that for sure. If someone were to tell Markham that there were other copies, he would probably believe it, because it actually seems more improbable that O'Reilly would never have made copies."

Marcia Sullivan stopped. She flushed slightly, embarrassed that she had never thought of it. "You're right."

Reggie continued his devilish stare. "And I just thought what would happen if we were to let him know that we had copies of both. How would he react?"

"Try to flush him?"

"Yes."

Marcia's eyeballs nearly exploded. "I know what we could do! What Julianne said!"

"What?"

"What she saw in the article. It was about a protein. Protein B1B. We could mention it."

Reggie bit his lip. It was perfect. "But we need more."

Marcia was roaring on. "You're right. We still need a plan that would put the fear of God into him."

They both fell silent with their thoughts running in parallel. The FBI could not be trusted. They were sure that one of them had sold out O'Reilly. The local police? Who would believe a reporter and a teenager. No ideas leaped to mind.

"What about some kind of blackmail?"

"No way," said Marcia. "Even if it's about something illegal. Blackmail is still a crime."

"True."

They were both anxious and pensive. "Think about what he has to lose, Marcia. That's always where a person's weakness is."

"His money?"

"He's probably got $60 million. He's not gonna be afraid of losing a little."

"But, his family," Reggie began.

"A guy like him would probably sell his wife for a nickel and his kid for a dime."

Reggie laughed in spite of himself. Then another thought occurred to him. "Why not the police?" he asked.

"C'mon. You really think that they're going to be able to do anything with 'Protein B1B'? That's not proof. It's just a word. They need a lot more than that to go on."

She was right. Discouraged, Reggie slouched into his chair. "I don't know."

For five minutes, they sat without saying a word. They knew the lead was way too flimsy for the police and, without being able to trust the FBI, it seemed impossible to put any pressure on Markham.

Marcia Sullivan nervously bit into one of her fingernails. "We should be able to—"

As she started to speak, Reggie leaped up, banging his legs into the underside of the table. His eyes were wild. So were Marcia's. Both thought of it at the same time. "How many friends do you have at different papers around the country?" Reggie blurted.

Marcia started to write on her notepad furiously. "People from my class? I can think of fifteen or twenty off-hand, but I'll bet I could round up fifty names if I needed to."

Reggie laughed out loud. "He'll think he's been hit by a Mack truck."

Marcia's eyes looked like fire. "Every one of them will claim to have a copy of the article and the disks. Markham will think it's gonna be the lead story in *USA Today*!"

Reggie high-fived her as a couple of others in the cafeteria turned to see what the commotion was about. Marcia bit her lip, and then imitating a deep-voiced male reporter, said, "Mr. Markham, could I just get you to answer a few questions about Protein B1B and a few other things that were found on Dr. O'Reilly's disks?"

Reggie could barely contain himself. "He's the one who's gonna need new underwear!"

Marcia laughed so hard she snorted a couple of times, to the annoyance of some fellow customers. Finally controlling herself, she scribbled down a note and tore off the page of the notebook and handed it to Reggie. "I know what I'm going to do. This is what I want you to do."

Reggie read it, then crumpled the note and stuffed it in his pocket. "You got it. When?"

Marcia stood to leave. "Tomorrow. I'll have my friends call this afternoon."

"Beautiful."

In the years of his marriage, Troy Loomis had never been as nice to Molly as when she became a celebrity. He had always viewed his ex-wife as an average cook, below average in looks, and a terrible lay, but in his mind the sight of her picture on the nightly news served to quickly erase her deficiencies. In the hours after her story broke, Troy mapped out a plan. He noticed that in her version of the events he read in the newspaper, she glossed over their differences, a signal he knew could only mean she still held strong feelings toward him. It made him determined to act and to act rapidly.

He first appeared at the hospital on Tuesday. Reggie's attitude ranged from chilly to hostile. The others, whom he had never met before, reacted similarly at first, but after a while they were forced to admit Troy Loomis was nothing like the bum they were expecting. He stayed for four hours, drew little attention to himself, and concentrated exclusively on Molly's and the others' needs. The only person he talked to at length was Sylvia Caspers, to whom he expressed regret about everything that had happened. On Wednesday, he reappeared and was equally restrained. He brought with him bagels and snacks and at all times seemed focused on Molly. He slipped out when Tracy Timlin and Gus LeClerc appeared, but otherwise he rapidly became one of the regular group of Peter Colder's friends and family occupying the waiting room. He was extremely careful around Molly. "I'm just here because I care," he told her.

Molly was dubious, but even she was surprised by the selfless manner in which he acted. She was spending most of her time in Peter's room, but on

Wednesday night she and Troy dined in the cafeteria. It was a cordial meeting as they laughed together about old times. After, they walked around the hospital and talked. It was all benign and friendly.

After the two days, Molly was surprised to find that her feelings about his presence changed from reluctance to acceptance. Although she had no desire to think about the problems between them, he never once brought up any old issues and instead seemed more subdued and supportive than she had ever seen him. Thinking again about a few of the good times they shared helped take her mind away from Peter's condition and the trial for a moment; as they shared long walks through the hospital corridors, she found herself welcoming the slight distraction.

When Troy left the hospital on Thursday, he headed for the bar. He was satisfied and elated. It was an extraordinary performance. His ex-wife, always a sucker for any type of sympathy, read his comments in the newspaper that day about his being there "out of love and support." Even though she had some feelings for Peter Colder, Troy knew that a professional man like that would never be interested in someone like Molly.

Troy noticed each day that she still wore the wedding ring. It pleased him, as he knew what it had to mean. His plan was simple. He would get her back. Then they would return to their old life. It was already good, and soon it would be better. Soon, he would have what he really wanted—someone to take care of his every need.

At 10 P.M., Thursday Lisa Ann Bowman died with her parents, husband, and two-year-old son Brady at her side. The cervical cancer from the missed pap smear killed her in less than two years. She was twenty-six years old.

Chapter Twenty-nine

August 22

The Friday afternoon press conference was the first time the ComHealthOne lawyers publicly addressed the coming lawsuit since Ace Farnsworth and T. Quentin Cox spontaneously pontificated to a pride of reporters after one of the earlier preliminary hearings. This press conference, following the last pretrial hearing, took place in front of an army of reporters in the ballroom of the downtown Hilton. Jackson Barnes, Harley Whitfield, Farnsworth, and Cox, as well as a throng of junior partners, fielded questions about everything from jury composition to O'Reilly's funeral. The press conference, televised live locally as well as nationally on Court TV and MSNBC, ran for nearly two hours. By the time it was finished, Briggs and Sanders had an even greater appreciation of what they were up against.

Barnes and Whitfield were beyond masterful. Consummate spin artists, they were silver-tongued snake oil salesmen with their pitches perfected after years of defending rich, white-collar sleaze. For two hours, they practiced their trade with a skill mastered only by the best attorneys and all politicians, winding their way through the minefield of managed care with a disarming ease. Briggs and Sanders knew of their opponent's talents, but now, watching them in front of the camera, they still marveled at the way Barnes and Whitfield could make two and two equal five and make everyone feel foolish for not knowing it.

Their media savvy obvious, they guided the reporters through a well-conceived strategy that deflected difficult questions, avoided impossible ones, attacked their opponent's credibility, and consistently reiterated that ComHealthOne was never to blame, only the doctors. They portrayed managed care as a health care savior, bringing some sense of order and fiscal accountability to a system run amuck. And they portrayed ComHealth as a victim, a lightning rod of criticism for those who profited most by the old system and whose petty personal agendas drove them endlessly. Lastly, they portrayed Molly Loomis as a tragic figure. A lost soul who lied to all those around her, regretted her actions, and now sought personal vindication by attacking the very system that saved her life.

It was tough work, even for skillful attorneys. Earlier in the day, Marcia Sullivan published another article. In a page-one story, she detailed the plight of Barbara Kuzel, a thirty-year-old mother of two. Six months of upper back pain had led only to X-rays early in her course of treatment that were read as normal. It was not until she lost thirty pounds and was experiencing shortness of breath that the ComHealth algorithm authorized an MRI. The study showed an enormous tumor in her upper spine that did not appear on a plain X-ray. Over six months it had grown to a size where it pressed into her lungs, causing the shortness of breath as well as wrapping itself around her heart and great vessels. The tumor was too large for surgery, and radiation and chemotherapy had been futile, leaving her husband a widower, and her children motherless less than a month after its discovery.

Strategically, Barnes and Whitfield stopped talking about Marcia's individual cases in their press conferences. Now that the trial was near, they had no interest in connecting the tragedies detailed in the paper with what they referred to as "Mrs. Loomis's frivolous claim." Despite repeated attempts by reporters to lure the two ComHealth attorneys into further discussion of these cases, they held their ground, and, as usual, they managed to put a spin on their remarks that made ComHealth sound like the victim.

Briggs and Sanders, sitting nervously in Tyler's office, watched the press conference with a sense of anxious detachment. All that Barnes and Whitfield said was predictable. But the question that plagued both of Molly's attorneys was, Why?

As the spectacle wound down and the cameras again turned to the commentator, Briggs flipped off the television set after making sure the VCR continued to record the event. Standing next to the TV that was propped up on a chair, Tyler looked confused.

"Those guys are good," Marcus offered. "Damn good."

"No, they're great," Briggs corrected.

Marcus stood and walked over to the window. In the distance, he could see a few people head toward the courthouse where the protest was being held. The newscast the night before estimated yesterday's crowd at five thousand, and before the press conference, the MSNBC reporter counted the morning crowd at nearly five thousand, including nearly five hundred anti-abortion protesters who arrived to demonstrate against Molly.

"Did you see the size of that pro-life crowd?" Marcus asked as he peered across the skyline.

"I guess there have already been a couple of arrests," said Briggs, stating what Marcus already knew.

"How's Molly gonna react to that?"

Tyler drew a deep breath. "She knows it's coming. I talked to her a couple of days ago about it. It's gotta be one of their strategies."

"Did you see the sign that had the picture of her in between Jeffrey Dahmer and Charles Manson?"

"Yes," Briggs grunted.

"There was another one, a caricature of her with a sword stabbing a baby."

Marcus shook his head. He could only imagine how Molly would feel seeing such a sign. "It's gonna get ugly."

"I know."

"This is way bigger than we imagined, Tyler," he said nervously. "*Way* bigger."

Briggs was barely listening. His thoughts were still on the abortion protesters. One of ComHealth's strategies would be to defame Molly by emphasizing the abortion. They wanted to portray her as a scheming woman who lied to her husband and chose to abort a less-than-perfect child. This would be done in an effort to muddy the water and hide from the real issue, which was their refusal to pay for emergency room services. Tyler knew it.

"You think that ComHealth arranged for those protesters?"

"Maybe. Could even be the lawyers, too," replied Tyler.

"Think we should dig into it? It might make an interesting story."

Briggs considered it for a moment. The thought of exposing a well-financed protest would unquestionably make for interesting headlines. It was tempting, but Tyler shook his head "Naw, we've got enough else to think about. Not enough time."

Sanders agreed. "You're right."

Briggs began to wander around the office, pacing like the proverbial caged lion. Neither he nor Marcus seemed able to mention the problem they knew they had to face. The tension seemed to mount as neither man spoke. Finally it became unbearable. "If you're not going to say it, then I will," Briggs grunted.

"I know."

Both men walked to the window and stood side by side. They listened to a two-hour press conference by ComHealth's lawyers, who never once mentioned a delay.

"How could they not?" asked Marcus. "You think they're really going to go ahead?"

Briggs let his frustrated thoughts spill. "It makes no sense at all. I know that Barnes and Whitfield love the cameras, but why in the hell would they possibly try this case at this time?"

Marcus looked at his friend. Tyler uttered what they both thought. It made no sense at all. If ComHealthOne were ever to have a disadvantage, it was at this moment, in the heat of the battle. Jury selection could be a problem; the press was against them, as was the bulk of public opinion. Seeking a delay, preferably a long one, seemed so obvious a strategy that it left both lawyers searching for an explanation as to why they wouldn't. They knew that before the publicity, the ComHealth lawyers probably considered the suit a minor annoyance, not worthy of even much thought. But now it was a national event. It seemed impossible they would try the case now.

"I can't believe it," Marcus muttered. "They're really gonna try it?"

"I know." Briggs stopped before he said any more. The thought nagged at him like an aching tooth. Why? It made absolutely no sense at all.

"I can only think of two explanations," Marcus said.

Briggs returned to his desk. "Try me."

"Number one. It's such a slam dunk that they want to do it in as public a fashion as possible."

"That's what we've been telling ourselves. And I'll buy that, except for the fact that even with a slam dunk, they still take their hits with this kind of media coverage. Big hits. No way. It would be better to take those hits a long time from now, when no one is watching."

"I know," Marcus agreed.

"What's number two?"

Marcus plopped down in the chair across from Tyler's desk. His dark expressive eyes looked almost sad. "I keep thinking back on that conversation with Pokey Mercer. We never did figure out what he meant. We just wrote it off."

Briggs looked down and carefully massaged his temples in a circular fashion as if suddenly struck by a migraine. "I know."

Marcus slouched deeper into the chair and folded his hands in front of his face as if he was starting to pray. "What in the heck could it possibly be? We've been over everything a thousand times. We've interviewed the witnesses. We've researched ComHealth's books and heard their dirt. We've covered everything we can think of, except for Fragile X."

"Which is gone."

"Yes."

"I don't know. But you know it and so do I. The only other explanation is that they want the trial to get *going* as soon as possible so it will be *over* as soon as possible."

Marcus looked troubled and confused. "That's the real question, isn't it? Do they want to get the trial over with because they know we've missed something?"

Tyler didn't answer. He just slid deeper into the chair, completely depressed.

Molly spent Thursday night at the hospital and, when the surgeons made morning rounds early Friday morning, she was the first to hear the news that Colder would not need dialysis that day. His kidney function was only about twenty percent of normal, but for the first time in three days he would be able to avoid the two-hour procedure of removing his body's wastes from the blood. She asked them why he was still not awake, and they gave a vague answer, but said that stroke had been ruled out and he might regain consciousness as his blood chemistries completely returned to normal. Molly listened carefully, but reading between the lines, she could tell that while the doctors were happy about his improving kidney function, they were growing increasingly concerned by his continuing coma. Both encouraged and discouraged by the news, Molly returned to the waiting room.

Shortly after, Peter's mother and Sylvia arrived. Exhausted after another night in the hospital, Molly gave them the update, which they accepted graciously and then prepared to leave.

"Use the side entrance to the lot again," Sylvia warned. "Reporters are everywhere."

Molly only nodded. For the three days since her story broke, Sylvia, Letisha, and Sandra had used various entrances and disguises to get her in and out. Reporters from newspapers and TV stations were clamoring to interview her, but she continued to refuse all requests. One reporter had gone so far as to sneak into the ICU dressed as an orderly, but when identified he was quickly dispatched. At Tyler's suggestion, she remained silent. "What's ahead will be rough enough," he said. "You don't need it now." Avoiding the reporters was becoming as big a problem as staying sane.

Molly sneaked out of the hospital unnoticed in a pair of glasses and a baseball cap. She took Sylvia Caspers' car, and within minutes was free from downtown. As she drove away from the morning rush hour traffic, she realized she had never felt so exhausted and confused. Peter. The trial. Troy. It nearly made her sick when she thought of it all. And soon it would be the cameras, the microphones, and a cross-examination on national TV. A cross-examination where Whitfield or Barnes would grill her on every failure, flub, or frustration she had ever had. She always expected that there might be a few reporters, but nothing like the coverage that continued to explode before her eyes. Reporters in campers outside the courtroom. Reporters in the hospital. Reporters in the women's room, and even a couple of reporters in helicopters overhead. They were researching everything about her. Her grades in school, her friends, her marriage, her divorce. Everything. Everything was public. Everything for the world to see.

As the thoughts overwhelmed her, Molly momentarily lost her concentration. She swerved into the neighboring lane and then overcompensated swinging wildly back, landing in the outside lane. Missing a flock of honking cars, she gathered herself, turned onto the Crosstown Highway, and left behind a convoy of road rage. Shaken and perspiring, her mind remained a blank. She didn't know where she would go. Tracy Timlin offered her a place to sleep for a few hours before she returned to the hospital. Molly didn't even know if she should bother to go. She knew that she would never be able to sleep. The heat was unbearable. The eyes of the world cast a scalding glare. And there was nowhere to hide.

He waited in the depths of the parking garage of the Hennepin County Medical Center and stood in the shadow of a cement pillar as he waited for her. One of his fellow doctors had tipped him off that she was usually in a baseball cap and driving an old red Toranado. The tip was good, and it was easier than he expected to find the most sought-after person in the country. He knew reporters were looking for her everywhere, but Dr. Eric Johnson's informant proved to be correct. The west exit, probably around 7:00 A.M.

She walked within twenty feet of him, her tired gait noticeable even to someone not paying careful attention. He had gotten only a brief look at her face, but it didn't matter. It was a face Molly's former OB/gyn remembered well. But this time it shocked him. Hollowed, haunted eyes, hidden in the shadows of the pale, white skin; she looked thinner than he remembered. Ten pounds at least, he estimated. He also remembered that Molly Loomis was happier then, too.

He recalled her exuberance the day she first walked into his office. Vibrant and vital, Molly was filled with the vigor of unblemished youth. A young woman in love. A man she was crazy about since high school. A man she couldn't quit talking about. Johnson even recognized the name, a football player, perhaps with professional ability. "A good man," she said. A man who loved her too.

Johnson remembered the statement, finding it odd. He remembered his vague sense of worry before her continuing enthusiasm muted any concerns.

"We'll probably start a family in a year or so," she told him.

"That will be fine."

At that point, he remembered he quit worrying about the husband, thinking instead about the new medical world. Yes, he recalled, Molly Loomis was the first time it happened to him. And after, they came with the frequency of April rains. And, like the spring raindrops, those patients disappeared, absorbed unnoticed into the vast expanse of the earth.

But even after she left his practice, her health plan mandating the change, Johnson's mind occasionally stumbled onto her memory, wondering what had became of the girl whose dreams he was sure had died. Now as he watched her gaunt frame struggle through the parking lot and her name spill across the headlines every night, he knew that his long-held fears had come true. Her face made him want to cry. The truth made him angry.

After she left, he walked back into the hospital, his stomach churning and his heart pounding. What could he do? he asked himself. In his mind he had been over it a million times. There was nothing he could do, he assured himself.

"No, Eric," he said to himself. "That's a chicken-shit lie."

By noon Friday, Gregory Markham was in a pure panic. His throat was so sore that it hurt to breathe, and every time he tried to speak, only an unintelligible sound croaked out of his mouth. His hands shook like falling leaves, and his stomach hurt so badly that his bowels seemed to have constricted into a marble-sized rock of muscle. The first phone call of the morning had been bothersome, a reminder from the ComHealth lawyer helping him deal with the annoying SEC, but the second through tenth calls drove him straight into a manic frenzy.

Operating in a wild state of random motion induced by panic, he straightened his office, washed the sink near the bar, stacked his computer disks, filed his stray papers, and even dusted his desk, trying to calm himself down. When the third reporter called about Fragile X and Protein B1B, he cursed at her with the viciousness of a man about to engage in hand-to-hand combat and hung up after his third and final "bitch" of the diatribe. He popped a Prozac, a Zoloft, and a Valium, and called his doctor to wail that his prescriptions were low and nothing worked. More phone calls came to him shortly after, but he refused them all, having his secretary take down numbers he never planned to call.

For an hour, he collapsed on the couch, listening as his respiratory rate neared his heart rate and watching as the ceiling seemed to spin. He couldn't think straight. It was impossible! How the *hell* had they found out? Reporters, everywhere! Atlanta, Philadelphia, New Orleans, Los Angeles, Seattle. Every paper! Every major city! The image was terrifying and paralyzing: young, ambitious reporters from all over the country descending upon him, dissecting and disemboweling him for all the world to see. And the police? Oh shit, he thought. He knew where they were. Standing right behind the reporters watching and listening, waiting until there was enough for a subpoena or, oh God, an arrest!

Markham put his hands over his face and tried to breath deeply, as if Lamaze techniques would allow the demon to be delivered from him. It was impossible. He couldn't even inhale.

A call rang through on his private line, and Markham staggered to his feet.

His shirtsleeves unbuttoned and his tie loosened so far it rode on his shoulder, he looked more like a man caught in a tryst than the distinguished chief financial officer of the country's largest HMO. He answered it breathlessly. "Yes." It was Hutchins.

"Forget the SEC," Hutchins reassured. "Harley assures me that there's nothing they can do. There's nothing down on paper that links you to anything."

"Jesus Christ, Carter. I made $25 million on three HMO transactions purchasing the stock just weeks before it went through the roof. You think they're not going to notice that?" Markham was nearly shouting, and his face was as red as an August apple.

"I didn't say they wouldn't notice. I just said they couldn't prove anything. Besides, Harley and Jack are in the same boat."

The news that the lawyers were just as guilty did nothing to reassure him. "Carter, with those numbers, they'll be hunting us until every head is hanging above a fireplace."

Hutchins did not respond immediately. Silently Markham cursed himself for being so stupid. Too easy. Too big. Too fast. All the classic warning signals and he had ignored them all.

"I just want you to know," said Hutchins. "And be confident, that it's going to be all right. I'll call you later."

"Thank you." As he hung up, Markham felt a jolt of lightning shoot through him. It was all surreal, a bad dream, like a recurring nightmare filled with bizarre colors in bizarre worlds. He couldn't believe it was happening. The whole IDS Tower seemed to be shaking as they spoke, and Hutchins' hollow reassurance now seemed disingenuous. My God! Did he know?

The entire scenario poured down upon him. Hutchins reassures him to disarm him. All the while, he erases any tracks he has to anything. Then Fragile X resurfaces—press—police—investigations—Hutchins needs a fall guy. "Oh shit," Markham exclaimed. It was so painfully obvious.

But what if he was totally wrong? The SEC. Wouldn't they need proof that he actually traded on insider information? Hutchins basically told him with a wink and a nod that nothing was ever written down. Maybe they couldn't prove it. Maybe Hutchins was telling the truth. And Fragile X. How did anyone find out? He had the last disks and the last journal. There were no other copies. He was sure.

Markham's knees buckled. He caught himself against the desk, but not before a light passed before his eyes as if warning him he was about to pass out. No other copies? How the hell could he have been so stupid! Why would O'Reilly have ever done that? Of course there were copies! It only made sense. And where would he send them if he couldn't trust law enforcement? Oh shit, oh shit, oh shit! The press! That's how they had learned about it!

Markham dropped to his knees and threw up into the wastebasket. For five minutes, he heaved like a parched man who had mistaken ipecac for oasis water. Finally finished and bathed in sweat, he collapsed on the floor, cowering into the fetal position and hiding his eyes behind his hands. He couldn't breath. He couldn't talk. He couldn't move. He could only pray the building would crumble and he would forever be entombed as a relic in the rubble.

An hour later, he still had not moved. He was still breathing, but barely. He was still sweating, but barely. The only part of his body that seemed to work was the deepest recess of his mind. Somewhere in there a logical series of thoughts, like a fine thread of silk, had emerged from his cocoonlike state. He came to the conclusion he was now down to only two choices. But he still had no idea which one to pick.

Despite the lawyers' polished showing at the press conference, H. Carter Hutchins' mood was deteriorating as the day progressed. His first phone call of the morning had been from state Republican Chairman Marvin Cook, who gave the unmistakable impression that the party was now beginning to distance itself from him. Chairman Cook reiterated that the governor remained "intrigued" by the possibility of Hutchins as a candidate to succeed him. But he now added the disclaimer that the continuing ComHealthOne difficulties may cause the governor to reassess Hutchins' viability as a candidate.

Hutchins was not fooled by the polite tones. The party chairman was telling him that he was dead unless the ComHealth situation was settled quickly and in a way that cast him in very favorable light. Hutchins was polite and thanked him for the call, but the news was nonetheless distressing.

The next call was from Harley Whitfield, who informed him that the SEC was now demanding more of his and several of the other executives' personal financial statements. According to Whitfield, it was part of a wide-ranging probe of hospital and HMO mergers and nothing to be worried about. Hutchins was relieved by this statement, as he knew that Barnes and Whitfield, as well as Cox and Farnsworth and all of his fellow senior executives had been tipped off to the pending mergers and had themselves profited handsomely from the stock surges. "It's a wide-ranging investigation, Carter, but the truth is most of this stuff was so widely discussed that there is no way that it could ever be proven it was truly inside information." Relieved, Hutchins thanked his friend and promised to call later in the day.

Then he called Markham and the other executives to deliver the lawyers' favorable assessment. Following that series of awkward chats, Hutchins took a call from Wendell Eastman, a director, and probably his best friend on the board of directors. Eastman's tone was instantly worrisome.

"Wendy."

"Hello, Carter."

"How are you?"

"Fine."

"Nice of you to call."

"Thanks, Carter. I'll get right to the point."

The tone caught Hutchins off-guard. Wendy Eastman was a chatty southerner who was rarely anything but long-winded. "Please do."

"You've still got some trouble on the board."

Hutchins anticipated that the statement was coming and in some ways was almost relieved to know that he was being told the truth rather than kept in the dark. "I appreciate your telling me, Wendy."

"Carter, this entire company is indebted to you for your performance, and I know you know that most of the board feels that way. But there is a growing feeling that this entire situation is mushrooming before our eyes. So much press, so much *bad* press."

"Wendy—" Hutchins started.

"Look, Carter," Eastman interrupted, obviously not interested in anything Hutchins would offer. "The board is not a bunch of fools. You know and I know that every single member on it was aware of what was going on as our profits soared. They all knew that everyone was being squeezed. But the board always felt that ComHealthOne was just doing what all the other HMOs were doing."

"We are."

"But even if that's true, *we're* the ones on the nightly news."

"What are you saying, Wendy?"

Eastman sighed. He had known Hutchins for many years and felt great loyalty to him. "It's thin ice, Carter."

"How thin?"

"Thick enough to hold you for a while, but it's melting."

Hutchins stroked his chin. "What about the trial?"

"Tell me about it."

Hutchins knew he did not want details, only odds. "It's everything you *haven't* read about. It's idiotic really. It's about her hospital bill. She didn't follow procedure and we denied her claim. Legally, we're right."

"Is there any chance of losing. Any chance at all?"

"No." Hutchins was firm.

Eastman sighed. "I see."

"It's a piece of cake."

"I still don't see why you don't delay it. It's a damn blood bath now."

Hutchins swallowed hard. He had to lie. "The attorneys are confident that they can not only make it a victory, but a full-fledged infomercial for us."

"I doubt it," Eastman disagreed. "The networks have this girl looking like a cross between Joan of Arc and Mother Theresa."

"She's hardly that."

"You're missing my point."

"No, I'm getting it. It's about public perception."

"Yes.

Hutchins could feel his head start to hurt, and he pinched the bridge of his nose almost in reflex. "Tell me what you really think, Wendy."

"I think it's dicey. Maybe you can try this case now and make it look like an infomercial, but if you try, you've got to pull it off. Anything else…" His voice trailed off.

"I got you."

"Look, Carter, I say this as a friend more than anything. I know of your political ambitions, and I know how much it all means to you. But if this gets much bigger, I don't know how much I can help you. I realize your goal has been to get this sorry little trial out of the way as quickly as possible. But all of the sudden, it isn't so sorry and it isn't so little."

"You think we should delay it?"

"You and the attorneys are closer to it than I am. All I'm saying is, for your own sake and ours, you need a solution that makes ComHealth look like an organization Jesus himself would be happy to have a policy with."

Hutchins sat down at his desk and looked out over the plush surroundings. "I appreciate the call."

"Talk to you soon."

When Hutchins hung up the phone, he flipped on the television set and began watching a replay of Barnes and Whitfield. With the volume high enough to hear easily, he strolled to the east window where fifty-two stories below and six blocks away he could to see the crow gathering near the courthouse.

Staring through the tinted window, he was aware that his head hurt, his body ached, and even his teeth seemed sensitive to the hot tea he had been drinking. He closed his eyes and clenched his jaw. "Incredible," he grunted loudly. "Incredible!"

H. Carter Hutchins felt a wave of anger wash through his body. Molly Loomis! He wanted to reach out and break her neck with his bare hands.

"All I've done," he said to his reflection in the tinted window. "And this goddam little bitch waitress—"

Hutchins closed his eyes and regained his composure. He knew he did not have time for emotion. Anger was a luxury he could no longer afford. The board had spoken to him through Wendell Eastman. He knew he needed a plan and he needed it fast. Without one, his political plans, and perhaps even his career, were over.

By late afternoon, Markham quit vomiting and his head cleared. After lying on his couch for over two hours, he finally felt good enough to get up. Laboring, he stood up, cinched up his tie, and put on his coat. Closing the office door behind him, he told his surprised secretary he was leaving for the day.

"Two more reporters called."

"Tell them I'm unavailable," he said with a directness that invited no debate.

"Yes, Mr. Markham."

"I'm on my cell phone, but it better be a nuclear war or the second coming of Christ," he growled.

"Yes sir."

Ten minutes later, Markham sat in the corner booth of the Uptown Bar, a swank yuppie tavern overlooking the Mississippi River. Attractive but conventional, the bar was replete with the mandatory '90s mixture of pseudoantique decor and yuppie clientele wearing expensive suits owned by a high-interest gold card company. It was a classic hangout for young lawyers and business types to scam on their partners' secretaries. Markham picked it intentionally, as he knew it would get busy as the afternoon wore on. More importantly, he knew a man not looking for a pickup would never be noticed.

He ordered a bourbon as soon as he arrived and within ten minutes had downed his second. With the flow of alcohol now securely in his veins, he finally looked away from the crawling darkness of the river which had held his attention to that point. He turned and looked at the bar filling with well-dressed young men and women, all nearly twenty years his junior.

He ordered another bourbon and stared at the surface water as it twinkled in the afternoon light. The river. Yes, the river was like a man, its surface seen by the world, but seen in the same way by no one. The river. Like a man. Its real world within. Known only by itself.

Markham slammed the bourbon. Its alcohol burned at his throat. He felt better. Better than he had felt in a long time. "What does a man do when the world he has built is destroyed?" he asked himself. "Then he is no longer the man he was," he answered. No, that's not true, he thought. "Shit," he mumbled. "What does anything matter?"

How could he face his wife? He couldn't. How could he face his daughter? He couldn't. The thought killed him. How had O'Reilly fooled them? he asked himself. Then he stopped, knowing that the answers didn't matter. It would soon be over.

Markham ordered another bourbon. He took a moment to stare at the young people. He remembered when he had first been married and he and his wife would meet after work at a similar place. Before money changed them, the Markhams had more order and simplicity in their lives. Where had they gone wrong? He laughed when he asked the question, as if his wife were somehow to blame.

The bourbon came, and he thanked the waitress and kept his eyes on the crowd. His last drunk, he thought. What else could he do? The SEC? Hutchins and the lawyers were being foolish. The commission wasn't going to go away. Fragile X? Forget it. "That's a life sentence."

This time he sipped on the drink, knowing he needed to be able to walk if he wanted to kill himself. His plan was simple. He would shoot himself in his Lexus. It would be a perfect ending of irony and tragedy—killed by a bullet in the lap of luxury. He couldn't decide if it was Shakespearean or Freudian, but it didn't matter. He was past analysis and fear. He only knew he was going to do it, and that he was rapidly getting very drunk.

The river, he thought. Yes, the river. He should do it by the river. He turned toward the water, but his view was obstructed. A shadow occupied the seat opposite him in the booth. No. It wasn't a shadow. It was a young man. Markham shook his head, trying to focus, but all he could see was that the man was Asian, or at least part Asian. And he wore a baseball cap.

"Hello, Mr. Markham," came the voice.

Markham found he could barely formulate words. "How d'ya know me?"

"Oh, I know a lot about you, Mr. Markham. Allow me to introduce myself. My name is Reggie Tan."

At 5:00 P.M. Pokey Mercer walked out of Tyler Briggs's office. The eminent vulgarian had been in rare form, setting an apparent world record of four "fucks" in one sentence and five "shits" in another. Pokey visited them for exactly fifteen minutes, and in that time Tyler and Marcus spoke only two sentences. When he finished, Pokey stormed out without allowing any questions.

Marcus and Tyler each scanned the document that the ComHealth lawyer left them. Neither one spoke; instead, they tried desperately to find meaning in all that was happening. It was happening so fast. It seemed unreal. They barely budged when two minutes later, Molly Loomis walked in and sat down.

"Wasn't that Mercer?" she asked.

"Yes," answered Marcus.

"I saw him across the waiting room," Molly continued. "I recognized the toupee and the cologne."

The lawyers did not reply. Molly could sense instantly that something was going on. She knew Marcus and Tyler well enough that their eyes could tell her most of what she needed to know. "What am I missing?"

"I have something to tell you," said Tyler.

"I knew it," she started. "They requested a delay. I knew it. Let me guess. A year, two?"

Briggs stood up and walked to the window. His line of sight to the Metrodome offered him a perfect view when its lights went on. He loved the view. It was his favorite characteristic of the office. "How's Peter?"

"Stable," she said, sounding relieved. "The doctors don't think he'll need dialysis tomorrow either, but they're going to make that decision in the morning."

"Waking up?" Marcus asked.

"No. Still in the coma, but he's moved a little on his own."

"That's good," Tyler said.

"That's great," Marcus offered.

Molly nodded. Her relief was obvious. "It's at least a start."

"And a good one."

"Yes."

Briggs returned from the window and sat down. His mind was still spinning. "Molly," he began.

"How long will the delay be?" she interrupted.

Briggs drew a long breath. "There isn't going to be a delay."

"What?"

"No delay," Marcus repeated.

Molly pointed to the papers Pokey had left, sitting in front of each of her attorneys. "Then what are those?"

Tyler glanced at Marcus and then back at Molly. An odd expression crept across his face. "ComHealth is offering us two choices. The first is to start the trial as planned. First thing Monday morning."

"Yes. And the second?"

Briggs put his chin in his hand; his quirky look remained. "They've offered you a settlement."

Molly fell back into her chair, stunned. "What?"

"Yes," Marcus said. "A settlement. And a generous one."

Molly was too surprised to even think. She could barely even conceive of the basic questions needed to be asked. "Why?"

"I presume they fear that the negative publicity of the trial would be worse."

Molly struggled with her spinning thoughts. It was simply too good to be true. "I can't believe it!"

Neither Marcus nor Tyler seemed to share her enthusiasm. Each of them continued to rotate their eyes between Molly and the paper. It took Molly only a second to catch on. "You said it's generous?"

"Yes, it is, Molly," Tyler replied. "No doubt about it."

"Then why don't you guys seem excited?" she asked curiously.

Marcus handed her the paper and Molly began to look it over. It was typed, but written in legalese. "Let me give you a summary."

Molly put the paper in her lap, not reading it. Instead she followed Tyler. "The offer is as follows. ComHealth will pay for all of your hospital bills."

"That's great!" Molly gasped.

"In addition, ComHealth will give you a lump sum settlement of $250,000 and will pay our expenses at a customary rate."

Molly jumped into the air. "Two hundred fifty thousand dollars!" she exclaimed. "Are you kidding me? Two hundred fifty thousand dollars?"

Tyler allowed himself one chuckle as Molly did some sort of uncoordinated dance step in front of him. She nearly fell. "I don't believe it!"

Briggs watched as the dazed girl continued to jig around the room. She repeatedly tapped herself on the sides of her head as if her brain was disjointed and needed a jolt to again be realigned.

"Molly," Tyler said.

The tone of her lawyer's voice was clear, and in that second Molly Loomis realized that neither of the attorney's were sharing her enthusiasm. Just as quickly as she had risen, she appeared to deflate. "There must be a catch."

Briggs nodded. "There is."

"What is it?"

Marcus put his hand on her shoulder. "The money is yours under two conditions: The first is that all aspects of the settlement are absolutely confidential. No exceptions. Secondly, ComHealth will have the right to say publicly that you have agreed that the lawsuit was without merit. In addition, they would have the right to say anything they want about it."

"What?"

"Yes."

"You mean they could say anything? Like they won and I quit, or that I agreed that they were right all along?"

"Yes."

Molly slumped into her chair and buried her head in her arms. Briggs walked in front of the desk and leaned his backside against it, facing Molly.

"And they want an answer by nine tomorrow morning," said Marcus.

"I don't believe it," Molly whispered. "I just don't believe it."

Marcus and Tyler looked at one another. Her words perfectly summarized their thoughts. "Neither did we," Marcus murmured. "Neither did we."

Chapter Thirty

Markham was too surprised and too drunk to react smoothly to the appearance of Reggie Tan. Instead, his neck flexed forward as if in spasm and his mouth fell open like a child watching a rabbit pop out of a hat. He nearly dropped his drink. Markham tried to say something, but his tongue felt as thick as a porterhouse and he managed only a feeble grunt.

"I know," Reggie laughed, barely above the noise of the bar. "You're thinking I'm not old enough to be in here."

Markham tried vainly to talk again. Despite the alcohol, he was in no mood for games. Obviously Reggie had followed him, and he reacted more with anger than fear. "Get duh hell oudda here," he grumbled.

Reggie laughed at him again. It was the hearty laugh of a man brimming with confidence. Instead of leaving, he waved to the waitress. He put a Coke on Markham's tab, still grinning. The ComHealth executive was incredulous.

"They never card Asians," he said as he sipped on the drink. "Think we all know karate."

Markham's left eye seemed to want to close. "Do ya?" he slurred.

"Black belt in Tai Chi."

Markham looked puzzled, and Reggie knew that the drunken executive had no idea that he had just made a joke. Markham took a napkin and dabbed at the corner of his mouth, where one drop of bourbon had been perched. His head was spinning wildly, and his weakening mind struggled between the competing thoughts of trying to avoid falling over and wondering what this guy was doing in his booth.

"Listen, Mr. Markham," Reggie began. "I know that even with a blood alcohol of point four, you can figure out that I followed you here."

Markham appeared annoyed. "Obvizly."

"And I also know that you know that I'm no friend of yours."

Markham's vertigo was trying to pass. He finally managed a clear thought. "Whaz your point?"

"I came to offer you a deal."

"What?"

Reggie pulled a computer disk out of his maroon bookbag and laid it on the table in front of him. "Let's be straight," he began, his patronizing grin vanishing. "Here's what I, and about seventy-five others in this town know. ComHealthOne took O'Reilly's discovery and were conning women into abortions. What they discovered could be detected in the pregnant mother in a blood test. Since Doyne Labs does nearly ninety percent of the prenatal testing in the area and ComHealth owns Doyne Labs, it made for a nice fit. The women were told that their babies had one of several conditions, each done only infrequently so as to not draw attention. One of those was Fragile X Syndrome."

Gregory Markham did not react visibly, but the alcohol that had nearly caused him to pass out five minutes before now seemed to be wearing off.

Markham remained attentive and did nothing to deny his claims. "I must admit," Reggie admired, "it was done well. These women received phone calls from the health plan. A doctor, or someone claiming to be a doctor, came right to the house. They thought they were receiving the best care in the world."

Markham grunted. "What a buncha shit."

Reggie ignored him. "It was actually better than well done. It was almost perfect."

Markham wanted to fight back. "Indulge me. What was wrong?"

"You only made one error. Fragile X isn't as severe a disease as your doctor portrayed it to Molly Loomis, and Peter Colder caught that."

"You're full of shit."

"Yeah, right." Reggie tapped on the disk. "You guys were close. The whole system was close to perfect. These doctors weren't real, but their names were. You used the names of recently deceased physicians so that if the patient called to check them out, their licenses were still okay. Next, you gave the patients a phone number they could call, and this was a number where someone masqueraded as an office nurse or secretary."

"Sure. Whadever. Sounds good."

"Oh, it was better than that. Every obstetrician or family doc in the area orders blood work, and most of it goes through Doyne. Whenever there was a positive test, ComHealth was notified electronically and your doctor appeared at the woman's door."

"For Christ's sake," Markham scoffed. "That's ridiculous."

Reggie continued. "Actually it's ingenious. Whenever there was a positive test, the computer was programmed to erase all record of it from the woman's record and from the Doyne records. No trail. Better still, the test was run as part of a routine lab profile, something every pregnant woman gets. Since the technician just puts the blood into the machine and the computer prints out the results, not even the technicians were aware it was going on. Negative results were not recorded, positive results were erased, and only the computer had any idea it was going on." Reggie's eyes narrowed. "Except for you."

Markham laughed out loud. The alcohol evaporated through his pores as Reggie's words warmed him. His head was now nearly clear and his poise intact.

"Like I said, you're full of shit."

Reggie was unfazed. He tapped again on the disk. "The positive results were forwarded to a terminal within the main ComHealth office. I even know which one."

Markham's amused grin vanished. "What the hell are you talking about?"

"Oh, I know a lot," Reggie said confidently. "And so do a lot of others."

Markham shook his head dismissively. "I know that you had O'Reilly killed and that the leak was probably FBI. I know that you had the other scientists killed, and I know you tried to have me killed."

Markham tried to avoid it, but he found himself swallowing nervously. He could see that Reggie had noticed.

"You missed, my friend," Reggie said, his voice dropping. "But you got my mother."

Markham put his hand over his mouth. Lost in the flurry, he had forgotten about Reggie's mother. He nearly started to apologize before he caught himself. "I'm sorry," he sighed. "You're just so far out in left field."

For a second, Reggie's temper flared. His cheeks flushed and his lips quivered. "How many has it been, Mr. Markham? How many more will there be?"

"What?"

Reggie tapped his finger on the disk a third time. He had no interest in picking a fight with a drunk. He wanted to convey a message and see a reaction. He took a deep breath and controlled his temper. "Listen. This disk has the reconstructed Doyne data. It shows the computer program that was in place. It shows how the test was done without any of the technicians knowing about it and how the results were erased. I was even able to partially reconstruct what you were testing for. It was coded, but I'm at least close."

Markham squinted to express doubt, but his heart nearly jumped out of his chest and his bowels seemed to constrict to the diameter of a pencil.

"It was a protein," offered Reggie. "It was called 'protein' such and such. The second part was a letter followed by a number followed by a letter. The two letters were the same."

Markham's shoulder twitched involuntarily and Reggie's eyes seemed to burn right through him. "Don't even think of telling me I'm wrong."

"You are," Markham said in a voice that would have caused a polygraph to explode.

Reggie sat back in the padded booth and stared across the table. Markham was a pathetic figure, half drunk and able to deny the truth with only the vigor of a whisper.

"But I still have one problem," Reggie said. "The Doyne records are conclusive, but without the journal and O'Reilly's data, I still don't know exactly what you were testing for. I'm guessing something like cystic fibrosis. I'm sure your HMO would have just loved it if they found a test that identified babies that would be born with cystic fibrosis. It fits the criteria. They would cost a lot to care for."

"What are you jabbering about?" Markham asked, with an edge of desperation. He was too weak to fight back. He was too drained and preoccupied with how long it would be before Reggie's information found the reporters who had been calling and might actually have copies of the journal and O'Reilly's data.

"Tell me I'm wrong, Mr. Markham."

"You're wrong. And I gotta go," Markham said, shifting as if he planned to stand up.

"Now listen," Reggie growled in a tone so fierce that Markham stopped. "There are three links in the chain. I have one. Right now my Doyne data looks like some complicated computer programming, but doesn't prove a thing. If I could get my hands on the first link, O'Reilly's stuff, you're going to need a lawyer so good he makes O.J. Simpson's Dream Team look like a bunch of Alzheimer's patients."

"You said three links."

Reggie nodded. "The third link is the ComHealth stuff, your data. I'm sure you have a copy. I know you'll never give it too me, but it might still be useful."

"What? Useful for what?"

Reggie reached over and grabbed Markham's shot glass. A half ounce remained, and Reggie slammed it down in the manner of an experienced drinker. Immediately he started coughing wildly.

"Useful for what?" Markham repeated.

"P-plea b-bargain," Reggie blurted out.

Makham rolled his eyes as Reggie sputtered and coughed. Finally, after half a minute, Reggie could talk again. Markham waited nervously. "Good stuff," Reggie chuckled.

"I'm leaving," Markham stood up and dropped a fifty on the table. He slipped out of the booth, but Reggie was too quick, standing in front of him and blocking his way. Five inches shorter, the young man's eyes radiated an intensity that scared the wobbling executive.

"Two final things, Mr. Markham. The first is I want you to remember that every day for the rest of my life I will be looking for what I need. You and I both know that somewhere O'Reilly probably left copies. I'll climb any mountain I need to, but I'll find it."

Markham tried to appear indifferent, but he knew Reggie meant it. "What was the second thing?"

"Don't bother with the gun in your car. I disabled the alarm system, and the gun is now mine."

Markham's face turned crimson. "You little shit!"

Reggie did not react. He stepped forward until his face was within three inches of Markham's chin. "Think of this, Mr. Markham," he began in a low tone. "I'll never kill *you* with your gun. It wouldn't hurt you enough. But unless you take my advice, I'll use that gun and God knows I will."

Markham looked rattled. Reggie's eyes looked crazed. "What are you saying?" he asked Reggie.

"I'm saying, do as I want."

"What's that?"

"Don't be an idiot."

"What do you want?" Markham pleaded.

Reggie stepped back. He couldn't tell if Markham was stupid, drunk, or scared. He also knew it mattered little. "Complete the chain," he said just loud enough to be heard.

"Or what?"

Reggie stepped back toward him, intentionally stepping on Markham's toes. "Who do you love more than anyone in the world?"

For the first time, true fear was seen in Gregory Markham's face. He had no reason to doubt that Reggie was serious. "You're daughter's a beautiful girl," whispered Reggie. "Very beautiful. And like I said, I wouldn't kill you."

Markham's throat seemed to tighten, and his mind went blank. He felt pressure on his feet, but his head seemed to spin. Almost by reflex, he quickly sat down and buried his eyes in the palm of his hand. Words came to him, and he started to speak, but when he looked up, Reggie Tan was gone.

Tom Brokaw ended the Friday newscast with a reminder. "And on Monday, we'll be coming to you from Minneapolis. It will be the first day of a trial that we reported on earlier in the week. Molly Loomis, the young woman whose emergency room visit, surgery, and hospital stay were denied by her HMO, will be in court fighting that decision. It promises to be a case that many observers will be watching closely, as managed care. That is the foundation of health maintenance organizations is challenged in the courts. Monday will begin the jury selection and—"

Briggs turned off the TV before Brokaw could finish. Flipping the remote onto his desk, he turned to face Marcus and Molly. Sanders sat glumly in front of the desk staring into space. Molly stood at the other side of the office, leaning against the door with her hands across her chest and gazing toward the ceiling. No one seemed willing to talk. Finally, Molly sighed heavily. "What would you guys do?"

It was not a question that Briggs had allowed his own mind to avoid. Since the moment Pokey delivered the offer, he continued to run through various scenarios, all of which came back to one fundamental fact. The offer was better than anything they had hoped for. Tyler took a deep breath. "Let me preface this by saying that when I answer that question I speak as your lawyer, not as your friend."

"Okay."

Briggs was torn and he hid it poorly. "Molly, there's nothing I'd like to do more than to take shots at these guys in court. The way Hutchins and his corporate raiders, well, it's the type of cause I always dreamed of fighting for."

"I know," said Molly.

"But it still boils down to your individual situation. Your needs. Your future."

"I know."

Marcus nodded. Molly saw it. "You agree, Marcus?"

"Tyler's right. It's a better offer than I ever expected."

Molly again flipped her eyes toward the ceiling, gazing at a spot of no particular importance. She seemed tired beyond restraint. "I don't know," she murmured. "It's like I'd be lying."

"No," Tyler contradicted. "You just couldn't say anything. It's they who would be lying."

"And that doesn't make any difference," Marcus offered. "They're so good at that anyway."

Molly took a deep breath and opened the door. Her indecision was written all over her face. "You guys going to be here tomorrow?"

"About eight," Briggs replied.

Molly picked up the offer, folded it, and put it in her pocket. "I'll be here about then."

Marcus Sanders stood and walked to her. He put his hand on her arm. "You know, whatever you decide."

Molly looked at the ground. "I know, Marcus, and thanks for everything."

A moment later, she was gone, the sound of the closing door a jarring reminder of the decision she faced. Marcus returned to his seat, and Tyler flipped on the TV. Now it was the local news and another replay of the Barnes and Whitfield press conference. It caused both men to bristle at the sight. "What would you do?" asked Tyler.

"Need you ask?"

Tyler grunted. "I know."

"That money would change her life. It may be chicken feed to these guys, but for her it would make all the difference."

"I know."

"Think about all she's lost in this."

Sanders and Briggs returned to the screen and saw Harley Whitfield take the microphone. Point by point, he repeated the familiar fiction. Briggs instinctively tightened his grip on the remote, his mind wandering to the imaginary scene he had played through so many times, a closing argument before a jury. He gritted his teeth.

"God, how I'd love to take on these bastards," Marcus gasped, his eyes glued to the screen.

Tyler could only shake his head. "Amen, brother. Amen."

By midnight Friday, the bustle of the ICU was diminished to a constant pattern of beeps, buzzes, and the low voices of nurses visiting among themselves. The twenty-bed unit, full except for two beds, was largely dark. Ten nurses congregated around a central station of cardiac monitors, charts, and flow sheets. A handful of visitors still lingered in individual rooms shielded from view by curtains behind the glass walls. Peter Colder's room was in the northwest corner of the large rectangular unit only a few steps from the centrally located nursing station.

There since ten that evening, Molly continued her vigil at Colder's bedside. Peter's mother and brother had come and gone. Sylvia, Julianne, Letisha, and Sandra had all been by earlier, as had Jayne McCall and Shirley Mitchell. Sitting in the darkened room lit only by the cardiac monitor and the various lights on the respirator gave her time to think, trying to make sense of all that happened.

Stephanie, Peter's night nurse for the past week, came in every few minutes to check on him and the various machines attached to him.

Some of the nurses befriended Molly. A few remembered her from her own stay in the ICU months before, but most knew her primarily as the person at the center of the ComHealth controversy. Most were reluctant to ask her directly about the suit and only three times in a week was it even brought up. In general, the nurses left her alone, their professional demeanor winning out over their natural curiosity.

Just after midnight, Colder's respiratory alarm sounded and Stephanie reappeared. The endotracheal tube had developed a slight air leak earlier in the day and needed to be changed in the morning. The pressure loss now caused the alarm to trigger about every fifteen minutes, but was of no risk to Peter. Stephanie adjusted the tube, refilled the cuff, and the alarm stopped.

Molly sat at Colder's right. It allowed her to hold the hand that was not hooked up to the IV or the arterial line. It also allowed her to see the cardiac tracing. The respirator sat underneath the cardiac monitor, and after she finished with the ET tube, Stephanie turned to Molly.

"My last night here for three days," she said. "I forgot to tell you."

"You deserve the days off," Molly replied. "You've worked like a dog this week."

Stephanie injected a medication through the IV and flushed it with saline. "Gonna take my little boy to the zoo on Sunday."

Molly had been sitting with her arms on the bed and her head resting upon them. She sat up. "You never told me you had a son."

"Yep, he's six."

"What's his name?"

Stephanie's scrub jacket had two hip pockets. She pulled out a picture. "Davey." Molly took it. "Very cute."

"Thanks. He's a good boy. Wonderful kid actually. But he's got Sprue."

"What?"

"It's a disease that affects the intestines. There are a lot of things he can't digest."

"Oh," said Molly. "I'm sorry."

"No," replied Stephanie. "Don't be."

The remark about the disease unnerved her. Molly struggled for something else to say. "He's a very handsome boy. He's got your eyes."

Stephanie laughed for a second. "Got his dad's attitude. Real rambunctious. He's a handful."

"I'll bet."

Stephanie produced another syringe and injected something into an IV bag that she carried with her. Then she started to change bags and replace the IV tubing. "I was eighteen when I had him. You know, stupid kid, it'll never happen to me."

"Yes,"

"The guy was in college. I don't think he ever really believed that it was his, but it doesn't matter any more."

Molly squeezed Peter's hand and he seemed to stir a little. "Must be hard raising him on your own."

Stephanie stopped. Over the course of the week, she was the only nurse to really talk to Molly, and despite her young age, she seemed to be both seasoned and sophisticated. "I guess it's been about what you'd expect."

Molly swallowed hard. She suddenly realized where the discussion might be headed.

"Yeah," Stephanie continued. "I was eighteen. Catholic family. What do you do?"

"I know," Molly said.

"I took one way out."

Molly looked hard at the unconscious Peter Colder. She didn't reply. She had no intention of discussing her past life and the reasons behind the personal decisions which now were public.

"But that's not what I'm getting at. When it comes to abortion, the easy thing to do is to take a strong moral stance, as if you have the only answer. I mean, quote the doctrine you believe, scripture, science, or church position, and take a strong position. That's the surest way to narrow-mindedness."

"You think I was wrong?" Molly found herself asking.

"Not for me to say," Stephanie replied. "I wouldn't have done what you did, but I have no right to judge you either. People forget that we don't answer to one another."

Molly sighed. The fact that Stephanie, like everyone else, knew so much about her life seemed strange and unsettling. She could see before her eyes what the trial was bound to be like. But now for some reason, she felt like talking. "You know what's always bothered me most about it?" Molly asked.

"What?"

"The fact that I've always looked at it like it was both a right decision and a wrong decision."

Stephanie continued to fiddle with a monitor. "Maybe that's exactly what it is. Sometimes there aren't perfect answers."

"Maybe."

Stephanie shifted and started to work with the IV tubing again. She turned to look at Molly. "Can I ask you just one question?"

Molly looked tentative. "Yes."

"You know, the abortion. Tell me, would you have done it if they had told you the baby would only be mildly handicapped instead of severely retarded?"

"No."

"Or scarred or malformed?"

"No."

"Or a girl instead of a boy or vice versa?"

"No."

"And do you think any of that makes a difference in God's eyes?"

Molly drew a breath. "No."

"Okay, but what about the reality? Your child. A lifetime in a nursing home? Vegetative? Unable to communicate with the world?" Stephanie looked squarely at Molly. "We're comfortable letting the elderly or the dying go when quality of life isn't there. What's the real difference? You can easily say that 'life' is always right. But is it? I don't know. I just know that God makes us *make* these decisions. He makes us make them out of love. He makes us suffer out of love."

"Yes," Molly agreed.

Stephanie leaned down and checked the urimeter. Molly looked at her pretty face, but Stephanie was expressionless. "Actually I mention my son for a different reason."

"What's that?"

Stephanie recorded the number on the flow sheet and then replaced the clipboard on the Mayo stand. "This sprue he has. The last two years I've spent nearly two thousand on lawyers just to keep our insurance."

"ComHealth?"

"Who else?" Stephanie activated Colder's automatic blood pressure cuff and waited for the reading. "The system is so screwed up now, I don't know where to go. Used to be that hospitals had an incentive to take care of people. Now no one wants to take care of anyone. Patients are looked at as expenses, and my son is too big of one."

"Have you kept the insurance?"

"So far. But they keep trying. Someday I won't dot an *i* or cross a *t* or they'll rewrite the policy so as to exclude him. It'll be done in a lot of fancy language, but the end result will be the same. Their bottom line won't be fat enough and the shareholders won't be happy."

Molly didn't respond.

"You know," Stephanie continued, watching Molly hold Colder's hand. "The problem is that what they do is legal."

"You're right."

"It may be unethical or immoral but that doesn't really matter to 'em."

Molly looked at her curiously. She was impressed. The nurse was a powerful mix of open-mindedness and strong opinions.

"I read in the paper about these people who have been hurt by the managed care cutbacks and I ask myself where does it end? Who is going to stop it?"

Molly didn't have the heart to tell her about ComHealth's offer.

"It will come only from someone who has the guts to stand up and say that the emperor has no clothes. From there it's up to the public to see that the clothes aren't there."

Molly bit her lip as conflicting emotions raged within her.

"I know you started this because of the bill they stuck you with. And I know it probably scares the hell out of you to think of walking into that courtroom with the eyes of the country on you."

Molly nodded.

"But when you do it, remember that it's not just you that's going to be there. It's going to be all of us—my little boy, my mother who had breast cancer a few years back, my uncle who has heart trouble, my cousin who has cerebral palsy. They'll be there with you. And when they call you a liar or a schemer or whatever, the patients of the world, like me, will be behind you. And they'll be that way because the issue is not what your life has been, but instead what ComHealth has done. You'll speak for all of the people, that silent majority who still know right from wrong."

Molly put her head back on her arms, leaning onto Colder's bed. His unconscious body seemed lifeless, his head was turned toward her, his eyes closed and his face impassive. "I don't know," she muttered.

Stephanie opened the curtain and prepared to leave. "And remember," she said, "this conversation never happened. I work here."

Just before sunrise, Molly Loomis sat alone, parked in front of her parent's house. The small Cape Cod home of her youth was dark and unchanged. In the months since she last spoke to her parents, not a day passed when she didn't think of the look on her father's face as he screamed at her about the abortion.

His eyes, wild with anger, hiding the hurt he actually felt. Her mother the same, her sullen gaze masking the feeling of betrayal of every principle she held dear. How could she hurt them again?

A light rain carried randomly by a howling wind whipped against the side of the car. She felt no chill despite the cool temperature outside. It was all too painful and all too real. She was no hero, she told herself. She was just a girl, a woman, one like millions who just wanted the life she planned. She was no crusader, no saint, no example for the young. She was only herself, flawed, wanting, and filled only with the same simple goals she'd always had. She was nothing special, she told herself. Nothing special at all.

And her parents. She couldn't do it again. She could only imagine how humiliated they were when the newspaper article came out mentioning the abortion again. And then the TV news. The pain she caused them and continued to cause. She imagined them walking into Mass surrounded by the gossip and the shame. She could hear the words being said. She could hear what they called her. How could she put them through more?

Tears welled in her eyes. The windshield was covered with a light film of water, with innumerable drops swirling about in the wind. Only a shadow of the house could still be seen, with the silhouette of the large oak tree guarding the small front yard. Molly dabbed her eyes. The tree, she thought. That crazy old tree.

It stood like a sentinel in the front yard, a sturdy remnant of her childhood. She remembered so much about that tree, now a mature oak reaching high into the night sky. The front yard tree. Planted by her parents when they first bought the house, it was always a way to gauge time, view the passing seasons, and watch the inevitable change from youth to beyond. She guessed that every home had one. Where the children once played, under which the neighbors paid calls, and through which the winds gave warning of the intentions of the sky.

She had grown older looking at that tree. Grown into a woman. It was her friend and companion. She could see it through her tears. It spared her no judgment as it swayed in the wind, its limbs reaching and signaling, obscuring different portions of the house as it beckoned in the darkness. What did it say?

She wiped her eyes again. How could she hurt them more? Was that it? Was that her fear? Yes, she knew it was. That was part of it. Sitting in a courtroom on TV telling a jury how she lied to her husband and aborted her child. The pain she would cause her parents. That was part of it. But was that it? Or was it more pain to herself?

A quarter million dollars. That was school and a home. That was savings and a future. That was even enough money for in vitro and a child of her own. The others could fight the HMO, she told herself. They were too powerful, too clever. Too many lawyers with too many good businessmen. Who was she? She was just one person, one small soul, about to be crushed by the weight of publicity, microphones, and public scrutiny. She was not a hero. She knew that. There would be protesters and critics, analysts and experts. It was all so easy to see. Her name, a symbol of abortion on demand; she would be vilified by the righteous, lauded by the crusaders, dissected by the media, and examined by the world. Her life would be one of microanalysis by each and every person, all ultimately passing judgment upon her. Harsh judgment.

She had no wish for fame. Just a life, her life, simple and plain. The money would buy her that. Security and invisibility, a return to the existence she dreamed of. The others could fight the battles. Those who were smarter, richer, and less afraid. Who was she to fight these men? She was no opponent for them. She was a laughingstock, a pipsqueak, a runt. They would crush her, she told herself. She was no spokesman for the cause that Stephanie Randall had talked about. She couldn't do it. She could never be a hero.

The wind continued to swirl the rain, and with it the old oak seemed to wave its mighty limbs. Molly dabbed her eyes, watching as the silhouette continued to speak in its own sign. The tree. The old tree, standing alone against the wind and the rain. The tree, free in its life and its place secure, but fixed and given never to choose, let alone to choose against fear.

What would Peter do? she wondered. What advice would he give? He would want the best for her, she knew. But what was that? Peter, lovely Peter. What he had done. What he had given. And O'Reilly, exiled and executed for some cost-effective cause. And the patients. All the patients. Dead or dying, hurt and hindered, their lives reduced to an entry in a cost–benefit worksheet. Stephanie Randall and her son. A boy who would need lifetime care. Rudy Jalowicz, a blood count would have saved him. Zach Lawton, the eight-year-old who died when discharged too early. Molly started to cry. A boy, eight years old.

She stepped out of the car and onto the street. The howling wind greeted her with a blast of chilling rain. She walked to the curb to look at the house, careful not to step on the property where she was not welcome. She closed her eyes and settled into the rain. Now she could hear the tree speak. Creaking like an old door, it moved with grace and speed, contradicting its sound.

Why her? she asked herself. Why? Why not someone rich or powerful? Someone articulate or eloquent. Her eyes stung as she opened them and tried to look at her parents' house again. Her clothes soaked in the rain, she shivered. "Why?" she asked out loud. "Why me?"

A strong gust of wind blew her hair across her face, and Molly swept it away, pausing in the middle of the street. Behind her, she could still hear the tree creaking in the wind. Or maybe it was another; her tree was one like many. Then a thought came to her. It was not about heroes, it was about truth. It was not about fame, it was about infamy. It was not about individuals, it was about a cause—a burden for which the pride of sacrifice may be the only consolation.

She stopped and turned. Peter's words returned to her. "I just hope that whatever happens to me, someone better and stronger will pick up the baton." Better? No, she thought. Stronger? Impossible. But her tears ceased. The wind and the rain stopped, and the tree appeared to stand still. She turned and walked down the street. The night became eerily silent. As the rain passed, the sky became clear.

When the first hints of dawn appeared on the horizon, H. Carter Hutchins was awake, sipping a café au lait in the solarium. The late-summer sunrise offered a rare view of both night and day, with a stream of pastel colors tucked beneath a star-lit sky. Looking north, he saw a single great star shinning brightly. Closing his eyes, Hutchins slid deeply into his chair and relaxed.

It had been a long night—rain until nearly dawn and then a rapid passing of the clouds. Hutchins, awake through it all, reviewed everything in his mind, time after time. He opened his eyes again, staring at the star. It was a signal, he thought. The clouds of night, yielding to a clearing sky. And the star, the North Star, used by the explorers as their guide, now used by him as God's signal. The devout Hutchins said a prayer. "God will provide," he assured himself when finished.

Hutchins sipped on his coffee. A damn waitress, he thought to himself. How in hell could God side with someone like her? It was not meant to be. His actions were inspired. Hers were self-serving. His future was that of legend. Hers was useless insignificance.

"A little girl who wants to steal money and then live on the dole," he muttered to himself. Hutchins stared at the twinkling star. The sight reassured him. God always heard his prayers. H. Carter Hutchins always won. Both he and God always saw to that.

The pious Hutchins said another prayer just to be sure and then finished the coffee. They would pay her off in a few hours and from then on she would be out of his life. A quarter million for silence. A no-brainer. He knew no greedy little bitch would ever refuse it.

Just before nine, Molly Loomis walked into Tyler Briggs office. Still dressed in the damp clothes she had worn walking the streets throughout the night, she looked ragged and half dead. Her moist hair hung limply on her shoulders, her eyes were bloodshot, and her pale skin appeared whiter than snow. She took two steps into the office and then stopped, listening as the door closed automatically behind her.

Tyler was seated behind his desk. Marcus stood by the side window. Both were nonplussed at her appearance. "You should know," Briggs began, "that our friend Reggie has been bluffing Mr. Markham. Trying to get him to confess."

"Will it work?" Molly asked, her voice shaking.

"I wouldn't count on it," he replied.

Molly took one step forward. "I've been doing a lot of thinking."

"I guessed that," Marcus said.

Molly appeared on the verge of tears. "All my life, every time I ever came to a big decision, a decision that would affect my life, a decision that would affect others' lives, I always seemed to make the wrong choice." She choked slightly. "There never were a lot of things I wanted for my life. I wanted simple stuff mostly, but for whatever reason, I let most of it get away. I don't blame anybody for my mistakes, but it only makes it more important that I do the right thing here."

"I understand," Tyler said.

"The way I see it is that maybe deep inside, somewhere, there is a purpose to what I did. Some hidden meaning, some sort of silver lining."

"Maybe."

"But whatever the case, the truth is this really isn't about me anymore. It's more. It's about what's right."

Briggs and Sanders gazed at her carefully, trying to read her.

"I guess that many years from now when I look back I'll hope that I made the right decision, but I know that I'm comfortable with it now."

Briggs stood up. His hands shook as he folded them together.

"The money. It could set me up for life. A house, school, no more debts, everything."

"Yes."

Two tears rolled onto Molly's cheeks. "It's more money than I ever dreamed of."

"Yes."

"But," she continued, "you know, you can't lose what you never had. I've never had money, and I probably never will." Molly coughed and cleared her throat. "But more important. Self-respect. Dignity. They come only from within. Nobody can take it away, but you can sure give it away." She paused, tears rolling onto her cheeks.

Neither man showed any hint of reaction.

Molly turned away. "And I won't. I never will."

Marcus and Tyler glanced at each other.

"I can't take the money," Molly sputtered. "I just can't."

Briggs walked toward her and took her firmly in his arms. Molly tried desperately to stop crying, but it was hopeless. Both attorneys knew that from a legal point of view, it was the wrong decision. Both men also knew they had never been so happy that a client disregarded their advice.

No one spoke or moved, each of the three lost in their own thoughts. From now on there would be no turning back. The preliminaries had come to an end.

Shortly after nine, H. Carter Hutchins, who was in his ComHealth office gathering with his fellow executives, took Jackson Barnes' call. All the executives looked anxious except for Markham, who appeared hung over. "What?" yelled Hutchins, turning on the speaker phone.

The other executives listened in astonishment as they heard the news that Molly Loomis turned down the settlement.

"The little cunt!" roared the CEO.

"That's what I said," Barnes repeated. "No deal."

Hutchins was furious. "That little bitch will do anything to get famous, won't she?"

The attorney was soothing. "Doesn't matter, Carter, it's her loss."

Hutchins sat down. He inhaled deeply three times, slowly regaining his temper. "Where do we stand then?"

"Monday morning. Ten o'clock."

"You're ready?"

"Of course."

"Good."

"I'll see you then."

The click signaled that Barnes had hung up. Hutchins gazed up at the four executives standing before him in front of the desk. He noticed that Markham looked ill. "You okay, Greg?"

"Fine. Little flu."

Hutchins dismissed it. He reached across his desk and picked up a pencil while the other executives watched. "Here's what we're gonna do." He viciously snapped it in half and hurled it into the wastebasket. No one missed the inference.

"We're gonna absolutely destroy her," Ross laughed.

"And better yet," Bolger continued, "in front of the entire world."

Hutchins' eyes narrowed eerily. "Just what she deserves."

Chapter Thirty-one

August 24

Sunday began with bad news. The steady improvement of Peter's kidneys ended during the night, and dialysis was scheduled for noon. The unexpected backward slide disappointed the doctors, who gave the news to Molly, Julianne, and Peter's family by early morning. His liver function tests were also worse, and he still showed no sign of waking up. To compound the problem, he showed signs of a pneumonia and would need to start on antibiotics. Any lessening of ventilator support would need to be delayed until the pneumonia was resolved.

Normally the usual group of friends and family was full of questions for the doctors, but this morning they were subdued. The week in the ICU depressed them, watching many people die and seeing families come and go as their loved ones struggled for life. Although an experience they never cared to repeat, it was also enlightening enough to make them realize that Peter might never leave his room.

After the doctors left, Bryan Colder and his mother went into the ICU to be at Peter's bedside. Molly remained behind in the waiting room with Julianne. Molly's relationship with Peter's ex-wife started when Molly visited Julianne in her hospital room. The initial conversation awkward, their shared concern for Peter made the situation easier. After several days of seeing each other regularly, they now talked easily, becoming friendlier, but always focusing on Peter.

A short time later, Sylvia, Letisha, and Briggs arrived. Within a few minutes they were updated on the bad news and the somber mood that swept through the waiting room now engulfed them all. Briggs, his hair still damp from the light rain outside, flopped into a chair near the window. He stayed for half an hour, speaking briefly with each person in the room before leaving to return to the office. He hugged each of them and they all wished him luck, knowing his day would be a long one and his week even longer. Briggs made a point to tell Molly he would call her later to go over the details of the trial's first day. She told him she would be at the hospital the entire day.

After he left, the group mingled in the waiting room, talking and watching the Sunday morning news programs. NBC's *Meet the Press* and ABC's *This Week* each mentioned the trial, as did CNN. CBS showed video from Friday of downtown Minneapolis with over eight thousand protesters outside the ComHealth offices in the IDS Tower. They also showed clips of several speeches, including Tyler's Thursday press conference and the Barnes and Whitfield press conference from Friday.

As the report concluded, the reporter announced that the trial would start at 10:00 A.M. tomorrow and finished by saying, "Although only expected to take a week, this trial pitting one young woman with a checkered past against a health-care giant may do more to shape the future of health care in this country than any legislative action ever will."

Molly swallowed hard at the words. The slight insult aside, she could clearly see the magnitude of what was happening. Reporters, politicians, administrators, insurance executives, businessmen. Doctors, lawyers, nurses. The elderly, the young. The insured, the uninsured, the sick, the well. All would be watching. A nation of two hundred and fifty million gazing upon her, analyzing her and the nation's trend toward managed care. The sight of the crowd in the video was terrifying. Her strongest impulse was still to run and hide.

Letisha walked over to the TV that hung in the corner of the room and turned it off. No one objected. They were depressed enough about Peter. Thinking of the trial only added misery to the sadness. Letisha stood behind Molly and without a word started to massage her shoulders. It all seemed to be a nightmare. A nightmare that would not end.

Everyone knew what was about to happen. It was going to be the longest week of their lives.

Markham was still slightly hung over when the doorbell rang at 8:00 A.M. Sunday morning. The nagging throb that beat at his temples seemed to increase as he threw on his robe and slippers and made his way down the stairs to the front door. He responded with an irritated "coming" when the doorbell rang again.

Markham had attended a black tie benefit for the American Cancer Society the night before. Although both he and his wife, Deborah, wanted to decline, Hutchins had insisted and once again they were treated to a Celia Hutchins fashion show and a H. Carter Hutchins award. Markham felt it was totally inappropriate for anyone from ComHealth to be accepting an award from the ACS when the HMO had worked diligently to cut back on mammograms, prostate screening, and colon cancer screening in the past year. It had nothing to do with an increased interest in curing cancer. It was pure public relations, an award for a very public monetary donation.

The evening was a disaster. Preoccupied with the continuing calls from reporters and the SEC, Markham was distracted and distant. He ended up spending most of the night listening to Hutchins spew forth another "affordable, quality health care for all" speech that was now sounding more and more like "a chicken in every pot." With the other executives and their wives attired in thousand-dollar suits and ten thousand-dollar dresses, it all seemed a bit gauche. The Markhams left early, pleading illness, but not before Greg downed four whiskey sours, the residual of which he now felt knocking on his skull.

Before he opened the door, Markham turned around. It was almost as if he anticipated a problem. At the top of the semicircular stairs Deborah stood in her white cotton robe. Her look was one of concern. She knew her husband of twenty years well, sensing for weeks that something was seriously wrong.

When Markham opened the door, the warrant was thrust in his face. The first man introduced himself. Markham only heard "SEC." It did not surprise him. Barnes and Whitfield told him it was probably coming. Seven men followed him into the house and began opening cabinets and drawers and checking his computer. A shocked Deborah tried to object, but her husband gently put his arm around her and walked her back into the bedroom, asking her to change into clothes. Ashley, their thirteen-year-old daughter, appeared, and Markham instructed her to do the same.

As the SEC men continued to rummage through the house, poring over anything that appeared financial, Markham asked if there was one room he and his family could be alone in. The SEC's group leader offered them the front living room. They accepted.

When Markham closed the door to the living room five minutes later, with his miffed wife and his mystified daughter inside, he had on his face the look of a man already feeling the relief of a burden lifted. "I need to talk to you both," he began. Markham closed his eyes and began to speak. Before him sat the two people in the world he loved more than his own life. It killed him to hurt them the way he was about to. "These people are from the Securities and Exchange Commission. They're here to search the house, but actually that's only part of it." Markham bowed his head. "Let me start from the beginning."

Eight hours later, Deborah and Ashley Markham sat side by side in the twentieth row of a DC-10 on their way to Los Angeles. Their final destination was not determined, but they both knew they would not be back in Minneapolis for a very long time. At the same time, Gregory Markham poured himself his first drink of the day. The SEC and his family now gone, he plopped onto the couch and turned on the TV. He would watch the last half inning of the Twins game and then he would make the call. He knew that the time for being reactive was over. His only chance now was to take action and to take it fast.

Stanton Ross, T. Wilson Bolger, and Preston Cooley felt they had been hit by tornadoes. All three of the remaining ComHealth senior executives were also met at their front doors by the SEC investigators Sunday morning. Despite the continued assurances from their lawyers that nothing would ever be provable, the three men were now, more than ever, sure that they were in for a long fight. In addition, several reporters called each, asking about O'Reilly and Fragile X. None of them felt like the questions were idle curiosity.

That evening, on the eve of the trial, the three executives met at the Twin Cities Club and talked about what they were facing. They talked for hours. As they downed the club's expensive liquor, they became convinced that their only chance for salvation was a decisive victory in the trial. "Crush Molly Loomis!" they slurred many a time. They knew that would be the first step in the healing process. It would need to be followed by many years of their lawyers obstructing justice for them, but it would at least be a first step. In a drunken stupor, the executives agreed to pursue their plan with all the vigor they could muster. Success was an imperative. The only other possibility was humiliation, disgrace, and jail.

Dr. Eric Johnson was never a particularly religious man. The great-grandson of an immigrant Lutheran minister, he had never lived up to the devout man's expectations for his descendants. Instead, Johnson's own life was plagued with the agnostic questions so intimately interwoven with the cold objectivity demanded by the scientific world. Despite his ambivalence, Eric long before concluded that as a virtue, silence always outshone knowledge, and he was always a regular at Trinity Lutheran Church. His wife, more vocal and more committed, insisted that the two children be raised in a church environment. Rather than allowing it to be an issue between them, Eric learned to enjoy it and in the process developed some friendships with other parishioners and attended a few church functions.

The early Sunday morning was plagued by clouds and a light shower. Just as Pastor Youngberg launched into his morning sermon, the clouds parted and the sun began streaming through the stained glass windows. Eric, sitting with his wife Diane, reached over and held her hand. She turned and smiled at him. It seemed to be turning into a wonderful day.

The sermon, which began with a brief tribute to a fellow church member, an old WW II veteran who had died earlier in the week, was moving. Youngberg had a way of discussing death that incorporated both the joy of human life and the gift of the life after. Sitting patiently, Eric held the old family Bible he always brought with him. Originally his great-grandfather's, the old, beaten book had survived four generations of teaching, but now was nearly too fragile to use. The binding had long since disintegrated, and free-floating pages fell from the book if it was held the wrong way. Johnson gripped it tightly in his left hand, but as Pastor Youngberg came to the end of the sermon and everyone stood to pray, Eric shifted it to his right hand. With the movement, one page fell free and floated to the ground. Eric eyed the page as the congregation completed the prayer, keeping one foot near it in case some unseen breeze tried to carry it away. When the prayer was finished, Eric reached down and retrieved it.

"That old thing's shot," his wife whispered to him.

"I know."

The page was from Obadiah, a short book of the Old Testament that Eric knew nothing about. He checked the page number and set about to replace it in its proper spot. As he fumbled through the old Bible, searching for the proper place for the page, the choir burst into a hymn. His wife joined in, but Eric, always embarrassed about his terrible voice, was glad to have an excuse to avoid singing. His mind wandered as he flipped through the book, intentionally taking much longer than necessary. He found that recently his mind wandered constantly, a trait his wife noticed and reminded him of with great frequency. She also knew why.

It did not bother Diane Johnson that her husband's thoughts were about another woman. It was not someone he loved, or even knew very well any more, but someone he simply couldn't stop thinking about. Diane Johnson couldn't stop thinking about her either. All the time, they talked about her, his former patient Molly Loomis. It was so long ago, yet still so vivid. Both Eric and Diane knew they would never forget her.

He remembered the first time Molly had come into the office. Since seeing her in the parking lot two nights before, that's all he'd thought about. The symptoms and the signs. It was unmistakable. Any physician would have known. But the force of the new rules was formidable. In its wake, Molly's life's dream was washed away. He saw it coming. Any doctor would have. Tragic, he thought. Simply tragic.

He looked at his wife as she continued to sing the hymn. Beautiful as always, her blue eyes shone in the multicolored light passing through the giant stained glass window. He loved her more than the day they married. No, he thought. The trial. The lawyers must do it without him. His life was about his family. It was about Katie. It was about Robby.

Johnson could feel himself start to sweat. But the trial. Beginning tomorrow. The trial he had hoped for. The trial without him.

He found the correct page in the Bible. He thought about it long and hard. He and his wife had discussed it. If he said anything it could cost him everything he'd ever worked for. It could cost him the life they'd planned. His wife was right. It was impossible, he said. He was just one man. Who was he to fight the trend? It was impossible. He knew it. He'd fought and lost so many little battles against it already.

But his conscience ached. Molly. Molly Loomis. He could still see her face. He could still see her eyes. Young and hopeful and at least deserving of basic rights. The recollection tortured him. Where was his courage? Where was his honor? Where was the man he had once vowed he would be?

He held the book open and looked at it. His stomach churned. The trial. How he wanted to tell the truth! The whole truth and nothing but the truth. Eric thought of Hutchins, seeing him on the news again the night before. Another award for H. Carter Hutchins. The great CEO, the eloquent salesman; Hutchins, maybe a governor, a senator, or a president. Hutchins, the man himself, like an eagle set to soar to new heights after flying through the trial. "Hutchins," he caught himself muttering.

His thumb was positioned over a verse. He had not noticed it before, but now he saw the light pencil marks underlining the passage made years before. Perhaps his mother drew it, or maybe her mother, or even her grandfather. The line was faint but straight, coming from a steady hand that drew meaning from the space between the words. Eric read it. Obadiah 1:4 *"Though thou shall exalt thyself as the eagle, and set thy nest among the stars, thence I will bring thee down—"* Johnson blinked.

The hymn was finished, but Johnson read it again. Hutchins was the eagle in real life and in the verse. He was meant to be brought down. A simple message read by generations before was now passed to him by the slim line of a faded mark, its lasting impression a lesson all men must know.

Perhaps it was his great-grandfather who had read it first. The message. The trial would begin tomorrow, and with it the lies of the past and present would be rewritten as truths for the future. The message. Maybe it was written for someone else. Maybe it was not. It made little difference. The message was for him.

Rudy Jalowicz died eight hours before the trial was to begin. The kidney cancer detectable by blood tests ComHealthOne refused to authorize had spread to six different sites by the time it was diagnosed. It claimed his life in less than seven months. He left behind a wife, two sons, and two grandsons. He was fifty-five.

Chapter Thirty-two

August 25

The first morning of the trial broke with a spectacular sunrise in the east and a full moon in the west. Molly woke early and spent the first hour of her day doing nothing more than watching the sun come up. By seven, she was getting ready, and within an hour the phone began to ring continuously. The night before the trial was the first one in a week she'd spent in her own apartment, and she regretted the mistake. Living at Sylvia's allowed her to hide, but as she unplugged the phone to avoid any calls, she again realized that her arrival into the media spotlight was going to be anything but pleasant.

Drying her hair and applying makeup, she felt the growing anxiety. In her mind she visualized the microphones, the reporters, and the protesters. She could see the people staring at her. The thought was worse than nauseating. Never in her life did she seek the limelight and never in her life had she had it. Speeches in high school were terrifying. Even talking to customers at the restaurant wasn't easy, but this was like nothing she had ever experienced. This was national TV.

She walked into the living room and flipped on the TV. The *Today Show* was on, and she turned up the volume in order to hear the local weather as she returned to her bedroom. She was only there a minute when the forecast finished and Katie Couric gave a brief introduction of the next half hour's segments. Molly held her breath.

"And we'll be going live to Minneapolis to—"

Molly plugged her ears. She didn't even want to hear. She started to return to the living room to turn off the TV, but she only got a few steps before the wave of queasiness forced her to run to the bathroom. For the next ten minutes, she threw up.

When she finished, she was already exhausted. Worse yet, she felt no better, just fearful. The thought of being interrogated by Whitfield or Barnes about her life while the cameras focused on every blemish on her face sent chills through her. She doubted she would even be able to talk, let alone think. She wanted to cry. She wanted to scream. She wanted to run. But she couldn't do any of them.

The nausea better, she returned to the living room where the TV was showing the outside of the courthouse, with reporters standing on the steps. In the background, she could see the media camp, trailers and tents with call letters prominently displayed and reporters mingling about. But more impressive was the crowd. People were everywhere. Molly turned off the TV. She didn't want to see more. She knew she would see it in person soon enough.

Just as she was about to return to the bedroom, the doorbell rang. Peering through the peek hole, she was surprised by what she saw. A delivery man with a huge bouquet of flowers. "Thanks," she said as she accepted them.

"Are you *the* Molly Loomis?" asked the eager young man of about seventeen.

"Yes," she replied, her face flushing in embarrassment.

"Let me shake your hand," he said, grabbing her one free hand and nearly shaking her arm loose. "My mother says you're a hero, and I think so too."

"I don't think so."

The boy ignored her. "Last year she found a breast lump. Scared the hell out of her. And then these bastards wouldn't authorize nothin'. She had to pay herself for the doctor to stick a needle in it. Wasn't cancer, but for almost a month she thought she had it. And then they never paid a thing 'cause she didn't follow their rules."

"I'm sorry," she said.

"I'm glad you're fighting them. I don't understand all this insurance stuff, but I know what happened to my mom was shitty. Something's gotta change."

"You're right. It does."

He let go of her hand. "You just remember this. Jimmy Pierce. That's my name. You can get ahold of me at the flower shop. Any of those fancy lawyers give you any crap, you call me. Me and my friends will come and beat the shit out of them for you."

Molly laughed once out loud. She found his enthusiasm enjoyable and his attention flattering. She needed it. "Thank you, Jimmy Pierce."

"You're welcome, and I'm serious."

"Thanks again."

"I'm gonna tell my mother I met you," he said, walking away. "She'll be psyched!"

Molly closed the door. It seemed very strange to have people know her name. She was not at all sure she liked it despite Jimmy Pierce's adoration. She opened the card. *Good luck today, Emma Toselli.* Molly closed her eyes and held the card over her heart. Emma Toselli was an old woman with almost no money who lived on the ground floor. "Oh, Emma," Molly murmured, fighting back an emotional surge. She carried the vase into the bedroom and put in on the floor beside the mattress. "You shouldn't have, but it's very sweet."

Forty-five minutes later, the doorbell rang again, and when she opened it, Marcus Sanders stood before her. "Ready?" he asked.

"Ready as I'm gonna be."

"You look good."

Molly ran her hands down the sides of the plain blue skirt. "Thanks."

Marcus plunged in with the update. "Peter's labs are a little better this morning. No dialysis today. Maybe tomorrow. He's still not awake, but he's moved around a bit more. I knew you'd want to know."

"Thanks, Marcus," she said as she put her keys into her purse. "I did."

"I talked to Dr. Asadourian. He wanted to wish you well."

Molly grabbed his arm and started to leave. "Thanks."

Marcus closed the door behind her, and together they walked down the hall. Both took deep breaths, knowing it was time to face the crowd.

By the time Molly arrived at the courthouse an hour later, downtown Minneapolis was at a complete standstill. Nearly seven thousand spectators, camera crews, reporters, and protesters lined the streets and stalled the traffic. Police blocked off a ten-square-block area in preparation, but even that proved woefully inadequate as even more than expected university students and spectators flocked into the area, clogging the streets.

MSNBC, Court TV, and CNN positioned their booths across the street from the courthouse, in the center of a block that quickly became known as "Media Central." Local stations were positioned nearby. To the north, the abortion protesters stood with "murderer" placards in hand. To the south stood a large group of anti-managed care protesters organized by the two University of Minnesota law students. Only the fifty feet in front of the long wide concrete staircase leading up to the courthouse was empty, the police roping it off for the arrival of the participants.

Throughout downtown, all restaurants and cafes were packed and televisions turned on. Seats within the trendy restaurants were at a premium, some people having arrived as early as seven. The coffee shops and union at the nearby U of M were also filled as people scrambled to see any television. At the Hennepin County Medical Center, the waiting rooms were lined with people, the TVs offering different channels but all with continuing coverage of the trial. Families and patients milled about in the halls, listening overhead as the radio described the unfolding events.

At 9:00 A.M., a great cheer went up as the jumbotron TVs set up at varying positions throughout the crowd showed the *Today Show* going live to the MSNBC reporter in a booth at Media Central. A minute later, CBS *This Morning* did the same, followed by ABC's *Good Morning America*. The networks' live coverage was brief, but MSNBC and Court TV continued to broadcast live, interviewing the two U of M law students as well as two abortion protesters and two managed care victims.

As the minutes ticked toward the starting time of 10:00 A.M., the tension was visible. A fight broke out between several anti-abortion protesters and a small band of students. All were arrested and removed within minutes, but the incident seemed to add fuel to an already volatile mix. Many shouts and chants about managed care and abortion began to echo throughout the area.

When the two black limousines carrying the ComHealth lawyers arrived, a wild mix of boos, cheers, and gasps arose. The four dark-suited lawyers barely looked at the crowd as they bounded up the seventy-five steps into the courthouse. T. Quentin Cox and Ace Farnsworth stopped long enough to assure themselves the entire nation had seen their glorious physiques. The junior partners were obviously relishing their opportunity for glory, but Whitfield and Barnes were more discreet, turning to wave briefly to the sound of the cheers, heard exclusively from the anti-abortion protesters. Cameras bore in on each of them, but they paused for only a moment and refused all questions, heading directly for the courtroom.

Tyler Briggs arrived next in a Yellow Cab. On his way to the courtroom earlier, he spilled coffee on his tie when a spectator crossed the street in front of him, which forced him to return to the office to retrieve another. Molly and Marcus arrived less than a minute later.

As they emerged from their cabs, the noise was shocking. From seemingly everywhere, the cheers fell upon them like an avalanche, ringing through their ears and nearly knocking them over. Tyler and Marcus smiled wanly. It was even more than they expected. The two attorneys positioned Molly between them as they started up the steps to the courtroom. Reporters descended upon them, but they all waved off any questions. Molly instinctively partially covered her face as the cameras bore in. Then, thinking better of it, she dropped her hand and tried to look sturdy.

As they hurried up the steps, the massive crowd and the television cameras for the first time got a close look at the young woman who within a few weeks had become a household name. It was obvious to all that she avoided looking at the cameras as she made her way up the steps, but this only made the massive crowd cheer harder. Her face was grim, but when she finally reached the top step she turned, as Tyler had advised her to do, and waved once. The crowd roared its approval, and for the first time, Molly saw the masses that had turned out. The TV booths, the protesters, the cameras, and the TV screens. The banners, the flags, the fliers. Reporters were everywhere. The sight was incredible. She felt faint. Her wave was tentative, and the air she breathed seemed to scorch her lungs. She struggled to walk any further.

With the deafening cheers slowly pushing them forward, a dozen anti-abortion protesters suddenly broke through and ran toward the three. Screaming "Murderer!" and "Butcher!" they threw a mass of crumpled paper balls at Molly, a couple of which glanced off her. Two cameramen jumped in front of them and caught footage of Molly protecting herself from the barrage with her hands. Marcus and Tyler pushed in front of her as the police tried to rein in the protesters. A reporter trailing them caught all of their shouts of "murderer" on his open mike and then opened up one of the crumpled papers and showed it on camera, a drawing of a nearly full-term fetus with Molly driving a stake in its heart. Marcus and Tyler yelled at her to ignore it as they wrapped her under their arms, drove through the remaining people at the top of the steps, and barreled inside.

Inside the courthouse, the crowd was smaller and more subdued. Government employees, police, and others with any type of access lined the hallways leading to the courtroom. A few reporters mingled in the crowd but Tyler, Marcus, and Molly passed by rapidly, no one bothering them with any questions. In no time, they reached the door to the courtroom.

"You okay?" asked Marcus.

Molly appeared shaken. A little worse than she expected but not much. "Yeah," she replied, nodding nervously. "I'm okay."

"Piece of cake," said Tyler.

Molly looked at him like he was crazy. Tyler caught it, and the three enjoyed a momentary laugh. "Sorry," he replied. "I guess it wasn't."

"Get in there," said Molly, pushing his back.

Marcus pulled open the door. At the sight, Molly took a step back in surprise. The preliminary hearings were in a smaller courtroom that was all plastic and tile. This courtroom looked like ones seen on TV. Everything was a heavily polished, dark wood, cast in a pale yellow light streaming through the two tall windows to her left. The judge's bench sat at the front beneath a seal of the State of Minnesota, and the jury box was to her right. The courtroom's one camera sat above the jury. Allowed by Van Gilder in one of the pretrial hearings, it followed Molly as she entered. The spectator seats were filled, with one hundred of them given to reporters, family members, and friends and the rest assigned by lottery to the public.

The crowd murmured audibly when Molly, Tyler, and Marcus took their seats. Barnes, Whitfield, Farnsworth, Cox, and their phalanx of expensively clad assistants paid no attention. As soon as Molly sat down, she turned to those behind her. Sylvia reached over the rail and touched her hand. Letisha followed, as did Sandra. Tracy and Gus were there, and Jayne McCall sat beside them. Troy sat beside Jayne. Molly was ambivalent about having him at the trial, but both Marcus and Tyler agreed that it might send the jury a better message. She greeted each of them with a handshake. Troy briefly touched her shoulder.

They had barely taken their seats when the bailiff, a middle-aged man with a high voice, approached. "Judge wants you guys in chambers," he whispered to Marcus and Tyler. They nodded and left.

A minute later, Marcus Sanders, Tyler Briggs, Jackson Barnes, and Harley Whitfield stood before Judge John Van Gilder in his small office. The judge, seated behind a great desk, peered at the four as the lawyers respectfully shook hands. The silver-haired Van Gilder, looking relaxed, cleaned his bifocals as he talked. "Gentlemen, I just want to make sure there is nothing left to chance here. Are there any issues you wish to bring up?"

Van Gilder looked squarely at Briggs. Tyler could think of a million things he would like to bring up. ComHealth's arranging of murders and suppressing evidence would be good starters, but he knew that it was no use. He was more interested in his relationship with the judge. There was no point in poisoning it over something he couldn't prove. Tyler merely shook his head.

"How about you, Mr. Barnes?" asked Van Gilder.

"No, your Honor," he replied.

Van Gilder looked bemused. "Mr. Barnes," he began, "I've been doing this for thirty years, and I must admit I've never seen anything quite like this. I would have bet my life savings that you'd seek to delay this trial. I guess I'm glad I didn't make that bet."

Barnes remained formal. "Your Honor, the defense is well prepared to vigorously fight these allegations. We have no interest in a delay, despite what would appear to be problems in public relations."

"Very well." Van Gilder put on his glasses. His voice turned serious. Throughout all of the hearings, he had attempted to force a settlement, but now he gave up. "You're all four good attorneys. I understand the pressures of this case, but this will not be a Simpson-type affair. Is that understood?" They all nodded. "We will at all times conduct ourselves in a manner consistent with the ideals this institution represents. Are we agreed?"

"Yes, your Honor."

"Then let's go."

Five minutes later, the courtroom stood as the bailiff's cry rang out. Judge John Van Gilder walked in. Looking almost regal in his long black robe, the judge showed no reaction as he took his seat. Molly could see the camera turn to face him. He gave a few minutes of opening remarks and then announced that jury selection would begin.

For Molly, the morning was a mix of excitement, fear, and anticipation, but it took little time for the excitement to fade. Just as her attorneys warned, jury selection was laborious and boring. She watched as the first ten potential jurors filed into the jury box. As they took their seats, Molly turned around one more time, hoping vainly her parents would appear. She scanned the room, but did not see them. Until that moment, she held out a quiet hope that somehow they had forgiven her. Obviously, they hadn't.

She started to turn her head back as the potential jurors took their seats. Her eyes crossed back through the courtroom. She stopped when she saw him. He was seated in the front row behind the defense lawyers and gazing intently at her. It was the first time she had ever seen him, but his gaze was unmistakable. It was H. Carter Hutchins.

Molly gulped and turned. She glanced at the first group of ten potential jurors. All were staring at her. Molly could feel herself flush slightly, but before she could react further, Jackson Barnes walked across the courtroom and started talking. Molly sighed as the ComHealth attorney first introduced himself to them and then began his questioning.

Tyler sat in the middle. Molly was nearest the jury. Tyler leaned over to Marcus, who was busy with some notes. "How much do you think they spent on the jury consultants?"

"Probably a mill."

They both chuckled behind their hands. The "jury issue" was a standing joke for them. They knew that Barnes and Whitfield worked closely with a handful of jury consultants who each billed five hundred dollars an hour and supposedly could provide a sketch of the perfect jury for every case. At times they proved useful. At times they were a joke. Tyler's and Marcus's entire jury consulting consisted of their discussion with their junior partners, Michael Barker and Stephon Reed, as well as calling a handful of attorney friends around the country and asking their opinions. It probably cost nearly a million dollars less, and they suspected that they'd ended up with the same conclusion as Barnes and Whitfield. No one knew who to pick in this case.

By the noon recess, things were dragging. From the questioning, it was obvious that Barnes and Whitfield were preoccupied with avoiding anyone with a bias against HMOs, but this appeared to be their only real issue. They were as apparently unsure of race, gender, and age as were Tyler and Marcus. The process labored through the afternoon, and the TV cameras stopped broadcasting live because of the tediousness of the process and the need to keep the jurors confidential. By the end of the day, the jury was in place. They were a mixture of ages, races, religions, and educational backgrounds. With no clear victory for either side, all of the attorneys privately felt that jury selection was a toss.

Judge Van Gilder welcomed them and gave them his opening instructions.

Leaving the courtroom, Tyler stopped to talk with reporters. Molly offered the statement that Tyler instructed her to make, "I'm happy to finally begin this process and look forward to the truth being told." She declined any questions and was whisked away by her friends. Tyler then completed a full press conference while Cox and Farnsworth competed for air time a few feet away. Barnes and Whitfield left without a word. Marcus Sanders also escaped, heading home to practice his opening statement.

When Sylvia's car finally eluded the log jam downtown, they all breathed easier. Molly sat in the middle of the back seat between Troy and Letisha. Sandra and Jayne were in front. All except Molly were a mixture of exhilaration and exhaustion. They chattered continuously about the reporters, lawyers, judge, jury, and the crowd.

Molly leaned her head back and discovered that Troy's arm was behind her on the seat. She was too tired to even think about that. She closed her eyes and listened as the others droned on, still thrilled to have been part of such an event. Molly didn't share their excitement. She thought about Peter, as she had most of the day, wondering if his condition had changed. She wondered what he would have thought. And she thought about how much she wished he were part of it.

Molly nearly fell asleep as they drove away. She realized she had never felt so tired. Her prevailing impulse was to simply crawl into her bed and sleep for a month. But as they drove farther from the courthouse, she knew that was impossible. Tomorrow, the trial started for real. And with it, the fireworks would come.

At midnight, long after the local news ended, Tyler still sat in front of the TV. His second margarita melting in his hand, he gazed toward the set where an old rerun of *Bonanza* was showing. His otherwise empty house was quiet, his wife and children having left for her mother's the day before when the crush of reporters became too much. After he arrived home, he made a macaroni and cheese dinner, talked to his wife, talked to Marcus, and talked to Sylvia, who informed him that there was no change in Peter's condition. He was still in a coma, but his labs were stable and he hadn't required dialysis. Tyler took both as a good sign.

Tyler sipped at his margarita again. He could feel his stomach quiver. The more he ran over the day's events, the higher his anxiety mounted. He decided to talk to Marcus again. Sanders was still working on his opening statement.

"What do you think?" asked Tyler.

Sanders groaned audibly. He was beginning to think Tyler was obsessed. "Same as twenty minutes ago, Ty. I don't know."

Tyler started to pace inside his house. For two weeks, the same nagging thought continued to haunt him. There was nothing in the ComHealth lawyers' behavior that seemed conventional. All logic dictated that they would try to draw the case out as long as possible. Even Judge Van Gilder had been surprised. "Dammit, Marcus, they could have filed a zillion motions, tied this case up for eight years, and broken us. But they didn't."

"They did file a couple."

Briggs recalled the final pretrial hearings from the week before. There hadn't even been skirmishes, let alone wars. "Yes, let me list them. A summary judgment motion, which we knew Van Gilder would deny."

Marcus interrupted him. "Tyler, we've had this conversation at least a thousand times."

Briggs mind continued to run wild. "Even the jurors today. They fought, but they could have fought harder."

Sanders became firm. "Tyler, man, you gotta stop this. All this stuff is over. We've got a trial to do."

Briggs sighed and sipped from his margarita. "I know."

Marcus knew that his partner was castigating himself. Deep down they were both convinced that they had missed something. Despite ComHealth's claims of wanting good public relations to emerge from the trial, it seemed like little more than a lame excuse for getting the trial over as quickly as possible. But what could they have missed? They reviewed everything a million times. There wasn't a hint of anything strange.

"Work on your opening statement," said Briggs. "I'll pace around my house."

"I was working on my opening statement," replied Marcus with emphasis.

Briggs laughed at himself and his descent into paranoia. "And I was already pacing."

"Later."

Tyler hung up the phone and returned to his margarita. He knew he would not sleep at all. Paranoia or not, his mind continued to race. Where was it? What was it? It still didn't come to him. He got up and again started to pace. Somewhere, something was missing. What made him nervous was that for the first time, he began to doubt it was Fragile X.

Chapter Thirty-three

August 26

The second morning of the trial began as a repeat of the first. By mid-morning, most of the entire central city was crawling with people. Even the return of brutal heat and humidity offered no deterrent. People were everywhere, filling the cafes and coffee shops and scrambling to obtain any position that would allow them to see. Signs, banners, and cameras were standard attire. Lack of opinion was nonexistent. Passion was everywhere.

Media Central was in full swing. As advertised, Tom Brokaw and the NBC *Nightly News* had broadcast from Minneapolis the night before, devoting the first eight minutes to the trial, but as the second day started, the coverage was even greater. The *Today Show* and CBS *This Morning* both had live reports. *Good Morning America*, CNN, and MSNBC offered their own segments, while Court TV offered detailed analysis and insights into possible lines of questioning of the witnesses. Local coverage was nonstop.

As before, the ComHealth lawyers arrived first. Emerging from their limousines to a rousing chorus of cheers from the anti-abortion protesters and chants of "Com—Death! Com—Death!" from the university students, they paused only to answer a couple of reporters' questions before hustling into the courthouse. Tyler, Molly, and Marcus arrived next. The cheers overwhelmed the boos, while crumpled paper balls with grotesque pictures flew everywhere.

Once safely inside the packed courtroom, Molly surveyed the scene. Sylvia, Letisha, Sandra, Jayne, Tracy, Gus, and Troy were all in their same spots. Dr. Frissell and Dr. Larter were there. Disappointed, she noticed her parents were not. Molly greeted each of her friends with a smile or a nod and took her seat.

Judge Van Gilder entered quietly and right on time. After a few last-minute preliminaries, the real trial began. Van Gilder took a sip of water, signaled the court reporter, and pointed.

"Mr. Sanders. You may begin."

"Thank you, your Honor."

Marcus Sanders rose and began his opening statement. A deliberate, but skilled speaker, his ebony eyes flashed as he warmed to the task in only a few sentences. He started by defining the concept of insurance, how it was in fact a bond of trust between the insurer and the patient. He talked of how necessary insurance had become in an age of great expense and medical sophistication.

Sanders mentioned several insurance advertising slogans—the "Good Hands People," "The Rock," as well as ComHealth's two familiar jingles, "Our Doctors' Doors are Always Open" and "You're Number One with ComHealthOne." As his voice started to rise, he referred to the case for the first time when he said, "The defendants are the men behind the slogans, the men who have sought to change the world of medical insurance, the men who have exacted great fortunes in the reorganization of health care delivery, the men who have described the work as a 'mission' to save health care from ruin." Marcus paused and took a breath. "I stand before you today to say that we will prove to you that the cost of this 'mission' has been great. That the health-care delivery system we now see evolving bears no resemblance to the one this nation just a few years ago proudly referred to as the finest on earth. In the wake of the HMO revolution, we have seen the destruction of medicine as the HMOs restrict access to specialty care. We have seen the destruction of academic medicine as teaching centers nationwide are forced to close, deemed too costly by the powerful insurers. And we have seen the destruction of the once-mighty research centers, again viewed as too expensive by the HMOs in the new medical world."

Marcus' voice trailed slightly for effect. "But the cost has not just been in buildings and machines. It has been far more. In their quest for profit, the HMOs have wrestled to control every aspect of health care, from the medications patients use to the tests that are ordered. They have done it under the charade of 'cost effectiveness,' when the truth is they have merely pursued the cheap. Their formula for success has been simple: Restrict access to doctors, restrict medications prescribed, and restrict tests ordered while at the same time denying that any of these profit-producing tactics affects quality of care."

Marcus paused as H. Carter Hutchins and Stanton Ross entered and took seats in the front row behind their attorneys. Marcus walked away from the jury and stood in front of the ComHealth lawyers and the executives. Gesturing to the expensively clad crew, he started again. "These men would have you believe the opposite. That they merely shuffled a few papers here, changed a few rules there, and in the process they just happened to make a few hundred million dollars, while making health care affordable and effective for all."

At least half of the jurors and most of the audience laughed loudly causing the late arrivals to blush. The ComHealth lawyers, as expected, bore no discernible expression. If anything, there was a faint hint of condescension and amusement. Van Gilder quieted the room and Marcus continued. "But as I said, the cost has not just been in been in buildings and machines. It has been in human lives. People like you and me. Everyday citizens who have put their trust in their doctors and put their trust in their insurer that the care they receive will be safe and thorough. Everyday people who walk this earth, breathe this air, and carry with them the simple hope that the efforts of their lives will lead to health, prosperity, and a better future for their children. I say to you now, this is who has been affected. You and I. Our parents. Our children."

Marcus moved away from the jury railing. He gazed toward a window and then back at the ComHealth lawyers. His voice rose. "In this case, we will prove that this defendant has ruthlessly and recklessly acted in pursuit of only one thing—money. We will show you how ComHealth created loopholes in their contracts that allowed them to deny and cancel coverage at will. We will show how ComHealth forced doctors to choose between good medicine and cheap medicine. And we will show how ComHealth has consistently acted in bad faith, portraying itself as a kind, benevolent figure, while in truth acting exclusively in its own financial interests."

Marcus coughed once. It was a nervous gesture he had had since law school. It helped him think. "And remember that in the world of medicine, the axiom of Hippocrates is first, do no harm. Ladies and gentlemen, there has been harm to Molly Loomis and there will continue to be harm to others unless ComHealth is held accountable."

Marcus cleared his throat one more time. He wanted to keep his opening statement short so as not to lose the jury, but he still had one more thought. "The harm has been widespread. To patients young and old. To families, friends, and neighbors. We can now safely say that it has been our fate to watch the once-noble field of medicine reduced to broken promises and misleading advertising. Medicine, once the one institution we could trust, I'm ashamed to say, is now captive to the hucksters and the scam artists."

When he looked at Barnes and Whitfield, they remained expressionless, but for the first time a trace of fire could be seen in their eyes. "But let it be the result of this trial that the higher purpose to which these executives profess will actually be a higher level of accountability to which they will be held."

Marcus concluded with a handful of less inflammatory remarks and took his seat. Molly turned to him, but Marcus looked away. Instead of greeting her, he was eyeballing Hutchins' crimson face. By the time Marcus turned back, Jackson Barnes was starting to rise.

"Mr. Barnes," Van Gilder commanded.

"Thank you, Your Honor."

Jackson Barnes looked magnificent. The epitome of sartorial perfection, he was dressed like a mannequin out of a Fifth Avenue men's store. His suit was dark gray with a lighter gray pinstripe, and his polished leather shoes glimmered in the light. His hair was immaculately styled and the expression on his handsome face seemed both serene and thoughtful. He looked every bit the part of the prosperous senior attorney.

Barnes began by removing his wire-rimmed glasses and putting them in his breast pocket as he approached the jury. "You know, I've known Mr. Sanders for several years. I've always considered him an outstanding lawyer and an even better storyteller. But today, I think he has surpassed himself. Never in my thirty-plus years in law have I ever seen the equivalent of what we just heard." Barnes stopped and looked at Marcus. "A wonderful story. A fairy tale better than anything Hans Christian Andersen could write. It's just too bad it isn't true."

With that introduction, Jackson Barnes began a long-winded, but highly effective, defense. Also for the first time, the ComHealth lawyers began to behave as Marcus and Tyler had expected. Barnes completely ignored the accusations about HMO impropriety and instead focused on Molly. "We will show that this is a young woman who has lied consistently. Lied to her husband, lied to us all. This is a young woman who after choosing an abortion for her unborn child and lying about the reason seeks to destroy not only the reputation of one of America's most respected and innovative health maintenance organizations, but to *profit* from her errors." Barnes shook his head like a disappointed father and muttered something that sounded like incredible. The jurors looked attentive.

Barnes continued to criticize Molly and in doing so finally seemed to be revealing a strategy. He blasted Molly with all barrels. "There is no legal support for her claim. We will prove that Mrs. Loomis wantonly pursued an unauthorized procedure, an abortion, terminating a pregnancy she did not want. And when she experienced a complication, she expected her insurer to pay." Barnes looked at the jury disbelievingly. "Ladies and gentlemen, the moral equivalent of this would be if a homeowner were to burn down his own house and sue the fire department for not coming quick enough. Neither you nor I could, or should, get away with such a thing."

A couple of jurors seemed impressed by the analogy. Molly flushed. She could feel her cheeks turn warm and her palms start to sweat. The way that Jackson Barnes phrased his statement, she almost started to feel guilty. She glanced at the jurors and they too seemed to be leering at her. She looked up at the camera and saw the lens bear down on her face. Suddenly, she wished there was a hole she could crawl into and hide from the whole circus.

"But then," boomed Barnes, "not only *sue* the fire department, but also libel them, and slander them, all in an effort to save face over a bad personal choice."

Molly could feel her throat tighten. Jackson Barnes stood right over her, looking down upon her like God about to cast a sinner into the fires. "But, members of the jury, even that is not enough for her. No, she also seeks to destroy the reputations of many fine men. Men who have dedicated their lives to the pursuit of finding a solution to the crisis in health-care costs. Men who are innovators and visionaries. Men who instead of being placed on trial should be properly regarded as national treasures, saviors of a health-care system run amuck with inflation and waste." Barnes shook his head disapprovingly, still glaring at Molly, his eyes threatening her with a trip to perdition. "But no. For her there is nothing of importance other than saving face. She will stop at nothing to do it, destroying anyone or anything in her way."

Molly felt as if her neck was about 110 degrees. She was perspiring noticeably, and she could feel herself chewing on her lip involuntarily. The camera continued to alternate between her and Barnes, but at every pause, the lens seemed to go right up to her nose.

Suddenly Tyler turned to her and whispered in her ear. "You know, I forgot to tell you, my wife wants to have you over for a barbecue next weekend. Would you prefer burgers or steaks?"

Molly blinked. She turned and looked at him incredulously. Tyler was as cool as a January breeze and the message in his eyes was clear. "Relax," they said to her. "There's going to be a lot of this bullshit."

"B-Burgers," she managed weakly.

"Burgers it is."

At that point, Barnes became philosophical, equating H. Carter Hutchins to business sainthood and a combination of Hippocrates and Henry Ford. Tyler and Marcus both thought he was overplaying it a bit, but the jury seemed interested. He spoke for nearly a half hour more, ending with what sounded like a platitude-filled commercial for ComHealth. When he finished, the jurors looked impressed, and even Tyler had to admit that Barnes had been effective.

Jackson Barnes returned to his seat, and Judge Van Gilder looked at his watch. "Mr. Briggs. It is 11:45. Will your first witness take longer than fifteen minutes?"

Tyler stood. "Yes, Your Honor. I expect so."

"Very well. This court stands in recess until 1:30."

The gavel sounded. The morning session was over.

Gregory Markham watched the trial from his office. Court TV had carried it live, and he had watched in embarrassment as Jackson Barnes portrayed the ComHealth executives as shining crusaders. He knew it all sounded good to a jury, but was far from the truth. As the noon hour passed and the commentators reflected on the opening arguments, it was clear that many observers wouldn't buy it either. They were uniform in their praise of Barnes as a speaker, but dubious of every one of his claims. Markham felt himself sweat as he listened to the criticism. More than ever before, he was sure they would regret trying the case so fast.

The phone rang, and Markham picked it up. His secretary informed him that another caller identifying himself as a reporter, this time from the *Miami Herald*, had called and wanted to ask him about Fragile X.

"You know I'm not taking any calls from reporters," he growled.

"I know," she replied. "But you wanted me to let you know if they called."

"Yes, of course."

Markham hung up the phone. He felt like a great noose had been tied around his neck and was now gradually beginning to choke him. He could barely sleep any longer, even with sleeping pills. Food had lost its taste, and he had lost ten pounds in the last two weeks alone. The circles under his eyes were so dark that it looked like eye shadow. Even his mouth seemed to have a funny taste. He knew he was beyond exhaustion.

This call was the sixth reporter to ask about Fragile X. He had informed Barnes, Whitfield, and Hutchins that reporters were calling, but they had advised no reply or action. Their guess was that there was a good chance it was all a bluff, but Markham was not so sure. It seemed only logical that O'Reilly would keep copies and, if so, the most logical place to send them would be a news organization. More than ever, Markham had become convinced that O'Reilly had an "in case of death" plan. That thought alone was enough to nearly send him over the edge.

"There's no point in being proactive," Hutchins had reassured him. "They have nothing. It will pass."

"But what about this Reggie Tan?" he had asked.

"If that little chink had anything, he would already have turned it over. No way he has anything. We went through those Doyne files with a fine-tooth comb."

Hutchins' words had been slightly soothing. What he said was true. It was indeed unlikely that anything about Fragile X could be tracked through the

Doyne computers as Reggie claimed. It would require both cracking the code and obtaining the data before it was erased. It was doubtful Reggie had it, or Briggs and Sanders would somehow have tried to introduce it in court.

"Look," Barnes and Whitfield had said, "as it stands now, Molly Loomis will have to get up in front of the jury and explain that some doctor, probably in a trenchcoat and out of the blue, called her and told her to have an abortion, based on a nonexistent test and a disease that she incorrectly described. The only way to avoid that wonderful scenario would be if they had some evidence that suggested it was true. If they had the evidence, they would have had to introduce it before the evidentiary hearing. Because they didn't, it means Reggie is bluffing. Pure and simple. And Molly Loomis is going to look like a fool."

Markham had been glad for the reassurance, but he was only partially relieved. He was well aware that winning the trial was not the only issue. Fragile X could haunt them forever unless it was stopped, and the reporters were not likely to just drop the story. They needed a permanent solution.

The phone rang. It was Stanton Ross, his fellow executive. "See the trial?"

"Yes," grumbled Markham as he rummaged through some papers.

"Barnes was great, wasn't he?"

"There's a long way to go, Stan. I wish we were trying this case about thirty years from now."

"They're going to make the girl look like an idiot."

Markham stood up straight and stared out through the window. He could feel his ire rise. Sometimes he was convinced he was the only one of the executives who could see past his nose. He was sure Ross never saw past his eyelashes. "Stanton, there are eight thousand people downtown who think we like to barbecue patients for our Saturday night feasts—and there are millions around the country who are going to find out we've made millions of dollars while grandpa couldn't get a blood test for his prostate that would have saved his life. Jack Barnes may have a twenty-four carat tongue, but Briggs and Sanders are not exactly idiotic stutterers. We're gonna take some hits."

Ross became quiet. He did not appreciate being lectured by anyone except Hutchins. "Gregory—" he began evenly.

Markham started regretting his remarks as soon as they leaped off his tongue. "I'm sorry, Stan," he interrupted. "I don't mean to tell you what you already know. I realize you're doing as I am, looking out for the company."

Ross immediately backed away from his planned retort. "You've been under a lot of stress. I know how heavily Carter counts on you. We all do."

"Tough times for all."

"Yes, it is." Ross paused, and in the background Markham could hear someone enter the office. "I called to tell you," Ross began again. "The new PR campaign will begin tonight. The first set of ads will air on KSTP and WCCO between eight and ten and during the news."

Markham recalled the ads. He had seen them at their screening the week before. They were beautifully done and, in the face of the trial, terribly cynical. Scenes of young parents with their newborns. Healthy-looking senior citizens dancing and picnicking, while a soothing baritone voice talked of low premiums, low co-pays, quality care, and specialist access. The campaign had cost over two million dollars to produce and was little more than exactly what Ross called it. Public relations. "You think it's a good idea to show them now?" asked Markham. "You heard what Sanders said in his opening. Those guys could have a field day with this."

"Both marketing and Hutchins say go ahead. Full offensive. TV, radio and all."

Markham groaned. "Thanks for reminding me. I'm on tomorrow."

"That's right. You have the radio show at ten. Then you fly to Fargo to tape that talk show."

Markham sighed. This part of the plan was his own. There was little doubt that public relations were important, and television and radio were better ideas than print. The newspapers would always editorialize, whereas electronic media allowed the speaker better control. They largely quit talking to the papers except in scripted press releases. TV and radio would be their offensive. "I'll get that ready tonight."

"Good."

Markham hung up and turned the TV back on. The camera showed the courtroom and was focused on Van Gilder's empty bench. The afternoon session was apparently about to begin. The phone rang again. It was his secretary.

"I have the Assistant D.A., a Wesley Christensen, on the phone."

Markham's throat tightened. "What?"

"I have the Assistant District Attorney, a Wesley Christensen, on the phone."

Markham panicked. He tried to think. Why would someone from the D.A.'s office call him? Fragile X? O'Reilly? It had to be. But how? Markham gritted his teeth. It was so obvious. The perennial pain in the ass, Reggie Tan.

"Should I put him through?"

Markham was tempted to have her put him off, but decided against it. He was sure it would be better to deal with attorneys or police up front. "Yeah, put him through."

Wesley Christensen had a deep, raspy voice that sounded much like a long-term smoker's. "Mr. Markham?"

"Yes, sir," he replied pleasantly. "What can I do for you?"

"Well, sir," the Assistant D.A. began, "I received your letter today, and I must say I was quite surprised. I thought I better check it out with you."

"What?" asked Markham, sitting down fast.

"Your letter, the one you sent to me."

Markham stammered "I-I, never sent you a letter."

For a second there was silence. Then Christensen's raspy voice returned. "That's sure strange," he said. "It's on ComHealth's stationery and it looks like your signature."

Markham was beside himself. "How do you know what my signature looks like?" he asked, his voice clearly strained.

"That ad in the paper. That one where you say 'Our Doctors' Doors Are Always Open.' You and several others have signed it at the bottom."

Markham exhaled, slightly relieved. What the Assistant D.A. said was true. "I can assure you that any letter is a forgery." In the background, he could hear a door shut.

Christensen did not sound impressed. "Boy, oh boy, Mr. Markham. Sure is a damn good one. Must admit that. Your signature. Your letterhead. Someone really took an interest in it. Even seems to know a lot about you."

"What does it say?"

"Well, I gotta admit, that's the most interesting part. Says you'd like to seek immunity from prosecution. That you have information regarding the murder of Dr. James Patrick O'Reilly as well as several other scientists. Also says that you have proof that ComHealthOne has engaged in illegal acts, deceiving pregnant women into having abortions based on the discovery of Dr. O'Reilly. It states that you were not criminally responsible, but that you have intimate knowledge of the acts as well as proof consisting of several computer disks and a journal, that you have stored in a safety deposit box. It also states that the entire episode was referred to within ComHealth by the code name Fragile X."

All of the blood seemed to drain from Markham's brain, and he felt like he was about to fall to the floor. He struggled to say anything. "That's n-not true," he garbled.

Christensen sounded skeptical. "It's a little strange, Mr. Markham. Oddest practical joke I've ever seen. People usually play them in April, not in August."

Markham coughed, his heart rate blazing past one-twenty.

"Don't mind me asking, but you sure there's nothing to it?"

"Positive."

There was a long pause. In the silence, Markham could hear the Assistant D.A. taking a drag from his cigarette. "Well, now, I know a respectable man like yourself would never have anything to hide, so I'll just assume my other caller was having a little fun too."

"Who was that?"

Christensen took another drag. "Reporter by the name of Edward Kerr from the *Houston Chronicle*. He wanted to know if we had started investigating you and your link to Fragile X."

Markham's heart felt as if it was going to leap out of his chest. His throat was so dry it hurt. His reply sounded ridiculously insincere. "I think some kid is just having himself a good time with the computer."

Christensen laughed twice before speaking. "Maybe so. Maybe so."

"I appreciate your call though," Markham offered, desperate to get off the phone.

"I'll be in touch. And by the way, if something happened to pop into your mind, well, how can I best say this? We can certainly continue this discussion."

Markham didn't answer. He hung up. His clothes were soaked, and his head felt like it was in a vice. His eyes were blurring, but he managed to see the TV. It showed Tyler Briggs walking toward a witness. Gregory Markham ignored it. He walked to the bar and poured himself a straight gin.

Marcia Sullivan and Reggie Tan watched Briggs question the first witness, a psychologist whose entire role was merely to establish that Molly Loomis wasn't crazy. Sitting next to each other in Marcia's cubicle at the main office of the Minneapolis *Star Tribune*, they stared at the screen, one of several dozen TVs scattered throughout the newsroom. Marcia twirled a pencil in her right hand and continued to glance at the names written on the notebook paper on her desk while the uneventful testimony proceeded. She turned her head and shook it in disbelief. "I can't believe you threatened Markham's daughter!"

Reggie was repentant. "I know. That was bad. But being near the guy, it just, like, pissed me off."

"I'm glad you were kidding. I'm not much into murder."

Reggie nodded. He had no interest in hurting anyone either. He knew his real satisfaction would come from seeing Markham, Hutchins, and the rest of the ComHealth crooks in eight-by-ten cells.

Marcia shoved a new list of names in front of Reggie. "What do you think of 'em?"

"It's unbelievable."

"I know. Right after this, I'm going to meet with the families. These doctors are calling me left and right."

Reggie sat back and listened as the psychiatrist continued to talk about how Molly Loomis was perfectly sane. Reggie's mind was still on the letter he had sent requesting immunity for Markham. A different thought occurred to him. "Look, by now that Assistant D.A. is going to have figured out that the letter isn't real. But he'll also have gotten the call from Houston, and he's going to be wondering what the hell is happening."

"He'll have also heard the rumors about Fragile X, O'Reilly, and their connection to Molly. I mean, off the record everyone is talking about it."

"Yes," admitted Reggie. "The D.A. will be interested, but you know and I know that there is no proof right now. It won't take him long to establish that."

Marcia sighed. She knew that realistically their bluffs could be called easily and with it any chance of getting Markham to confess. "This had better work," she said sadly.

"If we only had one more punch to throw at him."

"The disks, the journal. Anything," Marcia agreed.

Reggie stood up and walked around. The problem nagged him for a week. He hoped against hope that a copy of the journal or the disks would appear in the mail, a posthumous gift from O'Reilly, but none appeared. If copies existed, Reggie didn't know where they were. "That Protein B1B remark I made really threw the guy for a loop. He could barely talk when I met him at the bar."

"If we only had something more like that. If a reporter called him with say, more detailed knowledge of it."

Reggie stopped in his tracks. His jaw dropped. "Other publications!"

Marcia Sullivan stood up as the gravity of her own words struck her. "I can't believe I didn't think of it before. There has to be something else on Protein B1B."

"I'm a complete moron," gasped Reggie. "I should have thought of it the minute Julianne said it."

Marcia turned on her computer, and within a minute had the list of James Patrick O'Reilly's prior publications. Reggie crowded into the computer screen. It took them a moment to scan his previous articles, but nothing showed anything resembling the protein.

"Nothing there," said Reggie. "Try the other guys."

Marcia obediently drew up the bibliographies of the other scientists that they had largely forgotten about. The process took only ten minutes, but when they had finished they were no better off than before. Their heart rates returned to normal. It was another dead-end. "Nothing," Reggie grunted.

"It's gotta be someplace," said Marcia.

Although they were disappointed, neither one was discouraged. They were both on the same track. Reggie spoke. "If they found it in humans, they almost undoubtedly found it in animal models first."

"That's true," said Marcia.

"Let's scan the web," said Reggie gleefully. "It's in there someplace. Protein B1B didn't drop out of the sky."

Marcia's eyes twinkled. She handed the keyboard to Reggie. "You're better at it than me. Go ahead."

"At your command."

Marcia turned away from him and picked up the phone. "While you work I'm going to make some phone calls. I've got to get ready to meet this next set of patients."

"Do it."

Marcia was giddy. "And after that I'll try out my favorite new hobby again."

Reggie was already diving into the Web. "What's that?"

Marcia laughed. "Just throwing a few little bombs ComHealth's way.

By 9:00 P.M. Marcia Sullivan met the families of three new patients. The stories left her numb. The first was a grandfather who died of a ruptured aorta when his abdominal pain failed to meet criteria for testing. The second was a thirty-year-old man who died of a ruptured blood vessel malformation when his headaches failed to conform to a testing protocol. And the third was a twenty-four-year-old pregnant woman who died with her child when her placental–uterine separation was written off as "normal bleeding" by the ComHealth 800 line.

Marcia cried as she wrote the articles. Three more people, she thought. Three more victims. Three more sacrifices for cost efficiency. Her grief was real, but as she wrote, she realized that she never felt so good about her choice of profession and never was so eager to have her words read. She only hoped that with each story, her words, like their lives, would come to stand for something.

Chapter Thirty-four

By midnight, Reggie Tan was discouraged. Six hours of searching the Internet for any sign of Protein B1B had been useless. There was simply no trace of anything resembling O'Reilly's work. It was another dead-end. Sitting in the darkness of his bedroom, he slapped off his computer and leaned far back in his chair, covering his face with his hands. He was frustrated beyond imagination.

"Shit, shit, shit," he grumbled. "How can that be?"

The phone rang and Reggie answered it. "Give me something good." he sighed, knowing it would be Marcia.

"I can't," she replied. "But I got the articles done."

"That's better than me. All I got done was to send the next letter to the Assistant D.A."

"There's a start. But what about the protein?" she answered.

Reggie sighed again. "Nothing. I can't believe it."

Marcia was prepared for the answer. The thought had seemed too easy. "It just means that it was purely a human discovery."

"Yeah," he agreed. "Must be."

The background noise from the *Star Tribune* offices was stifling, but Marcia did not seem to miss a beat. She talked to Reggie well past noon, the new partners needing to catch up. "You see the last part of the trial?"

"It was just legal wrangling, wasn't it?"

"Yep."

"Who's tomorrow?"

"Someone from claims and that old ComHealth executive. The one Hutchins fired."

Reggie pulled out the newspaper. He remembered now. An executive fired ten months ago who had been an integral part in building the ComHealthOne giant. "This guy is Molly's best chance, isn't he?"

"This is the guy. What he says could be explosive."

Reggie left it. Both he and Marcia vowed they would concentrate little energy on the trial. They knew that there was nothing they could do to influence it unless they found O'Reilly's records, and all their efforts now focused on that thought.

Reggie opened another can of Coke and let the sting of the carbonic acid against his throat give him a jump start. "Let me ask you this," he started. "If you were O'Reilly, what would you have done?"

"Made copies," Marcia said sarcastically.

"Agreed, but what else?"

Marcia did not reply right away. It was a question she had already considered but one for which she did not have a perfect answer. "I think you either send them or store them or both."

Reggie agreed. "Yes. Now let's assume he sent them. Who would he send them to?"

"Newspapers, police, attorney general's office."

"Right."

"But he hasn't."

"Not that we know of."

Marcia was thoughtful. "We know he made copies. It only makes sense. That leads us to another conclusion. He stored them."

"Probably."

Marcia started jotting down notes again. Most of it was idle doodling. Her mind was largely blank. "But after that, I don't know," she grumbled.

Reggie gulped down the rest of his Coke, turned on one light, and tossed the can in the wastebasket. As it landed, it splashed a drop on a used manila envelope. The sight shocked him. It seemed so obvious. "Dammit!"

The verbal blast nearly deafened her. "What?" she asked, holding the phone away.

"O'Reilly arrived at the mall with a manila envelope. Three hours later, that envelope is opened and it doesn't contain the right stuff. That same day, a similar envelope arrives at Julianne's. It contains the disks and the journal, *the originals*. So we know that at the very least he was playing with the stuff and planning some fancy switcheroos."

Marcia continued to doodle. She was worn out and trying not to yawn. "I don't see what you're saying."

"Don't you get it? We've been assuming that O'Reilly came to the mall with nothing but fakes. But what if he was carrying more than one envelope when he arrived at the mall."

Marcia was tired but the idea jarred her back to life. "The mall! The lockers!"

"Yes."

She sat up straight. "O'Reilly gets cautious or senses that something is wrong. He stores the copies in a locker and carries only the fakes. In the meantime, he's already sent the real stuff to Julianne. He's covered himself."

Reggie was twitching with excitement. "It's perfect. I should have thought of it earlier."

"Me too," Marcia grumbled. "We're always one step too slow!"

Reggie was still rolling. "If I'm right, they only clean out those lockers once a month. So in about three weeks, the locker gets opened and whatever is in there goes into a lost and found."

"Yes."

"Unless it is something addressed and ready to be mailed."

"Yes." Marcia was still mad at herself. "He could've left the stuff sitting right there. Why didn't we think of it earlier?"

"Forget it. We thought of it now." Reggie started up the computer and headed for the Web. "I'll get us a map of the mall. We gotta check every locker."

"I wonder how many there are?"

"Probably hundreds, but I'll bet he thought of that too," said Reggie.

"You think he'll leave us a clue?"

"I sure as hell hope so."

August 27

The third morning of the trial began with a near riot. Marcia Sullivan's newest article on the death of Vernon Hanson, the sixty-four-year-old grandfather who died from the aortic aneurysm, was like adding rocket fuel to an already blazing fire. All the remaining smoldering pockets of the city seemed to explode as it became clear that the deaths of Lisa Bowman, Rudy Jalowicz, and Zach Lawton were not the isolated incidents the ComHealth lawyers implied. Suddenly, it was more names, more faces, and more grieving families. For the city, it was the last straw.

As a loud and boisterous crowd of several thousand gathered downtown, the local and national networks began broadcasting Marcia's newest story. Within an hour, the picture of the man who died because his abdominal pain had not met any ComHealth protocol for testing was everywhere. The crowd went wild as the reports were shown on the large TVs placed by the networks near their booths. Several fights broke out, and one car was tipped over before police reinforcements arrived and slowed the escalating anger.

But while the crowd and the city sizzled, ComHealth's troubles worsened. For the first time, Marcia Sullivan and the doctors were no longer the only source of news. Other anonymous tips from the Minneapolis–St. Paul area led CNN to identifying two other ComHealth-induced tragedies, and the network wasted little time in picking them up. First, CNN reported the death of Dylan Brustad, a five-year-old boy who fell off his bicycle one week before, bumping his head. Taken to an emergency room, he was discharged without workup, in accordance with ComHealth protocol. Since the boy was awake in the ER, according to the ComHealth algorithm, no CAT of the brain was indicated. But a slowly bleeding vein resulted in a subdural hematoma, a blood clot between skull and brain. The boy died later that night from a problem that would have been detected by the CAT scan and corrected with surgery. In years past, CNN reported, when doctors were allowed to act exclusively on clinical judgment, the problem would have been detected. But now, with doctors hamstrung by the HMO's rules, the boy died in his sleep while the million-dollar machine and his paralyzed doctors sat idle.

CNN's second case was that of Marion Whalley, a fifty-six-year-old widow. Working in the yard, she had developed severe back pain. Able to call 911 but unable to move further, she had been taken to the ER. With back pain as her only symptom and meeting no ComHealth criteria for workup, she was discharged. Taken home by the paramedics, she watched as her legs quit working during the night. Her paralysis complete by the morning, she was again taken to the hospital and finally admitted. Paralyzed from the waist down, she, too, was the victim of undertesting. An infection from a cut on the hand had spread to her spine, damaging her spinal cord and resulting in a permanent paralysis. An MRI scan would have found it. Surgery could have corrected it. But once again, the restrictive HMO algorithm dictated care, in essence handcuffing the doctors. With back pain so common, Marion Whalley became paralyzed because it was "cost-inefficient" to aggressively test.

Outside the courthouse, the growing crowd's reaction to each of these new cases was severe. Windows were broken in the IDS Tower, a car was overturned, and several fights led to arrests. By nine-thirty, the governor unleashed the National Guard, and within an hour nearly four hundred camouflaged and armed guardsman arrived to augment the already large police force. Shortly, the downtown situation was under control, but the passion that now flowed in the city had not ebbed. The downtown crowd of eight thousand, even restrained by police, created the atmosphere of a simmering volcano.

Despite some mild police efforts to curb the size of the crowd, protesters continued to arrive. They were now coming from everywhere. The two law students who had been the most vocal ComHealth opponents were now inundated with other student volunteers wanting to help. From the nearby universities, medical students, graduate students, and undergrads arrived to volunteer their time, as did nearly one hundred other law students. The growing army's first project was to print and distribute pictures of the newest victim.

In the midst of the growing peril, the participants arrived to the roars and boos of the primed, boisterous crowd. Barnes and Whitfield hurried in, guarded by a squadron of police. They held briefcases in front of their faces and appeared to be running for their lives. Even Farnsworth and Cox, who usually stopped to visit with reporters for as long as possible, wasted no time in getting inside. They, too, seemed to be trying to hide. Tyler, Marcus, and Molly arrived last and scurried through the crowd. The anti-abrotion protesters jeered wildly at Molly, but the National Guardsman kept them at bay and none of the paper balls got near her.

Inside the courtroom all was quiet, but Judge Van Gilder was in no mood for small talk. He was surly and perturbed. He spent only a moment in the court before retreating to his chambers with the lawyers. Once there, the judge laid down the law.

"Gentleman," he started as he cleaned his glasses, "this situation is bordering on getting out of hand. We've had six arrests this morning and about $30,000 dollars in damage to the IDS building."

Barnes interrupted. "Your Honor, I believe we should order the downtown cleared and the protests completely shut down. It's these violent, radical students, probably half of them drug-addicted, who are causing the problem. They're making it unsafe for everyone."

Tyler started to respond, but by the look on Van Gilder's face, he knew it wasn't necessary. The old judge's expression was one of a parent whose child had just suggested a Hershey bar instead of vegetables as part of dinner. "I'll take it under advisement, Jack. But the last time I checked, free speech was still part of the Constitution. Might be a little tough to explain why I decided against it."

Barnes tried to reply, but Van Gilder just glared at him and cut him off.

"Gentlemen, I'm ordering the jury sequestered. They'll stay at a downtown hotel yet to be determined. Any objections?"

"None, your Honor," offered a relieved Harley Whitfield.

"I'm not sure it's necessary," disagreed Tyler, thinking of how nice it would be to have the jury go home each night and read the newspaper and watch the TV.

Van Gilder turned on his evil glare again. "No, Your Honor," Tyler said, correcting himself. "No objection."

Van Gilder stood up, his towering frame dwarfing the lawyers. "Any other issues?" his commanding manner did not invite questions. No one stepped forward, and Van Gilder motioned them out. "Then let's go."

With the cameras rolling and most of the crowd outside watching on TV, Patrice M. Fallon took the stand. Tall with regally graying hair and a sinister sneer, she had been the head of claims for ComHealth for three years, after a decade in the same position for Blue Cross/Blue Shield. In the preceding weeks, she tried every maneuver possible to avoid testifying, and only after a conversation with her attorney regarding the penalty for refusing a subpoena did she relent. She was fiercely loyal to Hutchins, viewing him as a savior of modern medicine, and refused to answer most questions when she met earlier with Tyler and Marcus. Both Briggs and Sanders viewed this hostile witness as a necessary risk.

With the jury seated to Fallon's left, Briggs approached the steely-eyed woman dressed in an expensive black suit. Her eyes could not deceive; her contempt for Tyler was obvious to anyone in the packed courtroom. "Ms. Fallon," Briggs began, "how long have you been employed at ComHealthOne?"

"Three years."

"And during that time what has been your position?"

"Director of the Claims Department."

Briggs sought to warm up by leading her through a series of relatively innocuous questions merely to establish her position with the jury. Patrice Fallon answered them all evenly and succinctly, never once elaborating. When Briggs finished, he turned to the issue at hand. "Ms. Fallon, I'd like to ask you about your company's policy regarding processing of claims." Tyler held aloft a large volume that had already been established as evidence, ComHealth's official manual regarding claims.

"Certainly," she replied.

"Ms. Fallon, can you explain to me, in the ComHealth system, precisely how a claim is processed?"

"All care is preauthorized. It's not like traditional insurance."

"What exactly does that mean, 'preauthorized'?"

"Before a patient visits a doctor, he calls ComHealth. A screening nurse is responsible for evaluating the urgency of the situation. If she feels it is urgent, the patient is sent to an emergency room. If not, the patient is directed either to an urgent care center, to his own doctor's office, or nowhere if there is not believed to be a problem."

"So a nurse, over the telephone, without knowing or examining the patient, makes a decision as to if, when, and where the patient will be seen."

Patrice Fallon flushed. "Our policy dictates that our nurses have a very low threshold for referral to a physician."

"I'm relieved to hear that," Briggs offered, with only a hint of sarcasm. "And what if that 'preauthorizing' call is not made? Let's say the situation is urgent, a woman goes into labor, a man starts having chest pain, a child strikes his head and is unconscious. What then?"

"They are dealt with on a case-by-case basis."

"In other words, the coverage may very well be denied unless this call is made."

"We do not make a policy of denying claims merely because no call is made. It is simply a means of having some control over patient utilization."

Tyler paused. He wanted the jury to think about what she was saying. "So in other words, Ms. Fallon, in order to receive care and have the claim accepted in the ComHealth system, a patient must first call someone, a mysterious voice at the end of an 800 number, then accurately communicate his symptoms so as to sufficiently alarm the 800 number voice, and then depend upon the judgment and willingness of the person behind the 800 number to spend ComHealth's money and send the caller to the ER."

Patrice Fallon seethed through her teeth. "I wouldn't phrase it that way,"

"But it's true, isn't it? If this call isn't made, ComHealth has a builtin loophole to deny any claim, saying the service wasn't 'preauthorized.'"

"It's not intended to be a 'loophole,' as you call it. It's just access control."

"Access control? What in the world is that?" Many in the audience laughed out loud. A couple members of the jury snickered. Tyler looked incredulous. "Isn't it just a fancy phrase that means 'keep the patients away from the doctors'?"

Tyler remained expressionless. He moved in when a blushing Patrice Fallon did not reply. "I'm just curious, Ms. Fallon. What if an old man started having lower chest pain and got scared and called an ambulance. He is taken to the ER and much to his relief it is just a badly upset stomach. ComHealth would deny the claim, would they not, because he had not gotten preauthorization?"

Jackson Barnes flew to his feet. "Objection. Irrelevant, assumes facts not in evidence and calls for speculation from the witness."

The courtroom stirred, and Tyler continued without allowing Van Gilder to rule. "But even worse, say the man was having a heart attack and ended up in the ICU with a cardiac catheterization and a bypass. ComHealth would still deny the claim would they not? No preauthorization."

"Objection! Objection!"

Van Gilder sat up straight. "Sustained. Mr. Briggs, control yourself."

"I'm sorry, Your Honor." Tyler looked unperturbed. He paused and let things settle before moving even closer to Patrice Fallon. The old spinster who had ruthlessly denied hundreds of claims during her time with ComHealth now for the first time began to perspire. Briggs had her on edge. Her eyebrow twitched. Her mouth seemed to wiggle. She was not used to anyone challenging her like Tyler Briggs was, and she was not enjoying it. Briggs leaned toward her and then spoke softly, audible only to those in the front of the courtroom. "Tell the truth, Ms. Fallon, you'd deny it wouldn't you?"

Harley Whitfield leaped to his feet and roared as if a monumental indignity had been laid upon him. "Objection, your Honor!"

Van Gilder was less theatrical but equally succinct. "Sustained. Mr. Briggs, do not test my patience."

Tyler moved away from the bench. He allowed the jury to see his face, the slightest hint of frustration etched in his brow. It was intended to appear as if only a legal technicality was preventing him from exposing the truth. In fact, he knew a small point had been made. "Ms. Fallon, let me take you in a slightly different direction." He paused and walked around as if gathering his thoughts. "If a claim is denied, how does one appeal? Can you explain the appeal process?"

Patrice Fallon appeared to be relieved by the easy question. "The client may appeal by writing to the appeal committee requesting an appeal."

"And who serves on the appeal committee?"

"There are nine members."

Tyler waved his hand, gesturing. "And who might they be? Doctors? Nurses?"

Patrice Fallon flushed again. "There is one doctor and a nurse. The rest are not."

Tyler feigned surprise. "So do I have this right? Seven of the nine people reviewing medical claims, health care, life-and-death issues that we all face, have *no* medical education?"

Patrice Fallon's face was auburn. Her fists were clenched. "They are very experienced people."

Briggs turned to the jury. "Oh, I'm sure that's correct. I'll bet they've had millions of appeals to process."

The audience broke into loud laughter, and a few hoots came from the back rows. Several jury members smirked. Both Barnes and Whitfield were on their feet.

"Objection, Your Honor," they said in voices close enough to be clones.

"Order in the court," shouted Van Gilder. The judge was more amused than perturbed, but his practiced expression fooled all but those who knew him well. "Mr. Briggs, you will refrain from commentary and confine yourself to questioning the witness."

Briggs replied as if Van Gilder had just praised him. "Thank you, Your Honor. And now Ms. Fallon, who is the head of this committee?"

"I am," she replied.

"The ninth vote. The deciding vote."

"Yes."

"And do you have any medical training? Medical school. Nursing school?"

"No."

"You have a college degree?"

"Yes."

And what is your degree in?"

"A B.S. in business from the University of Illinois."

Tyler cocked his head. "And yet without any shred of medical training you are the one who has the deciding vote as to whether the care a person received was appropriate or not and whether the claim is accepted or not?"

"I have been doing this type of job for thirteen years," she replied, her resolve weakening slightly. "Our clients' interests have always been our greatest concern."

Tyler looked puzzled. "You call them clients. I thought they were patients."

"Th-they are patients," Patrice Fallon stammered, correcting herself.

Tyler walked toward the camera at the front of the courtroom, but he did not look at it. "That's what I thought you meant. Ms. Fallon, if a claim is denied and then denied again by the appeals committee, is there any other means of appeal?"

"No."

Tyler nodded. "So you are the final authority."

"Yes. In that regard."

Tyler picked up a three-ring binder and waved it toward the jury. Introduced during the evidentiary hearing, it contained the statistics regarding ComHealth's denials of claims. "Ms. Fallon, do you recall what percentage of claims overall are denied by ComHealth?"

"It's about fifteen percent."

"Does that strike you as high compared to industry standards?"

"Objection," said Barnes. "Irrelevant, calls for speculation."

"Sustained. Rephrase it Mr. Briggs."

"Ms. Fallon, when you worked for Blue Cross/Blue Shield, what percentage of claims were denied?"

Fallon blushed again. "I can't recall exactly."

Tyler began to fumble through the notebook. Both he and Patrice Fallon knew the denial rates of every insurance company in the Midwest were sitting right in front of the jury. "It was about two percent, was it not?"

"As I recall, yes," she admitted.

"And can you explain to me why there is this sevenfold difference?"

"It's, well—" she started angrily. "It's our system. We've tried to get some measure of control over costs."

Tyler quit any acting he had been doing. He was truly surprised. Patrice Fallon closed her eyes, regretting the words the minute she said them. Tyler could not have hoped for a stronger admission. "So this sevenfold increase in denials is a direct result of a financial motivation. More money for the HMO?"

Patrice Fallon looked shaken. She looked toward Barnes and Whitfield, but they were helpless. Her poise was gone. "No. No. T-That's not what I mean. Our goal has been to keep premiums down. We've done this by controlling access to doctors."

"That access control phrase again. So you admit you try to keep people from seeing a doctor?"

"N-no," she stammered. "That's not what I meant."

"What did you mean? You've admitted your access control is a financial scheme."

"No."

Briggs ignored her. "What it amounts to is a scheme: make sure every t is crossed or the care won't be paid for. The end result is a powerful disincentive to obtain care. The less people go to the doctor, the more money the HMO makes."

"No," she said helplessly. "That's not it at all. You're twisting my words."

"Then help us understand, Ms. Fallon."

She wiped her brow and rubbed her nose in a nervous manner, looking like she was developing a fever and a cold. "We've never meant to keep people who need care from receiving it. We've just wanted to make sure we had control over who was seen."

"In other words, if they don't have an emergency, put them off. If they do have an emergency, keep the testing and the treatment to a minimum so as not to spend too much of ComHealth's money."

Patrice Fallon looked desperate. Her mind was spinning, and she struggled for an answer. "Quality care at the lowest possible cost. That's what we strive for."

Briggs turned to the jury. "Hmmm. Quality care and low cost. Sounds a little bit like your friend the used car dealer selling you a Rolls Royce for five hundred bucks. You wonder why. Then you discover it hasn't got an engine, but it does have a nice little sticker inside that says 'Made in Taiwan.'"

The entire courtroom broke out laughing, and Van Gilder pounded the gavel for order. In the noise, Barnes objected and the judge sustained. The camera moved in on Molly, who did as Tyler had requested and avoided laughing. The rest of the courtroom enjoyed themselves immensely. Briggs let Patrice Fallon stew for at least a minute before he moved on. "Ms. Fallon, I'd like to ask you about Ms. Loomis's case. The case in question. Are you familiar with it?"

"Yes."

"You are aware that Molly Loomis was treated for a uterine perforation resulting in abdominal bleeding. She was taken to the Hennepin County Medical Center and underwent an abdominal exploration that resulted in a life-saving hysterectomy."

"I am aware of it."

"The claim was denied by ComHealth. Can you explain why?"

Patrice Fallon took a deep breath. Although the courtroom had enjoyed a laugh at her expense, she seemed to be slightly stronger with the brief break and the change of subject. "There were two reasons for the denial. First, Mrs. Loomis had undergone an elective pregnancy termination. This procedure is not covered by ComHealth. The complication, intra-abdominal bleeding, was a result of the uncovered procedure. Quite naturally, the complication would not be covered."

"Certainly," said Tyler, again with the faintest hint of sarcasm.

"Second, she had not obtained authorization for an emergency room visit. As such, the visit and all treatment is uncovered unless given retrospective approval. In her case, approval was not given because the procedure and complication were also uncovered."

"I see. Let me ask you this. A woman falling into shock, bleeding profusely, and unable to do anything other than pull the phone onto the floor and weakly call help to an operator. Do you think she should be penalized for her failure to go through a twenty-minute interview with an 800 number regarding her symptoms?"

"Objection," roared Barnes. "Argumentative and assumes facts not in evidence."

"Sustained," Van Gilder grunted.

Briggs had been standing in front of Van Gilder. He knew the objection was coming and that it would be sustained. He only wanted to make the statement.

He moved to a position in front of Barnes and Whitfield. "Ms. Fallon," he continued, "A different thought. You say that her claim was denied because she underwent an unauthorized procedure and then suffered a complication."

"That's correct."

"Suppose a woman underwent a D and C, a dilation and curettage, for continued bleeding. A common procedure. Would that be authorized?"

"In most circumstances."

"And if it wasn't, say the treating doctor felt it was necessary but ComHealth's nurse did not, in other words, it was not preauthorized, and then if she experienced the same complication Ms. Loomis did, none of her subsequent care would be covered either, would it?"

Patrice flushed again. "Probably not. But they could appeal."

"Appeal?" Briggs looked surprised. "And Ms. Fallon, remembering that your's is the deciding vote on the committee that handles appeals, could you tell us what percentage of appeals are successful?"

Patrice Fallon's face turned from auburn to lavender. She knew that statistic, too, sat right in front of the jury. "Six percent."

The audience gasped. "So what we're really saying is coverage of a procedure is based almost exclusively on what the *company* has decided is appropriate. Not what the patient's doctor has decided is necessary. Isn't that correct?"

Patrice Fallon stiffened. "Yes. Well, I mean, no." She stopped. "No, I mean yes, but you must know that most of our care guidelines had extensive physician involvement."

"Doctors employed by ComHealth." Tyler stated.

"Yes," Patrice Fallon replied.

"So then, these protocols you follow, are these for the patient's sake or for ComHealthOne's?"

"Objection, Your Honor." Whitfield was livid.

Van Gilder appeared to be weary of admonishing Tyler. His eyes narrowed and he glared at Briggs. "Mr. Briggs."

"My apologies, Your Honor." Briggs knew the judge was annoyed, but that he was also still on fairly safe footing. "Now, Ms. Fallon, let's go back a step. If a woman began bleeding spontaneously, say from a uterine rupture and failed to call the magic 800 number, her claim might be denied?"

"Probably not. It's an emergency."

"But it's possible."

"Yes," she admitted. "It's possible."

"And if a woman who had been bleeding and underwent a D and C but did not get preauthorization was found to have a uterine cancer, all of her cancer treatments might be denied. Is that not true?"

"Probably not, but it's possible."

"And if a woman was authorized for a D and C because of bleeding, but had to have it from a physician outside ComHealth because it happened to her when she was in another state at the time, her entire claim may be denied. Is that not true?"

"Not necessarily." Patrice Fallon looked ill.

"I must commend you, Ms. Fallon. It's positively ingenious. I've only mentioned a few, but there must be literally thousands of ways you've thought of to deny claims."

Patrice Fallon glared at him with a riveting hatred. Her face glowed with sweat.

"Your Honor!" boomed Whitfield.

"Mr. Briggs," the judge said pointedly.

"I'm sorry, Your Honor. Just one last question, Ms. Fallon. If a woman were told that the child she was carrying was to be so horribly retarded that it would never speak, see, or even know its mother, and this woman who had long desired a child underwent a pregnancy termination simply to see that child avoid a lifetime of suffering—"

Whitfield jumped to his feet, his eyes blazing with contempt. "Objection!"

Barnes was equally theatrical, pounding his fist into the table. "Objection!" he roared.

"Mr. Briggs!" shouted Van Gilder.

Tyler went and sat down. He knew full well the jury had read about the rumors surrounding Fragile X. He was unrepentant. "No further questions." He sat down.

Amidst the murmuring of the crowd, Harley Whitfield stood up and walked to the jury box with the confident strides of a medieval knight about to right a great wrong. His face was a perfect mix of shock and indignation. His attitude was one of piety and virtue. And his posture was that of a politician at center stage. He was ready not only to resurrect the witness but to convert her to sainthood while allowing her to spew forth the ComHealth fantasy that less care was better care. Whitfield knew he could do it, but inside, he also knew Tyler Briggs had scored a few hits.

Whitfield started by allowing Patrice Fallon to relax, discussing her background in greater detail, first reinforcing her qualifications as a claims analyst and then promoting the idea that nonmedical people working in appeals was considered an industry standard. Patrice regained her composure rapidly as Whitfield allowed her to talk freely and spurt out a series of well-rehearsed lines about the fairness of the appeals process and how financial issues were always secondary to patients' medical needs.

The discussion seemed slightly calculated, but it was a lengthy calculation and it allowed the dust to settle. It took nearly an hour, including a self-serving diatribe on the seriousness of the appeals committee task and the great care they exercised; then Whitfield focused on the claims themselves.

"And, Ms. Fallon, to your knowledge, at any time has there ever been a deliberate effort at ComHealth to deny claims, large or small, purely to increase profit?"

"No."

"And is it not true that the policies set forth in this manual, so aptly cited by Mr. Briggs, are given to every patient who enrolls with ComHealth?"

"It is."

"And that acceptance or denial of any individual claim is based exclusively on information that is given to every patient at the time of enrollment?"

"Yes."

"And that every patient is informed that they will be required to seek preauthorization before receiving care and that unauthorized procedures may not be covered?"

"All patients are informed of this, yes."

"And that Molly Loomis's claim was denied simply because she had a complication resulting from an unauthorized procedure and that she had never sought authorization or even consultation with ComHealth regarding potential coverage problems?"

Patrice Fallon breathed heavily. She was feeling much better. "That is true."

Whitfield sat down. "No further questions."

A rumble swept through the audience. Whitfield had been effective, and everyone in the courtroom knew it. "Anything further, Mr. Briggs?" asked Van Gilder.

Briggs stood back up. "Ms. Fallon, one last thing. You have testified that at no time was there ever a deliberate effort to utilize 'loopholes' or 'exclusions' in order to save ComHealth money."

"Correct."

"There was never any external pressure placed on you from any of the executives to deny claims in order to benefit the company's bottom line."

"That's correct."

"No meetings ever took place that included you, no phone calls were ever made to you, or no memos ever circulated to you that suggested claims should be denied more aggressively in order to improve the company's financial performance."

"That is also correct."

Tyler raised his eyebrows as if questioning her truthfulness. "Thank you, Ms. Fallon. No further questions."

Patrice Fallon left the witness stand. Van Gilder glanced at his watch. It was 11:55. "Court is adjourned until 1:30." The jury filed out, and the audience rose and left.

As the TV announcers warmed up, reciting the morning's events, they started by discussing the fact that the strategies of the opposing attorneys could now be clearly seen. ComHealth's lawyers would try to slide along, citing the legality of the contract and the intentionally large vacancies between the lines. Tyler and Marcus would fight the contract itself. As everyone watching could see, for Molly's attorneys, it was very much an uphill battle.

Reggie Tan was wrong on two counts. His first error was his estimate that there were about two hundred public lockers in the Mall of America. There were 2500. His second error was the thought that they were cleaned out by authorities once a month. It was actually every day.

By the time he and Marcia finished rummaging through the unclaimed items that sat in the Mall of America's lost and found, they were again disappointed and discouraged. There was nothing that even remotely resembled a package, a journal, or computer disks. They left completely dumfounded and depressed.

"Is it really possible that O'Reilly left no copies of any kind?" Reggie asked.

"I can't believe that," Marcia grumbled. "But I just don't know."

Reggie stared blankly at a wall. So did Marcia. They were out ideas. Fragile

X was a dead-end. And without something concrete, Markham would soon know that the letter to the D.A. and the reporters' calls were a bluff. Reggie and Marcia were at the end. ComHealth had beaten O'Reilly. Likewise, ComHealth had beaten them.

Gregory Alan Markham hurried into his office and closed the door. By the look on his face, his secretary knew better than to even say hello. His TV was still on, and as the noon recess continued, the local commentators were remarking on how effectively Harley Whitfield had rebuilt Patrice Fallon. Markham heard none of it. His interest in the trial was fading quickly. His interest in self-preservation was now consuming him.

Earlier in the morning, he had canceled all the public appearances on his schedule, assigning them to more junior executives. This came on the heels of two more reporters' calls, one at home, still wanting information on Fragile X. The Assistant D.A. also called him back. Markham had not yet returned the call.

Markham rushed to the bar and poured himself a bourbon. One shot later, his mind spun a little slower. As far as Markham could tell, there was still a slight chance. What the Doyne files contained was incriminating, but not fatal. The same with O'Reilly's journal. Taken together, they were explosive, but perhaps still not fatal. Also, he was sure that any pirated Doyne files that Reggie Tan stole were almost certainly inadmissible and the O'Reilly material by itself proved nothing. In all likelihood, if it ever came to a trial, he could probably be saved by technicalities. But personal reassurances meant little. He had no doubt that the Attorney General's office was now interested, and with a case of this magnitude they would probably fight right to the end. To make matters worse, Markham was sure that Reggie Tan wasn't kidding. The kid was undoubtedly a psycho and he would always be a shadow lurking in the corner. He poured another bourbon. This time the room started to spin.

Markham took a seat, trying to figure out a strategy. He thought about the reporters' calls and considered the possibility that the calls were bluffs. He checked and was relieved to see that nothing was printed in any of the reporters' newspapers. It was certainly possible that Marcia Sullivan or one of the other *Star Tribune* reporters had tipped off colleagues in an effort to apply pressure. But a bluff could probably not be proven, and it was illogical that O'Reilly had made no copies. There was nothing that could be truly reassuring.

Markham glanced at the TV. The commentators were still analyzing Patrice Fallon. He ignored it. His mind was on something else, his biggest worry. For all his fellow executives' loyalty, there remained the possibility that one of them would sell out. Markham had no idea what the others really knew of Fragile X, but as the rumors continued to circulate faster and faster, their lack of curiosity made Markham believe that they had known a great deal all along. If so, it was both a cause for indictment and a powerful bargaining chip for a plea bargain. The thought made him sick. The reporters might be bluffing. Reggie Tan's Doyne files might be illegally obtained. But testimony from another executive would be the end.

He thought about the other executives. The mood in the ComHealth offices had become subdued over the preceding days. The old cowboy, can-do spirit of an omnipotent organization was gone. The protests, editorials, television commentary, and the unending avalanche of bad publicity were taking their toll. Initially, they had met the criticism with denial and anger, but now even organization loyalists were faced with the shocking realization that the allegations ComHealth's critics made appeared to be true.

With the dour mood overall, it was difficult for Markham to read the thoughts of the other executives. Although Bolger, Ross, and Cooley seemed slightly more distant, he could not be sure that this was not simply their way of reacting to the stress and strain of the SEC investigation and the trial. None of them said anything to him regarding contact with the D.A. No one mentioned Fragile X. But this fact meant little. He had not mentioned it to them either. A sellout could come without warning.

Markham picked up the paper and skimmed the headlines. All the articles were either about dead patients or the trial. He felt sick. He tossed it in the wastebasket. He opened up the *Wall Street Journal*. ComHealth stock had dropped to 27½, down 3⅛. "Another few million," he sighed. He threw it away as well. Markham rose, walked to the front of the desk, and looked out the window. Cloudy. He shook his head, leaned over, and put his hands on the wood, his back now to the TV. Looking down, he noticed that the newspapers covered a manila envelope that he had not seen before. He picked it up. It was addressed to him. There was no return address but a post office sticker was attached. It read "To be delivered after August 26 unless other instructions received from sender J. P. O'Reilly." Markham ripped opened the long envelope and withdrew a sheet of paper. It was a handwritten note.

Dear Mr. Markham:

The fact that you are reading this means that I am dead. Congratulations. But understand that what is contained in this envelope will now begin to appear. You are just the first recipient. You won the battle, but you will not win the war, I have seen to that. This little present is just a preview of the noose that is about to start tightening around your neck.

O'Reilly

Markham felt his eyelids twitch. His hand plunged into the envelope and he ripped out the contents. He felt a wave of dizziness splash through his brain, and his legs seemed to give way as he watched his worst fears spilled all over the desk. James Patrick O'Reilly, in death, had trumped Markham's ace. He tried not to faint as he watched his future begin to fade. On the desk were his worst fears, copies of the journal and the disks.

Chapter Thirty-five

Prior to the trial, a number of critical hearings were held. As in any civil litigation, the hearings were necessary to determine all procedural and technical aspects of the trial. In Molly Loomis's case, the contested issues were straightforward: the admissible evidence, the witnesses, the use of TV, and the timing of the trial. Of the pretrial hearings, only one had generated any controversy. Witnesses were easy and without disagreement. Evidence was essentially without contention once the Fragile X journal and disks disappeared. Television was a nonissue, with both sets of lawyers in favor of the medium for different reasons. And much to Tyler's continuing disbelief, both wanted the trial as soon as possible. But in a courtroom with an apparent vacuum of acrimony, two rulings in the final hearing had been crucial. Tyler Briggs and Jackson Barnes each argued with every skill and persuasive phrase they could muster. In each instance, the talented ComHealth attorney prevailed. The result was devastating for Molly Loomis.

The first ruling was about Fragile X. Briggs wanted great latitude in speculating about the source, motives, and identity of the Fragile X mystery. Instead, he received no latitude. Judge John Van Gilder ruled that everything regarding Fragile X was inadmissible with the exception of Molly Loomis's testimony. With an absence of corroborating evidence, Tyler knew that this was tantamount to hanging Molly out to dry, sentencing her to a testimony that sounded highly improbable and was without any type of proof. Barnes and Whitfield would likely crucify her. Second, Tyler and Marcus wanted to put a string of witnesses on the stand to testify how ComHealth's practices caused loved ones to die or be irretrievably harmed. All of those mentioned in Marcia Sullivan's articles agreed to testify, but Van Gilder agreed with the defense's contention that Molly's case was narrow and about finer points. The judge ruled that the testimony of these witnesses would be highly prejudicial and was, thus, inadmissible. The rulings were crushing blows. Neither one was unexpected, but it left Molly's lawyers with a case that was embarrassingly weak.

Marcus started the afternoon session by calling Arlene Ward to the stand. The Billing Manager for the Hennepin County Medical Center, she was put there simply to testify about Molly's bill. She explained that all services rendered were usual and customary and that the $114,000 bill had been reviewed prior to its submission to ComHealth. The exchange took only twenty minutes, and

Ward was dismissed when Barnes announced he had no questions for her.

Arlene Ward was followed by Austin Shea, the handsome head of Health Care Coordination for ComHealth. A thirty five-year-old MBA with executive ambitions and a loud mouth, he appeared more preoccupied by looking good for the camera than saying things that would protect ComHealth. His job at ComHealth had been to develop and implement the Access Program, the 800 number "dial-a-voice" that Tyler had poked fun at when examining Patrice Fallon. Shea was vain, shallow, and remarkably mediocre: but he possessed a body worthy of a *Men's Fitness* cover, and he spared no effort to display it. Not bothering with a sport coat, he opted for a tight-fitting European-cut shirt, of which the fabric appeared on the edge of explosion. Repeatedly he puffed out his chest and flexed his pectorals as he started to speak. Twice, he raised his arm, ostensibly to scratch his ear, but more likely to allow the camera to focus on the size of his biceps. And as he spoke, he routinely turned to the prettiest of the jurors, smiling seductively, as if expecting her to faint at his animal magnetism.

Although Shea appeared to consider himself America's foremost fornicator, Tyler Briggs considered him a dunce. Tipped off by C. Boyd Messenger, the fired executive who would testify next, Tyler subpoenaed him, and in no time the former executive's recollections proved to be true. Shea easily showed himself to be an ineffective defender of the system he had helped to create. Tyler had no difficulty getting him to admit that gaining access to care through the ComHealth 800 number dial-a-voice system was at times nearly impossible.

"The caller first encounters a verbal menu of seven options." Shea beamed with pride. "Each of those options has seven more options to choose from, and each of those options has at least three more."

"Sounds very complicated," Tyler said.

"Only to morons," Shea laughed.

The audience broke up, and Van Gilder quieted them with his gavel. Barnes and Whitfield both looked a little pale. Shea tightened his tie and flexed his muscles. He beamed to the crowd, relishing his role as a comedian, but obviously unaware the audience was laughing at him.

"I see," Tyler continued. "So out of this menu of, as I count it, over one hundred choices, how does a caller actually talk to someone medical?"

"Well, that's the very idea. We want to keep the patient from talking to someone medical as long as possible."

Tyler and Marcus could barely believe their ears. Shea was even better than they had hoped for. "Really?" Tyler asked, incredulous. "Can you elaborate?"

Austin Shea for the first time seem to realize what he had said. Nervousness cracked through the testosterone. "I mean we do that for maximum efficiency," he replied. "Direct the calls appropriately. Make it easier for the answerer to answer, I mean for the questions to be answered."

"Certainly," said Briggs.

Shea's muscles seemed to shrink a bit before everyone's eyes and he slunk a little lower in the chair.

"Now, Mr. Shea," Briggs continued, "since we have established that ComHealth has a remarkably efficient system for patients seeking care, let me ask you this. Your system is built around touch-tone phones, is it not?"

"Yes."

"And what happens if someone happens to have an old rotary phone? How do they finally get to the voice that will allow them to seek care?"

"They simply hang on the line. They get connected to an operator."

"But isn't it true that ComHealth has had over 1000 complaints in the last three months alone, and a large number of these are from rotary phone users because of disconnections? They get disconnected rather than transferred to an operator?"

Shea blushed. "There are some bugs in the system."

"And if these people did not get through to a voice it's entirely possible that their claim would be denied if they did go to the ER, is it not?"

Barnes stood. "Objection. Calls for speculation."

"Withdrawn," Briggs said, having made his point.

Shea's initial cockiness was fading. His self-possession was not. He turned again to the pretty juror, but now his look was one that appeared to solicit sympathy. She looked at him as if he were truly pathetic.

Briggs was enjoying this. "Mr. Shea, are you aware of the type of phone Molly Loomis had in her apartment?"

"No."

Briggs walked to the bench and produced it, holding the black phone aloft for the jury. "1972," he said in a low voice. "Rotary."

There was a murmur in the courtroom as Briggs walked toward the witness stand holding several papers in his other hand. "Mr. Shea, are you aware of how many calls Ms. Loomis made to ComHealth in the hours preceding her admission to the hospital?"

Shea wanted to lie, but he couldn't. "Yes."

Briggs put down the phone for Shea to stare at and held ComHealth's and Molly Loomis's phone records aloft. "How many times?"

"Fourteen," he said in a near whisper.

"And how many times did she talk to a voice?"

"Zero."

"Fourteen times she was disconnected?"

Whitfield rose quickly. "Objection. Assumes facts not in evidence. Calls for speculation."

"Sustained."

"Fourteen times she failed to get through?"

"Objection. Beyond the knowledge of the witness. He did not answer the phone."

"Sustained, rephrase."

"Fourteen times she called and never once got through to an operator, yet each time she was on the phone for several minutes." Briggs stared down at the records. "Do you have any explanation, Mr. Shea?"

"Like I said," Shea managed weakly, "a few bugs."

Briggs lowered his head "I see. Molly Loomis tries fourteen times and never once gets through. But in the meantime, while she tries desperately to follow your rules and negotiate through these 'bugs'—all that time she is bleeding to death." Briggs paused. The courtroom was still. "Mr. Shea, I'd call your system a little less than 'maximum efficient.'"

"Objection. Argumentative."

"Sustained."

"No further questions." Shea's face was pale. He looked crushed. The courtroom was abuzz.

Jackson Barnes rose and asked a handful of innocuous questions that made Austin Shea look a bit more presentable and his system of phone menus look a bit better. He then quit, conceding another small point to Briggs. When Tyler declined to ask any redirect questions, Austin Shea stepped down and walked briskly from the courtroom, heading straight for the nearest bathroom.

Van Gilder ordered a ten-minute break that allowed Media Central and the crowd outside a little time to buzz and speculate. It was brief, and C. Boyd Messenger took the stand at 2:55. The former ComHealth executive, dismissed by Hutchins several months before, had been talked about by the media for most of a week as the most eagerly anticipated witness of the trial. A man close to Hutchins. An "insider." An intimate builder of the ComHealth empire. He was unquestionably Tyler Briggs's biggest gun. He was also a potential liability. He had been fired for a reason. Short, fiftyish with a stocky build and a drill sergeant's crew cut, Messenger looked more like a bulldog than a wealthy corporate executive. A graduate of public schools with an MBA from the University of Michigan, he had worked for insurance companies since graduation. He had been with ComHealth since its inception in 1985 and had risen to the role of Senior Vice President. Assumed to be a logical candidate for CEO, he was passed over for H. Carter Hutchins and relegated to a more insignificant, dead-end position.

A man with strong opinions and a fierce will, he remained a thorn in Hutchins' side throughout his stay. Hutchins' insistence on a draconian approach to insurance infuriated Messenger, especially when contrasted with ComHealthOne's carefully constructed public image of the benevolent, patient-loving, "friend of the family." His conflicts with Hutchins were legendary, and his firing was of little surprise to anyone within the company.

Tyler knew he was taking a risk by using him . Despite the constant base of idealism from which Messenger operated while at ComHealth, his career was checkered. There was little doubt that Barnes and Whitfield would make this a point. He was also Tyler's and Marcus' only real hope. Other interviews of executives at ComHealth via subpoena had been utterly useless. The silence was complete. Other than Messenger, the doors into ComHealthOne were completely shut.

The courtroom was hushed in anticipation as Messenger took the stand. As in all trials gathering media attention, the witnesses were briefly media stars. The camera zeroed in on him as he sat down, and most in the courtroom strained to see the man they had read about in the papers for several days.

Sanders began the questioning. He led Messenger through a series of questions establishing his background. After discussing his past, Marcus led him through his employment history with ComHealth up until his firing six months before. Reciting his past, it was clear to everyone that this man had been part of ComHealth's top level. Finished with the groundwork, Marcus took the problem head on. "Why were you fired, Mr. Messenger?"

"Alcoholism."

"Would you care to elaborate?"

"I had a problem dating back two or three years. ComHealth was supportive during that time. I took two leaves of absence to try to get it under control."

"Did you?"

"No."

"And it resulted in your firing?"

"Yes."

"Do you blame ComHealth?"

"No."

"And now? Is your drinking controlled?"

"Sober for four months."

Marcus nodded. He hoped to plant this positive spin on the firing with the jury knowing that the ComHealth lawyers were certain to exploit it. He had no interest it trying to give the appearance of hiding anything.

"Now, Mr. Messenger, I'd like to ask you more about your time at ComHealthOne."

Sanders now led C. Boyd Messenger into the heart of his testimony. Within minutes, Messenger established himself as a strong, articulate speaker and a damaging witness. He, like the buffoonish Austin Shea, was better than either Marcus or Tyler had hoped. He was truthful and organized in this thoughts. The courtroom and jury seemed to hang on every word. Even Van Gilder, often prone to appearing disinterested, was completely attentive. Messenger started by describing for the jury the beginnings of prepaid health care. Contrasting it with old-fashioned "fee for service," he carefully explained that the entire origin of managed care was based upon the idea of containing costs.

He continued by explaining ComHealth's explosive expansion, promising low premiums to employers, cutting reimbursements to providers, and as they grew, forcing competing HMOs to merge by undercutting them. Once competition was eliminated, premiums were allowed to rise, resulting in soaring profits.

"The same system John D. Rockefeller used to build Standard Oil into a monopoly, we used to crush any competition," he said. "And as we did it, we explained it to the public as consolidation, as making the system more efficient, leaner, and less costly."

"And was it?"

"To some degree. To employers our alternative was cheaper. That was all they really cared about."

"What about the patients?"

Messenger didn't hesitate. "I think you'd be hard-pressed to find an example anywhere, with respect to insurance, where cheaper is better."

Marcus let Messenger continue. The fired executive explained how ComHealth's initial success, like that of most HMOs, came from restricting redundant and superfluous care. Forcing the elimination of all but essential services pushed their profits even higher, resulting in greater power, expansion, and market share.

"That sounds much like the American business ideal," said Marcus.

"It was," admitted Messenger.

"Then where was the problem?"

Messenger took a drink of water and then went into greater detail explaining the perils of the prepaid system. "The problem was simple. Community Health One, like most HMOs, is a publicly traded corporation. The old indemnity companies like the Blues were nonprofit. The difference is monumental. The motive of a corporation is pure and simple—profit. Although executives and advertisers will talk easily about various platitudes, there is only one thing in a corporation of that size that is truly important, and that is profit."

"And how did the drive for profit effect ComHealth?"

"The savings we extracted from the system resulted in enormous profits for us, but they were unfortunately a one-time savings. Shareholders expect yearly growth, an increase in profitability, a ten or fifteen percent rise in the stock price per year. What happened was that once the easy money was wrung out of the system, we had nowhere to turn."

Marcus appeared deep in thought. "So what did you do?"

"There were two options. First, we could raise premiums. We did that to some degree, especially when much of the competition was eliminated, but that strategy still runs the risk of allowing others to undercut. It was smarter to keep the premiums low and go with the second strategy, work on the expense side."

"By that do you mean putting a tighter squeeze on the doctors and the hospitals? Lower their reimbursements?"

"Yes."

Messenger explained how ComHealth began cutting approval for procedures and tests on a more extensive basis. "It was all carefully conceived," he said. "Here's an example. Say we cut out all routine blood counts, which we did. Each of those labs runs fifty dollars. With two million patients per year, that is a savings of $100 million. Even if ten of those people ultimately died because something was missed and their families collected a few million dollars in lawsuits, we would still be way ahead."

"And this was discussed at the executive level?"

"These plans were formulated and implemented at an executive level."

Marcus glanced at the jury. They looked appalled. "What other strategies did you employ?"

"Our next strategy was simple. Make sure the doctors did not order tests or treatment unless it was absolutely necessary and make it difficult to get access to the doctors."

"And how did you go about this?"

Messenger explained that they first sought to raise the age of routine testing such as mammography, EKGs, and PSAs. They then sought the elimination of some tests altogether such as blood counts, urinalysis, stool for occult blood, and routine chest X-rays, explaining how this was part of a greater system that forced doctors to preauthorize nearly every procedure or test. Preauthorization criteria were made so rigid that almost no tests were initially authorized, requiring physicians to engage in lengthy, difficult appeals. Messenger went on to describe how this had been called "passive profits," in that this passive resistance would force fewer tests, because doctors would never have the time to appeal all denials. He concluded by describing the last strategy, rewarding doctors for ordering fewer tests and fewer specialist referrals.

"So physicians are compensated for ordering fewer tests or for ordering fewer consults from specialists?"

"Some are, yes. It was called our incentive plan."

"And how did they respond to this?"

"Initially, most resisted, but physicians are human. If they're working on a salary, have no financial incentive to work harder, but do have a financial incentive to work less, they will respond as any human being would."

"Even at the expense of patients?"

"The sick patients still got cared for. It's just that there were a lot more hoops to jump through to get into the system and the patients were often sicker when they finally got in. And truthfully, a few died."

Marcus nodded. The silent jury looked incredulous. "And yet your advertising, your public pronouncements, your brochures, all talked of cost-effective medicine."

Messenger looked amused as he continued. "The term 'cost-effective' was always a ComHealth executive favorite, but it is a totally meaningless term. Anything could be justified under that heading. Think about it. To an insurance company, a bullet to a patient's head is a more cost-effective option than an operation on a terminally ill patient, especially if that patient is going to live quite a while before they die."

Marcus let him continue. Messenger paused to take another drink of water before he started again. "You have to remember the mood of the country in the early nineties when this was being developed. The nation was concerned about rising health-care costs and they wanted something done and done fast. ComHealth stepped forward with an alternative. What our marketers knew was that we couldn't say cheaper; we couldn't say better. We had to make it sound as if the care was the same, just less costly, hence 'cost-effective.'"

"You would say the term 'cost-effective' was largely a scam then?"

"Absolutely, it was a scam. I gave you the example of eliminating blood counts earlier. Cost-effective? Hardly. Just cheaper. Raise the ages of starting mammograms, eliminate prostate tests, restrict routine EKGs. Is that cost-effective? Only to the people who never needed those tests before and happened to be lucky enough to need them just at that time they received them. Otherwise it is a life-and-death gamble and has nothing to do with effectiveness, just less cost."

"What about childhood vaccines?"

"ComHealth gave strong consideration to eliminating routine childhood vaccines. It is a perfect example of the ridiculousness of the cost-effective concept. The theory was this: For most children, if you don't vaccinate, it's no big deal. They get their mumps or measles, miss a little school, and get well. The cost-effective thing to do would be to not vaccinate all children. Instead, vaccinate only children at risk, say kids who have some other condition that would place them at greater health risk if they got one of these viruses."

"And if ComHealth had implemented this plan, how much would this 'cost-effective' strategy save?"

"Nationwide? Worldwide? Hundreds of billions."

"And how many children would die?"

Whitfield rose. "Objection. The witness cannot possibly answer."

"Many," interjected Messenger.

Van Gilder turned to the jury. "Sustained. The jury will disregard the answer."

Marcus ignored it. Whitfield's objection was justified. He moved on. "So what were the limits of ComHealth's 'cost-effective' strategy?"

Messenger leaned forward and turned toward the jury. "There were none," he said ominously. "It was simply what the market would bear and what the public would tolerate."

Several members of the jury gasped.

Messenger continued for several more minutes, providing even greater insight into ComHealth's machinery. He talked about how the contracts were drawn up. How innumerable broad exclusions were built right into the contract to give the HMO the right to deny claims nearly on demand. He detailed how ComHealth had intentionally made it difficult to access the system in order to deny claims if people proceeded to receive unauthorized care.

"So, ComHealth created enormous loopholes, exclusively for the purpose of finding ways to deny claims."

"Absolutely."

"And these were discussed at executive meetings?"

"Yes."

"And was by chance Ms. Fallon present at any of these meetings?"

In the audience, the austere Director of Claims looked faint. "Yes, she was," Messenger said. The crowd rumbled, remembering Patrice Fallon's earlier denials. Van Gilder calmed them instantly with his gavel.

Marcus let her lies sink in for a minute before he continued. "One final thing, Mr. Messenger. As part of your duties, you oversaw executive compensation, did you not?"

"Yes,"

"And can you tell me exactly how much you were paid in the last tax year?"

"$2.4 million."

The crowd rumbled again. "This was your base salary?"

"No. My base salary was $1.4 million. I was given a million dollar bonus for thinking up the vaccine elimination program even though we didn't use it."

The crowd's anger rose. Booing and hissing could be heard throughout. Van Gilder slammed his gavel a half-dozen times and rose to his feet. "I will have no problem clearing this courtroom," he said forcefully. The warning worked slowly. The courtroom's anger went back beneath the surface.

As the people in the courtroom quieted, Sanders continued. "And do you know any other executive salaries for last year?"

"All of them," he replied.

"Mr. Hutchins?"

"He was paid a salary of $12.1 million."

The crowd gasped. "Anything else?"

"He received stock options worth in excess of $40 million."

"And he was paid that kind of money while people were dying because they couldn't get a fifty dollar blood test?"

"Objection!" yelled Barnes. "Not in evidence!"

"Shut up, you prick!" screamed a man in the crowd at Barnes. "Let 'im talk! They're all bloodsuckers!"

Van Gilder slammed down his gavel and attempted to silence the courtroom. Security descended upon the man and whisked him away while he continued to scream obscenities at the defense attorney. Many in the crowd stood as security wrestled with the man. Under-the-breath profanity could be heard everywhere.

When the man was gone, Van Gilder took control again, "My last warning. Any further outbursts, and I will clear the room." An angry silence followed as Van Gilder and the audience exchanged glares. Finally the judge spoke again. "Mr. Sanders, you may continue."

Marcus took a few seconds before continuing, letting the ejected man's "prick" and "bloodsuckers" hang in the air. Satisfied that everyone in the court now associated the words with ComHealth and their lawyers, he continued. "Only one more thing, Mr. Messenger. The situation at hand. Molly Loomis. Was this precisely the type of claim you were attempting to avoid paying?"

Messenger was unperturbed. "Absolutely. Our two big loopholes were one—make it difficult to get authorization, and two, deny the claim on the basis of unauthorized care. It was all beautifully done. Hire the finest lawyers, write the cleverest contracts, and then blame the patient, even if they try to follow the rules."

"Thank you, Mr. Messenger."

Marcus sat down. The crowd was rumbling, but Van Gilder ignored it. He reached for his glass of water and let a bit of the room's steam blow off. Tyler looked across Molly and winked at his partner. Marcus was outstanding, and everyone watching knew that the plaintiff's attorneys had just enjoyed their finest moment of the trial. The only problem was that despite the stinging indictment, there was still no proof that ComHealth had broken the law. They were guilty of many things, but none of them appeared to be illegal.

The impromptu break over, Van Gilder quieted everyone. Harley Whitfield rose and walked deliberately toward the witness, wasting no time. "Mr. Messenger, you said you were fired for alcoholism."

"Yes."

"Weren't you actually fired for lying about drinking while on the job?"

"Yes, that is more accurate."

"That you showed up drunk for work and then proceeded to lie about it until your appeal? And only admitted it when confronted with the testimony of six people who had seen you drunk?"

"Yes."

"And that is not the only time you lied about your alcoholism, is it?"

"No," responded Messenger to a dead-silent courtroom.

"What do you mean 'no'?"

"I mean what you say is correct."

"In fact, if we look in your file, it will say that part of your dismissal was due to, and I quote 'a persistent pattern of lying dating back several years,' unquote. Doesn't your ComHealth file also document several other problems, such as tardiness for meetings, false explanations of absences, denials of drinking on the job when coworkers clearly smelled the odor of alcohol, and sleeping at meetings?"

"That's true. That's how the file reads."

"You mean the file is not accurate?"

"It's embellished a bit to make me look particularly bad, but basically it's true."

"How is 'sleeping at meetings' embellished? How is 'alcohol on the breath' embellished? How is 'erratic behavior' embellished?"

"You've read the report. I was referring to the adjectives used to describe me personally. I don't dispute the rest."

"So you admit that you were a drunk when you worked for ComHealth."

"I had a serious drinking problem that is now well controlled."

"Thank you for correcting me." Whitfield walked toward the jury and positioned himself right beneath the camera. "Now, Mr. Messenger, would it be fair to say that at one time you were considered a prime candidate for the job of CEO of ComHealth."

"Yes."

"And that Mr. Hutchins was given this job over you?"

"Yes."

"And can you describe your relationship with Mr. Hutchins?"

"I believe it was one of mutual respect. We did have our differences regarding the direction of the company. We were not social friends."

"Diplomatically stated," complimented Whitfield. "Isn't it true that you had nearly a pathologic jealousy of Mr. Hutchins following his appointment? A jealousy so deep that you assaulted him one day outside his office."

"I grabbed the lapels on his suit."

"And you shook him violently?"

"I pushed him slightly."

Whitfield produced the official record of the event. "It says here you shoved him. And at the bottom you've signed it."

Messenger's cool demeanor cracked slightly. He was nervous, but he had long known these questions were coming. "I signed it under duress. Mr. Hutchins' version would be the accepted one, and I was allowed to keep my job."

"I see. You lied about your drinking. You lied about stopping your drinking. You fell asleep at meetings. And yet he kept you on."

"Yes."

"And now you blame him for a version of events that happens to conflict with yours."

"Mine is true."

"Sounds to me that he was more than supportive of an employee with a problem over some length of time."

Messenger took another drink of water. He had been under fire many times, and despite his history, he was determined to fight. He desperately wanted to tell the jury every single lie Hutchins had ever concocted, but he followed the advice Briggs had given him to keep his cool, answer everything truthfully, and never appear vindictive. He was succeeding. "I understand that that would be ComHealth lawyer's viewpoint."

Winfield ignored it. "And tell me, Mr. Messenger. Do you recall the night of last August twenty-second?"

"Yes."

"What happened exactly?"

"I went out after work. I had several drinks, and when I got home, my wife was upset."

"And you struck her?"

"Yes."

"And you initially denied it to the police, did you not?"

"Yes."

"And only the large bruise on her face kept you from keeping up the lie, did it not?"

"No. It was realizing what I had done that made me tell the truth."

"Are you still married, Mr. Messenger?"

"No."

"And what about the events of this past January nineteenth."

Messenger blushed. This time his composure seemed to wane. Whitfield was asking about an event that was supposed to be confidential and sealed. "I-I," he stammered.

"Let me refresh your memory. Sexual harassment," Whitfield growled.

Messenger stroked his chin. "It was near an elevator. It was crowded, and the back of my hand struck the side of a young woman's buttock. I instantly realized what had happened, and I reflexively smiled and apologized. She interpreted my action as intentional and filed a complaint."

"And you were reprimanded?"

"I chose not to contest it."

"Why would you not contest it, if you were not guilty?"

"To avoid it becoming a spectacle within the company."

"I see, and didn't you deny it when first confronted with the allegation? Lying again?"

Messenger flushed. "Yes."

Whitfield was becoming a bit more dramatic. "By my count, that makes four admitted lies, but I could be wrong. It may be more." A couple of the ComHealth attorneys smirked. The rest of the audience was expressionless and silent. Tyler and Marcus watched in agony as Whitfield continued the onslaught. "Tell me, Mr. Messenger, after you were fired, did you file suit against ComHealth?"

"I retained counsel."

"For what purpose."

"To explore my options."

"To file suit."

"Possibly."

"To file suit against a company that stood by you during three years of drinking, that paid for your rehab, stood by you despite the lies, stood by you despite the erratic behavior, and stood by you despite your jealousy and animosity toward Mr. Hutchins."

"It was an option we considered."

"And what was the result?"

"Objection. This is irrelevant. Attorney–client privilege."

"Withdrawn," said Whitfield. "But tell me, Mr. Messenger, when did you last meet with your attorney?"

"About a month ago."

"And tell me, Mr. Messenger. When did you first contact Mr. Briggs?"

Messenger swallowed hard. "Three weeks ago."

Whitfield stood right in front of the jury. He looked straight at several of them before he spoke again. "So let me make sure I have this straight. Lied about drinking, lied about not drinking, lied about hitting your wife, and exerted no effort to fight an in-house sexual harassment charge. In addition, there is this claim that the CEO of ComHealth pressured you into lying about another incident, the same CEO who stood by you throughout all of this. The same CEO whom you decided to sue, and when you found out there was no merit to any lawsuit, you took it upon yourself to get even in any way."

"No," Messenger said.

Whitfield walked away from the jury. He ignored Messenger's answer. He stood in front of the judge, but stared at the fired executive. "Mr. Messenger, you've made a number of extraordinary claims regarding ComHealthOne, but having seen the witness list, I must say that it appears that you will be the only one testifying in such a manner. Do you have any evidence to prove your claims? Any records, tapes, computer disks, anything?" Whitfield knew he was safe. The admitted evidence contained nothing like that.

"No. When a person is terminated, all records must be returned," Messenger replied.

"I see. What about personal record, a diary, notes, anything."

Messenger looked downcast. "No."

"Drunkenness, jealousy, history of violence, history of lying." He paused for effect. "No further questions, your Honor."

Sanders asked several questions on redirect that offered Messenger the opportunity to sound like something other than a scheming, lying, wife-beating malcontent, but it was largely useless. Whitfield's cross-examination had been brutally effective. At 4:45 P.M., a depressed C. Boyd Messenger left the witness stand.

Five minutes later, court was adjourned, with the sequestered jury being taken to the downtown Marriott and hidden from the breaking news. Sanders and Briggs left the courthouse, stopping briefly to speak with reporters in front of a throng of people and issue a few tepidly optimistic statements. Whitfield and Barnes did the same thing, and, as usual, the TV cameras covered it all.

Molly left the courtroom in her baseball cap and sunglasses via the perfected underground route and headed to the hospital to visit Peter Colder. The day had been a high and a low. Despite the strain of the trial and the chaos that surrounded it, at the moment she was only thinking about Peter. How much she missed him, how worried she was about him, and how much she wanted to be with him.

As she walked alone and unnoticed through the underground tunnels that connected downtown, her mind, for an instant, leaped back to the trial. Her stomach seemed to jump. She would spend the night at the hospital with Colder, but she knew it promised to be the longest night of her life. For tomorrow, in front of the world, she would walk directly into the fiery breath of the ComHealth dragon, taking the stand as the last witness.

Chapter Thirty-six

Before Thursday morning, ComHealthOne offered a variety of explanations for the growing number of cases that were finding their way into the press. Of these excuses, the most consistent were that the cases represented isolated incidents, they were all computer snafus, or it was all a conspiracy and a media "vendetta." These remarks, offered regularly by a variety of ComHealth executives and their attorneys, were widely circulated and vehemently stated, but as the third day of the trial arrived, even those within the ComHealth organization were privately forced to admit that their analysis was more wishful thinking than fact. While Barnes and Whitfield continued to maneuver magnificently in the courtroom, the rest of the country watched in a mix of agony and amazement as case after case was revealed that substantiated the protesters' claim that ComHealthOne was the ultimate "Just Say No HMO." In a word, the largest health maintenance organization in the country was caught between the lies of public relations and the truth of cost control. With every passing day, the pressure continued to mount.

The trial dominated the Twin Cities, and a riveted public digested every detail. Thursday morning's headlines were crushing. "Ex-Executive Testifies About ComHealth Cost Cutting" was the most gentle. "$12.1 Million for CEO—Death Sentence for Unlucky Patients" was the toughest. Four articles in each of the Twin Cities newspapers, the Minneapolis *Star Tribune* and the *St. Paul Pioneer Press*, were dedicated to the testimony of C. Boyd Messenger, as was each paper's lead editorial. And worse, every word in print was positively scalding. Despite Harley Whitfield's battering of Messenger's credibility, not a person outside the jury box had any doubt that the ex-executive was telling the truth. The information was now coming from too many different sources.

Thursday morning was also the official end of Marcia Sullivan's reign as the Woodward and Bernstein of managed care. For the first time, cases began to appear in newspapers outside the Minneapolis–St. Paul area, as doctors and patients came forward from other parts of the Midwest. The *Chicago Tribune* reported on five new cases of ComHealth neglect. The *Milwaukee Journal/Sentinal* reported on three, and the *Des Moines Register* reported on two. All the cases were clear-cut situations where patients lost their lives because needed tests were denied. The new cases varied from horrifying to tragic. Making them worse was the fact that several of the victim's families had already consulted attorneys and been told that since ComHealth had acted "legally," there was no case.

Despite the continuing heatwave, the Thursday crowd outside the courthouse was by far the biggest and the noisiest. Nine thousand people packed the downtown area before the gavel sounded. Nearly twenty new media trucks arrived during the night, and with each came a squadron of microphones and satellite dishes. With each passing day, the protests grew more organized. The joined forces of law students and medical students from the U of M formed a potent group of protest leadership. The students were responsible not only for distributing daily fliers, copies of the case histories that had found their way into the news, but for recruiting or locating others. It was now proving to be an easy task. Patients were calling a special 800 number in droves to volunteer their stories, while nurses and doctors everywhere were anonymously offering tips, names, and stories; all of it found its way right to the press. Before everyone's eyes, the walls of silence were tumbling down.

With all of the publicity, the implications for ComHealthOne were unclear; but for Molly Loomis, everything was perfectly clear. None of it helped. With a sequestered jury and pretrial rulings that prevented their mention, such "irrelevant" and "prejudicial" information would never be heard. Whitfield's and Barnes' legal maneuvering left ComHealth perfectly positioned in the courtroom, poised to deliver the final blows to Tyler Briggs's case. With only three witnesses left before the defense began, a verdict in favor of ComHealth now appeared certain.

Molly Loomis was exhausted as she walked into the courtroom. She arrived by a back route and managed to avoid the crowd, the protesters, and the calls of "murderer," but the sleepless night in Peter Colder's room left her with a masklike face and dark rings underneath her eyes. She'd never felt worse. Peter continued to languish in a coma despite the improvement of his pneumonia, kidney function, and liver function. His failure to wake up was obviously concerning the doctors. Molly overheard several of the physicians speculating that the coma might be permanent.

Molly became even more depressed when Phyllis Colder told her that she had made arrangements for Peter to be transferred closer to her home. Dr. Asadourian and Dr. Wessman reluctantly agreed to her request and made arrangements for him to be flown to the Mayo Clinic in Scottsdale on Friday morning. Molly understood, but the news hit her like another death. His leaving felt like a stake being driven into her.

When Molly entered the courtroom, the camera followed her as it had every previous day. She took her seat without looking at the lens as Tyler and Marcus greeted her. The spectators continued to mill about, and the camera left Molly to follow the action. A moment later, the bailiff barked out his call to order and the camera turned to Judge Van Gilder as he entered. Van Gilder ordered everyone seated and called the attorneys forward. The impromptu conference was brief, and at two minutes after ten, the jury filed in and the court was in session.

Paul Pavelich was the first witness of the day. One of the two paramedics on the scene, he described in gory detail Molly's apartment when he and his partner arrived. His comment of "blood everywhere. On the floor. On her legs. On her body" made a couple of jurors visibly sick. Marcus Sanders milked it, trying to paint a picture of a desperate young woman, needing care and thwarted by a phone system that gave her only recorded voices. Each time Marcus mentioned the 800 number voice, Harley Whitfield objected; but judging by the jurors' looks of comprehension, the strategy of exploiting people's frustration with technology appeared to work.

Molly listened, but was slightly detached. Her mind was elsewhere, for a while on Colder and then on her own testimony later in the day. Tyler had gone over every question in detail and given her good advice on how to answer, but the thought of walking right into Barnes' or Whitfield's cross-examination was nauseating. The morning paper described it as "walking into the fiery breath of the dragon." Molly knew the paper was right. Every part of her body already felt as thought it were burning up.

The paramedic finished, and Dr. David Frissell took the stand as the second witness of the day. Molly's surgeon had been eager to testify. He volunteered his services as soon as her lawsuit became public, and his testimony was critical, establishing medical necessity beyond any doubt. It would also have the effect of showing to the jury a reputable doctor testifying against the insurance company.

Frissell slipped past the attorneys when his name was called and headed toward the stand. He appeared immaculately groomed. His usual tired appearance was gone, hidden beneath a haircut, freshly pressed suit, and a new tie. He took a long look at Molly Loomis as he sat down and took his oath, remembering the night her husband and parents abandoned her in the hours after she nearly died. He'd always hoped he would have a chance to help her. He relished this chance now.

Sanders began with the usual series of establishing questions. Dr. Frissell was a board-certified surgeon with an academic appointment and a member of all of the important medical organizations. He spoke easily in response to Sanders' questions, quickly establishing himself as a medical expert and effortlessly listing his accomplishments, but doing so without even a hint of bragging. To each set of attorneys, Frissell showed himself a nearly perfect witness.

"Dr. Frissell," Sanders began after the five minutes of introductory questions, "you were on duty as the attending surgeon at the Hennepin County Medical Center this past June 4 when Molly Loomis was brought to the emergency room, where you not?"

"Yes, I was."

"Would you describe her condition at the time of her arrival?"

"She was in critical condition. She was in hypovolemic shock."

"Can you explain that in layman's terms?"

"Shock is another word for very low blood pressure. Her blood pressure was falling fast. In layman's terms? She was bleeding to death."

The courtroom was attentive and hushed. For the first time, the jury was about to consider how close Molly Loomis came to dying.

Sanders approached the witness stand. "Can you tell us the sequence of events as they took place in the emergency room that night?"

"Certainly," replied Frissell, looking calmly at the jury. "Ms. Loomis was brought in by ambulance. She was unconscious with a very low blood pressure.

The paramedic noted significant vaginal bleeding when she was found at her apartment and en route to the hospital. At the time of her arrival, she was given normal IV fluids to try to elevate her blood pressure and she was prepared for a blood transfusion. As this was occurring, her heart briefly stopped, and she required a short course of CPR, medications, and shocks to restart a normal heart rhythm. Because her condition was so fragile, we had no time to do any further workup, realizing that the bleeding must be stopped, immediately. She was taken to the operating room where her bleeding uterus was removed."

Most of the jury looked white. For Frissell, candid talk of bleeding, life and death was a daily matter. For the jury members, it was anything but a daily occurrence. Sanders eyed them. He could see the doctor's testimony was effective. He continued without hesitation. "And what did you find at operation?"

"Her abdomen was full of about two liters of blood or nearly half her blood volume. She was bleeding from two sites, or perforations, in her uterus. One small artery was also bleeding, as well as a couple of veins."

"And what was your impression of the cause of the bleeding?"

"She had undergone at least a D&C, or a dilation and curettage. More likely, she had undergone an abortion."

"And were you able to confirm that it had indeed been an abortion?"

"Since she was unconscious, she was unable to tell us, but her pregnancy test run in the ER was positive. We felt confident it had been a pregnancy termination."

Sanders walked by the jury box. He made a point not to look directly at any jurors. He had wanted to mention the abortion, but not dwell upon it. "And what was required surgically to save her life?"

"Well, first of all you must understand that the primary goal of the surgery was just that—to save her life. Any other consideration was secondary. Only after some time were we able to understand what exactly was bleeding. At first, we were just staring into a pool of blood. I say this because some might ask why we didn't try to save the uterus. The answer is we would have if we had been convinced her life was not in danger. As this was not the case, we were forced to remove the uterus."

"But because of that she will never have children," Marcus asked.

"That is correct," Frissell affirmed.

Sanders paused. He knew that to some the question might seem preposterous. A woman terminating a pregnancy wanting children later. But he knew what Molly would say later, and he also knew that any discerning juror would ask the same question.

"And how long would you say she had been bleeding?" he asked.

"Several hours, minimum."

"And do you think that during this time that Ms. Loomis would have been capable of understanding what was happening to her and acting accordingly?"

"For a while, she would have been lucid. I believe she acted in that manner, trying to get through the ComHealth telephone maze."

"Objection," grunted Whitfield. "The witness has no way of knowing Mrs. Loomis's thoughts at the time."

"Your Honor, the witness is testifying as to Ms. Loomis's ability to act rationally in the face of active bleeding, not as to her precise thoughts at the time."

"Overruled."

Marcus looked squarely at one of the female jurors. He wanted them all to imagine what it had been like to be bleeding so severely that nothing could stop it. He wanted them to imagine what it had been like to think they were going to die. "I'm sure it had to have been just a little terrifying when you're bleeding to death and all you can get is a recorded voice on the phone, don't you think Dr. Frissell?"

"Absolutely."

Barnes was condescending. "Objection, Your Honor. Counsel knows better."

"Withdrawn," said Marcus.

"Strike it from the record," Van Gilder muttered.

Marcus walked back to the witness stand. "Is there any chance that Ms. Loomis would have survived without the surgery?"

"No."

"Is it possible that if she had received treatment earlier that a hysterectomy could have been avoided?"

"Yes. I would say that is probable."

Marcus nodded and returned to his seat. "Thank you, Dr. Frissell."

Van Gilder took off his glasses and wiped them. He took a drink of water. The courtroom was quiet. "Mr. Barnes."

Jack Barnes was already standing. "Just a couple of questions, Dr. Frissell. First of all, isn't it possible that if Ms. Loomis had undergone the pregnancy termination by a more skilled practitioner, such as any of the board-certified ones employed by ComHealth, that this situation could have been avoided?"

"Objection, Your Honor," Tyler scoffed. "The witness is an expert in surgery, not obstetrics and gynecology."

"Sustained," Van Gilder said. "You do not have to answer, Dr. Frissell."

Barnes furrowed his brow. He knew the objection would be sustained, but he'd made the point. "And one other thing. Is there any possibility that the bleeding was from anything other than an abortion?"

"No."

Barnes sat down. "No further questions, your Honor."

"Redirect Mr. Sanders?" asked Van Gilder.

"No, Your Honor."

The judge turned to Frissell. "You may step down."

The two witnesses took nearly an hour and a half. Rather than start Molly's testimony, Van Gilder recessed the court for lunch. Most in the court went to eat, drink, and analyze. Molly went to a bathroom and hid.

Three ComHealth executives, Stanton Ross, Preston Cooley, and T. Wilson Bolger held an impromptu press conference on the steps of the IDS Tower during the noon hour. Trapped by the TV cameras before they could get in the limousine, the three indignant executives, who'd spent most of the morning making sure there was no trail of their illegal stock trades made months before, appeared surly and preoccupied. They dismissed Molly Loomis's case against ComHealthOne as a "joke" and complained that Judge Van Gilder's refusal to dismiss the case "represented the height of judicial incompetence." They called Molly malicious and vindictive, and predicted that not only would ComHealth prevail in court, but that "every medical tragedy the media insisted upon exploiting would be shown to have been unavoidable and appropriately handled." They resisted further comment and finished by pointing out that "no court of law has ever found ComHealth liable, because we have always acted within the law."

Reporters battered them with questions, but they refused and scurried off. No one noticed that the fourth senior executive, Gregory Markham, was not present.

When Molly Loomis took the witness stand at 1:30, she looked gaunt. Her eyes were red, and her hands shook even on camera, but for the first time since the trial began, the young woman who'd succeeded in becoming the first person ever to bring the great HMO to battle was prepared to speak. The crowd outside the courthouse was quiet, but the air was electric. People were everywhere. The large TVs set up for those mingling in the streets could be heard easily, and in the neighboring restaurants and offices, nearly everything came to a stop. All TV stations in Minneapolis–St. Paul went live, as did CNN, Court TV, and MSNBC. The moment Molly Loomis long dreaded had finally arrived.

As she sat down, the courtroom was so quiet that the squeak of her shoes could be easily heard. She leaned forward slightly, her white blouse and blue blazer making her look pretty. Her hair was the same as it had been throughout the trial, straight with a slight curl and no highlights, but her nervousness was obvious. Her soft voice shook audibly, and her eyes darted between the lawyers, crowd, and floor.

Briggs began with questions about her life. She talked of her upbringing, her schooling, and how she had given it up after her marriage to Troy. After five minutes, she began to relax slightly and her quivering voice began to sound better. She continued, talking in detail about the marriage, how they had met in high school, dated in college, and married shortly after Troy injured his knee. She talked about how the marriage had been failing and mentioned, but did not exaggerate, Troy's drinking and his affairs.

"Did he ever strike you?" asked Tyler.

"Yes," said Molly.

"How many times?"

"Three."

"And did you ever suffer any broken bones or other injuries as a result?"

"A broken nose."

Troy Loomis was sitting in the second row, and both the jury and the camera found him staring at his shoes. Tyler asked a few more questions, establishing the fact her marriage was obviously in trouble before moving on. Tyler knew Molly's testimony was critical, and he would not risk losing the jury's interest for even a second. It was time for the important events. "Ms. Loomis, do you recall a phone call you received on May thirtieth of this year?"

"Yes."

"Can you describe it for us?"

"At about one in the afternoon, I was called by someone identifying himself as a Dr. Roland Michaels. He said he wanted to personally talk with me about a result on a blood test they had run. He said I could come to the office or he could come in person to our apartment. I was concerned by what he said, and since I had worked all night and didn't look ready to go out in public, I thought his coming over would be a good idea."

"And he came over?"

"Yes."

"And can you describe him?"

"Maybe five-eleven, not fat, black hair parted on the right, brown eyes."

"And his demeanor?"

"Very professional. Knowledgeable."

"And what happened?"

"He described for me how my blood test had revealed that my baby was going to have Fragile X Syndrome. He said this was a genetic disease that resulted in severe retardation. He said my baby would be in an institution and would never see or think or hear." Molly paused. She had been talking freely, but as the thoughts came pouring back she started to struggle. She choked slightly, but managed to get out the sentence. "He said that a child like this would never even know his name."

Tyler stopped. He let her gather her thoughts. He wanted her to be truthful, but too much emotion might cloud her thinking. Molly nodded at him and he continued. "And what was your reaction?"

"I was stunned, like, horrified. I didn't know what to do. I wanted a baby more than anything in the world, but Troy insisted that we not. I knew he'd be furious that I was pregnant and even madder that the baby wouldn't be normal."

"Then what?"

"I don't know. I was confused. I didn't know what to do. I guess I just tried to think about the baby, living alone, living in some institution, never able to even know me." Molly stopped again. She was on the edge. She bit her lip and took a deep breath. "And I just couldn't do it. I couldn't let a child suffer like that."

Tyler moved close to the jury. "And would you have terminated the pregnancy if you had not been told that the baby would be so severely retarded?"

Molly seemed almost shocked. "Absolutely not. I'd have done anything for a baby. Only if his quality of life was so bad that it seemed almost selfish on my part would I consider what I did."

"And what about Troy?"

Molly looked down. Her voice was even softer. "He didn't care what I did. He didn't want a baby with me."

The jury's eyes turned to Troy Loomis. Even without his testimony, his pale face and guilt-ridden look told them she was telling the truth about their relationship. He looked stricken.

"So you never told him about the pregnancy?"

"No."

"Tell me, Molly. Were you afraid of Troy?"

"A little."

Tyler moved back to his table and leaned against it with his backside. "Let me move in a different direction," he started. "Did you call ComHealth to verify that the abortion was covered?"

"No."

"Why not?"

Molly blushed slightly. "I guess I assumed it was."

"Why?"

"ComHealth had authorized the pregnancy test. And the way this Dr. Michaels talked, well, I thought it would be, since he recommended it." She looked sheepish. "Seems foolish now."

Tyler narrowed his eyes. They had not scripted her testimony, but he certainly did not want her to offer spontaneous opinions of her actions. She caught his look and its meaning. "Tell me what happened after the abortion."

"I got home about four in the afternoon. About an hour later, I noticed that I was continuing to bleed." She blushed even more, not accustomed to talking frankly about feminine matters, but recalling Tyler's instructions to talk freely, she continued. "I replaced the pad, but the bleeding continued. At that point, I started to get concerned and I called the clinic, but they were no longer open and their calls were routed to the ER. I remembered that with ComHealth any ER visit needs to be preauthorized, so I called their number. I couldn't get through to a person right away so I kept trying."

"And what happened? Were you concerned about the bleeding?'

"I was getting more concerned. They warned me that there would be some bleeding afterward, but this seemed to be a lot. As I kept calling, I started to get concerned."

"And did you get through?"

"No. We had this old dial phone, and I kept getting busy signals and this menu that was supposed to connect me to an operator. It didn't. I always got disconnected."

"Did you think about calling 911?"

"I did, but I knew that they would never cover an ER visit if it wasn't preauthorized. My dad had gotten burned on that a couple of years before when he had chest pain and ended up with a big bill. At that time, I thought I was still okay, so I just kept trying to get through to ComHealth."

"Then what happened?"

"It kind of hit me like a truck. All of the sudden I got real faint, and when I tried to walk, I fell down. I got up, but everything was spinning. I was still thinking pretty straight, but at that time I knew I was in trouble."

"What did you do?"

"I stood up again and fell back to my knees. There was blood running down my legs and onto the floor. I remember feeling panicky at how much blood I was seeing and how hard it was to breath. After that, I start to get fuzzy. I remember thinking I had to call 911 and starting to crawl toward the phone, but I don't remember anything after that."

"And your husband found you?"

"That's what I understand."

Tyler walked toward the jury box. The camera followed him. "What do you remember after you woke up?"

"Dr. Frissell was by my bed. He told me what happened."

"And how did your family react?"

"Troy was upset. He said he was mad because I never told him I was pregnant and because he wanted the baby, but I was pretty sure it was just because he wanted an excuse to leave."

"Did he leave?"

"Yes, he moved out of the apartment and in with a girlfriend."

The camera zoomed back in on Troy Loomis. His face was the color of a ripe plum, and he slouched as far down in his seat as he could.

"And what about your parents?"

Molly looked down. She had not wanted Tyler to ask about them. "They're good Catholics. The abortion and everything, well, it was all hard on them. They yelled at me for a little while. Then they left."

Tyler turned his focus to the jury. He could see by their faces that Molly's simple truths were compelling. "And have you had any contact with them since?"

Molly's eyes filled. "No. They haven't returned my calls. I tried about a week ago. It was my dad's birthday."

Tyler let it hang in the air for a minute before he moved on. Even Whitfield and Barnes looked moved. "How long were you in the hospital?"

"Four days."

"And when you got home, Troy was gone?"

"Yes."

"And what is your marital status now?"

"We're divorced."

Tyler wanted Troy Loomis present for the jury to see both for his reaction and as a sign of support. Judging by the jury's faces, it worked. He changed the subject. "Can you tell us about your dealings with ComHealth when you got home?"

"Soon after my discharge, they sent me a letter." Molly stopped as Briggs produced it for the jury. "It said that all of my bills were uncovered. The reason was that I hadn't followed their policy. I hadn't gotten approval to go to the ER."

"And did you appeal?"

"Yes. It was rejected."

"And then what?"

"The billing department from the hospital called wanting the $114,000. I knew I could never pay that, so I went to your office. I figured I'd probably have to go into bankruptcy."

Tyler was pleased. Molly had held up well and delivered her testimony even better than he expected. She wasn't totally polished, but he didn't want that. He wanted her to be as she was. Straightforward, credible, and truthful. She had done it. "One last thing. Did you ever hear from the doctor again? The one who had told you about Fragile X?"

"No. But a few days after the hospitalization I went to Dr. Peter Colder's office." She stopped, realizing the jury might not know who Colder was.

"For the record, Your Honor," said Tyler, reminding the jury of the well-publicized murder attempt, "Dr. Colder is the physician who was shot and wounded in an assault a week and a half ago." Tyler turned back to Molly. "Please continue."

"I knew he took patients who couldn't pay, and ComHealth had canceled my policy. Well, I just wanted to ask him a few questions regarding hormones and things after a hysterectomy. He told me he had never heard of a blood test that detected Fragile X. He also told me that Fragile X resulted in mild retardation, not severe."

"And what about the doctor, Dr. Roland Micheals, who had visited you?"

"Dr. Colder recognized the name. It was the name of a doctor who'd died a couple of months before. He figured whoever was doing this was using the names of doctors who died because their licenses would remain active until they were not renewed the following year. That way if anyone from another state checked—"

"Objection!" Whitefield jumped to his feet. "Witness is speculating!"

Van Gilder nodded. "Sustained. Strike it from the record. Jury will disregard."

Tyler gave a hint of a smile at Molly. It had gone very well. "No further questions."

As Briggs sat down, the courtroom was abuzz. Van Gilder let it go as he conversed briefly with the bailiff and took a drink of water. Outside, the spectators watching on the TVs turned to one another and began openly speculating about Fragile X. For weeks it had been the subject of rumors and a few small Marcia Sullivan articles in the paper, but now ComHealth would be forced to deal with it on the record for the first time. After a two-minute delay, Van Gilder quieted the court. "Mr. Whitfield?"

Harley Whitfield stood and pored over his notes. He knew he had to be careful. Molly Loomis and her testimony were filled with explosives just ready to go off. He knew millions viewed her largely as a sympathetic figure, and he could never be seen beating up on her. References to her past, her parents, her ex-husband must all be done in a way only to cast a shadow of doubt upon her. Anything else was too risky, despite Hutchins' intense desire to crush and humiliate her. The threats and the saber rattling were part of the pretrial posturing. Now he knew he would have to let her beat herself. "Mrs. Loomis, do I understand this correctly? You at no time informed your husband that you were pregnant?"

"That's right."

"Despite the fact that it was his child?"

"Yes."

Whitfield moved around the table. "It was his child, wasn't it?" He asked it without even a hint of condescension, but Molly still blushed.

"Yes, it was."

"I see." He paused and walked toward the jury. "Now let me go back to before you ended the pregnancy. The man who came to visit you. Had you ever seen him before?"

"No."

"Ever talk to him before?"

"No."

"How about since?"

"No."

Whitfield turned to the jury. "When's the last time you had a doctor make a house call for you?"

Molly cleared her throat. "I never have."

"Did it strike you as odd that a doctor would make a house call in this era?"

"Maybe a little."

"I see," said Whitfield, moving toward her. "And after this *mystery doctor* calls you out of the blue, comes to your house and tells you that your baby is going to suffer from this horrible disease, did you check on him? Did you check to see if he was licensed in Minnesota? Did you ask your regular doctor if he knew him? Anything?"

Molly was red. "No."

"Perhaps the biggest decision of your life, and you just took the word of a man you had never met before?"

Molly looked down, "Yes. I thought my regular doctor referred him."

"Did this man say he had been asked to see you in referral?"

"No."

"Or did he identify himself as being employed by ComHealthOne?"

"No."

"I see." Whitfield moved on. "Now, Mrs. Loomis, you say that your husband was prepared to leave you and that he did not want to have a baby with you."

"Yes."

"Did you want to have a baby with him?"

Molly paused to consider her answer. "I wanted to have a baby, yes."

"But with him?"

She looked down. "He was my husband."

Whitfield was cool. He made sure to not sound annoyed. "But did you want to have a baby with him?"

"If the relationship was okay."

"And was it?"

"No."

"I see," said Whitfield thoughtfully. "So you found yourself pregnant and in a bad relationship."

"Yes."

"And what would be your options? One, you could have the baby, but that might bring you back closer to your husband."

"Troy did not want me to get pregnant."

"But in the past, he'd wanted to have children, hadn't he?"

Molly couldn't help it. She flushed. She knew where Whitfield had gotten that information. Troy had warned her that Whitfield had interviewed him. "Yes, he had."

"So you were afraid that having the baby might bring you back closer?"

"No, I didn't feel that way."

Whitfield continued. "Isn't it true that all of your friends advised you to get out of the relationship?"

"Yes."

"And that you, too, thought of leaving?"

"Yes."

"And this baby might have thrown a big curve ball into those plans wouldn't it?"

"I didn't have a plan."

"I see." Whitfield was dubious.

The courtroom rumbled as he returned to his table and glanced at his notes. He stood there only briefly before turning again to his witness. "Mrs. Loomis, what religion are you?"

"Catholic."

"A practicing Catholic?"

"Yes."

"Married in a Catholic Church?"

"Yes."

"And how did you think your parents might react if they found out about an abortion?"

"They would be upset."

"But if there were a reason, a plausible story, perhaps some horrible disease that the child would have. Wouldn't it then be easier?"

"I doubt it."

"Isn't that really what happened, Mrs. Loomis? You found yourself in a predicament, a relationship you wanted to get out of? An unwanted pregnancy that you terminated without telling anyone and then got caught because of complications? Then you had to come up with a story to make it more palatable for your parents, and meanwhile your husband did just as you said, used it as an excuse to leave?"

"No," she said firmly. "I never would have chosen an abortion if I hadn't been told those things."

"I see. So there's no possibility that perhaps you just made this up, this cloak-and-dagger doctor stuff. No possibility that it was actually *your* error, that Fragile X wasn't as serious a disease as you thought."

"I had never heard of it."

"That perhaps you overheard it in the hospital corridor and decided to use it when your abortion scheme was found out."

"No," she said. "That's not true."

"I see," he said. "And what did the mystery doctor wear when he came to your house? Trench coat? False nose and mustache?"

Farnsworth and Cox chuckled out loud. The audience stayed silent. "No," Molly said through her teeth. "A suit and tie."

Whitfield didn't listen to the answer. He had returned to his notes. As he looked down, he saw nothing. He didn't use the time to prepare questions. Instead, he tried to gauge the audience and jury reaction. He was treading lightly and was sure he had pushed just hard enough. "Let me go back to one thing," he said, turning around. "You said you assumed that ComHealth would pay for the abortion because you felt you had been 'referred.'"

"That's right."

"And when you got to the abortion clinic that day, did they accept your insurance?"

Molly gulped. "No. They insisted on cash."

"Why didn't they accept your insurance?"

"They said that usually insurance won't pay for it."

Someone in the crowd groaned audibly. "I see," said Whitfield. "Well, Mrs. Loomis, you obviously knew the preauthorization rules. You called several times to get authorization to go to the ER. But did you call to get authorization to get the abortion?"

"No. The doctor, Dr. Michaels, he said it was taken care of. That's what I mean by I thought it was authorized. I was surprised when the clinic wouldn't take insurance, but I figured I would take care of that problem later."

"The mystery doctor again," said Whitfield with a strong hint of a joke.

"Yes," she admitted.

Whitfield stood right above her. He was now very intimidating. "Mrs. Loomis, can you offer the court any evidence that this mystery doctor actually exists? A photograph, a business card, a telephone number, another witness—anything?"

"No," she said.

"And yet you still hold to this notion that this mystery doctor telephoned you out of the blue, then made a house call and led you to the abortion."

"Yes."

"Ms. Loomis. You're under oath," he said.

Molly tried to sound confident. "I know."

"And that's still your story?"

"Yes."

"Despite the fact that you admit you lied, or at least never told your husband, and the fact that you knew your parents would be upset, so upset that they might disown you."

"Yes."

"That would be very strong motivation, wouldn't it, Mrs. Loomis?"

"What I said is true," she said.

"Certainly," Whitfield replied.

Molly looked at the jury. Their faces reflected the fact that Whitfield planted a seed of doubt. Even she realized her story sounded strange when cast in his light.

The ComHealth lawyer took one more trip to the notes. In his mind he debated. It was a debate that had raged in his mind for days. Finally he decided to gamble. "Tell me Mrs. Loomis, do you believe in abortion?"

The question caught her off-guard. "Not really," she heard herself say.

"Only in certain circumstances then?"

"I guess, maybe."

"Is that a 'yes' of a 'no'?"

"It's a yes, I suppose."

"Certain circumstances then, say when a child doesn't fit your definition of a perfect child, or when a father doesn't fit your definition of a perfect father."

"That's not true. It was about quality of life."

"Whose? Your's or the child's?"

Molly felt herself flush again. Her voice wavered. "The child's."

He hovered over her again. "I see. And what does your church say about abortion?" he asked.

"I think you know that," she replied, her temper flaring a bit.

"And yet you still decided to take this innocent, unborn child's life?"

Molly paused. She turned to Tyler Briggs who was shaking his head back and forth very slightly. He had warned her not to get angry under any circumstances. Whitfield would unquestionably trap her if her mind was anything less than perfectly clear, and no one thought clearly when angry. But the fatigue and strain had weakened her, and she could feel herself burn inside. Molly made a snap decision. She ignored Tyler's advice.

"Mr. Whitfield," she began. "There are many things in this world that I am not. I was not born a great athlete or a great student. I was not born beautiful or funny. I never stood out in anything I ever did. But as I grew up, I accepted the fact that despite all the things I wasn't, I could still do one thing well, or I at least wanted to do one thing well. Maybe I wouldn't be a glamorous movie star. Maybe I wouldn't be rich or famous. Maybe I wouldn't cure cancer. But I was determined to do that one thing as well as anyone had ever done it. I was sure that I would be a good mother." She paused for only a second. She squinted at Whitfield. "Maybe in this day, it isn't cool to have that as a goal. But I don't care. It was all I wanted and all I dreamed of."

Whitfield started another question but Molly interrupted him. Her eyes were filling and she could still see Tyler shaking his head back and forth. But all the months of horror seemed to crush down upon her an she could feel a surge rise within her. All the losses, all the deaths. Every hope and wish she had ever had, taken or destroyed. She continued to ignore Tyler.

"Mr. Whitfield, when I stopped that pregnancy, I didn't do it because I was afraid of my husband or my parents, or afraid of being inconvenienced. I did it out of love for a child who was destined to suffer an unspeakable life. And someday, when I die and I'm asked to account for all I've done, I'll stand there and say again all that I've said today—because at this point in my life I have only the truth to stand on. And it's all true. What I lost from that decision, my whole life's dream, I know no power on earth can give me back. But my heart knows the love I felt. And I know all too well the loss I've caused myself. So, you can judge me if you want, but no man can ever judge me more harshly than I've already judged myself."

Molly stopped talking and looked down as one tear dropped down on her cheek. Harley Whitfield looked pale with anger, not at her, but at himself for such a stupid blunder. For the entire trial, he had considered her nothing more than a mouse, but his underestimation cost him dearly. The mouse had roared.

"No further questions," he grunted, heading back toward his table.

His retreat set off a celebration. The audience leaped to their feet and applauded wildly, cheering Molly. Several in the jury appeared to want to do the same. Meanwhile the entire building quaked as outside, the crowd watching on TV shouted, stomped, and clapped its approval.

It took nearly a minute, but finally Van Gilder, with the help of the bailiff, silenced the court. Only the courtroom was silent; the noise outside never dropped a decibel. With the day at a close, the judge called the lawyers to the bench. It was merely for housekeeping purposes, and two minutes later, day four of the trial ended. Tyler Briggs and Marcus Sanders rested their case. Van Gilder retreated to his chambers. The ComHealth lawyers escaped through a side door, for the first time avoiding the press outside.

Tyler, Marcus, and Molly stayed in the courtroom to confer and prepare. All of them were happy with what had happened. Molly's performance had exceeded anyone's expectations, and her impromptu speech was an added bonus. Both were glad she'd ignored them and taken the risk.

As they sat in the emptying courtroom, Sanders and Briggs made plans to talk to the reporters and build up what had happened as much as they could. But everyone on Molly's team knew that there was now one very big problem. Molly's speech was the end of their case. Now, it was ComHealth's turn.

Chapter Thirty-seven

The reaction to Molly's testimony was spectacular. Her picture was on the front page of every newspaper from *USA Today* to the *Los Angeles Times*, and her testimony was on every newscast from Alaska to Alabama. Despite Tyler Briggs' admonition not to speak freely, Molly Loomis's pleading statement to Harley Whitfield, "Judge me if you will, but no man will ever judge me more harshly than I've already judged myself," had touched everyone who heard it. It was featured prominently as a sound bite on all three of the national network newscasts. In addition to Molly's remark, the national networks devoted more time than ever to the trial, nearly ten minutes apiece. The slant in several of the stories was obvious, because for once everyone who had been watching—legal experts, laymen, and even cynical journalists—were all in agreement. Molly Loomis was telling the truth.

The city's reaction was speedy. In the hours after Tyler closed his case, the Minneapolis Police Department launched a formal investigation into the identity of "Dr. X" as did the St. Paul Police Department, but neither agency had any idea that the FBI was a way ahead of them. Molly's tentative identification of Luke Henry as the man posing as Dr. Michaels was now supported by four other women. In the preceeding days, they had called the police reporting that they, too, in early summer had been advised to have abortions because they were carrying Fragile X children. Within hours, the police learned of the FBI breakthrough. Only with great effort did they manage to keep this story from the press.

At the same time, Assistant District Attorney Wesley Christensen, under advisement from the District Attorney placed a call to Minneapolis Chief of Police Roger Sanstead and relayed the story of his strange communication with ComHealth executive, Gregory Markham, two days before. He faxed him a copy of Markham's letter asking for immunity and provided him all the information he had gathered so far on Fragile X.

At 6:00 A.M., Markham appeared at the Minneapolis Police Headquarters. The officers requested that he appear for an interview with investigators. After a quick call to his lawyer, Markham agreed and spent the one-hour session not answering most questions and watching his lawyer dodge the others. Throughout, Markham could not stop staring at the picture of a man he wished he did not know. When the interview was finished, Markham and his lawyer drove home. During that car ride, and for the first time, Gregory Markham told the entire truth to his attorney.

Adrenaline kept Molly awake all night, but by sunrise she was finally tired. As she sat at Peter's bedside, the excitement of the preceding twenty-four hours was fading rapidly. Her exhaustion was complete, and the depression that had threatened to overtake her was now returning. The doctors were positive that he had suffered brain injury from the low blood pressure and openly stated that he might never wake up. The assessment appeared to be correct. The coma continued, unchanged. To make matters worse, it was time to say goodbye to Peter. The unthinkable moment had arrived.

Molly, her back to the door, put her chin on his bed and stroked his forehead. She gazed at him wistfully and let her fingers slide over his nose and chin. "You know, Peter," she sighed, talking to him as if he were awake, trying to put away the flurry of the past days, "I wish you could see what was happening. Even though all the people on TV say we can't win, ComHealth's stock has fallen way down. People are really paying attention." Her mind wandered for a moment. "Hutchins is going to testify today. I know Tyler's been looking forward to that."

A nurse breezed into the room, adjusted something on the cardiac monitor, and left. Molly barely looked up at her. She was still trying to think of things to say, but the thought of Peter's leaving for Arizona in a few minutes was the thought that was really on her mind. That nightmare of his loss was beginning to crowd in on her.

"I can't imagine you not here anymore, Peter," she said softly, forgetting the small talk. "I still can't believe what's happened, that you won't ever wake up. And, most of all, I can't believe you won't be part of my life anymore. I know you'd tell me not to feel guilty, but I still do, and I know I always will. If it wasn't for me, none of this would have happened."

Molly stopped as a few tears fell onto her cheeks. She wiped them away and stroked Peter's forehead again, leaving a trace of a tear on his skin. Cradling his hand, Molly continued. "You know, Peter, when I was about thirteen I wrote up this list of everything I wanted in a man. I know it sounds stupid, but it's true." She laughed briefly at herself. "The list was fifteen things, everything from a good sense of humor to liking animals. I still have it hidden someplace. You know, I hadn't thought about it in a long time, or at least not until the day you and I first went to have our sub sandwiches. It's strange, you were still technically my doctor, but I felt something. I suppose some would say it was a crush, or maybe loneliness, but that's not true. I know better. It's like the moment I met you I knew there was something different about you. You were the one. All fifteen things, everything, right there in front of me."

A respirator alarm sounded, and the nurse reappeared. She adjusted a knob on the ventilator and was gone again. "I guess what always worried me," continued Molly, "was me. I mean, you look at Julianne, and she's so gorgeous and everything, and then you look at me, and well—" Molly paused. She was struggling to say what she really thought. "I know what you told me about how the past means nothing and how my life is open to me, but it's hard for me to forget. I could never be like Julianne." Her voice trailed off to a whisper. "But then maybe that doesn't matter to you. Or at least I hope—"

A noise behind her made her pause, but she didn't turn around. "I guess I know one thing. That day Sylvia came over and bought me the groceries. I know she did that because she wanted to, but I also know she wouldn't have done it if you hadn't wanted her to. I guess I just can't give up this hope I have that you'll wake up and feel the same way about me as I feel about you. I know, maybe it's all crazy, but sometimes when you looked at me—I felt like maybe you did."

Molly looked up at the stand beside the bed. The transfer papers and the chart were sitting on it. She could hear the flight nurse and paramedics setting up just outside the room. "Peter," she started, "I don't know exactly how to say this, so I'm just going to try. It's like this—weird as it sounds. Before you, I had never known this feeling. I had lived my life thinking that love was only for others, like it was something won or earned, until you brought it to me. And when it came, I felt scared, realizing I had found the man I only dared to dream of deep in my heart. But now that I've had it, I'll hold it forever, until the last moment of my life.

All I know is how I feel, how much I've wanted to be with you, how much I care, and how much I'm going to miss you. You know, Peter, I'll think about you every minute of every day. I'll see your face on every ray of sun and hear your voice on every starry night. And why? Because your spirit will be with me forever. Inside me will be your dreams and all that you stood for. I'll go on knowing that my dream was real, while you can leave knowing that your dream will never die. Your life is now mine, Peter, and in my mind we'll always be together, bound by the memory of the time we had and sealed by a goodbye we'll never say. You saved me, brought me back from a world of despair that I'm glad you'll never know. But with that, I promise I'll live my life the way you knew I always could and maybe the way I always knew I could. I'll live with a feeling, a hope, and a purpose that only you could have given me. I'll never forget you, Peter. Never. Wherever I go or whatever I do, it won't be in memory of you—it will be because I love you, Peter. I love you, and I always will." Molly stopped talking, letting tears flow freely down her face. The room was silent except for the rhythmic sound of the cycling respirator. Outside, the ICU was filled with the usual activity of nurses coming and going, caring for the critically ill patients. Behind her, one of the paramedics coughed, apparently a signal that it was time to go. Molly did not turn around, instead she buried her head in Peter's hand. Molly had told him everything she wanted to say, but now she knew she had to let go. She held his hand until the paramedics gently pushed it away. A few minutes later, Peter Colder left the ICU and her life.

Molly remained in the room long after he was gone, feeling unable to move. Never had she felt so exhausted, so beaten, and so low. Never had she felt so completely aware of how she felt and all that surrounded her. The only thing she missed was that Julianne had been standing in the doorway, hearing everything she said.

Judge John Van Gilder looked exhausted when he took his seat on the bench Friday morning. His frown seemed to droop perilously close to his chin as he motioned for all to be seated. The paper reported the day before that Van Gilder was considering retirement after this trial, and by his demeanor and hunched-over posture, all who saw him found the report believable. He greeted the jury, the bailiff, and the audience and then turned to the lawyers.

"Any opening business, gentlemen?" he sighed.

Jackson Barnes approached the bench and Tyler, Marcus, and Whitfield followed. The four lawyers and the judge then spent ten minutes engaging in legalese while the jury and audience waited patiently. Cox and Farnsworth sat idle at the defense bench. Less prominent than they would have liked throughout the trial, they had privately complained to their bosses about their roles. As they sulked, however, the camera turned to them and the photogenic lawyers, previously bored, began discussing in earnest with each other in hushed tones the important documents before them.

Molly Loomis sat alone at the table as her lawyers talked with the judge and Farnsworth and Cox preened for the cameras. Their photo-op sideshow, once amusing, now annoyed her, and she turned away. She remained expressionless, aware that most of the jury members were watching her while the camera watched the lawyers. The break allowed her to think briefly about the trial for the first time since her testimony. She knew the strengths and weaknesses of the case and how each probably played to the jury. She understood that ComHealth simply intended to wrap itself in its contract and say "the law is the law." There was little question that losing was probably inevitable especially with a sequestered jury, but she still harbored hope that all who had seen and listened to the trial had heard the truth about ComHealthOne.

The legal meeting finished, Jack Barnes called the first defense witness. Harding Pesch IV was a partner at one of Minneapolis's largest legal firms. He was the first of four attorneys who took the stand in succession to testify about the same thing—the HMO contract. Each of the four lawyers was heavily involved in the writing of the contract, and all four provided in excruciating detail the history and nuances of what ComHealth covered and why. All said the same thing. The contract had been created to provide maximum client benefit for minimum expense. Never was there any deliberate attempt to create a contract that made money at the expense of patients. And never was there any attempt to conceal exclusions or conditions not reimbursable. The contract, they said, was straightforward and easily comprehensible for anyone who bothered to read it. Under cross-examination from Sanders, they consistently explained away the fourteen pages of exclusions, exceptions, and uncovered conditions by saying that it was either "an industry standard," or "considered experimental." They also defended the preauthorization program, stating it was essential for cost control and easily understood by all clients.

All four were highly effective witnesses. They were credible if not believable. Although any observer would question the statement that money was of no greater concern than in any other business, they said it consistently and each seemed to believe it himself. All four lawyers spoke well, and none played to the camera or bored the jury. As their testimony went on, they explained the contract in layman's terms, and after three hours, all who listened had a strong understanding of the fundamentals of ComHealth HMO insurance. Their point was simple, reinforced by Jack Barnes at every possible opportunity. "The contract is in writing. The rules are clear. Molly Loomis broke the rules." The strategy was simple, and each of them had known it was coming, but there was still little that Briggs or Sanders could say.

By the end of the morning, the emotion and passion that surrounded the managed care issues and Molly Loomis's personal tragedy seemed peripheral. Even Tyler and Marcus sat in admiration as Jack Barnes continued to lead his witnesses into hammering home the core point, "The rules are the rules." Marcus did not even cross-examine the last lawyer, the points he had made having been made three times before. As the noon hour approached, even the most biased observer knew the morning session had been a slaughter. ComHealth was just pouring it on. Over the noon recess, the legal experts interviewed on TV stated that the trial was over, and for the first time, the outside crowd's enthusiasm was diminished as the afternoon session began. Even the most ardent Molly Loomis supporters were forced to admit, ComHealthOne was legally invincible.

Harrison Carter Hutchins took the witness stand after the noon break. It was the first time that most in the room had ever seen the person long-rumored to be their next governor. His appearance, once long-anticipated, now seemed almost anticlimactic. Hutchins was dressed perfectly in a tailored navy pinstripe suit, and he sat in his chair with the relaxed manner of a man who did not have a care in the world. His act was beautifully deceiving. The jury had no idea of the turmoil swirling throughout the ComHealth executive suites as they listened to the distinguished-looking man speak.

Harley Whitfield controlled Hutchins' testimony carefully. Although Hutchins was a natural in front of a camera and good on his feet, the lawyer knew there was no reason to take chances. The morning session had established all the legal foundation they needed. Hutchins was appearing only to refute the testimony of C. Boyd Messenger, the dismissed executive, nothing else. Methodically, Whitfield led him through a series of answers that portrayed Messenger as an intelligent, ambitious executive destroyed by alcohol. Hutchins talked of how ComHealth had gone "beyond all normal limits" in providing him help and how he was personally hurt that Messenger would make up such lies.

Whitfield winced slightly when Hutchins rolled on for a few sentences about his feeling "hurt." He wanted the CEO to be careful and not overplay anything. It was Hutchins' only error, however minor. Overall, he was an extraordinary and convincing speaker. A true politician, he was able to make anything sound believable.

Briggs cross-examined him. "Only a couple of questions, Mr. Hutchins."

"Certainly."

"You think twelve million a year is appropriate compensation for an executive whose primary accomplishment is providing less care to needy patients?"

"Objection. Irrelevant."

"Overruled."

Hutchins did not blink. He had been warned by his attorneys that such a question was probably coming after Van Gilder had indicated in an early hearing that he would be lenient in allowing questions about ComHealth's finances. "My compensation is determined by the board of directors, not myself."

"What about stock options worth forty million?"

Hutchins cocked his head. "Thanks to you, Mr. Briggs, my stock options aren't worth much anymore, are they?"

Several in the audience laughed. Tyler did not react. He moved closer to the witness stand. "My apologies about the stock price," he said evenly. "But I asked if it was appropriate, and I don't recall receiving an answer."

The courtroom fell quiet. H. Carter Hutchins crossed his legs and folded his hands in his lap. He appeared completely unperturbed. "CEOs of corporations are rewarded financially for performance and profits. No one disputes that in general they are well compensated by a system that favors those at the top. At times, profitability is not pretty, and I would say that when wealth is contrasted with poverty, wealth is the ugly one. But it is a system that I did not create. I sought only to do the job to the best of my ability. My compensation is based solely upon that."

"And your 'profitability,' as you call it. It was based primarily on cutting back care, wasn't it? Care that could have saved lives?"

"We made health care more affordable by evaluating it in terms of cost effectiveness and implementing these strategies. That was the source of our profitability."

Tyler turned to the jury. He let them think for a minute, hoping they would consider all that they had heard. "And Mr. Messenger? He committed perjury then?"

Hutchins balked. Tyler's question was stronger than he had expected. "I harbor no ill will toward him. And I hope he can reconstruct his life and career. But, yes, I would say so."

Tyler stopped cold in his tracks. He looked flabbergasted. "So, Mr. Hutchins, none of the meetings he described took place? There was never any discussion at an executive level as to how to reap greater profits? There was never any pressure felt from the board or the shareholders to increase profit margins? All of what he said was a lie?"

"Yes."

Tyler leaned against the jury box and rubbed his hand over his mouth. He looked perplexed. "That's odd. It seems to me that makes no sense at all."

Hutchins' eyes narrowed. Briggs looked thoughtful. "Think about it, Mr. Hutchins. Why would he do it?"

Hutchins looked surprised. "What?"

"Why would he do it?" he repeated. "Why would he lie?"

"I don't know, revenge?" Hutchins replied.

Tyler turned to the jury. "Commit perjury? Risk going to jail?"

"Revenge," Hutchins reiterated.

"Revenge?" asked Tyler. "For what? He already admitted he deserved to be fired. He stated he had no animosity toward you personally or any of the other executives. His compensation at ComHealth has left him wealthy beyond most of our imaginations, and he's comfortably retired before the age of fifty-five. Why, Mr. Hutchins, would he now risk going to jail after getting his life together and facing a very bright future?"

"I don't know."

Tyler stared at him and let the jury hang on his point. "I didn't think you did." The courtroom was deathly quiet. "No further questions, your Honor."

When Carter Hutchins left the courtroom, Jackson Barnes requested a ten-minute break. Van Gilder granted it and retreated into his chambers while the jury returned to the jury room. Almost immediately, Hutchins reappeared in the courtroom and sat between Whitfield, Barnes, Cox, and Farnsworth. Molly watched as the five men talked. No one could miss what was going on. There was a disagreement. For five minutes, they shook their heads, pointed, and talked in hushed whispers. Hutchins appeared to adamantly disagree with something the two senior lawyers were saying. Cox and Farnsworth appeared to agree with Hutchins, and the vigorous discussion continued for fifteen minutes instead of the expected ten, but finally all was settled and Hutchins left. Most in the courtroom had paid little attention. Molly had no idea what it had all been about.

Van Gilder reappeared, and the jury returned to their seats. Now accustomed to the routine, the obedient courtroom fell silent. "Mr. Barnes," said the judge.

The lawyer stood. "The defense calls Dr. Clyde Jarman."

Tyler leaned across Molly to talk to Marcus. "What's this guy gonna say?" he asked.

"Weird they would bring him on now," Marcus whispered recalling his briefing with the doctor. "I thought they would use him only if they were going to dispute medical testimony. What I know is he's gonna testify that the bleeding might have been slower than Frissell said."

"Yeah, that's right," said Tyler remembering.

Molly Loomis looked up at the lanky, silver-haired pathologist as he took the witness stand. Patrician and austere, he looked as if he could have been a brother to either Harley Whitfield or Jack Barnes.

"Dr. Jarman," began Barnes. "First let me ask you about your training."

"Certainly."

Barnes carried the pathologist throughout the now familiar routine of establishing a witness as an expert. Jarman was a doctor of medicine, had graduated from Washington University School of Medicine and trained in pathology at Northwestern. He was board-certified in pathology and had worked at the Hennepin County Medical Center for seventeen years. After ten minutes of credentials and biography, Barnes proceeded with the important questions.

"Now, Dr. Jarman, you conducted the pathological examination on Molly Loomis's tissues after her emergency hysterectomy on June fourth, did you not?"

"Yes, I did."

"And what specifically were your findings?"

"Two uterine perforations caused by sharp instruments."

"And these perforations are an accepted complication of an elective pregnancy termination?"

"Fortunately they are a very rare complication, but it can happen."

"And the perforations were the source of the bleeding that caused Mrs. Loomis's near-fatal event?"

"I feel that they contributed, but in all likelihood, an associated vascular injury or injuries also played a major role."

"Can you explain?"

Tyler felt nauseated. He looked across Molly at Marcus. His partner's eyes said the same thing. Something was wrong. There was no need for this testimony. Barnes had something up his sleeve, and it was scaring the hell out of them both.

"The uterus can contract powerfully, helping to stop bleeding," started Jarman. "Because of this, I am doubtful that it alone caused all the bleeding. I would guess that one of the small arteries and/or veins in the pelvis were also injured."

"Dr. Frissell testified that an artery and two small veins were injured. Does that seem reasonable?"

Tyler nearly objected. The question was out of line, but it was also inane and harmless. He was more interested in trying to figure out what was going on. Marcus looked at him again and they exchanged confused and frightened glances.

"Yes, it does," answered Jarman.

"And Dr. Frissell also testified that he thought it would have taken several hours to bleed to the degree that Mrs. Loomis did. Does that also seem reasonable?"

"That might be a little short, but overall, yes."

Tyler was worried, very worried. Jarman was not saying anything expected. It was a lawyer's worst nightmare. Unexpected testimony. Even the audience seemed to realize something was up.

"Now, Dr. Jarman," Barnes continued, "let me ask you about the pathological examination of the tissues. What specifically did you do?"

"We examined the uterus and fallopian tubes both grossly and microscopically."

"And what did you find?"

"Grossly the structures looked fairly normal, and I'm sure to a surgeon trying to save a woman's life and operating in a pool of blood they would have appeared completely normal."

"But they weren't?"

"No," said Jarman. "Mrs. Loomis had what is called an ectopic pregnancy."

"Can you explain that for us?"

Molly looked quickly at both her lawyers. This was news to her. Marcus and Tyler tried to remain calm.

"For the jury, the eggs are produced in the ovaries. They then proceed down the fallopian tubes where they are fertilized by sperm. After fertilization, the egg, now called a zygote, continues to the uterus where it lodges along the wall and develops. An ectopic pregnancy means that the zygote lodged at some spot other than the uterus and started to develop."

"And where was this?"

"Near the distal end of her left fallopian tube."

"Far from the uterus."

"Yes."

Barnes nodded. "So is it possible that the doctor performing the abortion was particularly vigorous because he did not get out exactly what he expected, thus causing the perforations of the uterus?"

Tyler should have objected, but both he and Marcus were thrown off-balance by the line of questioning.

"That scenario is logical. When an abortion is performed at a very early stage, the zygote is quite small, but usually detectable grossly. I would guess that the doctor became concerned that he had not seen exactly what he was looking for and continued, using curettage that ultimately resulted in the perforation."

The courtroom was hushed. Van Gilder looked fascinated. Cox and Farnsworth looked proud. "And was there a reason for this ectopic pregnancy?" asked Barnes.

"There was," replied Jarman. "Mrs. Loomis had severely scarred fallopian tubes. Only a small amount of normal mucosa remained, and this is where the zygote lodged."

"And what was the source of this scarring?"

Clyde Jarman looked at Molly sympathetically. He knew what he was about to do. "Mrs. Loomis had sometime in the past suffered from pelvic inflammatory disease, PID as it is called. It is a severe infection of the female genital tract that scars the fallopian tubes and often results in infertility."

"Isn't PID just another name for VD, doctor? Venereal disease."

Jarman nodded. "Yes, it is. Sometime in her past, Mrs. Loomis had PID."

The crowd gasped. The jury stared at Molly. The camera bore down on her and she blushed to a near purple color. Barnes continued. "And it rendered her sterile."

"Almost certainly."

Barnes was relentless. "And, Doctor, isn't VD the type of disease that a woman contracts through multiple sexual contacts, multiple partners, or other indiscriminate sexual behaviors?"

The question caused a minor roar in the crowd. Molly was too shocked to move. She felt nauseated, and the whole room seemed to spin. Tyler reached over and held her hand. He was still trying to act as if this was expected.

"It is contracted through unprotected sexual intercourse with an infected partner," answered Jarman. "Multiple partners increases the risk of obtaining the disease."

Van Gilder had to pound his gavel twice to quiet the crowd, and Barnes turned toward the audience standing right in front of Molly but looking over her. "So, Dr. Jarman, what we have here is a woman who has a past of promiscuous sexual behavior, an unwanted pregnancy with undetermined paternity, that she decided to terminate without even informing her husband and then concocting a story about a mystery doctor and some disease to cover her tracks."

Marcus leaped to his feet. "Objection!"

Van Gilder looked at him with an 'it's about time' face. "Sustained," he said. "Strike it from the record. Mr. Barnes, you will refrain from offering your personal commentary."

"My apologies, Your Honor," he said humbly. "No further questions."

The jury members glared at Molly Loomis. Never had she felt so humiliated. Never had she felt so completely crushed. She wanted to scream. She couldn't. She wanted to cry. She couldn't. She wanted to die. She prayed to die. It didn't happen. The camera seemed to be coming closer every second. "Mr. Sanders," she heard the judge say.

Marcus tried to think. His mind was blank. He heard the crowd behind him still murmuring. He looked at his partner, but Briggs was obviously lost too. "Mr. Briggs," said Van Gilder.

Tyler stood. His knees nearly buckled. "No questions, Your Honor."

The judge nodded. He too wanted to mercifully end it. "Anything more, Mr. Barnes?"

"No, your Honor," Barnes stated. "The defense rests."

"Court stands adjourned until 9:00 A.M. tomorrow."

In an instant, Molly Loomis was gone. She bolted through the side door before anyone could stop her. She ran past a gaggle of reporters who had guessed correctly she would leave through that exit. For an instant, they had her trapped and they battered her with questions about who she had contracted it from and how many partners she had had. Molly, her eyes covered by her hands, tried to barrel through the crowd of reporters. They struggled to hold her back, still hammering away with questions about her sexual preferences but she managed to push through, never answering any questions. More reporters arrived as she began to run. They screamed at her as she passed by, but still she offered no reply. Only the cameras caught her, beaming her tears across the country as she flew out of sight. Sylvia, Letisha, and Sandra ran through the same side door and tried to catch her, but she was gone in an instant. Tyler and Marcus stood by in the courtroom, dumbfounded, angry, and equally humiliated.

Standing behind the defense lawyers, H. Carter Hutchins could barely contain his delight. He had returned for Dr. Jarman's testimony, having relished the chance to watch Molly Loomis be destroyed. It had been even more beautiful than he imagined. First they won the case. Now, her destruction was complete. Annihilation on national TV. He laughed out loud. It was absolutely glorious.

"Take that, you little bitch," he sneered. "Take that!"

Chapter Thirty-eight

In their living room, Dr. Eric Johnson and his wife, Diane, watched as a tearful Molly Loomis bolted from the courtroom, a stream of reporters hot on her tail. With spectators and reporters milling about in the aftermath, and television commentators openly speculating about Molly's sordid past, Eric leaned forward and covered his face. Diane began to cry. For two weeks, she had been the one who held him back. Her family, their future, had been her reasons, but now that decision seemed painfully selfish. For ten minutes, Diane cried in his arms. Finally gathering herself, she looked up into her husband's own tear-stained eyes. "Make the call," she choked. "Go."

Eric kissed his wife on the lips and held her tightly. A minute later, he reached over to the end table and picked up the phone. Dr. Steven Royce answered on the second ring. "My car isn't working right," said Johnson.

"I was afraid of that."

"I'm bringing it in."

"I'll be waiting," said Royce.

Johnson hung up. He stood up and walked to the front of the living room. He looked out the window and into the darkness. The anonymous car that had watched him for the past month was still there, barely hidden in the shadow of a tree down the street. "I love you," he said to his wife without looking over his shoulder.

Diane Johnson did not hesitate. "I love you too."

Halfway through the ten o'clock news, Tyler was floating from the light buzz of two margaritas. Comfortably seated in his favorite chair in the den, he raised his glass in a mock toast as Marcus Sanders joined in. "To destroying someone on national TV," he said

"Quit it, Tyler," Marcus said. "It isn't your fault."

"Yes, it is," moaned Tyler. "We should have known. All along there was something weird. They killed her. They absolutely killed her."

"Has anybody seen or heard from her?" Marcus wondered.

"Sylvia's still looking, but no."

"I hope she doesn't do anything rash."

That thought crossed Tyler's mind for the first time. "She won't."

Marcus sipped his margarita. "I don't know if I've ever felt worse. They absolutely killed her. They absolutely killed us."

"Six witnesses," Tyler grunted. "Six damn witnesses, and they crush us like flies." He stopped and threw his head back, opening his eyes toward the ceiling. "It doesn't matter. I just wanna find Molly."

Marcus nodded. "What did the news say about it? I was making drinks."

Tyler still looked at the ceiling. The alcohol relaxed him, but caused the room to spin slightly. "They called her a scheming slut, or something almost that bad."

Tyler stood up. He walked to the kitchen to retrieve the pitcher of margaritas. There was no point in not drinking. All that was left of the trial were the closing arguments. They had nothing to offer in rebuttal. He freshened his drink first and then poured for the others.

He was just about to take a sip when the phone rang.

"Tyler," came the voice.

"Hello, Reggie," he said, taking the drink.

Reggie Tan sounded excited. "Something's going down."

"You know where Molly is?"

Reggie paused. "Yes."

"Is she okay?"

"A little better, but she doesn't want to talk."

"I'd like to," Briggs said.

"I don't think so. I think she's had enough today. They kinda dissected her."

"I understand. Tell her I'm sorry." Tyler said.

"She doesn't blame you. She knew the risks. She knew it could be ugly."

Tyler Briggs's intestines felt like curdled milk, rotten and poisoned. Never before in his life had he so badly wished a client had not acted courageously. Never had he felt so lousy. "I know, but still—"

"If you can believe it," continued Reggie, "that useless ex-husband of hers is actually being nice to her. I think the guy has just about drowned in guilt."

He did not press Reggie for details or her whereabouts. He knew Molly deserved privacy, and he changed the subject. "What do you mean something's going down?"

"Markham's been with lawyers all day."

"ComHealth lawyers?"

"No. Other ones. They've been meeting in secret spots."

"Reggie, I don't even want to know how you know this."

"I won't tell you."

Tyler thought about it. "That could mean anything."

"Uh-uh," replied Reggie. "It's something 'cause Hutchins has been looking for him."

Suddenly Briggs was interested. He knew Reggie had been listening in on Hutchins' cell phone conversations for a couple of weeks. "How long?"

"Twenty-four hours."

"No one's talked to him?"

"He's like, completely disappeared."

"Keep me posted," said Tyler.

"Will do."

Briggs hung up and told the others. Just as Marcus was about to reply, the phone rang again. "Yes, Reggie?" Briggs asked, assuming something had been forgotten.

"Mr. Briggs?" came a female voice.

"Yes?"

"I am calling to tell you that you have a very important doctor's appointment tonight."

Briggs looked baffled. "What?"

"There is a cab outside your front door to take you there."

Tyler carried the cordless phone to the front door. Sure enough, there was a Yellow Cab in his driveway. Briggs had no idea what to think, but he played along. There was nothing left to lose. "And what doctor am I going to see?" he asked.

"One who will shed some light on your condition," she replied.

Tyler stopped. The alcohol was gone, and his mind rapidly raced through possible scenarios. He thought of many, but none that would suggest some sort of trap. "I'll be right there."

"Thank you."

When he hung up the phone, Marcus looked at him quizzically. "What the hell was that?" Marcus asked.

"Don't know," Tyler said forgetting about his margarita. "But don't go to bed. Something's going on."

The night was gloomy, with a hazy fog obscuring the higher downtown lights as the cab carrying Tyler Briggs passed from the western suburbs of Minneapolis and into the concrete forest of downtown. The cabby had been prepaid and drove him without a word to the emergency room entrance at the Hennepin County Medical Center. Tyler turned occasionally to watch the tail behind him as they drove. It was the same brown sedan that had been parked outside his house for days and it continued to follow him now. He worried little. As he told himself again, any kind of trap made no sense after this day.

As usual, the ER was busy. Three ambulances arrived simultaneously, and an army of paramedics and nurses were scurrying about, wrestling with three critically ill patients. The cab drive drove past them and stopped right in front of the canopied trauma room entrance. Tyler opened his own door, and as he got out of the car, a large black woman with a mane of red hair approached him. "Tyler Briggs?" she nearly yelled above the commotion.

"Yes,"

She extended her hand. "I'm Dolores Smith."

"Pleased to meet you."

"Won't you follow me?"

Dolores pushed her way through the door that abutted the electronic entryway. Tyler followed. Inside, people clad in scrub suits moved rapidly in every direction. Behind the main nursing desk, a large board listing patient names and room numbers was completely full, and the telephones seemed to be ringing three times per second. A full waiting room was to his right. X-ray and the examining rooms were to his left. In the distance, Tyler heard a scream and a crash, and from his right, an orderly took off to investigate as if on command. Wading through the chaos, Dolores Smith never blinked. She moved forward, leading Tyler away from all the action.

As Briggs walked behind her, many paused to look to look at him. Some nodded, other waved. Most politely looked at him for less than a second before returning to their task. In an odd way, he had become a celebrity within this small world. A world he set about to protect without ever having been part of it. A world he now felt he had let down.

Dolores Smith took him to the second floor and pointed to a door labeled Surgeons' Lounge.

"He's in there."

"Thanks," Briggs replied.

"I'll get you a cab for when you go back."

Dolores was gone before Briggs could reply. Suddenly he found himself alone in the hall. He opened the door in front of him tentatively, as if not knowing what to expect. "Come in, Mr. Briggs," came a voice. Tyler pushed the door open the rest of the way. "Please sit down."

He sat in the corner of a spartan lounge, decorated only with a handful of chipped plastic chairs, a battered couch, and an old Remington print. He was average in size, with brown hair and emerald eyes that seemed to pierce through the dim light. His roundish face was boyish, but the crows feet and hints of gray hair spoke of at least thirty-five years. "Glad you came," the man said. "The name's Steven Royce."

Tyler sat down on one of the chairs, and Royce offered him a can of Diet Coke he had hidden in his long white lab coat. Briggs refused.

"Habit," Royce replied. "What can I say."

The intercom clicked on, and a man's voice sounded. "Dr. Royce?"

"Yes."

"ETA ten minutes."

"Thanks."

Briggs watched him sip on his Diet Coke. The doctor looked tired, but more than that, he was a man apparently consumed by a thought. Briggs knew the look. The heavy eyelids beneath the wrinkled brow. It was the look of a man possessed by a demon he could not rid himself of. It was a look Briggs himself had worn often lately.

"You had a tough day," said Royce.

Briggs could feel his intestines churn again. "The worst."

"The jackals ate her."

Briggs was mystified as to what was going on. He had hoped that there would be something helpful at the end of the mystery, but he was in no mood to discuss the case with a total stranger. "Yes, they did, but Dr. Royce—"

Steve Royce waved at him. "Sorry, my mind is in five different spots. I'll get to the point."

"Maybe I should have that Diet Coke."

Royce chuckled and tossed him the other one. "Follow me," he commanded. "That's why you're here. I want to give you a tour."

For the second time in five minutes, Tyler Briggs became a follower. His presence in the hospital, being led around by a strange physician, both seemed odd, but he was convinced of only one thing: he was there for a reason. Briggs walked right behind Royce as they left the surgeons' lounge and headed down an empty hall. A minute later, they entered the cardiac care unit.

The two men stood outside a room protected by a large glass window. Inside, an unconscious patient lay on the bed, hooked to several monitors. A woman of about forty sat beside the bed. Two teenage boys sat beside her.

"Forty-three years old," said Royce. "His third heart attack. He's had two bypass operations, four angioplasties, and now a stroke."

"Oh, God," said Briggs.

"No man in his family has lived past forty-five." Briggs just shook his head. He looked at the patient's family. He could see the sadness in their eyes, the end of their dreams. "Know what the cost-effective thing to do would be?"

"What?" asked Tyler.

Royce looked impassive. "Just what Messenger testified. A bullet."

Briggs did not blink. "Don't get me wrong," the doctor continued. "I'm not recommending that. If it was my patient, my friend, my family, I'd go to the mat for him. I just say that to illustrate that these business concepts have no basis in the reality of medicine. They're just the fantasy in some MBA's thesis somewhere. These are human lives, real people, not abstract ideas about profit and loss."

Briggs couldn't stop looking at the patient's family. He could see the weariness in the wife's eyes, confronting widowhood and the questions surrounding the fate of her family. Her life was written in her eyes, and her fears were etched in the lines around them. "C'mon," said Royce tugging at him.

They walked to the elevators and then down a long hall to the pediatric ward and into the oncology section. They passed through a series of glass doors and by a nursing station where one lone nurse barely looked up as they ambled by. At the end of the darkened hall, an Exit sign hung adjacent to a room. Briggs and Royce stopped before it and looked through two sets of glass windows. A boy about five lay asleep in the bed, curled under a sheet. He was completely bald, and the cap he used to cover his head had come off and lay beside him. His skin was a ghostly white, his hands and body so thin the bones could be seen through his pajamas. The room was decorated with sports posters. Karl Malone and Shaquille O'Neal; Randy Moss, and an autographed helmet of Brett Favre.

"Born with AIDS," said Royce. "His father was the carrier. Never saw him again. Mother died two years ago."

"Oh, God," muttered Briggs.

"Poor kid. No one's ever wanted him. Couple of foster homes, in and out of hospitals. Originally from Illinois, but most hospitals don't want him because he's too expensive to care for."

"How's he doing?" Briggs asked with the tentative voice of someone who knows the answer.

Royce shook his head. "I'm not really his doctor. I just come here every night to talk basketball. That's the sport he likes best. He got an autographed card from Shaquille O'Neal when the Lakers were here to play last winter. He hides it in his dresser so it doesn't get stolen." Royce's voice seemed to shake a bit. "He says when it happens, he wants it to be buried with him."

Tyler Briggs looked at the limp white hand of the little boy whose name he did not know. The hand's smooth skin belied the coarse reality of the protruding bones beneath. This boy was a statistic the bureaucrats could quote with callous ease. He was an expense, a cost, a throwaway.

"He doesn't have long," Royce said.

"I want to know," Tyler said honestly.

Royce nodded. "I will. I'll let you know."

The doctor tugged at him again, and they moved through a series of halls to the other side of the building. A minute later, they were in the neonatal ICU. Standing again behind a glass window, they saw two exhausted-looking parents napping on each other in front of what looked like a plastic cage. Royce wiped a strand of hair back that had fallen on his forehead and looked inside. "Baby was born yesterday. A preemie. Twenty three hundred grams."

Tyler didn't know medicine, but he knew that twenty three hundred grams was very small. "What are the chances?"

Royce cocked an eyebrow. "Ninety–ten against."

"Shit," Briggs grunted. He could see the expressionless face of the tiny infant hidden beneath the tape of an endotracheal tube.

"Parents tried for eight years. Mom's got problems herself. This may be it." Royce became philosophical. "Think about it. What do you say to people? 'Sorry, it's too expensive to care for this one? We won't treat him. You go have another.'"

"No," Tyler said.

"Mr. Briggs, that's a baby there. If he lives, he'll probably have problems all his life. If he dies, he'll save ComHealth boatloads of money." Royce's eyes narrowed. He looked almost menacing. "Mr. Briggs, look at the parents, look at the child. Then look me in the eye and see if you can tell me that their incentive is to provide good care."

Briggs never budged. "I can't."

Royce's pager went off while Briggs watched the mother stroke the tiny child's chest. The father, who had been sleeping, lifted his head up and did the same. The tiny infant twitched slightly, his head rolling toward his father and his eyes cracking open. "I've got five minutes," Royce said after the phone call.

"No problem."

Dr. Steven Royce led him back to the surgeons' lounge, where they took the same seats they had occupied minutes before. Royce leaned back against the wall. "I wanted to show you those people just to illustrate a point I think you already know."

"The business of medicine," Briggs replied.

"Think about it," sighed Royce. "The business of medicine is medicine. When it becomes money, it becomes only a perversion of what it was intended to be." Royce looked sad. He took a sip of the Diet Coke he had left behind on the chair.

"That why you asked me here?" Briggs asked.

Royce stared through him at the wall. "No. A friend asked me to talk to you."

"Why didn't he ask me?"

Royce didn't answer right away. He seemed to fade into his own world. "Mr.

Briggs, you're an excellent lawyer. Everything you've said or thought, is true. You've stood for a cause that a courageous man needed to fight, and I commend you. But I want to ask you a question about all this. It's a question you need to answer—Why?"

"What?" Tyler asked.

"Why?" Royce repeated.

Briggs was perplexed. "I felt it was worthy."

"No, not the case. Molly Loomis."

"What about Molly?" he asked, completely baffled.

Steven Royce stood up and peered into the operating suites. He could see his operating room gearing up for his case. "What I saw this afternoon with Whitfield killing her with that PID stuff in front of the world."

"Yes."

"And I asked myself, Why?"

Briggs nearly shook when he thought of it. "It was a brutal tactic, but they played it well. Conniving, promiscuous liar, money-hungry pervert. Hey, they went for the jugular and got it."

Royce stopped him. "That's not what I asked, Mr. Briggs," he said pointedly. "I asked you, Why?"

Briggs bit his tongue. He had no idea what Dr. Royce was talking about.

"You're a lawyer," said Royce. "A good one. But therein lies your error. You have to change hats for a minute. Think like a doctor, and then ask yourself, Why?"

Briggs put his head down. His brain seemed dead. He started to speak, but before he could say anything, a frightened-looking intern flew through the door with a CT scan in his hand. He was panting and he handed it to Royce, who held it up to the light. "Twenty-nine-year-old male," said the dark-haired young doctor. "Roughhousing with his son. He clipped the side of his head on an end table. Fine initially, his wife found him unconscious twenty minutes later. Now he's fixed and dilated on the right, hemiparetic, upgoing toe on the left."

Dr. Steven Royce looked at the brain CT. A large biconvex area of hyperintensity could be seen displacing the right temporal lobe. "Big epidural," said the neurosurgeon Royce. "We'll decompress through the first burr hole while we turn the flap."

"Gotcha," the intern said, preparing to run off.

"And Tony," Royce said.

"Yes?"

"Put a move on it."

"Yes, sir."

In a flash, the intern was gone. Royce stood and took a surgical cap out of his lab coat and tied it around his head. Next, he took off his lab coat, revealing the surgical scrubs he was already wearing. "So, Mr. Briggs, here I was, watching the trial like any spectator. And I asked myself, Why?"

"Why the ectopic pregnancy?" asked Briggs.

"No. He told you that. PID."

"Why the PID?" Tyler guessed.

"No. He told you that. Sexually transmitted."

Briggs put his head down. He was no doctor, and he didn't pretend to be. Royce walked over and put his hand on the lawyer's shoulder. He opened his mouth, but Briggs leaped to his feet, nearly knocking the doctor back. "Why the infertility?"

Royce broke a hint of a smile, stepping away. "Getting warmer. Go on."

Briggs's mind began to shift gears. "What percentage of PID goes on to such severe scarring?"

"Very small," nodded Royce.

Briggs could feel his heart pound right through his chest. "And what percentage causes infertility?"

Royce shook his head. He could almost see Briggs's thoughts. "What do you know about her medical history?" asked the doctor.

Briggs started to pace, trying to recall the first part of Molly's medical file. Only hours ago, it had seemed so totally irrelevant. "History of a previous miscarriage."

"When?" questioned Royce.

"Shortly after she was married."

Royce opened a wooden box and pulled out his surgical loupes, draping them around his neck. "You're getting warmer. What else? Could something have caused the miscarriage?"

"I-I don't know."

Royce shook his head. "Keep thinking."

Briggs struggle to think. It was there, somewhere. His brain had gone from paralysis to random thinking. He was too excited to think clearly. He struggled, but nothing came.

"Anything else she ever told you. Anything you remember in the record?"

Briggs closed his eyes. Something came back: a vague memory. He could almost hear Molly's voice. "She told me about it. Something a few years ago. Think it was a bladder infection."

Royce's green eyes narrowed again. A sardonic smile crossed his lips. "Bingo."

Tyler stood in the center of the surgeons' lounge. As soon as Steven Royce said it, the lawyer felt his knees buckle. The image became perfectly clear. For the first time since he had met his client, everything made sense.

Tyler could barely breathe. His head hurt. His chest hurt. He tried to talk, but he couldn't. His thoughts were flying. The ComHealth strategy. The strange behavior of the lawyers. The quick trial. The lack of motions. No delays of any kind. Even the settlement offer. In retrospect, it seemed obvious. In foresight he had misunderstood. In hindsight, he knew now he had underestimated them.

"One final thought, Mr. Briggs," said Dr. Royce, looking at his hyperventilating friend. "There is a famous thought of Hippocrates that might shed some additional light on this. Would you like to hear it?"

"Yes."

Royce retied his scrub pants tighter as he heard the commotion coming down the hall. "Hippocrates advocated concealing most things from the patient while you are attending to him, revealing nothing of the patient's future or present condition." Steven Royce chuckled. "Fortunately, like bloodletting, such patronizing treatment became merely an embarrassing part of medical history." The doctor stopped. He looked deep into Briggs's eyes. "Or has it?"

Briggs appeared to visibly shake. Months of work and a day of agony seemed to crash down upon him. Royce put his arm around his shoulder. Together, they looked out the room's lone window. They could see the hospital's front entrance. Royce spoke. "In fifteen years of medicine, I've learned a million things, but perhaps the most important is also the simplest." He pointed toward the entrance. "White, black, old, young, male, female. There are more differences than similarities and there always will be. But as you walk through this building and meet the patients that bring it life, you remember them for the humanity that they represent. The old people from the nursing homes that no one comes to visit. The abandoned boy in the oncology ward with his Shaquille O'Neal card. And the little preemie, fighting for his life. It's all about them, and the only thing in this world that we all share."

"What's that?" asked Briggs.

Royce still pointed at the hospital's front door. "That we're all the same. That one day, we all walk through that door."

A great crash sounded outside the lounge, and Tyler turned. A group of nurses wheeling a gurney carrying an unconscious man whirred by. The still-panting intern appeared at the door. "Family?" asked Royce.

The intern cocked his head to the side. "Right outside."

Royce turned back to Briggs and extended his hand. "Gotta go."

Tyler shook his hand and then peered around the corner. He could see a pretty woman in her late twenties with tear-stained eyes. She held a daughter of about two whose arms were wrapped around her neck. A son of about five was crying fearfully and stood behind his mother's leg, his arms wrapped around her.

Tyler spied the young family. At that instant, he knew he would have done anything to help them. Steven Royce leaned toward him. "Tell you one last thing," he whispered. "Never, ever is real medicine about the money."

Briggs tapped him on the shoulder. "Go."

The door closed behind him, and Steven Royce was gone. Through the door, Tyler could her his first words to the patient's family. "I'm Doctor Royce. I'm the neurosurgeon who's going to help see your husband through this."

Briggs began to walk the other way. The determined words warmed him. He made a mental note to visit this patient in the next couple of days, but at the moment, he was too scattered to even write down the name. He tried to think clearly, but all he could comprehend was that he needed to get going and quickly. He ran out the surgeons' lounge side door. Dolores Smith was standing right outside, and he nearly sent the big woman sprawling as the door flung open.

"In a hurry?" she asked coyly.

"Gotta go."

"Your cab is ready."

Tyler leaned over and impulsively kissed the woman on the cheek. "Too bad you're married," she laughed.

"Thanks again," he said, as he started to take off. He took two steps and suddenly stopped. He turned. "One thing, Dolores, who sent you?" he asked.

"Dr. Royce."

"Who sent him?"

Dolores Smith grinned. "The doctor who took care of Molly Loomis four years ago."

"Who was that?"

"Dr. Royce's medical school roommate."

"His name?"

"Dr. Eric Johnson."

"Love ya!" Tyler Briggs touched her on the cheek and sprinted off down the hall. He could barely breathe, but breathlessness had never felt so good. He felt like he could fly.

Dolores Smith had not lied. The cab was waiting for him right outside the ER. He hopped in and breathlessly gave instructions to return to his home. The cab took off and headed away from the busy ER. Settling into his seat, Tyler reached into his pocket and pulled out his cell phone. He punched in his home number. In only seconds, he was talking to Marcus Sanders.

"Sanders," he gushed. "Put down the margaritas. Get the coffee on the burner."

"What? Whattya got?"

Tyler looked behind him, out the back window. He could see that the same car that had followed him to the hospital was following them as they sped onto Highway 35W. "We had it all along, Marcus," he said, his voice shaking. "We just missed it."

"What?"

"I'll tell you when I get there."

"Wattya know?" Marcus asked.

"Damn," Tyler grunted. Suddenly the idea of talking on a cell phone scared him. "I wanna tell you, but who knows who's listening?" He looked out the windows. The car was still there. He also noticed that two more Yellow Cabs had joined them, one on each side, driving at the same speed.

"I hear ya."

Briggs took out a notepad and scratched down a few lines. "Marcus, listen to me. We've got to find a doctor. Tonight."

"Who?" asked Marcus.

"Guy named Eric Johnson."

There was a long pause before Marcus replied. "You've got to be kidding me."

Briggs could feel his adrenaline surging as the cab blazed along the freeway, his tailing sedan two cars back. "No, I'm not. Gotta be tonight. No other way. We gotta dig to China if we have to."

"Can't be done, Tyler," said Marcus confidently. "No way."

"Why the hell not?" Briggs nearly screamed.

"Because I know! You're not gonna believe this, but that guy has disappeared."

"What?" bellowed Briggs nearly blowing out the cab's windows.

"I'm serious. The guy is gone. History. No one knows where he is."

"Shit!" boomed Tyler. "How in the hell?"

"Swear to it. I just got off the phone with Reggie. Says Hutchins and his boys have been in a panic. And that's the guy, Eric Johnson. Seems they lost him a little while ago and have been burning up the airwaves. They've been following him for some time I guess."

Briggs was almost panicky. "No way! I don't care what we have to do! We gotta find him! Call anybody and wake up everyone! Hell! Put it on TV!"

"Okay, okay," said Marcus soothingly. "I'll get everyone I can think of. We'll go to work. But what exactly does this guy know?"

Tyler closed his eyes. "I'm not sure. But I've got a pretty damn good idea."

"How long will you be?"

Briggs was beside himself. Thoughts overwhelmed his brain. He was twitching as he spoke, straining to think straight, but he managed to look at where they were on the freeway. "Oh, I'll be at the house in twenty."

"All right. I'm on it. I'll start making calls."

"Go," said Tyler without hesitation. "Don't waste any more time talking to me."

Briggs punched the End button and hung up. He closed his eyes. Never had he felt so frustrated. He had to talk to Eric Johnson. He had to. "Damn." He grunted.

"Excuse me?" the cabby muttered.

"Nothing," Briggs said as he opened his eyes. He looked out the window. The bizarre sight struck him like a fist. "One, two, three," he counted. "Six, eight, nine." Yellow Cabs were everywhere, surrounding them and rapidly switching lanes. Just then, two more cabs joined them, while two exited off a left ramp. Tyler looked behind them. He could make out the two men in the brown sedan pointing furiously. The car switched lanes, swerved back toward the middle, and then wildly swung to the left and followed the two cabs off the side exit. "What the hell?" Briggs said out loud. "Ten Yellow Cabs?"

The cabby did not respond. The cabs that had surrounded them honked, waved, and then rapidly dispersed, exiting at various sites on both sides of the freeway. The cabby seemed oblivious to it all, staring straight ahead. He drove a half-mile further and exited on Diamond Lake Road. At the first intersection, they stopped at a red light. "What the hell is this?" Briggs demanded.

The cabby turned around. "Hello, Mr. Briggs," he said extending his hand and pulling off a baseball cap. "I apologize for the inconvenience."

"Just who are you?

"My name is Eric Johnson."

Chapter Thirty-nine

August 29

At 9:00 A.M. in Judge John Van Gilder's private chamber, the great lawyer Jackson Barnes was in a fury. With a fervor usually reserved for a religious revival, his voice rose and fell like the crescendos and decrescendos of a magnificent symphony as he pontificated about everything from legal issues to his philosophy of life. His eyes were as big as baseballs. His neck was as burnt as a robin's breast. His speech was pressured and frantic. And his thunderous words were a cacophony of verbosity: big words, with as many impressive syllables as he could muster. It was a spell-binding performance and rich in the tradition of legal excess. But Tyler Briggs knew that none of it mattered. There was little doubt what Van Gilder's ruling would be.

"No way you can let him testify, John," roared Barnes, inadvertently slipping into the friendly vernacular of golfing buddies. "No way."

"Thank you for telling me my job," grunted the judge, looking ever wearier, and nursing a carton of orange juice he carried with him throughout the morning.

Harley Whitfield stood up next to his partner and put his hand across his chest. He wore his best wounded expression. His eyes were serene and pastoral. His voice was as sweet as an expensive liqueur. "In all my years of outstanding legal service to this community." He stopped, blushed, and looked at the judge. "Er, I mean, in all *your* years of legal service to this community—"

Van Gilder interrupted, his irritation beginning to show after Barnes' half-hour soliloquy. "Put a lid on it, Harley. Take a seat."

The two lawyers obediently sat down. It was obvious to all. The judge had had enough grandstanding. Briggs and Sanders, sitting patiently across from Van Gilder, never moved. They were perfectly content to let the defense lawyers flail and wail.

The judge stroked his chin. "Dr. Johnson will be a witness used to rebut the testimony of Dr. Jarman. Plain and simple."

"But your Honor!" whined Whitfield.

"You introduced it, gentlemen."

"John!"

"Forget it. End of discussion, gentlemen. This one is, what do the kids say? What is it—a no-brainer?"

"I must protest, Your Honor," complained Whitfield.

"Noted."

"I most *vigorously* protest," he howled.

"Should we put 'vigorously' in capitals in the official record?" asked the judge. The flippant remark caused Sanders to giggle and the ComHealth lawyers to fume.

"Your Honor," began Barnes, ridding himself of the judge's first name. "We'll need months, perhaps even *years* to adequately depose this witness."

Van Gilder groaned. "Listen, Jack, since this trial began, I've been asking myself every single day what you guys were up to. You've had a million chances to delay it, and now you want a decade's delay over the testimony of one witness?" The judge was clearly dubious of their supposed need. "I can smell something. Smell something bad. And that something is telling me that you already know every word this man is going to say."

"Your Honor," protested Whitfield.

The judge turned red. He would listen to no more. "You have two hours, gentlemen. Court will be in session at 11 A.M. That is the end of the discussion."

For the first time since the trial began, the crowd outside the courthouse was small and quiet as the morning session opened on Friday. The two-hour delay went largely unnoticed as the once-massive show of public support for Molly Loomis completely evaporated. Harley Whitfield's direct examination of Dr. Jarman portraying Molly as a calculating, lying, gold-digging, nymphomaniac was so convincing that the city abandoned her as readily as it had once embraced her. Most in the media criticized her openly, now buying completely Whitfield's reasoning that Molly fabricated the entire story to cover up her lies. A few resisted the temptation to openly criticize her, but even in these reports, the suspicion and innuendo were clear. Most reporters directly stated that she had been a poor choice to lead such an important fight.

Molly arrived at the courthouse in Gus LeClerc's old Bonneville ten minutes before the trial resumed. She stayed the night in her boss's basement apartment and had done her best to make herself look presentable for the morning session. Her eyes still appeared bloodshot, and her hair was lifeless, but as she walked the long stairway to the courthouse alone, she did so with her head up, trying to ignore the catcalls of "slut," "murderer" and "VD Queen" that were launched at her. The cheering crowds were long gone, but the protesters were not. They continued to howl at her as she walked by, showering her with paper balls while a handful of cameras caught the spectacle on tape.

Inside the courtroom, the atmosphere was different as well. When Molly entered and sat down, few in the courtroom seemed to notice. The spectators seemed cold and indifferent. The press almost ignored her. Even the camera, once nearly always focused on her, now wandered away. Only her lawyers and her friends seemed to remain solidly in her corner, rising to greet her when she approached her seat.

At one minute after eleven, Van Gilder strode in. He looked more exhausted than ever, but as usual he was businesslike and methodical. He waved, called, and signaled. Everyone was seated, and without any delay the court was in session. "Mr. Briggs," the judge grunted.

Tyler Briggs was already standing. "We call Dr. Eric Johnson, your Honor."

An expectant hush fell on the courtroom as Eric Johnson appeared through the great front door. His face was grim. His walk was purposeful. But to the surprised audience, his intent was unclear.

The name caught Molly Loomis by complete surprise. She had not talked to Tyler since the day before and had no clue that her former doctor would be called as a witness. She caught a good look at him as he strode by her. It had been four years since her visits to him, and she thought he now looked much older. She remembered that his eyes had once been a Scandinavian blue. Now they seemed almost gray.

Johnson sat down and unbuttoned his suit coat. He took a deep breath and wiped a bit of sweat from his upper lip as the bailiff swore him in. Johnson nodded throughout the oath. His simple "I do," finished it. He barely had a chance to say it. Tyler Briggs was already approaching the witness stand.

"Dr. Johnson, I'd like to begin by discussing your education."

"Certainly."

For ten minutes, Tyler ran him through the "establish the expert" questions. Johnson was a board-certified OB/gyn who had trained at the University of Wisconsin. He belonged to all the expected professional organizations, and he had worked for ComHealth for five years. There were no objections from the defense. But as Johnson answered the questions, the defense team was in complete chaos. Barnes and Whitfield were jotting notes to each other. Cox and Farnsworth were busy shuffling a pile of papers between them. Three other associates were also behind the bench attending to their bosses' needs, while all seven men kept whispering to each other like children in a classroom.

Suddenly a voice from behind the ComHealth lawyers interrupted their disorganization. The attorneys all turned to H. Carter Hutchins as the CEO took his usual seat in the front row. Hutchins could barely speak, his anger was so extreme. "I want this fuckin' sonofabitch fired this afternoon," he hissed.

Barnes shook his head. "Can't do it, Carter."

"And why the hell not?"

Barnes looked pale. "Because he resigned at 8:00 A.M. this morning."

Carter Hutchins fell back limply his chair. For the first time in his life, the great medical tycoon was speechless.

"Dr. Johnson," continued Tyler, "for the past five years, you have been in the employment of the defendant, Community Health One, have you not?"

"Yes."

"And are you still employed by them?"

"No."

"When did your employment with ComHealthOne end?"

"At eight this morning. I resigned."

Surprised sounds reverberated in the courtroom. Van Gilder quelched the noise.

"Was there a reason for your resignation?"

"To avoid being fired."

Tyler walked toward the witness stand. "Why would you have been fired?"

"I think you'll know in a few minutes," he replied.

The courtroom laughed nervously. Even Barnes smiled a bit as he continued to scribble notes. Van Gilder tapped his gavel and restored order. "You will answer the questions, Dr. Johnson," he warned.

"I'm sorry, your Honor."

Tyler strolled in front of the jury and stopped. He knew there was little doubt that everyone in the courtroom was already hanging on every word. Johnson's appearance was unexpected, and even the reporters in the back row, disinterested ten minutes before, were scrambling for any information they could find on Eric Johnson.

"Dr. Johnson, at any time in the past were you Molly Loomis's physician?"

"Yes, from July through September four years ago."

"At that time were you in the employment of ComHealthOne."

"Yes."

Molly leaned forward, her elbows on the table. She couldn't help staring at Johnson. She tried to remember the exact conversation, but she couldn't. It had been too long ago. She always thought it was a bladder infection. She was sure it was a bladder infection.

"And can you describe the nature of her first visit to you."

"It was July thirty-first of that year. I saw Ms. Loomis in the afternoon for complaints of abdominal pain, fever, and vaginal discharge."

"And what did you do?"

"I was very concerned and immediately suspicious of pelvic inflammatory disease, or PID as it is often called. Because PID is a sexually transmitted disease I asked for a detailed sexual history from Ms. Loomis."

"And what did she tell you, Doctor?"

"That she was married. And that she had had one sexual partner in her life."

"One sexual partner?" he asked, as the crowd murmured loudly.

"Yes."

"And who was this?"

"Her husband."

Tyler Briggs tried hard not to glare at Jack Barnes. He understood legal maneuvering, but he was still angry at his character assassination of yesterday. He relished the chance now to shove the truth down the ComHealth lawyers' throat. "So in the confidence of your office, with her own health on the line, this was Ms. Loomis's confidential history? Her true sexual history? One partner, her husband?"

"Yes, it was."

"Thank you." Briggs still glared at the defense table. The ComHealth lawyers were way too busy staring at their important scribbles to look up. "Is it true, Dr. Johnson, that with PID, the male is often the carrier and that he often has few symptoms?"

"That is correct. I felt confident that Ms. Loomis had contracted it from her husband."

"And did you ask about her husband's sexual past?"

"Yes, I did."

"And?"

Dr. Johnson looked a little sheepish. "She implied that her husband had—

er—um—*dated*—extensively before their marriage."

"Certainly," said Tyler. "And following the history what did you do?"

"I performed a pelvic examination."

"And your findings?"

"Ms. Loomis had purulent vaginal discharge as well as adnexal tenderness, tenderness in the area of the fallopian tubes and ovaries."

"What did this mean to you?"

"She had acute PID. There was no question about it."

The room was so quiet that Van Gilder could be heard putting his water glass down. Tyler turned to the defense lawyers. He remembered his own ghostly gaze as Dr. Jarman had testified the day before. Barnes and Whitfield now looked like twin sheets hanging on a clothes line. It was wonderful "What did you do next?"

"In the gynecology community, there is mild controversy over the management of PID. Some mild forms can be managed safely on an outpatient basis with antibiotics. Others require inpatient management with antibiotics through the vein."

Molly was baffled. She turned to Marcus. She remembered none of this.

"And what category did Ms. Loomis fall into?"

"There is complete, I repeat, *complete*, agreement that patients who manifest the most severe signs and symptoms, those being pain, fever, and vaginal discharge, be admitted to the hospital."

"Which Ms. Loomis had."

"Yes."

"So she was admitted to the hospital?"

Eric Johnson took a deep breath. "No, she wasn't."

Briggs was now zeroing in. He moved right in front of the jury "And why not?"

"That afternoon my office nurse called ComHealth for authorization to admit her to the hospital. It was denied. I called back and appealed. The admission was again denied. I was informed that according to new policy, inpatient treatment would be authorized only if the patient failed outpatient management."

"Admitted only if the symptoms continued while the patient was taking pills, oral antibiotics."

"Yes. You must remember that antibiotics through the vein are much more potent, but they are also much more expensive."

"So ComHealth was trying to save money?"

"Yes," said Johnson.

"Objection!" roared Whitfield. "The witness cannot possibly know the intentions of the defendant."

"Sustained."

Briggs didn't care, having made his point. "What happened next?"

"I was furious. I had never heard of anything so outrageous in all my life. This was a young woman, clearly ill, needing large doses of powerful antibiotics as an inpatient and it was not being allowed."

"What precisely were you concerned about?"

"Inadequate treatment results in scarring of the fallopian tubes and a high incidence of infertility." Briggs was watching the jury. Their eyes were glued to

Johnson. "And then what happened, Dr. Johnson?"

"I got into a shouting match with the nurse who was handling the case, accusing ComHealth of inappropriate interference in medical decision making."

"And next?"

"I was informed that according to policy, inpatient treatment was not warranted. And I was informed that according to my contract, I was forbidden from even *telling* her that I was recommending inpatient treatment. I would be fired if I told her."

The crowd gasped. The jury looked thunderstruck. Even Van Gilder looked amazed. "What did you do?" asked Briggs.

"At first I didn't know what to do. I was just a year out of training. I couldn't afford to get fired. It would be like being blacklisted. I still had $150,000 in educational loans. I had a newborn baby, a house, a marriage." Eric Johnson looked distraught and the room sensed his torment. Johnson looked toward the back of the room. His wife Diane stood alone, egging him on. The jury spied her as she shifted nervously from foot to foot.

"So what did you do, Doctor?"

Eric Johnson couldn't seem to speak. "I wanted to tell her."

"What did you do, Dr. Johnson?" repeated Briggs.

"I swear to God, I wanted to tell her the truth." He stopped. He seemed almost to choke. "She was so young. She was just married. She wanted kids."

"What did you do, Dr. Johnson?"

"I wanted—" His voice drained off.

"What did you *do*?" boomed Tyler.

Johnson turned pale. The years of torment still turned courage to fear. But now, the dreams, the nightmares, the horror of what he had done—it all seemed to descend upon him. He couldn't stop sweating. He could barely speak. "I lied to her."

"What?"

He sighed. "I told her what ComHealth wanted me to tell her."

The crowd let out a collective gasp that ascended into a dull roar. Barnes and Whitfield both sat with their lips quivering like an amorphous gel while Cox, Farnsworth, and Hutchins appeared apoplectic. Even the judge seemed to forget his job, letting the noise continue for half a minute, while his eyes bulged out in disbelief. Outside, chaos came quickly with Johnson's admission. The TV stations, which had started to abandon the trial, scrambled to switch back on. Reporters on the streets were suddenly running everywhere, tripping over cords, colliding with each other, and screaming at everyone.

Inside the courtroom, behind their table, Molly's eyes swelled with tears. Suddenly she knew. Suddenly she understood. The years of abdominal pains and strange sensations. The inability to get pregnant and all the other oddities. Now it made sense. The tears continued, but anger surged within her. Fury! How could he? raced through her mind. How could he? A doctor! A doctor who lied to her! A lie that had cost her everything she had ever wanted. Tears fell fast. She bit hard into her cheek, trying to keep from calling out.

She felt Marcus' arm on her neck, pulling her toward him. She leaned into his shoulder for a second and then jerked away, returning to her spot and looking at him. Marcus' eyes were soft and he mouthed some words she could not make out. She burned. She hurt. She felt dizzy and dazed. Marcus said something again. All she heard was "Molly." The noise in the courtroom was deafening. Reporters and spectators were nearly wild. Van Gilder seemed paralyzed, and Johnson looked devastated.

Molly turned from Marcus, wiped away her tears, and stared into the distraught doctor's eyes. He was looking straight at her. He, too, appeared on the verge of tears, his voice repentant and his soul pleading. Molly closed her eyes. But it made no difference. This was *her* life, her dreams, that had been dashed. A lie! Nothing but a lie! Tears welled in her eyes. She could feel her lips twitch and her stomach churn. Anger surged inside of her. She ached to rise and scream. She felt Marcus' hand on her shoulder again. Molly ignored him. She turned to the back of the room to avoid the camera that bore down upon her. She wiped her eyes. The audience all stared at her with looks ranging from sympathy to shock. Marcia, Sylvia, and Jayne looked white.

Molly's face had no expression. She let her eyes roam as she breathed deeply and tried to calm the fire that burned inside. Finally she saw a woman standing at the back. Diane Johnson, Eric's wife. She was slight and pale and looked enough like Molly to be her sister. She gazed at Molly looking sad and remorseful, her eyes filled with anguish and relief at the same time. Molly abruptly turned away.

"What happened next?" asked Tyler.

"Ms. Loomis went home with the antibiotic pills."

"And then?"

"Two weeks later, she returned. Her symptoms were slightly improved."

"What was your recommendation?"

"I still felt she should be admitted, but it was denied. My concern was that the disease often burns itself out, but not before the damage is done. The fact that she was getting a little better did not surprise me. But I was truly afraid she would be infertile."

"And how about after that?"

"She saw me one final time, in September. She said she was having only occasional pain and discharge."

"What did that mean to you?"

"That the disease was indeed burning itself out. I was sure there was a strong chance that she would never be able to bear children."

"Remind me, why is that?"

"Because the infection scars the inside of the female organs. The fertilized egg is either blocked from getting to the uterus or it fails to lodge anywhere."

"If it is blocked from getting to the uterus and it lodges in the fallopian tube it is an ectopic pregnancy, is it not?"

"It is."

"Precisely what Dr. Jarman found on pathological exam."

"Yes."

"And the scarring Dr. Jarman found. This is what you would expect to see from inadequately treated PID?"

"Yes," said Johnson.

Everyone in the jury leaned forward. Some were scribbling notes. Tyler continued to hammer it home. "So, in summary, Dr. Johnson, it is your expert opinion that Ms. Loomis was suffering from PID for which she received grossly inadequate treatment, rendering her infertile."

"Yes."

"Treatment contrary to the norms of gynecological practice. Treatment dictated to you by her insurance company and treatment forced upon you with the threat of losing your job."

"That is correct."

"And do I have it right? Ms. Loomis never even knew the truth of her own condition, the risks of her treatment, or the possibility of infertility."

"That is correct," he said. "She never knew until this moment."

The courtroom was in an uproar. Several jurors looked ill. Carter Hutchins looked ghostly. Barnes and Whitfield looked worse. They were even paler, and their gelatinous faces could only manage concocted smiles. Van Gilder shook his head disgustedly.

"No further questions, Your Honor," said Tyler.

Van Gilder tried to muster some force in his gavel. He tapped it only lightly, and the noise refused to die down. Outside the courtroom, the small crowd was wild. The handful watching in front of the ComHealth offices started to chant and scream. Cars honked their horns, and on all local stations "Special New Bulletins" hit the air. Meanwhile, the TV cameras continued to roll, the most important one bearing right down on a weakening Molly Loomis.

"Mr. Whitfield, Mr. Barnes, I presume you have some questions," grunted Van Gilder, his inner thoughts nearly boiling to the surface. Whitfield stood up. He rubbed his eyes like a man wishing he were anywhere else in the galaxy.

"Sit down!" screamed someone from the audience. Paper flew everywhere, and the placid court of an hour before disappeared in an instant. The mood turned ugly, and it threatened to degenerate further. Several men stood, screaming at the defense table, one pointing a finger menacingly at Hutchins.

Van Gilder shot up and slammed down the gavel. "Enough!" he screamed. A moment later, all four of the men and one woman were escorted forcefully from the courtroom. After, the judge warned everyone that there would be no more outbursts of any kind. His burning cinder eyes told everyone he wasn't kidding. "Mr. Whitfield," he said after a minute, "you may continue."

Molly Loomis missed the beginning of the cross-examination and the outburst. Her eyes had found Hutchins, and for the first time she gazed for some time at the great CEO. Through his pale face, his fiery eyes stared straight ahead. Looking at him, Molly felt nauseous. Her stomach churned as if fighting a poison he had inflicted upon her. Never had she felt so used, so deceived, and so betrayed. She couldn't cry. She couldn't scream. Her whole life. Everything she had ever wanted. Taken, manipulated, and thrown away by a man who personified the cliché that great fortunes were often great crimes. He, a man she didn't even know, a man who cared nothing about her. Her mind spun with rage. She felt dizzy.

"Dr. Johnson," continued Harley Whitfield. "Do you have any documentation of any of this?"

"No," replied Johnson. "When I went to check on these records after I first heard of Ms. Loomis's lawsuit, I found that all of the records pertaining to her illness and my appeals to ComHealth were missing."

"I see," said Whitfield sarcastically. "Flew off on a magic carpet? Eaten by your dog?"

"Actually," replied Johnson, "I thought you or Mr. Barnes might have them."

The courtroom broke up in hysterical laughter. Even Van Gilder chuckled for a moment, disregarding his forceful admonition of a moment before. Whitfield turned beet red with anger. It took a full minute before the courtroom was quiet enough to proceed. The ComHealth lawyer decided not to push the records issue too far. He was well aware that they had been destroyed by his junior partners. "But you can offer no physical proof that these visits took place?"

"No," replied Johnson, doubting that it mattered.

"And can you say conclusively that Ms. Loomis was rendered sterile from the treatment she received?"

"I'm not sure what you mean."

"Tell me, doctor, isn't it possible that the treatment of oral antibiotics was effective, and that she contracted PID at a later time, long after she had left your care?"

Johnson thought about it for a minute. Whitfield was trying hard, but he was reaching so far his arm was nearly halfway around the globe. Medically, the lawyer's thought was ludicrous. "Yes, I suppose it's possible. Just like I suppose you and Mr. Hutchins got VD from each other and later gave it to Molly after drugging her with some of your favorite illicit substances, but I doubt it."

The courtroom broke into hysterics. Van Gilder bit his tongue. The bailiff covered his face.

Only angry Harley Whitfield stood alone in the middle of the court. His mouth appeared to have been yanked sideways on a string, and his nose looked as though it could lead Santa's sleigh. A heat wave seemed to radiate off his body. "But it is possible," he finally managed, "isn't it?"

"Yes, it is," grunted Johnson. "But try the lottery. The odds are better."

Whitfield paused to let the courtroom settle down. The jury was still laughing amongst themselves, but Van Gilder had recovered enough to issue another warning.

Harley Whitfield appeared lost. He had long known Johnson's testimony would be impossible to refute, and worst of all, the particulars of the doctor's testimony were unknown. Anything he asked would yield an unknown answer. "Dr. Johnson, it was established that Mrs. Loomis had an earlier miscarriage, shortly after her marriage."

"That's correct."

"Isn't it possible that Mrs. Loomis had had this condition long before her marriage and that she had simply lied to you as well? Couldn't that have been the source of the earlier miscarriage?"

The frivolity in the courtroom was gone. Just as quickly, it was tomblike. Whitfield's point was good, and even Van Gilder sat up straight. "No," replied Johnson.

"Why not?"

Eric Johnson looked embarrassed. Despite his verbal shots at Harley

Whitfield, he found it difficult to talk about a patient's past so openly. "Because Ms. Loomis's miscarriage was caused by something else."

"And how can you be sure?"

"Because it happened when her husband was drunk and threw her down the stairs."

The crowd gasped, and Whitfield stepped back. His tongue felt like melted butter. He wanted to quit. He knew he was digging himself deeper. "And she told you this?" he asked lamely.

"Yes."

There was a noise, and the audience and jury turned. Troy Loomis stood in the middle of the court. Pathos and grief radiated from him. His eyes were closed and he was shaking visibly. He appeared desperate to confess. "Oh, God," he said pitifully.

Van Gilder cut him off. "Not one more word, son. Sit down right now or you'll be removed from this courtroom." Troy sat down, his head buried in his hands, his guilt radiating forth like the breeze from a powerful fan.

The audience stirred loudly. Several jurors started to talk among themselves. Van Gilder silenced them. Whitfield walked toward his table, carefully considering his options. He struggled to think. The scene was getting worse by the second. It was tempting to try to humiliate Johnson. The doctor had wounded him, and it hurt, but he decided against it. It was time to cut his losses. The old lawyer was experienced enough to know that personal vendettas against a witness were risky. Legally ComHealth was still on good footing and that was all that was important. He reminded himself again that the case was still about whether or not ComHealth should pay for an unauthorized hospital admission, not about her care four years ago. He took a deep breath and waved at Van Gilder. "No further questions, your Honor."

Five minutes later, Judge John Van Gilder adjourned the court. As soon as his gavel sounded, the reporters bolted, as did the ComHealth lawyers and Hutchins. Despite the small crowd outside, the courthouse seemed to shake from the stampede of people running in a hundred different directions.

Molly tried, but she couldn't even stand. Perspiring and weak, she slumped over in her chair and closed her eyes. Tyler and Marcus stood close to her, and the friends crowded around her, shielding her from the camera and the audience. All of them spoke encouraging words. She heard them all and was grateful for the presence, but as she gathered her thoughts, her mind again drifted away from the trial. Involuntarily as always, she thought about Peter.

After five minutes, she was able to stand. Surrounded by her attorneys and friends, she made her way out of the courtroom and into the hallway. In a second, a battalion of reporters accosted her. Reggie, Sylvia, Marcus, and Tyler stepped in front, but Molly did not hide.

"Molly," screamed one, "did you know any of this? Did you know that Dr. Johnson had lied to you?"

"No," she sighed, looking down.

"How many sex partners has Troy had?" yelled another. Molly did not answer. "Is it true he threw you down the stairs and it caused your first miscarriage?" Molly looked away.

In the glare of the lights and surrounded by the microphones, her mind drifted away for a moment. She thought of Peter. She thought of her parents and the abortion. She thought of Jayne McCall, Lisa Bowman, Rudy Jalowicz, and the others. The anger that had consumed her in the courtroom slowly faded as she reminded herself what it had all been for. O'Reilly, Cynthia Tan, and every patient on earth against the ComHealth juggernaut. Medicine against money. Families and people against greed. And yes, for Peter.

"Molly, how many times did Troy beat you?"

"Did you suspect you had been inadequately treated?"

Molly did not answer. The questions continued to pepper her as she stared blankly into space. Tyler nudged her as if to signal "let's go," but she did not move. Her mind still clung to Peter.

Eric Johnson and his wife appeared behind the group of reporters. The flock, all concentrating on Molly, did not see him. Eric and Diane paused to watch the media spectacle. Again Molly's eyes met theirs. The couple's faces remained the same, sad and unforgiving of themselves.

"Molly, could you ever forgive Dr. Johnson?"

The question struck a strange cord in her, but in that instant her reverie was broken. Molly suddenly saw it all. Dr. Eric Johnson was no different than her. Manipulated by the system, he, too, was a victim. He, too, had been used. But to his credit, he had come to repay and repent.

"Could you ever forgive him?"

Molly stepped past Tyler and Marcus and into the throng of microphones. For a second, the reporters fell silent. Her eyes were on Diane Johnson. She, like her husband, looked as if her life had been lost, destroyed by guilt.

Molly's eyes never moved from Diane Johnson. Her voice was thoughtful. "Forgiveness? He could have that without risking his career or putting his family through all of this. Forgiveness is in the heart and granted by the only one who matters. Far be it from me to do any less."

Diane Johnson buried herself in her husband's arms. Eric bit his lip. The reporters sounded astonished. "But aren't you even angry?" asked a reporter.

"I'm angry at a system that forced him to choose between patients and his career. And I'm angry at what happened—good medicine dying and me getting hurt because of it. But I understand why a man would put his family first. Should anyone do anything less?"

It was the last question Molly answered. With a look toward the Johnsons of both absolution and thanks, she retreated behind the wall of her friends and attorneys and left the building, the reporters tailing her as she walked away. The cameras followed her to an awaiting car before scattering to begin the recap of the morning session.

In less than half an hour, the analysts were back into high gear. TV and radio both blazed on, as if they had never been away. With straight faces, most members of the media explained that they had known all along of Molly's truthfulness, revising their sanctimonious opinions of the morning as freely as they breathed. And through the noon hour it continued: speculation, opinion, finger pointing, and legal insight. Little of the hot air mattered. In the wake of Eric Johnson's testimony, no one was sure of anything. Only one thing was clear. The trial was almost over. All that remained of Molly J. Loomis versus ComHealthOne were the closing arguments and a verdict.

At 12:30 P.M., ComHealthOne Chief Operating Officer Gregory Alan Markham III entered the District Attorney's office by its underground entrance. Flanked by four criminal defense attorneys, he carried with him a briefcase. Inside it was the end of his career. The contents were the bomb that Reggie Tan and Marcia Sullivan had tried but failed to obtain—O'Reilly's journal, the disks, and Markham's own records and those of Doyne Labs. Markham also carried along financial records of the top executives that proved beyond a doubt that they had profited by trading extensively in the stocks of HMOs they acquired using insider information.

Markham was subdued as they rode the elevator. His lawyers chatted among themselves. They hammered out the basics of an agreement over a twenty-four-hour period. Two felonies, eight years, and a fine of $10 million. It seemed minor, and Markham now seemed unconcerned. His conscience would at least start its cleansing, and one small hope would be realized: he would see his daughter graduate from college.

When they arrived at the large room, fifteen chairs were filled with attorneys and investigators. Markham sat at the head of the table. He lit a cigarette. He hadn't smoked in years. He pulled out the contents of the briefcase and put the materials on the table. The investigators hungrily devoured them. Without even a greeting, the first question was asked.

The inquiry took seven hours, but when it was done, the plea bargain was complete and no secrets remained. As Markham spoke, every person in the room knew what they were witnessing. The foundation of ComHealthOne, the largest HMO in the nation, was beginning to crumble before their eyes.

Chapter Forty

The morning session stunned the city. In the aftermath of Dr. Johnson's testimony, the Twin Cities nearly came to a halt, and every TV station replayed it three times before the afternoon session began. Throughout the noon hour, downtown Minneapolis was filling rapidly while reporters worked in high gear, sending their reports to both regional and national networks. "News Bulletins" were everywhere, and the networks blasted forth with all barrels open. Reporters were crazy. Hyperbolic adjectives describing Johnson's testimony buzzed in the air like a horde of mosquitoes. Astonishing! Shocking! Scorching! Blistering! "Molly Loomis was never even allowed to know her true condition," gasped one reporter in her live segment. "ComHealth bound and gagged its doctors," panted another a few feet away. "And then put a gun to their heads, ordering them to ignore everything they ever learned!"

But as the reporters beamed their message across the country, from downtown Minneapolis, the second major event of the hour hit with the force of a nuclear blast. "Special News Bulletins" interrupted the "News Bulletins," and the wild-eyed reporters ran like stampeding buffalo to get the scoop. Three thousand miles away in Santa Monica, California, Chief of Police Benton Abrahms announced before the cameras the arrest of a Mr. Luke A. Henry with a plan for extradition to the state of Minnesota. Once in Minnesota, Chief Abrams continued, the prisoner would be charged with three felonies, including impersonation and practicing medicine without a license. Mr. Henry, according to the police chief, was a convicted felon who had already admitted to the crime.

Following that press conference, breathless reporters continued to put the story together in front of the nation as more details of the conspiracy came pouring out. By the end of the noon hour, the truthfulness of Molly Loomis's Fragile X story had been confirmed, and all America knew it. Her vindication was complete. The only injustice was that the sequestered jury members sat unaware.

It took ten minutes to settle the court when the afternoon session began. Six extra policemen were now positioned in the courtroom, and any angry humor that punctuated the morning was gone, degenerating to simple anger. Before the jury was brought in, Van Gilder warned the audience that even one peep about what was taking place outside would result in his ordering the court cleared. The severity in the judge's voice and the police presence were convincing. When the jury came in, the court was silent. Only the judge uttered a word.

"Mr. Briggs, you may begin your closing statement."

Tyler Briggs rose when called. His eyes were barely open, and he drew a deep breath and held it. For a second, he was trancelike as he seemed to ready himself for the speech he had planned for weeks. All knew it would be the speech of his life. He'd considered many options as he prepared his closing arguments. Philosophy, history, money. Life, death. Truth and lies. It all seemed appropriate. It all seemed inadequate. As he opened his eyes further, he made a split-second decision and discarded half of what he'd planned. He would talk from the heart. Perhaps, he thought, it was an act of desperation. It was at least unconventional. But he knew no other way.

He began with a summary of the case, but within a few minutes he moved into his own, innermost thoughts. "You know," he said, "awhile ago I was sitting on the couch with my daughter watching TV. And as we watched, along came two commercials. The first was for medical insurance. Scenes of healthy, happy people with soaring music and a clever slogan that implied that you and I will always be safe with their insurance plan. Effective." He paused. "Amazingly effective.

"And then I thought about how much the ad had cost. Maybe half a million dollars. Maybe more. And I thought about what the ad really was. An illusion. Nothing real."

He looked impassively at the jury. "The second ad was for automobiles. Some guy in a suit talking about selling a Cadillac for a couple of thousand bucks. Big smile, lots of teeth, and then this disclaimer at the end that whips by so fast not even a computer can figure it out." He looked at one of the older jurors, a gray-haired black woman. "But ma'am, you and I know what that disclaimer is. That's where the other forty grand is located."

The jury and the audience laughed. "You know, as I sat with my daughter watching these typical illusions and lies, I asked myself some simple questions. One we all ask ourselves from time to time. What have we become? Where are we headed? And what is the fate of a people, of a nation, who not only promote lies, but *accept* them as well?"

Briggs moved to the center, in front of the judge. The sunlight now fell directly upon him. He shook his head as if in resignation. "I must tell you, members of the jury, with all attempts at humor aside, there are days when I am embarrassed to be considered a member of the legal system. You see it as well as I do. Ambulance-chasing lawyers, ridiculous verdicts, and a seemingly endless stream of justice purchased and justice denied. It makes me sick. It makes you sick."

The jury seemed interested. "But once in a while, a moment arises when I know why I chose to become a lawyer. Once in a while, there is a case or a cause, an injustice or a service, a hope or a help. Something legitimate. Something real. Something that makes me proud to be an attorney again. He moved and stood right in front of the jury, gazing intently at one man. "And it happened to me one afternoon a couple of months ago when Molly Loomis walked into my office."

Tyler was talking effortlessly. Sincerity was easy. Heartfelt truth was easier yet. "Most of the story you now know well. Abortion under deception. A history of managed medical care that strikes fear in us all. But there is part of the story you do not know. And that is how she came to my office. She came as a young woman just wanting to start over. To declare bankruptcy and start over. It was I who took it from there."

Tyler paced slowly back an forth in front of the jury. "And I tell you this for two reasons. Because first, if you ever want to think this is about money, then blame the lawyer, not the client. Secondly, I tell you to simply tell you the truth. It was never about money. It was always about two words. Two very ugly words. An oxymoron, and a terrifying one. It was about managed care."

The camera continued to move with Tyler's graceful pacing before the jury box. "Oh, their lawyers will tell you it's about one line in a contract. They'll tell you this is an open-and-shut case. They'll tell you this is about a rule, or a policy, or a waiver, or an exclusion, or some such other fancy term that allows them to do whatever they want. But I'll tell you differently. I'll tell you it's not an open-and-shut case. I'll tell you it's not a cleverly written phrase deep in the fine print. I'll tell you what it really is—it's about cost containment that leads to massive profits. It's about burning down the medical system that was once the envy of the world. It's about unapologetic CEOs making twelve million a year while people die or are maimed. It's about lying to a nation that less care is better care and using clever slogans and thirty-second ads that sell the lie. It's about blaming the doctors. It's about blaming the patient. It's about profits. It's about the greatest single moral dilemma to face this country in this century—care dictated by someone other than your doctor. It's about managed care."

Tyler was in front of the judge. He had expected Van Gilder to nearly snooze off, but he was as attentive as he had ever seen him. Briggs turned to the jury. "You people are smart. In the days before this trial I know you read about how no HMO has ever lost a case like this." He grinned at the jury. "Trust me. The thousand dollar an hour attorneys who write those contracts make it tough." The remark brought smiles. "But grant me something else as well, that this isn't about writing some insurance policy for a window that can be replaced or a car that can be repaired. This is about human lives. You, me. All of us. This is about the irreplaceable. And the responsibility that goes with caring for what is irreplaceable. Yes, members of the jury. It is about everyone. It is about the lives we want, and the lives we deserve. It is about the hopes we all have, and the future we all hold dear.

He paused for a moment. Not a sound could be heard. "Yes, my friends, the ComHealth lawyers will tell you how it is about one line in a contract. About honoring that contract. They will not tell you how that contract absolves them of all responsibility, how it doesn't matter who dies, or how many.

"No. They will tell you that the only thing that matters is the fine print in the contract. The contract their lawyers wrote. And after that, because of the way it was written, they will insist to you that they are just insurers, not doctors, and as such, they are never, ever responsible."

Tyler sighed. He wiped his hand across his chin. "Oh, yes, when it benefits them they will say the opposite. We've all heard their ads. They claim their job is to care for people. In those ads, they compare it to a holy calling. They say their care is just as good or even better than what we had before HMOs. They'll say they've made care more efficient and leaner. They'll say that modern medicine must be run by modern business methods. They'll say that cost savings help patients. Yes, they'll be free with all the corporate clichés trying to justify their massive profits. But I'll say this to them. Tell that to all the people we've come to know who have been hurt. Less care is just less care. Nothing else. And with less care, people suffer."

Tyler moved over to the witness stand and leaned against it. He looked squarely at the jury. He did not want to be too long or too short, but as he surveyed them, he was sure he still had their attention.

"And what will we say to them? Will we ask what has happened to the world of medicine? The once-noble profession now reduced to programmed robots following cookbooks written by insurance companies, often against patients' best interests. Will we ask what has happened to the world of medical research? Now deemed too expensive. Will we ask what has happened to our teaching hospitals, crushed to death under the weight of the managed care monster? And will we ask what has happened to real preventive care, like pap smears, urinalysis, and blood counts? Preventive medicine, supposedly managed care's focus, which is, in reality, too expensive to assure profitability."

Tyler moved to a spot in front of Van Gilder. The sunlight was on him again. "How have we allowed it to happen?" he asked. He held his chin in his hand. "It's like the car salesman on TV. He succeeds in deceiving us only because we don't fight back."

Briggs moved slowly toward the table where Whitfield and Barnes sat, appearing only mildly interested. Hutchins sat behind the lawyers and was glaring at him. "And if we don't fight back, then what will it take to make it stop? How many years must pass? How many millionaires made at the expense of the weak and ill? How much human suffering? And how many mothers, fathers, sons, and daughters must be sent to their graves before the fine print of rationalization and the large print of money are finally exposed for what they really are?"

Several in the jury nodded. "In this trial, you've heard from Mr. Barnes and Mr. Whitfield, lawyers of enormous skill, and their 'fine print' defense. It is a defense that has saved them before. But I ask you this. When you look at the defendants and think of ComHealth's advertising jingles, do they mean what they say? Or are their words like those of the car salesman? Hollow."

The jury looked at Hutchins and the lawyers. All appeared doubtful. The CEO squirmed a bit.

Briggs took a deep breath. He was winding down. He had no intention of reviewing testimony he knew the jury remembered well. "I would like to leave you with these final thoughts. I want to share with you the image that now haunts me. Me, not as a poor man. Me, not as an unsuccessful man. But instead me the lawyer, not good enough to tell the truth to the world. Me, tormented by my failure. Me, faced with living only with the hope that someday a man more skilled than myself will arrive and find the right word in the fine print or the right loophole in the right clause to bring it all to an end.

"But until that day comes, I will forever be condemned to a dream I believe all of us could share. Any of us, years from now, nearing the end of our own lives, sitting in a hospital next to our own grandchild. A little boy or girl, like we once were, but unlike us, not destined to live a long and healthy life. A little boy or girl, destined to die, because the need for profit made her too costly to save."

Tyler's voice began to rise. "And on that day when that child we love slips from our grasp, I ask you the question that I ask myself every time I have that dream. At that moment—when no amount of money, no amount of tears, and no amount of love, can rewrite the history we write today—what would we give to have one more chance to merge our destiny with our child's fate? What would we give to have one more chance to bring life to the child we ignored today?"

He closed his eyes. The dream of the dying child had indeed tormented him, but now he only searched for the right words. "And then as the years rolled by and the managed care giants drove on, impervious and omnipotent, and you, me, and all the Molly Loomis's of the world are steamrolled by the drive for profit that is hidden beneath the cynical veneer of their marketing magic, tell me, what would we give to have one more opportunity to rise above the technicalities and see justice as it was intended to be?"

The question lingered in the air. "But until the day comes, the day that we stop the bloodshed, we are condemned to live with the fear that our children and our grandchildren will live in a world not of right and wrong, but of fine print and illusions. A world not of compassion or care, but of cynicism, profit, and advertising. And a world not of material wealth, but one of moral bankruptcy."

Still standing in front of the jury, he pointed to the executives. "Ladies and gentlemen, make these men now take responsibility for their actions. Give health care back to those who have trained their lives for it. Give it back to the patients whose lives depend upon it. Return it to a system where quality and excellence are not an advertising jingle, but an expectation and a reality. Members of the jury, put an end to the shame and the hurt. Put an end to the cruelty and the lies. Put an end to all you have learned and all you have seen."

Briggs paused. He had only one thing left to say. His voice softened. "Yes, there are times when I'm embarrassed to be a lawyer. The system is flawed. What is right is not always what is legal. Justice sometimes appears never to exist. But from the depths of all that is wrong, one fundamental stroke of genius prevails. And that is you, the jury, the finest example of our founding father's faith in human nature, *are* justice.

"Ladies and gentlemen, that's what this is about. Justice. The most elusive concept known to man. But it's also about more. It is about independence from the tyranny that great power hides. It is about the basic rights we all cherish. It is about ourselves, our neighbors, our sons, and our daughters. It is about our hopes, our dreams, our futures, and our fates. And it is about one of the few common bonds that we all share—that in our humanity lies our mortality, and that some day we will all need care. All of us, black, white, old, young, man, woman, let destiny be our own. For the future, and for our children, let the choice you make today be a deliverance from the shadows into the light of justice. Let the choice you make today be remembered forever as your enduring contribution— that moment in your lives when you faced the challenge of the age and did not bow to wealth or power, but instead rose above it and exemplified the fairness, good sense, and foresight that our system was intended to foster. You, ladies and gentlemen, are entrusted with this challenge and this opportunity to let right prevail, to let hope prevail, and to let justice prevail."

Tyler Briggs sat down. The courtroom roared. Sanders patted Tyler on the back and Molly grasped his hand. She squeezed it and then released it. She was thrilled.

Van Gilder took a moment before he calmed them. He took a drink, and after the noise had stopped, he motioned to the defense table. "Mr. Barnes."

Jackson Barnes stood. The ComHealth attorney took a few seconds before he began speaking, but when he did he was brilliant. His summation took twenty-five minutes. It was a mixture of legal confabulation and indisputable fact. As usual, he was thorough, pointed, and exceptional. He reminded the jury that the case was unfortunately only about one small question. It was about whether or not an insurance company should pay the bill of someone who did not follow the rules of a contract she had signed. "Contrary to my esteemed colleague's opinion, this case is *not* about many things," he continued, before proceeding to list every witness's testimony. "It is only about one simple thing—the rules of a contract. A contract that was signed and understood."

He pounded that point home at every turn, all the while cautiously expressing a slight amount of sympathy for Molly Loomis. It was the only unexpected tactic in his summation, and it was beautifully done. Otherwise, Barnes was methodical, predictable, and precise. By the time he was done, he had diffused almost every bit of the emotion that had characterized the day. Even Briggs and Sanders could not contest that most of what Jackson Barnes said was true. This, they had long known. But the truth in Jack Barnes' argument had never been their argument.

By 4:00 P.M., Judge Van Gilder had given the jury instructions, and court was adjourned. The jury retired to deliberate. As they left the courthouse and faced the reporters, Tyler and Marcus were in a sober and reflective mood. Molly's friends and the others in the audience were the same. Only the ComHealth lawyers seemed upbeat.

As soon as the court recessed, most TV stations launched into interviews, specials, and continuing coverage, wildly speculating about the verdict and discussing the arrest of Luke Henry. Everyone in the media felt certain that the longer the jury deliberated, the better the chances for Molly Loomis. Everyone who had supported her now hoped for a long wait.

Within two hours, everyone knew that was not to be. Jury deliberations were scheduled to adjourn at 6:00 P.M., but the jury foreman asked the judge if they could continue, a bit longer. This fact was leaked to the press, and it fueled further speculation that the jury was close to a verdict. Van Gilder allowed the deliberations to continue, and decided to remain in his chamber. Tyler and Marcus, who had gone home, went to their offices when they heard the news, as did the ComHealth attorneys. Hutchins and his fellow executives, other than the mysteriously unavailable Markham, gathered at the top of the IDS Tower and tried to feel good with a few glasses of champagne.

Molly Loomis was the only participant not in the downtown area. She left, hidden in a cab, to find a quiet place where she could be alone. For her, the long nightmare was nearly over. A few moments of solitude were what seemed important. Long ago, she had fully accepted the fact that the verdict would not take long to reach.

Chapter Forty-one

Peter Colder's two-week coma odyssey ended at 6:00 P.M. in the ICU of his new hospital, St. Joseph's in Phoenix, Arizona. His mother and brother had been at his bedside, and when Colder first opened his eyes, they cried together and fell into his bed, welcoming him back. Within minutes, the three were joined by the entire ICU nursing staff, as well as his new doctor, Robert Maas. They were all ecstatic. The patient had been in the new ICU for less than twelve hours, and although no one knew how, the new surroundings had done the trick. Peter Colder was back. He had lived on the edge of death for a week and on the edge of a coma for seven days more, but it all ended with a wink of his eye and a squeeze of his brother's hand.

At first Colder spoke little, but within a half-hour of prodding, his earlier, confused, thoughts began to leave, and his humor started to return. The others asked him what he remembered. Nothing, only the fire. It was a blank after that. No one said anything more. He did not need to remember it now. A half-hour later, Peter Colder sounded like his old self. He was affable and curious, grateful and weak, tired and searching. He wanted to know about everything he had missed. The trial. The reaction. And most of all, Molly.

His family tried to fill him in as best they could, but there was too much information to relay or digest in such a short time. They talked about Molly's testimony and then one of the nurses began talking about Eric Johnson's. All of them laughed heartily when Bryan Colder recalled Johnson's remarks about Hutchins or Whitfield being a carrier for VD. They talked of the public response and the national coverage the trial had generated, and they related to him how much had been accomplished and how much about managed care had been exposed. No one needed to say the obvious. Everyone knew the verdict was a foregone conclusion. ComHealth had always had the upper hand.

"If only the jury could know everything," said one of the nurses.

"But even so," said Dr. Maas. "So much good will come from it. More than anyone could have ever imagined."

"Absolutely," agreed another ICU nurse.

Molly, thought Colder. He could only imagine what she had been through. How much he wanted to see her. How much he ached to see her. "How did Molly Loomis do?" he asked, his voice a bit hoarse.

"She was great. You'll have to see it. I have it on tape."

Colder grinned politely. He had no interest in seeing it. He only wanted to see her.

Just as Bryan Colder stepped forward to tell his brother more about the trial, the door to his room was flung open. A breathless orderly stood before them. The entire room came to a stop.

"The jury's reached a verdict," he gasped.

"Oh my God," whispered Phyllis Colder. "So fast?"

"Yes," the orderly said.

"When are they announcing it?"

"The judge is keeping the court open. They're calling everyone in. They think about eight central time."

"I wonder what it's like near that courthouse?" asked one of the nurses.

"It's unbelievable," replied the orderly. "I just saw it on the TV. The downtown has been filling all evening. The guy on CBS says there's already 65,000 people on the streets. They're expecting it to grow to nearly double that. National Guard has been called in."

The room fell silent. The jubilation was gone. They were grim and forlorn, all realizing that a quick verdict probably meant a ComHealthOne victory. "Why don't you turn on the TV?" asked Colder.

A second later, the TV screen was lit. NBC, in the middle of a special segment, appeared. Kelly O'Donnell, live from Washington D.C, was the reporter. She was talking with Tom Brokaw.

"That's right, Tom. The official word from the FBI is that the arrested agent will be charged tomorrow. They have not released the name, but sources within the Minneapolis Police Department, however, have confirmed that this agent, whose name is Thomas Hastings, was involved. He has apparently been implicated by the two men who will be charged with Dr. O'Reilly's murder. Hastings, according to these two, is alleged to have passed information to the accused murderers regarding the site of O'Reilly's appearance. He also allegedly helped arrange the accused murderers' escape from the Mall of America. And as I said, according to the FBI, formal charges will be filed tomorrow."

"Thank you, Kelly O'Donnell," Brokaw said, as the pretty redhead disappeared from the screen. "And now quickly to local affiliate KARE and news anchor Casey Kelly for a further development."

"Holy shit!" gulped Bryan Colder.

The screen flashed to the packed courthouse steps where the tall, blond reporter stood. All of the Colders recognized the scene, downtown Minneapolis in the heart of the growing crowd. "Tom, regarding what we were talking about earlier, we have now confirmed that forty-four corporations within the state of Minnesota have terminated their contracts with ComHealthOne within the past six hours. And I should note this, by our count, this will affect the health care of over 1.5 million people."

"Casey, this is obviously an enormous blow to ComHealth. Has there been any official statement from them?"

"The only word I have is from one ComHealth official who did not want to be identified. He told me that rumors of contract cancellations have been circulating for several days, but this is still far beyond his expectations. The only other thing we know is that the ComHealth board of directors is meeting at this hour in Chicago. We hope to have some more information as the evening progresses."

Information kept coming to Brokaw as he asked the questions. "Thank you, Casey Kelly of our KARE affiliate. And now quickly to Greg Jarrett for *another* development."

"Unbelievable!" crowed Bryan Colder.

The screen changed, and NBC's legal reporter appeared. He, too, was live from downtown Minneapolis right across from the courthouse. In the background, the mass of humanity that the orderly had described could easily be seen. People were everywhere. "Tom, the crowd here continues to pour in. By estimates, there are now over 70,000, and that number may swell to 100,000 by the time the verdict is read. The governor of the state has ordered an additional 5,000 National Guard Troops to the downtown area, and the mayors of both Minneapolis and St. Paul have called in all off-duty police."

"Any reports of violence?" asked Brokaw.

"None," said a surprised Jarrett. "In fact, I would describe the crowd as boisterous and loud, but orderly. Shouts and a lot of signs, but it has otherwise been uneventful."

"Any word on when the verdict will be read?"

"The best guess is about a half an hour," said the reporter. "All the participants were on pagers. Mr. Whitfield and Mr. Barnes were in their offices, and as I understand, are already outside the courtroom. Mr. Briggs and Mr. Sanders are supposedly on their way. The only holdup may be Molly Loomis. She had apparently left the immediate area and hasn't yet been reached."

"And what about this news conference at the D.A.'s office that is being talked about?" asked Brokaw.

"All we know is that the Hennepin County District Attorney's office has announced that there will be a press conference at City Hall following the verdict. We have no other details."

Brokaw looked curious. "Any guesses?" he asked, as if knowing the answer.

"The only other things he would say were that it *did* pertain to the Loomis case and that it would be to announce significant developments."

"Thank you, Greg."

"Unfriggin' believable!" exclaimed Bryan Colder.

Peter leaned back into his pillow as Tom Brokaw announced that NBC would continue to provide live coverage of the breaking story. Colder felt exhausted, weaker than he ever had in his life. The people in his room began to talk, but he allowed himself to fall into a light, fugue-like state. The voices talked around him, still buzzing about all the news. Colder let it all pass by him. Twice, he looked up at the screen, the TV still showing people pouring into the downtown area.

Colder ignored it all. Molly, he thought. Molly.

Julianne Purcell had guessed right as to where Molly Loomis would go. For five days, Colder's ex-wife had watched the trial from the back row, having used her legal partner's connections to get the sought-after seat. She watched as Molly had been alternately barbecued and eaten, with her entire life bared to open analysis, scrutiny, and judgment. For her, as a lawyer, it had been easy to watch, straight-forward, commonplace. As an acquaintance or friend, it had been brutal.

When she peered through the door and found Molly sitting alone in the darkness of Gus LeClerc's closed diner, she felt no pity. Pity was condescending. She felt much more, ranging from a humble respect to a touch of admiration.

Julianne quietly opened the unlocked door and slipped inside. Molly saw her right away. Although Gus had closed the diner for the entire week so everyone could attend the trial, Molly realized as soon as she saw Colder's ex that her hiding spot could have been better.

"I'm sorry to bother you," said Julianne.

"No, come in," waved Molly, her desire for privacy subdued by her desire for companionship. "I don't mind at all." Molly had come to feel a strange kinship with Colder's ex-wife. They had met at the hospital and spent many hours talking about the man they both cared about so much. In a strange way, they had become friends.

Julianne slid into the vinyl-covered seat across from Molly. "How are you?" she asked.

"Pretty good," sighed Molly. "Kinda glad it's soon over."

Molly's pager sat in the open on the table. Julianne could see the printed message. She knew Molly was just taking a couple of minutes before heading back to the courthouse.

"When are you going back?" asked Julianne.

"I've got a cab coming in a couple minutes. I just wanted a little thinking time."

"I understand."

Molly stood up. "Coffee? Sorry, I'm such a terrible host."

"Not at all," said Julianne.

"I have to admit I don't know a lot about the law, but I do make a mean cup of coffee."

"Forget it," said Julianne, "I'll be heading there too."

Molly plopped back down. Julianne could see the trial had taken its toll. Molly's face looked worn, and her posture was that of a body on the edge of exhaustion.

"You know," began Julianne. "I have to admit I didn't really come here to talk *with* you. I came here to talk *to* you."

Molly looked up, somewhat surprised.

Julianne folded her hands on the table. "I came because I wanted first of all to congratulate you,"

"No. I don't deserve that."

"Yes, you do. What you did took a ton of courage. Most people would never have exposed themselves in that way."

Molly looked down at her lap and rubbed her forehead in a nervous gesture. She felt awkward. "Thanks."

Julianne sighed. "It was a brutal trial."

Molly nodded at the obvious understatement. "Yes, it was."

"I wish…" Julianne's voice trailed off.

Molly didn't miss it. "What are you thinking, counselor?"

Julianne took a deep breath. She wished she could say something positive about the trial or Molly's chances. "I've known Tyler a long time," she started.

"and I have to admit I've never seen him better than he was today."

"He was beyond great," agreed Molly, knowing the "but" was coming.

Julianne sighed. "But the law is rarely about what's right. It's rarely about the present or the future. It's about what's printed on paper, the past."

Molly looked undisturbed. "I know."

Julianne paused. She held her next thought, a commentary on the fairness of the law. By the way Molly responded, Julianne realized she had misinterpreted her. Molly seemed not to be thinking about the verdict. She was strangely peaceful, as if she'd already left her past and the trial behind. "Actually, what I meant to ask," started Molly, "was whether you thought that the people had heard what Tyler said today, and what the witnesses said."

Julianne's face lightened. A faint smile crossed her lips. She had heard of the gathering crowd and the arrests, the flurry of activity and the media frenzy. On that point she was sure. "Yes, I do. I really do."

Molly was oblivious to the downtown chaos. "I hope you're right."

The pager went off, and Molly picked it up. It was the same message as before, and she put it back down on the table. She looked outside the diner just in time to see the Yellow Cab arrive. Julianne didn't flinch.

"You know how when you're a kid," Julianne started, "and your dad says something that sticks in your mind and you remember it the rest of your life?"

Molly laughed out loud. The question struck her as funny. She knew it all too well.

Julianne sat up straighter. "My dad always used to have this saying that there are only two kinds of people in this world. Those who underestimate themselves and those who overestimate themselves."

Molly stopped smiling. The words caught her off-guard. "And which am I?" she asked inquisitively.

"I would never presume to judge you," Julianne said. "Only myself."

Molly fell silent, considering the thought and what she meant.

"But then again, Molly, obviously I say it for a reason. A very good reason."

"I'll take it as a compliment," said Molly.

"It's even more than that," Julianne replied. "It's encouragement and a thought."

"What do you mean?"

"In the same way you forgave Eric Johnson, forgive yourself. Quit apologizing for what you haven't done in your life. And most of all, forget about the past."

Molly looked down. "You're probably right."

"Life is never neat. Let it all go, and I know what you'll find—that you're already more than you've ever imagined. And certainly more than most people could ever hope to be."

Molly seemed genuinely affected. "Thank you."

The cab driver honked, and the two women stood up. There were a million other things Julianne wanted to say, and an equal number that Molly wanted to ask. Julianne stepped away from the booth. Both seemed focused on the same thought. Neither one seemed able to bring it up. The settlement offer Molly had passed on. Finally Julianne said it. "You never asked me," she said. "But I want you to."

"What?"

"The ComHealth offer. I know about it."

Molly nervously ran one hand through her hair.

Julianne continued. "It's also what I was referring to. In part."

Molly looked down again. Despite all her certainty about pursuing the trial, the decision not to take the money still caused her fear. Molly knew she would now face the same financial problems and bankruptcy. "What would you have done if you were me?" she said.

Julianne moved a step toward her. "That's what I've been saying, Molly. I would have taken the money."

Molly didn't visibly react. "That would have been the smart thing."

Julianne took Molly in her arms. "Maybe. But also the wrong thing."

Molly held her tightly. Julianne had been someone she both respected and envied. Now she was someone she appreciated. "Thanks."

"Never regret your decision," Julianne whispered. "Never."

They stood immobile for half a minute before Molly broke the hold. She couldn't help her thoughts. "I think I always will, at least a little."

"Yes, I suppose that's inevitable. No one will ever blame you for having been tempted. Anyone would have."

"I suppose."

"What people will remember is that you weren't in it for the money."

Molly looked down. There was one more question she had to ask. With it, one final time, she yielded to the insecurity that had beset her all her life. "You think they thought—the people—everyone, you know—my life, my decisions—everything? Do you think they thought badly of me? And—I guess—more important, do you think I represented these patients well?"

Julianne thought for a second and measured her words. Stupidity was a curse. Ignorance was often a blessing. Molly Loomis was neither stupid nor ignorant, but Julianne knew Molly had more character than any who would chose to judge her. "You know, no life is without its mistakes—but show me someone without regrets and I'll show you someone you don't want to know." She hesitated again. "And yes, *no* one could have done it better."

Tears welled in Molly's eyes. In her entire life, no one had ever said anything nicer to her. Julianne's brief visit had been a gift, a validation. With a vigor reserved for a loved one, Molly held her again. Without uttering another word, the two women stood together for nearly a minute while Molly's cab driver looked on impatiently. Finally, Julianne broke and waved her away. "I'll see you there."

Molly took her hand and held it. "Thanks," she mouthed again as she prepared to leave. "I gotta go. Just one more trip into the breath of the dragon. One more time into the fire."

"I know."

Molly pulled away. "My fifteen minutes of fame are almost over." She laughed when she said it, as if relishing the thought.

Julianne Purcell released her, stepped back, and watched her walk away. "You know, I don't think anyone will forget you that fast," she said to herself, thinking of the huge crowd downtown that awaited Molly. "In fact, of that I'm very, very sure."

Darkness had fallen throughout the city, but by the time Marcus Sanders and Tyler Briggs arrived at the courthouse, the downtown crowd had swollen to ninety thousand and was still growing. Only by police car were they able to get to the courthouse steps. People were everywhere, milling about, listening to radios on headsets and watching the giant TVs. NBC, CBS, ABC, CNN, Fox, and CourtTV were live, their booths teeming with activity. Shops were closed, restaurants were packed, and students coming from the nearby colleges stretched as far as the eye could see. Police were on horseback and in cars. National Guard troops were positioned every thirty feet. Overhead, the national guard helicopters buzzed between the buildings like marine air command on D-Day. The noise was ear-shattering, but the people kept coming.

Enormous spotlights illuminated the courthouse steps, and as Briggs and Sanders emerged onto the pavement, a deafening roar of recognition and salute rang out from the crowd. Neither man reacted. They walked the seventy-five cement steps together under the glow of the giant floodlights while the cheering crowd grew louder. They called their names. They chanted. They waved. As the duo walked, the steps were theirs alone, the reporters and police keeping their distance as the two covered the steps one by one. Finally at the top, they turned and faced the crowd for the first time. The size of the crowd was frightening. Marcus waved once humbly, then again. The crowd only roared louder.

From the top step, Marcus and Tyler absorbed the scene. There were people everywhere, as far as they could see. People cheering. People waving signs. People chanting. Across the street, he could see the TV booths, alive with activity. Reporters, lights, cameras, microphones, and news anchors, all in full swing. They turned. Down the street, standing on a podium were several of the law and medical students who had organized the protests. The attorney spotted them and waved. The students waved back.

Next they turned to the vast army of people occupying the three streets that led to the courthouse. Cast in the shadows of the street lights, all in the growing crowd waved the papers that the students had distributed. Eight pages long, the booklet had been given to each person who arrived. It was the fine print of the ComHealth contract. The exclusions and waivers were now in regular print, for all the world to see. A student had given Marcus a copy. He held it up to the crowd, tore it in half, and listened as the cheers cascaded forth.

Tyler grinned as he watched his partner annihilate the ComHealth contract. But inside, it was the most humbling moment of his life. He knew the crowd cheered less for him than the words he had spoken about two important, but fleeting, ideals: justice and the needs of the patient in them all. Tyler knew that the ideals, not he, had touched them. And it pleased him.

The attorneys waved one final time, knowing they would remember the moment for the rest of their lives. They stood for less than ten seconds. Then they turned and moved inside.

From her spot in the crowd two blocks away, Molly could see her attorneys arrive. She could see the crowd wave the sheets of paper. She could hear the deafening roar. But with her cab stuck deep in the traffic and in the crowd, she could do little but watch and listen.

"Your lawyers are heroes," said the cabby, also watching. Molly looked out the window as Tyler and Marcus reached the top step.

"Yes," acknowledged Molly, feeling no twinge at not being part of it. "They would never think that, but they are."

"But it was you that did it."

Molly missed his remark. The cabby had opened his door, and the noise was too extreme for conversation. "I don't think I can get you any closer," he half-screamed as he closed the door again. Next, he honked, but the crowd failed to move.

"Don't worry. I can walk it."

More people were arriving every minute, and as the crowd continued to crunch closer toward the courthouse and past the cab, Molly opened up her handbag. "What do I owe you?" she asked.

The man waved his hand. "Forget it," he answered. "I only wanna favor." The ruddy-faced man turned to her. His face wore an odd expression, and Molly peered at him curiously. She couldn't tell if the Hispanic cabby was nervous or struggling with English.

"Got two daughters myself," he continued. "Me and my wife did a lot of things wrong as a parents. Probably more wrong than right. But love for 'em never changes."

Molly had no idea what this man was saying to her, but his English seemed fine. "What are you telling me?" she asked as she fiddled with her collar, her voice barely audible.

"I think as a parent, just as a child, when you're wrong, all you ask for is a chance to make it better. A chance to be forgiven."

Molly opened her wallet and pulled out some money. She was baffled by the cabby's sudden personal insights. "Fifteen okay?"

The cabby shook his head. "No money. But I gotta tell you something."

Molly was perplexed. She looked at him warily.

"It was on the radio just before I picked you up," he continued.

"What's that?"

The man paused. He took a deep breath. "They're up there. Your mom and dad are up by the courthouse."

Molly fell back. Her body shook, and she could feel a lump form in her throat.

"What?" she gasped.

"Yeah," he nodded.

Molly did not reply. She stared out the window and into the crowd. The thought of facing her father terrified her. After so many months, why now? Why here? She looked at the cabby and tried to speak, but nothing came out.

"Being a parent may be the toughest thing in the world," continued the cabby. "No one teaches you how to do it, and you never know if you did it the best you could. All you can do is try. And some of what you do is wrong."

Molly wasn't listening. Conflicting thoughts and emotions rattled in her brain. Her father. Her mother. She remembered their final words to her. Vile words. Hateful words. What would they say to her now? The same? On TV? In front of the world? Molly closed her eyes. Every thought seemed jumbled. What would she say to them? She tried to summon up the willpower to move on, but she seemed paralyzed. "They were on the radio?" she asked weakly.

"Your dad was."

"What did he say?" Molly bit her lip with fear.

The big man's eyes turned soft. "Not much, but enough."

"What?"

"I heard it. I know that sound."

"What?" asked Molly anxiously.

"The anguish in his voice."

Molly's eyes widened. "Huh?" she asked, surprised.

"He was only on the radio for a moment, but in it he said a lifetime's worth."

"What was that?"

"All he said was that he should have been here for you. And a long time before now."

The words hit her like an unexpected punch. Her father. Her mother. All that had happened. For a minute, she didn't move, as all the memories and all the fears flooded through her. Her eyes filled with tears, and she buried her head in her hands, struggling to breathe and comprehend. In her mind, she still heard his voice, his words saying goodbye forever, punishing her, destroying her. But now they had returned. Returned to seek the family they had once been. What would she say? What would she do?

"There is a saying, Molly, that your eyes can only look one direction at a time." The cabby's voice started to waver. "My one daughter, I haven't talked to her in five years. Instead of money, do me this favor. For the rest of your life, let that direction always be forward."

The cabby fell silent while the cab rocked softly from the passing spectators.

Molly's insides seemed to be locked in convulsions. Never for a minute had she expected it. Her father apologizing, her mother standing behind him. Her mind was a tangle of emotions, all extreme and powerful. She imagined how they must have felt, the anger, the all-consuming rage. But this was about something more. It was about love, loyalty, and forgiveness. It was about family. It was about everything that meant something.

Molly looked up. Her eyes were tear-stained, and her hand trembled, but she turned, opened the door, and stepped outside. She turned to the cabby. "Thank you," she said. He waved goodbye.

A moment later, the cab started to negotiate its way out of the crowd, and Molly found herself standing in the mass of people that continued to press forward toward the jumbo TV screens and the courthouse. She wiped her eyes and took a deep breath. Her poise was fragile, but she held on. She could see in the distance a man dressed as the grim reaper with "Hutchins" sewn on his back walking on the courthouse steps. The crowd cheered. The sight was needed. Molly laughed.

Molly stepped forward, but the crowd was too thick. She stopped and surveyed the massive, tightly packed crowd in front of her. She had no idea how she would get to the courthouse. Maybe they would start without her, she thought. She looked around, immobile within the mass. Less than a block from her and on her left was the large platform where most of the protest speeches had been given. She could see the student leaders. Two were being interviewed for TV. She could see others on the platform as well. Many were people she had met during the past month. Each member of these families held a candle. Richard Bowman, whose wife Lisa had died, and their son Brady. Pat Jalowicz, who had lost her husband Rudy. Shirley Mitchell and Jayne McCall. All the family members from the Marcia Sullivan articles were there, as well as more whom she didn't know. People, victims, who were now appearing in the national press every day. Over one hundred in all, they had come from as far away as California.

Molly started to try to make her way through the crowd. She nudged a man in front of her and slipped past him. Then she accidentally stepped on a woman's foot, and the roundish redhead turned angrily toward her. "Watch it," She stopped. She stared. Her eyes changed as she gazed at Molly as if she were seeing a ghost. "Molly Loomis," she uttered. "Molly Loomis."

Molly started to apologize, but people around had heard the woman and turned to see. All of them recognized Molly Loomis. A large man stepped forward and shook her hand. A young man patted her on the back. "Molly Loomis!" they both said loudly. More people turned.

"Make way," yelled another man and the crowd opened up slightly. "Molly Loomis!"

More people turned. Some touched her, others spoke words of encouragement. Some held up fists. Some waved. All moved back. "Molly Loomis!" yelled the two men again, joined by four more. The people turned and the crowd began to part.

Molly took several steps forward. Now all the crowd was turning to look. The whispers of "Molly Loomis" could be heard everywhere as people turned to gaze. To some, she waved in a modest fashion. To others, she nodded; all the while the crowd continued to split, allowing her a path. As she walked, cheers began to start. Cheers for her. Some screamed. Some chanted. Some waved. And most reached toward her in a gesture of affection for someone they barely knew. In seconds, the sound of her name flew through the crowd like great drops of rain, landing on all and calling everyone to attention. Molly was floored. It was overwhelming.

"Molly! Molly!"

She waved tentatively to a crowd that now turned to embrace her. Then she moved on, still skittish and shy, wishing she wasn't still a block and a half from the courthouse and that she hadn't been crying a few minutes before. She nodded to the crowd containing the group of young men who chanted her name. "Molly! Molly!" As she neared the platform where the patients' families stood with their candles, she turned, stopped, and waved.

One of the students on the platform stepped forward, and a spotlight found him. Holding his eight pages of exclusions in his hand, he produced a lighter, and in an instant the paper was ablaze. Holding it high above his head, he spoke one sentence into the microphone. "Let this light show us the way! We will be blind no more!"

Seeing him burn the ComHealth contract, the crowd roared again. Many in the crowd followed suit, and Molly Loomis watched as the flames spread as if blown by the wind. The police looked panicked and screamed for the fires to be put out, but the crowd was too large to maneuver and the ComHealth contracts continued to burn. The small fires lasted only for seconds before they were dropped to the ground and stamped out.

Molly began to move again. The path was open as she neared the courthouse, and she walked alone in the spotlight as the cheers pushed on. A young girl broke free from the unofficial barrier the crowd was obeying and ran toward her. Molly stopped. The girl, about five, offered her a paper flower. Molly accepted it and patted her on the head. The little girl beamed and hurried back to her father. Julianne had been right, she thought as she moved on. They had heard. They had read. And they had seen.

One step after another, she continued her walk while the chant of "Molly" grew ever louder. Many broke free to touch and greet her as she made her way to the base of the courthouse steps. When she arrived there, the spotlight blinded her, but one by one she ascended the steps. Light, flame, and cheers kept pushing her forward, and a few moments later Molly reached the top. Then she stopped and turned, gazing upon the mass of humanity before her. She gasped. It was incredible. People everywhere, packed in every corner, clamoring for her.

For a second, she did nothing as the cheers surrounded her. Her face was expressionless, and her hair blew softly in the wind. She turned left and then right, gazing near and then far, at individuals and then the crowd. The scene was staggering. Finally, her eyes growing moist and glowing in the light, she greeted them. She extended her arm and pointed deep into the heart of the crowd. The cheers only grew louder. She held the pose for several seconds before her hand became a fist that she shook toward them. It was a signal to never give up.

The crowd roared even louder at the sight, and the celebration appeared ready to go on forever, but Molly stayed only a few more seconds before the cheering mass. Like many before her, for one brief moment, Molly saw the magnificent view of the great height. But she knew that it was a place where no one should aspire to stay. The top of the world was a grand but uninhabitable illusion, a place from which all things must ultimately fall. Instead of lingering, she let her moment pass. With a long wave she said goodbye to those who had given her a lifetime's memory. Then she turned, disappeared from sight, and slid into the arms of her father and mother who were waiting for her at the front door.

At 7:55 P.M., Gregory Alan Markham III and his lawyers as well as the D.A. and his fellow attorneys watched as Molly Loomis arrived at the courthouse. From their negotiation room on the forty-fourth floor of the IDS Tower, they could see everything. With Markham's interrogation coming to an end, they had all moved to the window to watch the procession.

The day had moved quickly. Markham's information allowed for the arrest of FBI agent Tom Hastings by late afternoon, and as the verdict neared, police in Georgia and Florida were closing in on the gunman who'd killed O'Reilly.

Markham proved to be the perfect witness. His memory was good, his knowledge was thorough, and his documentation was complete. In a word, his testimony was devastating.

While Markham watched Molly arrive, District Attorney Winton Thacker and Chief of Police Roger Sanstead both stood behind the table and looked at the list of names that Markham's evidence was implicating. It was fifteen names long, and both men kept returning to look at the list. They could barely believe their eyes. Standing together, they stared down at it. Both seemed in a trance. Even these two seasoned veterans were stunned at the magnitude of what they were about to do.

Thacker and Sanstead moved next to Markham, who was standing by himself near the far end of a long window. The ComHealth executive was staring at the courthouse. Molly Loomis was on the top step, wrapped up by her parents. All three could see it clearly.

"It's over, Markham," whispered Thacker. "Doesn't matter. Even though you beat the girl, the public knows."

Markham turned to the D.A. His eyes were clear, his brow relaxed. He pursed his lips thoughtfully. Inside, he felt better than he had in a long time. His confession had been like wiping off his skin the first layer of dirt, two hundred layers thick. It would take years before he was clean. "She won," said Markham.

"What do you mean she won?"

Markham looked sublime. The arrogance of power stripped away, only the vacuousness of its core remained. "Funny," he said. "She's neither a hero or a saint, really. She's just what we want to see in ourselves: strong yet vulnerable, fair and honest."

The two men looked curiously at Markham. The executive kept staring at Molly in the arms of her father. "She never gave a damn about the money. And that's why we ultimately lost. Because everything we ever did was just about money. You know what I know. Big money is always about lies.

The D.A. and the police chief closed the notebooks that they were carrying. They started to walk away. They had no interest in his prisoner's philosophy of life. But before they were too far away, they stopped. Thacker realized he had forgotten a point. An important point, one that was probably of little legal significance, but one of great personal interest. "I almost forgot," the D.A. started. "What the heck was 'Fragile X' anyway?"

Markham smiled sardonically. "Just a code name."

Thacker looked annoyed. "You think I'm stupid? We know that."

Markham turned his attention from Molly, her parents, and the crowd. He had no intention of irritating the D.A. "It started when someone in Europe found that a high level of this protein in the mother's blood, an antibody I think, was associated with juvenile onset diabetes."

"You mean you could tell if an unborn child was going to have diabetes?"

"Yes."

The two men were flabbergasted. They thought of all that had taken place as a result of the discovery. "Quite a cure for diabetes," blurted out the police chief.

The D.A. would have laughed if it wasn't so shocking and pathetic. "Well, I suppose that would be the cost-effective solution," he said, sarcastically adopting the HMO vernacular. "Diabetics are expensive to treat."

"They are," Markham agreed.

"Indeed," Sanstead said, horrified. "My eight-year-old son is one."

Markham looked out the window. Below, the flames continued to spread. "They're burning something, aren't they?" he asked.

"Yes, they are."

Markham continued to watch. "What is it?"

The D.A. gazed out the window. He knew. He had heard. "Empty pieces of paper," he replied. "Empty pieces of paper."

Markham looked puzzled.

"And millions of dollars," the police chief added.

The two walked away from Markham, leaving him to gaze in wonder at the scene below. Markham never moved and said nothing more. He looked at only the fire and Molly Loomis. He had no idea what the D.A. and Chief of Police were talking about. Nor did he care. His only interest now was that with every flicker of the flame he could feel another layer of scum burn off his body.

As Thacker and Sanstead left the room, they encountered a young lieutenant waiting patiently outside. The Chief of Police handed him the list of those implicated by Markham's testimony. "Go get 'em," he said firmly.

The lieutenant's eyes popped open as he read the names. "Are you kidding me?" he asked. "You really want me to bring in all these guys?"

"Damn right," grunted Sanstead. "As soon as the verdict is read, arrest them all."

The noisy courtroom fell into a hush as Judge Van Gilder entered. The judge, who appeared to age a year every day, sat down and waved for the audience to follow suit. He talked briefly with the bailiff, and a moment later the jury was retrieved. Molly Loomis looked around the courtroom. Her parents sat right behind her. Beside them were Sylvia, Letisha, and Sandra. Jayne, Tracy, and Gus were second from the end of the row. Troy was at the end. Throughout the audience were the other waitresses and cooks from Gus's diner. Dr. Frissell was sitting with his wife. Dr. Johnson and his wife Diane sat with Dr. Royce. Dr. Larter sat with Dr. Asadourian. Reggie, Julianne, Marcia, and her boyfriend Rudy sat at the back. She looked to her left. Jack Barnes and Harley Whitfield sat with their toadies, Ace Farnsworth and T. Quentin Cox. No ComHealth executives were present. Hutchins was nowhere to be seen.

She turned back around. Marcus remained on her right as he had the entire time. Briggs was on her left. Each of them showed little expression. She looked at the jury. Two women appeared teary, as did one older man. Most showed no expression. All stared off into space or looked down. The sight was depressing. She had hoped against hope for some positive signal from the jury. But there was none.

With the TV camera on him, Van Gilder finished his conversation with the bailiff and turned to the courtroom. "Ladies and gentlemen, although this case has been short, it has been a case of extraordinary passion and emotion. It has been a case perhaps unprecedented in my long career. And for all of this, it will be remembered." The judge paused. He glared out toward the audience. "But I will say this, it will not be remembered for anything else. It is my duty to see that the finest traditions of the American legal system are upheld in this courtroom, and in those words are the reality that no passion or protests will be tolerated within a court of law. The courtroom is the place a civilized society seeks to uphold the laws written by its citizens through a democratic system. It is not the place for uncontrolled debate." The old judge paused. He put on his glasses. "Justice is not perfect, nor was it intended to be. Perhaps, in that sense, true justice does not exist. But the courtroom is not the place for philosophy. It is, in this instance, a place where your neighbors, your peers have come to judge, to the best of their ability, this case, based on the information allowed by the laws. Laws that our fellow citizens have written.

"Our system, our legal system, is a great one, however imperfect. And it always reacts in due time, but sometimes tardily, to the needs of our people. Please remember this as we hear our fellow citizens' verdict. And please grant this court, our courtroom, our system, the respect it intends to give to you."

Van Gilder stopped. The court was quiet. He turned to the jury. The appointed foreman was a black woman. "Madame Foreman, I have been informed the jury has reached a verdict. Is that correct?"

"We have, your Honor."

"Will you hand it to the bailiff?"

The wiry little man took the slip of paper from her and delivered it to the judge. Van Gilder opened it while the court breathlessly stared at him. The judge's eyes and face never moved. The lone wrinkle in his brow deepened. He closed it and handed it back to the bailiff, who returned it to the jury foreman.

"All rise," commanded the bailiff. Everyone in the courtroom obeyed. Briggs and Sanders closed their eyes. There were few phrases in the English language that were so paralyzing.

The jury foreman opened up the slip of paper. The other jury members turned to her without changing expression. The foreman took a deep breath. "We the jury for the following entitled action, Case Number 97-69546, M. J. Loomis versus Community Health One, rule on all counts on behalf of the Plaintiff, Molly Jane Loomis.

There was bedlam. The courtroom broke into a wild celebration as Molly stood trembling and too numb to move. Letisha burst into tears and crashed over the retaining rail into the arms of Tyler. Sylvia followed and hugged Molly. Reggie was next. He screamed some unintelligible babble and grabbed Marcus. Molly's parents wept openly, while Troy raised his arm like a touchdown signal. Marcia, making no attempt to remain objective, leaped over the railing, wrestled Tyler from Letisha, and nearly strangled him.

Van Gilder let all of it ride. For three minutes, the old judge sat back with the gavel resting in his lap while the courtroom cheered and slapped hands. He made no attempt to calm them. He took a drink of water. He took a pill. Then he watched the courtroom celebrate; he, too, was breathing a sigh of relief.

Finally Van Gilder spoke. "And you have awarded damages?"

"Yes, Your Honor."

"I am informed that you found with the plaintiff on Count Two, that the defendant has acted in bad faith."

"Yes, Your Honor."

Molly could barely listen. She was sure she was going to pass out. Most in the court could barely hear. The foreman detailed that ComHealth would be responsible for all of Molly's medical bills plus some additional money for pain and suffering.

"And in addition, we are awarding Ms. Loomis the equivalent of three years' salary for punitive damages."

The judge rolled his eyes; the courtroom was confused. Everyone wanted numbers. "I don't believe Ms. Loomis's yearly salary has ever been established in this court, Madame Foreman. You must provide a specific award."

The foreman looked surprised. "No, Your Honor. Not Ms. Loomis's salary. We are awarding her the equivalent of three years of *Mr. Hutchins'* salary—$36.3 million dollars."

The roar came from everywhere. There was pandemonium and triumphant delirium. Ecstasy and joy. It was in the court and in the city. It was in the hospitals and restaurants, sidewalks, streets and stores. It was everywhere. All at once. Chaos. Glorious chaos.

Molly's legs turned to Jello. She fell back into Sylvia's arms while Sandra, Jayne, and her parents crushed toward her. Marcia cried. Reggie and Letisha danced, while Troy Loomis fell numbly into his seat. The old courthouse shook like bridge in an earthquake. Outside, the cheering noise was like winds of a hurricane as the thousands gathered danced, screamed, and hugged while the cameras recorded the scene. For five minutes, it went on. Endlessly, noisily, and without a break. Van Gilder just sat back and watched the celebration. The trial of the old judge's life was over.

Finally breaking through the melee, Whitfield and Barnes walked over and shook the hands of Tyler and Marcus as the two winning attorneys continued to wrestle with their friends. Then both defense attorneys shook Molly's hand. Both could barely be heard, but both said "wish you well." Farnsworth and Cox stayed put, with petulance and pouting replacing surprise.

A moment later, everyone returned to their seats, and Judge Van Gilder quieted the crowd for one last time. "Do any of you have any final remarks?" he asked the lawyers.

They all said no.

Van Gilder stood up. He looked at Molly Loomis and smiled. The gavel came down. "This court stands adjourned."

Ten minutes later on the courthouse steps, the press conferences began. A visibly shaking Molly spoke only briefly. She said she was pleased with verdict but vowed to remember how ComHealthOne had earned its money—profits from the cutbacks that had hurt people. And she promised to remember it until her dying day. It was a statement she had not planned, but she meant it. Tyler and Marcus spoke longer, each saying he was pleased with the verdict but declining to say what actions they would take in the future with all the potential clients they had encountered. Reporters and questions were everywhere, but after only fifteen minutes, Tyler cut everyone off. He reiterated how pleased he was, but then the entire group left, disappearing into cars that slowly made their way through the still-celebrating crowd.

Only Marcia Sullivan remained behind. She stood near the back of the throng of reporters that surrounded Harley Whitfield and Jackson Barnes. The ComHealth lawyers were both wearing their best "offended lawyer" faces and putting on their best "miscarriage of justice" act. Marcia listened intently for a while as Barnes droned on. His speech was laced with vitriol and hyperbole, and during his discourse he got even better, ripping into the verdict with a total of seven different synonyms for the word "abomination." Finally Marcia had had enough. She walked back into the courthouse, and from a quiet corner she telephoned her editor.

"Any news today?" asked Ed Weinshel, laughing.

Marcia chuckled. "I might be able to find something to write about."

"When will you have it?"

"In an hour."

"Good."

Marcia had an idea, and she decided to press it. "Hey boss, you know how you never let me write a headline and I always complain?"

"Yes."

"Let me write this one."

Marcia heard his laugh again. "Try me."

"I got an idea. A couple of minutes ago someone in the IDS Tower turned out the lights on that great big dragon at the top."

"Really?"

"Yeah. It's back on now, but it gave me the idea."

"What?"

How about 'The Dragon Falls'?"

The editor's laughing continued. "I'll think about it."

"C'mon," she pleaded. Marcia was giddy and teasing him. He knew it.

The editor changed the subject. "Barnes and Whitfield are still going at it. I can see it on TV. Why aren't you there?"

Marcia sighed. "Heard all I need to. Everything else is just nonsense."

"What was that?"

"Under his breath, Jackson Barnes said the sweetest five words I've ever heard."

"What were those?"

Marcia closed her eyes. "He said, 'There will be no appeal.'"

The arrests began a little before ten, and by midnight most of the fifteen men on the list were safely in jail. They included all the senior ComHealth executives, several junior executives, and two managers at Doyne labs. Whitfield, Barnes, Cox, and Farnsworth had managed to disappear temporarily. The arrested group all went without a fight, some confessing as soon as they were put in handcuffs.

Just after midnight, with TV cameras still on, H. Carter Hutchins arrived at the police station. Two hours earlier, the ComHealth board of directors had announced sweeping changes that included the firing of the CEO and its twenty top executives. To Hutchins, Markham's betrayal had stung, but it was nothing compared to the firing and his arrest.

The CEO was brought in by the front door, hounded by reporters and escorted by five policemen. He was still in a suit, although the tie was gone and his hair was slightly messed. He was grim, ashen, and angry, and even as he walked, his fists were clenched.

As he was being led through the halls, Reggie jumped out of the crowd right in front of him. The group stopped, and the policemen drew arms. Reggie held up his hands. He was unarmed. In between his fingers he held two pictures. He flashed them to Hutchins and then thrust them in the CEO's breast pocket. The pictures were of Molly Loomis and Reggie's mother. Hutchins saw them.

"I thought you'd need something on your walls," Reggie said.

H. Carter Hutchins was typically condescending. "Young man, you'll never understand what all of this was about, will you?"

Reggie stood right in front of him. He glared up into Hutchins' eyes. "Tragic, but true." He said it so softly it was almost as if he were talking to himself.

"What?" grunted the CEO.

"You really believed all that nonsense you said, didn't you? Your ads, your speeches."

Hutchins didn't answer. Even in defeat, his arrogance refused to yield. He signaled to the guards to take him away. Reggie Tan was not worth his effort.

As Hutchins disappeared, Reggie shook his head, disbelieving. "No, Mr. Hutchins, it's you who will never understand. And maybe that's the scariest thing of all."

Chapter Forty-two

December 2

It was over three months later when Peter Colder first returned to Minneapolis. The "forgotten man" in the ComHealthOne battle, he completed his rehab in Arizona, with a six-week period of outpatient physical therapy. His stay in Phoenix, his mother's home for seven years, allowed him to miss three months of Minnesota autumn, the beginning of winter, and the aftermath of ComHealth's defeat. He kept abreast with calls from Sylvia and Julianne as well as an occasional segment on the news.

His recovery had been difficult. Despite his rapid emergence from the coma, his condition had been fragile for nearly another month. One brief bout of pneumonia was followed by a urinary tract infection and a blood clot in the leg. Also, his kidney required frequent labs to check on their function. It was not until his first week of rehab that his doctors completely cleared him to begin a full load of physical therapy. In addition, the surgeries left him nearly twenty pounds lighter and weaker then he had ever been. His chest remained sore, and he continued to walk with a slight limp, the result of a neuropathy that none of his doctors could explain. But despite the problems, none of it mattered to Peter Colder. He had been discharged with every expectation he would continue to improve. Overall, he was healthy, fairly happy, and eager to return to work.

On the return flight to Minnesota, Peter reflected on the past six months. So much had happened. ComHealth One was dead, and in its aftermath, the governor had launchd a probe into managed care tactics. Hutchins and his henchmen were behind bars, while O'Reilly's findings were to be published in the *New England Jornal of Medicine*.

His talks with Sylvia and Julianne told him of Marcia's awards and promotions, as well as Reggie's college plans. Peter smiled as he thought of the bright future ahead of Reggie. He knew of Tyler and Marcus, whose law firm flourished as a result of the trial publicity.

Peter turned to look out the plane window. He knew about them all. Except Molly. During his absence, they hadn't communicated. He'd heard updates from Sylvia and Julianne, but she never called. Nor had he. What had kept him from calling her? How many times had he started to dial her number and then hung up without waiting for her to answer? He didn't know. What he did know was he missed her. He missed her more than he could express. He wanted to be with her. He needed her, and he never needed anyone.

When his plane landed, Sylvia met him at the gate and drove him to his new apartment. A furnished two bedroom in a newer downtown building, it had a 180-degree view of the Mississippi river and a beautiful view of the city. Sylvia had picked it out. The apartment would serve as a "resting station" while his insurance claim on his burned home was ironed out. It was quaint, but comfortable, and the night view was nothing short of spectacular. Colder thanked her when he saw it. After unpacking, he and Sylvia had dinner and then he retired early. He was tired, and she had informed him that there would be no rest for the weary. She had scheduled patients beginning in mid-morning the following day. Colder was glad.

When morning broke, he was up early. He showered, shaved, and turned on the TV as he made breakfast. He watched it only out of the corner of his eye. Ever since his near death he watched the news less carefully. He found that his new habit seemed to free his brain. This morning was no different. The news was nothing but politics and accidents. The weather was nothing but variable. And the sports was nothing but free agent complaints about being insulted by multimillion dollar offers. Colder listened and let it go. The world was staying on its bumpy course without him. He was pleased.

Julianne picked him up at his apartment at ten. His only physical restriction was no driving. His right leg and foot were too weak for him to drive safely. She hugged him for nearly a minute when she saw him and wiped a tear from her eye when she saw how thin he looked. "You sure you're ready to go back?" she asked.

Colder kissed his ex-wife on the forehead. "Never been readier."

Julianne drove him the twelve blocks to the edge of Third Street, just out of sight of the Third Street Clinic. The traffic was light, and a few snowflakes fell through the thirty-degree air. Julianne pulled over to the curb and stopped. She turned to Peter.

"It's great to see you," she said, hugging him again.

"Thanks, J," he whispered warmly. "It's good to see you too."

Julianne let him go after a minute. Colder knew his ex-wife well. Even after less than five minutes, he knew she had something on her mind. "What do you want to tell me, Jules?"

Julianne turned away. "I hope you're not mad."

"About the money?" he asked.

"You know?" she said surprised.

Colder nodded. "Sylvia told me last night. Your boyfriend, Geoff, got me a low-interest loan to keep me afloat."

Julianne looked shocked. "You're not mad?"

Colder shook his head and looked out the window at the clouds. All false pride was long gone from his soul. He was convinced it had been removed with the bullets. "Naw," he replied. "I need the help. I appreciate it."

Julianne looked at him curiously. She had known him many years. It was perhaps the first time she had totally missed on her prediction of his reaction. "What happened to Don Quixote?" she asked.

Colder threw his head back. He closed his eyes and laughed. "I guess he found out it was better to try to enjoy the breeze than to fight the windmills."

Julianne looked out at the few flakes of snow that had landed on the windshield and were now melting into drops of water. She smiled warmly at him. "You know you were always the courageous one, Peter."

Colder chuckled. "Maybe. But courage and foolishness are neighbors. And you were the smart one."

Julianne's eyes filled with tears. She was clearly on the edge. "I'm really going to miss you," she said.

Colder was surprised. Her remark had not been expected. "What do you mean you're going to miss me?"

Julianne shook her head.

"You moving?" he asked. She didn't react. Then he got it. "You're marrying Geoff."

"I told him I would."

Colder didn't know what to say. She was his best friend, but he suddenly felt no right to even comment. "He's a good man, Julianne. Whatever you do, I know you'll do the right thing."

Colder saw a gentle gust of wind whirl snowflakes off the ground. The spiraling bands of white appeared to reach up, defy gravity, and twist toward the single stream of sunshine that was passing through the solid gray sheet of sky. Colder had dreaded this moment. He knew that he and Julianne would need to make a decision about themselves. They had been too close not to corrode any other relationship they entered. It just felt strange and depressing to have it happen now. He deftly changed the subject, knowing the message to both of them was clear. "We should have dinner."

Julianne followed. She already felt she had said enough. "That would be good." She paused and wiped a tear from her eye. "Besides, your lawyer thinks you should put on some weight."

Colder smiled. "I'm relieved to have such good medical advice."

Julianne tried to laugh, but she ached too much inside. Nothing seemed fair. Nothing was ever fair, but neither could reality ever be avoided. She took a deep breath, and like him, bravely moved on. "Why don't you ask me what you want to know?"

"How's Tyler?"

"He and Marcus donated some money to a pediatric oncology wing in memory of a child with AIDS who died a few weeks ago. Also they donated some to the ICU—in the name of a patient Tyler met the night before the trial ended. He had a blood clot on the brain. Was operated on. He's fine. At home with his wife and children."

"Is Reggie getting excited about school," Colder asked.

"Yeah. I guess CalTech really wanted him. The kid's amazing. They needed an altimeter to measure his SAT score," Julianne laughed.

"And?" asked Julianne. "Who else?"

Colder quit laughing and sighed. He had no energy to beg it out of her. "You know."

Julianne's eyes sparkled. She looked relieved and almost proud. "Molly's doing well," she said. "Geoff has helped her a lot with the money. She established an endowed chairmanship at the U of M med school. She also started a bunch of scholarships and a charitable foundation for poor kids and single moms. It will provide grant money for education and other needs. And she donated enough to build a new wing at the rehab that will be named after Cynthia Tan."

Colder couldn't help smile. "That's beautiful," he said.

"She even gave a speech the other night. Minneapolis chapter of the League of Women Voters. She was great."

Peter looked genuinely surprised. "Really?"

"Well, I'll admit I helped her write a little of it. But once she relaxed, she really did well."

"Way to go Molly," he said, trying not to sound too thrilled. "Way to go."

Julianne put her hand on his knee. "Let's go see the place."

"I'm ready."

Julianne fired up the car and turned the corner. Before they could react, they were in the middle of a crowd. Colder's eyes flew wide open at the sight. Patients lined the block all the way to the Third Street Clinic, and they waved furiously as they saw him coming. A large sign hung over the Clinic. "Welcome Back, Dr. Colder."

Julianne drove slowly, allowing Peter to see the familiar faces that had turned out to greet him. He waved back as they cheered him.

"They didn't have to do this," he said modestly.

Julianne knew he was happy. "Blame Sylvia for the sign. The patients came on their own."

The car stopped in front of the clinic, and Peter stepped out. The two hundred people standing out in the thirty-degree temperature swarmed around, shaking his hand and patting him on the back. Julianne drove a few yards away and watched.

Letisha flew out of the door and leaped into his arms. He was nearly bowled over, but managed to stay on his feet. She buried his head with kisses while the patients laughed. Sandra Becker was next. Formal as always, she shook his hand. "Good to see you, Dr. Colder," she grunted. "Now, we have financial concerns to discuss."

Colder laughed and put an arm around his dedicated accountant. In a crazy way, he had missed her more than anyone but Molly. "I'm sure we do, Sandy. I'm sure we do."

Reggie was next. Peter punched him lightly on the shoulder. "I hear it's CalTech," he said happily.

"Yeah," said Reggie modestly. "It's either gonna be rocket science or sex therapy to the stars. Right now I'm leaning toward the latter." Everyone around laughed harder. Reggie blushed.

Eric Johnson appeared and shook Colder's hand. The two had met only once before, but Peter had heard about his testimony. "Dr. Johnson has been helping out down here while you recuperated," said Sylvia.

"Thanks," said Colder sincerely. "Thanks for everything."

Before Johnson could respond, the honk of a large truck interrupted them. The crowd made way, and the moving van with the sign 'Whalen's' on the side stopped in front of the clinic. A grubby-looking man with a two-day beard and a stub of a cigar stepped out of the cab."

"Third Street Clinic?" he asked to no one in particular.

"Yes," said Peter.

"I'm here to take the equipment," he said.

A rumble passed through the crowd. Peter whirled to Sandra. "Sandy, are we broke?" he asked frantically.

Sandra Becker stammered. "Uh, no. No!" she said loudly. She put her hand on her head nervously. "We've had a minor cash flow problem. Actually a major problem, some creditor issues. But with Dr. Johnson and with First National—"

A large black man carrying his son in his arms stepped forward and looked menacingly at the moving man. "Over my dead body are you takin' our X-ray machine. My son hurt his ankle, and he needs that thing."

The moving man rolled his eyes. "I don't give a crap if you keep the old stuff," he growled. "But if you do, where in the hell am I going to put the new stuff? I've got an X-ray machine, couple of examining tables, and a whole pile of lab equipment."

Colder whirled back to a gray-looking Sandra who was supported in Sylvia's arms. "Sandy, did you order this stuff?"

Sandra's blood pressure was bottoming out. She could barely utter a no as she shook her head. Peter looked surprised. Then it came to him. Geoff and First National. He turned, and Julianne was standing about ten feet away. Financial help was one thing. But this was too much. "J, no way. You know how I feel."

She nodded understandingly. "Yes, I do."

"Then?" he asked, annoyed.

"Where do you want the stuff?" asked the irritated moving man, still munching on his cigar butt.

"It wasn't Geoff," Julianne replied.

"What?"

"I said it wasn't Geoff."

Colder was twitching. "Well then, who?"

"It was me."

The crowd parted and Molly appeared from behind the moving van. Peter turned, took a step back on his bad foot and nearly fell. Others caught him and propped him back up. Steadying himself, he gazed at Molly. Her hair was cut and her long black coat made her look almost regal. Her glasses were gone, replaced by contacts; for the first time since he had known her, her face looked full and healthy. Molly Loomis looked even more beautiful than he remembered.

"I never had an opportunity to say a proper thanks, Dr. Colder," she said, moving slowly toward him.

"You never needed to," he replied, his feet now firmly planted on the ground.

"Yes, I did."

Molly stood right before him. Colder swallowed noticeably. He was still shocked at how attracted he was to her. "You hungry?" she asked as she looked deeply into his eyes.

"What?"

Molly seemed slightly nervous. "I was hoping you were hungry. I never had a chance to buy you that sub sandwich I promised."

Peter seemed unable to speak. His lips quivered, but no sound arrived. Molly was holding a styrofoam cup of coffee in her left hand and she raised it to her mouth. Peter saw it at once—the wedding ring she had always worn was gone.

"We've got an entire office full of patients," said Sandra, who was finally recovering from the thought of new, expensive equipment.

"I can handle it," Eric Johnson said.

"Dr. Colder needs his nourishment," Sylvia said, stepping forward.

"We'll set up the new X-ray machine," the large black man said to the moving man.

Letisha stepped up to Colder. "I don't believe I recall any appointments for you, Doctor, until after lunch."

Colder put his head down. He wanted to go; any guilt over a full clinic seemed minor. Letisha nudged him. "Get your bony butt out of here."

Everyone laughed. "Oh," Molly blurted, "one more thing."

She disappeared for a moment, running to her car parked behind the moving van. She was gone only a few seconds, but when she returned, she was carrying an animal traveling cage. "By the way. I thought you might want this."

Colder looked at it curiously and peered in through the cage front. Inside he saw him. "Oh, God," he gasped, fumbling with the door.

"I thought you would want a new kitty, but when I heard about this one, I thought you might just want him back."

Colder opened the cage door, and the great beast Mortimer leaped out and into his master's arms. Molly was busy telling the story. "He must have gotten out through a window that blew out in the fire," said Molly. "He had some burns on his body, and he had two cut tendons in his front legs."

"Oh, Morty," gushed Colder, scratching the purring cat's neck.

"Someone found him a couple of hundred yards from your house. He could barely walk, but they took him to the U of M vet school. They're amazing there. He had to have a couple operations on his legs and then he had to go to therapy."

"He looks wonderful," sighed Colder, running his hands through the cat's fur.

"In therapy, he didn't like the treadmill much, but he loved the leg massages."

Everyone laughed. Colder held Morty tightly as the cat cuddled with his master like the dog he thought he was. Mortimer seemed a bit thinner, and his fur was short in the areas of his healing burns and operations, but otherwise he was perfect.

"It was lucky you had the collar on him. It had your telephone number on it. We had your home calls forwarded to the clinic, and Sylvia got the call from the man who found him."

"Thanks, Molly," he said softly. "Thanks a lot."

Julianne walked up and petted the cat. Peter knew how much she loved their pet as well. "He looks good, doesn't he?"

"Yes, he does." She leaned over and kissed Morty on the top of his head. "Take good care of him."

"I will, J. And thanks."

A moment later, Julianne was gone, and the crowd began helping to unload all the new equipment. Letisha waved at Colder to "get lost," and Sylvia did the same. Colder stood next to Molly, watching them work for just a minute. Then he turned to her. "I think I'm getting hungry," he said.

She took his arm. "Let me show you the way."

As Molly's blue Saturn drove down Third Street, away from the clinic, they passed a metal vending box of newspapers. With Morty tucked safely in his cage in the back seat, Molly slowed for a minute, only to glance. The headlines read, "Death of The Dragon—The Rise and Fall of America's Late, Great HMO." It was the paper printing excerpts from Marcia's upcoming book.

Peter and Molly paid no attention. It seemed long ago. At last, they were both where they wanted to be. Peter reached across the front seat and put his hand on hers. Molly, slowed, leaned over, and kissed him before returning her eyes to the road. Neither of them spoke, but both of them noticed it at the same time. The sky ahead was clear. Throughout the city, it had stopped snowing.

Acknowledgements

The idea of managed care and HMOs is not new. The horrors of managed care are real. Fragile X, born on a muggy night in northern Minnesota in July 1995, is an attempt to put real-life scenarios behind the concept of managed care. Since those first paragraphs were written, it has seemed to most who have helped me that several more millennia would arrive before a finished copy could be seen. After procrastination, excuses, three million rewrites, and one citywide flood with five feet of main-floor water in my house, it is finally finished. I thank you all for your patience.

While it seems very strange to be finishing a project that has been so much a apart of my life for these four years, I can honestly say that much of this book will forever be a part of me. Most of the medical histories in Fragile X are authentic and camouflaged only for privacy reasons. Their tragedies accurately represent the moral dilemma of managed care, and I hope that their lives will continue to inspire debate on the future of health care in the United States.

To say thanks to all the people who have helped me is truly an impossible task. The debt is too large. But I know that I owe a special debt of gratitude to my parents, brother, Maree Nelson, Judy Teske and my life-saving editor, Eileen Zygarlicke. Also, thanks are due Dr. Chris Schmidt, Dr. Lynn Stanco, Dr. Dan Schmelka, Dr. Susan Thompson, Ron and Brenda Gallagher and everyone at Century Creations: Glen and Jean Clayton, John Loukas and Amy Young. Lastly, a special thanks to Pam Brown. Without your support and encouragement, it never would have happened.

Stuart Rice, raised in Minnesota, graduated from the University of North Dakota and the Medical College of Wisconsin. He is a neurosurgeon in private practice in Grand Forks, North Dakota.

One man's discovery could change the world.

COVENANT

A hope too dangerous to be ignored.
BCL-2. The immortality gene.
The Holy Grail.

WITH

When man's final frontier touches the hand of God, reality meets fantasy and dreams come true.

ETERNITY

Never fail to dream.